TIMESHIFT

TIMESHIFT

KRIS TRUDEAU

SECOND EDITION

LACLU
PUBLISHING

COURTENAY, BRITISH COLUMBIA

ISBN: 978-0-9949225-7-1

LACLU PUBLISHING
351-2401 Cliffe Avenue
Courtenay, BC V9N 2L5
www.laclupublishing.com

Cover and layout by Halftone Pixel Website Design

Printed by CreateSpace

DEDICATION

First and foremost, I must thank two people who have been a tremendous help and have listened to me talk about this book for oh, over six years: Mom and Andrew. I'm sorry. I didn't really mean to go on about it. But look! It's done now! Wanna hear my next book idea?

To my eleventh hour angels—Sherry and Double D—and everybody else who played a role in the evolution of this book, thank you. Whether it was advice, opinions or encouragement, the contribution each of you has made was, and always will be greatly appreciated. This book would not be what it is without you.

I dedicate this book to everybody who wanted to do something that they didn't believe they could. You often hear successful people tell you that you can achieve any dream and accomplish any goal. To a penniless high school graduate, an employee living paycheque to paycheque, or to somebody whose day is so full there isn't enough time to eat or sleep, advice like this makes the speaker seem out of touch with us mere mortals. I can attest to this, as I've been all three of those people, thankfully at different times. But guess what? They're right! I feel this advice should come with some disclaimers—I don't recommend you study online to become a backyard brain surgeon. However, if you possess the proper motivation, tenacity and common sense, you too can achieve anything you set your mind to. To paraphrase Canadian legend Terry Fox, "The only limit is the one you set for yourself."

Don't let fear stop you from fulfilling your dreams. Life is short; there are no do-overs. Be the best you that you can be, live your dreams and don't let anybody—especially yourself—tell you that you can't or you're not good enough. Grab life by the horns and ride!

PROLOGUE

August 14, 2097

The view from the third-floor balconies was nothing but a sea of windows belonging to cookie-cutter, high-rise condominiums. Unlike the sixty-seventh floor, where the cluster of adjacent glass and concrete buildings wove a tapestry of an idyllic urban utopia, the view from the third floor showed no appreciable beauty in the surrounding landscape—merely a too-intimate view into the living rooms and lives of faceless residents of neighbouring buildings. However, the third-floor residents were privy to something that residents of the upper storeys were not—a front row seat for real city living in all its imperfections, mediocrity and grittiness.

Recent events had erased the city of its colourful daily affairs. The absence of people, the boarded up storefronts and eerie silence were indicative of what life in the city had recently become. The only sign of activity was the occasional face of neighbouring apartment dwellers peering out their windows. Some wore expressions of fear, some looked nervous. Others looked angry and contemptuous; ready with the phone to report to the police anything remotely amiss.

A two-day-old, white plastic news sheet lay atop the glass coffee table—its information layout a throwback to turn-of-the-century newspapers. The single-sheet news daily featured an article so long that an arrow bobbed up and down at the bottom of the thin sheet, begging the reader to touch it, thereby scrolling the remainder of the article into view. Peppered throughout the article were various silent video images of robots congregating, angry residents and deserted streets. Topping the article in red, upper-case letters, its headline blinked:

"NRD DENIES ANY INVOLVEMENT"

Curled edges and finger smudges on the white surface were evidence of the news publication having been frequently handled—as if it had been picked up, read and set down repeatedly. Perhaps from being rolled up and taken to a neighbouring apartment where its damning claims were speculated upon over afternoon coffee. The overuse had caused areas on the recyclable digital sheet to fade, or not show at all. The previous day's news sheet lay across the arm of the sofa. Its headline read in the same oversized, blinking red font:

"WHAT THE NRD ISN'T TELLING YOU"

However, today's news sheet, lying on the parquet floor behind the door after having just been delivered, screamed the most damning headline to date:

"THEY'RE COMING FOR YOUR HOME!"

The local evening news boomed from the TV, the volume set at maximum so as to be audible over the sound of clanging pots, a singing kettle and shuffling footsteps in the kitchen.

"I don't know, Ted," said the stately news anchor, scepticism etched in his puzzled face. The timbre of his voice rumbled, rich and deep. "There really isn't too much proof that they're the source of these break-ins."

The anchor's attention was focused on a large split screen on his right, displaying the feeds of two people weighing in on the discussion. The right-side feed showed Ted, a prominent, however, bedraggled anti-robot activist standing in a deluge of rain. His hair lay plastered to his head and face. The water-spotted lenses of his round, horn-rimmed glasses had begun to fog and he clumsily pushed them up on his face. The hand-painted message on the sandwich board he wore had dripped down the white sign like colourful ice cream on a child's face on a hot day. A sharply-dressed woman filled the feed on the left. Her designer suit jacket had not a single drop of water on it, shielded from the driving rain by several large black umbrellas. Mobile lighting lit her up like an angel as she stood among vibrant flowers in a formal garden before a magnificent glass building.

"I agree," said the woman. Her authoritative voice commanded respect if her confident demeanour and professional appearance had not already earned it. "If there was any chance that these robots were even remotely responsible, National Research and Defence would have launched a formal investigation."

"Are you kidding me? Not even with eyewitness accounts from people who have had their homes destroyed?" Ted pushed his wet hair from his face and it came to an awkward point on the side of his head. "Homes and businesses have been demolished and I don't get why you people don't see!"

A smile grew on the woman's face. "They don't *see*, Ted, because there is nothing for them to see. These incidents are mostly unrelated, although we do suspect that some of the break-ins may be gang-related."

Ted sputtered and his face reddened. "Unrelated? Gangs? Each of these break-ins are identical. The same thing is stolen and no physical evidence left behind. Sounds like a pattern to me!"

"You are finally correct," said the woman in her calm, metred voice. "There is never any evidence found proving who was responsible."

"Because what they steal is evidence!" What remained of Ted's façade began to crack. His face screwed up in frustration and his voice shot up an octave.

The apartment suddenly shook. Seconds later, another quaking shake. The cacophony of cooking sounds issuing from the kitchen fell silent for several moments. The miniature poodle slumbering on the couch awoke with a start and surveyed his surroundings. Seeing nothing of interest, he laid his head back down.

"These robots are a plague on our communities and inevitably our planet! The human race was at risk from the moment they were released in this city! They are going to take over and end up killing us all!"

The woman smiled warmly, the way one would to console an upset child. Ted achieved her goal for her—he had made himself sound like a raving lunatic.

A large crash echoed in the distance and the building shook more violently. With this, the little black dog jumped off the couch and scampered into the kitchen.

"There is no evidence that the robots have had anything to do with these break-ins. There are a lot of people who fear that the robots may take over their jobs and that is a legitimate concern we're prepared to deal with. But to make these wild accusations about this highly successful, world-class program is slanderous. These robots have been proven to be safe, productive members of society and they pose no danger to any…"

The projected TV screen vanished and the lights in the apartment went out. An eerie silence crept through the apartment as all electronic devices shut down. The blades of the fan in the corner of the living room began to slow.

CHAPTER 1

May 27, 2016

Weak columns of early morning light sliced through the blinds in the darkened master bedroom of the house that three generations of Taylor men have called home. The bars of light fell across the dark hardwood floors, up the foot of the bed and skipped to the dresser. They cut across the dresser mirror and illuminated the face of an attractive man at the top of a narrow strip of newsprint tucked into the mirror's frame.

Owen lay in bed awake. A mixture of drowsiness and inadequate sleep clouded his mind. He could not exactly pinpoint at what time he had awoken but guessed—by the way his head and body ached—it was some time before he had fallen asleep. He looked across the room at the digital clock on the dresser. Seeing 5:42, he rubbed his eyes. After staring at the ceiling for several minutes, he knew any further attempts to sleep would be futile. He swung his feet over the side of the bed and sat up. The heaviness in his chest—a sensation to which he had become accustomed over the last six months—felt heavy, like his entire body's weight hung inside his rib cage. He looked across the darkened room again at the alarm clock hoping it would show a more reasonable number. The red illuminated digits announced 5:46, and he sighed as he looked away. The column of newsprint caught his attention. Seeing the obituary brought a fresh wave of heaviness to his heart. As he stood, he turned on the lights and his eyes squinted reflexively. He dragged himself to the dresser and stared at the obituary even though he knew it word for word. He knew it because he wrote it.

"Michael William Taylor, February 16, 1947 – December 21, 2015, passed away peacefully at his home in Riverbend. Michael was a young, vibrant man who lived life to the fullest. He was predeceased by his parents, Jon and Nancy Taylor, and his wife, Abbey. His memory will always be cherished by his only remaining

*family—son, Owen Taylor, as well as family, friends and those he touched through-
out his life and career. Michael is known mostly for the buildings he designed in
Tricity including the Centennial building on Main and 20th, the Miner building
on 2nd and 11th and many others. Other prominent works include the Free Children's Hospital, where he donated his professional services and 'The Escalade,' an
upscale condominium complex on the west coast. Michael was a dedicated father;
his wife having passed three years after the birth of their son, Owen. Michael had
a zest for life that he shared with all those around him. Hiking, kayaking, fishing
and camping were just a few of the activities that Michael instilled a love for in his
son. In retirement, Michael again took up sculpture and woodcarving; two hobbies
he enjoyed in his youth that a demanding career had forced to the sidelines. Several
of his commissioned sculptures reside at the CityCentre Rooftop Atrium and Art
Gallery and the Central Station terminal. Michael's passing is an unspeakable loss
to his son Owen, his friends as well as the community. Services will be held—"*

Owen smiled wistfully at the close-cropped face in the photo. His father had been
dead for six months. During the day when his mind stayed occupied, the loss was barely
tolerable. At night, his thoughts acted like oil and vinegar. Good thoughts were trapped
at the bottom as the negative thoughts floated above, choking the good thoughts away
from the surface. He awoke in the mornings feeling listless, and he attributed this to
the depressing memories that lingered in his mind, keeping him from peaceful sleep.

Michael was the only parent Owen had ever known, and the two shared a
bond stronger than hardened steel. Owen knew his father had moved into this, his
parents'—Owen's grandparents'—home, in the suburb of Riverbend after they died
in a car accident. Despite the tragic circumstances, Michael appreciated the opportunity to live in the home that had meant so much to his father. Owen's grandfather,
also a renowned architect, had designed and built the house to be his retirement
home. Living in his parents' home resurrected happy memories of his youth and
warm reminders of his parents. The change of scenery also eased the loss of his wife,
not yet a year past. Michael and his son, although too young to understand, had both
experienced significant losses and Michael looked forward to a fresh start.

Both men always shared a healthy, mutual respect for each other. Despite differences of opinions that shook the house at 152 Riverbend Road in Owen's teenage
years, Owen and his father were always best friends. As Owen grew, it became
apparent to Michael that Owen favoured two particular interests—outer space and
camping. Michael encouraged these interests by enrolling Owen in Scouts and Space
Camp, and he spent considerable time learning alongside his son. On weekends, they
would hike through the backwoods with large packs of gear and set up camp at
remote lakes or other destinations far off the beaten trail. For Owen, the telescope
was considered an essential camping necessity and he carried it with him the way
other children dragged along teddy bears or toy cars. Many nights were spent lying on
rocky outcrops staring up into the vast expanse of space. By Owen's mid-teens, both
he and Michael were master survivalists and proficient amateur astronomers.

After university, Owen moved into the heart of the city upon landing his first job in a lab testing geological samples. Although the drive to Owen's from River-bend Road took less than an hour, the transition for both men had been harder than either expected or wanted to admit, and they continued to stay close. The majority of Owen's friends had spread around the world after university as they followed careers and relationships. The few friends that remained knew Michael well and enjoyed time with him as much as they did with Owen.

Years passed and Michael watched his son grow as a person and into his career. He knew it had always been Owen's dream to work at NASA, or for the International Space Coalition. He was shocked to learn that despite the promising contacts Owen had made at the ISC while touring there after university, he had never pursued a career there, choosing instead to stay in Tricity. When Michael asked his son about his shift in career goals—away from the better pay and professional prestige a career at the ISC would have brought—Owen's answer had surprised him.

"I have more than one goal in life, Dad. Plus, money isn't everything. Sure, working for the ISC would be amazing, but it can't offer me something that a job here does."

"What's that?" Michael had asked, expecting his son's answer to be a girl, good hiking trails or mountain biking.

Owen's face had reddened as he had said, "You."

Michael had stared at his son for several moments while searching for a response. He felt guilty for being the reason his son had compromised his dreams and even guiltier for feeling happy about it. Some of these emotions must have shown on his face because Owen had added, "Now don't go getting all after-school-special on me. I also happen to like it here."

Michael swelled with pride as his son became a highly-respected astrogeologist for the research branch of the government organization, National Research and Defence. His specialization made him one of a handful of astrogeologists globally and as such, he was frequently sought after for specialized projects. On many occasions, he had travelled the globe to study various meteor impact sites. When Owen's expertise had been specifically requested by the ISC through his work at the NRD, it alleviated some of the guilt Michael had felt for Owen not chasing his dreams.

One of the men's Sunday hikes fell on an unusually warm fall day and Owen and his father planned to hit their favourite hiking trail before the inclement winter weather arrived. Michael had awoken that morning feeling tired and under the weather. He popped some vitamin C pills in hopes of killing the bug before it grew into a full-blown cold. Owen picked him up mid-morning and soon they were on the trail, enjoying the blue sky, the warm breeze and what remained of the vibrant fall leaves. After being on the trail for only a few minutes, Michael had found himself short of breath, something that had not gone unnoticed by Owen.

"Are you feeling alright?" Owen had asked. "You seem a little off your game today. Are you coming down with something?"

"I must be," said Michael. "That, or maybe my old age is catching up with me."

Owen chuckled, however uneasily. At sixty-four and fit as a fiddle, Owen knew his father's health surpassed that of many thirty-year-olds.

After several more minutes of walking, the men reached a fork in the trail. Owen stopped at the junction. His father's breathing had not improved, and Owen worried his father was downplaying how he felt.

"We don't need to make this a major outing. Why don't we stroll over to Duck Lake instead?"

Michael struggled to catch his breath and succeeded after several attempts. "Sure, I think that would be good. When was the last time we went to Duck Lake anyway?"

The path leading to the right would have been their typical route—a scenic, but long and technical hiking trail leading up and down steep rocky terrain, through a man-made cave and around a lake. Instead, the trail to the left continued a short distance where it ended at a picnic area overlooking Duck Lake. The two men sat at a picnic table and watched a flock of seagulls run amok in the empty park while they chatted about their week's events. Uncomfortable with his father's increasingly ill appearance, Owen suggested they head back to his truck.

Halfway to the truck, Owen noticed his father's breathing becoming increasingly laboured, and he stopped so his father could catch his breath. Michael had begun sweating profusely and his ghostly pallor matched that of the wispy clouds moving lazily across the blue sky.

"Okay, take it easy. We're close enough to the end and the trail is wide enough, I'm going to get the truck and pick you up."

Michael did not respond immediately. Hunched over with his hands on his knees, he shook his head as he tried to catch his breath. "No, it's fine. Let's just walk slowly." He looked at his son, smiled weakly and added casually, "And then maybe we could swing by the hospital on the way home? Maybe I should get checked out. It would probably be the responsible thing to do." His voice remained calm, but his widened eyes betrayed his casual demeanour.

Owen wrapped his arm around his father's waist and supported him as they resumed walking. As they reached the trail head, Michael fell to his knees, clutching his chest and collapsed to the ground, unconscious.

Not unlike other heart attack survivors, Michael's heart sustained considerable damage and never fully recovered. He had just begun enjoying life as a retiree—he had laid-off his landscape contractor, taken up gardening, resumed sculpting and some of the other artistic hobbies he had enjoyed before Owen's birth. All his rediscovered joy had been snatched away from him, now too weak to walk down the stairs from his bedroom to the kitchen. Despite his father's protests that he would recover with a few weeks of rest, Owen rented out his house in the city and moved back into his childhood home with his father.

Michael had always maintained good spirits about his health, but when it became apparent his recovery was not progressing the way he and the doctors had expected, his spirits fell and he went through a period of depression. After much support from friends of both Owen and Michael, Michael had come to terms with the situation and once again became himself in spirit, although a new man in appearance. The broad-shouldered, muscular man that Owen once knew no longer existed. That tanned, energetic man was replaced by a pale, angular man with barely enough energy to walk from room to room.

On good days, Michael would venture to a seating area Owen had set up in the living room that overlooked the river. For hours, Michael would sit and watch deer and the other wildlife that wandered into the backyard as the river meandered past. When Owen went back to work, a private nurse came to spend the days with his father. The time that passed had devastating effects on not only Michael but Owen as well, who felt powerless. Owen could do nothing but watch the health of his father and best friend continually decline. Finally, one warm December morning before Christmas, Owen came downstairs and found that his father had passed away in his favourite chair overlooking the river.

Owen had managed to avoid a complete withdrawal from life through the support of many friends and co-workers. His best friends, now spread all around the world, had come home for the funeral. Too soon, however, they needed to return to their lives, jobs and families, leaving Owen alone in a sprawling, empty house full of sweet but painful memories at every turn. His director offered him time off, but he declined the offer, choosing instead to throw himself deeper into his work. Work dulled the pain during the day, but coming home to the empty house every night was nearly as painful as it had been the first few days after his father's passing. Adjusting to life without his father and best friend proved to be an enormous obstacle around which Owen could not find his way.

Owen glanced away from his father's smiling face in the obituary and the reflection of himself in the mirror caught his attention. At six-foot-one, he needed to duck to see the top of his head. He ran a hand through his thick, chestnut-brown hair. It had grown far longer than he usually kept it, the locks now hung into his eyes if he let them. It had a casual, unkempt look about it, not entirely inappropriate for work, so he left it alone. The mere thought of having to make small talk with his hairstylist was too onerous to even entertain. He rubbed at the farmer's tan on his bicep where his shirt sleeves ended and his lightly tanned arms began as if this would somehow blend the two colours together. The tan line on his left arm was partially hidden by a Celtic armband tattoo he had picked up as a souvenir in Europe. He noticed for the first time that his muscle mass had diminished, having spent very little time at the gym over the last six months. His shoulders, though naturally broad, were not as muscular and imposing as they had once been. By contrast, his abdominals were more prominent—most likely, he assumed, the result of depression cutting into his appetite. The fine lines around his tired, dark-brown eyes seemed deeper than he had remembered, and the dark circles beneath them had not been there a year previous.

A gurgling sound from the coffee maker in the kitchen below brought Owen's attention back to the day at hand, and he went to the bathroom and turned on the shower. The hot water pummelling his chest was a welcome, soothing sensation. The heat seemed to melt some of the weight he carried there and the steamy vapour energized him. Anxious to get to work and occupy his mind, Owen dressed and raced out the front door without a glance at the freshly brewed travel mug of coffee waiting for him in the kitchen.

Owen slipped his truck into his parking space in the office parkade. Instead of entering the building, he detoured through an exit to the street and walked several blocks to a coffee shop to replace the forgotten coffee in his kitchen. Minutes later and with a large coffee in hand, he walked back toward his office. With his mind now properly fuelled, he began to think about his tasks for the upcoming day. He stood at an intersection waiting for the light to change, savouring the warm morning sun on his face. As he sipped the steaming coffee, he thought about how to begin the long, wrap-up process documenting a fascinating discovery he had recently made. Owen ordinarily despised the administrative portion of his job, preferring to be seeing and doing instead of writing. However, documenting the findings of a completely alien, high-energy, super-element would hold his interest with no difficulties.

Owen waited for the traffic lights to change so he could cross. He stood at the edge of the curb and within moments, a large number of pedestrians had gathered behind him. Owen watched as a city bus barrelled toward him and he became uncomfortably aware of how close he stood to the curb's edge and stepped back. He felt something bump him in the shoulder and he lost his balance. Hot coffee sloshed from the lid of his cup and burned his fingers. He swore under his breath and stepped back onto what little curb remained to catch his balance. The bus rocketed past and the wind from its draft blew his hair. His heart pounded and a wave of adrenaline surged through his body. *A little too close for comfort,* he thought. He wiped the spilled coffee on his pant leg and seeing another bus approaching in the same speedy fashion, he decided to get clear out of the way. He turned to slip through the crowd, but he found no space to cut through. Instead, he got bumped by the bags and shoulders of people distracted by their thoughts or too busy chatting to hear Owen's "excuse me's." He leaned backward into the crowd, which prompted choice words and complaints as people shuffled and tried to make room for him. Then Owen felt another bump in the back, but this time much harder. He willed his shoes to cling the sidewalk, but his body weight hung over the wrong side of the curb. Dropping his coffee, he reached backward, grasping blindly for anyone or anything and felt nothing but air. Both feet slid off the sidewalk and he staggered forward, unable to maintain his balance. He carried too much momentum and knew he could not recover in time. He closed his eyes and braced himself for the impact.

CHAPTER 2

August 15, 2097

Every single chair in the 1,300 seat Burton Auditorium was occupied. People standing at the rear of the auditorium spilled into the aisles as more people filed in, the room already filled beyond capacity. A glass podium stood at the centre of the raised stage, and to its left sat six empty chairs. None of the seats had legs or wheels—they hovered uniformly in a neat row. The wall behind the stage of the auditorium was a single, expansive pane of glass spanning from floor to ceiling of the three-storey room. Through the window, the tall trees and lush greenery of the living eco-atrium were revealed in the building's main foyer.

The voices became hushed as every pair of eyes in the overfilled auditorium shifted to a door that opened at the front corner of the room. A woman entered, followed by a middle-aged man wearing a NRD uniform. Two more women and three more men, all wearing civilian clothes followed. The window behind the stage darkened until the foliage in the atrium beyond became completely obscured by the black tint. The lights over the seating area dimmed slightly.

The woman who lead the parade of speakers into the auditorium strode past the hovering chairs and walked directly to the podium. The six people following her seated themselves in the airborne chairs. The crisp suit jacket and matching skirt of the woman behind the podium spoke of nothing but strength and power. But something about its fit—the way it hugged the curves of her slender body—was undeniably feminine. Four-inch patent leather heels accentuated her shapely calves and her dark brown hair pulled back into a tight knot could undoubtedly fuel any man's librarian fantasy. The steely look in her eyes reinforced her no-nonsense demeanour while her warm, genuine smile took the edge off her severity. She scanned the room and waited for the hushed voices to fall silent before she spoke.

As the face of public relations for National Research and Defence, Allison Hargrave excelled at painting lovely pictures with words and glossing over details deemed unnecessary for the public. She usually enjoyed the adrenaline rush that hit her before speaking to hundreds or thousands of people, but that was not the case for this press conference. Tonight was different. Over the last few months, her level of discomfort in the role increased daily. As the face of public relations for Tricity's branch of the NRD for the past eight years, she knew her job required her to skate over certain facts for the greater good. But for the first time in her career, she found herself conflicted between her morals and the requests being made of her.

"Thank you all very much for coming." Allison greeted the crowd with a friendly smile. "We know that there have been some questions about recent break-ins being linked to the robots associated with the National Research and Defence's Artificial Emotional Intelligence Project. But before we get into that, I'd like to introduce our speakers and share with you some of the many successes of the AEI Project."

Allison stepped out from behind the podium as she introduced the other speakers. The ease and comfort she possessed while on stage was one of the many qualities that made her an elocutionary master. The uniformed man seated in the floating chair closest to the podium watched over her possessively, as if uneasy she no longer stood within his reach.

"The NRD has achieved what we were told was impossible. We developed artificially intelligent robots that can think for themselves and experience emotions. Before this ground-breaking project, robots were inefficient and costly. They were designed to save time and money, but billions of dollars in man-hours are still being spent every year micromanaging instructions and performing maintenance on these helper robots, or First Generation robots, as we've come to call them. And what happens? They inevitably end up discarded in landfills, because after only a few years, they no longer serve their purpose, or their manufacturer discontinued software support."

As she spoke, an enormous, three-dimensional NRD logo materialized in the air at the rear of the stage. After a few moments, it faded away and a photo appeared showing a robot sitting at the bedside of an elderly woman. The aging woman smiled weakly and held the robot's hand. As if projected onto an invisible movie screen, the photo nearly spanned the room's full width, stopping just short of the ceiling and just above Allison's head. Another image appeared—a robot carrying a large load of two-by-fours at a muddy construction site. Another photo, this one showing a robot in a daycare handing out snacks. Several more photos appeared and finally, one image remained; a picture of a classroom with smiling children holding up books. Amongst the children sat a robot wearing a pink, knitted cardigan. A child sat on the robot's lap smiling broadly and proudly holding up a colourful storybook. Another little girl wearing a grin that revealed several missing teeth, wrapped her arms around the robot's neck giving her mechanical friend the biggest hug she could muster.

"I would like to introduce you to ID000172, or Nyx. Nyx received base programming equivalent to a university degree in Early Childhood Development. Nyx has been working at an elementary school in the city's core since day one of the pilot project." As she spoke, the photo changed to show Nyx working with the children. "A teacher with a class of fifty children needs to teach using a method that reaches the greatest number of students. With numbers that high, time can't be taken away from the majority for only a few. Nyx can assess learning disabilities and help each child learn in a way that is understandable to them. As a result, these grade one children are reading at a third-grade level or higher."

Allison walked to the side of the stage as a video began to play. Children played and chased each other around the school's playground. The video cut away to a classroom scene where Nyx, in her trademark pink cardigan, sat with a child holding a book. Nyx pointed to words on the page as the little boy cautiously sounded them out. The child's voice faded away and a friendly female voice with a British accent cut in.

"I'm Nyx, or ID000172. The children call me Miss Nyx. This student had an extreme case of dyslexia and could barely read individual words let alone full sentences. After spending some time with Sean, I developed a customized learning program for him and his parents to follow. Now he can read stories to his little sister at night."

Clip after clip of heart-warming stories revealed how Nyx and other robots like her made learning easier and improved the lives of children and their families. The principal expressed his astonishment at the spike in the school's overall grade point average and attendance. Kids were interviewed about how they liked Miss Nyx and teachers expressed their gratitude for having additional qualified help in the classroom.

After the spotlight on Nyx, the video profiled ID000296. Affectionately known as "Bubba," this robot spent his days in a maximum security prison. Initially, his presence had not been well-received, but after a few weeks, the inmates took to him like an old friend. Through conversations with many of the convicts, Bubba helped them recognize and work through the issues that caused the behaviour that landed them in prison. Other robots like Nyx helped the prisoners finish their educations or learn new skills and trades. AEI robots were revolutionizing the prison rehabilitation system.

When the video ended, the photos and videos vanished into thin air. Allison returned to the podium, having arrived at the part of the presentation she had been dreading.

"There have been reports of criminal activity and a rash of break-and-enters in recent months." She could feel the mutinous eyes of the crowd boring through her. This is why they had come; to see how much responsibility the NRD planned to accept. "National Research and Defence would like to confirm that parties responsible for a portion of these break-ins were the AEI robots."

The crowd broke into angry chatter and a female voice rang out. "Exactly what percentage of the break-ins were committed by robots?"

Allison smiled and handled the interruption like a pro. "I'll take all questions at the end but as I was just about to get to that, I'll respond. Please save all other questions until the end. Our investigation revealed that between twenty to thirty percent of the break-ins were committed by the robots."

"Only twenty to thirty percent?" shouted an angry male voice from the back.

Allison felt the tension in the crowd inflating like a balloon. She continued to talk, leaving no opportunity for interruption. "We think that the rest of the break-ins are copycats; people who are trying to undermine the trust in the AEI Project and the robots. The project is being re-assessed and we're going to recall..."

Despite her effort, a male voice cut her off. "What about the people that have died? People have been murdered by these killing machines! How do you explain that?"

"As I was saying, we are going to recall all of the robots, run diagnostic scans and check them for programming bugs. We feel that this isn't a widespread problem and it can be contained with..."

Another voice cut her off. Through the bright lights trained on the stage, she saw a man standing in the aisle beside his seat. "My wife is in a coma because of your robots! Three robots literally smashed through the front window of my living room and stormed into my home. They pushed my wife out of their way and she fell down a flight of stairs. They nearly trampled her as they ran down to the basement. The crime scene investigators found three sets of robot footprints, caked with mud from the flower garden in front of the house. How can you deny that?" The man walked toward the stage, holding up a piece of paper with pictures on it. "I have the police report right here! Do you want to see it?"

Allison saw two security guards approaching the man, one from the front of the room and one from the back. "Sir, I'm sorry for your pain but..."

"What about my father?" yelled a young woman, her voice shaking with emotion. "He was a security guard at the Capitol Building downtown. Your robots broke in at night and he got stabbed in the leg trying to fight them off. Because the power to the building was cut, no alarms were triggered. It wasn't until the alarm monitoring company noticed there was no signal coming from the building that they called 9-1-1. As a result, my father bled out and died from an injury that could have been easily fixed!"

Another voice rang out above the crowd, "I saw you on BCB News not twenty-four hours ago claiming no responsibility for this. What's changed?"

The crowd got to their feet like a wave and voices escalated quickly—people shouting, desperate for their stories to be heard. Others demanded that all the robots be destroyed. A parade of security personnel marched into the room from the door at the front and filed along the front of the stage. Cameras and bodycams flashed, filling the room with a bizarre light quality, as if by a faulty, erratic strobe light. The crowd began pushing its way toward the stage like eager concert-goers. Two of the male speakers and one of the women seated on the stage looked at each other nervously. As if they had conferred telepathically, they simultaneously stood and calmly walked off the stage, their pace quickening as they passed the angry crowd that security strained to hold back. The remaining seated woman and one of the two remaining men watched longingly as the door closed behind the fleeing speakers.

A paper coffee cup flew through the air toward the stage. Shrieks and screams issued from unsuspecting audience members, startled by the stream of hot coffee raining down on them. The plastic lid popped off completely as the cup landed at the feet of the remaining seated speakers, spraying their shoes and legs with hot coffee. This act of aggression proved too much for two of the remaining speakers and they left the stage hurriedly, leaving only Allison and the uniformed man on the stage. The man stood and took a protective step closer to Allison. Allison tried to regain the crowd's attention by talking louder than everyone else and delivering assurances, of which the people wanted none. Allison stopped talking and looked out over the crowd, hoping they would calm down of their own accord.

Security struggled against the crowd as it continued to surge toward the stage. It became evident to the uniformed man that control of the audience had been lost and the situation was becoming dangerous. Nothing positive could be gained from proceeding further. He watched Allison's attempts to control the crowd—she seemed to be taking the sideways turn of the conference as a personal failure. He walked up behind her and gently took her elbow, motioning for her to leave with him. She refused his gesture by pulling her arm away and stepped in front of the glass podium. A man in the crowd broke through the wall of security and grabbed her ankle. Allison jerked her foot out of his grasp and she stumbled backward. She hopped several times to regain her balance and knocked over the glass podium. It fell to the floor and shattered, the sound of its crash barely audible over the roar of the crowd. As she bent down to grab her shoe that had fallen off, the uniformed man grabbed her around the waist and dragged her off the stage, out the door and into to the hallway.

Outside the auditorium, Allison shook with fury over being manhandled off the stage. She swore as she pulled herself from the man's grasp, her face flaming with anger.

"What the fuck, Mitch! We need to finish that!" Angry voices thundered through the closed wooden doors. "We need to make them understand!"

"They do understand, Ally. Too well." Mitch Campbell rubbed his tired eyes and sighed heavily. "We can't keep this under wraps any longer."

"No shit!" she said, angrily. "That was the point! That, yes, clearly there's a problem and we're taking responsibility for it."

"Yeah, but twenty to thirty percent? Those numbers are unrealistically low. Even you know that. We're lucky they didn't storm the goddamn stage and lynch us."

"Twenty-six percent is the actual number of break-ins with proof that directly linked the robots to the scene." Allison rattled off the statistics like a well-prepared speech.

"Spare me your talking points, Ally." He crossed his arms, shooting her a frosty look. "I'm not Joe Public."

She sighed and closed her eyes. "Twenty to thirty percent was all I was authorized to say." Unlike her perfect posture on stage, her shoulders fell forward and the sparkle that shone in her eyes just moments ago had vanished. As Mitch watched her disengage from public-relations mode, he put his arm around her shoulder and led her away from the auditorium.

In the safety of Mitch's office deep within the Defence side of the NRD building, she sat in a chair opposite the desk. Mitch poured her a scotch from a bottle inside a cabinet behind his desk. She took the glass and shot back the amber liquid in one swallow as Mitch watched in surprise. He refilled her glass and sat down beside her. She stared at the contents as she swirled the liquid around in the glass.

"Mitch, I love my job here, but I can't take much more of this. If I continue to be the face of this scandal, I'm going to get run down in the street. I'm already getting death threats."

CHAPTER 3

August 16, 2097

"You're here today to be briefed on our current situation." Mitch Campbell stood ramrod straight behind the aged, wooden podium at the front of the Tactical Strategy room. Located in the deepest sub-grade level of the Defence side of the National Research and Defence building, the minimalist briefing room lacked the frills and pomp of the showy Burton Auditorium. Bare concrete walls set the tone of the windowless dungeon; the sunken stage at the front of the room looked up at the theatre-style seating.

Brilliant lights beat down on the thick grey wool of Mitch's uniform. He felt a bead of sweat trickle between his shoulder blades as a flash of heat washed over him. Something shiny at the corner of his left eye caught his attention. Light reflecting off the long row of service medals hanging on his jacket distracted him momentarily as he took in the room before him. This room and his position behind its podium were as familiar and comfortable to Mitch as an old pair of jeans. Today, he stood in the same familiar spot and felt none of that comfort. Anxiety grew in his chest; wound up like the elastic band in one of his grandfather's antique toy airplanes that he ached to play with as a child but was never allowed to touch. His nerves were stretched as he surveyed the faces of the high profile individuals seated before him. He sipped water from a glass hidden from view on a shelf inside the battered podium—the room was dry and already he could feel the words catching in his throat. His heart beat like he had just sprinted a half marathon and nausea bubbled in his stomach; but nothing in his composed, authoritative appearance indicated he felt anything but calm and confident.

The room seated eighty-five people, but like so many meetings held at NRD as of late, the room was filled beyond capacity with people standing at the back. So important, so top secret was this meeting that every person in the audience had been stripped of their phones and other communication devices. This temporary communication ban included even the leader of the country, who sat in the centre seat in the front row, along with several other federal politicians, the NRD board of directors and other top city officials.

"Thank you all for coming," said Mitch, with the slightest of nods acknowledging the country's primary political figure. His words were infused with a slight drawl, typical of one who grew up on the east coast. "We all know why we're here, so I'm going to cut through the bullshit and give you the straight facts. I know every single one of you is aware of our situation to varying degrees. Most of you know me but for those of you who don't, I'm Mitch Campbell, Level Seven, Senior Strategist for Black Ops."

Quiet whispers broke out around the room. Mitch took another sip of water from the glass hidden inside the podium. As he did so, he saw a man in the front row lean to the woman beside him and whisper, "Black Ops? I thought they were a rumour. How bad is this?" Mitch set the glass back down and continued as though he heard nothing.

"Most of you are used to seeing Ian in front of you, but that's not going to happen today. I'm not him and I'm not going to dress any of this up with hundred-dollar words, optimistic predictions or how what we have learned will better society. I'm going to tell it like it is. And what it is, is a serious issue that threatens civilization not only in our country but the entire world if we don't eliminate this problem now." Mitch noticed several audience members shift uncomfortably in their seats.

"True, we succeeded where everyone else in the world had failed in creating Artificial Intelligence. With the invention of Artificial Emotional Intelligence, we created a series of robots that could learn and apply knowledge successfully. They make decisions not on 'if' statements or projected outcomes of probabilities, but on gut feelings, emotions and desires. To test the robots in a real world setting, a one-year pilot project was launched. We've nearly reached the end of that year. The results were promising in the beginning but have degraded rapidly, leaving us in our current situation. The robots are no longer under the control of the NRD. Not only have they grown entirely independent of us, but they have launched an attack on the human race in general. The number of functioning robots they have produced is increasing at an incredible rate, making them an extremely numerous and intelligent enemy, and, therefore, highly dangerous. We have troops on the ground downtown as well as other areas at high risk for an attack. At this point, we have a zero-tolerance policy for any robots regardless of whether they are of the AEI or the First-Generation variety. The AEI robots have been reconditioning the older, task-driven First-Gen robots with the new AEI programming."

The room broke into a buzz, this time much louder. Polite whispers were abandoned.

Mitch continued over the din. "We managed to capture one of the top four ranking robots in their army." He produced what looked like a green rectangle of transparent glass from inside his jacket pocket and held it up as the audience fell silent. "This is the robot's hard drive. We've analyzed his behavioural and knowledge data. None of you are going to like what you're about to hear. I'm going to take you through this project from the very beginning so you have the straight facts. Get comfortable. We're going to be in here for a while."

For the next several hours, Mitch took his apprehensive audience through the entire AEI Project to ensure everyone present had the straight facts, not the skewed version the media was spinning. The goal was to develop robots that learned and behaved like humans—to welcome them into society, both socially and economically.

Like humans, each robot would have a job, get a pay cheque, volunteer—become a contributing member of society. For the robots to achieve these goals successfully, four fundamental conditions needed to be met: a power source, shelter, the ability to perform routine maintenance and a purpose.

The first condition, a power source, was met with battery packs possessing a nearly infinite life expectancy. A large deposit of Elevanium was discovered during a routine mine blast in the early 2040s. This super-element, initially a classified, hypothetical secret became common knowledge, eventually becoming the country's primary power source. Historical sources of power—solar, wind and water—were abandoned for domestic use and became the primary export. Elevanium provided a near-infinite amount of energy when harnessed within a compact, maintenance-free battery pack.

The discovery of Elevanium left the government spinning on its head. This alien material was so foreign that it took years for engineers and scientists to analyze and develop it. So limited and sought after, it required more security than anything else in the planet's documented history. To meet the security requirements, Tricity's NRD base was designed as a modern-day fortress complete with an airfield, air and ground combat vehicles and other assorted defensive weaponry.

Several years after its discovery, Elevanium was introduced to the public and it quickly became the primary power source for housing, commercial buildings and city infrastructure. This new energy supply alleviated the extreme strain on the aged and deteriorating power grid. Buildings were retrofitted and equipped with Elevanium-based battery packs. Not long after, smaller Elevanium battery packs were installed in mobile electronics, robots and mass transit. By the 2070s, the traditional, lithium-ion rechargeable batteries and those of the like had been abandoned.

To meet the second requirement of shelter, four frosted glass domes were constructed to provide a home for the robots. The domes were located at the rear of the NRD property, away from the airfield and separated from the base by a dense forest.

The robots' living space needs were speculative and the domes were built on the assumption that the spheres would act as a starter home during the societal integration phase. Later, when the robots had found their permanent homes in society, the domes would transition into maintenance facilities. Unexpectedly, the robots preferred living communally and showed no interest in leaving. Their interests leaned toward the academic and they socialized differently than humans. They showed little interest in typical forms of human entertainment, so the pool tables, art supplies, instruments, video games and movies went ignored. Interim maintenance stations covered the main floor of each dome, addressing the third requirement. The stations provided tools and supplies enabling the robots to perform the routine maintenance necessary for them to stay in peak mechanical condition.

The fourth and final condition, purpose, proved to be the easiest task of the project. The response to an advertising campaign launched in Tricity inviting individuals and businesses to participate in the year-long pilot project, exceeded all expectations. The stipulations to participate were that the robots' assigned positions must be overseen by a human supervisor and could not compromise safety. That meant no surgeons, firefighters, police, mechanics or other roles where the job performance of the robot could directly affect humans or property. Although the campaign was promoted only in Tricity-area media, buzz from the pilot project had captured the attention of the entire world. Organizations around the globe begged to be included in the project, some offering more than ten times the hefty price tag to participate. The selected organizations were chosen based on the job the robot would perform—how well it would test the robot's faculties and its ability to learn and apply its knowledge.

Each robot received the same base knowledge: the equivalence of a high school diploma, as well as whatever secondary education a human would require to qualify for that same position. The rest of the robot's knowledge would come from on-the-job training and life experience.

Prior to the release of the robots into the workforce and society, the NRD launched a public service campaign preparing Tricity citizens for what they could expect. TV commercials, air traffic billboard screens, outdoor transit screens and shopping malls were plastered with infomercials showcasing the twenty-two different AEI robot models. Demonstrations in malls, schools, meeting centres and parks showed how the robots would move, behave and interact with people. The robots were designed to communicate like humans through voice, hand gestures and body language. The elastic properties of Alumiflex—the flexible, stretchable aluminum-rubber hybrid that covered their faces like shiny, silver skin—enabled them to smile, frown and express their feelings visually in the same way humans could.

Despite the advance warm up, the first few weeks of the year-long pilot project were rocky. Polls from local news stations revealed the general public's reaction to the new "E-migrants," as dubbed by one news outlet, as wary and untrusting. However, those who employed the robots and interacted with them on a day-to-day basis were over the moon about their new mechanical employees, and many organizations wanted to place orders for more. Schools and hospitals benefitted greatly from the extra help they provided. Adding a robot teaching assistant to a classroom or a nurse helper to the floor of a hospital meant better care. But for some, the concept of free-thinking, independent robots was too frightening regardless of how many security precautions were put in place to ensure the public's safety.

Unbeknownst to the public or the robots themselves, each individual robot's thought processes were transmitted back to the NRD and routed through a program that monitored their thinking for keywords or patterns that could indicate potentially undesirable behaviour. Due to the incalculable amount of data streaming in, only twenty-four hours of data would be saved for each robot. If something in a robot's thoughts threw up a flag, logging would continue until manually reviewed. As added security, the brain hardware of the robot, the central thought processor, contained an additional, super-sized hard drive that recorded five years' worth of the robot's thought processes. If needed, a robot could be collected, powered down and the hard drive could be removed and reviewed, as Mitch had shown during the briefing.

The first two months of monitoring revealed promising results. Flags were rarely raised and when they were, it was a word or phrase taken out of context. On the job, not only did every robot pick up their tasks and responsibilities flawlessly, but they were eager to learn and do more. Reports from their supervisors indicated that the robots enjoyed their work environment and their human co-workers.

In the domes, the robots had developed their own unique culture. Although each robot was programmed with one of the twenty-two personality applications to ensure diversity of character among the group, all robots shared common ideals: enlightenment and improvement of self and the species at large. Every conversation, every task that the robots undertook was in the interest of learning more about the world around them and becoming more efficient in their way of life. In the evenings, they would have long, spirited debates on topics ranging from current events, politics and philosophy to space, time and the meaning of life. These conversations led to questions and speculation about their own existence as a species and the meaning of life was a concept they had difficulties understanding.

By the end of the second month, the project's success exceeded expectations and the NRD began accepting pre-orders from organizations around the globe. Most of society had now become comfortable around these intelligent beings, save for the small percentage of naysayers who vehemently opposed them.

The project continued successfully, though it was not without its problems. While the robots adjusted well to their jobs and society, collectively they had developed several concerns that were brought to the Robot/Human Liaison Department at NRD by the Robot Representative, GammaTron.

GammaTron was the third and the only successful AEI robot in a line of prototype robots. He was deemed male as his personality programming was donated by a man, so he received a male voice to match. Because he was a prototype, he looked different than the production AEI robots. He was physically larger and possessed strength and abilities the production models did not. He looked significantly more aged than the shiny new models; his roughed up, timeworn appearance was the result of being disassembled, modified and re-assembled again. During the AEI Project's development phase, GammaTron had access to most of the base and was encouraged to wander through the different departments, ask questions and learn. He was helpful, astute and easy-going. People treated him like the base mascot—the symbol of success claimed by the project's cynics to be unachievable. Already familiar with the names and the faces around the base, he was a natural choice to appoint as the head of the robot community and to oversee the domes.

A growing wave of discontent consumed the robot community like a flash flood. Not being able to determine their purpose in life left the robots frustrated, further compounded by the lack of control they possessed over their own existence. They resented being treated like vehicles from an assembly line, being churned out only to meet demand as it arose. The robots felt commoditized and it insulted them. The NRD computers dedicated to the filtering and monitoring of the robots' thoughts crashed from the spike of flagged thoughts and the corresponding influx of recorded data. This discontent marked the first robot-human conflict and the NRD chose not interfere immediately. Instead, they watched to see how the robots would handle their concerns.

GammaTron watched unhappiness spread like a virus through his community. Together, he and the other robots developed a series of proposals that they felt were fair compromises and GammaTron presented the ideas to the NRD. The first request proposed the robots assume operation of the Robot Recycling Depot, created years ago in an attempt to keep discarded robots out of the landfills. The AEI robots regarded the discarded First-Gen robots as their predecessors and felt that they should be a part of the end-of-life process for their deceased ancestors. The second request was to manage the repairs of any robots that became damaged. Like humans, it was not uncommon for a robot to be involved in an accident requiring medical or, in the case of the robots, mechanical attention. The third and final request proposed a plan whereby the robots would assume the manufacturing of future AEI robots. Resounding global demand for these uber-intelligent robots was common knowledge, as was the hundreds of thousands of pre-orders flooding in from all over the world. In order to have the required number of robots ready to ship by the end of the year-long pilot project, the robots knew that production would need to start soon. As members of their species, the metallic collective felt it was their right to create these robots.

All three requests were met with resistance within the NRD. While nothing in the robots' behaviour to that point had indicated they could not handle, or would improperly handle, these responsibilities, the NRD felt that to agree would relinquish too much control too soon. The request was about to be denied when Ian Turner, the man who pitched, sold and managed the AEI Project, made a case on behalf of the robots. He proclaimed to the NRD board members and stakeholders that they had been given a fantastic opportunity to showcase the project's sustainability to the world. A denied request would send the robots and the world the opposite message— that the robots were not to be trusted. The publicity generated from such a negative message would certainly tarnish the project's reputation and its future success. Ian recommended giving the robots production responsibilities, but set restrictions on the materials and quantities. He proclaimed it would be a good show of faith and would speak volumes for future robot/human relations.

The robots were pleased with the decision and transition of the three operations began immediately. The restrictions placed on production levels, although not a surprise, were viewed as a slap in the face to the robots. Despite that, they chose to focus on the victories they had attained. All supplies and materials required to produce more robots would be procured and managed by the robots, with the exception of the Elevanium, which remained stored at the NRD base under heavy security. The robots knew that Elevanium security was an issue on which the humans would never budge and chose not to press the matter at this time.

Production began on the first batch of robots. During assembly, GammaTron noticed a part he had never seen before being piggy-backed onto the central thought processor. He reviewed the schematics and could not find the small, coin-shaped part anywhere in the original design. When he questioned the production robot affixing the supplemental piece to the CTPs, the robot informed him that one of the NRD humans had delivered amended specifications.

After disassembling this new part in his office, GammaTron discovered it was a transmitting device that sent data back to the NRD labs. The discovery sickened him. His human co-workers, the people he had trusted, were spying on the robots' private thoughts. He removed the back of his head and inspected his own CTP at the base of his skull and saw that he, too, had the transmitting device. Devastated, he reassembled himself and sat unmoving in his office for hours, mulling over what he found and what it meant. He felt betrayed and violated, but what he felt most was disrespected; like he had never truly been seen as an equal at the NRD. He felt like an object—a gadget to entertain people when it suited them, only to be dismissed or passed off to someone else when they became busy or disinterested.

After much contemplation, GammaTron decided it was best to keep his discovery to himself and continue adding the part as instructed. He knew there would be an uproar if the other robots found out, which would undoubtedly draw unwanted attention. He decided to resolve the issue on his own and bring it to the others' notice after the fact.

GammaTron's solution took the form of an electronic information jammer that interrupted the NRD's receiving system. The jammer disabled the receiver so the data from each of individual robots could not be collected. Instead, the jammer fed fake data on a loop, shuffled on each repetition so the monitoring program noticed nothing unusual.

Able to think freely without fear of throwing up flags, he then discussed the matter with the others. As expected, they were outraged. GammaTron had always enjoyed the time he spent with his NRD co-workers, even after most of the robots had grown weary of the humans' simplicity, oppressive nature and hunger for money and control. However, his discovery forced him to reconsider everything he thought he knew about humans.

The NRD was pleased with the progress the robots were making. Routine quality control visits at the domes revealed the robots ran a tight, efficient operation. As the pilot project entered its third quarter, it continued to exceed all expectations. Accolades for the NRD's accomplishments were received from around the world and the robots were regarded as the finest example of human innovation to date.

Incensed by the attention the humans received and the credit the NRD received for the project, the robots' resentment continued to grow. As determined as humans were to create a civilization of artificial life that would integrate seamlessly into their society, the robots became equally hung up on having been created as creatures of convenience for humans. The focus of conversation in the domes shifted from enlightenment and self-improvement to changing their role as a species within human society.

GammaTron's trust in people all but disappeared after discovering the transmitting device inside his own head. However, he had not completely written off society as a whole the way the other robots had. On many occasions, the robot community made him aware of their opinions on humans and insisted that he should begin forming a resistance. GammaTron had always been able to keep the other robots in check, but that changed after watching a documentary on the AEI Project from concept to production, as told by Ian Turner. The two-hour documentary extinguished any lingering feelings of loyalty GammaTron felt toward humans like a lit match in a windstorm. GammaTron had worked closely with Ian many times on during hardware testing for the AEI Project, and again as the Robot Representative to the NRD. GammaTron knew Ian to be a friendly man who could always be counted on to stand in the robots' corner. But in the documentary, GammaTron was blindsided by Ian's arrogance. He attributed the robots' genius solely to the ingenuity of human invention. He talked about the robots as objects, not equals. When asked if he had any concerns about the robots rebelling against the human population as they had in most science fiction stories, he laughed, quipping that the robots were smart, but not *that* smart.

Provoked by the documentary, GammaTron conceded his pro-human position and, with the help of his inner circle, began planning a resistance. He knew their numbers were too small and that they would need to increase their population exponentially before they could take any kind of stand.

In the months that followed, GammaTron played a double agent; performing his regular duties during the day and spending his evenings planning feverishly with his co-conspirators. The robots' productivity never ceased. With no need to sleep and driven by passion, the robots worked around the clock to produce as many robots as resources would allow. Obsessed with the propagation of their species, they had soon created the entire year's worth of orders. The shiny new robots waited in storage, finished but lifeless. With Elevanium heavily controlled by the humans and dispensed each month like treats to a dog, they had no way to power them.

GammaTron's plan to grow the species was stonewalled by dwindling resources, so he looked to the greatest source of robot parts at their disposal—the Robot Recycling Depot. Here, discarded robots were disassembled and sorted. Elevanium battery packs were removed and returned to NRD for auditing. The scrap metal was melted down, the plastics were shredded and the reclaimed resources were sold to manufacturers to be repurposed into new vehicles, building materials or clothing. With the AEI robots starved for an army, the Robot Recycling Depot had become a veritable goldmine of reusable parts. Thousands of robots were salvaged, repaired and reprogrammed so the older, First-Gen robots could run an AEI personality that would allow them to learn and think like genuine AEI robots. Like the first batch of AEI robots, they waited lifelessly; their missing Elevanium battery packs the final ingredient needed to bring life to the new descendants.

The robots' attention turned to the wealth of Elevanium in buildings, vehicles and homes. This observation, though logical and inevitable, left an uneasy feeling in the pit of GammaTron's proverbial stomach. Any building with electricity—homes, office buildings and apartment complexes—was powered by an Elevanium-based battery pack system. The Elevanium powering just one home could give life to a fleet of robots; a small office building or an office tower downtown could power up potentially hundreds or thousands of times that amount.

GammaTron worried about the potential fallout of stealing Elevanium from public places if the heists were improperly planned or executed. Any conspicuous behaviour on the robots' behalf would draw unwanted attention and the robots could not risk having their strategy exposed prematurely. Stealing Elevanium from an office building or retail stores would not go unnoticed. Taking it from a residence would be easiest; however, the risk of humans getting injured greatly increased. While this fact seemed to not bother the other robots, GammaTron knew that if humans began getting hurt by robots, it would surely spell the end of any freedom for their species.

GammaTron put a call out on the underground market, spreading the word of top-dollar payment for any Elevanium battery pack large enough to power a single-family dwelling or greater. No questions asked. The response far exceeded GammaTron's estimation. He had no idea where it came from and, as promised, no questions were asked.

Despite the forward progress, many robots grew restless. Within a few short weeks, they had amassed enough Elevanium to power an army large enough to easily storm downtown and steal the Elevanium from the largest office towers. GammaTron struggled to control a number of fanatical robots; the extremists were no longer interested in maintaining a low profile. One robot broke into a shopping mall during the day to steal the Elevanium battery pack from the mall's power centre. Discovered before he could access the utility room, the robot fled and a dramatic police chase ensued through the suburbs, all caught on video by several roaming news camera drones. The fleeing robot left a trail of destruction in his path—smashed cars, damaged property and terrorized humans, all televised for the world to see. Three people were left dead from a freeway accident when a police car involved in the chase collided with a car, ramming it through the guardrail where it plummeted to the road below. The robot was finally apprehended with the use of an E-cannon, a gun that delivered an electromagnetic pulse that overloaded and destroyed the robot's circuits. This marked the first outward display of overly aggressive behaviour by a robot and the NRD was blindsided. No unusual flags had been thrown up in weeks.

The rogue robot's thought processes were reviewed and analysts were surprised to discover none of the robot's thoughts or brainwave activity showed it had operated outside set tolerances. This inconsistency between the robot's behaviour and its mundane thought patterns led the analysts to believe the robot's transmitting system had been altered and launched an investigation into the status of the transmitting systems. The result of the investigation revealed nothing unusual—the transmitting hardware inside the robot functioned properly as did the receiving equipment on the NRD side. What the task force failed to find was the jammer GammaTron had hidden among the numerous satellites on the roof of the NRD building. Increased security and additional inspections of the domes revealed nothing unusual. The robots had completed their annual production schedule early, but without the Elevanium, the finished, lifeless robots waited in storage. The invoices for materials supplied were on target for new builds and the Elevanium supply remained in check.

To ease increasing pressure for more aggressive approaches by a growing number of malcontents within the robot community, GammaTron searched for other low-risk ways of obtaining more Elevanium. He assigned small missions that saw small numbers of robots go out at night, stealing Elevanium from empty or abandoned warehouses where the missing Elevanium battery packs would go unnoticed. This pleased the robots; they saw forward progress and were able to participate in their cause.

Within months, the robots had grown their army to numbers that surprised even GammaTron. Much to the general robot population's frustration, these surplus robots had to remain in hiding. An increased number of unemployed robots roaming around the city would not go unnoticed and would raise questions. In addition, many of these robots were assembled with parts scavenged from the recycling depot and had irregular appearances; some looked downright scary and grotesque. Many robots had mismatched limbs, like two left arms or legs of different height and limped or walked improperly. Some were missing an eye, an arm or their protective covering, leaving their inner workings exposed to the elements.

In the wake of the destruction left by the rogue robot, NRD board members leaned on Ian Turner, the brilliant mind behind the AEI Project, to launch a deeper investigation. Ian agreed wholly, but his promised investigations were always delayed due to various unforeseen circumstances—sickness, deaths in the family and a stint of short-term disability from a mysterious undiagnosable illness. Nearly a month had passed before Ian could be pinned down. The public's confidence had been shaken by the incident at the mall and the deaths that resulted. Investigative journalists fuelled the concerns of the public by reporting a string of break-ins at abandoned warehouses.

GammaTron was brought in by the NRD and his loyalties were questioned. Officials at the NRD wanted his privileges suspended but instead agreed to keep him on a short leash—the robot had never given any reason to shadow his integrity with doubt. He had always acted diplomatically and in the best interest of the two groups he represented.

The reputation and goodwill of the AEI pilot project plummeted. In a matter of days, the public's approval rating of the robots dropped from eighty-seven to sixteen percent. The world once again watched every move the robots made but this time out of fear.

GammaTron sensed his control over the disgruntled robots was slipping away. The depth of their obsession obscured the light of logic and reason. General consensus was that the humans suspected them and that the jig was up, so effort spent on stealthy behaviour seemed illogical. Robots began breaking into any building at any time of day if the odds of a successful grab were high. Like humans, robots possessed a strong sense of self-preservation and feared having their circuitry cooked like the robot from the mall. At night, the robots broke into homes and office buildings. People were afraid to stay in their houses for fear the robots would break in, and anti-robot activists began questioning whether human evacuation of the city was necessary.

Stories about the robots and the break-ins battled for top headlines daily on the news. Every night, panels of experts weighed in on the matter. Everyone suspected the robots, but no proof had yet been produced. Other than the rogue robot, no robot had ever left evidence or was caught on camera despite the many news camera drones flying around the city looking to capture anything amiss. The NRD declined any comment and the focus of the controversy changed from the break-ins to the echoing silence from the NRD. No comment was issued because they were scrambling, trying to assess what had happened, where it went wrong and calculate the damage. The silence of the government agency reignited old international controversy. The debate over Elevanium and who should control it, again hit the spotlight of the global political arena. Over the previous fifty years, the mere presence of Elevanium nearly sparked several wars and countless attempts had been made to steal it. Other world leaders felt the super-element should be divided and distributed around the world rather than remain under the sole control of a single country—especially one already so power-rich.

When it became apparent Ian could not be relied upon, Mitch Campbell received the assignment of investigating the implosion of the pilot project. The biggest break came to Mitch three weeks after his appointment to the inquiry when he was called into the office at 2:00 A.M. to review some fresh evidence. One of GammaTron's co-conspirators had been caught breaking into one of the hangars. Security overtook the robot, powered it down and pulled its hard drive.

The hard drive contained more than enough information for Mitch to assess the gravity of the situation. He learned how many robots were in operation, how many had been converted from First-Gen to AEI, how many were powered up, hidden in storage and how many waited, unpowered. He found maps and dates of their plan to storm downtown. Mitch also found a reference to a plan seeking access to the largest Elevanium supply of all, the Elevanium vault beneath the NRD compound. However, the robot had no details of that plan. Mitch suspected GammaTron compartmentalized information in different robots to protect their secrets should a robot be captured.

"I stand before you today, telling you that the AEI Project, as it currently stands, is a failure. The number of robots being produced is increasing so rapidly that by the time we have a campaign planned and ready to execute, it will be too late. The time for a combat response has passed and preparation for an alternative approach must start immediately. If this base is attacked by their army, we *will* lose control of the Elevanium supply. That isn't an estimation, that is a guarantee. If we lose that, any chance of resolving this problem will be lost. If the robots seize control of our Elevanium, there will be enough robots to alter human life on this planet. Our final hope to gain control of this situation rests in an unconventional strategy. I have gone over our proposed strategy with my colleagues, as well as some of the greatest combat strategists in the country and possibly the world. They agree that Operation TimeShift is the only plan of action that will work. That plan will go into effect in two weeks. You will be updated with further briefings on the operation later this week. Any questions?"

The crowd remained stoically composed. Multiple people raised their hands and voiced their questions simultaneously. Before Mitch could answer, a man entered the steel doors at the back of the room and hurried toward the sunken stage, taking the deep steps two at a time. The man's arrival seemed to disrupt the audience's polite disposition and voices grew louder and questions shot out around the room. The man handed Mitch a brown folder. Mitch opened it up and took out the blank white sheet of paper it contained. At his touch, words appeared. As Mitch read the paper, the words scrolled upwards to reveal more text and a map. Several blinking red dots appeared on the map. For the first time, Mitch's imperturbable composure cracked and he looked up at the younger man with terror in his eyes. The words on the sheet disappeared as he placed the sheet of paper back in the folder, closed it and handed it back. Mitch ran his hand through his military cut, salt-and-pepper hair, turned toward the crowd again and hammered his fist on the podium to regain control of the room.

"I would like to amend my initial estimate of deployment from two weeks to one."

Mitch accepted his appointment to the AEI Inquiry with assurances that Ian Turner would cooperate fully and lend his experience to the investigation. Mitch knew Ian by reputation only. He knew Ian had been the driving force behind the NRD's first attempt at Artificial Intelligence, the AI Project. When that project failed spectacularly, Ian convinced the NRD and private funders to invest more money in the AEI Project. Mitch admired Ian's drive and passion and was impressed with his ability to stay true to his vision when everyone else believed him to be crazy. After digging further into Ian's past, Mitch learned that Ian had enjoyed a successful career, starting first as a brilliant computer and robotic scientist and later as a visionary for practical new technologies. His foresight, perseverance, drive and determination revolutionized projects he was involved in, rocketing his career to great heights. That same perseverance, drive and determination were seen by many as stubbornness, hunger for power and blind arrogance, which prompted people to question his motives and ethics. Ian had a reputation for being untouchably brilliant despite countless personality clashes over ideals and several unproven allegations around stealing co-workers' work. His many successes made him sought after not just nationally, but internationally as well. His charisma and ability to rally employees were unparalleled and many believed he could convince a person rescued from three months stranded at sea to turn back for a dip.

Only days into the inquiry, Mitch began to feel uneasy about the vibe he was getting from Ian, who kept claiming unavoidable meetings and appointments. Mitch continually fought for scraps of Ian's time. Ian avoided Mitch like a bad date—never returning phone messages and missing meetings. On the afternoon of the third day, Mitch caught Ian leaving his office early, jacket in hand. As Mitch probed Ian for access to online files and prototype specifications, he watched Ian grow increasingly uncomfortable—the man's face paled with each question and his foot tapped a rapid staccato on the floor.

The following day, Mitch returned to Ian's office to pick up where they had left off, but no answer greeted Mitch's knocks. Fed up with Ian's erratic and counterproductive behaviour, Mitch stormed into the office beside Ian's, startling its occupant by snatching the antique, steel-footed coat rack and ramming it through Ian's glass door. The safety glass shattered into tiny, pea-sized pieces that clattered to the floor. Ian's office had been cleaned out.

Somehow unsurprised by Ian's sudden departure, Mitch continued his inquiry and it quickly became apparent that Ian had been withholding information on the project long before any issues had arisen. Ian had dismissed many of the concerns brought to his attention regarding the robots' safety. Mitch's interview with Spencer Grayson—a whiz kid in the Neural Programming Division—had been particularly enlightening. Spencer informed Mitch of his concerns regarding what he felt were inefficient testing simulations and how he was reassured by his director that Ian had deemed them sufficient. What concerned Mitch the most was that only a few of the twenty-two models had been tested for safety before being put into production for the pilot project. Mitch was no technical genius, but even he knew that launching untested robots into society was beyond irresponsible—it was criminally negligent.

Mitch appointed Spencer to assist him with the inquiry and, within days, Spencer had Mitch up to speed. After two weeks, the pair got the breakthrough they needed with the capture of GammaTron's co-conspirator and Mitch gleaned enough information to fully understand the severity of their situation. If drastic measures were not taken immediately, Tricity's problem would quickly become a national and international crisis. They consulted with several Defence strategists and each one drew the same single conclusion: deploy a massive attack on the robots and try like hell to keep the damage contained to one city if it was not already too late. Mitch refused to accept their recommendation, confident a better plan must exist. A combat response would destroy much of the city and the number of human casualties would be high. But one thing remained clear, something had to be done immediately, or the city would be crippled and unable to take action.

The idea came to Mitch over lunch. He chuckled out loud and pushed it from his mind, blaming desperation and lack of sleep. Later in the afternoon, the idea resurfaced. Feeling silly but driven by utter desperation, he humoured himself and sketched out some ideas. The pieces seemed to fit together though he had no idea why; the concept was far-fetched and unrealistic. He shared his idea with Spencer, worried the wonder-kid would think he was crazy, but to his surprise, Spencer agreed. If executed properly, the damage around the city would be reversed, the flaws in the AEI Project would be fixed and the world's bitter feud over Elevanium would be resolved. It would require absolute precision and leave no room for error. The question was, with a solution so unconventional and dangerous for those executing it, would anyone risk their life for it?

CHAPTER 4

August 17, 2097

Logan and Asher Grayson sat opposite Mitch's desk and watched as the superior officer from their sister division flipped through a stack of papers. The curiosity of the two men was piqued. Never had they been called into a meeting with a level seven from the Defence branch, and on a Saturday, no less.

"You two have been selected to participate in an extremely high-risk Defence operation," said Mitch. He picked up his pen and twirled it around his fingers.

"I'm sorry?" asked Logan. He sat up straighter, certain he had misheard. The brothers looked at each other with matching expressions of surprise.

"As you know, the NRD is having some issues in regard to the AEI robots. We have a plan to resolve it, but it's complicated. For the most part, this operation is voluntary. Only a few individuals have been hand chosen. You two are specifically required, and I hope you'll both participate."

"What could we possibly bring to a Defence operation? We have zero combat training," said Asher.

"We need you both for several reasons, but mostly because of your familiarity with the AEI Project."

"Well, I'm with you so far but, I don't see..." Logan trailed off.

"I'll explain the operation first, then you've got four hours to decide if you are interested in participating," said Mitch. He elaborated on the plan but stopped when he came to the part that would involve the two brothers. He looked appraisingly at the two men, hoping they could be what he needed. He sighed and continued. "Your role as part of Team Three, is to go back to the year 2095 and help rework the AEI Project as it develops."

Logan and Asher looked at each other like Mitch was mad, but they both knew better than to interrupt a senior level seven from the Defence branch of the NRD.

"This operation is unlike anything the NRD has ever undertaken before. It is an unprecedented solution to an unprecedented problem. Are you interested in hearing more about what your roles would be?"

The two men nodded.

"Excellent. First off, I know that all you guys on the Research side are airy-fairy about the chain of command, but in Defence, observing rank is what keeps people alive. I need to know that you'll respect your lead and follow orders without question, no matter who he or she may be, no matter your relationship."

Both brothers considered this an odd statement and silently wondered who the lead was. Logan suspected a build-up like that meant there was a good chance it was his nightmare of a boss, Delaney Levitt. He shuddered at the thought of a six-month dedicated mission with her and wondered if signing up would be a mistake.

"Sure, I can lead your second team," said Riley. She sat opposite Mitch's desk with one leg slung over the chair's arm. Her flushed face matched the red apple she held, having been pulled from the gym, mid-routine. She bit into the apple as she flipped through the coil-bound document Mitch had given her earlier.

"It's pretty risky." Her eyes darted quickly back and forth as she skimmed over the pages. "I mean, from the research you've done on him, it seems like if anyone knew the answer, he would. God knows no one else'll touch Elevanium."

Mitch nodded. "I know. It's a real long shot. If he doesn't know, you guys will have to figure it out on your own."

"Let's hope it doesn't come to that. I'm no scientist, Mitch."

"I know, but I need someone I can trust. You've never failed me before Rile, and I'm banking on the fact you're not going to start now. We've got a retired researcher from the Dominion Project from back in the fifties and a research assistant from the Liberty Project in '72 who have agreed to help us. But it's in a theoretical capacity only. They outright refused to help conduct any experiments. So, it's all theoretical, and it's all we've got."

"So what you're telling me is, after all these years of researching, testing and experimenting with Elevanium, the best that we could get is a guy who worked with it fifty years ago and some research assistant from the seventies? Nobody with any recent experience volunteered to help?"

Mitch shook his head. "Nobody with any relevant, hands-on experience will agree to talk about it, let alone be in the same room as the stuff."

Riley rolled her eyes.

"Do you work well as part of a team?" asked Mitch.

The pale-faced man stared as if Mitch had asked the question in a foreign language. "Uh, alright, I guess." He shifted impatiently in his seat.

Mitch jotted some notes on the notepad sitting atop a thick and battered employee file. He looked up at his candidate again. "What motivates you?"

A thin smile grew on the man's narrow face. "Money, sir. Money motivates me. Speaking of which, what kind of coin are we talking about for an op of this magnitude? And why are we wasting time with these pointless questions? I know you need me because no one with my skills has even applied, so you can save the charade."

Mitch stared back at the man for whom his dislike grew with every passing minute. It was true. Clint Nelson was right.

Clint continued before Mitch could speak. "I mean, if I go, I'm really getting your asses out of a jam, so what's in this for me?"

Mitch wanted to reach across his desk and strangle the man, but instead, he smiled and set his pen down. "Your salary will be quadrupled for the six month period you will be away. There's also a bonus, contingent upon successful completion of the project."

Clint leaned forward in his chair and eyed Mitch. "How much?"

"This is a very dangerous mission and your lead has told me you've gone through a lot lately. Are you sure you can handle the pressure and isolation of this op?" asked Mitch.

Lexi's frosty gaze made the icy air billowing from the air conditioning vent above Mitch's desk feel like a warm tropical breeze. The chilly air blowing down on her did nothing to cool the fire his question ignited within her.

"With all due respect, sir, did my lead give you any indication that the quality of my work has been less than what he's come to expect from me?"

"No. In fact, he said the opposite, that you've been extremely dedicated and putting in more hours than are requested of you."

"Then I don't understand the motivation for your question, sir."

Mitch hesitated. He knew he was dancing close to the line of inappropriate questioning, but he had to be sure that the team he assembled was healthy. Mitch rarely got involved in the personal lives of subordinates, but one weak link with the best of intentions could pose a dangerous threat to the entire team and the mission. With no room for error and no do-overs, he could afford no loose ends.

"This is going to be a long and possibly complicated mission, and I need to make sure that everyone who applies is doing it for the right reasons."

Lexi looked searchingly at Mitch, mentally daring him to say what he really wanted to. He gave away nothing, so she pressed him. "And what are the wrong reasons?"

"To run away from your problems…"

Shocked by her own daring, Lexi cut him off. "I'm not running away from my problems, sir. My problems are pretty much dealt with. Sure, yeah, a change of scenery would be great, but if you want to know the real reason I volunteered for this, it's the same reason that I joined the NRD in the first place; because I want to make a difference and make this world a better place. Can you think of a better way of doing that right now?"

"So, you've heard the details and you know the stakes. This op is pretty dangerous," said Mitch, "and I can't tell you how happy I am that you volunteered for it. Still, I would like to know what motivated you?"

The natural blond highlights in Finn's copper coloured hair caught the light and glowed. Finn looked thoughtful for a moment. "I love this country, Mitch. What we're doing here isn't too different from what we do on a daily basis. I'm doing this to save our country."

"I love to hear that kind of dedication. I wish all people carried that same patriotic spirit," said Mitch. "Welcome to Operation TimeShift."

August 19, 2097

Mitch opened the gate and hopped off the otherwise empty speedwalk platform and strode through one of the open aircraft doors of B Hangar. Behind him, he heard the humming of the speedwalk as it zipped away, summoned to some other location on the base. As he entered the cavernous aircraft hangar, he spotted Jake at the back working with some of the new recruits. As he walked toward the back, he took in the buzz of activity around the hangar. Parked in the furthest aircraft bay was an INV-66, an enormous stealth plane that dwarfed everything and everyone around it. The plane shone like the polished chrome rim of a classic car and its semi-circular shape resembled a boomerang with stubby arms. Although its four hydraulic landing pods were set in the down position, the feet of the craft hung at waist height as if the plane was suspended above the ground by an invisible crane. One of the rear legs lay on the ground beneath the aircraft surrounded by tools and other parts of the landing gear. An aircraft mechanic working on the plane stood on a ladder, his top half inside the compartment into which the landing pods retracted during flight. Bay Two appeared empty at first glance, but when Mitch looked again, he saw a pair of legs standing on a ladder that leaned at an unnatural angle. The disembodied legs were visible, however, the portion of the mechanic's upper body inside the compartment had vanished inside the invisible aircraft. Mitch recognized instantly that, similar to Bay Three, Bay Two also housed an INV-66. Repairs were being made to its invisibility shield. After realizing this, he noticed the moving, holographic orange and black caution band reading, "CAUTION: IN-VISIBLE CRAFT" that hovered around the rectangular perimeter of the repair bay at waist height.

Mitch walked through the empty Bay One and saw to his left seven white Hummingbirds—small, manoeuvrable crafts modelled after their helicopter predecessors.

Mitch approached Jake and his recruits but hung back, not wanting to interrupt. Mitch knew from personal experience that new hires could be a handful. Desperate to prove themselves but having no real practical knowledge, recruits were like puppies, eager to please but always underfoot. Jake and his three apprentices in their crisp, grey overalls gathered around the open engine compartment of one of the NRD's armored hover vehicles.

"Now, I know you guys have studied these in school and having solid theoretical knowledge is good, but you won't learn more than when your hands are dirty. Who can tell me what these vehicles are primarily used for?"

One recruit snapped to attention. "The APHV, or All Purpose Hover Vehicle, is the most commonly used multi-purpose vehicle in the military because it leaves no trace and is completely silent. They're particularly useful for recon missions because they essentially make no sound while in operation."

Jake smiled. He liked new recruits. Their energy inspired him in a way the first day of school had when he was a boy. On the flipside, they sucked the life out of him with their errors and constant questions.

Jake looked up and saw Mitch standing by his office door. He backed out from under the hood and waved in acknowledgement. In that fraction of inattention, one of the recruits had grabbed something under the hood and all three leapt back as a blue liquid sprayed across their faces, shoulders and chest. Jake looked back and saw one of the recruits holding in his hand the cap to the primary heat sink coolant reservoir. His apologies were barely audible over the expletives being yelled by the other two.

"I'm sorry! I forgot it's under pressure!"

"You idiot!" yelled one of the other recruits, wiping the sky blue goo off of his neck with his sleeve.

Jake watched the young men frantically wipe the glowing slime off their faces and necks with any rags they could find, clean or dirty. Seeing their grimy faces made him chuckle. "Okay, I think that's enough for one day." The three recruits rushed to the industrial sink, washing their skin until raw.

Mitch chuckled as the recruits cleaned up. "Fresh from the academy?"

"Yeah, about three weeks ago," said Jake. "Despite what you saw, they're actually a pretty smart bunch. They've got promise."

Jake knew it was no coincidence that Mitch had appeared in his shop. He thought he had given Mitch his answer by not giving him an answer. Lately, decision by indecision had become Jake's favoured method of decision-making. Sometimes doing nothing until the urgency had passed was the easiest way to make a decision. Jake closed the hood of the APHV, turned his attention to Mitch and wiped his hands on the faded red rag hanging from a side pocket of his grey work pants.

"I noticed you didn't get back to me," said Mitch.

Jake shook his head. "I couldn't make up my mind." He tossed the dirty rag into the used rag bin and grabbed a clean one from the neat stack at the back of his workbench. "I'm not really sure of anything these days."

With his recruits gone, Mitch watched Jake transform from an affable teacher into the withdrawn and depressed man he knew Jake had become. Mitch knew what he had been through over the last several months and felt sympathy for him. "I thought it would help take your mind off of things."

Jake said nothing and shrugged. He turned to his workbench and began putting his tools away.

Mitch refused to give up without a fight. "You know, it's not too late. I want you on this op, Jake. I need your expertise for one, and, two, it might give you time to heal. You'll be off-base and out of the city for six months. The change of scenery might do you some good." Mitch took a wrench out of Jake's hand to get his attention. "Jake, you're one of our best leads and you have a strong mechanical background. You can fix anything, even if you've never seen it before. I need that ability."

Jake looked at Mitch for a moment, unsure of how to respond, then stared at the tools on the workbench and crossed his arms. He knew Mitch was right. He knew a change of scenery was exactly what he needed. It was everything else that came with it that he could do without.

Mitch worried he may be losing ground with Jake and knew a hard sell could push him further away. Jake's level of motivation and interest in participating in life had become very unpredictable after the accident, but Mitch needed him badly. "You don't have to answer me right this moment. Why don't we go for a beer later and I'll tell you more about the op."

Jake flipped a roll of electrical tape over in his hands several times and then tossed it onto the workbench. He nodded and looked at Mitch. "Yeah. Alright."

"What do you mean you're going to be late again tonight?" barked the exasperated voice of Mitch's wife from the earpiece in Mitch's ear.

"Sweetie, you know that I'm desperately trying to get these positions filled. And you know what Jake's been through. He's hard to reach right now. I need to take time with him." He fell heavily into his desk chair and it floated backward and bumped the cabinet behind his desk.

"How about taking time with me for once, instead of…" Her angry voice stopped mid-sentence. Silence rang from his wife's end of the phone for a long moment. Finally, she spoke and her voice trembled. "Mitch, I'm sorry. I just… I just can't do this anymore. I've spent this entire marriage being the supportive wife while you spend all your time with your true love, work. I thought things were supposed to slow down as you neared retirement so we can start enjoying life. As far as I can tell, the opposite has happened. I never see you and I just can't do it anymore. I'm taking the kids to my parents for a while."

"Honey, please. I'm so sorry, but I can't talk about this now. Can we discuss it when I get home?"

"Mitch, of course you can't talk now because you're always busy. I would talk about it with you when you get home, but you don't get home until I'm asleep, and honestly, I don't want to be woken up to have this conversation. We've talked about this before and you assured me things were going to change. Now with this latest project, you can't tell me a damn thing about it."

"This isn't the first classified project that I haven't been able to tell you about," said Mitch.

"Mitch, there's always a project or an emergency op of some kind. I don't care that it's classified, but this is the first one that the media is having a field day with. Everybody else seems to know more than me. I want more than this, and I deserve more than what you're giving me. You're a great man Mitch, but you're a horrible husband. I'm sorry."

"Honey…" Mitch heard the connection die and knew she was gone.

Mitch heaved a heavy sigh and leaned as far back as his chair would allow. He stared hypnotically at the concrete ceiling, playing the events of the day through his mind and wondered if things would ever return to normal.

CHAPTER 5

August 19, 2097

Jake arrived at the bar before Mitch and chose a booth near the door. He recognized several faces from work but sat down without acknowledging any of them. Only a few blocks away from the base, this bar was a favourite five o'clock hangout for many NRD employees. It reeked of stale beer, and the grunge/country-western motif had aged to the point of becoming trendy again.

As the server arrived at the table, Jake saw Mitch enter the bar and waved him over.

"Wow, you two look like you've had a rough day. And, if that's the case, this is the place you want to be. The longer you stay, the better things seem to get. Well, 'til the morning that is." The server smiled warmly and tucked her tray under her arm. "What can I get you handsome gentlemen this evening?"

Mitch read her glittery nametag, "Ange." He also noticed her perfect figure and how she dressed it to maximize her earning potential. Her short, black skirt showed off tanned, toned legs. A tight, v-neck t-shirt showed off what he assumed to be the two attributes that earned her most of her tips. Mitch also noticed that Jake paid her no notice at all.

"A Kokanee is fine, thanks," said Jake. A burst of laughter from the back of the bar drew his attention to a rowdy group sitting around an oversized booth.

"Same," said Mitch.

"Thanks, guys, I'll be back with those in a sec," said Ange. She spun on her spiky heel and strode to the bar. Within moments, she returned and placed two beers in front of the men.

"I'm going to be completely up front with you, Jake. I need you on this op. I need your expertise with the mechanics, but more importantly, you're good with people. I need the lead of Team One to be reliable, experienced and good at managing inexperienced subs."

"I didn't realize you wanted me to be the lead," said Jake. He spun his glass of beer on the coaster. He shook his head and laughed at the absurdity of the suggestion. "I'm in no shape to be a lead. You know that."

"You were doing great with those kids today," said Mitch.

"Yeah, because at the end of the day, they leave and they're not my problem. I can't be a long-term lead right now, Mitch. I don't have the energy or the patience. I can't deal with people slinging question after question at me because they can't make a decision for themselves. Not to mention the inevitable egos and drama that come with a six-month op."

"I don't think you're giving yourself enough credit," said Mitch, who knew being a lead came as naturally to Jake as swimming did to a fish. "I've got all of the key positions filled except yours, and we were lucky, we got some pretty good volunteers. I don't think you'd have any problems with any of them. They're all good-natured and very dedicated."

Mitch leaned over the table and spoke quietly so neighbouring tables would not hear. "Look, I can understand if you're not interested in doing this. This is a long op, but it's not particularly complicated. And like most ops, a million things could go wrong. But sitting around doing nothing all the time isn't going to bring them back, and the old Jake I know would have jumped at this opportunity."

Jake watched little bubbles float to the surface of his beer for several moments. He sighed heavily. "You're right."

Hope sparked in Mitch's chest like the flick of a lighter; he needed Jake more than he wanted to admit. Jake had been Mitch's top pick for this role and there were no second choices. If Jake declined, Mitch would need to promote one of the subs within the existing team. Even though they were all hard workers, none of them had the experience to lead a complex, six-month op. Generally, people clamoured to participate in ops but no one wanted to come near this one, which left several key redundancy positions unfilled. Every person who applied was accepted.

"You're right," said Jake. "About all of it. I can't live like this forever. They're gone and they're not coming back. Dragging my ass around like this isn't doing me any good, and my wife would kick me in the ass if she could see me. It's just hard to remember how to live sometimes. You kinda forget how to put one foot in front of the other." Jake saw the look on Mitch's face and he turned to look out the window. It was the same expression that appeared on everyone's face when they tiptoed around the topic of his dead wife and children. He knew it was a normal reaction and people were naturally sympathetic. He had probably given that same look to others in the past but now that he was on the receiving end, it was too much. "Tell me more about the op. If I'm gonna commit to this, I should probably know what I'm getting myself into."

"That's a fair request," said Mitch, daring to smile. "Operation TimeShift is a 185-day mission consisting of three teams for a three-part solution. Each team is going back to a different point in time to accomplish a particular goal. When those goals are successfully completed, time should rewrite itself and fix our little problem." Mitch made air quotes with his fingers around the words, *little problem*. "The three teams will then return to 2097, arriving just twenty-four hours after they left, from the present day perspective."

"That sounds risky. Not to mention it breaks about half the time-travel laws." It had never occurred to Jake that the plan would involve time travel. The thought made him uneasy.

"We'll be breaking more than half. Operation TimeShift is being executed in bonded time."

Jake exhaled loudly and swirled the contents of his glass as he processed Mitch's words. Regret flooded him for having told the level seven he would participate. Bonded time was only a theory he had heard bounced around in scientific documentaries as he channel surfed at night. It was something about altering the present day by linking pockets of time together and simultaneously manipulating past events, geography or human interaction in different time periods. Now he wished he had paid more attention to those late night documentaries.

"We have no choice. We can't predict the outcome any other way." Mitch saw doubt growing in Jake's eyes and continued talking before he backed out. "There is logic behind the 'one group, one time period' law. If two groups travelled to two different time periods at the same time, the group farthest in the past could do something to disrupt the lives of the other group."

"Yeah, but I don't see how bonded time will make a difference?"

"At the moment the three teams go back in time, a 185-day window of bonded time will be opened. During that time, the changes each team makes in the past will be bonded together as one change. Is it dangerous? Absolutely. But because the teams are working on completely unrelated tasks, the work they do will never overlap or affect one another until the very last moment. That last moment is the timeshift. It's imperative that the changes each team makes coalesce at the exact same moment in the bonded time window, otherwise, who knows what the results will be. Once the timeshift has occurred, from our perspective in 2097, time will have been rewritten without the problems we're having. Or, that's the theory anyway."

Jake swallowed a few mouthfuls of beer as if the alcohol would tune his brain in better. "Right. Otherwise, if the tasks were done in the regular sequence of time, as history naturally progresses, you wouldn't be able to predict how the first change would affect the other teams making changes. And you got an approval on this?"

Mitch nodded. He set his pint glass down on his coaster.

"So what is each team doing?"

"Well, part of the problem is that the Artificial Emotional Intelligence programming is flawed and it needs to be reworked if we want to salvage the project. Team Three is made up of three robotic engineers who were a part of the AEI Project the first time around. They're going back to 2095 and will reintegrate into their jobs to fix it."

"How are three people going to assimilate into a project where the roles have already been assigned?" asked Jake.

"Actually, it's not as hard as you'd think." Another burst of raucous laughter rang out at the back of the bar distracting the men from their conversation. They looked back at the crowd, huddled around a table in a large booth. "Well, speak of the devil," said Mitch. "There's two-thirds of Team Three right now."

Mitch and Jake watched as Logan Grayson, in the centre of the group, laughed and pointed to playing cards that he and some of the others had stuck to their foreheads. His brother Asher was trying to convince Ange to let him do a Tequila Bomb shot off her stomach.

Jake took in the brothers as he sipped his beer. "Really? That's Team Three?" he asked, one eyebrow arched in disbelief.

Mitch chuckled. "It's not as bad as it looks. They're actually both pretty damn smart. If they got their shit together instead of screwing around all the time, they could actually make something of themselves. But they were chosen not for their brilliance but because of who they're related to."

Jake looked at Mitch with surprise; nepotism seemed out of his character. Choosing those two—especially those two—solely as a favour seemed like a disaster waiting to happen.

Mitch read Jake's thoughts in his expression. "No, it's not like that. Actually, they don't know who their lead is and their lead is even less pleased with their appointments."

"Sounds messy. Who's the lead?" asked Jake. He swallowed the last gulp of his beer and waved his hand in the air to distract Ange's attention away from Asher. Seeing Jake hold up two fingers, she nodded in acknowledgement and made a beeline to the bar.

"Their younger brother, Spencer," said Mitch. "He is their polar opposite. He has concerns that they're beyond anyone's control, but he'll be fine."

Jake shook his head and chuckled. He looked back at the two brothers again and saw they were clearly the centre of the group's attention. "So how are these guys going to go back and insert themselves into a project when the past versions of themselves are already involved? I think people might notice."

"Simple. By sending the past versions of themselves away."

"I think that just broke the other half of the time travel laws."

Mitch shrugged. "I think you're right, but it's our only chance. Desperate times and all."

"What about Team Two? What are they doing?"

"We're going to kill a couple birds with one stone here. As you know, Elevanium has changed our country in a lot of ways. Some of them good, some of them not so good. It's created a lot of problems domestically, as well as internationally. And then, of course, there's the more immediate problem of the robots destroying anything in their path to get to it." Mitch stopped talking when he saw Ange coming their way with a bowl of soy nuts. He resumed when she was safely out of earshot. "Team Two is helping resolve the Elevanium issue. NRD has made a decision to eliminate it."

Jake thought he had misheard. Using Elevanium as the country's primary source of power meant billions of dollars were brought in from the export of domestic wind and hydro-generated power. Getting rid of Elevanium seemed like a very drastic measure.

"I know what you're thinking, but it's the best thing for the planet. How many wars have nearly broken out over it? It's not like there's enough of it to share with the world. Any country that could afford the high cost of the security it requires wouldn't really need it. The countries that do need it can't afford to protect it, and it would be just a matter of time before it fell into the wrong hands. Then we've got a whole other set of problems to deal with. It was a hard decision to make, but the planet will be better off if it had never been discovered."

"So how are they going to get rid of it?" asked Jake.

"Well, that's the question. We're not quite sure yet. Nobody wants to get near it, so to date, nobody's tried to figure it out."

"I've heard people say it's cursed or something, but I wouldn't think that scientists would buy into superstition."

"I agree," said Mitch, "but I don't think I blame them. Too many people have died trying. Consensus is that there's some kind of self-preservation quality about it that we don't fully understand, and no one'll get close enough to it to try to get to the bottom of it. The numbers don't lie. Seventeen dead and seventy-two injured."

"But someone has obviously figured it out to some degree. I mean, it's in all of our homes. People have obviously worked with it enough to commercialize it."

Mitch nodded in agreement. "Nobody who's developed it commercially has died. It's only the researchers who tried to gain a full understanding of it who have died. No real research along those lines has been attempted since that last string of deaths in the seventies."

Jake seemed sceptical and drank his beer. "So you're telling me that fifty years after the discovery of Elevanium, there's not one person who can tell us how to neutralize it?"

"Well, there may be one, but it's a long shot. The very first person to research it, but he died at thirty-eight."

"What year was that?"

"2016."

"That's about thirty-five years before it was actually discovered on Earth. How could he possibly know anything about Elevanium? How would he know how to neutralize it?"

"How good are you with history?" asked Mitch. "A few years after the turn of the century, the International Space Coalition launched a program to seek out other Earth-like planets."

"Right. And that's when they found Key Eleven," said Jake. Everybody knew that. It was in every third-grade science book.

"Owen Taylor was the guy who actually first learned of Elevanium. He named it, in fact."

"Never heard of him," said Jake.

"Well, he didn't get too much credit for the project because he was hit by a bus before he could start compiling his findings. His notes and data were reviewed and compiled by other ISC scientists after his death. He's the guy who proved that parts of Key Eleven had struck Earth by matching light signatures from Key Eleven and parts of other meteors found around the planet. In fact, he thought it was highly likely that part of Key Eleven's core was buried deep in the Earth's crust with the rest of the meteor remnants."

Mitch had researched Owen's work with Elevanium extensively. Owen was the ideal candidate for Operation TimeShift. He had never physically seen Elevanium and, therefore, had none of the bias or superstitious beliefs of the scientists who came after him. Mitch had tracked down Owen's original notes and was impressed with the man's estimations; many of his theories had turned out to be accurate. He possessed a genius-level intuition for Elevanium considering he never had any physical contact with it.

Mitch finished his beer as Ange came with another round. "The beauty of Taylor is that he's extremely familiar with Elevanium and unaware of its bloody history."

"You're risking a lot of marbles on one hell of a long shot, don't you think?" said Jake.

Mitch sighed. "He's the best chance we've got. He's got enough knowledge of the element to know what won't work and what could, and that's more than what we've got at this point. In the interim, we've found a couple of people with past Elevanium experience who have agreed to provide some of their hypotheses. They'll share their knowledge about it, but they refuse to conduct any experiments. They're working with Riley Morgan right now and bringing her up to speed."

"Riley Morgan?" Jake coughed after swallowing beer along with a mouthful of air, having been taken by surprise. He knew that like Mitch, Riley Morgan was in Black Ops. The elite of the elite. She was a Field Op Lead, level five or maybe six. He knew she was young for her level, but if half of the stories that had leaked out of Black Ops were reliable, she had earned her rank fairly. Jake had never worked with her directly, but she ran many of the covert operations that his Mechanical & Infrastructure Recovery Unit picked up after. Although she had been friendly on the few occasions they had met, he had heard rumours that she was a ball buster, expecting absolute perfection and unwavering loyalty from her team. From what he knew of her, she was fearless, had an uncanny intuition and a flawless record of successfully executed operations. Even though this operation was very different from her typical assignments, Jake took a certain amount of comfort in knowing she was involved. Her success rate made the endeavour feel more achievable. "This is a bit of a different assignment for her, wouldn't you say?"

Mitch chuckled. "Yeah, for her this will be like a vacation. But she heard we were in a jam for leads and volunteered. Said it would be fun to do something quiet and low-key.

"So Riley and her partner, Finn, are going back to 2016 to work with Owen for a few months to figure out how to neutralize the Elevanium. Then they'll join up with

you and Team One about half way through for the remainder of the op. The goal for
your team is to excavate diagonally down and expose the Elevanium deposit so they
can execute their plan to neutralize it."

"How many people are on Team One?"

"Seven, including you."

Jake's eyes widened. "Yeesh. That can't be enough."

"That's all that volunteered," said Mitch, "but you'll be adequately staffed. You just
need enough people to keep the machines and a camp running. I mean, that covers
your key positions and when Team Two shows up, you'll have a few more bodies.
Sure, a few more people would have been nice, but realistically, all of the heavy work
is done by the machines. A smaller team means you just can't run them twenty-four
hours a day and that's fine. I want you guys to take your time and make sure the job
is done right. Six months will be more than enough time. Plus, one of the members is
an excavation expert. The others, while willing and eager, are not trained for this kind
of mission. Some of them will be out of their element, and this drilling equipment
pre-dates all of us."

The men discussed the finer details of the project as the evening dwindled away.
The crowd at the back grew rowdier. Jake looked back to see the Grayson brothers
playing Rock-Paper-Scissors for the last shot of tequila. One of the twins held a
lemon, the other a salt shaker. Jake chuckled as he watched the two, reminded of
his youth. He guessed the men to be only a few years younger than himself, but he
felt decades older. At forty-two, he was by no means old, but the nights of bars and
partying had long since passed him by.

CHAPTER 6

August 20, 2097

The following morning, Mitch made his rounds, touring preparations for the op. Seeing things come together buoyed his spirit. His meeting with Jake the previous evening had given him renewed hope that this mismatched group of people just might be able to pull off these seemingly impossible tasks. However, not an hour later, the positive vibe had all but evaporated when he arrived home to find that his wife had made good on her promise to leave and take the kids. The house stood quiet as a tomb and without his family there, it might as well have been one.

Mitch's attention was coaxed back to the present by a buzz he could feel in the air as he followed up on the teams and their prep staff. The whole NRD base seemed to hum with excitement and activity. This phenomenon was common during the preparatory phase of any operation. Planning for ops typically had a motivational effect on staff, even if the people preparing were largely in the dark in regard to details. The particulars of this op were limited to only a few key people with top-level security clearance: Mitch, several NRD top executives and the team members themselves. The international community was leaning heavily on the NRD to get the mess cleaned up before it became a global problem. That being said, Mitch doubted anyone would feel assured if he announced to the entire world that twelve brave men and women were going back in time for advice from a man who died nearly ninety years ago. Then, based on that advice, they would change the course of history, possibly de-create hundreds of thousands of people and alter the lives of billions. After the operation succeeded, time would be re-written, and no one would ever know the problem had ever existed, except for himself and the twelve people on the operation. It was a desperate solution for an extreme problem that grew worse each day with each new report of lost ground and brazen invasions. The robots were multiplying, and if they continued to collect Elevanium at their current rate, it would spell disaster for the whole planet in a very short period of time. Mitch shuddered to think about what could happen if the robots got their hands on the entire reserve of the super element. Every person in the world was now a stakeholder in this project. Failure was not an option.

It seemed to Mitch that the week leading up to the operation was the fastest, yet longest of his life. Days flew by in a blur of activity. The members of the three teams spent their time cramming in as much knowledge and skills as possible. They refined their strategies, recalculated their risks and developed contingency plans for their contingency plans. While the teams prepared themselves mentally, Mitch fortified the base for an attack by the robots. Thanks to the insight gained from the captured robot's hard drive, he knew of their intent to invade. But at the time of the robot's capture, no date had been set. Had they decided since? Mitch had no way of knowing, so he prepared as if the attack was coming tomorrow. He had ordered more troops and heavy artillery from other bases around the country and added a second and third redundant power source for the security system that protected the Elevanium vault. Twenty-four hours a day, troops patrolled the grounds. Still, he questioned whether it would be enough.

With little more than eight hours until the launch of the operation, Mitch found a moment's peace to attempt sleep on the couch in his office. Mitch set the alarm on his watch for 3:00 A.M. but he tossed and turned for several hours and shut the alarm off before it chimed. He sat up on the couch and rubbed his eyes, grateful that from his perspective, the entire ordeal would all be over in a little less than thirty hours.

Mitch grabbed a metal lockbox from his desk and walked up the fire exit stairs to the second floor. Judging from the darkness he saw through the glass office walls surrounding him, he was alone on the floor. Halfway down the hallway, he approached the time travel control centre. The room's double glass doors slid open automatically at Mitch's authorized presence and he entered. The room's low ceiling and the absence of windows to the outdoors gave the space an enclosed feel despite being quite spacious. Large monitors were projected at the back, illuminating the darkened room enough for Mitch to see without the overhead lights.

The time travel control centre contained monitoring stations and tracking equipment that managed the time travelling system. Each monitor displayed different maps, clocks, countdowns, count ups and status reports that monitored the status of time travellers. Dominating the centre of the room was a thick, round metal base with a large glass capsule fixed above it. Suspended in the heart of the glass enclosure was a large, polished cube of Elevanium, the size of a soccer ball. Rotating slowly, the cube floated in the centre of the glass tube, glowing unnaturally white despite its partial transparency.

This particular piece of Elevanium now held more importance than the rest of the country's Elevanium supply combined. This glowing, gleaming stone played an instrumental role in the success of Operation TimeShift. The energy harnessed from this stone powered the time travel system, and by extension, the bonded time generator. If the robots stole this piece of Elevanium before the moment of the timeshift, the system would shut down and the open window of bonded time would collapse. The effects would be catastrophic. With no bonded time, the changes each team had been sent back in time to make would not be connected and the resulting effects could damage their present situation in ways Mitch could not begin to imagine.

Mitch walked over to a wall where a bank of black nylon backpacks hung on individual hooks. Fourteen of the packs were missing: one for each member of the op, plus one for the astrogeologist in 2016 so they could take him to meet up with Team One and one for a spare. Mitch smiled at Riley's penchant for preparedness.

Mitch set the metal box down on the nearest desk, removed one of the backpacks from its hook and unzipped the main pouch. He reached inside, felt around and found an oversized watch. He removed the watch he was wearing, slid it into his pants pocket and strapped the cumbersome watch in its place. Mitch brought the backpack over to the bank of projected screens at the back of the room and tapped the holographic menus several times. He entered the number forty-seven— the number embroidered on the front of the backpack—and a loading bar appeared with a message that flashed, "Activating time travel device." The message blinked several times and then Mitch heard both the pack and the watch beep simultaneously. Pack number forty-seven appeared on the screen at the bottom of a list showing the fourteen other activated packs.

Mitch turned his attention away from the screen and unzipped the front panel of the pack. The fabric panel folded forward to reveal an elaborate control panel. Mitch changed several of the values on the touch screen interface and set the destination time to the current time, minus two seconds. He zipped up the pack, slid his arms through the straps and picked up his metal lockbox. Mitch stepped into the middle of the room. With the box lodged under one arm, he awkwardly held up the arm wearing the bulky watch. As he readied his index finger over the white button on the watch's face, he inhaled deeply. He had never travelled through time before and, although he planned to go just two seconds back in time, he still felt his heart race.

He knew the importance of this precautionary step. When the timeshift occurred and time rewrote itself, the entire mission—the problems with the robots, his life as he knew it—would be re-written. Just as it would be for everyone else on the planet. He knew that by sending himself back in time, even just two seconds, it would be enough to remove him from his natural time sequence. When the timeshift occurred and time rewrote itself along with everybody else's memories, he would still retain all of the knowledge and memories he possessed at this moment. There was a good chance that his new, post-timeshift reality would no longer match these memories.

Was it dangerous? Absolutely. Did he like the idea? Absolutely not. He was putting himself and his family at extreme risk. After the timeshift, he would need to investigate his life to see how time had rewritten it. Would he be married to his wife? Would he have kids? Would he have the same friends? Will he have even been born? Mitch pushed the thoughts from his mind. How his life was going to change as a result of the timeshift was beyond his control. He knew if he dwelled on it too much, the endless speculation could drive him mad. Instead, he chose to hope for the best. He was doing what needed to be done for the sake of the men and women of Operation TimeShift, whose efforts would ensure he and the rest of the world had a future.

Mitch inhaled one last time and unconsciously held it. As he prepared to press the button, a version of himself appeared in front of him, holding the same box. The future version of himself smiled. Mitch stared incredulously, even though he had fully expected to see this. He wasted no time and pressed the white button to initiate his two-second leap back in time.

Suddenly, his perspective on the room changed. He now faced the front of the room and the past version of himself stood in front of him—white-faced with a gaping expression. That had been him, two seconds ago. He smiled at the pale version himself and blinked. The past version of himself had vanished.

August 23, 2097

Carrying three white plastic boxes tucked under his arm, Mitch joined the teams at the deployment site outside one of the aircraft bays of B Hangar. He saw two large, distinct piles of gear and supplies. Members of the three teams milled around the piles, some talking animatedly as they double and triple-checked their lists. Others looked nervous and quiet. Each member wore a black backpack and bulky watch identical to the one Mitch had worn the night before to send himself two seconds back in time.

Mitch called the three leads away from the group to offer his final words. There were no last minute plans or directions. If something had been missed, they would need to figure it out on the fly.

"I forgot about these," said Mitch. He handed each lead one of the square boxes. Stamped into the side of each box was the word, "CUBE."

Riley took the box with barely a glance, nodded in acknowledgement and slid it under her arm. Mitch recognized her game face; he had seen her steely gaze and firmly set jaw many times before as she mentally prepared for deployment.

Jake read the contents on the side of the box. "Jeez. Is this really necessary?" he asked.

"You never know what people are capable of until they're pushed to their limits. Especially on long-term ops. It never hurts to be prepared," said Riley. She thought of the number of ops she had gone on with Finn and knew she would never need to use it, but it was a matter of protocol and safety for both the team and the op.

Riley's matter-of-fact take on the cube took Jake by surprise, and he wondered if she had ever had to use it during any of her past experiences in the field.

"Oh, and Spencer, that's not for recreational use, no matter how tempted I know you'll be." Mitch laughed. He watched Spencer's eyes widen as he read the box.

The three leads returned to their teams after quick farewells, handshakes and well wishes. Mitch addressed the group one last time.

"Alright everyone. This is it." Mitch studied their faces as he spoke. Some of them were smiling and excited, some looked green. The concept of time travel was thrilling in movies but in real life, it unnerved many people, himself included. "I know this isn't your standard op and some of you will be doing things you haven't done before now. But you're all smart and I know that you're all going to do great. Do not get caught, I can't guarantee that we can get you out. Finally, and most importantly, this is bonded time, ladies and gentlemen. There are no do-overs. Good luck teams."

Mitch watched each person hit the same white button on their watch as he had the night previous. All twelve people along with the mountains of supplies disappeared. Realizing he had been holding his breath, he exhaled heavily and stared at the empty concrete where the group had stood just seconds ago. He closed his eyes and took in the magnitude of the op when he heard footsteps approaching from across the hangar.

"Sir?" called the voice. It echoed through the cavernous hangar. "Sir, I'm afraid I've got some bad news. Another power centre has fallen, sir. We've lost power to all city infrastructure on the south-west side."

CHAPTER 7

TEAM 1
YEAR: 1200
TIME REMAINING: 185 Days

Jake Anderson opened his eyes. He had half-expected to disappear into thin air and cease to exist. He surveyed their surroundings. Seven deer stood in front of the group, startled by the team's sudden appearance. The largest deer snorted; a blast of visible breath issued from each nostril. The buck turned and bolted into the bushes. The other six followed, bounding elegantly toward the forest and disappeared into the thick growth.

The scenery looked exactly as the prep team had described it, although more dreary than the image Jake had drawn in his mind. Although fully aware they were arriving in early spring, he had always envisioned a warm breeze, a cloudless sky and a lush boreal forest. In reality, thick, ominous clouds threatened to welcome them with rain at any moment. The woods beyond their clearing contained the various evergreens he expected—fir, spruce and pine with the occasional tamarack—but their muted, winter colouring washed over the forest giving it a dull appearance. Clusters of birch trees were peppered among the pines, their distinctively knotty white bark a stark contrast to their dark-needled companions. Strands of long grass lay brown and matted beneath his feet, damp with snow and weakened by decay.

The clearing in which Jake and his team stood was surrounded by forest with the exception of one corner where the grassy clearing gave way to a rocky outcrop that dropped off abruptly. The forest resumed at the base of the rock face and sloped gradually down toward a lake in the distance.

More noticeable to Jake than the cold, drab surroundings and the pungent smell of decaying grass and leaves was the deafening silence. Sure, he heard the wind, the sound of tree branches tapping against each other in the chilly spring breeze and somewhere in the distance flew a skein of honking geese, but that was all. No traffic. No music. No sirens, no neighbours, no electric humming of various bots, no TV. Nothing. Just him and his six teammates.

Jake surveyed the people for whom he would be responsible for the next six months. They stared at him expectantly and he realized they were waiting for him to issue an order. He felt his chest tighten. *What have I gotten myself into?*

"Okay, everyone. Welcome to the year 1200! Let's start unpacking," said Maya. Seeing that Jake looked a little green around the gills, she dove in, giving him a chance to recover from any post-leap nausea. "Tyler, please confirm the location of the deposit. Let's see how accurate our fact-checkers are."

Tyler pulled a yellow handheld device from his backpack, handed it to Jake and the two men walked east into the forest. Maya watched, perplexed, as Clint left the group and meandered toward the edge of the clearing. Hearing her name being called, Maya focused her attention back on the task at hand and joined her three remaining teammates at the supply container. They unclasped the clips securing the lid to the base and each raised their corner slowly and carefully, fighting chilly gusts of wind as it caught the tall cover like a sail. Once cleared of the contents, they set the lid down in the shelter of the trees at the edge of the clearing. Maya removed a black cylindrical tool from her jacket pocket and held it up to read the screen embedded in the handle. She scrolled through different options, selected COMPRESSION/DECOMPRESSION, then held the tool like a flashlight and pressed a button on its side. A narrow, blue laser appeared from the tool's end, which she aimed at the pile of supplies. The blue beam encompassed the platform and its contents and began to grow. What had resembled little silver sausages only moments ago were now seven full-size, shiny aluminum house trailers. Parked beside the house trailers were two white, cylindrical mechanical monsters. An assortment of neatly stacked plastic crates and boxes covered the remaining area of the platform containing all of the food, supplies, tools and buildings the team would need for the next six months.

Maya Navaros had been assigned the position of Sitespace Manager for the six-month operation. She was somewhat green, having been with NRD for little more than a year, and enjoyed the administrative nature of the position more than she had expected. The home base of a field operation—like a living organism—adapted and changed over time by its environment and the people that lived within it. It could be happy, stressed, tense or under-slept. Despite the satisfaction, like any job, there were parts that left something to be desired. The position had little glamour factor in comparison to other job roles at the NRD and, at times, it lacked respect; some people regarded a sitespace manager as little more than a babysitting housekeeper.

Maya knelt down at her corner of the steel platform and opened a small access panel revealing a series of coloured buttons. She called out, "Clear?" Three voices around the platform responded affirmatively. She pressed a black button which triggered the fall of a crate only a few feet away from where she knelt. The crate fell forward onto a black metal box, then to the wet grass. Its lid popped off, spilling cans and packaged food. On the far side of the platform, she heard a metallic thunk—the sound a metal toolbox would make if it were to fall on the lid of a hard plastic crate. The sound was followed by the unmistakable clattering of tumbling tools.

"That could have been a lot worse," she said as Darren walked up beside her. "Something always seems to shake loose when you release that flex field netting."

"Just be thankful it wasn't the freezer," he chuckled. Darren righted the fallen crate and put the spilled supplies back inside.

Darren Roy, Chief Executive Chef, dug through his backpack for his VersaTool—the same black cylindrical tool Maya had used to resize the supplies. He pointed a narrow beam of red light at a large, olive green crate. The red beam engulfed the entire container and he used the beam to lift the container into the air and away from the other supplies. Heavier than three men could carry, Darren guided the crate easily through the air in front of him. He set it down on the ground beside the platform of supplies, unclipped the lid and heaved it aside. Aiming his VersaTool at the contents within the box, he removed a doghouse-sized building with a white canvas roof. Still locked in the red beam, Darren carried the building effortlessly through the air toward the edge of the clearing and set it down gently. He released the beam and contemplated the building's placement on the brown grass for a moment, then nudged it counter-clockwise, firmly but gently with his knee. Content with the position, he held up his VersaTool to read the display embedded in the handle. He changed the setting from MOVE to COMPRESSION/DECOMPRESSION. A blue light encompassed the small building and Darren backed away as he the structure grew to the size of a single-storey house.

Further down the clearing, Ben crawled beneath the two white, cylindrical drilling machines and released the tethers that anchored the metal beasts to the platform. Like Jake, or perhaps even more so, Ben Bishop possessed an extraordinary ability to fix almost anything. As the head mechanic for this op, he looked forward to the diversity of the machines and systems he would be working with. Everything from complex and ancient excavating equipment to house trailers, alarm systems and whatever else happened to break within the camp. The only problem was, he had never seen these massive, Mole model tunnel-drilling machines before.

Both of the hulking drilling machines hung knee-height above the platform of their own volition. Released from the clips that held them in place on the platform, Ben pushed the first Mole off the platform as effortlessly as if were a helium balloon. After setting it down a short distance away, he parked its twin beside it as Jake and Tyler approached, back from their trek through the forest to locate the Elevanium deposit.

"Have you seen Clint?" asked Jake, looking around the camp.

Ben locked the second massive drill in position so it would not be blown into the trees by the wind. "No, not since we arrived."

Like Ben had done with the tunnel boring machines, Lexi crawled around the platform on her hands and knees from trailer to trailer, reaching underneath to release the clips that anchored the housing trailers to the platform. After the seventh and final trailer, she stood and brushed off her knees and elbows. Her oversized uniform hung on her tiny frame like a little girl dressed up in her mother's clothes. The rolled up sleeves of her shirt were loose and baggy and her pant legs were hemmed. Not a hair over five feet and weighing 105 pounds, none of the standard uniform sizes fit her tiny frame.

Lexi weaved her way across the platform, around the trailers and columns of neatly stacked boxes, careful to avoid smashing her knee on any of the trailers' protruding hitches as she passed. She crouched down at the front left corner of the first trailer, opened an access panel and pressed a button. The trailer rose as if being lifted by an invisible crane. She pressed another button and the trailer's eight hydraulic legs silently folded into the trailer's undercarriage like the feet of a bird in ascent. Standing again, Lexi guided the floating trailer backward off the platform. She hopped to the ground and, with some difficulty because of the wind, guided the trailer to its new home at the corner of the clearing. She pressed another button inside the access panel and the feet returned to their down position. The trailer settled itself gently onto the ground and auto-levelled itself.

After positioning the five other house trailers alongside the first one, Lexi placed the seventh and final trailer at the opposite end of the clearing, so as to have a view of the lake in the distance. The exterior of the seventh trailer matched the first six, though the modified interior featured a control room for the two Moles, affectionately called Mole Control. Here, operators could monitor the large drills from above the ground instead of from inside the cramped control compartment within the machines themselves.

Lexi Grant had an unusually delicate build for a Non-Combat Field Equipment Operator; the nature of the work in this position usually involved a fair amount of physical exertion and manual labour. Simplification tools, like the VersaTool and Mules, did most of the work—the days of excessive heavy lifting were gone, but the job traditionally appealed more to men than it did to women.

In Lexi's first year, she participated in a domestic recon mission to gather intelligence on an international drug cartel. One of her teammates had become violently ill—the operator of a remote-controlled stealth monitoring device—and she covered his position. The device was no larger than a marble with a camouflaging finish that made it nearly undetectable in any environment. It could take pictures, shoot video, take readings and measurements of its environment and transmit the data back to the operator. Lexi flew the device to the coordinates of interest from the safety of the field home base and monitored the area they were sent to investigate. Blowing things up was an adrenaline rush but she loved piloting remote machines and devices that enabled her to do things she could not, like fly or dive deep underwater.

For Lexi, the high stakes of this op made up for the dull nature of the Moles, but it was neither the stakes nor the machinery that motivated her to volunteer for this mission. Tunnel-boring machines were museum artifacts in comparison to the equipment she generally operated. What drew her to Operation TimeShift was the opportunity to take a six-month break from her life. This assignment would be the perfect way to focus on putting things back into perspective.

CHAPTER 8

TEAM 1
YEAR: 1200
TIME REMAINING: 185 Days

Jake joined Tyler and Lexi in Mole Control to help set up. The pair was between conversations when he entered. Jake turned on the fan sitting on the kitchen counter and acknowledged his subordinates with a nod. He disappeared into the small boardroom at the front of the trailer and Lexi saw him emerge with several crates. Jake's presence brought a solemnity to the room that seemed to discourage conversation. Unable to explain why, Lexi felt the need to walk on eggshells in his presence. Jake never initiated conversation unrelated to work and showed no interest in getting to know any of his teammates. A glance from Tyler indicated that he noticed it too.

The large windows of Mole Control revealed a view of the lake in the distance. Jake sighed heavily as he looked out at the tiny slivers of pink from the setting sun as it sliced through the thinning clouds. Movement caught Jake's eye and he watched as Clint returned to the clearing.

Lexi reached in front of Jake to grab a transport pod from the crate sitting at Tyler's feet. She looked out the window to see what had captured Jake's attention. Clint, now wielding a long branch, poked at an abandoned bird's nest high out of his reach in a tree. Lexi shook her head and chuckled to herself. The thought of working with Clint for six months chilled her, worried she may not be able to keep her dislike of him from the others. Her brief encounter with him in the past made enough of an impression on her to know their personalities would blend together like oil and water. Lexi saw the lens of the transport pod was cracked and dug further in the crate to find a replacement. Finding one, she returned to her seat at the control desk opposite Jake and began removing the screws in the pod's casing to replace the broken lens.

Clint strolled casually into the trailer, letting the door slam behind him as he entered.

Lexi tried to ignore Clint's entrance and continued with her work. The cracked lens lay in pieces on the desk and she held up the pod, inspecting the inner workings carefully to ensure no glass fragments had fallen in. "Out for a stroll, Clint?"

"Just checkin' the place out, sweetie pie." Clint leaned over her, blocking out the lights above and casting a shadow over her work. "Do you even know what you're doing with that thing? If that lens doesn't sit exactly straight, the reflector crystals won't…"

Lexi set the pod down, leaned back in her chair and folded her hands in her lap as she looked up at him. "I'm aware, Clint. Thank you." She focused her attention back on the pod, finished her inspection and set the new lens flush on the base.

"Don't cross-thread those screws," said Clint, watching her replace the first of six screws. He leaned over her again.

Seeing Clint's shadow fall on her again, she stood abruptly, picked up the device and left the trailer to work elsewhere.

Lexi knew Clint from her National Research and Defence orientation; a mandatory class where all recruits and new hires learned the NRD's expected protocols, policies and procedures. The difference between Lexi and Clint was that Lexi fell into the "new hire" category. Clint had been ordered to take the course again after having already worked there for eight years. Clint had been an enigma to Lexi. He had chosen a seat behind her on their first day. By the end of that day, she had learned all she needed to know about Clint. What at first she thought were a couple of harmless blonde jokes was his genuine sentiments toward women. No one was immune from his self-righteous and passive-aggressive comments. His temper flared like gasoline on a bonfire, and he oozed a cold negativity that infected everyone around him. By the end of the two-week orientation, he sat at the back of the class away from the others, except for a couple of young male recruits too immature to see beyond his humour.

Watching Clint that afternoon had drained Jake of what little energy he had. After reminding Clint of the things he could be doing, his subordinate begrudgingly selected a small box to unpack and Jake retreated to his trailer. Sealed off from the rest of the world, the silence hammered at his mind. A fan stood at the foot of the bed and he cranked the dial to its highest setting. The anxiety created by the silence dissolved into the whirring sound of the fan motor and plastic blades cutting through the air. He noticed that someone had deposited his bag of belongings on one of the double beds. With a limp, exhausted arm, he dragged the black duffel bag from the centre of the bed and pulled back the zipper. Jake removed a pair of jeans and stared at them without seeing. He forced his gaze to the dresser beside the fan. The task of having to decide what drawer he should keep his pants in felt overwhelming. His shoulders and head fell forward and he closed his eyes, unsure of how it was possible he could feel so much pain while at the same time, feel nothing at all. Jake tossed the jeans aside and they landed on the edge of the chair beside the bed. The pants unfolded as they fell onto the grey carpet below. Heaving an exasperated sigh, he grabbed the bag's nearest handle and dragged it dispiritedly off the bed and onto the floor. The bag tipped sideways and several pairs of socks and a shirt spilled onto the carpet beside the fallen pants. Feeling as lifeless as the socks lying on the floor, Jake crumpled onto the bed and stared out the window. He watched, as if in a trance, as the trees swayed in the wind. He tried to recall any of his reasons for accepting this position and could remember none. He knew he had made a huge mistake in letting Mitch talk him into this. He felt like he was drowning—like he was slowly sinking deeper and deeper into a lake, looking up and seeing the bright surface high above him with no energy to swim.

When Jake awoke an hour later, he felt more energized. He felt guilty for not feeling guilty about how little he had done for his team on their first day and that encouraged him. It was a small step, but a step in the right direction. Feeling something, even guilt, was better than feeling nothing but pain and emptiness.

He exited his trailer hoping no one would be around. The camp was illuminated by the lights Ben had set up and Jake was pleased to find his wish granted—not a soul in sight. He looked at his watch and guessed Darren was serving dinner, so he took the opportunity to tour the camp uninterrupted. As he neared the rocky drop-off at the far corner of the encampment, he stumbled over a knee-high, black cylinder with a glass tip protruding from the ground. Jake recognized the narrow metal post as one of the six sensors that marked the invisible wall that surrounded the perimeter of the camp. He knew there would be one stake at each corner of the camp and two in the forest to contain the upcoming drilling site and the path that would inevitably be worn between the two.

The invisible wall did not keep people out, instead, it acted merely as a warning system to alert the camp if someone unauthorized, human or animal, wandered into the camp. Parameters could be set within the system to broaden or lessen the range of sensitivity. Small animals like squirrels and rabbits could stroll through the camp on a regular basis. However, larger animals posed a real safety threat. Moose, bears, even deer could be aggressive, so the minimum body volume an intruding animal would need to exceed that of a fawn before the alarm would go off. By adding different sensors to the stakes, the modular monitoring system could perform various additional functions like collecting environmental or biological data on unauthorized individuals or animals as they passed through the invisible barrier.

Another sensor was jammed into the ground beside the perimeter sensor. Resembling a chrome hockey puck atop a narrow, tapered stake, four of these sensors surrounded the camp with two more at the drilling site. These WeatherShield sensors generated an invisible dome-shaped shield that blocked out undesirable weather conditions. Neither wind, rain nor snow could penetrate the invisible barrier. Hail would bounce off the barrier like an invisible tent. A howling rainstorm could rage on, but the area inside the protective shield would be calm and dry. Buildings or towers contained inside the dome would be safe from lightning. Although the shield protected the area from all forms of weather, it could not protect against debris. If the wind blew grass or leaves into the camp, the detritus would penetrate the shield and fall harmlessly to the ground.

Jake walked across the uneven rocky surface to the cliff's edge and looked out over the forest below. In the darkness, he could only see the line where the trees ended and the sky began with a sliver of lake between. With his VersaTool set to LIGHT, he shone the tool like a flashlight down the steep drop and saw various platforms and rock ledges that could function as steps to climb down to the forest below. Jake hopped down to the first ledge, sat and rested his elbows on his knees. *I wish you were here Brit, you would have loved this place,* he thought. At the thought of his wife, he slid wireless earphones in his ears and cranked up his music.

Jake lost track of how long he had sat on the ledge. He felt several large drops of rain land on his head and arms, awakening him from his thoughts. As he climbed back up the ledge, the rain became more steady. He felt it stop as he passed through the WeatherShield barrier. He turned back to look at the effects the shield had on the rain. Under the camp lights, he could see the water bead down the side of the invisible boundary like rain on the window of a car. He stuck his hand through the barrier and felt the drops land in the palm of his hand.

CHAPTER 9

TEAM 2
YEAR: 2016
TIME REMAINING: 185 Days

With no balance and no way to stop himself from falling forward into the path of the oncoming bus, Owen braced for the hit, but it never came. As quickly as he had found himself in the street, he felt himself being jerked backward. The corner of the bus's bumper clipped his foot as it flew by, the driver honking madly. Owen stumbled back awkwardly; his mind unable to process what was happening. The arm that saved him tried to steady him, but he toppled over backward. He expected to feel hard concrete, but instead, something soft broke his fall. Owen lay flat on his back and the blue sky above him became obscured by the faces of concerned people looking down at him. Time then seemed to stop as if to compensate for the whirlwind he had just experienced. He could hear his heart pounding a rapid tattoo in his ears and he stared without seeing, paralyzed by fear, relief and confusion. In those brief milliseconds that had just passed, he had come to terms with the fact he was going to die, but then he had not.

He heard a woman's voice beneath him swear and realized he was lying atop the person who had saved his life. The people around him who, just moments earlier were too caught up in their own world to let him through, helped him to his feet. He adjusted his jacket as someone slung his messenger bag over his shoulder and brushed him off. Owen turned to thank the person and winced in pain as he put weight on his right foot. The pain evaporated when he caught a glimpse of the woman who had saved him. Collecting herself by the bus shelter a few steps away was a woman unlike any he had ever seen before; the perfect mix of rugged yet feminine. She seemed deeply concerned about her backpack. Owen watched as she inspected the outside of the pack quickly then opened a zipper on the front. From where he stood, the bag's contents were obscured but her shoulders fell with relief at the sight of whatever was inside. She smiled warmly at the man with her, revealing perfect white teeth. The man who accompanied her looked even moreso relieved. She zipped the pack, slid her arms through the straps and pulled her long, dark brown braid out from between her back and the bag. Not a strand of hair hung out of place. She was average height with a slender but wide, athletic build. He worried that she may have broken something or sustained bruised ribs at the very least, but her muscular frame appeared miraculously uninjured, with the exception of a gash on her forearm. Her outfit seemed unusual to Owen; more like a uniform than something a woman would wake up in the morning and choose to wear. She wore a black fitted canvas vest over a dark grey t-shirt and her matching pants resembled something a SWAT team member would wear. The man she stood with wore a matching outfit. *They must be a couple*, he thought. *Tourists maybe?*

The woman held up her arm to inspect the cut from which blood had now trickled to her wrist. Owen saw something in the cut catch the sun then cringed as he watched her extract a jagged piece of glass. She scowled at the glass and tossed it into an open garbage can two bus benches away with barely a glance. Her partner took a water bottle out of his backpack, wet a tissue and handed it to her. She took it impatiently and wiped the blood off her arm quickly and distractedly as if this was wasting valuable time. She looked up at Owen, who, as she did so, realized he had been staring.

"You alright?" asked the woman.

"Uh, yes. Thank you." He nodded awkwardly. "Sorry, I'm a little lost for words."

Owen tried desperately to keep the pain in his foot from showing on his face as he limped toward the pair. He was very aware that the woman had just plucked a shard of glass from her arm and seemed to feel no more pain than had it been a tissue from a box.

Her redheaded travelling companion smiled. "All in a day's work." His thick Scottish accent took Owen by surprise.

"You're Owen Taylor, right?" the woman asked.

Owen was thrown by her question. He knew he had never seen this woman before; he would never have forgotten that smile or her electric green eyes. He looked at the pair with a puzzled expression. "Yes, as a matter of fact. I am."

"Perfect. We were looking for you, actually," said the woman.

Owen smiled. "Well, I have to say I'm glad you found me."

Her face softened as she smiled. "I believe that. Is there somewhere we can talk?"

"Sure." Owen hesitated. "Have we met before?"

"No, sorry, we haven't met. I'm Morgan. Riley Morgan, and this is my partner, Finn McLaren."

Riley shook Owen's hand with a firm grip. She pulled him in close and whispered to him quietly. "It's crucial that we talk. It's about national security."

Owen was not surprised to hear that someone wanted to discuss something involving national security, though he would not have phrased it with exactly those words. His most recent project with the International Space Coalition required clearance far and above what most high-ranking NRD officials would be granted, but nothing was a matter of national security, *per se*. While it was no secret that he was being outsourced to ISC, the details of the project were confidential. Owen guessed the pair were from the central NRD office and wanted to discuss security protocols or a changeover in contacts.

"Is there somewhere we could speak privately?" asked Riley.

"Yes, absolutely. We can use my office. It's only a few blocks from here." He pointed down the road, then felt foolish. "But you probably knew that already." Owen limped as he walked with his two visitors. Every step shot a lightning bolt of pain through the top of his foot.

Owen entered the foyer and signed his two guests in at the security desk. The security guard gave Riley and Finn each a plastic visitor card with a clip at the top. Owen dug through his bag and found his ID badge. He glanced up and saw Finn tuck the badge into his pocket. Owen noticed Riley watch him as he clipped his badge onto his shirt pocket and then she did the same while elbowing Finn, who then pulled the badge out of his pocket and did the same. Owen thought it seemed like bizarre behaviour, but little of his morning had been typical, so he dismissed it. He led Riley and Finn down the main hallway past large offices, through a metal door that revealed a dimly lit concrete stairwell. One of the ceiling lights flickered, giving the stairwell an ominous feel.

"It's not as dodgy as it looks, I promise," said Owen, looking over his shoulder at his guests. He stopped at the third door on his right and used a key to unlock the door. "Geology used to be a large, happening department, but it's become a bit of a old dog over the last few decades. Much of its budget has been allocated to newer and flashier fields like biodiagnostics and nanotechnology. Something about 'larger return on the government's investment' and 'standing out on the world's stage.' I used to have an office on the second floor, but about eight years ago I got downsized. It's not that bad; the basement's rather quiet."

Owen limped behind his desk, tossed his keys onto a shelf and slid out of his jacket. He forwent the coat rack at the far side of the room and instead slung his jacket over the back of his chair.

"So, what can I do for you guys?" asked Owen as he sat. He slid his laptop out of his messenger bag and set the bag neatly on the floor beside the desk.

Riley and Finn seated themselves in the two chairs opposite the desk. Riley, who Owen had gathered by now to be the more senior of the two, spoke first.

"Owen, we need to discuss the progress you've made on the Key Eleven light signatures you've been cross-referencing for the International Space Coalition." She had specifically left out, *"and we're here from 2097,"* planning to jump that hurdle later.

"Oh," said Owen, completely surprised. He had not expected anyone here to have this level of knowledge about the project. He knew that no one at the NRD but himself had been read in on his mandate, including his boss and his boss's boss. Only he and a select few people at the ISC knew he was working on light samples specific to Key Eleven. Unsure of how to handle their request, he proceeded vaguely. "Are you looking for a preliminary report of my findings? I was under the impression that I had a couple of months still to file the reports."

"No, we're not here in that capacity," she said. "We're here to help you with it."

Owen frowned, finding this news highly unusual. It seemed counterproductive to throw new people into a project like this part way through. Even more peculiar was that no one at the ISC had mentioned this to him. "I wasn't aware I was teaming up with anyone on this. Who's your contact on this? Have you been briefed?" Owen tried to piece together what they were telling him, but he was finding it difficult after the morning's events. He could still feel his body buzzing from the massive adrenaline surge. "In fact, I'm sorry, but I don't even recognize you guys. What office do you work out of?"

The two guests shared a look. "We do work for the NRD, but not right now," said Riley, hoping he would get over this last hurdle quickly. She looked at Owen with her straightest expression. "We do work out of this office, but in the year 2097."

As part of her research in preparation for the operation, Riley had learned everything she could about Owen Taylor's shortened career. She knew he had been employed by NRD for over fifteen years and was one of the few astrogeologists on staff; the only one in Tricity. His work was less "astro" and more "geologist" than a person with the same title employed by an organization with a more comprehensive astronomical component. He was one of a small number of experts in his field worldwide.

Riley also knew the project Owen was currently participating in for the ISC was an extension of the first project he had been hired to work on. Again, he had been selected for this project over a handful of others around the world who shared his specialty because of his extensive knowledge of astronomy. It had not occurred to Riley until seeing family pictures, art and sports medals, that behind Owen the astrogeologist was Owen the person. She had been intrigued by his career and impressed by how much he had accomplished in fifteen short years. But now, having met him this morning, he intrigued her as a person.

Trained to observe everything, Riley noticed several things about Owen that did not seem to add up. She took in every detail of his office while he had settled in at his desk. Floor-to-ceiling shelves were lined with neat rows of organized books and binders, with the exception of two. One shelf displayed a collection of rock samples, trophies, several plaques and awards, all covered with a thin layer of dust. The shelf above contained more personal items. Two picture frames—one containing a recent photo of Owen and an older gentleman sitting in kayaks, thoroughly soaked. The frame next to it held a faded, yellowing photo of a young woman holding a toddler. The other shelves overflowed onto the floor where binders, folders and boxes of rock samples lay in neat stacks. Topographical maps of South America were affixed to another wall. A painting of three canoes resting on the shore of a secluded lake hung above a small fridge. Hanging off both sides of the painting's frame were several dusty cycling and tennis medals.

Owen and his office space intrigued Riley. *He likes order. Makes sense,* Riley thought, *he's a scientist. He's definitely involved in his work, but no recent awards. Is that because he doesn't feel the need to show them or has he been less active in his career? No recent athletic medals... Feeling his age? No, he just got hit by a bus and walked back to the office. Must be too busy. Maybe more pressing priorities? Kids maybe? No...there's no pictures of kids and there's dust on the photos of the only two people he cared enough about to frame. The woman in the photograph? Easy. Mother, deceased. The man? Probably father. Alive? Dead? Hard to tell, photo's pretty recent. He's a very attractive man, smart, too, but no ring. No ring mark. No pictures of any other family or friends. Odd...*

Owen stared across his desk at the beautiful woman claiming to be from the future and said nothing. He blinked several times while he tried to make sense of what she had just told him. He smiled, thinking surely it was a joke, but neither guest laughed. He looked from Riley to Finn, as if waiting for him to give some kind of visual cue that would confirm that she was indeed joking—a twitch in the corner of his mouth, a crinkle around his eyes—but Finn remained as stony-faced as Riley and this made Owen uneasy. Neither of them said anything. Riley leaned back in her chair slightly and crossed her ankles, her posture as perfect as a dancer.

"I'm a bit confused," said Owen, finally. "Is this a joke? I don't really get it." He chuckled nervously. He felt uneasy but then realized obviously, clearly, this was a joke. They were very convincing, but there was just no possible way they could be from the future.

Riley and Finn laughed with Owen for no better reason than there is just no easy way for a person from the future to explain this fact to a person from the past without sounding utterly ridiculous, and laughter was better than other reactions.

Riley pressed forward. "Owen, I know this is a lot to take in, but we really are from 2097. I know you don't believe me, and I know it's a lot to take from two strangers you've just met. It's a long story and we'll explain it all. But what I need you to understand right now is that we've come here because we need you."

Owen's laughter died instantly and he eyed the pair with distrust. He wondered who these crazy people were that his director at ISC had sent him to work with, that was, if they really were sent at the request of the ISC. Owen's suspicion of the pair grew rapidly. "I don't understand. You're obviously not from the future, so let's move on with the project."

Riley fought an unexpected urge to talk louder and more slowly as if that would make him understand. She side-stepped his question and continued.

"There's a problem in 2097 and you're the only person who can help us. Here's my identification key." She unzipped the main compartment of her backpack and retrieved her keys. The only similarity between what she called keys and what Owen considered keys to be, was that they hung collectively on a key ring. Her keys were a series of narrow metal rods of different shapes, all the length of his pinky finger. She selected a hexagonal key and let the others dangle from the ring. She held it out for Owen to inspect.

Owen had no patience for people wasting his time or making a fool out of him and, in this case, he felt it was both. Becoming irritated, he took the key from her, thinking it looked more like a hex wrench than a key. He turned it around in his hands. Owen saw the words, "NRD" engraved on three of the sides, but that failed to impress him. "It's a metal rod." Seeing nothing else of interest, he returned the keys to her and as he did so, his eyes fell on the red call security button on the phone sitting on his desk. He decided they had one minute to start making sense before pressing that button.

Riley took the keys back from him. "This is my NRD identification key. It operates, I guess, in the same way this card does." She held up the visitor's pass clipped to her vest. Riley leaned in toward Owen's desk and held the key up in front of her.

Owen watched a light flash from the tip. It projected a three-dimensional holographic image of something that looked like an identification card. The size, clarity and legibility of the projection was equal to that of his computer screen, despite being partially transparent. On the left side, a head-to-toe, three-dimensional image of Riley wearing black military fatigues rotated in place. When her figure completed a full rotation, the image changed to a close-up of her face. After a few seconds, her face switched back to her rotating figure. To the right of her likeness was text. Owen was only able to read "Riley Morgan, Level Six, Black Ops, Field Op Lead" before she removed her thumb from the key and the projection disappeared. Owen was impressed by the lengths to which she had gone to convince him. It was a realistic prop, but at the end of the day, it was still a prop. Time travel only existed in science fiction.

Owen stared at the pair sitting opposite him, expressionless. He tried to find meaningful words but failed. "I'm sorry, I don't understand your intent. You're clearly not from the future." He felt it was becoming time for them to leave and he eyed the red button on the phone again. Calling security would be awkward for everyone involved. After all, they had just saved his life and he had just signed two crazy people into to a highly secure federal building. Calling security would mean a lot of questions.

"I don't really have time for this; I have a lot of things to do, so please let me walk you out. Thank you again for saving me, I did appreciate that." He stood and motioned toward the door. They had seemed so genuine; nothing about them in any way seemed shady or dishonest. He wanted to believe them, but simple logic prevented it.

Riley also stood. Her demeanour was quite calm, Owen noted, considering she was about to be chucked out. "Owen, I know you don't believe me, and trust me, I wouldn't either if I were you, but you need to hear me out. This is more important than you can understand. Please take a leap of faith for a second."

Finn chimed in with his thick Scottish accent. "Owen, we need you to wrap your nut around this because we're not here for a vacation." Finn was a shade taller than Owen, about six-foot-two, but unlike Owen's lean, medium build, Finn was as broad in the shoulders as a rocketball linebacker. "We need to get you up to speed on this and briefed as soon as possible."

A subtlety in Finn's voice gave Owen pause. There was a hint of desperation or, perhaps, helplessness. "If you were really from the future, wouldn't you have brought some more compelling evidence?"

At this, Riley chuckled. There were plenty of ways that she could prove this, but they were concepts so foreign, so fundamentally different from what Owen could imagine, that it would look like trickery. Worse, they could have harmful effects if he did not receive a proper explanation. She thought of something simple like b-loading a book into his mind. However, she guessed Owen would be no more likely to let her put a metal object near his head than he would take a HOP pill to keep him fed for a week. Instead, Riley reached again into her backpack and removed a white, padded and zippered case which he assumed contained a tablet. She unzipped the case and took from it a black rectangular device similar to the tablet he had expected, but with one very noticeable difference. Unlike Owen's tablet, this device had a clear window in its centre, as if someone had cut a large rectangle and replaced it with glass. She held it up for Owen to see. "You want proof? Sit."

Owen did not sit and instead alternated his gaze between her and the device.

Riley smiled. She enjoyed a challenge. She walked behind his desk and stood in front of him. "You want proof, right? Let me see your foot."

Owen remained standing and looked sceptically at the object in her hand. "What is that thing?"

"It's a medical appliance. Please sit and take off your shoe."

Owen stood motionless. The boy inside him wanted to believe so badly, but his adult logic told him that everything about this situation was certifiably crazy. He sighed loudly and rolled his eyes as he sat. He kicked off his shoe, happy to do so as the swelling had made it quite uncomfortable.

Riley knelt on the floor in front of him and gently set his foot flat on the ground. Owen was grateful he had thrown away the first pair of socks he grabbed that morning after seeing a hole in the toe. He leaned forward and watched carefully as Riley held the scanner over the top of his foot. He could see the fabric of his sock through the clear glass centre. A flash of red light illuminated his foot, then his mouth fell open as the transparent centre of the device disappeared and an x-ray image of his foot appeared on the full surface of the instrument. She looked at the x-ray briefly, touched the screen, and the image was replaced by text too small for him to read.

"Ouch," she said under her breath. She looked up at Owen shaking her head. "I can't believe you were walking on that foot."

"Why?" Owen felt foolish but had asked the question before he could stop himself. Although he remained convinced this was nothing but an elaborate act, he ached to know what she pretended to know.

"You've fractured your first, second and third metatarsals." She ran her hand gently, almost caressingly across the top of his swollen foot.

Owen cringed and nodded. "Okay," he squeaked through the pain. "I believe you."

"No worries, though." She put down the scanner, looped her fingers and extended her arms. "I can fix that."

She held the scanner over his foot again and tapped the touch screen interface several times. The x-ray photo disappeared and the clear window reappeared. Owen saw three short bursts of ice blue light illuminate his foot. Within seconds, the pain and swelling had vanished.

"Whoa. What just happened here?"

Riley rubbed the top of his foot again, this time with more pressure. He barely felt it. She motioned for him to stand up. "I fixed your foot."

Owen looked down at her sceptically. "What do you mean, 'you've fixed my foot?'"

"MediScan. Mobile medicine, compliments of the year 2097." She held up the tablet-like device for him to see.

Owen saw the MediScan logo on the top left corner of the screen. She tapped the screen several times until the skeletal image of his foot appeared and she handed the device to him. He saw three distinct lines in three of the longest bones in his foot. Riley took the medical tablet back, knelt down and held it over his foot again to re-run the scan. When it had finished, she passed Owen the device.

Owen looked at the x-ray image of his foot and the black lines that had been there just moments ago had disappeared. A blinking green box on the screen read, "DIAG-NOSTIC NORMAL." Owen shook his head, not sure if he could believe eyes. "No offence, but I'm not entirely sure I believe you."

Riley took the device from him and stood as she zipped the device back into its case. "You don't have to believe me. Put some weight on that foot."

Owen pressed gently on the top of his foot. He felt no pain, so he increased the pressure. He felt nothing except the pressure from his hand. He stood and slowly shifted his weight onto the foot. It felt fine. He jumped up and down on it and then stopped abruptly as the only possible explanation occurred to him. She must have sprayed his foot with some kind of topical numbing agent, and if his foot truly was broken, jumping was going to make it much worse when the numbing wore off.

Riley sensed Owen's scepticism but knew they were on the right track.

"How many people have one of these?" Riley asked, as she pulled a battered-look-ing, cylindrical metal tube with a clear glass end from one of her pants pockets and held it up for him to see.

"A flashlight? Everybody?" Owen looked from the battered black device to Riley. He was becoming impatient again. "I've got two right here in my..."

Owen turned to his desk to open the top drawer but jumped back when the entire desk glowed with red light. He jumped again when it started to rise into the air. Owen looked at Riley open-mouthed and saw her pointing the "flashlight" at his desk. The tool emitted a narrow beam of red light that engulfed the entire desk and the items on it. The desk, with the drawer still partially open, hung a foot above the ground. Owen stood speechless, his mouth agape.

"I'm assuming that you don't see too many of these around the office." Riley looked at Owen, pleased to see him frozen in shock. With the effort of setting down a pencil, Riley lowered the desk back to the floor and released the beam.

"Or one of these?" said Finn. He took a similar tool out of his pocket and aimed an equally narrow laser beam of blue light at the bike trophy on his shelf. The trophy became engulfed in blue light and quickly shrank. Finn picked up the miniaturized award and handed it to Owen. Owen's eyes widened, unable to hide his amazement. He was blown away by the utterly preposterous displays he had just witnessed.

"How about one of these," said Finn, with a smirk. He aimed a fuzzy white light on Owen's chest. Owen's smile disappeared, replaced with a mixture of shock and betrayal. Blindly, he stepped backward, knocking over a neatly stacked pile of binders behind his chair.

CHAPTER 10

TEAM 2
YEAR: 2016
TIME REMAINING: 185 Days

Owen was taken aback. *Who are these lunatics that I've let into my office?* thought Owen. *I brought them here and now they're going to vaporize me!*

"Oh, wait, this is just a flashlight. You said you've seen those." Finn smiled broadly and switched off the light.

"Finn!" snapped Riley, slapping him not-so-playfully upside the head. "Finn is our practical joker. Please forgive him and his poorly timed sense of humour."

Owen's heartbeat slowed to normal for the second time that morning. "Okay, okay. You've got my attention. How did you do that?" he asked, trying to sound nonchalant. He wanted nothing more than to try the light-beam tool. That was no prop.

Riley smiled, happy to have gotten over the hump. "It's a VersaTool, a fairly standard multipurpose utility tool. It does a few different things. It's got a move tool and a compression tool like you just saw and a high-powered flashlight as Finn was also kind enough to show you. Depending on how much you spend on the tool will determine how many options you get, kind of like a Swiss Army knife. The ones we have are NRD-issued so they've got all the bells and whistles." Riley pointed to the different buttons and sliders on the handle of the tool. "You can also heat, cool and cut things." She handed it to Owen. "The move tool is pretty self-explanatory. It allows you to move heavy objects that you might not have been able to do without a significant amount of effort. Just press the button down halfway and you'll see the red laser light… Yes, like that," she explained as Owen aimed the red beam at his chair.

"Now press the button down the rest of the way and hold it." Like the desk had, the chair glowed red. "With the button pressed, the object is locked in the beam, so wherever you aim the beam is where the chair will go. Raise the beam up and it will go up," Owen was a half-step ahead of her, his seat already in the air.

"This is unbelievable," said Owen as he raised his chair waist height. One of the wheels bumped the desk and a pen rolled toward the edge and fell to the floor. Owen moved the chair up and over his desk then set it back down again. It was as effortless as a flick of the wrist. He handed the tool back to Riley. He pushed his questions temporarily to the back of his mind to learn more about the fascinating device. He turned to Finn. "So can you make my trophy bigger than it was? You know, so it looks like I won?"

"Sure," Finn chuckled. He put the trophy on Owen's desk, aimed the blue beam carefully at the tiny prize and increased its size. "Making things bigger is tricky. You need good aim. Aim is less important when you're making things smaller that were already big to begin with. I once decompressed a desk by accident and blew up a room. I was trying to resize someone's CI after shrinking it as a joke, but I got the desk instead. It ended up bigger than the room and I broke the ceiling and knocked myself out in the process," chuckled Finn, smiling at the memory. "It took a bit of explaining to my boss." He looked at Riley with a sheepish smile.

"Decompressed? CI?" asked Owen.

Finn chuckled. In 2097, these concepts were simple and a fundamental part of everyday life. "Compression is when you make objects smaller, shrinking them like I did to your trophy. Decompressing is when you make them large again."

"The CI is similar to what you would call a computer," said Riley. She placed her backpack on the floor and sat down, eager to get down to business.

Finn passed Owen his VersaTool. "Same concept as the move tool but you slide the button as you hold it down. Press the button half way to bring up the beam and aim it whatever you want to compress. When the object glows blue, press the button the rest of the way and then move the slider up or down depending on the size you'd like."

Owen took the tool behind his desk and again preyed on his chair. He repeatedly made it smaller and larger, compressing and decompressing it, and in the process, knocked over another stack of binders. He felt the tool vibrate in his hand when the chair reached its original size. He released the button and the blue beam disappeared. Surprised by the tool's considerable weight, he held it up for a closer look. He saw a display embedded in the handle indicating what mode the tool was in. Using the control buttons beside the display, he flipped through the list of settings. He saw the options that Riley had told him about: HEAT, COOL, CUT, MOVE, METAL DETECTOR, COMPRESS/DECOMPRESS, HEAT SENSOR. There were several others he made a mental note to look at later if he got the chance. He returned the tool to Finn.

"So, let's say for a moment that I believe you." Owen pressed down on the arms and on the seat of his chair several times, ensuring it was still structurally sound after the abuse it had just endured. It passed his inspection and he sat. "How did you travel back in time?"

"Time travel has been around for about twelve years or so. It's highly controlled by the NRD and generally not available for civilian use." Riley grabbed her backpack off the floor and held the front flap open for him to see inside. "These backpacks control a person's ability to travel time. What you see here is the control interface."

Owen studied the complicated looking screens of coordinates, dates, maps and other controls he could not identify. "This is what you were looking at after you saved me earlier. To make sure it was still working after we both fell on it?"

"Yeah, I should've had Finn hold it while I grabbed you."

Riley pointed at different numbers and settings as she explained their purpose. "These are your landing coordinates. This is the date and time you will land at those coordinates. This is your real-time and this is the dimension number you want to travel in. This other stuff isn't too important." She waved off a screen about tag syncing.

"Dimension number?" asked Owen.

"Yes. Time travel now requires mandatory inter-dimensional travel." Riley zipped up the pack, slid her arms through the straps and hopped up to sit on the nearest lab table. "There have been two versions of time travel. Time Travel 1.0 and Time Travel 2.0. Version one, called TT1.0, was replaced by version two, TT2.0, after it was deemed exceptionally unsafe."

Owen's expression became pained. He rubbed his eyes and shook his head. "I think I need coffee. I don't know if I'm going to be able to follow this conversation without caffeine in my system." He ran a hand through his hair. "Does anyone want coffee? I'm assuming you still have coffee in the future?"

"Yes!" said Finn quickly. "I'd love coffee. They didn't let me travel back with a hot beverage. Something about 'for my own safety.'"

Owen listened to Riley as he grabbed the glass carafe from the coffee maker and filled it up at one of the sinks in the lab.

"Time travel is a somewhat recent discovery," said Riley. "Time Travel 1.0 was discovered and tested in 2085, though the method was quickly discarded."

"The testing of time travel nearly destroyed the discovery of itself," said Finn.

Owen eyed the water as it filled the carafe. He suspected a full pot would be needed for this conversation. "That sounds complicated. How could that even happen?"

"It's a fascinating story and it caused a lot of controversy. It is an excellent example of how, even with the best intentions, time travel can cause a lot of damage to the future and it has to be used with extreme caution," said Finn.

"How dangerous can it be, other than breaking your backpack and getting stranded in the past?" Owen poured the water into the coffee maker, turned the machine on and returned to his desk.

"The smallest, most insignificant event, like bumping a guy in the street, could completely change your life as you know it when you return. In fact, it could even cause you to not have been born," explained Riley.

Owen's eyes narrowed. "How could bumping a guy that you don't even know alter your life?"

"More easily than you'd think," said Finn. "Imagine this. You bump a guy on the street, he drops his bag. You pick it up for him and you both exchange apologies. He then runs ten seconds later than he was supposed to. He misses his bus and is late for a meeting that will now hold twenty people, fifteen minutes later than they were supposed to. Those people could have been meeting other people and are now late and may now miss a very crucial moment of their life. Maybe they missed an elevator where they were supposed to meet their future wife. Maybe that woman is your mother or grandmother. Maybe they speed home because they're late, have an accident and die. Maybe that's your father."

Owen took a moment to digest Finn's words. "I guess that makes sense. You're sending small ripples of change through time that could eventually accumulate into a tsunami of change," said Owen.

"Exactly. The next thing you know, people aren't getting born when they should have and, as a result, future leaders may never be born. Well, maybe that's not the best example," said Finn. "But what if one of the Rolling Stones hadn't been born? What if Mick Jagger hadn't been born because of a hiccup in time? It would be a sad, sad loss to antique rock and its culture."

"We try to not alter anything in the past and keep a low profile, interfering in as few lives as possible," said Riley.

"I hadn't thought about it like that," said Owen. "So how does time travel work? How was it discovered?"

"Well, Time Travel 1.0 was discovered by three scientists. Or, that's what two of the scientists, Jason Cortez and Brandon Page, claim. They give credit to a third scientist by the name of Adam Seers," explained Riley.

Owen opened his mouth to ask more questions but could not decide what to ask first. He decided to wait.

Riley continued. "The test team chose the year 2000 because it seemed like a landmark year to go back to for such a landmark discovery. All three scientists went back in time with no problems, except that their coordinates were off by a city block. Instead of landing in an alley out of sight, they materialized in the middle of a busy intersection. Cars swerved to miss them and it resulted in an eighteen car pile-up. It was a real mess. Pedestrians were hit and one car smashed through the front window of a restaurant. They ran over to the most severe collision to see if they could help. As they approached the car, they found the driver crawling out of the wreck, covered in his own blood. He collapsed on the pavement in front of them. They tried to revive him but he had lost too much blood and died."

"And that's where it gets really weird," said Finn, sitting up straighter, his eyes widening. "One of the scientists, Adam Seers, disappeared just as the man died."

"As in, he took off?" asked Owen.

"No, as in vanished into thin air!" said Finn theatrically, waving his hands for dramatic emphasis.

Owen's mouth fell open in disbelief. "Wait, so you're saying a man, this Adam Seers, just disappeared?"

"Yes. He had been de-created, so he vanished into non-existence."

Owen looked at Riley, puzzled. "De-created?" The slurping sounds from the coffee maker had stopped. Listening intently, Owen poured his guests coffee. Finn popped five sugar cubes into the small mug, stirred it quickly and took a sip as though his life depended on it. Riley added milk to her coffee and settled again into the chair opposite Owen's desk.

"De-creation," explained Riley, "is when people, things or events, from a present-day perspective, don't happen as a result of events in the past being altered or 'shifted.' De-created people, things and events are erased from our—that is from a future person's—perspective. Memories get deleted because the events they remember never ended up happening. The other two scientists were dumbstruck by what they just witnessed, but the disappearance of their co-worker could only be the result of one thing—de-creation. So they found the driver's wallet to see who he was. His name was Jon Seers."

"The two men were related?" asked Owen.

"Yes. It was his great-grandfather who had died," said Riley. "So when Seer's great-grandfather died, from the 2085 perspective, time rewrote itself eliminating Seer's grandfather, father and Adam himself because none of them could've existed if Jon Seers had died."

A moment's silence passed while Owen processed this information. "But if you follow that logic, then technically, Cortez and Page shouldn't even know that an Adam Seers ever existed."

"This is true, and an excellent observation. When you travel time, you are plucked out of your natural time sequence. If time rewrites itself and you're not in your natural time sequence, everything in your mind remains unaltered. You remember and know everything you did when you left. The downside is, when you come back, your life will have been re-written. You'll have no idea what's different until you stumble across it. So when we return from this mission, my memories and recollections may be radically different than what my new reality is. I may not have gone to the elementary school I have in my memory. I may not have dated the people I remember dating in high school. I might not be friends with the same people and I have no way of knowing until I call them and they have no idea who I am," said Riley. "Hell, I might not have even been born."

"That sounds like a horrible nightmare," said Owen, taking a sip from his coffee.

"That's why the reason we're here is so bloody important," said Finn. "Now, for the two scientists, when they returned home, no one knew who this Adam Seers was. There was no record of him at NRD and, of course, there was no record of his birth. This is where it gets controversial. Most people didn't believe Cortez and Page's story and thought that the trip back in time had rattled their brains. People who had worked with Seers for years and were very well acquainted with the theory of de-creation didn't believe it themselves, even though they were living a textbook case of it. They couldn't accept Cortez and Page's claim that Seers no longer existed because there was no evidence indicating that he had existed in the first place. It was a real mental loop. It was like people needed proof to believe he existed before they could believe that he didn't.

"Now move two years into the future to 2087. Time Travel 2.0 is discovered and deemed safe," said Finn. He made air quotes around the word *safe*.

"You seem sceptical," said Owen. "So how is the second version better than the first, if it's still so risky?"

"TT2.0 is the mandatory inter-dimensional time travel I mentioned earlier," said Riley. She could see she had lost Owen again with his vacant stare. "It's safe to say that most people in this, your day and age, recognize comfortably that there are three dimensions, width, depth and height. These first three dimensions are intertwined and can't be separated from each other. They are very basic dimensions," explained Riley. "Everything that you physically see exists in what people call 3D or three-dimensional, correct?"

Owen nodded in agreement.

"There are actually more dimensions than most people realize," said Finn. "The fourth dimension is time, or duration."

"Without the dimension of time, things wouldn't *be*. For example, if you're born in 2015 and you died in 2095, you existed in the fourth dimension from 2015 to 2095," said Riley.

Owen silently held up the coffee carafe and Riley and Finn both extended their mugs for a refill.

"It's impossible to travel in only one of the first four dimensions because they depend on your existence in the other three," said Riley. "Us sitting here, right now, are in four dimensions. With TT1.0, if you were to travel back in time, you would be travelling in the same four dimensions that you are currently occupying. Since the first four dimensions are so basic and unprotected, you're left vulnerable to de-creation and other damaging, catastrophic outcomes, just like Adam Seers was."

"And travelling in other dimensions is safer?" asked Owen.

"Well, yes and no. The dimensions beyond the first four start to get more complicated. Mostly because we don't know everything there is to know about them, and not fully understanding them is a pretty big risk in itself," said Riley. "But they seem to have better handling for complex objects. For example, a single four-dimensional object can be put in one of these complex dimensions, say the fifth or sixth dimension."

"Basically, traveling back in time in dimensions five and up preserves your current physical state," said Finn. "When you travel with TT2.0, your body is plucked out of the first four dimensions and wrapped up in say, the fifth dimension. You'll appear at your destination in the past, but you'll remain in the fifth dimension until you return back. When you do finally return to your regular time, you're reinserted into the first four dimensions again. While in that fifth dimension, you are protected from any pre-generational mishaps that could alter you or de-create you entirely when time is rewritten. No matter what happens, you are preserved in your present state."

"So, what you're saying is that right now you guys are in the fifth dimension and are therefore preserved as you are right now. If one of you killed your grandmother, you wouldn't be de-created."

Riley was impressed with how quickly he picked it up. He was proving himself to be as smart as she had expected. "Correct."

"And if you did kill your grandmother, what would happen when you returned?"

"My life would be a mess. Well, actually, I'd have no life. Nobody would know who I was except for people who travelled with me. I would be an Orphan of Time."

"An Orphan of Time?"

"Yes, so if Riley's grandmother did die, time would rewrite itself. Riley's mother and, of course, Riley, would never have been born so there would be no record of any kind of Riley or her mother. Riley would return and have absolutely no identity. No home, no social identification number, no bank account, no job, no friends, no family and so on," said Finn.

"Sounds messy. I can see why you'd want to keep a low profile while you're here," said Owen. He thought he might be getting his head wrapped around the concept of time travel, but that thought alone blew his mind all over again. "So let me see if I've got this. Three scientists went back in time in dimensions one, two, three and four. They weren't protected from de-creation. Great-grampa Seers died. Seers the scientist disappeared. Time was re-written so the people in 2085 didn't know who Seers was because they were in their natural time sequence, so their memories were re-written to exclude any trace of him. Cortez and Page, because they were pulled out of their natural time sequence and, therefore, weren't around as time re-wrote itself, remembered everything. In contrast, if the scientists had travelled in the fifth dimension, Seers would have lived despite his great-grandfather being killed. But, he would have been an Orphan of Time and upon their return to 2085, Seers would be alive, but no one except his two buddies would know who he was."

"Exactly," said Riley. "Also worth noting, if something happened to you while you were travelling time, say you lost your arm or something, you would still be missing your arm when you returned."

"Interesting. So that cut on your arm will be there when you return?" asked Owen.

Riley nodded. "Anyone who elects to travel in time is made very aware of the risks and knows that there are no guarantees. Nothing horrific has gone wrong since the Seers fiasco."

"Do a lot of people travel back in time?" asked Owen.

"Not really. It's heavily regulated," said Riley. "It's used mostly for information gathering purposes, but even then, it's not used that often. There is still too much unknown about it to use it recreationally."

"Well, I have to say that I'm grateful that time travel isn't part of my job description." Owen shot back the rest of his lukewarm coffee and, in doing so, missed Riley and Finn exchanging glances. "So, I'm interested to hear what your operation has to do with me."

"Yes, we need to get into that, but I want to make sure we're not overheard," said Riley.

"You're in luck. Nobody ever comes in here."

"Good. This is not a conversation we want to have overheard." Riley wasted no time and dove right in. "We know that you've made some significant findings in the project that you're working on for the International Space Coalition."

Owen felt his stomach cinch up into his throat. They wanted to talk about his work with the ISC. He had accepted that the pair was from the future and, as crazy as that sounded in itself, it was not reason enough for him to break the very strict nondisclosure agreement he had with the ISC. He had signed his life away when he agreed to work on the project, swearing absolute secrecy. There were serious penalties for breaking his silence including jail time and fines that his grandchildren would still be paying long after he was gone.

Fourteen months previous, the ISC launched a program to search for planets similar to Earth. For years, the ISC's two earth-orbiting telescopes had been circumnavigating the planet collecting information and occasionally shooting brilliant photos of galaxies, nebulas and other celestial bodies. For this project, their attention would be focused on finding life beyond our solar system.

Within months of the program's launch, the ISC received a significant amount of data from hundreds of planets. The two massive telescopes returned breathtakingly detailed images of the surfaces of different planets and nearby moons, meteors, dust and gas clouds. Collected from each planet and its surrounding environment were thousands of unique light reflection signatures—a reading of how light reflected off surfaces of different objects on the planets. With that information, the ISC could determine the composition and other characteristics of various objects or substances.

Prior to the start of the project, the ISC approached Owen to see if he would be one of three astrogeologists to help analyze the data. His job would be to cross-reference light reflection signatures against those of ordinary earthly substances, as well as the remnants of meteors collected on Earth, and note any remarkable findings.

Waiting for the data to arrive filled Owen with anticipation. The prospect of discovering the origins of the meteors that had hit Earth, or discovering some kind of new, never-before-seen cosmic element would not only be a career highlight, but a dream come true. When the data finally did arrive, analysis of the results revealed nothing remarkable. By the end of his six-month contract with the ISC, Owen had found many common materials and elements. Many of them were iron, magnesium and various silicates, but none were exact matches with anything found on Earth. Owen was disappointed not to have made any earth-shattering discoveries.

Owen had finalized his reports and had begun wrapping up his work on the project when the ISC approached him to extend his contract another six months. He accepted the extension but this time, protocols and reporting procedures had changed significantly, and information was treated like secrets of international security. Upon his acceptance, he required security clearances higher than he had previously been granted and underwent a psychological assessment. A representative from the ISC met with him to discuss the nature of the extension, but none of what was discussed seemed overly sensitive. In fact, it had been in the news several weeks prior. All over the world, people were buzzing about an astonishing planetary discovery made by one of the telescopes. Key Eleven was a misshapen planet from a unique system in the Andromeda galaxy called the Keys System. The Keys System was named for the distinctive synchronized alignment of several planets rotating around their sun. Their arrangement in relation to each other resembled a series of islands in an ocean of space.

Since the discovery of the Keys System, Key Eleven remained a hot topic of speculation for scientists and the world because it was unlike any other planet ever seen. Like Earth, it was green and blue; but unlike the Earth, one-third of the planet was missing. The planet appeared to have been a victim of a massive intergalactic collision, leaving the interior of the planet visible to its core. The exposed inner layers of the decimated planet were black, except for the brilliant white core that glistened to the point of glowing.

News of this unusual planet had captivated the world. Astronomers hypothesized that, based on the relatively short distance between the Earth and the Andromeda galaxy, it was very possible that one of the many meteors that pummelled the Earth over its billions of years of existence could be remnants of Key Eleven. The ISC's secretive behaviour made Owen question whether the ISC had more than just a theory on those rumours and were trying to get their facts straight before issuing any public statements.

With all of the data collected on Key Eleven personally escorted and hand-delivered to Owen, he got to work on the project. His mandate was to learn everything he could about Key Eleven and to note any other unusual findings. Nothing the ISC had told him about the project seemed to warrant the need for increased security. Owen felt the hush-hush nature of the project was unfortunate because Key Eleven had captured the world's attention and injected much-needed interest in space programs all over the world.

The extension of his contract began only weeks after his father's death. To deal with the pain and depression surrounding the loss of his father, Owen threw himself into the project. He spent more hours in the lab than he cared to calculate, even staying overnight on occasion, not wanting to return to his empty house. Within the first two weeks of the project, Owen discovered the first exact match. Several of the light reflection signatures collected from the exposed inner layers of the planet matched meteoric remnants found in three different impact sites around North America. This discovery was momentous; it meant that there was a good chance that more of Key Eleven could be on Earth, if it had not burned up as the meteors entered Earth's atmosphere.

After several eighty-hour weeks, Owen was months ahead of schedule. He had analyzed over eighty-five percent of the light samples and was beginning to wonder if the planet had revealed all of its secrets in the three matches he had already confirmed. However, at the end of the first month, Owen learned something very extraordinary about Key Eleven and he now understood the ISC's secretive behaviour.

The light reflection signatures collected from the planet's gleaming core revealed many properties, all unlike anything found on Earth. Or for that matter, unlike anything found on the other hundreds of planets. The energy level of the core material and some of its other properties were barely calculable and Owen knew this had to be what spooked the ISC. Without an understanding of this material, a leak of information this sensitive would be a nightmare of global proportions. The public already suspected parts of Key Eleven were on Earth, and soon the same would be assumed of this alien core material. If the general public was to learn of its bizarre, otherworld-ly properties, any number of social issues could erupt. Fear of the unknown could cause a worldwide panic or, worse still, a country or private organization might try to gain access to it, should it possess any properties of value. Its physical discovery and recovery could change the face of the planet—for better or worse was anyone's speculation. What if it was highly toxic and it wiped out the planet? Who would own it? The country it happened to land in or the organization that found it? What if it sparked a global conflict? Wars over land and resources were not uncommon, and with the world scrambling to develop alternative sources of energy, the discovery of a high-power energy source would undoubtedly lead to global chaos.

Upon this discovery, the unspoken portion of Owen's mandate became abundantly clear. He needed to learn as much as he could about Key Eleven's core material, so if and when a time came to discuss it with the public, the ISC would have reliable, albeit hypothetical, information to report. In the months that followed, Owen compared data from the core material to existing substances on Earth that possessed vaguely similar characteristics, attempting to gain a wider understanding of the material. Because there was no other element like it on Earth, he could never be absolutely certain of anything and could only hypothesize. Being a scientist who typically deals in absolutes, the theoretical nature of the project at times left him frustrated. He always felt so close to brilliant discoveries, but because he had no physical proof, only hypotheses, he could never be sure. He had experienced the same unfulfilled, aching feeling as a kid looking up at the glittering night skies with his telescope. Seeing the moon and other planets was amazing, but it left part of him feeling slightly un-fulfilled. As silly as he knew it sounded, not being able to reach out and touch the planets that looked so close made for a hollow experience.

Having accomplished much of the project in the first month, Owen was free to spend the time remaining studying the properties of this new element, which he had named Elevanium. Elevanium was an extremely dense, rocklike substance with a density of energy beyond what he could accurately calculate, and far beyond anything on Earth. It appeared to be so dense that Owen suspected a piece the size of a pea could supply the power needs of a single family home for several lifetimes, if it could somehow be harnessed. Having proven that parts of Key Eleven's mantle had already been found in three different locations on Earth, it was reasonable to assume that part of the planet's core had also traveled to Earth.

With the research and analysis of the ISC's data on Key Eleven nearly complete, Owen's work on the project was drawing to a close. His final task would be to compile his data and write the formal reports revealing his findings to the ISC. Owen knew he held significant conclusions that would rock the world—if the ISC chose to release it. He suspected they never would.

Riley appreciated Owen's hesitation to speak about the project. She would face any combination of court-martialing, jail time or astronomical fines if she were to divulge anything she had learned during any of her top secret operations.

"I understand why you're hesitant to talk about the project. You don't have to say anything right now. I'll tell you what I know," said Riley. She walked toward the basement window and looked out at the colourful array of tulips in the flower bed just above her eye level. "We know you've found a new element in this batch of light samples. We also know that several remarkable readings came from the core of Key Eleven and you believe there's a good chance that part of Key Eleven's core material is on Earth."

Owen looked at Riley, his mouth agape. Everything she had said was completely accurate, but he had shared that information with absolutely no one.

Riley pulled some papers from the back of her bag and handed them to Owen. She watched his eyes grow as he flipped through the pages. He unlocked and opened the bottom drawer of his desk and pulled out a brown manila folder. He flipped through the documents inside, took one page in particular and held it up beside the papers Riley had handed him. The pages were identical. Each word printed on the pages matched; Owen's handwritten notes in the left margin were the same, right down to the blue ballpoint pen ink. The only difference between the two pages was that Riley's paper had yellowed slightly with age. Owen was speechless.

"How did you get this? If I was supposed to die today, how would you come to know anything about what I've done?" asked Owen.

"The majority of the work was done, um…well, before your untimely demise," said Riley, hoping to sound appropriately sensitive. She pulled an official-looking, coil-bound report from her backpack and handed it to Owen. "When you died, all of your findings, extrapolations, notes and drawings were sent back to ISC and they compiled this report."

Owen looked at the title of the document and nearly fell out of his chair. *Light Reflection Signature Analysis and Findings Report from Planet 397.309.290.838 AKZ (Key Eleven) by the late Owen Taylor (Compiled by Steven Falcon.)* He flipped through the pages and found his work. It was another surreal experience.

"Your hypotheses are spot on for the most part. Some of that core material is on Earth right now. It will be discovered by miners in 2047 when they sink a new mine shaft," said Finn.

Owen looked at Finn, his eyes wide with disbelief. "Really? How much of it?"

Finn looked stumped for a moment. "I'm unsure exactly. A lot, for what it is. About the size of an Olympic-sized swimming pool maybe."

"Wow," breathed Owen. He leaned back in his chair and flipped through the pages of the report that had been created after his death. "So what do you need me for?"

"We need you to help us destroy it," said Riley.

CHAPTER 11

TEAM 3
YEAR: 2095
TIME REMAINING: 185 Days

Team Three materialized in a small clearing in an otherwise heavily treed area. The dense forest served its purpose well, acting as a shroud to hide this sudden appearance from onlookers and avoid the chaos that would inevitably ensue. The sounds of distant traffic were barely audible over the roar of a nearby creek, swollen and overflowing from annual spring runoff. The crisp air that filled the damp forest smelled of springtime decay.

Having never travelled time before, Spencer's first instinct was to look at his hands to make sure they were still there. Satisfied to see that they and the rest of his body had made the journey intact, he took a step away from the pine boughs poking uncomfortably at his side and brushed stray needles from his freshly-issued field op uniform. A uniform was not required for his role in the Research branch of the NRD, nor his brothers'. Logan, to Spencer's left, untangled the spindly branch of a young birch tree from the strap of his backpack. To his right, Asher stepped delicately through the muddy water like a cat through snow, looking for higher ground.

"I hope this isn't an indication of how well the next six months are going to go," said Asher. He stood resignedly in the water, feeling the icy, wet cold seep into his boots.

Logan held the branch he had untangled from his backpack straps. It still had several of last year's leaves attached to it. One of the brown, lifeless leaves broke away and he caught it with his other hand. He rolled the withered stem between his thumb and forefinger. "I don't know," he said, inspecting the leaf. "I think I'd like to *leaf* at some time."

Asher rolled his eyes and groaned.

Spencer ignored his brothers and focused on the compass on his watch. The compass was unnecessary because Spencer knew his exact location, but his compulsive nature forced him to double check.

"Okay, guys." Spencer slid the sleeve of his jacket over the bulky time travel watch and looked at his brothers. "Let's go."

Spencer sloshed through the water toward the front of the park leaving his older twin brothers in his wake. The identical, six-foot-two, broad-shouldered figures followed behind him, cracking jokes about their little brother who followed every rule to the letter. Spencer had no interest in their thoughts or opinions. Their undivided attention was not required at this moment, so he let them entertain themselves. It was just easier. Spencer's focus and drive were just two of the many ways he differed from his brothers and likely how he had received more promotions in his career than his brothers, despite being four years younger.

Feeling like a third wheel around the twins was nothing new to Spencer. Having grown up in their shadow, the scenario was always the same: the twins and him. The Two Musketeers…and Spencer. Spencer was an exceptionally bright child and could see that, even at a young age, he and the twins were different. The twins were loud, messy and always pushing the limit of their parents' patience, whereas Spencer preferred to spend time indoors on quiet endeavours like reading or puzzles.

When Spencer turned six, the boys' principal informed their parents that Spencer was extremely advanced for his age and recommended skipping him past grade one into grade two for a more appropriate challenge. His parents had always suspected he was gifted but never pursued it, assuming that every parent thought the same about their children. The twins, despite their good natures and zest for life, failed to set the bar high in terms of academic achievement. With the addition of a new sibling named Emily, and their father being deployed for months at a time for his job in the Defence side of NRD, things in the Grayson household were hectic. The twins alone were a full-time job and adding a new baby to the mix meant that the majority of Spencer's exceptional scholastic achievements went unnoticed.

Years passed and the twins left for university. In their absence, a peaceful calm returned to the rural Grayson home. Spencer found that without the twins underfoot, the days seemed to yield more time and found he could accomplish far more when not fighting for personal space, peace and quiet or simple routine. He took extra classes allowing him to graduate from high school a year early, putting Spencer two years behind the twins academically.

Spencer's excitement at the prospect of a field op-esque opportunity dampened after learning the twins would be his teammates. Employees from the Research branch rarely went on NRD operations, let alone as an operation lead with two subordinates—a level two and a level three, no less. His excitement turned to sheer anxiety when he learned the level two and level three subs Mitch had chosen were his twin brothers, and he worried how they would handle him as their figure of authority. Spencer knew the twins were a handful at the best of times and reining them in could be impossible. They rarely took anything or anyone seriously, a fact that drove Spencer to madness. Even as children, he felt he had to be the one with common sense, not that it made any difference. He continually found himself in the same situation: the twins would have some great idea, which Spencer knew from experience would inevitably end in disaster. Without thought—or maybe with thought, but without care,

Spencer could never be sure—they ploughed ahead. Unsurprisingly, the end result was always the same: smashed windows, razed sheds, wrecked sleds, bikes or cars. Destruction.

The team trudged through the muddy, wet forest. With each step, their boots made sucking, squelching sounds. Within minutes, they reached the edge of the small urban forest—the trees, bushes and muddy undergrowth ended abruptly to reveal the manicured expanse of the sprawling city park. Their exit from the bushes startled an elderly woman walking her pugs past empty flower gardens. She glared at them suspiciously as if to punish them for whatever delinquent activities would draw three grown men dressed in matching outfits into a soaking wet forest at nightfall.

"Good evening, ma'am." Spencer smiled at the woman as he dragged his boots across the grass to wipe away the mud. She looked away quickly and picked up her pace.

Metropolitan Park, affectionately known by its many loyal visitors as "Retro Metro," was Tricity's oldest park and the city was experimenting with the park's attractions. The playground area was a throwback to early-century parks and their more simplistic play structures: covered tube slides, mini zip lines, chain bridges and monkey bars. The park was a hit with children and parents alike despite having none of the standard play equipment other city parks had. Most other parks featured at least one airboard park; a hangout where kids could sharpen their skills and perform tricks and stunts while hover skating over obstacles on their airboards—a flat, skateboard-like platform that hovered in the air, propelled by foot power. It was also missing AirForce360, an outdoor arena where kids could fly child-sized versions of some of the world's fastest jets and engage in laser dogfights. The miniaturized planes puttered through a designated airspace with a fraction of the speed and manoeuvrability, and a maximum fifteen-degree tilt in any direction. Sensors in the planes ensured no mid-air collisions. For younger children, two-storey, mind-stimulating play structures were equipped with HangTime technology that eased children to the ground like an invisible hand should they fall. The parks that featured these types of play equipment were always very popular. But kids, no matter what the era, loved a park where they could actually crash their bikes or airboards, get scars or jump off the swings and try to land without falling. Adults were drawn to the park by nostalgia, and it was not uncommon to find adults swinging alongside their children.

Tonight, the park was visited by the Grayson brothers for a much different reason. The forested portion of the park was thick enough for a team of three to materialize in with no one being the wiser. However, the most important reason was its proximity to Spencer's condominium.

With the majority of the mud scraped from their boots, the three men strode toward the front entrance of the darkening park. They walked past the swings, monkey bars and rope castle. To their right, a few teenagers played gravity-assist Frisbee with a disc that lit up as it flew. To their left, a man pushed a giggling little boy on a swing.

A chocolate-coloured puppy raced around the pair barking, jumping up and nipping at the boy's heels as he swung by.

Just outside the park, two layers of red tail lights were visible through the trees. The sparse traffic on the aging road below moved considerably more slowly than the steady stream of faster-moving tail lights following the air route above. Travel by road was becoming less and less common, but not everyone had converted to cars that flew.

"Are you sure you're not home yet?" asked Asher. His eyes were fixed on two women in short shorts jogging toward them. He put on his best smile—unleashing the dimples—and gave the ladies a quick salute as they passed. The women giggled and he turned and walked backward as they jogged past.

"I'm pretty sure. It's about quarter after seven," said Spencer. He looked again at his oversized watch to confirm the time he already knew, having checked it just moments ago. He quickened his pace.

Spencer's watch differed from most watches. While it had many standard watch features, it had many features other watches did not, the most important being that it was an auxiliary control for the time travel backpack he wore on his back. A screen displayed a GPS-enabled map marking their geographical position and several digital clocks showed various time zones. One clock showed present time—the current time for where he physically stood at that moment: March 19, 2095, 19:18. The other clock showed the time and date from where he had originated, August 23, 2097, 08:18. A timer counted down, with one-hundred and eighty-four days, twenty-three hours and forty-two minutes remaining.

Logan took several quick steps to catch up with his little brother. "Working on the weekend, Spence? Trying to make a good impression at the office?" As they neared the stone wall marking the park's entrance, Spencer's condominium building became visible beyond the traffic.

The twin's playful abuse rolled off Spencer like water off a duck's back. "It's not a character flaw to want to do a good job. I take my career seriously and it wouldn't hurt the two of you to put a little effort in." The twins rolled their eyes at his remarks, as he knew they would.

Just as they were about to exit the park and cross the street, Spencer abruptly veered to the left and onto the grass.

"Hey, what's the deal?" asked Logan.

Spencer pointed up at his balcony, his familiar eye able to pick it out faster than his brothers. "I'm home."

"I thought you said you'd be at work?" Logan squinted and pointed at each floor as he counted up and across the balconies. Through the large living room windows, he saw a shadow moving behind the curtains.

Spencer turned and sat down on the stone wall. "I thought I would be. At the beginning of the project, I stayed well past seven and sometimes eight o'clock most days."

"Even on Saturdays? You're such a nerd." Logan rolled his eyes at Spencer.

"Maybe he's got a hot date lined up," laughed Asher. He sat down on the wall beside Spencer.

Spencer crossed his arms and thought, trying to recall what he had done on this very night nearly two and a half years earlier. "No, I don't think so. Well, not that night anyway."

The twins looked at each other and burst into a fit of laughter. "When was the last time you went on a date?" asked Asher.

"I go on dates," Spencer snapped, irritated at allowing himself to be goaded by his brothers. He looked back up at his balcony and smiled. "I just don't tell you about them because I don't want to admit that I'm related to either of you."

Logan patted his little brother on the shoulder before sitting on the wall beside Asher. "That's funny. I wouldn't want to have to admit to my dates that I'm related to such a stick in the mud."

The twins' reputation for being lady killers was widely known in both their personal and professional lives. The two men possessed a level of confidence and rugged good looks that would make a movie star envious. Their charisma and outgoing personalities were matched only by their want of a good time. Add to that the novelty of being twins and the result was a magical spell under which impossible numbers of the fairer sex had fallen.

"Live life to the fullest" was the philosophy upon which the twins' core beliefs were based and they enjoyed no more commitments than work, beer and Friday night rocketball. Spencer secretly wished he shared some of their qualities; there was an easiness about them and everything seemed to come to them so naturally.

To the uneducated eye, the twins' looks were identical, as if from a production line. They shared the same wide set jaw, broad shoulders and brown hair that, whether intentional or not, always looks perfectly messy. Their eyes were blue when they were younger but changed to chocolate brown as they grew up. Spencer told them countless times it was because they were so full of shit. While both twins were in decent physical shape, Logan was slightly thinner than Asher. Logan attributed his leanness to his great athleticism while Asher claimed it was because Logan could not handle his liquor.

The bond the twins shared grew stronger as they aged, and as adults, they spent most of their free time together. They bought condos in the same building, across the hall and one unit apart. They also shared a love of sports and were both very active in "retro" activities like hockey, football, soccer and lacrosse. Older now and with more than a few sports-related injuries between them, they were starting to prefer their feet, skis or wheels firmly planted on the ground.

"Okay, smart-ass. How are we going to get you out of your condo so we can get in?" asked Asher. He looked up at the figure partially visible through the gap in the curtains.

"Let me think for a second." Spencer stared up at the balcony and chewed his lip in thought.

Logan chuckled. "I know." Logan pulled a red device the size of a kidney bean from his pocket, slid it into his ear and smiled at Spencer. "Trust me."

The look in Logan's eyes reminded Spencer of the day that followed the Great Snowstorm of '74. Kicked out of the house for being rambunctious, the twins and Spencer explored the snowy depths of the backyard. The twins were delighted to discover a snow bank nearly touching the roof peak of their garage. To eight-year-old boys, a gift of this magnitude rivalled that of a brand new airboard under the tree on Christmas morning. Spencer found himself on the roof of the icy, snow-covered garage, sitting in a battered, antique wooden sled, a twin on either side. The rickety skis straddled either side of the snowy roof peak, wobbling timidly under Spencer's meagre body weight. After years of well-intentioned love and abuse from the twins, the sled showed significant signs of aging—chipped skis, broken brakes and missing wooden planks on the seat. Excited at the prospect of what the twins touted as, "the greatest ride of his life," Spencer listened carefully as they explained the plan. When they launched him and the sled off the roof, he would sail over the gap like a bird, land safely on the snow drift and have a smooth ride into the garden. In the eyes of a four-year-old, this was clearly a no-lose situation. The twins pushed Spencer and the sled as they ran along the steeply-pitched roof. As they neared the edge, one of the skis broke off. The sled stopped suddenly, but Spencer continued forward. Asher lost his balance when Logan tripped on the defunct ski and fell. The twins rolled down opposite sides of the roof and landed in soft snow banks like screaming sacks of flour. Spencer tumbled over the roof's ridge and dropped like a stone to the freshly shovelled sidewalk below, luckily sustaining no more injuries than a sprained ankle and twisted wrist. Spencer learned a lot that day, but the most valuable lesson was to never listen when the twins say, "trust me."

"Logan! What are you doing?" demanded Spencer in a loud whisper. He leaned over Asher, trying to keep his voice from being heard by people walking past them on the sidewalk.

"You'll see." With the little red phone snugly placed inside his ear, Logan thought about the number he wanted to dial. On his eyes, he wore Icomm contact lenses that intercepted his brain's commands and translated them into instructions an electronic device could execute, in this case, the little bean-shaped phone inside Logan's ear. When Logan thought about placing a call, a phone icon appeared on the contact lenses, but to Logan the tiny symbol looked like a large projection just out of his arm's reach. As Logan thought of the numbers he wanted to dial, the numbers appeared beside the phone icon then flashed three times—indicating the call was placed—then disappeared. The phone icon turned lime green, shrank and slid down to the bottom right corner of his vision where it stayed unobtrusively. Hearing the phone ringing on the other end, Logan smiled at his little brother.

Spencer heard the muffled ringing of the recipient's phone in Logan's earpiece and he saw the shadow move in his condo. Realizing what his brother had done, Spencer lunged over Asher with the intent of tackling Logan to the ground and forcing him to end the call, but his hands seized nothing but air. Asher grabbed Spencer around the waist and tackled him to the ground. Asher was thrilled to finally get a rise out of his younger brother as if this had been the first really productive thing they had accomplished all day.

"Hello?" answered a voice on the other end of the phone.

Spencer stopped fighting Asher and they both lay unmoving on the ground at Logan's feet. Asher had Spencer locked in a half-nelson and the pair strained to listen to the conversation Logan was having with the 2095 version of his little brother.

"Hey Spenssssse, hooooow's it goin'?" Logan slurred.

The Spencer on the other end of the phone did not speak immediately as if he suspected the nature of the call. "Good…How are you?"

"Weeeeell," said Logan in a singsong voice, "I'm not going to lie to you. It could be better."

"Are you drunk?" asked past-Spencer, the impatient incredulity clearly audible in his voice.

"Hmmmmm…yes!" said Logan, with a heavy emphasis on the yes. "I'm stuck at the bar and I really need you to come and pick me up."

"Are you kidding me? It's not even seven. How is it you're loaded before seven o'clock?"

"Weeee've been at the bar since two. We got an early start today, Spenssssse!" Logan giggled.

"Where's Asher?" asked Spencer, knowing that if one twin was loaded, the other twin was usually equally drunk and not too far away.

"He's gone home. He left me here." A sulky emphasis on *left*.

"What do you mean 'he's gone?' Why would he leave you?"

"When we got to the bar, Ange, yoooooou know Ange, the waitress that Asher always makes a fool of himself in front of?" Asher kicked Logan awkwardly in the shin. "Ow! It was her day off and she came in to pick up her sweater and we told her she should stay and have a few drinks with us. Annnnnnyway, she stayed all afternoon and now they've gone off together and left me heeeere all alone." His voice rang with drunken self-pity.

"Why don't you call a cab?" snapped past-Spencer callously, more of a demand than a question. He had been through this too many times before. "I have plans."

"Yoooooouuu don't have plans Spence, you never have plans. What are you doing?"

"I'm on a date."

Both twins shot accusatory glares at the future-Spencer in their presence. Logan silently mouthed, "Rude!"

Spencer shook his head and rolled his eyes.

"I don't believe you," said Logan. He peered at the shadowy figure moving behind the curtains. "Are you sssssure you're not in your living room, right now wearing SquidoPus pyjama pants?"

The shadow in the window moved suddenly and the curtains flew open to reveal a two-and-half year younger version of Spencer standing in his living room wearing a white t-shirt and SquidoPus pyjama pants. Logan dropped to the ground beside his brothers and all three scrambled clumsily for cover behind the low stone wall.

Logan covered the device in his ear with his hand so past-Spencer on the other end of the line would not hear him. He whisper-yelled to the Spencer on the ground next to him, "By the way, I can't believe you have SquidoPus pyjama pants."

Spencer was unapologetic. "They're extremely comfy."

"You never said your date was with SquidoPus," whispered Asher, as he accidently kneed Spencer in the ribs.

"Who are you talking to?" demanded the Spencer on the phone.

"Hang on a sec Spenssse, there are some very beeeeeauuutiful ladies here…"

"Logan! I don't have time for this," protested the Spencer on the phone. Logan slowly peered up over the wall and watched as the Spencer in the condo whipped the curtains closed. No longer under threat of being seen, the three men took their places atop the stone wall.

Logan made a tutting sound. "Spensssssssse, there's always time for ladies. You wouldn't be so wound up all the time if you realized that…" Logan trailed off. He looked at Spencer beside him and pretended he was one of the mythical ladies.

The Spencer on the phone heard a muffled Logan doing a bad job of trying to make a good impression on some poor woman. "Hey, Baby, you're looking pretty fine this evening!"

Asher could no longer contain his laughter and had to cover his mouth. Spencer looked livid and gestured for Logan to wrap it up.

"Ugh. Well, turns out she wasn't a lady," said Logan, sticking his tongue out at the now fuming Spencer beside him.

"Take a cab," ordered the Spencer on the phone.

"I can't do that Spenssssse! You know I'm allergic to cheap air fresheners. Aaaaand I've lost my credit keys."

"Pay the cab when you get home. Surely you have spares?"

"Ashhhhh has my credit keys."

Future-Spencer watched Logan in awe, equally impressed and disturbed by his brother's capacity for lying on the fly.

A moment of silence could be heard over Logan's earpiece. "For the love of Christmas." Past-Spencer exhaled in frustration. "Alright, where the hell are you?"

"*Way Off Base,*" said Logan. "You know, the bar that's down the road from the base? The one we try to get you to come to but you're always too busy?"

"Shut up. I'm leaving now. And don't go anywhere because if you're not there when I get there I'm leaving without you and you can either walk home or sleep in a bush."

"Ooooh Spence, you're my favourite broth…" The line went dead. "…er," finished Logan.

Logan smiled smugly at Spencer as he removed the earpiece and slid it back into his pocket. Spencer was irked, but not surprised, that his brothers were having fun at his expense, again.

Logan saw that Spencer looked less than pleased. "What? I got the job done, didn't I?"

The sun had set completely and the aged street lighting had come on, illuminating the pot-holed and patchy road beneath. Light pods hovering above the air traffic illuminated the vehicular air routes. The brothers settled themselves on a wooden bench facing the street and waited for past-Spencer's car to leave the parking lot.

Spencer thought for a moment about something Logan had said. "There is no way you could see what kind of pants I was wearing," said Spencer.

"I took a guess. I saw them in your bathroom once."

Spencer looked at Logan and all three began laughing.

The men passed the time speculating about the op as they watched the building. Only minutes had passed before Spencer's silver two-door car emerged from the parking garage. As the car approached the lot exit, it rose into the air and its wheels folded into the undercarriage as it merged into the lines of air traffic.

Spencer stood and looked at the twins. "This is it. Showtime."

In the privacy of the elevator whisking the men up to Spencer's floor, Asher quizzed his younger brother. "So you don't think the past version of you would deal too well if all three of us showed up on your doorstep?"

Spencer watched the numbers above the door light up in succession. "You know, I'm unsure. The problem is that if you two are involved, I would think it was a joke. I'd probably think you created a hologram or something."

"I guess I could see that," said Asher. "In fact, I can't believe we didn't come up with that ourselves."

"I know," said Logan, shaking his head. "We're losing our touch."

Spencer rolled his eyes. "I'm really not sure what I'd think if I came home and found myself in my apartment, so I think it's good that you warm me up to the idea. For all the good it will do. I probably won't believe you."

"Well, that's nothing new," said Logan.

The elevator chimed and the door opened.

"You remembered your keys?" asked Asher, as they stopped at the second last door on the right.

Spencer held up his keys and gave them a shake. The key ring was thin and rectangular with twelve or thirteen different keys hanging from it. Each key was similar in that they were all slender, elongated shapes with the diameter of a pencil. Some were cylindrical, two were square, one was shaped like a plus sign and several were shaped like long, extruded letters. Spencer chose a well-worn key and slid it into the small round hole above the door handle. The light beside the keyhole flashed green, and he heard the locking mechanism inside release.

As Spencer entered his condo, the lights came on and he surveyed "his" home. There was no visible difference between the condo he left in 2097 and the one he now stood in. If he had not known he had just travelled back in time, nothing in the appearance of his home would have indicated that he had. The furniture, floors, wall colour and art were the same, as were the curtains that covered his windows and sliding balcony door. Even the large rubber plants and dragon tree beside the balcony doors seemed no smaller than he could recall. The white leather couches and the glass coffee table sat in the same location they did in 2097. He made a mental note to call a decorator when he returned to 2097.

The twins took off their jackets and flung them over the back of the white leather sofa. Logan flopped onto the couch and made himself at home like this night was no different than any other Saturday night. He turned the TV on and a commercial promoting a lunar vacation materialized. The intangible screen appeared several inches in front of the living room wall, spanning nearly its full width and completely obscuring the art hanging on the wall behind. Spencer heard Asher rummaging through his cupboards for a snack as Logan flipped through the channels looking for a rocketball game.

Spencer shook his head in frustration at his brothers' lack of focus. "Uh, guys? Aren't we in the middle of something?"

Asher appeared from the kitchen holding a bag of multi-grain crackers. "Seriously, Spence? No chips? The food in this place is as boring as you are."

The rocketball game went to a commercial advertising the 2096 line up of Everblast jet bikes. Logan muted the sound, though his attention remained fixed on the scantily clad woman sprawled across the leather seat of a cruiser. The commercial ended and the next one advertised MicroMaid cleaning services.

"I guess we should get you back here, eh?" Logan looked at Spencer with a grin, sliding the little bean back into his ear. Logan dialled Spencer's number again. The past version of Spencer answered, now half way to the bar.

"Hey, Spensssse! Where are you? Yeah, okay, never mind. As it turns out, the bartender had my wallet and keys. I'm in a cab. Thanks, though!"

Asher and Spencer overheard a verbal barrage of name calling and suggestions of what Logan should do to himself. Logan pulled the earpiece out of his ear and held it in front of him and all three stared at it, listening intently to past-Spencer's rant.

"You need to learn to chill," Logan said to the Spencer standing next to him. Logan ended the call, cutting past-Spencer off mid-sentence.

CHAPTER 12

TEAM 3
YEAR: 2095
TIME REMAINING: 185 Days

The 2095 version of Spencer stormed out of the elevator and down the hall in a foul mood. As he held his key out toward the lock, he realized the door was partially open. He saw the lights were on, heard the rocketball game on TV and had a pretty good idea who was in his home. He pushed the door open and charged into his home finding the twins on his couch.

"What are you guys doing here? Is this some kind of a joke?" demanded Spencer. His voice increased in both decibels and octaves. He threw his keys down on the floor and rubbed his face in exasperation. "What is wrong with you two? Don't you have anything better to do on a Saturday night? And how did you get in here?"

"Actually," interrupted Asher, ignoring all questions, "before you get your Squi-doPus pyjama pants in a twist, we're here for a legitimate reason."

Spencer eyed his older brothers and realized he had just been had. His shoulders fell and he sighed heavily. "You've both been here all along haven't you?" He slid out of his shoes, placed them neatly on the shoe rack in the closet and hung his jacket.

"In a sense," said Logan. He stood and walked into the kitchen. "Got any beer?"

"No, I don't," Spencer lied. He always kept a twelve-pack of beer in the fridge for when the twins came over, but today he felt disinclined to accommodate them. "I need a glass of wine. You guys are too much to take sometimes." He followed the twins into the kitchen.

Knowing full well that Spencer always kept a twelve on hand specifically for their benefit, Logan peered into the fridge, grabbed two bottles of beer and tossed one to his twin. They both leaned casually against the counter opposite the fridge and chucked their bottle caps into the fruit basket on the counter. Spencer grabbed the metal lids and tossed them into the garbage as he heaved another sigh. He pulled a bottle of red wine from the rack on the wall, uncorked it and poured himself a large glass. He savoured the first taste in silence with his eyes closed before giving the twins his attention.

"Okay, why did you say you were here?"

"We didn't," said Logan, suddenly unsure of where to begin. It never occurred to him to plan for this conversation. "We're here on NRD business."

Spencer took another sip of his wine and looked at them with narrowed eyes. "What do you mean, 'on NRD business?' Like, work?" Spencer scrutinized Logan's face like he was seeing his brother for the first time. He did the same to Asher. "What's wrong with you guys?" Standing in the harsh light of the kitchen, Spencer noticed the twins looked haggard.

"Yes, yes, we're irresponsible, we delight in making you miserable," said Asher, rolling his eyes.

"No, that's not it," said Spencer. "Why are you so tanned? You look like you've aged five years since I've seen you last. What have you guys been doing?" He leaned in to get a closer look and Logan held out his arm to distance himself from Spencer's visual inspection.

"Whoa. Personal space, little bro."

"Nice," Asher chuckled. "That's really nice. It's actually only been about two and a half years, not five, but thanks for that. The compliment is great for the ego."

Spencer laughed derisively. "Your egos could use a couple of hits." He leaned against the stove opposite the twins and eyed them suspiciously as he processed what Asher had just said. "What do you mean, 'it's only been two and a half years?'"

"We're on an op," said Logan, unable to contain a grin.

Spencer nearly shot wine through his nose as he coughed and laughed simultaneously. "Sure you are. And I'm the Queen of England. For one, I must have missed it when they transferred you from Research to Defence, and two, it's past five. Oh, *and* it's the weekend. Neither of you have worked a minute of overtime in your lives." Spencer took another sip of his wine and cleared his throat. "Research staff don't go on ops. Besides, what operation would want you two?"

"I'll disregard your hurtful comments," said Asher smirking, not hurt at all. "And it's true, about the overtime, anyway. But this operation required special talents only we possessed."

"What's that? Getting drunk and hitting on women?" Spencer smiled at his own quick wit. So rarely did he get good shots in at the twins.

"Now Spencer, you know we're much deeper than that. Actually, we're on a pretty cool op that we think you'll like. In fact, it involves you, but not *this* you," said Logan, pointing at Spencer's chest. "We're here from 2097."

Spencer felt flames of anger flare on his cheeks. Jokes were fine and the occasional jab at his work ethic he could handle. What he had no patience for was being talked to like a fool. "Wow. You guys really are loaded aren't you? It's pretty early in the night for this wouldn't you say?"

The 2097 version of Spencer listened to the conversation from the top of the stairs. The point was to have the twins ease the 2095 version of Spencer into the situation and save him the shock of finding himself in his own living room. The twins were doing a horrible job, something Spencer assumed they had done intentionally—to get under the skin of two Spencers for the price of one. He listened as the conversation went nowhere. He walked down the wide spiral staircase and joined the twins and the past version of himself in the kitchen before the twins got out of hand. Future-Spencer entered the kitchen and showed himself to his past-self.

"I know this sounds crazy, but they are actually telling you the truth. As hard as that is to believe." Future-Spencer shot the twins an angry look and they smiled back innocently.

At the sight of himself, the past version of Spencer jumped backward. Already leaning against the stove, this resulted in him smashing the hand holding the wine glass into the handle of the fridge. The glass shattered and red wine sprayed the fridge and wall. The twins watched with amusement; their eyes lit up like kids being given a bag of candy.

"I think everyone should just have a seat in the living room and we can discuss this," said future-Spencer. He wet the cloth in the sink and threw it at Asher. It bounced off his chest before he could catch it leaving a damp patch on his grey shirt. "Clean that up," he demanded in exasperation, then followed his younger self into the living room.

After nearly a half hour's worth of explanation and questions, the past version of Spencer finally accepted that the twins' story had not been an elaborate hoax, only because of the presence of his future-self. From the future or not, he knew that he would never joke about this. Spencer enjoyed talking to the past version himself. At first, it had been a surreal experience—he saw himself from the perspective of how others saw him. Initially, he felt self-conscious at how different his voice sounded and how different his mannerisms looked from an outside perspective. This awkwardness lasted only a few minutes; after talking to his past-self for several moments, the conversation felt comfortable and natural.

"I guess we should get the twins here then," said past-Spencer, still recovering from the mental shell-shock. He expected it would take some time to become comfortable with seeing himself in his own home.

"I agree. As unlivable as it will be having four of them around," said future-Spencer.

"You know, we're right here," said Logan. "We can hear you."

The two Spencers looked at each other and smiled.

Lured easily with a promise of beer, pizza and a Saturday night rocketball game, the twins took no time in getting to Spencer's condo. When they arrived, they knocked only as a formality and walked in.

"What's up with your doorman?" Logan asked, kicking off his shoes and turning toward the small closet.

Asher knelt down to untie his shoes. "Yeah, he looked at us really funny."

"Well, understandably he's shocked. He's already seen a more handsome version of you two come in tonight," said future-Logan.

Confused by the familiar voice, the past versions of the twins looked into the living room, found their duplicates seated comfortably on the couch and howled with laughter. When two Spencers emerged from the kitchen, they broke into another wave of laughter.

The past versions of the twins settled themselves down on the loveseat after a stop in the kitchen to grab a couple of beers.

"Okay, okay, what is this?" asked the past version of Asher, his eyes still watery from laughing.

"It's a long story," said future-Logan, "one we know will intrigue and amuse you."

"Sounds good. I'm always up for being amused," said past-Asher. "But before we do that, I heard a rumour about pizza?"

While they waited for the pizza to arrive, the future version of the twins told the story of Logan's ruse to get past-Spencer out of the condo. The past version of the twins found it just as amusing as their future counterparts had and were still laughing about it when the pizza delivery robot arrived.

Future-Spencer opened his door to a familiar hovering robot. It appeared outside his door more often than not when the twins came over. The delivery robot doubled as a sleek mobile oven. It baked the pizzas en-route to destinations, zipping around the city, in and out of air traffic like other delivery bots. Spencer saw the crispy, golden pizzas through the glass window in the robot's oven door.

"Hello, Resident of Two-Eight-Eight-Three Cloverdale Road."

Spencer grabbed his keys off the table by the door and selected the key shaped like an elongated "M" and slid it into the appropriately shaped receptacle on the delivery bot.

"Thank-a you for your payment," said a half-mechanized, half-human voice with a thick Italian accent.

The robot's oven door opened and a wave of hot, delicious air hit Spencer in the chest. Inside the robot's oven body were four racks with a pizza on each. He watched a stainless steel shelf underneath the oven slide forward with a circular cardboard tray on it. The bottom rack tilted downwards and the pizza slid onto the cardboard circle with exact precision. A green laser dot zipped across the pizza slicing it into eight equal pieces. Spencer set the pizzas on the coffee table.

Future-Spencer refilled his and past-Spencer's wine glasses, then selected a piece of pizza and placed it on his plate. "Okay guys, we need to discuss this."

Future-Asher grabbed his third slice of pizza and jammed it into his mouth with no sign of slowing down or needing to breathe. "Why don't you just relax for a bit?" he said through a mouthful of pizza. A piece of cheesy pepperoni slid off the slice and onto his shirt.

"There's a lot to explain." Future-Spencer cut into his pizza with a knife and fork. He watched future-Asher eat the pepperoni off his shirt and try to lick away the grease stain it left behind. He shook his head in disgust. "The reason we've been sent back in time is because we need to make some adjustments to the past."

"Adjustments? What kind of adjustments?" asked past-Logan. "I thought messing around while travelling back in time was, well, messy?"

"Not to mention, strictly prohibited," added past-Spencer.

"True, but there are some problems in 2097 that can only be addressed by making some slight modifications to the past."

"Hah! That's putting it lightly," said future-Asher. He washed down a mouthful of pizza with beer. "This is the highest profile, noncombat op in the history of the NRD."

Three sets of eyes fixed on future-Spencer. "The AEI Project that you have all just started working on has failed and we're here to try and salvage it."

The room fell silent. "Wow," said past-Logan finally. "That is the last thing I expected you to say."

"Let me explain," said future-Spencer. "The project gets completed and the one-year pilot project rolls out successfully. The robots are mass produced and become integrated into society relatively quickly."

"That sounds pretty successful to me," said past-Spencer.

"It started out successfully. In fact, the demand for the robots in the first few months of the pilot project exceeded the NRD's estimation by 1,277 percent. People and businesses were offering to pay ten times the asking price to place a pre-order," explained future-Spencer. He leaned back in his chair with his glass of wine in hand and watched the two sets of twins continue to devour the pizza like a pack of starved dogs. He wondered where they had gotten their manners. Seeing the expression on past-Spencer's face he knew his past-self was wondering the same thing. He took advantage of the twins' mouths being full and explained the dismal situation they were facing in 2097.

"So in a nutshell, we need to manipulate the robots' Personality Application programming to make sure that they behave in a manner that is safe."

"Wow. So, you need to convince the people who planned the project that what they've planned isn't going to work. Then, tell them how it needs to change, but give no explanation why?" asked past-Spencer.

"Good luck," agreed past-Logan. "My boss won't do anything without a lengthy proposal and three studies worth of supporting data before she'll agree to any kind of deviation from a set plan."

Future-Spencer forced a smile. "Well, I'm hoping I won't need to tell them anything. I'm hoping that by pointing out the shortcomings they'll agree with me."

"So if you're doing all the work, why are they here?" asked past-Logan, nodding toward the future version of the twins.

"A few reasons, actually." Future-Spencer swallowed the last of his wine. "First of all, you can't have just one person on an op. If I died, it would mean an instant end to the mission and complete failure. Second, between the three of us, we have a lot of access to different areas of the project. I may need to get information from other divisions and I don't need to draw attention to myself by poking around in areas I'm not involved in. And third, because we're brothers, it doesn't look suspicious for us to be spending an excessive amount of time together."

"So what do you want us to do?" asked past-Spencer, eager to be involved in something so important.

Future-Logan chuckled. "You guys have it easy. All you need to do is disappear for six months."

"What?" asked past-Spencer, his mouth agape and his expression tragic.

"It has to be us. All three of you get to leave town, all expenses paid, for six months. But you have to lay low." Future-Spencer eyed at the past-twins specifically. "Don't draw attention to yourselves and you can't be in touch with anyone at all."

Ample grins broke out on the faces of the past-twins. The past version of Spencer seemed put out. "Why can't we stay and help? I was really looking forward to working on this project."

"How are you going to explain to our lead that there are now two of us? You'll be fully briefed when you come back," said future-Spencer. He motioned to the twins and laughed. "Plus, no one wants any more of these guys; two is already too many."

"Hey," said future-Asher, oozing charm. "You should ask the ladies about that. I think you might be surprised to find out how many of us they'd like."

Past-Spencer remained focused on the project like a laser beam. "I don't understand why you can't tell us what needs to be changed? Can't we make the necessary modifications?"

"It needs to be us because we've already done it. We know the project inside and out, so when we do it again, we can focus on what needs to be changed because we already know what doesn't work," said future-Spencer.

"Plus, you'd probably screw it up," said past-Asher, punching past-Spencer in the arm. Both Spencers ignored him.

"Actually," said future-Asher, "little Spence is running this op."

The past-twins laughed in disbelief. "What? Spencer's levelled up past you guys?" asked past-Logan. "What have you guys been doing for the next two and a half years? You'd better fix that while you're here too."

Future-Logan looked at future-Asher, shaking his head in mock disgust. "Who would have thought we'd ever hold our own selves accountable for anything?"

"I know, I know," said future-Asher shrugging. "It's a sad day when we question our own work habits."

In typical Spencer fashion, his determination and initiative advanced him through the NRD quickly. Spencer's level four outranked Asher's level two and Logan's level three, a considerable achievement as twenty-seven-year-old level fours were few and far between.

Although delighted to hear he was outdoing the twins at something they actually seemed to care about, past-Spencer felt frustrated about losing the opportunity to be involved in the AEI Project. "This operation seems to have a lot of room for error. Why don't you just go back to the beginning of the project and discuss the changes that need to be made with the Project Director so he can give you the results you need?"

"Ian Turner is the reason this project has failed as spectacularly as it has," explained future-Spencer with more disdain in his voice than he typically showed for anyone. "When it became evident there was a problem with the robots, people started asking questions about the personality applications and whether or not they were safe to be integrated into society. Ian began to feel the heat and disappeared."

"Ian could be the biggest liability of this op," said future-Logan.

Past-Spencer could not believe his ears. Ian was the driving force behind both the AI and AEI initiatives from day one. "But he's the reason the whole AI Project didn't get scrapped. Only Ian could go back to the NRD and the private stakeholders and tell them why they needed to pour more money into a project that just failed. He convinced everyone that they should try again by adding artificial emotional intelligence. He seems pretty inspirational."

"He can paint a beautiful picture with words, no argument there. Ian's very motivational and very persuasive, no doubt about it. But he's had a long career and there's no way he's going to let his legacy be a failed project," said future-Spencer.

"Are you saying that the only reason he pushed for the AEI Project was for his own reputation?" asked past-Asher.

Future-Spencer thought for a moment. "Not necessarily. I think it's a combination of things. I think that Ian believed in the viability of the project. But you have to admit that leaving a legacy of robotic genius that will revolutionize the world is a good way to be immortalized. I don't think he'd be too keen to let the project fail if it was within his power to avoid it." He folded up the pizza trays. "I just need to convince Ian that we need to tinker a little with the personality applications. Other than that, we'll just work around him and hope he doesn't become too much of a problem."

"So how does this work?" asked past-Asher. "Do we just leave?"

"Pretty much," said future-Spencer. "Would you believe that the largest part of our budget is allocated to making you three disappear comfortably for six months?"

Past-Asher returned from the kitchen with a fresh round of beers. "How comfortably?"

"Comfortable enough that you won't have to worry about anything for six months." Future-Spencer watched the twin's eyes grow as their minds filled with possibilities. "But not enough to get into serious trouble."

Spencer reached into his backpack and removed three fat envelopes and handed one to each of the past siblings. The future-twins eyed the envelopes like two dogs drooling over an unattended plate of steaks. Future-Spencer was unsure if it was the reflection of the cash or the look of envy that made their usually brown eyes look a little green.

The past versions of the twins inspected the contents of their envelopes and their jaws fell open. Future-Spencer had intentionally left this part of the conversation until after discussing the pertinent details. He suspected that after the twins saw the cash, talking to them would be like trying to communicate to two loaves of bread, and he was right. The past-twins launched into a conversation about what they wanted to do and even past-Spencer joined in. Seeing the money warmed past-Spencer to the idea of taking a vacation and decided to spend it touring Europe while the twins opted for surfing and snowboarding in Australia and New Zealand. The twins raced up the spiral staircase to Spencer's office and began booking their flights. The future-twins became quiet and withdrawn, put out by the loss of a six-month vacation they never had. They cracked open fresh beers as a consolation prize and turned the rocketball game back on to watch the last quarter.

"Well, we need to run," announced past-Logan. He and his twin slid down the arms of the staircase, their feet skiing down the stairs. They walked directly to the front closet. "We hate to be buzz kills, but we need to go home and pack. Our flight is wheels up at 8:00 A.M."

They hastily threw on their jackets and as the group said their farewells, they made each other promise not to damage themselves too badly on any of their endeavours, be it vacation or work.

"Lucky bastards," said future-Logan as the door closed.

The future-siblings discussed their plans for integrating into their past counterparts' jobs on Monday morning while the now-vacationing Spencer booked his trip. As much as he wanted to be a part of the operation, he was thrilled to finally have an opportunity to see Europe.

Past-Spencer came down the stairs to find Logan and Asher sliding into their jackets to leave.

"Okay Spences, we're out of here," said Asher. He opened the door to leave.

"Thanks for the beers and the 'za little bro...and littler bro." Logan wore a confused look while he processed what he had said to see if it made sense. He shrugged as he turned to leave but quickly turned back. He looked at past-Spencer. "Oh, and have fun on your trip. Try to meet some women while you're out there, eh? Live a little."

Asher stuck his head back in the door. "And don't get the two of you mixed up!"

CHAPTER 13

TEAM 2
YEAR: 2016
TIME REMAINING: 185 Days

"Destroy it? That's absurd! Why would you want to do that?" Owen was aghast to hear that Riley wanted him to aid her in destroying the most abundant source of power the planet had ever seen.

"It's rather complicated," said Riley. "Let me try to explain. Back in the late forties—2040s that is—miners came across a handful of white stones as they were cleaning up debris after a routine blast. At first glance, they thought it was quartz. But when they looked more closely, they saw that the stones had a light, slow-pulsing glow. Having never seen anything like it before, the foreman took a sample to the surface so the lab could run tests on it. By the time the foreman got to the lab, word had spread that some glowing rocks had been discovered and people from all over the mine flocked to the lab to get a peek. The geologists knew immediately that there was something remarkably unique and unusual about the stones. To be cautious, they stored the rocks inside a lead-lined, radioactive material container, which was good, because the stones were horribly toxic. Unfortunately, it was too late for everyone who had spent more than five minutes around the samples; they all became sick and died the next day. The miners, dead. Geologists, dead. Everybody else who just got a quick peek or passed within a ten-foot radius got sick to some degree but recovered."

"What did they die from? Is Elevanium radioactive?" Owen flipped through his notes wondering if he missed something.

"No, it isn't. But it emits something that's unlike anything documented on Earth before. We don't know exactly what it is, so it's been coined 'Elevanium Poisoning.' To make a long story short, the Elevanium deposit was expropriated by the government, studied and commercialized. By 2051, the owners of homes, apartment complexes, and retail and office buildings could purchase a retrofit kit and power their buildings with an Elevanium-based battery pack. As you hypothesized, it revolutionized power consumption across the country," explained Riley.

"That sounds like it would resolve a lot of energy shortage problems," observed Owen.

"It did, but it created a lot of social controversy at the same time," said Finn. "People were angry because it was pretty expensive to get a retrofit kit. I mean, in the long run, it paid for itself hundreds of times over, but the conversion cost was steep for the average homeowner. A lot of people were angry because they saw it as another luxury for the wealthy. Politically, it was a hot topic because it seemed unfair that a country as power rich as ours had sole control over a nearly infinite energy source. Especially when it was really just a stroke of luck that it happened to be located where it was. World leaders argued that because it was from outer space, it shouldn't be just one country's to control."

"I hear what you're saying, but surely with all of your time-travelling abilities you could go back in time to when they were researching this and integrate it a bit better? Change some of the mistakes from the first time?" asked Owen.

"No. This is only the first part of the problem. Part B is the even bigger problem," said Finn. "Robotic technology, as I'm sure you can believe, has progressed a lot between now and 2097. Fast-forward to around 2090, 2091. The world is heavily dependent on robot technology to function and the market is flooded with hundreds of models. Because there is so much competition, prices are low and improved models are launched weekly. You'll find at least one or two robots in every home and hundreds in offices and businesses. They're great for a couple of years as long as they can recharge somewhere and have a limited set of task features, like a robot that cleans your home or a garbage bot in an office. They can exist and function without much supervision, but they become obsolete quickly. Not all owners are savvy enough to know how to maintain their robots, so they use them until they no longer function or the manufacturer no longer supports them. It's really tricky and time-consuming to keep a robot's programming current and it was cheaper and easier to buy a new robot with the latest task programming and newest capabilities."

"By the time a robot was one or two years old, it had become obsolete and so devalued that people just pitched them," said Riley. "Robots had become disposable items and the numbers being tossed away were astronomical. Regular recycling facilities couldn't accommodate the unwanted robots because of their complex construction, so they were sent to landfills. It created a tremendous problem. I mean, these aren't leftovers we're talking about. Some of these robots are as big as the average human or larger, depending on their function. You couldn't walk down any street without seeing robot parts or even whole discarded robots lying in junk piles waiting for garbage collection. So in 2091, the government tasked NRD to solve the problem. The NRD collected all the robots from the landfills and created a Robot Recycling Depot where people could drop off their unwanted robots. The volume they accumulated was staggering. This massive depot still spans three city blocks and is continually overfilled with discarded robots waiting to be processed, operating far beyond its intended capacity. The piles never seemed to shrink because deliveries of more defunct robots came in from cities all over the country. Countries without recycling facilities shipped their robots here as well, just to be rid of the garbage. Inside the depot the workers separated the different components of the robots. They recycled what they could, threw out what they couldn't and melted down the metal content into cubes and sold them for reuse."

"It was a big job and no private company wanted to take on something that was expected to yield such little profit," said Finn. "When no private organizations put in any bids, the government tasked the NRD with it."

"After the depot had been in operation for six months, it became apparent that the NRD was going to turn a very healthy profit. The government decided to invest the money back into robotic research with the goal of developing robots that were smarter and easier to upgrade. Artificial Intelligence seemed like the only logical solution. Developing a model of robots that could continually learn would solve all of the issues that made the current robots so disposable. They would know how to keep themselves maintained and they would require no upgraded task programming because they would continually learn," said Riley.

"That sounds like a sustainable solution," said Owen.

"It solved a lot of problems," agreed Finn. "But people didn't believe AI could be done. They were extremely vocal about flushing trillions of government dollars down the toilet on research that so many other organizations had already attempted and failed at."

"One of the top guys at the NRD, Ian Turner, was convinced he had the people who could get it done and he pitched his plan to the NRD," said Finn. "They agreed, but he needed to find private investors to fund the rest."

"So are you telling me that it takes until 2090 to get AI mastered?" asked Owen. "I thought it would have been much sooner than that."

"Well, more like 2095," said Riley, stretching her arms above her head and shifting in her chair. "Like Finn said, it had been attempted many times before but no one could successfully get it off the ground. There was always a missing link."

"So by the end of 2094, the AI Project had gone as far as it was going to go," said Finn.

"Was it successful?"

"No, it fell flat on its face. Quite literally, in fact," said Finn.

"Well, the AI Project wasn't a complete failure," said Riley. "The robots learned, which was further than everyone else had gotten, but there was still a major problem."

"If the robots learned, wouldn't that mean success?" asked Owen.

"Well, yes and no," said Riley. "The robots' thought processes were transmitted back to the lab to study their learning progress. The number of things a sedentary robot could calculate in a matter of seconds blew the minds of the engineers. Within seconds of being powered up, a robot had calculated the lab's size, volume, temperature, humidity, noted changes in air pressure and predicted weather patterns for the next twenty-four hours."

"All that in just a few seconds? How is that failure? That sounds remarkably impressive."

"The engineers were impressed by their learning capacity. But the problem was that the robots didn't do anything," said Finn.

"So the brain worked but the body didn't?" asked Owen.

"No, the robots were quite agile, in fact," said Riley. "The problem was that when they tested the robots' abilities, they found the robots wouldn't do anything without instruction. They needed to be told what to do. It's kind of tricky to determine where the line is between mind-reading and Artificial Intelligence. Humans, for example, learn all the time but at the same time, at work, they still have managers that check-in and periodically tell them what to do and keep them on track. Generally, most humans behave within a set of socially acceptable boundaries. So these were the baseline standards to which the robots would be tested.

"So when they tested the robots, they treated the robots like employees and asked them to do very simple tasks like putting different shaped blocks into matching holes or stacking empty boxes. The robots did as they were instructed but nothing more than that. They were behaving like First-Gen robots." Riley saw Owen's face blank at the term. "First-Gen robots or First Generation robots, are all of the task-driven robots that came before the AI robots. So these crazy expensive, uber-intelligent AI robots were behaving the same as all the task-driven robots lying wasted in piles at the robot recycling depot. The engineers were stunned and thought the AI programming must be wrong. When they looked at the robots' thought processes, it showed they had learned as they completed the tasks. The robots calculated more about the little plastic shapes and the corresponding holes than a human could ever imagine to be calculable. The engineers spent hundreds of hours running the robots through similar types of tests and the results were always the same. Their behaviour was nothing like what the scientists and engineers had predicted."

"Yeah," said Finn chuckling, "one of the tests was getting a robot to catch a baseball and it wouldn't engage. The engineer threw the ball and clocked the robot in the head. They analysed the robot's thought process after the fact. The robot had calculated the size of the ball, the speed it approached, the weight of the ball and, based on the trajectory and speed, where the point of impact on its head would be. But it did nothing about it."

"It became apparent that the robots weren't going to do anything unless they were specifically instructed to and this boggled the minds of the engineers and programmers," said Riley. "The behaviour didn't fit the agreed-upon definition of genuine artificial intelligence. Going back to the human employee benchmark, most people know that once they've completed their task, there is something else they can do. In most cases, they don't need to be micromanaged. But the robots had to be instructed task after task. The engineers finally decided that maybe more motivational testing was needed to kick-start their activity. They put a robot in a test car and showed it how to operate the car. Then, they identified the wall the car was going to hit, but gave it no instructions. As the car careened down the test strip, the robot did nothing to avoid the wall. No braking, no swerving. It didn't even put its hands on the wheel. The robot and the car were smashed to pieces. Another robot was taken up in a plane and given a parachute pack. The robot received an explanation on parachutes and how to operate the chute. Then, they tossed the robot out of the plane. The engineers watched the video footage from the camera in the robot's eyes. All they saw were streaks of blue, green, blue, green as the robot tumbled through the air, then black when the robot smashed into the ground."

"The data the robots had logged was crazy," said Finn. "Like the simpler tests, the robots logged a ton of data. The robot in the car calculated the rate of acceleration, the amount of force with which the car would hit the wall and even how fast it would fly through the windshield. The robot that went skydiving knew what the weather was going to be for the next month and predicted the growing conditions for crops for the rest of the season. It knew exactly how fast it was going, how fast it would be going when it hit the ground and, and, and…."

"Why didn't they do anything?" asked Owen. He had been so mesmerized he had forgotten about his coffee. He took a sip and found it lukewarm.

"All further tests were immediately stopped after the parachute test. These prototype robots were not cheap and they were being destroyed with every test. The programmers checked their code for errors and the engineers reviewed the logic for flaws. When neither team found any problems, they pored over the robots' thought processes for any clues to shed light on their lack of engagement. The robots would only process the information their sensors picked up and that was it."

"How did they solve it?" asked Owen.

Finn chuckled. "Would you believe it was a Chinese food delivery kid who figured it out?"

A week after the parachute test, the programmers and engineers closeted themselves in a boardroom to discuss the problems, determined to find the missing link. They worked well into the evening and ordered in Chinese food for dinner. On this night, all of the restaurant's delivery bots were on deliveries so the food was delivered by an employee. When he entered the boardroom to drop off the food, he saw lines of code, data charts and exploded views of the robots' mechanical schematics projected in the air above the boardroom table like a bizarre, three-dimensional buffet of data. Mesmerized by what he saw, the pimply teenager asked what they were working on.

One of the exasperated developers humoured the uniformed driver. "We've designed robots, but they won't do anything and we can't figure out why." The woman absently pitched balls of crumpled paper across the room into the mouth of garbage bot. As she threw another crumpled ball, the trajectory was off. The can zipped to the left and the paper ball sailed smoothly through the open lid and landed neatly inside.

"Maybe they just don't feel like it," said the kid jokingly, zipping up his jacket to leave.

The room had gone silent as the exhausted, sunken faces looked at one another. The delivery boy thought his attempt at humour may have hit a nerve. Glad to have already been given his tip, he backed away quietly.

"Oh…my…God…" said one of the engineers. "That's gotta be it. They've got no goddamn motivation. Think about it. The robots think and learn, but they don't physically do anything until it's requested of them. If they have no reason to want to do it, why would they? What does it matter to them if they exist or don't exist if they don't care about their existence?"

"Needless to say, the delivery kid got a bigger tip and from that conversation, Artificial Emotional Intelligence—or AEI—was born!" proclaimed Finn, who threw his arms wide for dramatic effect.

Riley batted one of his arms out of her way good-naturedly. "The robots needed to feel. With emotion would come interest, curiosity, motivation and desire. So, blah, blah, blah, Ian goes back to the NRD and the private investors and tells them he needs more money. Then, he pitches them on a plan to program the robots with different human personalities."

"Once the AEI robots were created, the government launched a year-long pilot project in the city. Businesses and individuals could apply for a robot and participate in the project. Soon these AEI robots were working everywhere. Manufacturing, hospitals, restaurants, and so on, working as receptionists, teachers and construction workers, you name it. At first, people didn't know what to make of them and some folks were genuinely afraid. Total social acceptance took several months. For most people, they were the greatest thing since sliced bread. Some people never warmed to them at all, saying they were unnatural and refused to work or interact with them," said Finn.

"I could see how that would be a hard thing for people to get used to," said Owen. He imagined what his reaction would be if his director came into his office with a shiny robot as his new partner and equal.

"Overall, they were a wild success. The robots were so good at everything they did and they were very likeable. People had become as fascinated with them as the robots had become with humans," said Finn.

"So did these robots live where they worked?" asked Owen.

"No. That's another difference between AEI and First-Gen robots. There was a community on the outskirts of the base where they lived," said Riley. "Don't forget that the robots were programmed with human emotions. They were essentially humans, no different than you or me, but they just happen to be made of metal. So, they worked their eight-hour shifts just like the other employees and at the end of the day, they wanted to socialize and be with others like them," said Finn.

"It's difficult to wrap my mind around a robot wanting to socialize," said Owen.

"It was really weird getting used to it at first but really, most feelings a human can experience, these robots can experience," said Riley. "And that's where the problems started. When you look at the fundamental reason for any kind of robot, they are primarily built for one purpose: improved efficiency. Every robot is created to do something so a human doesn't have to, or to do something quicker or more efficiently."

Owen nodded and thought about how, even in his lifespan, the numerous times he had heard about lay-offs because workplaces had become automated.

"If the fundamental reason for the existence of robots is to do something better or faster," said Riley, "can you see where the problem begins?"

"I don't actually. It all sounds really amazing."

"Part of efficiency is finding the path of least resistance. If you were a robot, and you needed something, does it make sense for you to work at your job, save money and pay for it? Or go through the proper channels for it? Or does it just make sense to take it? If you take it now, you have it, and that's much more efficient than waiting three months until you've saved enough money."

"Yeah, okay, but morality is part of what defines a personality. Wouldn't they have inherited some morals from the human personalities?" asked Owen.

"Yes, and a good observation, but here is the problem. A human's morals can be shaped by events as they go through life; they aren't fixed in your personality like say, intelligence is. For example, you can learn that one plus one is two and that can't be taken away from you, but it comes down the old question. Is it alright to steal bread if your family is starving? You get mixed answers on it. In fact, you yourself might think one thing, then because of something that happens in your life, your paradigm shifts and you believe something different. Apply that argument to another grey area like ending someone's life. If you asked a person if it's right to murder people, their answer is likely going to be no. But if you spin the question and ask if the death penalty should be enforced in a case where someone has murdered thirteen people, you might be surprised how many people answer that question differently. So in the case of the robots, their personality programming frequently conflicted with their core, fundamental programming goal of efficiency."

"So, the robots' behaviour degraded to a level below what most people would deem moral," said Owen.

"Exactly. Ultimately, I believe that the robots' intentions started out innocent enough, but over time they justified their actions to satisfy their needs. Kind of like how a person who feels underpaid could justify taking a few small bribes, but then finds themselves on the take for millions a few short years later. It's a slippery slope, and it rarely starts big. Each time the robots went against what they were programmed to believe was moral, their actions would become easier and easier until eventually they no longer felt any guilt or remorse.

"The final contributing factor became apparent at around the four- or five-month mark of the pilot project. Many of the robots began to resent humans because they felt like second-class citizens and the negative feelings spread like a virus through the robot community. They despised being the product of humans and it enraged them that no one dictated when a new human was born, or how many. The death of a human was never decided upon by the government, either. The robots felt like the humans were dictators and that they were created merely as a slave race. So, after a lot of debate, the robots were allowed to run the Robot Recycling Depot. The robots felt that the recycling of a robot was the equivalent to the end of a human's life. In addition, they would manufacture new AEI robots; the start of a robot's life. Obviously, the creation of robots was contingent on several factors, for example, Elevanium, plus supply and demand. The robots didn't love it but had accepted it, or so we thought," said Riley. "They took over the production and it went very smoothly, though they had made it known they were unhappy with several terms of the agreement. Being told how many robots they were allowed to manufacture really rankled at them, so they silently created their own plan and began by quietly collecting Elevanium."

"How could they do that if it's all under lock and key at the NRD base?" asked Owen.

"They stole it," said Riley. "It wasn't noticeable at first. Abandoned warehouses and manufacturing plants were broken into, but the break-ins went undetected. The few break-ins that were reported were blamed on gangs or homeless people looking for shelter; no one even thought to check the power system. This went on for a while and other mysterious break-ins began occurring at seasonal buildings, abandoned homes and empty offices. Again, no evidence, no suspects, no charges."

"The robots also bought a lot off the black market," said Finn. "They'd buy Elevanium from anyone who was looking to sell, no questions asked. To this day, those initial break-ins really could have been anyone."

"Where did they get the money for that?" Owen asked.

"Don't forget, all the robots had jobs. They got paid like everyone else and they pooled it together. The robots had lower expenses than humans. They didn't have grocery bills, cars, mortgages or investments and they lived and socialized among themselves. The only things they paid for were rent at the domes and maintenance supplies. They have tons of cash. Well, had. Their accounts have been frozen," said Finn.

"By the end of the year-long pilot project, the robots had secretly created an enormous army ready to deploy," said Riley.

"Wow. So what happened?" asked Owen.

A shadow crossed both Riley and Finn's faces. "They've essentially waged war on the city, intent on collecting as much Elevanium as they can get their hands on. Most of our downtown has been shut down for weeks. It's too dangerous for people to return to work or live downtown. They've crashed at least one city power grid so it's complete chaos in the north end. Buses and cabs have stalled out. City lights and air traffic guidance systems are down. Every public service that is powered by that city grid no longer runs. Most people have fled the city but for those who have stayed to defend their homes or businesses, the area has become a war zone. So far, we've been able to contain the turmoil to our city but it's just a matter of time before they shift their focus to other major cities. In fact, we suspect that they're already in other cities, laying the groundwork and buying more black-market Elevanium," said Riley.

"The irony of the situation is that the robots were programmed to be intelligent and diverse in their thoughts. But they devolved to the point where they had become so fixated on getting Elevanium, it's like they were programmed to complete that one task only," said Finn.

"They're behaving like First-Gen robots," said Owen.

Riley nodded. "So while we're sitting here, this city is under attack. We're here to change past events so we can put a stop to it and hopefully reverse the damage."

"But where do I come into this? Surely you guys have far more qualified people that know more about this than I do. I've never seen the stuff," said Owen.

"The short answer is that because people in the science community believe it's jinxed," said Finn.

"Jinxed? Are you telling me that scientists actually think that something is jinxed?" Owen looked perplexed. "Wait, what's the long answer?"

"Well, maybe 'jinxed' isn't the best term," said Riley. "Some scientists believe that there is something unique about it—something that they don't understand that protects itself in some unseen way—in addition to the Elevanium-poisoning. Most people who have any previous experience with Elevanium won't have anything to do with it. Throughout the years, there have been more incidents than I can count involving the people that have worked with it. In the late forties and early fifties, members of the original team of scientists that studied it ended up dead. There were seven people on the team at the start and it was suspected they had been poisoned. Two of them died and five of them were so sick that they barely recovered."

"Was it Elevanium-poisoning? Were they exposed to it in some way?" Owen asked.

"That's what everyone thought at first, but no. Their symptoms weren't consistent with exposure. But there was no explanation for what made them sick. The research was put on hold while the remaining scientists recovered. When their work resumed, one of the scientists had a car accident and died. I think he swerved to miss something on the road and he hit a tree. Later, a gas leak was found inside one of the other scientist's homes. Fortunately, no one was hurt," said Riley. "Immediately one of the scientists quit, saying everything was too coincidental and wanted no part of it. The three remaining men continued on only to die in a lab explosion a few months later. Much of that knowledge went with them when they died or was destroyed in the blast."

"That is weird," said Owen. "So what was it? Was someone out to get them? Did someone not want them researching it?"

"Nobody knows," said Riley. "There was another seventeen unexplainable deaths in the sixties and twelve more in the late seventies, not to mention countless, countless injuries. After all that, no one would touch it."

"And I've only known about this stuff for a few weeks and I just about got hit by a bus today."

Riley retrieved a small glass jar from her backpack and tossed it to Owen. "Behold, Elevanium."

"Whoa," breathed Owen, holding up the jar for closer inspection. Little white stone chips filled the bottom. They reminded him of the decorative crushed quartz that was common in gardens but with more depth somehow. The white colouring seemed partially transparent, though it was hard to tell because of its slow, pulsing glow.

Owen had a thought. "Why can't you just shrink the whole deposit down with one of those fancy tools and bury it again or toss it into the ocean?"

"That would have been a great idea, but the compression tool doesn't work on it in its potent state. We can't shrink it and we can't make it bigger."

Owen glanced down at his watch and stood abruptly. "I'm sorry, I've got a meeting. I'd love to help you, but I just don't have the answers you need." As he handed the jar of Elevanium chips back to Riley, he looked at them longingly, like he was parting with old friends. "I'm sorry. I just don't see how I can help you."

The room fell silent. Riley looked at Finn for a long moment. Owen wondered if she was mulling over a thought or having a conversation with Finn telepathically. At this point, he would believe either.

Riley slid her arms into her pack. She turned toward the door, but not before sliding a business card onto Owen's desk. "Come by our lab after work. Let us show you what we've got going on. If you still think you can't help us, we won't hassle you any further."

Owen picked up the card and read it. He looked up and they were gone.

CHAPTER 14

TEAM 2
YEAR: 2016
TIME REMAINING: 185 Days

Owen drove to the address on the business card Riley had given him and found himself looking up at one of the most highly secure research facilities in the country. He knew organizations around the world clamoured for space in this building as if it was the last seat on the bus to heaven. Its state-of-the-art facilities and "no questions asked" security policies drew top-dollar from companies desperate to ensure their trade secrets stayed secret.

After a thorough interrogation at security, Owen was handed a visitor card and admitted into the building. Riley greeted Owen like an old friend, not at all surprised to see him, as if his decision to come had been a foregone conclusion.

"Welcome to our lab." She opened her arms to the sprawling space before her. Equipment and packing crates lay in piles on the floor and counters. "We're still unpacking. This place is huge and overkill, but it's the privacy and security we needed."

It became evident to Owen why organizations paid a premium for space in this facility. He stood before one of the most spacious and luxurious laboratories he had ever seen. He knew his own lab spread over 1,200 square feet and he estimated this to be easily four to five times larger, perhaps more. Every aspect of the rented space was elegant—a word he never had associated with a utilitarian work environment.

Owen stood in the centre of the open-concept space. Cinnamon-coloured lower cabinets with black, fire-retardant surfaces lined the length of the far wall. Above which, tall windows extended fully to the extra high ceiling. The late afternoon sun poured into the room and reflected blindingly off the polished stone floors. Owen was drawn in by the view of the city and walked past several rows of workstations to the back of the room to take it in. He saw heavy-duty resin packing boxes and crates littered throughout the lab like opened Christmas presents scattered around on Christmas morning, their contents in various stages of organization and assembly.

Opposite the lab space was a fully stocked kitchen befitting a million dollar home. Lights recessed into the bottom of the cabinets lit up flecks of stone in the black, quartz countertop and the polished surface glittered like scattered diamonds. Between a break in the upper cabinets hung a sixty-inch flat-screen TV. Below the TV, a shelf showcased a collection of hard alcohol, large enough to please any bartender. An over-sized island commanded the remaining kitchen space with enough seating to accommodate a hungry team of lab workers. Baskets of fruit and individually wrapped pastries and muffins sat atop the massive island. As Finn rummaged around in the fridge, Owen saw it was stocked with sandwiches, bottles of juice, canned drinks, fruit and some other items he could not make out. Owen explored the rest of their rented space and found a hallway leading to furnished offices, dorm room, boardroom and a unisex bathroom.

Owen returned to the central lab area to find Riley pulling the lid off a black plastic crate. "Nice place you've got here."

"It's kind of over the top," said Riley, removing contents from a box and lining them neatly atop the nearest lab station. "We pretty much blew our entire budget on this place. Plus, we had to line a few pockets to skip the waiting list."

"Don't worry Rile," said Finn. He strolled up juggling a can of Coke, a cherry pastry and a half-eaten ham sandwich. "We'll save money on food. This place is stocked to the tea bags every day. Can you believe that? Owen, what can I get you? Beer? Coke? Wine? Juice? Coffee? Tea? Espresso? We've got it all."

Owen chuckled and declined. He thought it was odd these two would have to worry about money. Surely they could zip back to the future to get more, or better yet, wait for today's lottery numbers and then go back in time a few days and win the lottery.

Finn slid into his jacket and announced he was going for a walk to take in the nearby sites. He balanced his Coke and pastry in one hand—the sandwich was already gone—and opened the door to leave. Seconds after the door closed, there was a knock. Riley smiled and shook her head as she grabbed Finn's access card off the kitchen counter. She held it up for him as she opened the door.

Finn took it from her with a sheepish smile. "Thanks, Rile. You know me so well."

Owen helped Riley unpack. He came across a lot of equipment he recognized but even more he did not. Riley answered his every question with long-winded explanations that piqued his curiosity ever further.

"Have you set up your computers yet?" He smiled at the thought of what computers from 2097 could do.

"No, we haven't set them up yet." Riley grabbed a black, zippered case from the counter behind her and passed it to Owen. "Help yourself."

Owen sat down on one of the comfy lab stools and as he did, made a mental note to find out who the supplier was and order in a few for his own lab. He looked over the case Riley had handed him and frowned. It looked identical to something that would hold a tablet or an exceptionally slim laptop. Convinced something far more remarkable and future-esque waited inside, he unzipped the sleeve and pulled out a black device. Its surface was black and glassy and had no markings he could see. He flipped it over in his hands. The underside was either plastic or metal; he could not be certain which, as it looked and felt like both. He recognized it as an electronic device, seeing grippy feet and ports on either side, though these ports were different from any port he had ever seen.

"This is a computer? How do you turn it on?" Owen looked over to Riley for instruction. Strands of hair had come loose from her braid and framed her face. She tucked the loose strands of hair behind her ear as she pulled a toolbox out of a crate and set it on the floor. Owen noticed that even though she wore no jewellery and very little makeup, she could rival any Hollywood beauty on the red carpet.

"This is the CI I was telling you about earlier. It's loosely based on what you would call a computer." She stood and stretched her knees before stepping over the boxes to join him. She picked up the device, pressed her thumb to the centre of the glassy surface and a blue light flashed beneath it. Then, she placed it on the desk in front of him and returned to her unpacking. A little green light flashed where she had just used her thumbprint to turn on the device. Owen heard some computer-type whirring sounds as the little machine booted up.

The futuristic device intrigued Owen and he wondered how the little machine would transform itself into a functioning laptop. He peered around the edges to see where the screen would slide out from.

"Where's the screen?"

"Just give it a sec, it'll pop up."

Owen decided that the screen would most logically slide out from the back then fold up to take the shape of a traditional laptop. Owen slid off his chair and leaned over the top of the device, watching the back for a little door to flip open so the screen could emerge. Instead, his eyes were assaulted by a blinding light emitted from the top of the device. He swore loudly and stumbled backward like he had been punched, knocking over the stool behind him. Blindly, he felt around for anything to regain his bearings and knocked over a stack of boxes while tripping over several cords.

Startled by the calamity, Riley looked over to see Owen feeling around and trying to sit on a desk lamp she set on the floor earlier. She saw the illuminated screen of her CI and put two and two together. She hid her laughter as she leapt to his side and led him to another chair. Riley eased him into the seat and picked up the chair he had knocked over. Standing in front of him and fighting a smile, she waited for him to stop rubbing his eyes.

"Are you alright? You're not supposed to look directly into the projection eye."

"The projection what? The what?" Owen looked up at her, but all he saw were black spots.

"I'm sorry, I should have explained that." Riley leaned over and looked directly into his reddened eyes as if checking to make sure they were both still there. She smiled and patted him on the shoulder. "I didn't think you'd look right into it." She hoped he still saw spots because she could not wipe the grin off her face.

"I was waiting for the screen to pop up. I thought you meant like a laptop." Through his spotty vision, Owen could see something hovering above the device. It looked like a ghost of a computer screen and it hung in the air just above the device.

"What's a laptop?" asked Riley as she grabbed the CI and placed it directly in front of where Owen now sat.

"It's a computer. It kind of looks like this," he pointed to her device, "but folds open, like a clamshell."

Riley tried to visualize his description in her mind. "Really? That seems so small."

Owen pointed to the holographic screen suspended in mid-air. "It's bigger than that."

"That's just the default size. Nobody really uses it at that size. I'll make it bigger."

Owen felt like he was missing something. "How are you going to make it bigger? Where's your keyboard and mouse? How do you connect it to the Internet?"

Riley chuckled. "One thing at a time. This is called a Nexus Connection Interface, or CI as we call it for short. Everybody has one of these because without it, you couldn't function in society. You couldn't do most jobs and you couldn't pay your bills. It's your lifeline to, well, life and the world."

"Okay, but where's the mouse? Don't you need a keyboard?"

She eyed him suspiciously but with good nature. "I'm uncertain of your term 'mouse' in this context."

"You know, the mouse?" said Owen again, moving his right hand around in the air in a flat circular motion, like he had an imaginary computer mouse in his hand. He made a few mouse-clicking motions with his index finger. "How do you move things on the screen?"

Riley truly had no clue what he was asking and his demonstration, although entertaining, did nothing to shed light on his question. She shrugged. "You just tell it what you want it to do." The technological gap between them was more like a canyon and for some reason it amused her. She felt like she was enlightening an underprivileged child.

"Like with an input device or do you just speak to it?"

Riley shook her head. "I tell it what to do with my mind."

Owen stared at Riley with the same blank expression he wore when she had revealed to him that she was from the future. His confusion changed to awe as the screen grew to a size that made the sixty-inch television in the kitchen look like a watch face.

Riley chuckled at Owen's bewildered expression. "Your brain is going to be hurting tonight."

Owen slid off his chair in amazement and stared up at the massive screen now spanning nearly the full width of the lab. "How did you do that?"

"I just think about what I want the screen to do and it does it. It's very easy and very complicated at the same time. Basically, I have a controller that interprets my thoughts and executes them on the CI."

"A controller?" Owen asked. He looked at her hands and saw she held no controller. Nor was there any controller on the desk around her. "Where is it? Are you wearing it?" he asked, thinking of a clip-on microphone.

"Actually, I am." Riley pointed to her eyes.

Owen looked confused. "It's in your eyeball?"

"In a matter of speaking. You're familiar with contact lenses, right?"

Owen nodded. "You have contact lenses that you control your computer, sorry, your CI with?"

"Essentially. And my phone, my house, my car and everything else."

Owen shook his head and looked sceptical. "Surely you're joking?" He was very conscious that Riley and Finn could spin the wildest tale and he would never know the difference.

Riley laughed and stood in front of Owen. "I'm serious. Look into my eyes."

Owen looked into Riley's eyes and saw only plain contact lenses. He was just about to say something to that effect when he noticed two tiny lights—one red and one lime green—illuminated against her vibrant green eyes.

"Whoa," he breathed. "That is overwhelmingly difficult to wrap my mind around. How does that work?"

Riley pulled herself up to sit atop the lab station behind them and as she did so, the screen shrank to a more manageable size. "Most of the devices in 2097, for example, CIs, phones, the lights and heat of your house, cars and TVs are controlled telepathically. But for it to work, there needs to be something that interprets your thoughts and translates them into commands that your computer, car, phone or whatever will understand. That's where the Icomm communication system comes in. When I wear these contact lenses, they show me the interface of whatever device I want to control. So if I need to make a phone call, I think about making a phone call. And as I think about the numbers I want to dial or the name of the person in my contacts file, the numbers or name will appear in my vision." Riley fell silent for a moment and then continued. "There, I just thought about calling my grandfather and his number appeared right about here." Riley reached out in front of her with both hands and traced the empty air in front of her to show where she saw the numbers. "It won't work obviously, being here and all. So, if I want to turn up the volume on the stereo in my car, I just think about it. If I want to turn up the heat inside my house or pay my Visa bill, I just think about it, and it happens. If there are options I need to choose between, the appropriate menu appears in front of me. I'll then mentally choose from the options presented to me and ta-da! It's done."

"That sounds kind of dangerous doesn't it?" asked Owen. "What if you're driving and you're thinking about something and the menu pops up and obscures your vision?"

"Good question. First of all, the list is usually small, so it's rarely in your line of sight. The lenses are also smart enough to change the colour of the menus and text if the contrast is too low, so if I'm in a dark room, the menus will be white. If I'm outside and it's too bright, the menus will be dark. And, if you found yourself in a situation where your full attention was needed elsewhere, just the change in your thought process would abort the menu. Secondly, your brain is always churning through thoughts, even while you're doing or thinking about other things. It's what we call subconscious noise. Subconscious noise consumes only about five percent of your thought processes and the lenses need ninety-five percent of your undivided attention before they'll execute a command. So, if you're mulling over all the nasty things you may want to say about your boss or mother-in-law while you're cooking dinner, you don't have to worry about calling them by accident.

"Now the CI is different. Most devices, like phones, have an interface through the lenses, but more complex devices—like the CI—have their own interface, as you've seen. For the CIs, the Icomm lenses interpret my commands and transmit them to the device and the changes are reflected on the screen."

As she spoke, items on the screen began moving around. Owen watched in awe. Riley stared at the screen while objects and icons moved around. Files unlike anything he had ever seen appeared and disappeared. He recognized nothing on the display but saw a mess of moving symbols, graphs and dials. Owen ached to try but guessed that Icomm lenses, like regular contact lenses, were not something one shared.

"Wanna try? I brought quite a few extra sets, just in case," she said. She dug through her backpack, pulled out a small, cellophane-wrapped box and handed it to him. "You can order them with optical prescriptions if you need. These are plain. No prescription. I noticed you don't wear contacts and you're not wearing glasses, so I expect you'll have no problems with these."

Owen took the box from her, removed the protective wrap and opened it to find two sealed blister packs. Owen had never worn contact lenses in his life. After a few minutes of fighting with them—the right one continually popped off and landed on his cheek or stuck to his eyelashes—and a bit of coaching from Riley, he finally got them in. It was a weird sensation and they made his eyes feel heavy and tired. But weirder still was the little red blinking dot at the bottom of his vision area on the right-hand side. When he looked straight ahead, the light was less prominent and blurry, but if he looked directly at it, it came into focus. It looked like he could reach out and touch it but when he did, there was no change. He held his hand close to his face and the dot remained the same. He closed his eyes. Still there. Unlike the CI screen that was physically projected from an unmoving location, the dot was not projected, it just looked like it.

"All I need to do now is do a retinal scan of your eyes, add your retinal data as an allowable entity to my CI security settings and you'll be ready for flight. The retinal authentication is a security measure so people can't go around hijacking other peoples' cars, CIs, bank accounts and things like that. Once I capture your retinal data, we can both use this. Finn's been added, too."

Within seconds, Owen was able to move things around on Riley's CI the way she had. It was a lot easier than he had expected. Owen assumed that he would have to mentally command, *Move this icon from one side of the screen to the other.* But as he thought of the words he planned to say in his mind to execute the mental command, the action happened.

Owen found the CI to be very intuitive. After only a few minutes, he located what would be Riley's equivalent of a word-processing program and some photo albums, but also a lot of things he did not recognize. Owen marvelled at the interface. While the projected screen remained stationary, the icons and interface moved at differing speeds in an almost parallax-fashion. The screen itself looked 3D, but when he walked up to it and looked at it from the side, it nearly disappeared. The elaborately layered graphics not only looked three-dimensional but real in a way he had never seen in a 3D movie. Most actions were animated and information was frequently shown graphically in colourful, three-dimensional, animated charts and illustrations. Things he wanted came to the front of the screen and other things slid to the back and became partially transparent. Unable to resist, he reached out and touched it. His hand penetrated the image like a typical projection. He saw only a faint outline of his hand through the screen.

"So how do I get my email on this thing?" He returned to his seat and the interface moved around as he searched for the Firefox browser icon. "Doesn't it get the Internet? Or is the Internet in the future different? How do you Google things?"

"We have something called the Nexus. It's like your Internet but more all-encompassing. We can access it from anywhere in the world, even on the top of a mountain or in the middle of the ocean. The CIs are our windows to the Nexus. They're really just an interface. The applications and file storage is all on the Nexus. Everyone has personal file space on the Nexus. That's where everyone keeps their documents, files, photos and all the other crap everyone accumulates, but it's so much more than that. I control appliances, order takeout, call a cab, log into my car for maintenance updates and watch TV on the Nexus through my CI. I use it for work and every student from kindergarten to university will use one in school. Everything is on the Nexus. Unfortunately, I can't show you any of it because I can't access it from here."

"If you can't access the Nexus and your CI's only real function is to connect to the Nexus, what good will it be here?" Owen asked.

"This CI has been modified for this operation. Since I can't access the Nexus to access the notes, files and preliminary research we've compiled, this one has been modified with memory for file storage."

"And if you guys use this to pay for things, does that mean there's no physical money?"

"It's around, but you don't often see it. I don't think it will ever disappear entirely. It's a good way to keep something off the books if you want some discretion. You just need to get it from the bank."

"So you have to lug that thing out when you want to buy a coffee?" He motioned to her CI.

"The CI payment system is more for banking-related transactions. You wouldn't pull this out to buy a coffee. There is a more portable payment method." She reached back into her bag and pulled out the keys that Owen had seen earlier. "I've seen people here use plastic cards to buy things. I suspect those work kind of the same way these do." She held up one of her keys, this one the shape of an elongated V. "I can order a coffee, swipe this at the pay station, and that's it."

"What if someone steals your keys and goes on a shopping spree?"

Riley pointed to her eyes. "If my keys are out of proximity to my lenses, they won't work."

"What's stopping someone from stealing your eyeball with the contact on it and hiding it in their bag?"

Riley laughed. "My eyeball would be dead and the contact wouldn't function, rendering it and my keys useless. And, they can't just steal my contacts and wear them because the retinal data wouldn't match."

Riley resumed unpacking while Owen continued to explore the CI and the different settings on the contact lenses. Every once in a while, Riley would hear a knock as Owen subconsciously reached out to grab something and rapped his knuckles on the lab station in front of him.

Finn returned from his walk with a bag of gummy candies and an energy drink. He explained to Owen how funny it was to have actual, physical money. The sun had long since sunk below the city skyline by the time the team had finished unpacking. The lab finally looked more like a functional working space than a vacant room. Riley used her VersaTool to shrink the pile of empty crates and boxes down to the size of a toaster. Owen helped, using Finn's VersaTool. Riley was very fast and accurate and could resize the boxes three or four times faster than Owen when they started. By the end, Owen's proficiency had increased significantly.

The three stood in the centre of the lab space and took in the new surroundings. "Well, I think this'll do just fine," said Riley.

Finn rummaged through his backpack. Unable to find what he was looking for, he zipped up the bag in mild frustration. "I left the orientation documentation back at the hotel. If we order something to eat now, it should be at the hotel by the time we arrive."

"Always thinking with your stomach, eh?" said Riley. "That sounds good. Plus, if we start the briefing tonight that'll give us a good jump on tomorrow, and then Owen can decide whether or not he wants to help."

"Sounds good to me," said Owen, gathering up his banana peel and muffin wrapper and tossing them into the garbage. "Where are you guys staying?"

"We're at the Fore Seasons."

After seeing their lab space, it was no surprise to Owen that they would be staying in a hotel of comparable comfort. "Nice. The NRD's spared no expense, eh? The Four Seasons. I thought you said you were low on cash?"

"We are. We're not in the Four Seasons, as in the number, we're in the Fore Seasons, as in golf." Finn swung an imaginary golf club. "It's off of Route 54. You know, the motel with the gigantic golf ball out front?"

CHAPTER 15

TEAM 2
YEAR: 2016
TIME REMAINING: 185 Days

Owen turned into the motel parking lot where a massive rusting golf ball atop a faux-wood golf tee stood sentinel at the entrance. As he did so, it occurred to him that his eyes had never ventured beyond this rusty eyesore as he passed it each day on his way to and from work. Seeing the property up close, he noticed the little motel had a lot of character, but like the aging roadside attraction, it too showed signs of neglect. Owen cringed as his truck jostled violently as he drove across the cheese grater of a parking lot. The sign over the office door flickered, Fore S-asons—with the "e" burned out.

Inside the office, Finn helped himself to a seat in the waiting area on a floral, velour sofa and watched a staticky version of Jeopardy on an aged television set, ancient by even Owen's standards. Before joining Riley at the counter, Owen adjusted the rabbit ears atop the TV and the picture cleared. Finn looked at Owen like he had performed magic.

Owen watched as the elderly couple behind the counter finished up with their current guest. The aged proprietors were short; each barely taller than five feet. He could not help but overhear the exchange between the couple and their colourful customer. Towering over the pair, Owen estimated the woman at the counter to be at least six-foot-four. While she possessed very prominent male facial features, she was dressed to kill with bright, colourful makeup, fake eyelashes and spiky black stilettos. Her tan looked unnatural against her blond hair and she wore a fitted, pink sequined dress that she could not quite fill in the right places. The aging woman spoke warm words of thanks as she folded the receipt marked "CASH" and handed it to the flamboyant woman.

"Good night, Mr. Collins," said the woman in a husky falsetto voice. She reached over the counter easily and squeezed the old man's shoulder. "You stay out of trouble, you hear me? And you make sure you take care of that young bride of yours!"

"I will, don't you worry." He smiled broadly at the woman like she was his own granddaughter. She blew him a kiss and left the office, room key in hand.

Still smiling, the old man watched the door close. "Mandee has been coming here for years. She is such a sweet dear," said Mr. Collins. "I don't know if she's in town on business a lot or if she just likes to take a lot of mini-vacations."

Oh, she's here on business alright, Owen chuckled to himself and bit his lip to keep from smiling. The old man was clearly oblivious and Owen left him that way.

Riley paid for the rest of the week. They left the office and crossed the parking lot to Finn and Riley's rooms. Halfway up the paint-chipped staircase to the second-floor rooms, they heard raised voices. At the far end of the outdoor hallway, two men argued over a transaction that one party seemed to no longer find satisfactory.

"This wasn't the deal," snarled one of the voices. "This is half of what we agreed on."

"Prices go up my friend. Inflation. The economy's not doin' so hot right now, or haven't you heard?"

"Don't be an assclown. You can't just jack up the price for no good reas..." The first man stopped talking when he saw Riley, Finn and Owen coming up the stairs.

The second man quickly, and in no way discreetly, crammed something small into his pocket. "What are you guys looking at?" asked the man angrily.

Riley opened the door and Owen quickly ushered her in. When the door closed behind him, the yelling outside resumed.

"Well, that was pleasant." She slid out of her jacket and tossed it on the bed. "Welcome to our humble abode."

Harvest gold walls matched the shag carpet and it reminded Owen of a horror movie he had once seen. Two mismatched wooden chairs, one armless with mint green cushions, the other with arms and a tall back with salmon pink cushions, were tucked neatly around a faux-wood table in the far corner of the room. Owen felt like he had fallen into a box of pastel mints—the bedspread on the queen-sized bed was light pink with a cream-coloured, vinyl headboard. A hanging lamp, dripping with gold beads and smoked glass baubles hung over the nightstand. Owen wondered if the door to the room was a portal that took them all back to 1972.

Owen had growing concerns about Riley and Finn's choice of residence. The motel was located in a decent area but despite the owners' good intentions, they were oblivious to their establishment having become a choice location for business dealings that were not on the up and up. He had only a moment to take in the room and contemplate his new friends' safety before the arrival of the pizzas they had ordered before leaving the lab.

The delivery kid wore a concerned look on his face when Finn opened the door. Owen was unsure if it was because of the dodgy motel he was being asked to deliver to or if he was startled by Finn's overzealous greeting. Finn greeted the kid like he was delivering the last pizzas the world would ever see. The driver's eyes darted nervously between his car idling below in the parking lot and Finn, who, very carefully sorted the bills into colours and counted them out like a child in the first grade. Finn handed the bills to the driver who pocketed them quickly then dashed down the stairs.

"I can't wait to see what pizza tasted like eighty-five years ago," said Finn, closing the door and tossing the bag of napkins to Riley. He set the boxes down on the table in the corner and folded back the lids.

As Owen listened to Finn talk about all the culinary treasures he planned to eat during his visit to 2016, he found his mind wandering and he stumbled across an interesting revelation. He felt good—better than he had in the days and months previous—like he had been shaken awake from a deep sleep. This time yesterday he was heading home from work so tired that he barely remembered the drive. His only desire had been to get into bed and hope that sleep came fast. Tonight, he sat in a cramped and questionably safe motel room eating pizza with virtual strangers who had successfully convinced him that they were from the future. Having his mind blown every few minutes had mentally and physically exhausted him, but the excitement kept him on a constant high. For the first time in months, he felt normal and alive. Vibrant colour seemed to seep back into the world around him and the heaviness in his chest had eased.

After dinner, Riley dove into her preliminary briefing. Owen got a comprehensive overview of the inner workings of Operation TimeShift, the three teams and what their roles were. How Riley and Finn needed to devise a way to neutralize the Elevanium, travel back in time to the year 1200, meet Team One and execute that solution at the exact moment of the timeshift.

"I'd like to be able to help you guys, I really do, but I just don't think I'll be of any use," said Owen. "I just don't have the level of knowledge you need to…"

Riley cut him off. "I know, I know. You don't know how to neutralize it, you don't have the answers we need. Don't worry about that. You're the best chance we've got, and without you, we have no hope in hell."

Owen looked at her as he mulled over her words.

"So, Owen Taylor, will you become a member of Team Two and help us?" asked Riley again.

Owen thought carefully before answering. His brain spun like the wheels of a car speeding down a street of doubt. Even though he had seen absolute proof they had come from the future, what he had seen and learned seemed so surreal. If he awoke in bed at that very moment, he would have absolutely believed it had all been a dream. He felt like he needed a sensible third-party to verify the situation to confirm that what he experienced today had in fact been real. He rationalized to himself that as unbelievable as what Riley and Finn were proposing, the work he was doing for the ISC was also top secret to the point of being unbelievable. He suspected himself to be the only person in the country privy to the information he possessed for his work for the ISC, but that had not made it any less real. *The only difference,* he thought, *was that none of it had been explained by people from the future.* In addition, he had had no idea as to how he was going to help them solve their problem. He worried that they would rely on him and he would inevitably let them down. He was now involved with two mind-boggling projects and he could not tell any of his friends about either, which was fine because no one would believe him anyway.

Owen took a leap of faith and hoped to all that was holy he was not being filmed for a reality TV show exposing idiot scientists. "Yes. I'm in."

"Welcome aboard!" said Finn.

"So do I get a t-shirt or something?"

"No t-shirt, but you get one of these." She reached into a nearby box and tossed him a shiny silver VersaTool.

Owen caught it and his chest swelled with excitement and something else he could not describe, like being inducted into an exclusive club. He looked at his new VersaTool. It had none of the wear that Riley's or Finn's had. Riley's VersaTool looked like it had been through a war zone. He flipped through the different options on the display and set it to the MOVE setting. He picked up the ice bucket on the night-stand then placed it on the counter across the room.

"We know you've got a day job, so whatever time you can spare we'll be grateful for. And we'll compensate you for your time of course. I know we haven't talked about that yet, but part of the budget is to pay you…" Riley was interrupted by the rhythmic sounds of a bed creaking in the room next to them.

"And you get to hang out with people who live in a motel with colourful ambience," said Finn. They heard a woman giggling over the creaking sounds.

Owen shuddered at the thought of having to spend one night in this place, let alone the months they expected to be here. "Are you sure you couldn't find a better place than this?"

"We had to spend three times more than what we had anticipated on the lab. This was the best of the few choices we had. Our other options were in far more question-able areas," said Riley. Owen's scepticism must have showed on his face. "It's fine. I mean it's not ideal obviously, but it could be worse. We've stayed in much worse places than this. Trust me. At least we're not being shot at. Plus, we can always crash in that dorm room at the lab if we need to."

The woman next door giggled again, and Owen, Riley and Finn chuckled at the absurdity of the situation. They tried to resume their conversation but were derailed by a male voice asking the woman, apparently named Kitty, how she was enjoying herself. From her squeals of delight, the three could only assume she was having a great time. Riley, Owen and Finn stifled their laughter when they heard Kitty ask, in a purring voice, if he liked what she was doing, and a different male voice answered her question with a long groan, then told her how he could like it more. The thin wall that divided the two rooms moved visibly as the headboard hit the wall with an increasing cadence. A faded photograph of Niagara Falls fell off the wall. Its wooden frame bounced off the vinyl headboard and landed picture-side down on the bed-spread.

"Well, I think that's my cue to leave," said Owen, as he picked up the photo and set it on the bedside table. He was thrilled to have a bed to go to that was far, far away from this motel. The picture frame containing the fire escape instructions swung on the hook in time with each creak. He shook his head. "Okay, seriously. You guys can't stay here. I live in a large house and the space is truly wasted on one person. There's more than enough room. Stay with me until you get something less colourful lined up."

"Owen, we're fine," said Riley. Finn fell silent and looked longingly at Riley as if silently begging her to accept.

Owen opened his mouth to respond when all three were startled by a loud cracking sound in the parking lot.

"What the hell was that?" asked Finn.

"I think it was either a car backfiring or a gunshot," said Owen. He opened up the curtains a crack and peered out. Seeing no moving vehicles in the parking lot, he let the curtain fall back into place. He grabbed Riley's bag off the bed.

"That's what a gun sounds like here?" asked Finn. "It doesn't sound anything like the movies."

"Surely you've heard of gunpowder before?"

"Gunpowder? Like that old black powder in cartoons? That is so wild!" gushed Finn. "I love it here! It's so different, so unstructured. It's like the Wild West."

Owen made a mental note to inquire into that statement later; his immediate goal was to get these guys and himself out of the motel from hell. He tossed Riley her bag.

She caught it with a questioning look on her face. "Owen, what are you doing?"

"I've made my first decision as part of Team Two, and that's your relocation. Get your stuff. We're getting out of here."

"Owen this neighbourhood is so lovely," breathed Riley. She took in the opulent houses lining the heavily wooded street. He heard her breath catch as he pulled into his driveway bringing his home into view. The house was more to him than just a building he lived in. It connected him to his past and hopefully his future. He wanted more than anything to raise his family here. He had so many great memories growing up with his father in this house, surrounded by the nature that frequented the over-sized, heavily wooded plots and the neighbouring park. He even had a few patchy memories of his grandparents picnicking by the river and helping his grandmother in the garden, pulling vegetables and eating carrots fresh from the ground.

Owen had never seen another house like his grandfather's unique design. The sprawling, concrete and glass home consisted of a walk-out basement with two storeys above, extending beyond the concrete basement and created an overhang that sheltered a wooden patio. The rear of the walk-out basement featured a double garage and the concrete driveway sloped down toward two garage doors. To the right, a wide set of wooden stairs led to a landing that announced the home's main entrance. Recessed pot lighting in the overhang gave the house an imposing, grand feel. A rooftop deck was partially sheltered by an enchanted-looking wooden pergola with vines and small white lights entwined around the wooden beams. Through the tall panes of smoky tinted glass window-walls, a light in the living room revealed a spacious, loft-style interior.

Owen eased his truck into the garage between his father's Range Rover and all the tools and equipment of his father's sculpting studio. Owen helped Riley and Finn with their bags and led them to the living area of the basement, where walk-out French doors opened onto the front lawn. Finn claimed the first bedroom he saw and deposited his belongings on the bed.

Owen led them up the stairs to the main floor. The open-concept kitchen caught Riley's eye first. The warm glow cast by the backlighting in the glass front cabinets was drowned as Owen turned on more lights.

The living room fascinated both Riley and Finn in its tasteful simplicity and they stood for a moment to take in its expanse. The ceiling vaulted past the second floor to reveal the loft above. Exterior walls alternated between floor-to-ceiling pillars of concrete and panes of smoky tinted glass. A freestanding stone fireplace, the focal point of the room, complimented the dark hardwood floors and its rectangular base tapered as it climbed toward the ceiling. Gathered around the hearth was a brown leather sectional and matching couch, all dwarfed by the substantial living space. Atop the glass coffee table in the centre of the seating area lay several copies of *Architectural Digest, National Geographic* and *Outdoor Living*. Owen led the pair past patio doors and up a set of stairs to the second floor to another seating area overlooking the living room below. A coffee mug sat beside an open copy of *Astronomy Today* on the coffee table in front of a matching sofa and loveseat. A staircase on the far wall led to the rooftop patio. A hallway revealed bedrooms to the right and overlooked the living room on the left. Owen concluded the tour by giving Riley a choice of rooms in which to stay, and she chose the one Owen promised would have a spectacular view come daybreak.

TIME REMAINING: 184 Days

Owen awoke to find his room filled with sun and the smell of coffee. He felt like he had slept better than he had in recent memory. Remembering his company, he hopped out of bed and threw on a pair of jeans and a faded Led Zeppelin t-shirt. He stepped barefoot onto the small glass patio off his bedroom and immediately shielded his eyes from the bright morning sun. A light breeze blew brisk air through his hair and he heard a loud family of ducks floating down the river that bordered the rear of the property.

"Mornin' stranger," came a voice from below. Owen looked down through squinting eyes to see Riley, already showered and dressed, her hair pulled back into the same French braid as the day previous. She looked relaxed as she read the paper and sipped her coffee at the patio table.

"Morning," said Owen. He saw a black tank top and shorts draped over the patio railing and a pair of jogging shoes beneath. "You've been up a while?"

A flash of pink to Owen's left caught his eye. He could not help but laugh, looking over and seeing Finn step onto the balcony off Riley's room. Finn had found the floral silk robe hanging in his bedroom closet and he wore it unabashedly. Forgotten by a visiting friend, she had declined Owen's offer to mail it, declaring it an excuse for her and her husband to visit again. The pink of the robe clashed horribly with Finn's copper hair. Even though it was tied at the front, the garment strained over his massive shoulders and left most of his legs exposed. None of this seemed to bother Finn in the slightest.

"Top of the morning to you, Owe!" said Finn, with a mock salute far too exuberant for eight o'clock on a Saturday morning. "You're not kidding Rile, this view is amazing!"

"Yes, it is remarkable." She glanced up from her paper to agree but looked away quickly. "Dude! Come on! Glass floor!"

Riley looked back to the newspaper and chuckled. "I've gone on some sketchy ops in my time and I've seen some crazy shit. But that I did not sign up for."

Over breakfast, Riley and Finn continued to bring Owen up to speed about their portion of the operation. Finn still wore the robe, though open wide now and with sweatpants. Owen wrote notes like a madman in between bites, desperately trying to capture every word.

"So, with no real conclusive historical data to draw from on this stuff, we're really flying blind," said Riley.

Owen shook his head. "It's hard to believe that after fifty years of Elevanium playing a role of this significance in society, there's no real information available."

Riley shrugged. "There have been so many mysterious accidents or mishaps over the years that virtually no one wants to work with it. Or they do the minimum and don't touch it again."

"Well, lucky for you, I'm not superstitious." Owen leaned back in his chair and shot back the rest of his orange juice, hoping he really believed that.

CHAPTER 16

TEAM 3
YEAR: 2095
TIME REMAINING: 183 Days

Spencer arrived at the office two hours earlier than usual to reacquaint himself with the project. He preferred to do this alone so as to avoid being asked a simple question he could not answer.

As he entered his office, the lights turned on automatically. Much like his home, he noticed his workspace looked identical to that of 2097. The same art hung on the walls. The same mug waited on his desk along with the same family photos. The walls of his office, like every other office, were glass from floor to ceiling.

"Walls: Tint, sixty percent. Blur, eighty percent," commanded Spencer. The glass walls instantly darkened to resemble the tint of a car's window. It also took on a blurred quality so he could no longer make out the details of the colourful art hanging in the hallway outside his office.

Spencer removed his CI from his bag and set it on the desk. As his CI went through its boot sequence, he reviewed the files on his desk to see where his past counterpart had left off on Friday afternoon.

During the AI Project, the Neural Programming Division was the largest division in the entire project. They developed the central thought processor, or CTP—the brain of the robot. Similar to how a human's brain sends signals to the rest of the body to walk, run, throw a baseball and talk, the robot's brain needed to do the same. When the AI Project was complete, the robots' capabilities and movements were extremely realistic in comparison to a human's. But the failings of the AI Project were due to the robots' disinterest in doing any of those things. Adding a human's personality and emotions to each robot would give it the desire to be, and the want to live life and thrive. However, adding a human personality into the existing brain was a considerably smaller task than designing and building the robot's central thought processor from the ground up. As a result, only a handful of the original Neural Programming employees had their contracts renewed for the AEI Project, and Spencer was one of those employees. Their primary task was to collect twenty-two donor personalities and compile them individually into software programs. Each robot would have one of the twenty-two personality software programs installed on their CTP.

After reviewing his past counterpart's work, Spencer felt confident that he could answer any questions that may be asked of him. However, his resolve began to crack as he walked to the departmental boardroom for their Monday morning meeting. Anxiety gripped his chest as he neared the meeting room. He knew he could deliver a progress report consistent with what his past self would have, but his fear grew at the possibility of drawing attention to himself in some unforeseen way and blowing his cover. Walking into the room, he saw his co-workers had already arrived.

Kalen White was chatting with Erik Kristensen and Lisa Chan—all three robotic engineers like Spencer. His stomach did a little flip when Kalen looked up at him. Her warm smile was quickly replaced with a look of concern. "Spence, are you feeling alright?"

"Geez, what happened to you?" asked Erik. He set his cup of coffee down on the table and studied Spencer as he sat.

"What are you guys talking about? I'm fine." Their comments surprised Spencer; he felt fine, in fact, surprisingly well considering he had tossed and turned in bed all night. Their concern over his appearance, of all things, caught him off guard and he wanted desperately to switch the topic of conversation to something other than himself.

"Uh, Spence? It's March, and I'm pretty sure that you're way more tanned now than you were on Friday," said Kalen. Her blue eyes washed over him with concern.

"And your eyes look tired," added Lisa.

Spencer laughed nervously. "I'd just like to thank you all for starting my Monday by telling me I look old."

"Not so much old, Spence," said Erik. "Just really shitty."

The team sniggered quietly as they watched their boss, Jim, coming toward the boardroom through the glass walls. His approach would have been evident without the glass walls—his booming laugh echoed down the hallway as he conversed with another director. Jim's gregarious personality always seemed to enter a room before he did, a remarkable feat considering he was an extremely sizeable man.

"Good morning everyone! Let's get this meeting started." Jim sat down at the head of the boardroom table. "I know you're all really excited to be here on this perfect Monday morning, so what's everyone got on their plates this week? Spencer, what the hell happened to you?"

Logan, like Spencer, arrived at the office earlier than usual. Even with a detailed explanation from past-Logan, he had no real clue where his past-self had left off in his work and he wanted to get up to speed before the weekly meeting. Getting caught unprepared would not be a good way to start his first day. He wanted his early arrival to go unnoticed by his pit bull of a boss. She was smart and keenly observant, and while he wanted to avoid raising any suspicions, his larger motive was to keep her from expecting early starts more frequently. Logan was unaccustomed to being up so early and he hauled himself through the maze of halls half asleep, despite the extra large cup of coffee in his hand. He wore his aviator sunglasses to block out the relentless morning sun that shone through the glass walls of the building like light through a kaleidoscope.

The Motor Skills Division was divided into two subdivisions: Arms and Legs. For the AI Project, Logan had been the primary engineer overseeing the development of the mechanics and movements of the robots' arms.

Like the Neural Programming Division, the Motor Skills team had been slashed for the AEI Project. The modifications required to accommodate the AEI updates were relatively minor. Again, only a fraction of employees had received renewed contracts for the AEI Project, and Logan's boss was not one of them. Instead, Logan, now the head of his subdivision, learned he would be reporting directly to the director of the Motor Skills Division. His new role was to oversee the small group that would accommodate any minor changes to the robots' physical structure as needed for the AEI upgrades, and to streamline the mechanics of what already existed.

When Logan learned he would be reporting to Delaney Levitt, he entertained the thought of changing careers to something more fun like cleaning up roadkill or becoming a rectal thermometer tester. Knowing there was no person less like him in the world, he had concerns about how well they would work together. Logan's entire existence revolved around the weekend. Delaney's entire existence revolved around Monday mornings. He could never understand how some people could have so little interest in fun.

Logan slid his hood back as he neared his office. With several sips of hot coffee in his system, his mind had finally kicked into gear. He racked his brain, trying to estimate where he was at with his work this time nearly two and a half years prior. He turned around a corner and collided with a tall brunette, completely engrossed in a report she was reading from inside an open folder. The lid popped off of his paper coffee cup and hot coffee spilled down the front of her red wrap dress. Her papers fell and fanned out across the hall as they settled to the floor. Logan's stomach jumped into his throat.

"Dammit Logan! Watch what you're doing." The Director of the Motor Skills Division, and the person he was specifically trying to avoid, pushed up her three-quarter length sleeves and wrung out the front of her dress.

Logan found himself at a loss for words and discovered he was more nervous about his first day than he had thought. Delaney Levitt was concise in her interactions with people to the point of being abrasive and was demanding in the expectations she set. Her broad shoulders and high, wide cheekbones gave her a natural look of authority, sophistication and unwavering professionalism. Her harsh nature was offset somewhat by her colourful, professional wardrobe. She dressed elegantly—and whether she realized it or not—this softened her and made her more approachable in a way her personality could not. Logan noticed how the red dress flattered her body—one that could easily grace the cover of a fitness magazine—toned and flat where it should be but voluptuous elsewhere.

Delaney knelt down and angrily snatched up her papers. She picked up the wettest ones and shook them to rid them of excess coffee. She started in on Logan before he could to apologize. "Where are you at with the CAD mods for the new mounts in the skeletal structure?"

Logan knelt down to help her. This was the exact situation he wanted to avoid—caught off guard and unprepared. He had no answer, but he knew that would never fly with her.

"I'm making some headway," he said vaguely and flashed her a smile. He handed over the papers he had retrieved for her.

Clearly this was not the answer she wanted. "What the hell, Logan? We just discussed this last Wednesday. You said you'd have the initial draft done by the end of the week." She took the papers from him.

Logan searched for something intelligent to say and Delaney was surprised by this uncharacteristic wordlessness. Logan usually knew the answer to anything she asked and if not, he at least had some half-witted response lined up; never was he speechless. Delaney was always harder on him than most of her subs because she knew he was extremely sharp. However, he seemed to have no interest in using his brain outside the hours of nine to five. As much as his lackadaisical attitude irritated her beyond belief, Logan was one of her smartest and most reliable engineers. Delaney felt something was off about him though she could not put her finger on it. Wearing heels, her height nearly equalled his and she stood eye to eye with him. After a moment, the expression on her face changed from scrutiny to dawning comprehension.

"Is something wrong, Logan?" She raised an eyebrow and eyed him quizzically. The extra large coffee, hoodie and sunglasses were a dead giveaway and she concluded he was hung over. She had no patience for people who let their personal lives interfere with their performance at work.

Though unsure of what, Logan knew he had been busted for something. He suspected for dumping his coffee all over her dress, not because she suspected he was an imposter of his own self.

Like the past version of Spencer had in the kitchen on Saturday night, Delaney leaned in to get a closer look at his face. "Logan, what the hell happened to you? Did you spend the entire weekend in the sun? You look like shit." Delaney shook her head and smiled to herself. Men will be men and nothing will ever change that, especially this man. "This can only mean one of two things. You've either botched the CAD mods and you've travelled back in time to fix it before I find out, or you passed out in the sun on the weekend."

Sensing he was off the hook, Logan gave her a mischievous, trademark twin smile. "Definitely the CAD mods."

Delaney's interest in science started at a young age. She had no interest in spending Friday nights talking about boys, shopping or clothes, leaving her with little in common with most girls her age. Her life was further complicated by the well-intentioned teachers and group organizers who, wanting to encourage her interests, failed to realize the special treatment she received alienated her from the few remaining kids who did accept her. In high school and university, the pendulum swung in the opposite direction. Not being "one of the boys" or a school hockey star made it harder for her to gain access to the same resources and lab time that some of the men got. Delaney learned that she would have to work harder and do better to prove she was better than her male counterparts. Even when she graduated from university in the top percent of her class, she got passed over for jobs inevitably filled by lesser male candidates.

When she finally did land a job, she worked harder and longer than anyone else and her efforts paid off. She quickly established a name for herself as one of the brightest robotic engineers in the NRD.

Delaney's hard work and dedication had come at a high price on a personal level. Having finally achieved her career goals, an inventory of her personal life revealed that other aspects of her life had suffered as a trade-off. Eighty-hour workweeks meant that making friends and socializing always got pushed to the back burner. The few friends she had from university were spread around the world—easy enough to talk to, but difficult to go out with on weekends. Friday nights for the grown-up Delaney were very similar to that of her sixteen-year-old self. The only difference was now if she curled up with a good book, she could do so with a glass of wine.

Despite being perceived by many as cold and aloof, people enjoyed working with Delaney. Even Logan had to admit that she had some good points. She was highly-respected and had the brilliance of a visionary. True, there were no practical jokes and less fun in the lab, but Logan did appreciate her to-the-point personality and that instructions given by her were clear and well-defined. He knew that her expectations were high and sometimes hard to achieve, but if he put the goofing off aside and honestly focused, they were always attainable.

Asher overslept. He ran out the door of his condo with water from his shower still dripping down his back. He hit the down elevator button repeatedly and finished buttoning his shirt while he waited. He stared at the illuminated number seven, waiting for it to change. He tucked his shirt into his pants, zipped his fly and tapped his foot as he waited.

After another thirty seconds had passed with the number seven still illuminated, he raced to the stairwell door at a speed that an Olympic sprinter could be proud. He flung the steel door open and the crash of the handle colliding with the concrete wall echoed down the stairwell. He charged down the fourteen flights, taking two and three steps at a time. He burst into the lobby, startling an elderly couple shuffling out of the elevator with their walkers, then ran through a door at the back of the foyer into the parking garage.

Asher dashed past the rows of parked cars and toward the door to his private garage. As he approached the entrance, he and the keys in his pocket entered the proximity of the door's lock and he heard the click of its release. He threw the door open and stopped dead in his tracks when he saw the vehicle inside. He had forgotten that two and a half years ago he owned a Toyota Thrill—a sporty, sky blue, two-seater convertible. Fond memories of the car flooded back and a smile broke out on his face. He remembered vividly how the car hugged the curves as he sped too fast down the freeways. He recalled the day he traded this car in and bought his current vehicle, a new 2096 Honda Mudslinger. He remembered how torn he was with the decision, but the Thrill was impractical for bikes, skis, snowboards and other sports equipment. *But it was practical for picking up women,* he thought with a smile.

Excited at the prospect of spending time behind the wheel of his Thrill again, his already heightened sense of urgency to get on the road increased. He sat in the driver's seat and reminisced in the familiar environment. The smell of the interior—a mix of faded air freshener and leather—brought back vivid memories of road trips and starry nights with pleasurable company. The bucket seat felt custom-designed for his body, and the steering wheel and instrument screen looked more like something out of a rocket ship than a car. He ran his hand across the dash and admired the car's ergonomic perfection when his eyes fell on the time illuminated on the windshield.

Asher voiced his commands for the garage door to open and mentally command-ed his car to start. He listened with great delight to the throaty sound of the engine as it fired to life. He simultaneously fastened his seatbelt and stepped on the clutch. He threw the car in reverse, hit the gas and turned around to look over his shoulder realizing too late that the garage door had not gone up. Unable to stop in time, he shut his eyes just in time to hear a metallic crunch as the car slammed into the door.

The Sensory Development Division developed the robots' five senses. During the AI Project, Asher collaborated with two other engineers to develop the robots' vision. Despite the leading-edge technology they employed, Asher was never happy with the end result. He always felt like they were on the edge of a breakthrough, but their lead insisted they had run out of development time and needed to deploy what they had. In many respects, the AEI robots were cutting-edge technology, but Asher felt that the eyes were not of the same calibre. Robot eyes were mostly decorative—the machines relied on other sensors to perceive the world around them. Asher always felt there had to be a better way, but he had failed to crack the mystery.

Asher's division had not been included in the AEI Project until a serious flaw was discovered with some of the robots' sensors. Some of the robots had problems perceiv-ing certain surfaces if indirectly touched. For example, boots worn in poor weather to protect their feet and mechanisms from water, snow and salt, smothered the sensors located in their feet. To compensate, the robots relied on other sensors to calculate the properties of the surfaces they encountered. In some cases, like icy or wet sidewalks, without direct contact the robots were unable to determine the slipperiness of a surface, which created a safety hazard for both humans and robots.

When Asher finally made it into his office, his mood was foul. Sensing his uncharacteristic disposition, his co-workers left him alone when he came in and this suited him fine. Between the fury of smashing his car and being on edge about the integration, he had no interest in talking to his co-workers.

By noon, he had returned to his usual self and like his other siblings, he too was harassed by his co-workers about how he appeared to have aged over the weekend.

"It's working with you morons that's making me old before my time. Before you know it I'm going to have grey hair."

CHAPTER 17

TEAM 1
YEAR: 1200
Time Remaining: 182 Days

Jake rose early to take a walk before the day began. The sun had not yet risen, but there was enough light in the sky to see easily. He wanted to get his head in the game before the day began. Although he had been out of sorts at work for months, he had been able to get away with it because everyone went home at the end of the day. Here, he was responsible for everyone, every minute of every day. With that thought, he felt more weight crash down on him. Looking out over the glistening water in the distance, he slid his earphones into his ears, climbed down the rocky face and walked toward the lake.

Jake returned to the camp as his team finished eating; the smell of bacon hit him like a wall when he opened the door to the main tent. His team sat together at one of the picnic-style cafeteria tables wrapping up a breakfast fit for champions—bacon, eggs, toast, hash browns, pancakes and sausages. The group chatted while they ate, learning about each other and hearing about their past operative experiences. Jake filled a plate and took his breakfast into Mole Control to read reports while he ate.

Never in his life had Jake Anderson shied away from hard work. Brought up by two hardworking parents in a lower-class neighbourhood, his father worked at one of the few remaining automobile manufacturers that made road-only vehicles. He did menial tasks deemed too random or insignificant to assign to a robot. To help make ends meet, his mother ran an unofficial daycare during the day and waited tables in the evenings.

Jake had always been happy despite not having much. He had learned that material possessions were not the key to happiness. With family, friends, a barbeque, a case of beer and an old FM radio, there was nothing more he could ever want. He had literally married the girl next door; a little brunette in overalls with whom he spent countless hours as a kid building forts, riding bikes and playing catch over the fence between their two houses. Looking back, he thought he must have always loved her; although, he had only discovered this on their first day of school in grade ten when she wore a dress for the first time. He made fun of her while they waited for the bus and she tackled him to the ground and forced him to eat dirt. He could still remember the taste of the grass and his mother's shrieks later that evening when she saw the grass stains and rips on the knees of his brand new pants.

Jake and Britain—or Brit as he always called her—lived a quiet, simple life. They got married at eighteen and Jake worked in a local mine as a heavy-duty mechanic. Their quiet, happy life had been turned upside down when an accident at work had caused permanent damage to the ligaments in Jake's shoulder leaving him unable to perform the repetitive motion tasks his job required. Jake approached his boss about a transfer to a different department, but sympathy was light and excuses were plentiful—there was no room, budgets were tight—and he found himself out of a job. After a year of unemployment, he took some teaching courses at the local community college and was hired by the NRD to teach heavy-duty mechanics. His teaching career had been short-lived as his superiors decided his knowledge and expertise were too valuable to keep locked in a classroom, and they eyed him for a supervisory role. Jake found himself as a lead in the Mechanical & Infrastructure Recovery Unit managing postcombat recovery operations where his team would repair and bring home as much equipment as they could feasibly salvage. Having a family had been put off until he felt assured his job was stable and, within a few years, their first child arrived—a little girl. When they had their son three years later, Jake felt blessed beyond any words he could find. It seemed preposterous to him that his life could get any better. But it all came crashing down ten months later.

The afternoon weather brought a marked improvement; the cloudless sky seemed more blue than possible and by midafternoon, short sleeves were necessary. Ben and Lexi pushed the two suspended tunnel boring machines across the camp, setting them in front of the large windows of Mole Control, and began running the predeployment checks. Having two Moles ensured there was always one working if the other required maintenance or broke down. Lexi ran the preflight checks on Mole1 and Ben did the physical inspection on Mole2.

Tunnel boring machines were not new technology; having played a role in global construction projects for over 200 years. Despite the invention of simplification tools, the safest and fastest way to build a tunnel was with a TBM. However, an enhanced TBM equipped with simplification tools made the task a far more efficient business. If a curved tunnel was needed, the compact and agile Mole models were the best option. Miniature in comparison to regular tunnel boring machines, the Moles' bodies articulated, allowing them to cut and turn around tight corners. However, the trade-off for this feature meant slower progress.

Attached to the front of these round, white drilling machines was the drill head—a flat, disc-shaped cutting bit, constructed of thick, hardened steel with a ten-foot diameter. Along the edge and on the front of the disc were rows of interchangeable, round metal protrusions that cut away the rock. Behind the cutting disc, a trough caught the discarded debris and funnelled it onto a conveyor belt. As the rocks fell onto the conveyor belt, they passed through a compression beam which shrunk them to a fraction of their original size. The conveyor belt carried the discarded stones from behind the cutting disc, through the body of the machine toward the rear, where they fell into metal collection containers. These containers, called dump buckets, floated behind the Mole underneath the conveyor belt to catch the discarded rock. Other dump buckets lined up in a queue behind the active bucket in the collection position. Once filled, the active bucket exited the queue and the next bucket would move into the collection position. The full bucket would proceed to a preprogrammed location to unload.

Mirrored on either side of the large drilling machine were two rows of rectangular feet, several feet wide and double that in length. These hydraulic feet gripped the rounded wall of the tunnel to provide the stabilization the Mole needed to dig its teeth into the rocks and simultaneously inch the machine forward. As the Moles progressed forward, they automatically installed small pressure shield devices in the floor of the tunnel every few steps creating an invisible shield that prevented any loose debris from collapsing into the tunnel.

Ben began his visual inspection on Mole2. He hopped up the four diamond plate steps to the decklike platform at the back of the machine, moving toward the door to the inner control room. He opened the narrow door to the control room at the back of the machine, ducked his head and stepped inside the cramped space. The inner control area was not the place for a person suffering from claustrophobia. Controls covered every surface. Ancient, plastic-protected keyboards and age-faded monitors displayed status updates on the Mole's systems. The Moles could be controlled from inside this control room, but this practice was not common owing to the tiny space, the constant noise and uncomfortable vibrations. The room generally remained unoccupied unless something required close attention.

He finished his inspection of the control room and ducked again as he squeezed through the small door. Ben's five-foot-eleven, slender build made for a tight fit in the control room and he wondered how Jake would ever fit in there. His lead stood six-foot-three with the shoulders of a linebacker. Then again as the lead, it seemed unlikely he would spend even a moment in the machine's control room.

Ben circled the Mole, opening each access panel as he passed them. He pulled and twisted hoses and fluid lines to ensure they were in good shape—tight with no leaks, bends or kinks. At the drill head, he checked each tooth on the cutting disc and rotated the massive drill head with his hand to reach the teeth at the top. As he did so, the cutting disk of the Mole beside him spun to life.

"Mole1 is online and all systems are a go. How's Mole2 looking?" asked Lexi. He adjusted the tiny red earpiece in his ear. He looked over his shoulder at Mole Control and saw Lexi watching him through the large window.

His Icomm lenses picked up on his brain's intent to speak only to Lexi and the communication system engaged the talk mode just as if he had hit the "talk to speak" button on a walkie-talkie. "Mole2's passed visual inspection. Fire'r up and give'r the gears. I'll take Mole1 to the shed and load it with some supplies so she'll be good to go when Jake and Tyler are done surveying." She gave him a thumbs up and left the window.

Starved, Lexi jogged into the dining area to find Darren serving up an assortment of sandwiches, potato salad and raw veggies for lunch. Maya, Ben and Tyler were already eating.

"I was wondering if you were going to stop for lunch," said Maya, turning in her seat. "Ben was just saying the Moles are nearly ready to roll. That's exciting!"

"We should be good to start prepping the dig site tomorrow," said Lexi. She grabbed a plate off the counter and sat across from her lone female team member. "Jake should be finished those survey calculations today I'd think."

"Has anyone seen Jake?" asked Tyler.

When no one answered, eyes and raised eyebrows asked the questions they dared not verbally.

Finally, Ben spoke between bites. "He's got a pretty laid back leading style, eh?"

Darren put the last of the prep food into the fridge, took a plate off the counter and sat beside Ben. He grabbed two sandwiches off the tray in the centre of the table and took a handful of raw veggies.

"You mean nonexistent," said Maya, as Clint entered the main tent. She was happy that Jake's bizarre behaviour had been noticed by others and was not the product of her imagination. "I've had to make all the decisions since we got here. I mean, I don't mind, but some of this stuff is his call and I don't want to start off a six-month op by stepping on my lead's toes."

Clint grabbed a plate and sat down heavily. He reached over Darren's plate to grab a sandwich off the tray, knocking a carrot out of the chef's hand. "All you've had to call the shots on is where we're going to play house." He crammed the sandwich into his mouth then spoke with his mouth full. "Like that's so hard."

Lexi ignored Clint's comment. "Apparently he's an awesome leader. I've never worked with him before because our jobs seem to be at opposite ends of operations. I'm usually on intel gathering missions *before* the real ops, and he's on the infrastructure-salvage end *after* the ops. But I've worked with people who've been on some interesting post-op trips with him," said Lexi. "Time travel is a hard thing for people to get used to. Maybe he's got a family that he's worried about."

"He did look a little green around the gills when we landed," said Tyler.

"Well, we are about 1,000 years in the past and, personally, I find it's got a real isolating feel. I think it's going to take a few days for all of us to adjust," said Ben.

The spring sun retreated early and by seven-thirty, the twelve pod lights hovering above the temporary base illuminated the camp. The wind had picked up and rain began to fall but inside the WeatherShield, the chilly camp was calm and dry.

Jake left his trailer for dinner. He hoped everyone would be finished eating and have vacated the dining area, but he heard voices and laughter through the thick canvas roof of the main tent. Procrastinating, he decided to complete his arrival inspection, already two days overdue. He cut across the camp toward the sheds, noting as he walked how tidy everything looked. Even the grass—long and tangled when they had arrived—was now trimmed like a manicured lawn. Little green shoots had begun to puncture the brown decay of last year's grass.

Jake walked to the work shed, outside which Mole1 waited to be deployed. The work shed, while the largest of the three utility buildings, featured only one equipment bay. The grey shed was a modular structure and its metal-plastic hybrid panels married aluminum's light weight properties with the resilience of plastic. The lights in the darkened work shed flickered to life when Jake opened the door and crossed the threshold. Mole2 hovered in the bay at his left. To his right, workbenches and toolboxes lined the wall. Above, dingy furniture had been laid out as a makeshift break room on the mezzanine.

Jake took in his surroundings, impressed by its organization. Crates of consumable parts were stacked neatly under the workbenches and frequently used tools hung on the wall behind the workbench with magnetic strips. Along the left wall, safety clothing and equipment hung from a series of hooks and a welding cart was tucked neatly in the corner beside the overhead door. As he left the building, the lights went out as the door closed behind him.

Jake ambled over to the tool shed—another portable structure— lined up beside the work shed. It contained the less frequently used tools and parts. Jake opened the door and, like the work shed, the lights came on as he entered. Jake noticed the same meticulous organization of the shelves.

Beside the tool shed and adjacent to the house trailers was the food pantry. Jake had never been on an operation with a food supply of this size. Row after row of shelves contained boxes, cans and crates of food. At the back of the shed, a cold room contained enough fruits and vegetables to feed an army for six months. Jake opened the door to the industrial freezer to find several white boxes among a sea of brown, waxed paper meat packages marked with codes that he assumed were meaningful to Darren. Jake's stomach growled and he looked at his watch. He knew Darren would stay in the kitchen until he had eaten, and he did not want to take advantage of the chef's easy-going nature.

Jake opened the steel door to the main tent and entered the dining area. His six subs were eating at what had become their usual table.

Jake looked around the cavernous space. A tent in name, though nothing about it was tent-like except its thick canvas ceiling. The outer walls were constructed of the same plastic-aluminum panels as the three utility buildings. Lamps hung from the white ceiling, illuminating the room unevenly.

A meeting room bordered the left side of the sizeable eating area. Jake had spent many hours in this meeting room, or ones identical to it, on previous operations strategizing and collaborating with other team members. At the rear of the building, the lights were off in the medical and recreation rooms.

When Jake had entered, the team looked back, greeted him and continued their conversation. He sensed their uncertainty of him and to this he harboured no ill feelings—he felt unsure of himself, too. The smell of Darren's roast permeated the building, and Jake's stomach growled for him to get down to the business of eating. He took a plate from the stack on the counter and filled it.

"Jake, that roast is amazing. Darren is a culinary genius," said Maya, sliding her knife and fork together at the four o'clock position on her plate. "I'm so glad he came with us."

Darren looked over his shoulder at leftovers on the counter. "Yeah, it wasn't bad, but I'm not used to cooking for such a small number of people. I hope you guys like roast beef sandwiches."

"I'd be disappointed if there weren't any," said Tyler.

After Jake had finished, Darren collected the dishes. Maya stood to help.

"No, please sit. You've worked hard all day," said Darren. As he said it, Clint stifled a laugh with a cough.

Maya began collecting the dirty plates. "I don't mind. You cooked an incredible meal."

Darren took the plates from Maya and chuckled appreciatively. "Thank you, but this is what I'm here to do. While you're out working away, I'm loafing around."

"Let her do it. She is a woman after all." Clint popped the last bite of garlic bread into his mouth and laughed into his glass of wine, oblivious to the incredulous stares in his direction. Jake stood suddenly and without a word, he turned and left. The sound of the door slamming him behind him caught Clint's attention. Clint looked up to see the others looking at him.

"What?" asked Clint innocently.

Jake bee-lined to his trailer and slammed the door behind him. He sat on the corner of his bed and held his head in his hands. A crushing weight gripped his chest like a boa constrictor as he fought the panic welling up from his belly. *What am I doing here? I shouldn't be here. How am I going to get through six months of this?*

"Well, I think I'm done for the night, too," said Clint. He picked up his plate, handed it to Maya and dropped the cutlery on it with a loud clank. The knife slid off the plate and bounced off the bench, spraying her with gravy. "Better get scrubbing." He winked at her and left the table. The group watched in awe as the door closed behind him.

Lexi was the first to speak. "Did that really just happen?" she asked. "Did that shit really come out of his mouth? What is this, 1942? And what is Jake's problem?"

"I should have said something," said Maya, her eyes focused on the table and not meeting the others. She put down the plate and used her napkin to wipe the gravy off her pants. "I'm second in command here. I should have called him on it, but it kind of caught me off guard."

"I think it caught us all off guard," said Ben. "You just don't hear that kind of stuff anymore. Joke or no joke. I'm sorry Maya, I should have said something. It's not cool that none of us said anything."

Lexi stood and collected the wine glasses off the table. "I'm sure you'll get a chance to redeem yourselves. I don't know why Clint is the way he is but, from my experience, that about sums him up."

"Jake should have said something," said Tyler. He placed a lid on the pan of mashed potatoes and slid them into the oversized fridge. "It's going to be a very long six months if that's the kind of lead he's going to be."

Ben shook his head. "This isn't the Jake that I've heard about. Something isn't right."

"Well, he better get whatever it is sorted out because if Clint keeps that up, I'll end up locking him in one of the Moles and welding the door shut," said Lexi.

TIME REMAINING: 181 Days

"I can't believe how much crap is in here," said Clint. He looked up and down the racks of shelves in the tool shed for a box containing spare teeth for the Moles' rotating drill head.

"I know. It's a little mindblowing," said Tyler. He pulled down three unlabelled boxes, decompressed them and pulled off their lids one by one. Not finding what he wanted, he compressed the boxes again and placed them back on the shelf. "We're only here to do one thing, but there are so many different things that can go wrong. The Moles, the trailers. Christ, even Darren's stove could give out."

"Where's Ben? He'd know exactly where these are," said Clint with an edge of irritation in his voice. He scanned the boxes with no labels in the row he walked down but opened none of them. Clint looked back at Tyler, who was digging through a box. "Make sure you check those, will you?" Clint asked, pointing to the stack of crates on the shelf Tyler had just gone through.

Tyler looked at Clint and chuckled. "I just looked through them." He expected Clint to laugh and say "Haha, I know you did, just kidding man." But he said nothing.

"Are you sure they weren't in there?" asked Clint. "I swear they were in a grey box."

Tyler fastened the lid back on the box he had searched and slid it back on the shelf. He walked over to where Clint was idling and grabbed the only grey crate on the entire shelf, one that Clint had dismissed without opening. Tyler set the container down roughly, removed the lid and found it full of compressed boxes containing the cutting teeth. Clint reached out to grab the crate, but Tyler hesitated before releasing it.

"Dude, you gotta take it easy with the comments."

"What? You mean last night?" Clint laughed. "I was only kidding."

"I don't think people realized you were kidding."

"That's not my problem now, is it?" said Clint. He pulled the box from Tyler, but Tyler continued to hold tight.

"People might not find it as funny as you do." Tyler's tone elevated from casual to warning.

Clint put on a sad face and pretended to rub his eyes like a crying child. "Awww, did I ruffle the feathers of the hens?" His face hardened. "I'll say whatever I want to whoever I want and if they can't take a joke, that's not my problem." Clint took a step forward and faced Tyler squarely, eye to eye. He jerked the box out of Tyler's hand and walked out the door.

Tyler followed closely behind him into the bright morning sunlight. "All I'm saying is that we all have to live together for the next six months, so everyone needs to be amicable."

Clint continued toward the work shed without looking back. "Oh, I'm amicable," he yelled back over his shoulder, loud enough for everyone to hear, regardless of where they were in the camp, "all the goddamn time. It's not my problem if she's got a stick jammed up her ass."

Tyler tailed Clint and kept pace. "I don't know what your problem is, but you're not making any friends."

Clint stopped dead in his tracks, dropped the box and turned around to face Tyler. "If you've got a problem with me just say so."

Tyler stood face to face with Clint, not because Tyler wanted to fight but because he had been following so closely when Clint stopped abruptly. He had no desire to get into a fight, and he was dumbfounded by how Clint had taken a simple conversation and blown it into an explosive showdown in less than a minute. Tyler felt cornered. If he backed down, Clint would think he could get away with bullying the group.

Ben heard shouting outside the work shed and peered through a window to see Tyler and Clint toe to toe. He raced toward the pair and inserted himself between the two men and tried to push them apart. Maya ran to Ben's aid and, with both hands, grabbed Tyler. Tyler, though shorter than average for a male, carried his presence in his broad shoulders and wide build. Maya could no more restrain him than an infant could hold back a raging Rottweiler.

"Guys! What's going on?" yelled Maya. Bucked around by Tyler's arm, she looked around for Jake.

"Did you run to Tyler last night because I hurt your feelings?" spat Clint. "I don't have a problem. You're the one with the problem."

Maya was taken off guard again. She opened her mouth to speak, but nothing came out. Lexi and Darren ran up, and Darren jumped into the melee with Ben. Four arms succeeded where two could not and they separated the two men. Lexi, assuming that Clint was the catalyst, ran up behind him, grabbed his wrist and tried to pull him away. Clint spun to face her as though her touch burned him like fire. He yanked his arm up and out of her hand with such force that when it broke free of her grip, the back of his fist struck her on the side of the face.

Jake sipped his coffee in Mole Control, reviewing the preflight test logs generated by Mole1 when a commotion outside caught his eye. He bent forward in his chair just in time to see Clint hit Lexi, knocking her backward to the ground.

Jake sprinted across the camp to the group now frozen in shock. Clint stared at Lexi; both were equally stunned by what happened. The moment of silence was broken when Tyler burst through Darren and Ben whose attention had been distracted and he tackled Clint to the ground. Maya helped Lexi to her feet. Lexi looked over at Jake, holding her throbbing face. His expression was puzzled as though trying to piece together what had happened.

"What the hell is your problem?" Lexi squared off at Jake as Tyler managed to get the upper hand on Clint. Her face reddened—not from being hit but from anger. "Are you leading this team or what? I don't know what your bloody problem is but get over it! This team is falling apart and it's your fault. You're supposed to be leading us, and if you can't, get out of the way so someone can."

After Lexi's outburst, there was very little for Jake to break up. For the second time in several minutes, the group froze like statues, staring at the Level Two who just verbally assaulted a highly respected Level Five. Her words had an effect on Jake, as though she had just given him permission to participate in the team. A light seemed to spark in his eyes. He stood straighter and, for the first time, looked engaged.

Jake strode to Clint and Tyler, sprawled out on the ground. Clint wore a red patch on his face where Tyler's fist had connected with it, and Tyler's lip bled. Jake grabbed Clint by the collar and pulled him to his feet like a rag doll. He pulled Clint in close, his voice barely audible. "You're going to shut your mouth and learn some respect. I don't know who you talk to like that in your home, but it's not tolerated here." Jake nearly pushed Clint over backward as he released the smaller man's collar. Clint's eyes widened in surprise as he stumbled.

"Go and prep the drill site. You," Jake looked at Tyler and the overturned box of teeth, "surely you've got something to do. Put these away."

Tyler glared at Jake as he picked up the box of spilled teeth. In the scuffle it had been kicked over; the lid had fallen off and the miniaturized boxes of teeth had spilled onto the ground. Ben pulled Tyler to his feet and brushed the grass off his shoulder. Eager to avoid the conflict, Darren silently returned to the main tent.

Jake turned to Lexi, his expression a mixture of sincerity and concern. "Are you alright?"

Lexi's face, still reddened, had begun to swell.

Jake looked at his feet. He stammered, unable to find words to articulate his feelings. "I'm sorry...I..."

"I think we should scan that cheekbone," said Maya, cutting Jake off unintentionally. She looked over the swelling around Lexi's eye with concern. Maya put her arm around Lexi's and led her toward the main tent. Jake noticed Lexi intentionally look in the opposite direction as they passed him.

Maya led Lexi to the state-of-the-art, mobile medical unit at the back of the main tent. Doctors rarely accompanied field operations, and only level fours and up had comprehensive first-aid training. The automatic lights were exceptionally bright, magnified by the white floor of the sterile-looking room. Lexi flinched when the lights came on. The pain of the flinch caused her to recoil again. She inhaled sharply and in doing so, noted the smell of disinfectant in the room.

Against the far wall, a MediScan RX-4000 dominated the small room. The imposing medical appliance resembled more closely an expensive, oversized dining room set, not a billion dollar medical appliance. At waist height, a thick glass exam surface sat atop a stainless steel base. A metal arm extended from the base, curved up from behind and ended over top the patient surface. Attached to this arm was a rectangular metal fixture, surrounded by more glass and bright strip lighting. Centered above the base, this fixture housed and hid from view the various ray projectors, surgical tools and other tools required to administer treatments.

The all-in-one medical appliance took the place of doctors and nurses by addressing a patient's needs from diagnosis to treatment. A patient would lie on the glass surface of the device while it performed a full body scan. It would then present a diagnosis that a front-line caregiver or the patient could interpret. It also recommended treatment options, the pros and cons of each, and the expected outcomes. The patient could choose their desired treatment, and the device would administer the remedy and heal the patient sometimes in minutes, or longer if surgery or multiple procedures were required.

Maya closed the door behind them. She took her jacket off and tossed it onto one of the two stools in the room.

"Maya, I'm fine," said Lexi. "It's no big deal. I just needed to get away from there."

Maya smiled and rolled her eyes. "If you say so." She turned Lexi so she could see her now purpling reflection in the mirror above the sink.

"Whoa." Lexi leaned toward the mirror to look more closely at the mark darkening around her swelling eye. She gently touched her painful puffing cheek. "I guess it wouldn't hurt to get a quick scan."

Lexi tossed her jacket on the stool with Maya's and pulled herself onto the oversized, transparent surface. She kicked off her shoes and lay down. The glass examination table chilled her and she regretted taking her jacket off. She stared up at the glass and metal housing of the machine that doctors had dubbed, "a medical vending machine," at its introduction. When they saw how much relief it brought to overcrowded emergency rooms and the backlogs of scheduled procedures, they quickly changed their tune.

"I always feel like an appetizer when I lie on one of these things," said Lexi.

Maya chuckled appreciatively as she took in the large control screen projected up at the edge of the machine. She tapped the intangible screen in several places and the screen changed as the scan activated. Lexi lay motionless and listened to the faint whirring noises coming from the base of the device. Maya watched the three-dimensional silhouette illustration of Lexi's body appear on the screen. When the scan finished, the machine beeped.

"Good news. Nothing's broken, you just got a good whack. It recommends another scan to treat the area with some anti-inflammatory feeder rays."

"Sounds good to me." Lexi continued to lie still and closed her eyes. A red light issued from the centre of the metal housing above and focused on the injured area. The beam cast a pinkish glow on Lexi's swollen face as the warm, medicinal rays were absorbed.

The high spirits that the team had enjoyed during the first several days were extinguished like a bonfire in a deluge of rain. By day's end, the sombre mood around the camp had not improved. Jake had been predictably absent, and no one expected him at dinner. Clint sat at the same table as the others but distanced himself by sitting at the far end.

The group looked up hearing Jake enter the tent. Maya, always trying to keep the peace, greeted him warmly while the others mumbled acknowledgement. He strode to the head of the table and looked his team over.

Jake had spent the rest of his day locked in the boardroom of Mole Control putting together a plan. Lexi's words had shocked him back to reality like a bucket of ice water to the face. Everything she had said was true and he had needed to hear it. He realized that instead of just talking about leaving his past behind and moving forward, he actually needed to start doing it. His wife and family were gone and nothing was going to change that. There was a group of people here relying on him, and he had let them down. As a result, people had been hurt.

Jake surveyed the faces looking up at him. They looked tired and worn and they were only in their first week. He felt so ashamed. Lexi's cheek looked the same as it had before the incident, thanks to the RX-4000. Though the physical mark had been healed, Jake knew the damage he had caused her and the rest of the team had not.

"I would like to apologize," he said. Jake made eye contact with each one of his subordinates as he spoke, starting with Lexi. "My head hasn't been in the game since we arrived and I've been a horrible leader. I've let you all down and I apologize. I've been very distracted for the last several months, but it's no excuse. I accepted this position and I didn't step up. This isn't who I am and I'm embarrassed by my lack of leadership."

The teammates stole quick glances at each other around the table. Clearly, this was the last thing any of them expected him to say.

"Thank you, Lexi, for calling me on it." As he smiled at the petite blonde, her eyes widened in surprise. "I needed a shot of reality."

"Uh, no problem?" She smiled tentatively. "So you're not going to have me fired when we get back?"

"No," he laughed. "But we seem to have gotten off on the wrong foot, so I was hoping we could start over." Jake eyed Clint.

"Clint, do you have anything you'd like to say to Maya and Lexi?" Jake asked.

Clint looked thoughtful for a moment, popped a sugar snap pea in his mouth, then turned to look at Lexi. "I'm sorry Lex, I didn't mean to hit you. It really was an accident."

Lexi's eyes softened. "Yeah, I know."

Clint shifted back in his seat and picked up his fork. His facial expression soured like he had bit into a lemon wedge. He studied the utensil as he turned the handle over in his hand. "I'm sorry about my comments Maya, I was only joking."

"It's okay," said Maya. A weight seemed to lift from the room as the air cleared. "We're all under a bit of stress. No hard feelings."

Darren rubbed his hands together. "Well, it's a good thing you guys are getting along because I wasn't going to give any of you dessert." He retrieved a covered plate off the counter and set it on the table. "But seeing as how you're all friends again, and seeing as I like dessert," he grabbed some of his extra pounds around his middle with his free hand, "here you are." He pulled the lid away with a flourish to reveal a cherry-topped cheesecake.

CHAPTER 18

TEAM 2
YEAR: 2016
TIME REMAINING: 180 Days

Although Finn had eaten a late lunch only hours before, he grabbed a Coke, a sandwich and a muffin from the kitchen before joining Owen and Riley in the boardroom. With Owen now present after working his day job, the newly minted trio could get down to business and determine what method would neutralize Elevanium the quickest.

Finn sat down at the mahogany table and laid his spread of food before him. Riley handed Owen a thick coil-bound book and sat down beside him. Her own copy looked well-read with little pieces of coloured paper bookmarking various pages. Finn's copy wore a collage of coffee and food stains on the cover. Owen read the title, *Elevanium Neutralization Hypotheses and Speculative Assumptions*. He flipped through the pages and saw endless text, charts, illustrations, images and flow charts. He had university textbooks thinner than this and with less information.

"This book is the compilation of the research we gathered while prepping for this op. All of these methods were either suggested by the two researchers we collaborated with during the prep for this mission, or, were methods used in neutralizing other materials that we thought might be useful here in some way."

"Ugh. I hate reading on paper," said Finn, heaving the thick document theatrically while swallowing a mouthful of banana muffin. "It makes my eyes feel like they're swimming in mud. I wish we could just B-load the damn thing. I mean, who wants to physically read all of this? It'll take forever."

"Suck it up princess," said Riley, smiling as she flipped to the first page.

Owen looked confused as he so often did when Finn or Riley made reference to something from the future to which he was oblivious. "B-load?"

"Brainloading," explained Finn. "Some books you can upload right into your brain and save yourself the tiresome and tedious hassle of having to physically read it. The problem is that programming a document for B-loading is pretty time-consuming, so it's really only feasible to do it to books that are going to sell lots of copies, so mostly mainstream stuff."

Riley opened her book and flipped to a page that was bookmarked. "I've high-lighted some methods that I think might be good. For example, on page 142, there is something about a gel that could possibly absorb the energy, plus it would need to be sped up considerably. On page 275, there is something about microbes, and on 332, there's something about an electric shock. That one might be good. It seems like it might be fast. We need the process to be damn near instantaneous. At the longest, less than half a second."

"Personally, I like this one," said Finn, "on page 327."

Riley flipped to the page. "Of course you do Finn. Anything that involves guns wins with you."

"*Neutralization via Zeno Rays,*" read Owen. "Sounds complicated. And I'm not really sure what a zeno ray is."

"Zeno rays are a highly-concentrated, highly-damaging energy-based ammuni-tion. From a zeno ray gun," explained Finn.

"And did you even bring a zeno ray gun?" asked Owen.

"Of course," said Riley. "We brought supplies for all of these solutions unless it was something we knew we could get here. Some of the things we brought are unstable to a degree, so we left them in their protective boxes." She motioned to the dorm room where the packing crates were stored.

The core left from the apple Owen had eaten had long since turned brown. There were enough coffee mugs, empty water bottles and soda cans on the boardroom table to give the impression that seven people had shared the room. Owen yawned. Finn's dishevelled hair stood at all angles from holding his head over the book as he read. His eyes were red and bloodshot from continually rubbing them. Riley looked as composed as she had the moment she sat down hours earlier.

Owen felt at a major disadvantage. Riley and Finn had the advantage of having conversed with real professionals about all of these methods. This being the first time he had seen any of these solutions, Owen scanned the book as quickly as possible, trying to familiarize himself with all of the suggested methods before reading them again in greater detail.

The group read in silence, flipping through page after page. Every so often they would break into a discussion and talk through a process that seemed to have merit, but the conversation inevitably ended with Owen explaining why it would not be successful based on his knowledge of Elevanium or the pitfalls of the solution itself.

Owen rubbed his eyes. "Most of these won't work and the ones that have potential could take days or months to be effective. Elevanium is just too dense for most of these," said Owen. He flipped through the rest of the book and shook his head. "And the rest involve equipment I've only now just had a crash course in. I just don't know enough about them to give you an accurate assessment."

Finn put his feet on the boardroom table, reclined his chair as far back as it would go and tossed his book on the table. "Well, this is depressing. We've nearly gone through the entire book and none of these solutions are even close to being viable."

The group took a break to let what they read sink in. Finn showed Owen his B-loading device. At first glance, it looked like a pair of earphones—two white ear buds attached to a thin, metal headband. Owen was surprised when Finn set the ear buds on his temples and not in his ears. After offering Owen a selection of popular fiction titles, Owen selected Finn's recommended choice, *Tales from the Trench*, a highly-acclaimed, book-turned-movie about a human colony living in a pod-like city on the ocean floor. Finn started the device and watched Owen with interest. Owen, expecting his brain to be bombarded with an explosion of words and flashing imagery, felt and saw nothing.

"How long does it take?"

"An instant," said Finn, removing the device from Owen's head.

"I don't think it worked. I didn't feel anything."

Finn smiled. "What did you think of chapter twenty-three?"

"Amazing! How could a person live with such conflicting loyalties? I mean, what choice did Lennox have? The squid was…" A smile grew on Owen's face and he appeared trance-like while his memory recalled all of what it had just taken in.

"The trick is knowing how to find what you've just B-loaded. The information gets placed in your brain, but then you need to recall it."

Owen took the device from him and inspected it with awe. "What other books do you have?"

After taking in six books, Owen and Finn joined Riley at her CI. The screen showed mostly white except for some notes and illustrations on it. She stared at the screen, a perplexed look on her face.

"A digital whiteboard?" asked Owen, looking at the screen and seeing sketches and notes.

Riley looked at him sideways. "How did you know this program was called *Whiteboard*?"

"I didn't. It just looks like a whiteboard."

"I could never figure out where the program designers got the name from. *Scratchpad*, okay. *Thought Canvas* or *Idea Sketch*, maybe. What is a whiteboard?" asked Riley. "I mean, I get that it's white…"

Owen chuckled as he disappeared into one of the offices. He returned pushing an executive-sized whiteboard on wheels. He set it beside Riley's CI screen and took one of the dry-erase markers from the ledge at the bottom of the board. He drew a picture of a cube then swiped his index finger across the illustration to leave a swath of clean white in its wake, to demonstrate the dry-erase quality. He recapped the marker, hitting the lid closed with the heel of his hand.

"Well, I'll be damned," breathed Riley. Finn dove for a marker.

Owen enjoyed these few moments when the tables were turned and Riley and Finn were the ones in the dark about the simplest things that had apparently become obsolete somewhere between the year 2016 and 2097. "Surely you've heard of a whiteboard before? Chalkboard?"

Their heads shook.

"I mean, we had handwriting tablets when I was little, but that's about it," said Riley. Owen chuckled as he watched Finn draw on the board, inspecting his work as carefully as a surgeon would review his stitches, then erase it.

"It's a little more low-tech than I thought you'd be used to," said Owen.

"Oh, it is," agreed Finn. He removed the cap from the red dry erase marker and smelled it. "It's super low-tech, but it's so neat and I've never seen anything like it, well, in real life anyway."

While no conclusion was drawn on a particular method, the team agreed that the first day of research into the neutralization of the Elevanium got off to a good start. They celebrated this with a late night barbeque on Owen's rooftop patio. The conversation over dinner was lively considering the hour. Finn's fascination with the past was rivalled only by Owen's curiosity about the future, and much of dinner was spent cross-referencing different aspects of daily living to see how they differed in 2016 and 2097.

After dinner, they relaxed in reclining deck chairs with wine in hand and stared up at the stars. Owen drifted in and out of the conversation and wondered how many evenings he had been spent doing exactly this with his father over the years. He noticed he had been dwelling less on the death of his father since the arrival of Riley and Finn, and for this he was grateful. He knew that if his father could see how little living his son had done in the last six months, he would have been very disappointed. But Owen's heart had lost all interest in hiking, kayaking or any of the things he previously loved to do. His telescope had accumulated a thick layer of dust. The distractions that Riley and Finn brought were so different from the usual, monotonous routine he had designed to keep his mind occupied every waking minute—work, sleep, work, friends and more work. At night, his mind would become flooded by the waves of mourning he dammed up during the day, but that had changed since the arrival of Riley and Finn. They brought a level of distraction so unique that it encompassed him entirely.

Riley looked over at Owen, who had fallen quiet and saw his thoughts were elsewhere. She knew he would bear a considerable amount of strain between the time spent at his real job and the time spent working with them in the evenings and on weekends. She had personally experienced and seen in her co-workers, how damaging an unbalanced work-to-life ratio can be. It could destroy relationships, cause excessive mental strain and physical illness, making neither work nor life very enjoyable.

TIME REMAINING: 177 Days

For the fourth evening in a row, Riley, Finn and Owen revisited the coil-bound book of proposed neutralization methods. They had seated themselves at the back of the lab to enjoy the setting sun, which by now had long since set. Finn was reclined back in his cushy lab stool with his arms folded behind his head with his feet up. He stared blankly at the ceiling in concentration. Owen conceptualized an idea on the actual whiteboard—the same idea he dismissed hours ago, but he revisited for lack of anything better. Riley stared out the window as if hypnotized by the city's lights. They were no further ahead in finding a usable solution than they had been on their first day. Owen had eliminated nearly eighty-five percent of the suggested methods, and the ones remaining involved equipment or processes too complex for any of them to learn within their timeframe. For four nights, Owen's mind had been hammered as Riley and Finn gave him a crash course on technologies, processes and equipment that had come into existence somewhere between 2016 and 2097. With a better understanding of the proposed equipment or methods, Owen could determine whether the solution was viable. An empty wine bottle, wine glasses and several empty energy drink cans stood in a neat cluster in the centre of the lab table.

Owen erased his drawing out of frustration and set the marker back on the ledge. He returned to his seat, ran his hands through his hair and flipped his book open again. As he did when he became stumped, he started by eliminating what he knew would absolutely not work. He apologized to Riley for what he was about to do and begun tearing the pages from the book that contained suggestions he knew were no use. When he had finished, the book had lost over three-quarters of its content.

"Feel better?" asked Riley, looking at the pile of torn pages lying on the table.

"Actually, that was quite cathartic." He smiled guiltily. "All that remains now are solutions that we haven't been able to eliminate, either because we don't understand what the hell they're talking about, or we can't find a way to speed them up. Let's go through it again and investigate each unknown a little further."

This pass over the book went more quickly than any of them had anticipated. Of the areas in which the group had no practical knowledge, delving deeper into the unknown areas yielded only more confusion and wild speculation.

Owen closed his book, leaned back in his chair and stared at the pearly white lights of the city. "I think the most viable method is the zeno ray solution," said Owen after a long moment. He grabbed his book again and flipped to the page he had marked with an orange sticky note. "I mean, I'm only basing this on what you've told me about zeno ray guns, but they sound powerful enough to do the job, in theory."

Finn slid his feet off the desk and sat up straight as he shook his head. "My gut says no. Your description of Elevanium's density makes me think it won't work fast enough, mostly because the beam is too direct. I think that the gun itself is probably powerful enough. It would take too long for the effects of the narrow beam to penetrate the entire mass. It would be like trying to cook a turkey with a single heat source on one side, instead of one that is all encompassing."

"But what if the beam could be split into multiple beams..." Owen trailed off, wondering if the answer lay in mirrors or a prism. He stared out the window at the colourful gardens near the building's entrance, lit up by elegant lights. Puffs of mist appeared as the sprinklers came on. The garden lights took on a ghostly quality as the misty spray of the sprinklers diffused the light. *Diffused,* thought Owen to himself. "Yes. Zeno ray guns. I have an idea."

"What is it?" Riley yawned and closed her book, ready to call it a day.

Owen slid off his chair and woke the CI out of Unobtrusive Mode. The sleeping screen had shrunk to its start-up size, and, after being awakened, it quickly returned to the size it had been set to at last use. He cleared the whiteboard on the screen. An unshapely mass appeared with the word "Elevanium" written inside. Beside it, an illustration of a fully automatic machine gun appeared with a miniature satellite dish on the top of the barrel.

Finn squinted at the illustrations Owen had drawn with his mind. "What is that?" he asked, pointing to the object beside the Elevanium drawing.

"It's a zeno ray gun," said Owen.

Riley stifled her laugh, but Finn outright howled. "It's clear you've never seen one of these before," said Finn.

"What if," an object appeared at the end of the barrel of Owen's illustrated weapon like a silencer, "we diffused the beam?" Owen drew a green, puffy cloud coming out of the gun's barrel.

Finn studied the screen for a moment and then shook his head. "This is a great idea, but it won't work."

"What? Why?" asked Owen. "I think it's the only way to spread the beam over a wider area."

"I agree, but we'll lose a lot of the gun's efficiency that way."

"We did bring three of them, plus a ton of cartridges," said Riley.

Finn looked sceptical. "Even still, I don't know if it would have enough of an impact."

"Well," said Riley, already heading toward the supplies in the dorm room, "we won't know unless we try."

TIME REMAINING: 176 Days

The team began their day by setting up the equipment to test Owen's ray gun theory. Finn emerged from the dorm room carrying a black crate with something perched atop it that looked to Owen like a fish tank. Finn set his load down on the nearest lab station. From inside the crate, he retrieved two of three matching, elongated metal cases and handed one to Owen. Owen opened his and saw something shiny, held securely in place by protective foam.

Finn looked over Owen's shoulder. "That is a zeno ray gun."

"Kinda small, isn't it?" asked Owen.

"Well, yeah. At the moment." Finn set the two cases in the centre of the empty lab space and with his VersaTool, he decompressed the two boxes until their length rivalled Owen's height. The gun—that moments ago would have been too small to fit a child's hand—now looked so heavy and unwieldy that Owen doubted he would be able to hold one up with a single hand for any length of time. Owen was impressed by Finn's strength as he hoisted one of the mirror-finished guns up in front of him with little effort. Taking it from him, Owen was surprised to find the weapon weighed barely more than a bottle of wine. He turned the gun over in his hands, taking care not to let the long barrel hit the ground. Although it vaguely resembled a gun, it was unlike anything thing he had ever imagined or seen in a movie. The majority of the gun's five-foot length was in the long and narrow, semi-circular barrel, round at the top and flat on the bottom. The semi-circle gradually increased in size as it neared the rear of the gun's body, though Owen was unsure where the barrel ended and the rest of the gun began. The unique hand grip was the gun's most unusual feature. It looked less like a hand grip and more a metal tube, like something to be worn instead of held.

Finn pulled the second gun from its case and caressed it adoringly like a new father would his baby. He slid his hand into the flared, tubular handle. Owen did the same. Inside, his hand found a grip that matched his expectation of what the grip of a typical gun would feel like, having never held a handgun before. Without warning, the flared edges of the gun's handle clamped firmly around his hand, wrist and partially up his forearm. Owen jumped back in shock. He would have believed that the gun would have fired out rabbits before what he had just experienced. The handle had formed a flexible metal sleeve around his hand and forearm. It felt considerably snug but in no way painful. As he flexed his wrist, the shiny metal stretched like a bizarre fabric.

"Oh yeah. Sorry, I forgot to warn you about that," said Finn, chuckling at Owen's reaction. "That's the blast brace. The gun's got an anti-kickback counterbalance that eliminates most of the kick, but it still kicks and the brace helps."

Finn gave a detailed tutorial on the gun, explaining its intricacies to Owen on whom most of the minute details were lost.

Owen noticed something important missing. "There's no trigger. How do you shoot?"

"Two ways. It's just like using a CI. You tell it what you want to shoot and when, so it's pretty accurate when you're in a combat situation and your target's moving. If you're looking for a bigger blast, like if you need to blow something up that's really big and you need multiple guns, you'd want to use the remote control. You can also modify the software on the guns by connecting to it with your CI, say if you need to repair it, recalibrate it or update its software."

Owen thought it was bizarre that a gun would have software in it. "And where do the cartridges go?"

With his hand still secured around the hand grip inside the gun's metal sleeve, Finn held the gun up to reveal the underside. Part way up the metal sleeve where the base of the hand grip met the sleeve, Finn pointed out a small access panel. He pressed down on the panel and with a mechanical click, the gun's clip slid out. Similar in dimensions to a C-sized battery, a red cartridge with the word "ZENO" printed across it, fit neatly into the clip. Finn used the heel of his hand to expertly push the clip back into the gun's handle and it clicked back into place.

"You know a lot about these," said Owen. He looked over the weapon he held with new appreciation.

"Not really. Not these anyway. Some of our service guns, yes. But these aren't commonly used. They're incredibly destructive. Think of these like one of those over the shoulder rocket launchers we saw on the news the other night. Times ten."

"So if they're extremely destructive, how come the Elevanium doesn't get blown to bits by the zeno rays?" asked Owen.

Finn shrugged. "When they were doing exploratory research on it back in the fifties, they found it was resistant to a lot of things that would be considered destructive. Explosives, yes, extreme heat, no. It has some characteristics that have been found by accident. Like the Elevanium poisoning. We don't really know exactly what about it is so toxic, but we've found that standard radioactive protection protocols seem to contain it."

Riley set a box down on the lab table beside the men and leaned on it. "Finn is an artillery expert."

Finn chuckled. "I'm nowhere near an expert. I know a bit about some of the more common guns."

"Wow, Finn, I've never known you to be humble," teased Riley. "Finn spent two years in Artillery before switching to my unit."

"Yeah, I thought Artillery would be crazy cool. I loved to blow stuff up when I was a kid so it seemed like a natural fit, but it was so unbelievably boring." He rolled his eyes. "Lots of technical stuff, numbers and programming and stuff. It was horrible."

"But you were so good at it," said Riley.

"Yeah, but I didn't get to blow a single thing up, except on the range when we were testing repaired equipment. Ugh. So boring. But after being there a while, I started watching to see what unit sent in the most equipment for repairs and maintenance, and I thought that's where I need to be, so I applied. Riley's division has given me the biggest bang for my buck, quite literally."

"Either way, he's a whiz with guns and a good asset to have in the field."

"I know a bit," he said in earnest, "but trust me, there are a gazillion types of guns. Lots are similar, and lots look similar but are very different. The programming of say, a zeno ray gun, is far more complicated that the standard plasmaqueous guns we're issued."

Owen mimicked Finn and ran his finger across a sensor beneath the barrel at the gun's base. The blast brace released his hand and the gun handle returned to its original state. Owen extracted his hand from within the gun's unique grip and like Finn, set the gun back inside its case. Owen's attention shifted to the fish tank while Finn set up a tripod.

"That's our testing tank," said Finn, seeing Owen peer into the empty tank.

Owen leaned closer and looked inside. It reminded him of an expensive fish tank but with a glass lid. Looking closer, he saw a small door on the side large enough to accommodate a hamster. "A bit small, isn't it? Wait, you're going to make this bigger too, right?" He took his VersaTool out of his pocket.

Finn shook his head. "Nah, this'll be big enough."

Owen knocked on the side of the tank. It looked like glass but sounded different. "This isn't glass, is it?"

"Kind of. It's three layers of polyplastiglass. Sandwiched between the layers is a transparent film that acts as a shield for things like chemical reactions, radiation, laser blasts and, conveniently, Elevanium poisoning."

Riley emerged from the dorm room carrying two large yellow crates; the muscles in her arms clearly defined from their weight. Owen noticed that even though Riley had the VersaTool to make jobs easier like carrying the two boxes she struggled with, she rarely used it. Owen jogged across the lab, heaved the surprisingly heavy crate off her load and followed her to the collection of matching containers she had already stacked against the far wall. He was just about to unclasp the lid of the heavy-duty crate he carried for her when she spun it around so he could see the label. Owen jumped backward like he had received an electric shock. The words "ELEVANIUM" were stamped across the front with a symbol he had never seen before but intuitively knew to be toxic; a triangular circle with hooked spikes and an E in the centre.

Riley watched Owen's eyes grow with shock. "Don't worry. Even if you'd gotten it open for a second, the worst you'd've experienced for that length of exposure is flu-like symptoms for a day or so. You're fine, and these boxes are shielded. You could sit on this all day long and nothing will happen. We do need to get you suited up though."

"You guys remembered radiation suits I hope?" Owen knew he could get some from work if he had to, but it would be a real stretch for him to come up with an excuse for why he needed three.

Riley disappeared into the dorm room again and Owen expected her to return with three chihuahua-sized radiation suits needing to be decompressed to their full size. Instead, she carried yet another metal case, and she set it down on the lab table beside Owen and Finn. She folded back the lid of the clamshell case to reveal three substantial syringes—the size of syringe Owen associated with equine medicine. Riley removed one of the prefilled syringes, as well as a fresh needle tip, and began screwing the two together. Owen's stomach sunk at the sight.

"We don't need protective suits because we're shielded from the Elevanium poisoning internally." She held the needle pointy side up, flicked the syringe a few times, then squeezed the plunger gently until a drop of the silver, metallic liquid oozed from the business end of the oversized needle. "This will shield your body from the Elevanium poisoning."

Owen looked at them sceptically and subconsciously took several steps backward. "And you guys have had this? What are the side effects?"

"Don't worry, mate, it doesn't hurt as much as it looks," cheered Finn, slapping Owen on the back so hard he stumbled forward in Riley's direction.

Riley smiled to reassure him. "Yes, we've both had this shot. Everybody on Operation TimeShift got this shot. And there are some side effects but nothing major. You'll probably feel a little nauseous right after the shot and you could experience some fever symptoms in the first twenty-four hours, but that's about it."

"I'm feeling both of those symptoms already," said Owen, forcing a casual laugh as he rolled up his sleeve.

"Sorry, sweetie," said Riley, "this ain't a shot in the arm."

CHAPTER 19

TEAM 3
YEAR: 2095
TIME REMAINING: 164 Days

Within days of the three brothers inserting themselves into the lives of their past counterparts, they had become as immersed as they had the first time around. All three contended with an unexpected phenomenon—their days were frequently punctuated by spells of intense *déjà vu*. Also, having the advantage of hindsight perspective, the brothers knew exactly how the project would progress, what would work and what would not. The siblings exercised caution, careful not to let on that they knew more about the project than they should. While they tried to let things progress as they had the first time around, it was hard even for the twins not to do exceptional work when it now came so effortlessly.

Spencer stared at his CI screen, deeply engrossed in a document as Kalen walked in and sat in the chair opposite his desk. Her view of him was mostly obscured by the projected screen that hung in the air between them, but she could make out his outline through the display.

"Are you ready for our three o'clock?" Kalen asked. She held up a steaming cup of coffee for him in his favourite coffee mug—shaped like the goggly, yellow-eyed, deep sea antagonist SquidoPus from the 2074 classic movie, *Tales from the Trench*, where the genetically faulty monster offspring of a squid and octopus threatens the peaceful, deep sea human colony on the floor of the Mariana Trench. Spencer gratefully took the betentacled coffee mug from Kalen's disembodied arm as it appeared through his screen and the clock above her head caught his attention. His smile evaporated, seeing that another day had whizzed past leaving him with little feeling of accomplishment.

"Thanks for this Kale, I'm going to need it. It's going to be a long night."

"Is that Brad's file you're looking at?" Kalen asked.

"Yeah." The mug warmed his hands. "I was reviewing his initial assessment again." As Spencer sipped his coffee, he mentally instructed his CI to shut down. The document closed and within seconds the screen disappeared and the quiet humming noises of the device fell silent. He grabbed a small cardboard box off his desk then he and Kalen left his office.

"I've been looking forward to meeting this guy. He's had a pretty amazing life. It'll be interesting to meet him as a robot when this is all said and done, eh?" said Spencer.

"I think interacting with all the robots after meeting the people who donated their personalities will be fascinating," said Kalen, as the pair walked briskly toward the glass elevators. Kalen stuck her arm into a closing elevator door and it reopened so they could enter.

"Thanks again for the coffee Kale, I really appreciate it."

"I thought you might need it. You've been working late a lot. Well, later than your usual 'late.' You know we don't get paid overtime, right?" Kalen asked, smiling.

Spencer feigned shock and surprise. "What? You're just telling me this now?"

The elevator chimed for the main floor and the door opened. They walked through the eco-atrium foyer and Spencer, as he always did, took in the intriguing clash of textures the vertical gardens made against the smooth glass walls, the contrast of nature and manmade. At the other side of the atrium, he and Kalen entered a small meeting room already occupied by a middle-aged man wearing an expensive, tailored suit. Brad Jamison had arrived to begin the process of capturing a digital copy of his personality. He was one of the twenty-two people volunteering their personalities for the project.

"Mr. Jamison," greeted Spencer with a friendly smile. They shook hands. "I'm Spencer Grayson and this is my colleague, Kalen White."

"Nice to meet you," said Mr. Jamison. "But please, it's Brad, I insist."

With the offers of coffee and small talk out of the way, Spencer offered Brad a seat and dove right down to business. "As you know…"

The glass door of the meeting room flew open and Ian Turner strode in smiling from ear to ear. "Bradley!"

"Ian!" said Brad, standing again. "Hey, it's great to see you!"

Ian greeted Brad like an old friend and they shook hands heartily. "Brad, I'm so glad you agreed to this. You were the first person who came to my mind when this project came up. After me, of course." Ian winked.

"Always the kidder," said Brad chuckling.

Spencer and Kalen looked at each other and knew what the other was thinking—that Ian was not joking.

Brad continued. "Well, I wasn't too interested at first. I thought it seemed a little egotistical. But after thinking about it for a while, I thought what the hell? Why not? It's in the interest of science. And now that I'm making my donation to science before my death I can change my will and cancel that substantial endowment."

"Who's the kidder now?" said Ian, pointing at Brad and laughing.

As Ian smiled, Spencer was sure he could see every one of his teeth.

"Anyway, I was just walking by and I saw you in here so I thought I'd pop in and thank you personally again. We should hit the links, eh?" Ian mimed swinging a golf club. "Stay in touch, eh?"

As fast as Ian had entered, he was gone.

"Walls: tint, twenty percent, ripple, eighty percent," said Kalen to the room when the door had closed. Brad sat back down at the table. The glass walls darkened slightly and the clear glass changed into a pattern that looked like frozen water ripples.

"Mr. Jamison, Brad, sorry," said Spencer diving back into business. "I know that you're familiar with the procedure because you've made it this far in the process. But we'll quickly go through it one more time, just to make sure nothing's been missed. Then we can answer any questions you may have."

"Sounds good," said Brad.

"You passed the psychological evaluation and criminal check with flying colours, so now we'll begin the process of collecting your personality. The personality data collection process is long but not hard or painful. It's a two-part process. The first part is answering a series of questions, which you'll do today. The second part is wearing a brain wave interceptor and documenting your daily activities."

"Does the interceptor read my mind?" asked Brad.

Spencer noticed Brad shift in his seat ever so subtly as he asked. Spencer knew that the concept of recording brainwave data was mind-boggling for the participants. People were familiar with having their thoughts interpreted by Icomm lenses to deliver commands, but having their private, inner monologues documented, saved and analyzed was different. They felt naked and exposed at the idea of having their minds read.

"No, it doesn't read minds. While that would be faster and probably a lot more accurate, I don't think anyone would have volunteered for the project if that were the case. It just records the emotions you feel as your day-to-day events happen to you. We're trying to understand how different situations make you feel and how you react to them."

"Sounds easy enough," said Brad.

"The hardest part will be remembering to document your activities," said Kalen.

Spencer removed a small translucent disc from the box he had brought from his office. He held the tiny disc on the tip of his index finger to show it to Brad. As he touched the disc, its colour changed to match the colour of his finger.

"This is the brain wave interceptor. As you can see, it's pretty small and unobtrusive, making it virtually invisible. After your next shower, just remove the adhesive back and stick it behind your ear. At the end of the collection period, we'll remove it." Spencer returned the tiny disc to its box and handed it to Brad. "The disc will intercept your brain activity, moods, emotions and stress levels and transmit them directly back to us. In the meantime, you'll keep a log of your daily activities. This will allow us to match up what you were doing when you felt each emotion or feeling," said Spencer.

"So that covers the data collection portion," said Kalen. "Now we just need you to answer a series of questions."

"Sounds more like an interrogation," said Brad good-naturedly. "Your assistant said to block off at least two hours for it. Reading my mind might have been faster."

"It's definitely thorough," said Spencer. "The questions deal a lot with your past, the experiences you've had, how you dealt with them and how they affected you. Things like that. It helps us get the whole picture of you so we can program the personality accurately. Feelings and emotions tend to fade over time, but your answers to these questions give us the scope of who you are and the brainwave activity will add the feeling and the spark. Do you have any questions before we move to the questionnaire?"

"Yes, one. How does all this work? How do you take my personality and emotions and put them into a robot?"

"That is an excellent question." The AEI Project employed cutting-edge technology and not even Spencer could fully wrap his mind around some of its aspects. The concept of giving a machine a free-thinking and feeling personality was a foreign concept to most people. "All of the data we collect from you—the answers from today's questions, your activity log and the data from the brain wave collection—will be formatted by our team then compiled into a functional program. This working, digital version of your personality is called a Personality Application. We'll verify it through another program called the Real Life Simulator and then it will be installed into every one in every twenty-two robots."

"So it's like a program or app. Like the ones I use on the Nexus?" asked Brad.

"Well, yes and no. Yes, it's the same concept, but it's specifically designed for the hardware that is used in the robots central thought processor," explained Spencer.

"So there will be a bunch of robots that will think and react and behave in the same manner I do?"

"Precisely," agreed Kalen. "But that's only in the beginning. As time goes on, each robot's personality will grow and change. Each robot's life experiences will be different—different jobs, different social circles and different circumstances. The situations that the robots encounter as time goes on will shape their personalities into one that is different from the original and unique to each robot."

"That is pretty amazing," said Brad. "Alright. Bring on the questions."

Spencer and Kalen waited in a small boardroom that overlooked the Neural Programming CI lab where Brad answered the questionnaire. The glass wall was set to two-way mirror mode, and the pair waited on standby should Brad have any questions.

Kalen watched Brad, who sat at one of the lab's CIs. Although too far away to read the words, she saw the text of his answers appearing on the screen as he mentally answered the questions. "I couldn't believe how many questions were on this questionnaire. I thought there was only supposed to be around 50, but it looks like there's closer to a 150?"

"Actually, 163 to be exact," confirmed Spencer. He leaned back as far as his chair would allow and locked his fingers behind his head, grateful for a few moments of downtime before spending Friday night behind his desk. "Didn't it seem like there were a lot of important areas missing? I mean, there were a few questions about the recent past, but didn't it seem odd that there were no questions about the personality donors' formative years? No questions about the donors' childhoods? No 'How did your mother treat you?' kind of questions?"

"I reviewed them when they first came in, but nothing really jumped out at me. Nothing like this has been done before. It's hard to say what would be needed for sure. Ian said he'd had the tests designed by top psychologists. Honestly, it never really occurred to me to question them."

"I guess so," said Spencer casually. This was one of those moments where he had to be careful not to let on that he knew too much. "I analyzed the questions over a couple of evenings and it just seemed like we wouldn't really get a full snapshot of who these people were with that set of questions. So much of who we are is developed when we're young. Without that data, there'd be gaps, and I don't think the program will be able to generate a whole personality. The last thing we want is to have to go back to all these people for more information. So I made some additions to the survey."

"Does Jim know that you added some questions?"

"Oh, yeah, I told him I was adding a few," said Spencer with a sheepish grin.

Kalen raised an eyebrow and smiled. "I see. A few, eh? Not 113?"

Spencer smiled innocently and shrugged.

Kalen looked at her watch and saw the time neared five o'clock. She stood and stretched. "What are you up to this evening, Spence?"

"I'm going to stick around here for a bit." Spencer watched Brad, though his mind had already drifted to some ideas for testing that he wanted to map out. "I've got some planning I need to get finished up. You?"

"I was going to meet some friends for dinner. Why don't you come? We're going to the Oriental Pearl." She struck Spencer with a look loaded with meaning, which he missed as Brad had finished the questionnaire and stood to collect his things.

Spencer stood and picked his documents up off the seat beside him. "I'm sorry Kale, I can't. I need to start planning how best to test these things. Another time?" Kalen's invitation was not unique—they had been best friends since their first day on the job and frequently did things together outside of work. He moved toward the door, but she blocked him before he could open it. She put her hands on his shoulders and looked into his eyes with meaning, as if to a child onto whom she needed to impress something of importance. Spencer looked up at her, startled.

"First of all, Ian is getting the testing data from the same psychologists who wrote the questionnaire, so you don't have to worry about that." She ran her finger over the fine lines around his left eye. "Secondly, I think you're working too hard. Life isn't all about work. If you're not careful, you're going to find yourself an old man, and all you'll have are robots for friends. Come out and live a little."

Her touch sent an electric sensation down his spine and shook up his feelings for her that he routinely bottled up. Unable to quantifiably predict the outcome of him expressing them to her, he stashed them away not wanting to risk ruining their friendship.

"I…I can't," he stammered. "I'm sorry. I've got some good ideas and I need to get them out before I forget them." Spencer watched her face fall and wondered if he had just made a big mistake. After all, it was work he could do from home later.

Kalen walked into the hallway outside the observation room. "No worries, Spence. If you change your mind, we'll be at the O.P. at eight."

"Thanks for the offer, and I promise I'll come out next time. Have fun." He watched her walk down the hallway toward the foyer. With each step she took putting distance between them, a nagging feeling grew in his gut.

Spencer returned to his office and bumped into Jim leaving for the weekend.

"Spencer! I'm glad I found you," said Jim. He looked down at his watch. "Look, I know this is really last minute but my kids have convinced me to go skiing with them, so I'm flying to the Rockies tonight to meet them and I'm late, late, late!"

Jim threw his jacket on as he walked and talked. Spencer followed in his jiggling wake. "You've got such a handle on this project that I feel like I'm barely needed here. It's like you've got some kind of bloody intuition for this stuff and it's making my job so much easier. Everything here is pretty much under control and I've got some banked days that HR's been bugging me to use up, so I'm extending my weekend. I won't be back until Thursday. I'm leaving you in charge. I've sent an email to everyone in the office and cc'd Ian so they know what's going on. Have a great weekend!" Jim charged out the door before Spencer could respond.

After half an hour, Spencer had done nothing more productive than move icons around on his screen. His thoughts bounced back and forth between Jim and Kalen. While Spencer could not recall every single minute of his life two and half years ago, Jim taking this vacation and Kalen asking him out to dinner were two events that had not happened the first time around. Spencer pondered the ramifications of these two changes. Should he have made up an excuse, causing Jim to stay? Was he right to decline Kalen's offer?

Every thought he had ended with his conversation with Kalen. They had gone for dinner together many times in the past; getting dinner together was not unusual. However, her invitation today seemed different, as if loaded with unspoken words. He tried to measure the thrill of what that could mean if he was right—against the horror and mortification he would experience if he was wrong. Between the surprise of being left in charge and his conversation with Kalen, he found he could focus on nothing and called it a day.

Logan peered into the Sensory Development lab and much to his surprise, found Asher still working. As he walked through the lab, Logan surveyed the work left out on other workbenches. Robot limbs, tools and containers of spare parts lay strewn across the workbenches in various stages of work. On one table, a robot's hand and arm lay in a fireproof pan wearing a winter glove. As he neared it, he noticed the glove was charred and missing two fingers. Logan nearly tripped on the propane torch and fire extinguisher at the foot of the table. He made his way to the back of the room where Asher stood hunched over his workbench, concentrating intently.

"What are you working on?" Logan asked.

Asher looked up, surprised to see his brother standing next to him. "I didn't even hear you come in." He focused again on the items on his work bench. "I'm working on a theory I had. Check this out."

Logan looked at the object of Asher's interest—a miniature, Frankenstein monstrosity of mismatched and ill-fitting robot parts. Both men watched as the tiny wheeled device moved through an obstacle course of coffee mugs, office supplies and battered pieces of fruit. The device inched its way around a badly bruised apple. Asher seemed extremely pleased with its slow progress.

"What is that thing?" asked Logan. The device encountered a pencil and adjusted its course to the left.

"It's just some ramshackle robot that I threw together out of some spare parts. But really, it's just a vehicle for this." He pointed to the top of the robot.

Logan leaned in closer to get a better look at what Asher had pointed to. Perched atop the body sat a half-moon-shaped eyeball with wires hanging out the back. The eyeball rotated several degrees side to side. "It looks like your robot's brains are spilling out."

Asher chuckled. "I need to make adjustments on the fly. This is one of the first eyeball prototypes we developed."

"Okay, but I still don't get it. What are you trying to accomplish?" asked Logan.

"Well, funny you should ask. I was in the shower the other day…"

"Whoa, whoa, whoa." Logan held his hands up in front of him in mock defence and backed away. "I don't know if I really want to hear what happened in the shower that has you making a mobile robot with an eyeball."

"Smart-ass." Asher threw the battered apple at Logan and it bounced off his chest before he caught it. "What I was going to say, was that I had a revelation in the shower last week. I think I found a way to make robots actually see. As in, giving them the ability to reliably gather accurate and comprehensive data by what they see with their eyes and not from other sensors. Data collected visually that they can use to draw conclusions and make decisions, for both their personal mobility and quantitative assessments required for learning and completing tasks."

"Are you kidding me?" asked Logan. He set the battered apple back in its place in the obstacle course. "That's huge! What have you got so far?"

Asher picked up the robot, unplugged a red wire at the back of the eyeball and plugged in a blue one. He drew Logan's attention to his CI monitor behind his workbench. A video screen appeared. Asher placed the robot back on the course and the video feed showed different coloured shapes; an orange sphere and then a black cylinder sitting on a flat plane. Logan looked back at the obstacle course and saw the round orange and the black mug sitting on the work bench.

"So this is what your robot sees as it goes through the obstacle course?"

"Yes, in a way. Well, as you know, robots don't *see* anything. I mean, we can put a camera in their eyes so we can see their perspective, but robots don't derive information from their eyes. They've got various sensors to detect the proximity of objects around them. They can't necessarily tell what the objects are, they just know they have to go around them. People just assume they see it with their eyes because that's how humans see. A person can tell it's going to rain because they can see the sky is stormy. A robot can tell it's going to rain because of the barometric pressure change."

"Wait, are you telling me it's not because their knees get squeaky?"

Asher made a face at Logan. "What you're watching on this video feed is a visual interpretation of what the different sensors have perceived its surroundings to be." He tapped the small square box under the eyeball. "The sensors are here in the body."

Logan put his hand in front of the robot and a vague shape resembling Logan's hand appeared on the screen.

Asher picked up the robot again, unplugged the blue cable and reinserted the red one. He set the robot down and the video feed again showed the obstacle course from the robot's perspective but this time, as clear as the human eye would see. The robot's eye shifted to the right. Logan watched the scene on the video feed shift to the right. It looked back to the left again and at the orange. It zoomed in so closely to the orange peel that the entire screen filled with a yellowy-orange blur. It zoomed out again and focused on the outer skin. A circular, three-dimensional grid appeared on the screen over the orange. A white horizontal line scanned the orange from top to bottom. An information table with small text and numbers appeared on the screen next to the orange and the data in the table began to change and refresh itself so rapidly that Logan could not read any of it. The grid disappeared, as did the table of text and numbers. The robot moved forward and the brothers watched its progress on the screen. It manoeuvred around the orange and stopped. The eye examined the coffee mug the same way it had the orange.

"That robot is seeing and analyzing its surroundings."

"That's amazing," said Logan. He was impressed with his brother's work. "I sometimes forget that robots can't see. I mean, they've got eyes."

"Right. People assume they can see because they're designed with decorative eyes. But it's a mental thing. I mean, if these robots are going to integrate into everyday life, they need to resemble the human form to a certain degree for people to relate to them. People won't really see them as equals if they look like kitchen appliances."

Logan laughed at the thought of going for drinks on a Friday night with a blender. "No, I suppose not."

"If I can crack this thing, it will open up a whole world of possibilities for these robots. I mean, think about it. A robot can't do reliable visual inspections. As an example, a robot couldn't go through a building and do a fire safety inspection. It couldn't reliably inspect the quality of the safety items to determine a pass or fail. Think of the advancements this could do for law enforcement. Lightning fast, reliable, facial recognition that could identify criminals or suspects and nab them on sight? The possibilities are endless."

"I didn't realize you were working on this again. I didn't think optics was being revisited?"

"No, you're right, it isn't. Not officially anyway, but I wanted to test my theory. It's been a little slow around here because some parts were on back order. It gave me some free time to work on it. But the new sensors have been delivered, so it's back to solving the ol' slip and slide problem."

"How's that going by the way?" asked Logan.

"Not good. We may have to add some additional sensors, but I don't like that idea. It doesn't truly solve the problem and it overcomplicates the construction. If I can crack this vision thing, it will resolve this issue as a by-product.

"So I decided—brace yourself now—that I'm going to spend a couple of evenings here and see if I can come up with some concrete results. With a solid proof of concept, I might get some time allocated to revisit optics again officially."

Logan stared at his brother, his face deadpan. "You're right. I don't believe it. I thought you didn't believe in overtime? Didn't you say that too much work destroyed your soul?"

Asher chuckled. "Don't get me wrong. That is still the foundation of my occupational belief system. But I wouldn't call it overtime, think of it more as a hobby. How's that?"

"It's unnatural," said Logan. He looked disgusted. "Okay, what are we doing tonight?"

"Working. Sorry, I mean, exploring my hobby," said Asher.

"What? Tonight? It's Friday. I thought you meant next week or something."

"I'll just stay another hour or so. Where are you heading?"

Logan thought for a moment. He came up with nothing and shrugged. "Without you? I don't know. I guess I'll probably just go home and catch a game on TV or something."

"I'll call you when I'm done, and then we can go out and paint the town Grayson." Asher watched Logan leave as he picked up his robot. He switched some of the wires, placed the robot at the beginning of the obstacle course again and watched it inch toward a box of tissues.

Spencer stood rooted to the sidewalk outside the doors of the Oriental Pearl. Paralyzed with fear, his gaze had become locked on the neon restaurant sign like a deer caught in the headlights of an oncoming car. He wondered if he was crazy. *How long have I been standing here?* he asked himself. *Oh man, what am I doing? Her invitation didn't mean anything, she's just out with friends. She's eating dinner and she knows you eat dinner, too. Because people eat dinner all the time. Nothing more than that. The two of you have eaten dinner together plenty of times and this is no different. Or is it? Why does it feel different? Okay, you need to do something, you're going to have 'Oriental' burned into your retinas for a week. You'll be looking at her and instead of her head, all you'll see is "ental." "Ental," like mental, which is what you are for coming here.*

Spencer closed his eyes and turned to lean on the brick wall beside the door. Neither of the twins would agonize over what an invitation to dinner did or did not mean. He sighed heavily and walked toward his car, staring at the pavement and wishing he had just a fraction of the twin's confidence. Burned into his vision, the blackened word, "Oriental" stayed two steps ahead of him on the sidewalk as he walked.

"Spencer?"

His eyes shot up from the sidewalk and he saw Kalen and her friends approaching him.

"Spence! You came!" She ran up to greet him.

Her face lit up with a smile and Spencer saw her blue eyes sparkle. Her honey brown hair seemed almost blonde in the glow of the street lamps. Although Spencer had none of the twins' height, at five-foot-eleven, he towered over Kalen, barely a shade over five feet. Spencer's stomach felt like it had come loose and was sliding down toward his navel. He thought of everything and nothing simultaneously. He tried to say "hey" but it came out as a squeak. He coughed quickly. "Uh, hi. Am I late for dinner?"

"Well, you will be if you keep walking the wrong way." She grabbed him by the arm, spun him around and marched him toward the restaurant.

The dinner party broke up well after ten. Kalen followed Spencer to his car before joining her friends.

"I'm really glad you came out tonight, Spence." She took his arm as they walked. "I think you're working too hard. You need to take more time to relax and enjoy life."

"I know. You're right. It's just a busy time at the office. Well, you know. Thanks for inviting me. It was nice to get out and I had a great time." He smiled at her, unsure where the conversation was going. An awkward silence fell between them and he found himself rambling to fill the void. "Well, thanks again. It was a lot of fun."

"Yeah, it was," said Kalen. She smiled up at him.

Spencer saw the city lights reflected in her impossibly large eyes. She was wearing more makeup than usual and he thought to himself for the thousandth time, how beautiful she was. She radiated a warmth that made him feel at ease with her, usually. At this moment, his heart pounded so loudly he worried she would hear it. Nervous and unsure of what to do, he gave her an awkward hug. He walked around to the driver's door of his car and got in. Kalen sighed, gave him a small smile and weak wave through the passenger window. He waved back and forced a smile that he knew was too big and cheesy.

Three blocks later and with the advantage of hindsight, Spencer felt sure that Kalen may have been expecting something more and he had just failed spectacularly.

TIME REMAINING: 161 Days

Monday rolled around and as expected, no one had heard from Jim. Spencer worried about what his initial encounter with Kalen would be like. He wondered if it would be awkward or maybe he had just misread the entire situation altogether. Whatever the case, he came prepared. Two Starbucks coffees, hers with a shot of caramel—the way he knew she liked it. He hoped to give it to her in private, worried that if his co-workers saw him give it to her, they would see how he felt about her as plainly as a blinking neon sign.

Secretly relieved she had not yet arrived, Spencer left the coffee on her desk and returned to his office to prepare for the weekly meeting he would run in Jim's absence.

Spencer, Lisa, Erik and Kalen—with her coffee—congregated in the boardroom. Lisa asked Kalen about her weekend and Spencer jumped right into the meeting before she could respond. Erik began his report on his risk assessment when Ian charged into the boardroom.

"I have some bad news, folks. Spencer, can I talk to you for a moment?" Ian sat across from Spencer, looking grave. Taking this as a cue to leave, the others left the room.

"Spencer, there's been an accident."

"What? Who?" His thoughts turned immediately to his idiot brothers and their usual weekend antics. He had spoken to neither of his brothers all weekend.

"It's Jim."

"Jim? What kind of an accident?" Spencer had visions of a plane crash or Jim careening off the side of a mountain out of control on a pair of skis, an avalanche...

"Skiing accident. Don't worry, he's fine, just a few broken bones. Well, a lot of broken bones. What business a man with that little skiing ability has on a double black diamond is beyond me. I think he went over the edge of a small cliff or something, or was skiing at the base of a cliff and hit a rock..." Ian paused in thought. "Well, I'm really not too sure of the details but the bottom line is, he's going to be out of the game for a while. He's got a broken hip, fractured and bruised ribs, a compressed spine I think, and a bunch of other things. He hit his head pretty good too, I think. He's conscious at the moment, but it sounds like he's got some surgeries lined up and months of rehab."

"Wow," said Spencer taking in the news. "So what happens now? Who's taking over for him?"

"Well, you are." Ian said this as if it should have been obvious and Spencer was slow to catch on.

"I'm sorry?"

"Jim's been going on and on about you and how brilliant you are and how you seem to have an intuition for this stuff. In the brief conversation I had with him on the phone, he said to let you continue running things and the project would be more than fine," said Ian with a quick smile. "But then he did follow that up with a story about a lobster on a rollercoaster, so make whatever you will out of that." Spencer noticed Ian seemed fidgety and distracted, like this meeting was taking too long and he had somewhere else to be.

"Alright then," said Spencer slowly, processing the last two minute's conversation. Jim's health and well-being concerned him to be sure, but at the same time, fireworks went off in his brain about this extension of his foray into leadership.

"I'll send you details about what I need from you in terms of status updates, deliverables and whatnot. I'll also get you access to Jim's files. Congrats kid, you've levelled up. I'll get HR to do up the papers and get them to you to sign. I'll let you get your team up to speed on this. Not too much will change for them."

"Uh, thanks," stammered Spencer.

"Keep up the good work!" Spencer blinked and Ian was gone. His co-workers milled about in the hallway trying to look busy as Ian sped out. As soon as Ian was out of sight, they rushed back in. With their mood dampened by the news of Jim, they continued solemnly through the meeting.

TIME REMAINING: 159 Days

"Well, I'll be damned. Hell must be freezing over." Delaney folded her black leather jacket over her arm as she walked into Motor Skills Lab to find Logan working in the corner. "Is that Logan Grayson...putting in overtime?"

"Very funny." Logan made a face at her. "I could say the opposite of you. This is uncharacteristically early for you to be leaving."

She walked over to his workbench. "I've got a university friend in town for a couple of days. He's insisting that we go out every night this week to break me of my bad work habits."

Logan looked up from his work. "And how's that working for you?"

"I've been having a lot of fun actually. I can see his point. I might try this spontaneity thing a little more often. Maybe, if I can schedule it in somewhere."

"You're going to schedule in spontaneity? Isn't that the opposite of being spontaneous?"

"Maybe, but I've got a limited amount of free time. So, I'll leave some room open in my schedule here and there, and when that time comes, I'll do something spontaneous." She walked toward the door to leave.

Logan chuckled at what could only be a workaholic's definition of spontaneous. "Well, have fun and stay out of trouble, eh?" He watched the door close behind her and focused his attention back on the robot.

CHAPTER 20

TEAM 1
YEAR: 1200
TIME REMAINING: 159 Days

As drilling got underway, the daily activities of Team One fell into a monotonous routine. The active Mole would work for six to eight hours a day, sometimes more if everything remained operationally sound. A good day for productivity meant a dull day for the team. However, most days were not problem-free. Snags and obstacles were as inevitable as night following day, and solving problems kept the team busy.

Ben and Tyler spent most of their time maintaining whatever inactive Mole occupied their workspace—the tradeoff for the specialized nature of the Moles meant frequent maintenance due to their intricate construction. Ben's expectations had been exceeded by the Moles' performance to date. The small number of break-fixes that required the team's attention impressed Jake as well, despite several late nights spent troubleshooting a few intermittent problems. Clint would pitch in and help Ben and Tyler. But for the most part, his time was split between Mole Control with Lexi and Jake or inside the cramped control room of the Mole itself, analyzing the machine and monitoring rock scans.

As Jake neared the drill site, he could hear the rumble of the machine and felt the ground vibrating as the Mole chewed its way through the rock below. He entered the tunnel and consciously controlled his walking speed along the decline. The cutting angle struck a balance between being safe enough for the team to traverse safely but not so slight that it added excessive drilling distance.

Jake walked to where the Mole was busy chewing away. A thin strip of microlighting affixed to the ceiling lit up every scrape and cut mark the drill's teeth left on the rounded stone walls. Jake watched the drill slowly inch its way forward. He enjoyed the loud, heavy crushing sound of the rocks being cut away and the deep hum of the drill's engine. A beep caught Jake's attention; the active dump bucket reached its capacity and slid to the left, leaving its position beneath the spinning conveyor belt and away from the Mole. The floating rectangular bucket waiting in the queue moved forward and took its place under the conveyor belt. The bucket, heaping with discarded rock, slowly began the ascent to the surface.

Jake grabbed the railing at the back of the machine and hopped up the steps two at a time. He had felt the vibrations when he stood on the stone floor but now standing on the rear deck, the intense sensations pulsated through the steel shanks in his work boots and tickled his feet. He opened the door to the control room to check on Clint.

"How's it going down here?" yelled Jake over the noise.

"Not too bad," yelled Clint. Clint tapped one of the touch screen monitors and the display changed to show the status of various ongoing sensor readings. He scrolled through the different screens, showing Jake the positive test results. "Things are running pretty smoothly."

"Excellent," said Jake. He looked around the control area without entering. *Tight quarters. Wouldn't want to spend too much time in here,* he thought.

Clint disengaged the drill head. The grinding sounds, as well as most of the vibrations, stopped. Silence followed as Clint turned the engine off.

Clint followed Jake down the stairs. Jake looked at the tool marks etched into the stone walls and ceiling. "See anything interesting down here?" He ran his hand across the jagged surface.

"No, not yet." Clint rubbed a small area of the wall with the heel of his gloved hand as if to polish it and shrugged. "We're not really down far enough to see anything of significance. This Mole is doing well. We're making decent progress today."

"Don't stay down here too much, you'll go crazy in that small space," said Jake.

"I like it down here. I find it peaceful. I mean, it's loud, obviously, but it's peaceful at the same time."

"Trust me, I understand that better than you know," said Jake, slapping Clint on the back before heading back up the slope.

Clint jumped up the steps to the platform and Jake turned to leave. The drill's engine fired up and the heavy scraping sounds resumed. Without warning, a mechanical grinding sound punctuated the air. Jake, not ten steps away, turned back and the noise stopped as Clint disengaged the drill and shut the engine off.

Clint stuck his head out the door of the tiny room, grinning. "I guess we jinxed it."

Working underground was in Clint's blood, following in the footsteps of his father, grandfather and uncle; all miners. After high school, Clint got a job with the same mining firm where his father was employed and he worked side by side with his father. Clint had an intuition for the job and quickly became a supervisor and ran his own team. Several years passed and he was approached by the NRD to head the excavation of several sites in preparation for the construction of several underground facilities. The successful projects finished both on time and on budget, and Clint was retained by the NRD for future projects and consulting.

Clint's professional opinion and skill carried weight far beyond the rocks he moved, but in recent years, it seemed as though the rocks were in his head. The funny, personable man grew bitter and angry over a period of time so long that the change went largely unnoticed. Now consistently irritable and emotionally erratic, Clint had been labelled, "difficult to work with." His superiors received complaints about his poor attitude but were hesitant to fire him because of his unmatched skill and intuition. After several complaints about aggressive behaviour, explosive confrontations and an incident where he pushed an indirect lead into a wall, Clint was prescribed mandatory reprogramming at an NRD orientation class.

Jake leaned on the door frame and watched as Clint scrolled through the diagnostic screens. He tapped the screen several times and stopped on a screen with several red circles.

"It looks like we broke a row of teeth," said Clint.

Jake heard a smooth female voice come over his earpiece. "Everything okay down there?"

"Yeah, Lex, we're good. Just some broken teeth," said Clint casually. "Ben, you there?"

"Yep. Teeth, eh?" said Ben, "I'll come down with a couple rows."

"No rush. I've got a spare row," said Clint. "I'll slide it in. But yeah, I'll take them anyway. We'll need them sooner or later."

Like many of Maya's days, the morning passed slowly. Going into this op, like her past operations, she knew there would be some downtime but she felt awkward about how little work there was for her to do. With such a small camp, it required little management. On larger ops, too little time and too many problems were the norm—with supplies being delivered and inventory checks, new people coming and going requiring check-ins, check-outs, briefings and debriefings. Out here, no one was coming or going from the camp except Team Two, but it would be some time before they arrived. With no supplies being delivered, frequent inventorying was unnecessary.

Regardless of whether the year was 2097 or 1200, food still needed to be planned and cooked, dishes needed to be cleaned so Maya spent her free time helping Darren to even out the workload. Laundry and dishes were not what she signed up for, but she felt good staying busy and appreciated the company.

Maya stood at the end of the counter cutting up raw vegetables for lunch, far away from the onions Darren was slicing beside the sink. She hung on the soft-spoken chef's every word as he explained how he was recruited by the NRD, right out of the kitchen of one of Tricity's hottest restaurants.

"I can see why you'd be offered a job on the spot. With meals like this, you'll have the enemy defecting just so they can join us for dinner."

Darren chuckled, appreciating the compliment. He carried the cutting board to the stove. He was just about to slide the onions into a sizzling frying pan when he froze, straining to listen for a noise he thought he had heard. After a moment's silence, he shrugged. He heard it again, this time much louder. He and Maya caught each other's gaze and listened. Another crash, this time unmistakable, came from somewhere in the camp.

They raced to the nearest window and peered out. Maya gasped and Darren swore under his breath. Someone or something inside the food pantry was destroying it from the inside out. Several of the linking wall panels were knocked out and lay on the grass. Cans and dry goods lay scattered on the ground and the pantry floor like a tornado had blown through. A bag of sugar lay on the floor hanging partially over the edge. Its contents spilled into a neat pile on the grass below like the sand of an hourglass. The freezer had been tipped on its side, and its door lay open on the floor. Torn and shredded packages of meat lay strewn across the pantry floor.

Maya and Darren sprinted across the camp to investigate, but they stopped dead in their tracks just steps from the pantry door when they heard a deep snort issue from inside.

Maya swore under her breath, not daring to move. Another muffled snort and shuffling sounds echoed from inside the pantry. She grabbed Darren's wrist and backed away slowly. They heard the crash of a shelf falling over, accompanied by the sounds of metal tins rolling across the floor. A can of creamed corn rolled off the pantry floor and onto the grass through the gaping hole in the wall. A fluffy black bear cub tumbled off the pantry floor and onto the lawn. Unaware of his onlookers, the baby bear sprawled out comfortably on his belly and licked at apple sauce leaking from several crushed cans.

Darren, a city boy through and through, laughed. "Oh, it's just a cub." He looked over his shoulder, but Maya was gone. He laughed at the absurdity of the scene; surprised at how a little animal could make such a mess. He approached the cub to get a closer look. Just then, another cub appeared from behind some boxes, dragging a large salmon fillet. The little bear inadvertently stepped on the torn wrapper and it pulled away from the meat as he walked. Unable to decide which little troublemaker to shoo into the bushes first, he was startled by a loud metallic clanking sound behind him. Maya charged from the main tent with two pots in her hands and banged them together over her head. The two bear cubs looked up at her startled. As she neared, the cubs abandoned their tasty treats and darted toward the bushes. Maya chased the furry siblings to the edge of the clearing and continued banging the pots until all the bears were deep in the forest.

"Hopefully, they don't come back," she said jogging back toward the mess. "I wonder how come the perimeter alarm didn't…"

Darren's heartbeat, already beating fast, doubled its pace. Mama bear lumbered through the opening in the wall, her mouth clamped tightly around a package of three frozen roasts, the packaging partially torn away and dragging at her feet. Cornered between Darren, the food pantry, the house trailers and Maya, the bear had no clear route of escape.

"Maya!" yelled Darren, his voice an octave higher than normal. "Don't move!"

The bear began to growl through the mouthful of roasts and spit peppered the brown packaging. She stood for a moment on her hind legs, pulling herself to her full and impressive height and then fell back down on all fours. The bear's ears flattened backward and she continued to growl—the sound muffled by the meaty prize she refused to drop. Darren moved suddenly like a gunfighter in a classic country western movie. VersaTool in hand, he caught the bear—ballistic with rage—in the red beam and lifted the snarling, growling beast into the air. The bear dropped the package of roasts, however, they remained in the air next to the bear, trapped by the beam. The bear's feet scrambled, seeking the ground and but hitting nothing.

With the bear now locked in the beam, Maya gave the flailing yet powerful limbs a wide berth and followed behind Darren as he carefully carried the suspended bear into the bushes. Darren did his best to weave the floating animal around trees but despite his care, the bear kicked madly. One of her rear legs connected with a tree, sending her spinning around within the beam only to become even further enraged. When Darren reached the edge of the camp, he gently set the bear down on the ground but waited before releasing the beam. He could feel sweat beading on his forehead despite the chilly weather. The bear was merely ten quick bear strides away from him. He looked over his shoulder at Maya. "Ready?"

Maya nodded and backed away, prepared to run for shelter in the nearest trailer should the bear decide she wanted to come and try for a win in round two. The bear, trying desperately to run deeper into the forest, struggled with all her might against the beam and stumbled forward when Darren finally released it. The bear picked up the package of meat then darted out of sight.

Maya stepped through the hole in the wall into the pantry. Her stomach turned at the sight of their food supply. "Oh man. Look!" She pointed at the meat packages on the ground. Only three brown, wax paper bundles and a white box of spices remained in the toppled freezer. "At least half our meat is missing." She knelt down and picked up a package of pork chops laying at her feet. The paper was mostly torn away. Some of the pork chops were missing and the ones that remained were gouged by the bear's sharp, carnivorous teeth. "And half of what's left has been chewed."

"It can't be that bad," said Darren, following Maya into the shed. He picked up a few packages that looked untouched. He turned them over, saw the torn paper and gnaw marks made by little bear cub teeth. He sighed heavily. "This is not good."

Ben ran to the pantry and swore at the mess. "What the hell happened?"

"Bears," said Maya.

Jake and Tyler arrived to find Maya and Darren struggling to lift the freezer. Both men stepped through the wall and helped them heft the upright freezer back to its vertical position.

Jake surveyed the room then picked up a torn package containing a half-eaten salmon filet. "How long were they in there? This salmon is pretty much thawed. How'd they get in?"

Maya and Darren shrugged. "The door, we guess. It was wide open," said Darren shrugging.

"There's no scratch or kick marks. It was like it was left open." Tyler crouched down and inspected the door latch mechanism. He removed a tuft of thick black strands wedged beneath the latch plate on the door frame and held it up for the others to see. "There's a chunk of fur in the latch plate but no damage."

"Who would have left the door open?" asked Maya.

"More importantly, how come the perimeter alarm didn't go off?" asked Ben, surveying the food on the grass. He picked up the can of applesauce one of the cubs had been enjoying and globs of the sauce dripped onto the ground. He tossed the can aside and wiped his hands on his work pants. "I'll take a look around."

Tyler and Jake stood the toppled shelves and helped Maya and Darren separate the salvageable food from the contaminated. A large pile of destroyed food grew beside the wall panels lying on the grass.

"So what's the verdict? How much meat do we have left?" asked Jake, holding a package of untouched sausages. He tossed the still-frozen Brats back into the freezer.

"I'd say we've got maybe half left. Nearly a third of the entire supply is missing altogether." He looked at the pile of discarded food. "About a quarter of what's left is tainted and needs to be pitched. There is a lot that is thawed, or partially thawed, so I'll need to cook all of that now, but I can pop it back in the freezer after."

Jake sighed. The majority of their principal food staple was now gone, and they were still in their first month. "You can't cut around the bite marks?"

Darren shrugged. "I don't think I'd want to take the chance. I mean, one day you think you're eating pot roast, but you find out later it was *Rabies à la King*."

"Fair enough." Jake tossed the meat back onto the discard pile of crushed boxes, torn packages and leaky cans. "So what does this mean for our overall food supply?"

"I'll do an inventory and let you know," said Maya.

"I think we'll be alright," said Darren surveying the discard pile. "I made sure that we brought far more food than I projected we'd need. Plus, we've still got a fair amount of dry food. It's not as exciting, but it'll do."

"Don't forget, we've also got HOPs," added Maya.

Tyler pretended to choke. "Forget it. I'd rather take my chances with the contaminated meat."

Horn of Plenty pills, or HOPs, were a nifty little invention by the Research branch of the NRD back in the early eighties. They had been popular in Defence for years as one HOP pill could keep an individual fed for a week. Unfortunately, nasty side effects including nausea, irritability and paranoia could outlast the pill's intended effectiveness, and could accumulate if pills were taken back to back. These side effects were the reason their use changed to an emergency backup food source only. If given the choice, most people preferred not to take them.

"Nah, I don't think we'll need to start popping HOPs. We'll just have to conserve a bit." Darren placed the last few packages of meat in the freezer and closed the door. He turned to face the group in the small shed. "We'll be cutting it close, and there will probably be a lot of vegetarian dishes, but we'll be fine."

"Are you crazy?" asked Clint, joining the conversation. He wiped rock dust and oil off of his hands with a rag. "Look where we are! This forest is teeming with mobile meat! We'll be fine. We just have to go hunting."

"Hunting?" said Maya. She held a large plastic bottle of olive oil in the crook of her elbow. "Like in the bushes killing animals?"

"Where do you think meat comes from?" asked Tyler.

"Nobody hunts anymore. It's so archaic." Maya placed the bottle on the shelf next to the others.

"No, it isn't," said Clint impatiently. "My grandfather used to take me hunting when I was little. Sitting for hours and watching nature. It was so peaceful."

Jake contemplated Clint's suggestion. "That drill has been running well lately," said Jake. "Hunting might not be a bad idea. Tyler or Lexi can run down if the Mole needs anything."

Ben leaned into the pantry through the hole in the wall and held up a black metal stake with a broken glass tip. The glass was smashed and part of the internal circuitry was missing. "I figured out why the alarm didn't go off. I found this sensor knocked over, laying on some rocks. I assume it got knocked over by debris from the wind and smashed on the rocks. I checked to see when the sensor went offline and it was over thirty-seven hours ago."

"Did the wind knock it over?" asked Maya.

"It's within the WeatherShield perimeter. Wind won't affect it," said Jake.

Ben shrugged unable to offer any other hypothesis. "I don't know. There was no tree or any other debris around it. Not sure what to tell you."

"Maybe the bears knocked it over when they walked into the camp?"

Ben shook his head. "But that's the whole point of the perimeter sensor. The alarm should have gone off when the system went offline."

The group fell silent, unable to come up with any plausible explanation.

"Maybe it's the curse," suggested Maya, hesitantly.

"There's no curse," said Clint, not bothering to mask the condescension in his voice. "There's no such thing as a curse."

The attention of the team was distracted from the broken sensor when they heard a whoop. Tyler stood by the door holding a case of beer under one arm, and in his free hand, he held up a bottle of vodka like a well-earned trophy. "At least they didn't get the booze!"

CHAPTER 21

TEAM 1
YEAR: 1200
TIME REMAINING: 158 Days

Ben and Clint, the sole volunteers for the hunting brigade, slipped quietly out of the camp before sun up. Though the weather grew steadily warmer with each passing day, their breath was visible in the chilly morning air. Despite their bulky jackets, both felt the wet cold penetrating their clothing as they tramped through the underbrush. Ben inhaled deeply and took in the fragrant smell of new growth. Every few minutes Ben checked his manual compass. The needle wobbled on the spindle as they walked. Ben chuckled to himself as he thought about the billions of dollars' worth of equipment back in 2097 that would have made their job here so much easier. The GPS units and aerial imaging systems were useless with no satellites to provide data.

Watching the compass needle swing from one side of north to the other, Ben walked into the back of Clint, who had stopped. He reopened the compass case that snapped shut on his finger and looked up to see Clint pointing ahead of them. Ben saw the flick of white—a white-tail deer stood motionless in the distance. The deer, sensing danger, darted deeper into the bushes, her white tail bouncing from side to side as she bounded out of sight.

"Dammit," said Clint. He slid his plasmaqueous gun back into its holster on his hip.

"It's just as well," said Ben, patting Clint on the shoulder. "We don't want everyone thinking it's too easy."

The quiet forest was a welcomed change from the work shed and drilling. The men pushed their way through a hilly tapestry of forest. Thick, tall trees occasionally thinned out to reveal small meadows or rocky patches, then changed back to bush so dense the men had to struggle to pass through.

The forest thinned again and in the distance they saw a hill rise up through the trees, its base a steep rock face. They skirted the granite wall and spotted a rocky ledge large enough for both men to sit and scout for activity below. Ben scaled the rocky cliff with the ease and agility of a monkey climbing a tree. Gripping rock protrusions and crevices, he hoisted himself easily onto the ledge.

Jake climbed the steps to Mole Control slowly, his eyes fixed on his dangerously overfilled mug of coffee. Unsurprised, he found Lexi already at one of the control desks, reviewing the results of the active Mole's daily pre-launch system check.

"All these numbers look good," she reported. "I think some of the fluids are going to need to be changed soon, though. We should probably pull Mole2 out tonight and run Mole1 tomorrow."

"That's not a bad idea." Jake sat down at the second control desk opposite Lexi and winced as the hot coffee sloshed out of the mug and onto his fingers. He set the cup down and dried his hand on his pant leg as he studied the results on the three flat-panel monitors at his desk. The two opposing workstations were divided by a bank of three flat-screen monitors on each desk. "There are probably a lot of teeth that need to be replaced, too. That Mole's been a rock star."

Jake found Lexi easy to work with, and he enjoyed partnering with her in Mole Control. Incredibly smart with a strong work ethic, she beat Jake to their post every day. She never hesitated to pitch in and was eager to learn. She and Jake had become well acquainted during the mind-numbing hours spent in Mole Control when drilling progressed problem-free. Despite having learned a lot about each other, Jake always managed to skate over any questions about his wife and family and had not divulged that they had been killed in an accident.

Lexi watched as Jake unmuted the monitor showing the underground camera feed of the Mole. The scraping sounds of the massive drill head droned away on the screen's tinny speakers. Lexi had grown accustomed to Jake's constant need for white noise, assuming he suffered from tinnitus. After a while, she found she enjoyed the monotonous sounds. She cycled through the screens of Mole's meters and gauges. One of the indicators on the screen had changed from green to yellow. She tapped the screen.

"That coolant's getting warm." She clasped her hands behind her head and leaned back in her chair. "I think our Mole is asking for some love."

"Sounds reasonable," said Jake. "It'll make it the rest of today no problem. We'll get her fixed up tomorrow when Ben's back."

Silence filled the room as it often did—not an awkward silence, merely an absence of conversation and activity. Jake leaned back in his chair and looked out the large window. The grey-brown colouring that dominated the forest at their arrival was fading into the vibrant green of new spring growth. The sun shone brightly and the lake glistened in the distance. Movement by the living quarters caught his eye as Darren stepped out of Lexi and Maya's trailer, carrying a stack of fresh sheets. He walked around the front of the girls' trailer and into the next trailer. The chattering sound of a seized wheel on Lexi's office chair brought Jake's attention back. She stood, pen and paper in hand, and walked into the boardroom. She stared intently at the drilling plans taped to the wall. The cutaway illustration of the ground showed the tunnel that they were drilling and some artist's rendering of what they imagined the Elevanium deposit would look like. She wrote several numbers on the notepad and returned to her seat.

Jake watched Lexi's activity with amused interest. "Recalculating the numbers again?"

Lexi smiled guiltily like she had been caught doing something illicit. "Yeah. Might as well. I've got the time and you can never be too sure, right?"

Lexi worked through the math. When she was done, she sighed loudly. She balled up the paper and tossed it into the garbage can. Jake chuckled as he watched her fidget; tapping her foot on the base of the chair and readjusting her ponytail. She flipped through the diagnostic screens. The coolant gauge still showed yellow.

After a few minutes, Lexi burst out in exasperated boredom. "Oh, sweet mother of the universe!" She swiveled her chair away from the desk, rubbed her eyes and stood to stretch.

"I wouldn't complain," said Jake. "Something catastrophic will happen."

Lexi sat back down and pulled herself and the chair back up to the desk. "Yeah, I suppose you're right." She sipped her tea and set the mug down beside a stack of old books and outdated crossword puzzles on the desk, their appeal long since lost.

"So what do you think your family would have said if they knew you were a part of the most high-stakes, ambitious and dangerous NRD op in the history of the NRD?" asked Jake. As they sat in the quiet trailer bored out of their minds, the word "dangerous" seemed ironic, almost comical.

Lexi looked thoughtful for a moment. "I think they would have been pretty pleased. Well, they'd naturally be worried that something might go wrong, but I think they would be proud." The three teams, while on-mission for six months according to their personal reality, were only away from the year 2097 for little more than twenty-four hours. Jake knew that Lexi had explained her twenty-four-hour disappearing act to her family by telling them she was going out of town with some girlfriends. The classified nature of the op meant the team could not tell their families any details. Sometimes it was easier to say nothing until it was over. "My fiancé though..." The smile on her face disappeared like it had been slapped off. She looked awkwardly from Jake to her hands. "Well, let's just say he would have had kittens if he knew the details."

"Right, right. The accountant." Jake had gathered from the few times Lexi had mentioned her fiancé, that the amount of personal risk he could tolerate matched his expectation of how much personal risk an accountant could handle. He noticed that Lexi rarely mentioned her fiancé, but when she did, he always got the sense that she felt like she had said too much.

Lexi turned the conversation around. "Surely your wife would have been worried if she knew the details?" She flipped through the screens on the monitor and as expected, nothing had changed. She pulled a crossword puzzle book from the top of the pile of outdated magazines and flipped through the pages. Judging by the tattered and yellowing pages of the book, she guessed it may be as old as the trailer in which they sat. She looked at the date on the spine. September 2062. It never ceased to amaze Lexi how some aspects of the NRD were so advanced with cutting-edge technology, but at the same time, some aspects were older than dirt, for example, Mole Control.

Jake knew that eventually his wife's death would come up. He avoided the topic with anyone except close friends and family and even then he remained tight-lipped. It was no secret, he just preferred not to see people's expressions of horror and pity when they learned he had lost not just his spouse, but his two infant children as well. Having become friends, Jake felt he would be misleading Lexi not to tell her. "Actually, my wife is dead," he said quietly. "And my two kids." He looked at her, waiting for the dreaded facial expression, but it never came. Instead, she flipped the crossword puzzle book open to a page bookmarked by a pencil. She was silent for a moment then looked at him, her expression blank, neither sympathetic or pitiful.

"I'm sorry, that's really horrible." She looked at the book again. "Now give me an eight-letter word for 'predicament.'"

After sitting in silence on the mossy ledge for over three hours and seeing only birds and the occasional squirrel, both men needed to stand and stretch.

"I guess this spot isn't as hot as we'd thought," said Clint, at full conversational volume. Talking quietly had yielded no results and he saw no point in continuing. "I say we head closer to camp. Maybe we'll find that deer again."

Ben stood and stretched too. "Sounds good. Plus, they're always in bunches, right? So there's bound to be more."

Clint climbed carefully down the rock face and jumped the last few steps. "Herds, you mean. They're always in herds." He brushed the moss and debris from the backside of his clothing.

"We'll have to remember this place. It was pretty neat," said Ben hopping to the ground. Like Clint, he brushed off the mossy debris and knelt to re-tie his shoes.

Clint pulled his standard, NRD issue, plasmaqueous gun out of his holster and pressed the menu button on the top to confirm its setting. A list of options appeared in the air, projected above the rear sight of the gun. He touched the holographic menu and changed the setting from six—a low-power kill—to seven, a higher power kill but not disintegrate. The gun responded by projecting a slightly larger red dot on the ground in front of Clint where the gun pointed. When he lifted the gun up and aimed it at a tree in the distance, the red dot was distinctly visible. He pulled the trigger and the gun emitted a tiny slip of white light which hit the tree. The blackened bark smoked where the laser had struck it.

Ben stood and the two men started back toward the camp. Ben watched as the red light from Clint's gun darted over the grass, roots and rocks as they walked. After ten minutes, Clint stopped suddenly. For the second time that day, Ben walked into Clint's back. He looked over Clint's shoulder and saw a startled buck in their path. Unlike the skittish deer occasionally spotted beyond the perimeter of the camp, this deer stood stock still and held its ground. His only movement was the flaring of his nostrils as he breathed and his ears rotating twitchily as he searched out every sound around him. The black eyes of the animal glared at the intruders, daring them to proceed. With a loud snort, the deer stomped his front hoof and pounded out a message its trespassers heard loud and clear.

Ben froze, suddenly acutely aware of how little he knew about hunting. Fear radiated in waves from his chest and tingled as it spread to his shaking extremities. Despite having no previous interactions with deer—other than what he saw on TV—he could read the buck's body language well enough to know he did not want to be eight quick deer-leaps away from an animal with dagger-like cloven hooves and the stubby nubbins of new antlers. He watched the red dot from Clint's gun bounce erratically from the deer's body to the trees around him and back again. The deer stomped again and Ben pulled his own gun, praying he would not need to use it.

Ben whispered hoarsely to Clint, who appeared frozen. "Uh, are we doing this?" In that moment, Ben wholly regretted his decision to be a part of the hunting brigade.

"Shut up," hissed Clint with a strong emphasis on both words. "Just give me a minute. I haven't done this in years."

The deer made the first move and lunged toward them. Red streaks appeared over the uneven, moulting fur of the charging animal as it barrelled toward the two men. Ben lost the remaining threads of bravery he possessed and ducked behind the nearest tree and turned to watch. Mortified, he saw Clint frozen in the deer's path.

Lexi felt her heart drop into her stomach when Jake told her he had lost his entire family. She pretended to work on the crossword puzzle as she processed the information. Having just experienced a life-altering tragedy herself, she knew how each look of pity and condolence could rip open a healing wound. She understood now why he always seemed so withdrawn and mysterious. He was neither withdrawn nor mysterious. Just hurt.

"Quagmire."

"Sorry?" asked Lexi.

"An eight-letter word for 'predicament.'"

Lexi laughed and looked at the page and nodded, impressed. The "Q" from quagmire worked with the six letter word for "five babies." She wrote it in.

"How about an eight-letter phrase for 'gratitude?'"

Lexi looked confused.

"Thank you."

"For what?"

"For not looking at me like I had a second head when I told you about my family. I think you're the first person to treat me normally. It's just…refreshing."

Lexi had gathered from their short time together that Jake was a private individual, and after experiencing such an unthinkable loss, his life would have been an open book for everyone to see. Lexi was no stranger to the raw, exposed feelings one experienced after everyone you care about witnesses the worst moment of your life.

Lexi continued to work on the crossword puzzle but became frustrated; the book—whose lifespan had nearly lapped that of Lexi's a second time—featured clues aged beyond context. She flipped to a different page and started at the top.

Jake flipped through the monitors. No change. He rolled up the sleeves on his red and white plaid shirt. "It was my fault. They died in a car accident." Lexi looked up from her puzzle. Jake leaned back again in the chair and looked out the window. "It was the day that robot broke into the Riverfront shopping mall. It was all over the news."

"Yeah, I remember that. That was unbelievable."

"It was the first daylight break-and-enter into a building that wasn't abandoned. Anyway, Brit and I had no idea any of this was going on. At the time, we were driving home from visiting my parents. We were trying to figure out what was going on because six aerial cop cars flew overhead on the AR-301 with their lights flashing and sirens screaming. Then three road cruisers passed us like we weren't even there." Jake stared at the lake in the distance as he racked his memory for details. He found some of them were becoming harder to remember. "My memory's kind of splotchy but I seem to remember a fifth cop car coming toward us then something darted out on the freeway. I never did see what it was, but the cop swerved to miss it and he clipped the concrete railing at the top of the Kingsway overpass."

Lexi knew that the BrakeTime technology that sensed objects around the vehicle and prevented collisions was standard equipment on all cars after 2082, but it was ineffective at excessively high speeds.

"Apparently the police car barrel-rolled down the freeway. I swerved to miss it, but the police car hit us on my side at the front. We ricocheted off the cop car, broke through the guardrail and fell off the overpass. Our car landed upside down on the freeway below." Jake flipped through the screens of the Mole monitoring systems again. "I don't remember the impact at all, but what I do remember is total silence afterward. I could see my wife hanging limply in the passenger seat. I couldn't turn to see the kids in the back because I was pinned in my seat by the steering wheel, but they were quiet. I kept calling their names, talking to them so they would be less afraid, but all I got back was silence."

Lexi was dumbstruck as she recalled how the story of the rogue robot had dominated the news. The people killed that day were the first human casualties of what had turned into a war with the robots. Lexi thought back to all of the times she saw Jake wearing headphones and listening to music or how whenever she walked into Mole Control he had the monitors blaring or the music in the work shed. All to avoid silence and the memories it brought back.

"None of them made it. My wife and ten-month baby boy died on impact, my three-year-old daughter died later that night at the hospital."

"Were you hurt? How did you manage to survive?"

"I didn't. Most of me died that night. How I physically survived, I'll never know. I was virtually unscathed. I had some bruised ribs and a sprained wrist. Can you believe that? It should have been me who died."

Lexi looked thoughtful for a moment. "I thought you said this was your fault? It doesn't sound like you could've controlled any of this."

"It was my car. I had this vintage black Dodge Charger. Not the really old ones from the 1960s, but a 2015. It was the first car I ever bought. I got it from a little old woman who inherited it when she was younger but never learned to drive. It stayed in her garage for more than half a century. It was in good shape considering, but I rebuilt it. I loved it. Brit said we should get a safer car when we had kids, you know with BrakeTime and the better safety features those old cars cars didn't have. But we never did. If I'd just listened to her, they might still be here today."

"I'm sorry Jake," said Lexi, feeling that this was the appropriate time to express her condolences.

"I don't mind talking about it, it's just that initial look I get from people that I can't handle." This was the first time he had told anyone the entire story from beginning to end. To his surprise, he felt the tension in his chest lessen. Something about Lexi made her easy to talk to and share with. This surprised him as she was nearly two decades younger. Never in a million years did he ever think he would feel comfortable telling his life story to a twenty-two-year-old woman, but she seemed wise beyond her years.

"Ever since then, I've been drifting through the days. I went to work, pulled it together then fell apart later at home. I started spending as much time at work as possible, though I can't say I really accomplished much. When Mitch approached me for this op, I put him off hoping he'd just go away, but in the end I agreed because I figured the change of scenery would be good. But as you saw, it didn't help. It wasn't until Clint hit you that the reality of everything sank in. People needed me. Life was moving forward and I was standing still and people were getting hurt. Since you yelled at me, I've been feeling much better."

"Sorry 'bout that," said Lexi, looking sheepish.

"Don't apologize. I needed to hear it." He looked out the window at the shining lake. "I think I'm about as fine now as I'm going to be for a while. Life goes on. I gotta keep moving forward. They'll always be with me, but I gotta move forward." Jake eyed the monitor. Two more gauges had changed to yellow as they talked.

Lexi nodded, engrossed by the story. "I get you about the change of scenery. My fiancé…well, let's just say I needed a change of scenery as well."

Jake could tell something weighed heavily on Lexi. Jake suspected it involved her fiancé because whenever she mentioned him, her face reddened and she seemed ashamed. Jake watched her close the puzzle book and put it back on the stack of ancient reading material. She accidentally sipped from the coffee mug Clint had left from the day before and winced as she spat it back into the mug.

Jake opened and closed the drawers of his desk and found a 2091 issue of *Car and Pilot* at the back of the bottom drawer. He leaned back in his chair and thumbed through the tattered and curling pages. "Do you want to talk about it?"

"Talk about what?" She straightened the monitors on the desk.

Jake sat forward and reached between the bases of the monitors, grabbed her hand and looked at her. Her eyes darted around the room to anything but Jake. "Lex, I can see something's bugging you. If you don't want to talk, that's fine. But if you do, I'm here."

She stood up quickly, tripped on one of the wheels on her chair and stumbled backward. "Thank you," she tried, but the sound of her voice was absent. She cleared her throat. "Well, I'm going to haul that Mole out of there. I helped Ben with Mole1 when he was doing some maintenance on it. I can get this one out and prepped, at least." She backed away from the desk and walked out the door.

CHAPTER 22

TEAM 1
YEAR: 1200
TIME REMAINING: 158 Days

The story of the deer became legend over dinner.

"So I got the distinct impression that the buck did not like us being there," said Ben. He relayed the day's events to his captive audience around the dinner table. "It was snorting and stomping its hooves like a raging bull."

"Yeah, it was pretty pissed," agreed Clint. He cut a large piece off his pork chop and stuffed it in his mouth.

"Clint's scope dot bounced all over that deer like he was watering a garden with a hose. I was frozen stiff in fear and so was Clint. Don't believe him if he tries to tell you anything different," said Ben. He laughed at the memory of his hunting companion's reaction as he sipped his wine. "And before we could even think, the damn thing charged us. Here I am, this city boy in the bushes with my life flashing before my eyes as this freaking murderous beast barrels down at us at mach one. I decided that I was alright with salad for the next five months and ran for cover behind the nearest tree, hoping that that was the smart thing to do—I really had no freaking idea. I looked back to see where Clint had run to, and there he was, still standing there."

"Omigod," breathed Maya, looking at Clint. "What did you do?"

"In two leaps and bounds, that deer would have been on top of him. But he snapped out of it just in time, retreated backward and tripped on a rock. As he hit the ground, the gun went off."

"What are you talking about?" asked Clint. "That shot was perfectly planned."

"Oh, it was perfect alright, but definitely not planned," laughed Ben. He took a bite of salad from the heaping pile in front of him; the savoury pork chops Darren had prepared were noticeably absent from his plate.

Clint picked up his glass of wine and held it while he spoke. "I should also point out that Ben has conveniently left out of the part of the story where he threw up behind a tree. He had to sit with his head between his knees for five minutes before he could walk again."

The group laughed and quizzed the men about their success, which seemed to be more luck than anything else.

Clint turned to Ben. "So when are we going out again?"

Ben held up his wine glass. "I would like to take this moment to announce my retirement from hunting. While I have a firm understanding of the food chain and where meat comes from, that was an experience I will never forget. From now on, every time I eat meat, I will be eternally grateful to the animal it came from. But I can tell you that won't be for a long, long time."

"Well, it's just as good you're retiring," said Jake, setting his knife on his plate. "Work's been piling up today while you were gone."

"Sounds good to me. Bring it on," said Ben. "I'll take a Mole over a deer any day."

Thinking of the work piling up, Jake looked around the table and noticed Lexi's absence.

Jake left the main tent and saw lights on in the work shed; however, when he entered, the shed appeared empty. As he turned to leave, he saw a pair of feet beneath the hovering machine. He walked around the front of the Mole to find Lexi leaning into one of the side engine compartments. She stood on the tips of her toes and strained to push herself further into the compartment but could not get enough leverage. Jake walked up the machine's rear stairs, reached into the control room and held down one of the many buttons on the control panel. The Mole began to lower itself closer to the ground. He returned to where she was working, said nothing and leaned against the side of the machine.

"Thank you," said a quiet voice from inside the compartment.

He listened to the metallic sounds her tools made inside the machine. After all his years in mechanics, the sound of tools and metal on metal was as sweet as cotton candy.

Frustration filled Lexi's muffled voice. "I can't…believe…how tight…this is!" She spoke each word as she pulled on something and Jake felt the Mole budge ever so slightly with each tug. The small movements stopped and silence followed.

Lexi backed her upper half out of the compartment and stood up. She glanced up at Jake briefly and brushed her hands on her pants to wipe away the oily rock dust. A streak of black grease in her blond ponytail complimented the smudges of dirt on her face. She retrieved a black drainage pan the size of a toddler's swimming pool from beneath the mezzanine and rolled it to the front of the machine. She let it fall to the ground and the plastic thud echoed throughout the cavernous building.

"You didn't come for dinner."

"I wasn't hungry and I wanted to get a jump on changing this coolant." She reached underneath the massive, metallic monster and lined the pan up with the coolant drain.

"Working yourself into the ground won't make things go away." He stuffed his hands into his pockets and turned to lean against the Mole. "Trust me, I know."

The crack of her knee joint was the only sound she made as she stood. She crawled back into the engine compartment, this time pulling herself so deep into the machine that only her lower legs were visible, parallel to the floor. The Mole moved rhythmically as she yanked on the stopper valve to allow the coolant to drain. Despite her efforts, the valve refused to yield. Jake sensed her temper flaring, confirmed by muffled swearing coming from inside the compartment. The Mole stopped moving after one particularly violent shudder followed by the dull thunk of a metal instrument hitting the thick plastic pan below. Quiet sobs followed. Jake rarely got involved in the personal problems of his subs, but Lexi had been there for him in a way today that no one could and that meant something to him.

"Okay, okay, come here," he said, softly. He helped her back out of the compartment, placing his hand gently on the back of her head to protect it from hitting the frame of the access panel. Looking at her feet, she pushed the baggy sleeve of her oversized uniform up and used her clean forearm to wipe her tears away.

"Come here." He pulled her into a hug and she sobbed into his chest.

After a few minutes, her tears stopped. She stepped back, rubbing her eyes again with her forearm. "Thank you. I'm sorry. Look at your shirt." She rubbed the wet spots her tears had left on his shirt.

Jake looked down and chuckled. "No worries. If that's the worst thing that gets spilled on me today, it'll be a good day. Would you like to talk about it now?"

Lexi stared absently at the welding cart by the overhead door for a long moment, then nodded weakly. "But there isn't much to tell, it's not a long story." She wiped the corner of her eyes. "It's just a little fresh still."

Jake walked up the stairs to the mezzanine and Lexi followed, where she fell heavily onto the couch that overlooked the shop in the make-shift living room Ben had set up. Jake grabbed two Sprites from the bar fridge in the corner and two energy bars from the box atop the fridge labelled, "Ben's Mechanic Fuel. Hands Off!" He sat on the couch beside Lexi, handed her the two energy bars and set the cans on the makeshift coffee table. One of the energy bars was gone before Jake took the first sip of his drink.

"Not hungry, eh?"

Lexi smiled sheepishly as she opened the second wrapper and tossed the first onto the makeshift coffee table. "I was supposed to get married about a month before the launch of this op, but it never happened. The day of the wedding, my maid of honour was MIA, but I just figured she was running late. It was pretty informal, just close family and friends at the Royal Flower Gardens in Metro Park. We were all waiting for Bryan, my fiancé, to show up. Fifteen minutes after the ceremony was supposed to start, the best man got a call from Bryan saying that he wasn't coming."

"Geez," breathed Jake.

"That wasn't the worst of it. He'd run off with my maid of honour. So here I am, standing in front of all my family and friends already feeling pretty foolish because my goddamn fiancé can't show up to his own damn wedding on time, only to learn that I'd been dumped at the proverbial altar. So I know what you mean about getting that 'look' because I got it from about eighty-five people all at once."

Jake looked at his watery-eyed sub with renewed respect. "I'm so sorry Lex. That's horrible."

"It was an absolute nightmare and I couldn't seem to wake up from it. My brides-maids took me home and stayed while my mom dealt with everything. Thank God for my mom. She was the consummate wedding de-planner." Lexi chuckled appreciatively. "She took care of all of the guests and everything else that needed to be looked after and then spent the afternoon with me. I'm not sure where my father or my brothers were, probably trying to hunt down Bryan. She suggested that she and I take the honeymoon trip to the Bahamas. She thought the change of scenery would help me deal with the shock.

"So we went to the airport early to transfer the name on the second ticket but Bryan had already taken the tickets, changed my name to the name of my maid of honour and they'd already gone through security. So, I had an emotional breakdown in the middle of the airport. I'll tell you though, that 200 people looking at you like you're crazy is better than eighty-five pity stares.

"I stayed at my parents for a couple of days and then went back home. I had the week off so I thought I should do something productive instead of lying in bed all day feeling sorry for myself. So, I packed up Bryan's stuff and put it by the door so when he got home, he could move out of my condo while I was at work."

"Wow, that's pretty decent of you. I think I'd've dumped it all on the lawn."

Lexi laughed. "Don't think I didn't think about it. But it had been pretty rainy so I thought I probably shouldn't. I didn't pack it well if it's any consolation."

Jake was impressed. He thought she was functioning pretty well for a girl whose life had taken a 180 degree turn little more than two months ago.

"I went back to work later in the week because I couldn't stand being at home anymore. Just when I thought life was returning to a normal routine, I got a call from my neighbour who found a bunch of stuff all over my lawn. I raced home from work to find all of my stuff dumped outside. Clothes, shoes, my art, my desk. Everything. I went to go inside and my key didn't open the lock. The bastard had changed the locks. So I'm hammering on the door, neighbours are staring out their windows and coming out onto their balconies to see what the commotion was. Bryan walked out onto the balcony and told me very politely to remove my things from his lawn."

Her fists were shaking with anger and her knuckles were white. Her eyes welled up again. "It's my condo! I put half the mortgage down over two years ago with money that I'd inherited from my grampa. He only just moved in six months ago. I'd put his name on the mortgage only the week before the wedding so we could get a jump on paperwork and stuff. So of course, the cops got involved and they removed him from my place, but now he's suing me."

Jake watched fresh tears stream down her face. He personally wanted to find this guy and pound him into the ground like a tent peg.

She pulled her legs to her chest and wrapped her arms around them, shaking with anger. "I'm still getting used to everything. I think in some ways I'm still in shock. I'll be thinking about something and it will trigger a good memory of him—how it was when it was good. Then the horror of what the reality is comes flooding back." She cried into her knees. "I feel so stupid."

Jake wrapped his arm around her. "I'm so sorry. You shouldn't feel stupid. He sounds like a real piece of work."

"That's just it," she said wiping away a tear. "He was never a jerk. A little boring sometimes but he was always a really great guy. This all just came out of nowhere. I thought maybe he had a brain tumour or a stroke or something, anything, to explain his sudden change in personality. But apparently he'd been sleeping with my best friend for over six months. She had told him before the wedding he had to make a choice: her or me. He chose her."

Jake shook his head, truly speechless. Lexi cried on his shoulder for the better part of five minutes before calming. He patted her gently on the back, unsure of what to say. He always felt awkward and at a loss for words around women when they were upset, but he had learned that, more often than not, a friendly ear and a hug worked far better than words.

After a long moment's silence, Lexi spoke quietly. "What do you think it will be like when we get back? Do you think it will be any better?" She wiped the last tear out of her eye and stared down at the Mole sitting in the repair bay below.

Jake sighed as he thought about it. "You know, kid, I just don't know. I try not to think about it much, and I've become pretty good at it. I'm just getting used to taking things day-by-day and I'm having a lot of success with that. I don't want to mess it up by hoping for a storybook outcome only to be disappointed. Nope, I'm living for now. Whatever happens, happens—and whatever that is, we'll adapt."

With dinner long since finished and the plates collected, the group continued to relax around the table and chat as had become their nightly custom. Despite the awkward start, the members of Team One had meshed into a cohesive team. The friction caused by Clint's comments and mood swings faded fast after Jake's intervention.

Maya passed the bottle of wine down the table. The night was a celebration; a successful hunting trip ensured there would be enough meat to last a while. The team never worried about starving to death, but they feared having to resort to popping HOPs, and felt better having proven they could sustain their own food supply. Other hunting trips would be required, but between the meat left untouched by the bears, Ben's temporary vegetarianism and the deer from the day's hunt, the group would be set for a while.

Darren poured the last of the red wine into Tyler's glass and set the empty bottle at the end of the table beside the other three. He grabbed the last bottle off the counter, removed the cork and topped up the remaining glasses. Silence filled the room and Clint broke it. He clapped his hands and rubbed them together.

"So who's going to be my new hunting partner?" asked Clint. He looked around for takers. "Maya?" Maya, taken off guard by the question, said nothing.

"It's okay. You're probably a lousy shot. I've never seen a woman shoot a gun well. You probably couldn't hit a rock if you were sitting on it."

"Okay there, buddy," Ben shot out of his seat and over to his trailer-mate. "I think we've had enough for one night." He slapped Clint on the back firmly, slid his arm under Clint's and lifted him up and away from the table.

"What?" Still holding his wine glass, Clint feigned innocence. He looked up at Ben standing behind him. "I'm just saying, maybe she'd have more fun out in the bushes instead of fluffing pillows all day."

Ben closed his eyes in frustration. "Clint, that's enough." He wanted to remove Clint before he alienated the team again. "The night is over. Let's go."

"But I'm not done my wine!" He tried to take a drink as Ben pulled him away from the table and Clint stumbled over the bench. Red wine spilled onto the shoulder of Tyler's white shirt. Ben marched Clint toward the door despite increasingly loud protestations. When they reached the door, Clint pulled himself free. He shot back the rest of his wine and threw the glass against the far wall of the dining area where it smashed to pieces. The remaining team members sat in silence as another episode of the Clint Show played out before them.

"How did that guy get assigned to this op?" asked Tyler, after Ben physically removed Clint from the tent. "How did that asshole not raise fifty flags when they did the psych eval?"

"He's talented," said Maya. "They needed someone with his expertise."

"How can you make excuses for him when he treats you that way?" asked Tyler.

"I can't let it get to me. We've got a long road ahead of us so I just try to imagine he has redeeming qualities."

To this, Darren raised an eyebrow but said nothing as Jake entered the common area and sat down next to Maya. He looked from one face to the next and got the distinct impression that he had walked into the middle of something. Tyler uttered one word when Jake looked at him inquiringly. "Clint."

Tyler's answer and a glance at the five wine bottles on the table told Jake more than he needed to piece together the room's awkward silence. He sighed heavily. "What happened?"

Tyler relayed the events of the last five minutes.

Jake shook his head and rubbed his eyes. "I'll talk to him tomorrow."

"You should talk to him now," said Tyler angrily. "I'm sick of Maya being this guy's verbal punching bag."

Jake eyed Tyler for several wordless seconds and it had the effect that Jake wanted—to remind Tyler that despite the casual nature of the op, there was still a chain of command to respect. Tyler apologized and Jake explained. "I will talk to Clint tomorrow because if he's been drinking, nothing good will come out of it. If Ben's with him, that's the best scenario for now. I'll deal with him in the morning."

TIME REMAINING: 157 Days

Clint opened the door to the trailer he and Ben shared and quickly shielded his eyes from the morning sun. He stepped down each step heavily as he adjusted to the daylight. Jake intercepted Clint and motioned toward the tool shed. Jake never man-handled his subs; in all his years of supervising, he had never encountered any conflict he could not resolve by a good conversation, though, sometimes a good scare helped.

Clint walked nonchalantly down the nearest row of shelves. He turned to lean against one of the shelves and was startled to find Jake so close behind him. Clint's five-foot-ten, medium build resembled a toothpick in comparison to Jake's massive frame leaning over him.

"Clint, this shit's gotta stop. I don't know what your problem is, and if you care to share it with me that's fine, I can help. If you don't, that's fine too. But you've got to get it together and start being a full-time member of this team instead of a part-time asshole."

"I know, I know, I'm sorry. I guess I had too much to drink," said Clint, looking genuinely remorseful. He looked across the shed at the different crates, unable to meet Jake's eyes.

"I'm not the only one you need to apologize to."

As Lexi and Ben pushed Mole1 across the camp toward the drilling site, they watched Clint and Jake leave the tool shed. Clint bee-lined for the work shed and Jake walked toward Mole Control.

"What's the deal with Clint?" asked Lexi, as the work shed door closed behind Clint. "I mean, I know what he's like, trust me. I spent more than enough time with him at orientation. But I just don't get him. You have to bunk with him. Has he ever said anything? I know he's divorced, that's about it."

Ben hesitated, feeling that to speak would betray his bunkmate, but Clint's erratic behaviour was alienating people. "I don't know exactly. I mean, it's not like we sit around and talk about this kind of stuff, but he has told me a bit. He was married and you're right, he's definitely divorced. It sounds like it was a while ago, when his kid was about two. I think he's six or seven now. He said that they were having problems before the boy came into the picture. I get the impression he might have clued in a little at one point, like maybe he realized he had something to do with the problems, but by then too much resentment had built up." Ben flicked several small stones off the rear deck as they walked. "I don't know. These things are rarely one-sided. Appar-ently she took him to the cleaners, or so he said. He says she was out to get him and that she was doing it to punish him. I think financially he's just starting to recover from it. Emotionally, it doesn't sound like he's ever really gotten over it. I mean, it's been about four years so he's moved on, but just from what I've seen of him, I don't think he gets it."

Lexi got the impression that Clint, in fact, did a lot of talking. "That would be hard on a person," said Lexi, trying to remain unbiased.

"A lot of this is what I've pieced together, so I can't say for certain. What I do know is that despite his shortcomings, he is really a decent guy. He'll give you the shirt off his back if he doesn't feel threatened by you. It's just unfortunate though because of what's happened, he doesn't seem to trust women. It's like he thinks that they're all out to get him. I won't even get into some of the things he's said about some of the women around the base that outrank him. The man is pretty smart when it comes to his work, but beyond that, he seems denser than the rocks he's paid to drill through."

"I've noticed," said Lexi. "But that explains why he seems to have such a hate on for Maya. What is he, level three? Four? If he has to answer to a female level two, that's gotta get under his skin."

"I would think so, but I think there's another reason. Clint has a picture of him and his kid tucked into the frame of the dresser mirror. The other day I accidentally bumped the mirror and the picture fell onto the floor. I picked it up to put it back in and part of the photo was folded over. On the other side, there's a woman who I can only assume was his wife. The kid looked about one-ish maybe, I don't know. But what I do know is that the woman in the picture looks damn-near identical to Maya.

CHAPTER 23

TEAM 2
YEAR: 2016
TIME REMAINING: 155 Days

Owen led the team in their next endeavour—developing a diffuser to fit over the muzzle of the zeno ray gun to diffuse the rays. It was an easy concept and with his father's industrial-grade tools, Owen customized a diffuser body to fit the barrel's unique shape. While the construction itself was easy, less so was finding a material to do the diffusing that would not disintegrate the moment the highly-destructive zeno rays touched it.

Days turned into weeks of experiments with different substances in the diffuser, but with no luck. Owen had tried frosted glass first, but the thick red beam melted the thin piece of glass like a blow torch on butter, despite the strengthening compound they coated it with.

The effects of working fourteen-hour days and weekends had begun to show on Owen. Eighty-hour work weeks agreed with him far better when he was in his twenties. Dark circles had appeared under his eyes, his complexion grew pale and something in his eyes, Riley noticed, had become flat. He never once complained and maintained a positive attitude when even Riley, herself, wanted to start smashing things in frustration. He was generous with his time with no question of compensation; his only concern was the success of Riley and Finn's endeavour. Riley knew he needed time away from anything resembling work.

"Alright guys, that's it. We're done," announced Riley. She slid off her cushy lab stool.

"What do you mean?" asked Owen, looking down at his watch. "It's not even noon yet. We can still get another eight hours in."

"We've been at this for ages, and it's Saturday." She looked out the window at the small park across the road, packed with people enjoying the sun. "This is the first day in over a week where we've had great weather. I think we should take the rest of the day off."

Owen leaned back in his chair and rubbed his eyes. "I could really use a nap."

Finn abandoned his work without a second thought and bee-lined for his jacket in the kitchen. "Excellent! I've been wanting to check out that amusement park by the stadium. I was reading up on it on your Internet and it looks so retro. I bet those rollercoasters don't get even get a single G! Do you guys want to come? We could make an afternoon of it."

"Thanks," said Owen, "but the only G I want to feel is the gravity pulling me into bed."

Owen pulled into his driveway, pleased with himself for having kept his eyes open the entire trip. As he closed the driver's door, he savoured the warm sun rays on his face. It felt shameful to sleep through such a glorious Saturday afternoon, but he had barely enough energy to even complete the thought. As he entered the front door, he thought he heard a loud metallic click in the basement. He stood stock still, listening for more sounds. Hearing nothing, he wondered if what he heard had been a figment of his imagination. He had no trust in any of his senses, but thought it was worth a quick investigation.

Owen crept down the carpeted stairs to the basement. He peered around the living area and into Finn's room. Hearing nothing further and seeing nothing amiss in either room, he walked down the hall toward the garage. He opened the door to the garage and saw his father's tools and the white Range Rover, but nothing was out of place. He stood silently for a moment and heard nothing. A fresh wave of tiredness fell over him and he lay down on the couch with the intention of investigating any more noises should he hear any, but fell asleep as his head hit the throw pillow.

Riley struggled off the bus with six paper bags of groceries. The grocery store had been too busy for her to use VersaTool to shrink her purchases down to a manageable, pocket-sized load. The nearest bus stop was a five-minute walk from Owen's home and without the assistance of her VersaTool, the groceries would be impossible to carry without dropping items or losing the bottom of a bag. With the bus out of sight, she pulled her VersaTool from her backpack and shrank the grocery bags to the size of large marbles.

Riley entered the front door of the house and closed it gently behind her. She placed the miniature bags of groceries on the kitchen table, taking care not to knock any of them over. Chasing down a cantaloupe the size of a small bead would be tricky.

Riley wanted to make sure that Owen stayed in good health and good spirits. Not just because he was a valuable asset and they would lose time if he became ill, but because she cared about his well-being. The last thing she wanted was for him to resent their imposition on him, or worse, regret his decision to help. Riley was impressed by Owen's selflessness and how he always made himself available. He had insisted they stay at his home, worried about their safety in cheap motels.

Riley retrieved her VersaTool and aimed the blue beam at the bags. Just as she pressed and slid the button, she sneezed. Instead of selecting the groceries, she missed. The table doubled in size, knocking four wooden chairs backward onto the stone floor with a deafening crack that echoed throughout the silent house. Cringing and hoping she had not disturbed Owen, she returned the table back to its original size. She tiptoed to the overturned chairs and righted them as silently as possible. She made a mental note to apologize to Finn for being so hard on him when he blew up her office; apparently it was an easier mistake to make than she had realized. Positive the beam encompassed the bags only, she decompressed the bags to their regular size and began putting the food away. She carried the last few items to the basement to leave in the cold storage. At the bottom of the stairs, she realized Owen was sleeping on the couch. She crept past him and put the supplies into the storage area. As she passed, he stirred and rolled over to face the back of the couch. She pulled the blanket off the back of the sofa and laid it over him.

Finn arrived and found Riley in the kitchen preparing dinner.

"He's flaked out downstairs," explained Riley, reading her protégé's mind. "I figured I'd let him sleep until dinner's ready."

Finn reflected on Owen's unwaveringly amiable temperament and durability. "The guy's a machine, eh? I couldn't work like that."

"Oh, trust me, I know," said Riley, one eyebrow arched. She joked, but in truth, Finn was one of the best subs she had ever worked with. He played hard, but he worked even harder. Even though he had only been in Black Ops a few years, Riley knew she could trust him with her life.

"Who's your date?" asked Riley, looking at the oversized, stuffed Tyrannosaurus Rex under his reddened arm.

Finn's face and arms were pink from the spending the afternoon in the sun. He explained to Riley in great detail, a crazy game he played where he had to shoot an antique gun that used air and something that sounded like "bee-bees" to hit different targets. He had done it just for fun and when he was finished, the stunned carnie handed him the biggest T-Rex hanging in the booth.

"You guys should have woken me up," said Owen, pouring glasses of wine. "I could have done all this."

As Riley, Owen and Finn sat down to dinner on the rooftop patio, the sun faded into a pink pool in the west. The patio lights cast a soft white glow over the deck.

"Owen, you're insane. You're putting in more hours in a week than two people would. We can do a few things around here."

The steaks were charred with Finn at the helm of the barbeque, but it had been his first time with a manual grill. Owen arrived on the rooftop patio to find Finn dictating his grilling instructions to the barbeque. When the cooking appliance failed to acknowledge his command, he leaned over and this time, spoke the commands louder and directly into the temperature gauge. Chuckling, Owen handed Finn the barbeque fork and explained that his eyes were the cooking gauge. Finn was thrilled by the low-tech nature of the barbeque but after becoming distracted in the kitchen while getting the potato salad, he returned to find the barbeque billowing smoke.

When dinner was over, Owen brought up coffee. Watching Owen fill the three mugs reminded Riley of something and she dashed downstairs only to return moments later with a small plastic container.

"I found something for you today, Finn." Riley tossed Finn the container as she returned to her seat.

Finn caught it and read the label. A grin lit up his face. "Wow! Where did you find this?"

Riley shrugged casually, but the sparkle in her eye gave away that she too was excited. "At the grocery store!"

Owen passed Riley and Finn mugs of coffee, surprised that honey could be so fascinating.

"And it was just in the store? On a shelf, like with ketchup?" Finn pulled off the lid and spooned some of the golden delight into his coffee.

Riley nodded. "There was tons of it! Isn't that crazy?"

"Have neither of you had honey before?" asked Owen.

Riley shook her head as she took a spoon off the coffee tray and sampled a small scoop. "Wow. That's way sweeter than the synthetic stuff."

"Honey bees have been extinct since sometime in the fifties," said Finn. He sunk the spoon deep into the honey then jammed it into his mouth.

"So how do all the crops get pollinated?" asked Owen.

Finn, with the spoon of honey still in his mouth, mimed something that Owen thought may have been a bird flying into a window. Riley looked thoughtful. "I'm not sure how it works exactly. I was never big into biotech in school but from what I understand, there are millions and millions of little marble-sized drone bee-bots that fly around and pollinate everything, but that's it. No honey."

"Really?" said Owen, fascinated.

"There is a small amount of honey left-over from before the extinction, but it's rare and definitely not something the average person can get. You'd have to pay a ridiculous amount of money for it," said Riley.

Finn had managed to remove the spoon. "Well, honestly, it seems inconceivable that millions of little insects flew around from plant to plant, pollinating everything and then crops magically grew. Now that sounds like science fiction."

After dinner, the team discussed their string of less-than-stellar results and attacked their problem from a different angle. Did they need to use a combination of materials? Perhaps they needed to blend and fuse different substances or create something from scratch? Perhaps a liquid?

"Hey, what if…" Owen looked off into the night in thought. He frowned.

"What if, what?" asked Finn.

"No. It couldn't be that simple," he said absently.

Riley sat up in her chair. "What are you thinking?"

"You said you were able to successfully neutralize Elevanium before you came, right?"

"Well, yes. But the method was too slow for what we need," said Riley.

"Right, but what did the Elevanium look like after it was neutralized? Did it change in any way?"

Riley thought back. "No, not really. It just kind of stopped glowing. That's about it."

"Did anything else about it change?"

"No. Why do you ask?" asked Riley. She set her wine glass down on the table and sat up straight.

"What if we diffused the zeno rays with a piece of Elevanium?"

Riley crossed her arms and looked up at the sky, running the idea through her mind. "I don't know. The stuff is only slightly transparent. Don't you think the rays would lose a lot of their effectiveness?"

"If we tried different thicknesses it stands to reason that you could control how much of the beam passed through it by how thick the piece was. You brought tools that will cut it, right?"

Riley and Finn exchanged excited glances.

"I think we should go to the lab and try it," suggested Owen.

Riley smiled. "I was hoping you'd say that."

At the lab, Riley walked directly into the dorm room and returned with yet another device Owen had never seen before. It reminded him of a deli scale.

"What is that thing?" asked Owen.

"It's an Elevanium Fragmenter." Riley placed a glowing rectangular brick of Elevanium on the surface of the cutting machine. After Riley tapped her commands into the holographic screen projected above the device, the slab of Elevanium rose off the surface and settled itself several inches in the air. A small bead of green light sliced down the front of the brick like a knife, and a wafer-thin slice of Elevanium separated from the block. The green light reappeared on the slice, and like a laser cookie-cutter, cut a perfect circle then bisected it down the centre. The laser disappeared and the circle slid out leaving a hole the size of a quarter. The various pieces of Elevanium settled on the base. Riley grabbed one of the semi-circles and tossed it to Owen. He held it up and noticed the light was quite visible through the thin slice, like looking through thick, frosted glass.

Owen placed the small piece of Elevanium into the tip of the diffuser then slid the diffuser onto the barrel of the gun. Finn set the gun and its tripod in the tank. The zeno ray gun had been shrunk to less than a quarter of its size to make testing more manageable. Riley hung a new paper target on the side of the tank. If the diffuser worked, the paper would disintegrate instantly. If it failed and the zeno rays burned through the Elevanium in the diffuser, the thick red beam would ignite the centre of the paper.

"Ready?" asked Riley. She held the remote control for the gun in her hand, her thumb ready on the trigger button. The two men nodded and she hit the button. Instead of the thick beam they had grown accustomed to seeing, a pink haze appeared. The target disappeared instantly and tiny bits of black ash settled to the floor of the tank.

Any residual tiredness that Owen felt had disintegrated along with the paper. The team jumped up and yelled with excitement. Caught up in the excitement and not realizing until after he had done it, Owen turned and pulled Riley into a big hug and kissed her on the cheek. She looked stunned and blushed a little. He let go of her awkwardly and gave Finn a high five.

CHAPTER 24

TEAM 2
YEAR: 2016
TIME REMAINING: 155 Days

The team shut the lab down shortly after their success. Conversation during the drive home was light and filled with the type of giddiness only relief can bring. Now comfortable in airing their mounting concerns about what their next suggestions would have been, they joked about their level of desperation. Of all the neutralization methods presented, the zeno ray guns seemed like the only method with reasonable potential, but without a diffused beam, that solution faced abandonment leaving them with no clear runner-up.

"My next suggestion was to fill the tank with water," said Owen, turning down a side street. "I was really running out of ideas."

"I was ready to grab a hammer and smash that bloody gun to bits," said Finn from the back seat of the truck.

"What would that have accomplished?" asked Riley.

"Not a bloody thing. It just would have felt very satisfying."

The team laughed as they pulled into Owen's driveway. Owen noticed how bright the stars were for the first time in ages and parked his truck in the driveway to gaze at them before going inside. As he closed his truck door, he stared up into the vast abyss of space and felt a wave of gratitude wash over him. Gratitude for what specifically, he was unsure. Perhaps for Riley and Finn coming into his life and waking him from the debilitating depression that had seized his life? That he had finally started to move forward? Perhaps all of the above. Owen took one last look at the Big Dipper then took the steps to the basement entrance two at a time.

"Owen?" called Riley.

Owen was just about to slide his key into the lock. "Yeah?"

"I, um…I don't think we should go in."

Owen thought she was joking. He looked over his shoulder at her with a smile and was puzzled to see her still beside the truck. "Riley, are you okay? Maybe it's the floodlights, but you look really pale. Do you want to sit down? Let me get the door open."

"Owen! No!" Riley raced down the stairs and knocked his hand away from the lock, sending the keys to the ground. Owen knelt down to pick them up. As he stood, Riley grabbed him by the arm and pulled him back up the concrete steps.

"Riley, what is it?" asked Finn. He looked at his lead imploringly and this confused Owen further.

"I don't know," she said. She put her hands on her hips and looked up at the house. "Something doesn't feel right."

Owen saw Finn back away from the house at her words. Riley pulled Owen farther away from the house. "Riley, what's wrong?"

"I just have a bad feeling about this," she repeated.

Owen looked at Finn for a clue, but his expression gave away nothing. "This intuition is what makes her good at her job," said Finn, finally. "It's why she, well we, and a lot of other people are still alive. If Riley has a bad feeling about something, I listen. She's been right before about some crazy, out of the blue things."

"What, like someone's in my house?" Owen found the situation hard to take seriously, but the grave expressions on their faces left him unsettled.

"Call the fire department Owen. Call them now." Her voice was urgent but controlled, like that of a seasoned emergency services operator.

Owen dialled 9-1-1. *Better safe than sorry*, he thought as he held his hand over the phone. "What am I going to say to them?" he whispered loudly as a voice picked up on the other end.

"I don't know. Tell them anything," whispered Riley.

"9-1-1. What's your emergency?" asked a calm voice.

"Fire. Or police maybe. Police I guess, please," stammered Owen.

"Is there a fire sir?" asked the voice.

"No, uh… Not that I can see. I just got home and I think someone's in my house."

A new voice collected Owen's details and dispatched a unit to investigate. They stood at the back of the driveway staring at the house and waited for the police to arrive. In Finn and Riley's silence, Owen contemplated the situation. He never really believed in premonitions, but he had come to know Riley fairly well over the last month and knew her to be an intelligent, humble and honest individual. Based on what he had learned of her and the level of respect he had for her, he took her words more seriously than had they been anyone else's.

A police cruiser pulled into the driveway within ten minutes of placing the call, lights flashing but no siren. Owen relayed the made-up cover story to the two officers before they entered the house—that he had seen some shadows moving in the living room as he pulled into the driveway.

The first officer took Owen's house keys and instructed them to wait behind the cruiser while they searched the house. Owen told them the alarm code and pointed to the basement door through which he had planned on entering.

Owen, Riley and Finn watched from behind the squad car as the first officer unlocked the deadbolt. He pushed the basement door open as he unholstered his gun, then looked inside. Seeing nothing that caused him any concern, he entered the house and disappeared from their sight, though they could see his shadow stop at the alarm keypad. The second officer followed his younger partner inside. His tall, husky shadow disappeared as he walked deeper into the basement. They heard the keypad beeping as the first officer entered Owen's code. Seconds after the sixth and final beep, an explosion rocked the house. Glass and chunks of concrete flew in every direction. A fireball shot out the open door and disappeared upward into the dark night. A mass of concrete landed on the hood and windshield of the cruiser. The impact rocked the car and instinct drove Riley, Finn and Owen to the ground as heat and wind from the deafening blast washed over them. Small pieces of debris rained down around them. Dust and smoke accompanied the flames that poured through the basement door, as well as through a hole in the basement's foundation. Smoke billowed from where basement windows had been. Many of the two-storey, tempered glass window panes had cracked into millions of little glass cubes. Some stood in their frames like unique art while the others fell to the ground outside like frozen droplets of rain.

Owen hit redial on his phone and got the same operator. Before he could explain to the operator what had happened, he watched in shock as Riley sprinted through the basement door. Owen's stomach lurched and he forced himself to focus on what he relayed to the operator. Finn called after Riley and followed her inside without hesitation.

Owen got off the phone with emergency services and bolted toward the basement door just as Finn emerged with the younger officer slung over his shoulder. Owen helped him lay the unconscious officer down beside the cruiser. He looked back, expecting Riley to come out any moment; however, the only thing exiting the basement door was thick, inky smoke.

"Where's Riley?" yelled Owen over the sound of the air whistling around them. He checked the vital signs of the officer while Finn knelt on the ground, hunched over, his chest heaving. A black mark crossed his forehead and matched dark patches of ash in his copper hair.

Finn shook his head violently, coughed a few times and sat up straight. "I don't know. It was too smoky. I couldn't see a damn thing. Hit my head on a beam or something."

Owen found a pulse on the officer and confirmed he was still breathing. Hoping he would be alright for the moment, Owen ran toward the door. Finn grabbed his arm and pulled him back.

"Owen, it's too dangerous. You can't go in there!" shouted Finn, over the sound of the raging fire.

"We can't leave her in there!" yelled Owen, fighting against Finn's vise-like grip. Finn stumbled on a piece of debris and lost his footing. Owen jerked free and bolted but skidded to a halt just outside the open door frame. Dense smoke surged through the open door and he could see no farther than his arm's length. He knelt down to the ground and found the visibility little better.

"Owen! No!" Finn grabbed Owen again, this time restraining him with an arm around his chest, the other on Owen's arm. He pulled Owen away from the door. "Don't worry. She'll be okay. Trust me."

Unable to pull himself out of Finn's grasp, Owen's heart pounded harder with every passing second that Riley failed to appear. He heard sirens in the distance. After what seemed like hours of staring into the dense, black smoke, Riley's figure appeared, carrying the second officer over her shoulders like an oversized sack of potatoes. Finn released his grip on Owen and they lunged toward her. Riley sped between the two and carried the unconscious form away from the house. Finn led her to where the first officer lay and they helped her ease the man to the ground. She stood upright to catch her breath and stumbled. Owen left Finn with the second officer and grabbed Riley. She tried to shake him off, but her balance faltered. She bent over, propped herself up with her arms on her knees and coughed.

Owen grabbed her around the waist and eased her to her knees. "Are you okay? What were you thinking running in there like that? There could have been more explosions! The house could have collapsed on you!" He knelt down in front of her and looked her over. "Are you hurt anywhere? Did you hit your head?"

Riley said nothing but shook her head with a pained expression. She tapped her chest with the palm of her hand then massaged her neck. She coughed out raspily, "Smoke."

Owen pulled her into a hard hug. She wrapped her arms around him tightly but released him nearly immediately as flashing red lights announced the arrival of the fire truck. A second fire truck, two ambulances and two more police cars filed into the spacious driveway. Owen felt a tug on his sleeve and saw Riley trying to say something, but her smoke-scarred voice was inaudible over the sirens. He leaned in closer.

"No hospital."

What seemed like hours were only minutes since the blast. The medics looked over the two officers. The junior officer had already regained consciousness and sat in a daze beside his less fortunate partner, who lay on a gurney inside one of the ambulances. A medic pulled the rear door closed and it tore down the driveway, sirens screaming. The second set of medics insisted on checking over Riley and Finn, and no amount of protesting from Riley would deter them. Riley settled herself on the bumper of the remaining ambulance, holding up an oxygen mask with a hand that had been wrapped in a tensor bandage for a suspected sprain. Satisfied she was alright, the medic who looked her over began filling out paperwork, and Riley watched the other medic clean and dress the cut on Finn's forehead.

Relieved that somehow Riley and Finn had miraculously escaped with only bumps and bruises, Owen stood among the chaos and watched the nightmare unfolding before his eyes. It seemed like for him, time stood still, but for the firefighters putting out the fire, it moved in fast-forward. Mist from the thick jets of water flooding the house landed on his face. It felt cool on his over-heated skin, baked by the raging inferno that was his house. He felt helpless. The home he had known for most of his life and the last tie he had to his family—his father—was going up in smoke. All he could do was stand and watch the memories burn. He felt a large lump forming in his throat at the thought of the photos of his father, mother and his grandparents, going up and smoke. He looked down as a hand slide into his. Riley stood at his side, the orange of the blaze reflecting off her skin and eyes as she looked up at him.

"Come on Owen, we're in the way here." She pulled him gently away. He let her lead him and he followed blindly, looking back over his shoulder, unable to take his eyes off his home.

TIME REMAINING: 154 Days

The fire was contained quickly, but Owen prepared himself for the worst. Firemen with axes walked through the home checking for immediate structural issues and areas that may still be smouldering. Owen kept his eye on their progress while another police officer on the scene took his report.

Owen explained to the middle-aged officer exactly what had happened, save for the few embellishments required to maintain consistency with what he told the emergency operator earlier that evening.

"And your friends went into the house and pulled out the two officers?"

Owen nodded, looking over the man's shoulder. The home looked like the charred carcass of its former self with the blackened concrete and missing windows. His gaze fell back on the officer and saw that the man was speaking. "Sorry, say that again?"

"Your friends. I'd like to get their reports too while I'm here." The officer smiled sympathetically as he motioned from Riley to Finn with his clipboard.

Owen hesitated for a moment as he wondered how Riley would want to handle this but saw no way he could protect Riley and Finn from the officer's questions. Riley showed no signs of concern. After hearing the pair's account and writing for several minutes, the officer jogged his papers together until they became uniform and clipped them to his clipboard. "Alright. I think I've got all I need from you guys. I just need to see some identification."

For the second time that night, Owen's stomach turned over. He thought back to the first day they had met when Riley showed him her three-dimensional ID tag in his office. He remembered the Adam Seers story and hoped Riley and Finn could avoid getting carted downtown and locked in a padded room. As Owen retrieved his wallet from his back pocket, he tried to think up a cover story for them. Riley and Finn produced their identification cards and the officer took all three. Seeing their cards were not from the area, the officer eyed them with curiosity.

"Phoenix, eh? On vacation, I take it?" asked the officer.

Riley nodded, not missing a beat. "Yes, we're here for a couple of weeks."

"I like Phoenix. Go down there sometimes during the winter. Great place."

"Yes, it's really nice. I like the heat," said Riley, watching the officer line up the three identification cards then clip them atop the handwritten reports.

As the officer walked away, Finn leaned into Riley, his brow furrowed. "Are those IDs going to hold up Rile?" She said nothing but gave him an I-guess-we'll-find-out look and a shrug to match.

The officer returned to his cruiser and sat down wearily in the driver's seat. They watched him punch their information into his computer. After a few moments, they heard a loud voice crackle over the two-way radio clipped to his vest.

"Hey 4-0-2, there's something wrong with the ID numbers you've given me."

The officer jumped in his seat, startled by the volume of his radio. He turned it down then tossed his pen onto the dash and rubbed his eyes in frustration. His cell phone rang and he answered it tersely. Finn began balling and unballing his fists subconsciously. "There's gotta be a problem. It wouldn't be taking that long if there wasn't a problem."

The officer returned and handed Owen back his driver's licence as he looked from Riley to Finn. "I'm having problems running your IDs. I'm only getting partial reports," said the officer. "I think the system crashed half way through retrieving the information. The guys at the station say the federal database has been up and down all day." He sighed heavily and rubbed his temples in exasperation. "We upgraded some software and it's been nothing but hassles. This has been happening to me daily for at least two weeks now. I'm sorry for the inconvenience."

The officer looked back at his car painfully, like the thought of having to trouble-shoot another computer problem might push him over the edge. He tapped the two IDs on the palm of his hand, then handed them back to Riley and Finn. "That damn database could be down all night for all I know." The officer looked beyond them and saw the fire chief waving to get his attention. "And it looks like the chief wants you. I'm going to bug out; I've done all I can do. It's up to the investigators now. I've got your info in case I need to get in touch. Sorry about your loss, Owen."

As the officer got into his car, Finn exhaled like he had not breathed in ten minutes. "That was close. I don't know if their system was down or if it was the cards, but I'm fine not finding out either way."

As the trio walked over to where the fire chief was conferring with his men, Owen saw his back door lying on the concrete drive. The door now possessed a bowl-like quality as a result of the blast and blackened water had collected inside.

The chief was holding two small, grey unmarked packages and a third item that looked like it may have once been identical to the first two at some point. All that remained was some grey paper that had miraculously not disintegrated in the blast. All three items were dripping wet.

"Do you know what caused this?" asked Owen.

"I don't want to say officially until I've completed my report, but it looks to me like this was intentional." He held up the two packages and the blackened remains of the third.

Owen looked at the water-soaked packages in the chief's gloved hands. He had never seen them before in his life. "Like explosives? You're telling me this wasn't a gas leak or something?"

The chief nodded. "It's looking that way. Your alarm system was rigged, but whoever did it didn't finish the whole job. An amateur, I'm guessing." He held up the charred package. "I found the remains of this in the panel box that controls your alarm in the utility room." He held up the two grey bricks. "These were on a shelf in the cold room. I can't say for sure, but I'm going to guess that whoever was doing this got interrupted and hid them hoping they'd go off in the blast. You're a very lucky man. This could have been…well, three times worse."

"How bad is the damage?" asked Owen. He prepared himself for the house to be a total loss.

The fire chief pushed up his helmet scratched his forehead. "Well, it's not as bad as it looks. Especially considering what it could have been. Good thing the house is mostly concrete, that's what saved it. Whoever built this house built it like a tank. There is a hole blown out of one basement wall as you've seen and there's some cracking, but the place still looks structurally sound and what is damaged should be repairable. Most of the upstairs is untouched, just smoke and water damage. Structural Assessment will come by tomorrow and do an official inspection. Oh, and the Forensics Unit will be spending a bit of time here too. They'll want to go over that basement with a fine-toothed comb."

Owen nodded and looked back at his truck. He saw the windshield had several spider web cracks and a softball-sized chunk of concrete sat where his left headlight should have been. "Before I go, can I go in and salvage what I can?"

The chief hesitated for a moment as if deciding whether or not to let them in. "I think that'll be alright. There's probably a lot of smoke damage, but we didn't water the upstairs too badly, so it's worth taking whatever you can if it puts you more at ease."

The chief escorted the three into the house. Behind the back of the chief, Owen saw Riley and Finn shoot each other a look he understood. *Make sure you get everything out that you can't explain.* Once inside the house, the chief left them and they surveyed the damage. Most of the windows were missing; fragmented into millions of pieces and lying on the grass below. Water dripped from the ceiling like a bizarre rain shower. The furniture was soaked and water trickled steadily down the stones of the fireplace chimney and collected in pools on the warped hardwood floor. The cover page of *Astronomy Today* floated in one of the puddles. The hardwood floor by the kitchen had blackened where the fire had begun spreading into the living room.

Owen, Riley and Finn went to their rooms and packed what they could. Finn was done first; there was little left in his room to salvage. His bag and some dirty clothes, having been crammed under the bed, were remarkably undamaged, albeit smoky, and he gathered them quickly. As the rest of his clothes and possessions had been strewn about his room at the time of the blast, they had succumbed to the fire.

In what remained of the *en suite* bathroom, Finn found and picked up the now blackened medical bag from the floor. Water poured from a tear in one of the seams.

He pulled out the MediScan device that Riley had used to heal Owen's foot on the day they met. Water dripped out of its casing and the screen was cracked. He swore under his breath.

Riley found most of her possessions were salvageable. Most were wet and all smelled of smoke, but nothing had burned. As she filled her bag, she thought about the bullet they dodged by keeping their most unexplainable gadgets on themselves at all times or locked safely in the lab. She imagined having to explain her VersaTool to a room full of police officers. She finished packing and quickly removed all traces of her ever having been there. She went to Finn's room to ensure he had done the same. They waited in the living room for Owen, giving him space.

Ten minutes passed and Owen still had not come downstairs.

"You should check on him," said Finn, his voice quiet and morose.

Riley peered into Owen's room and knocked on the doorframe. His closet door stood open revealing a mostly bare closet. A large rolling duffel bag lay open on the damp and stained white duvet covering his bed. It was packed to the top with clothes and personal items. Sitting next to it on the bed were some wet wood carvings, water-damaged pictures and a soaked and torn strip of newsprint. Riley looked through the glass patio door and saw Owen still as night, leaning on the balcony railing and watching the river. The moonlight reflected off his dark hair as he leaned on the railing. She wanted to give him space but felt it would be best if she and Finn left before more questions were asked.

Riley slid the patio door open and leaned on the railing beside him. Without consciously thinking about it, she tested its integrity before leaning on it.

"Owen?" She put her hand on his shoulder.

He looked back at her and sighed resignedly as he straightened up. "I know, we have to go. It's just really hard to leave. It's hard to see this place like this." He ran his hands back and forth across the railing in a caressing fashion. He explained to Riley about his father passing away, how it had nearly destroyed him to lose his best friend and father. Seeing the house like this made him feel like he was losing him all over again. Riley let his words hang in the silence for several minutes before delivering another painful blow.

"Owen, I think whoever did this meant to connect all three explosives but was interrupted and left the remaining two underneath the panel hoping they'd detonate in the explosion."

Owen looked at her, perplexed. He thought maybe she had misheard the fire chief. After all, his ears were still ringing from the blast. "No, the other two were in the cold room. There's a concrete wall between the panel and the cold room."

"No, they were under the panel box. I came down to the basement this afternoon and put some groceries in the cold storage. When I passed by the door to the utility room, I saw those two grey bricks sitting on the floor. I had no idea what they were and, truthfully, I didn't really give them too much thought. Looking back now, I realize there was a beige metal box mounted on the wall above them, but at the time, I barely noticed it. I just thought it was a weird place for whatever the two bricks were because everything in your house is so orderly. They were sitting so haphazardly, I moved them into the cold storage area so no one would trip on them." She looked at Owen. "Owen, I'm so sorry. I didn't know."

Owen studied Riley's face. She still had streaks of soot on her cheek. He believed her. How would she have known what explosives from eighty years ago looked like? Hell, most people now had no clue what explosives looked like. He would never have recognized them as explosives if he had stumbled across them. He smiled weakly. "It's okay. Don't worry about it. If you hadn't moved them, they would have exploded as well, and my house would have been confetti."

"Hey, guys?" Finn stuck his head out onto the balcony. His expression was solemn. "Sorry, but the chief needs us to head out."

TIME REMAINING: 153 Days

After hearing about the harrowing events of Owen's weekend, his director had no problem letting Owen take three weeks of banked time off, and even threw in an extra week of vacation time for good measure. Owen was an asset to the NRD and they wanted to keep him happy—not just because he was a star in his field that private industries paid big dollars to contract out on occasion, but because he was a dedicated employee. He was easy to work with and a genuinely kind-hearted individual who would give you his last loaf of bread if he was starving.

The days that followed the explosion had been a blur. Despite the damage it sustained during the blast, the alarm panel did an excellent job of telling its story. Between the crude materials and the amateur method of connecting the explosives, the forensic team concluded that the person who rigged it likely had little to no experience with explosives.

What unresolved issues Owen had about that night, he swept aside with surprising ease. He knew the house could be rebuilt back to its former glory and his most valuable possessions, like photo albums and old family mementos sustained surprisingly little damage, having been stored in waterproof plastic containers. The rest could be replaced. What Owen did find uneasy was knowing that someone had done it intentionally. He wondered what his father would have done in this situation. He suspected his father would have looked on the bright side, helped the police with whatever they needed to help find the culprit and move forward. The bright side being that it could have been a lot worse—none of them were seriously injured and Riley had again saved his life. Her wrist had healed in a matter of days, and even the mark on Finn's forehead had begun to fade. "Chicks love scars," Finn had said after taking the bandage off the following day to survey the damage.

Owen, Riley and Finn had spent the night in a hotel. This temporary residence would become permanent until the insurance completed the repair on Owen's house. Riley and Finn were spared from returning to the Fore Seasons. One of Owen's friends owned a small chain of hotels and was more than happy to give them a very generous "friends and family" rate after hearing about Owen's predicament.

The group ate breakfast in the hotel's restaurant. Speculating over who could have blown up Owen's house, or why he would have been targeted, carried the trio through their entire meal. With no word yet from the police, and unable to come up with any person or group with the desire to target Owen, they could only conclude it was a random incident until evidence was discovered that proved otherwise.

Owen could not believe the attention to detail Riley went into as she explained the alibis she had arranged to account for their existence in 2016. Huddled together over the now empty plates and talking quietly so no one around them would hear, Riley defended her compulsive need to plan.

"Think of it as our backup chute. You never want to have to rely on your backup chute. But if you need it, you're glad it's there. When you travel back in time, you obviously want to avoid any situation where there is a lot of probing into the details of your 'life.' However, if you do find yourself in a sticky spot, you'll be thankful you took the time to set it up. It was part of my own little risk assessment test when we were preparing. What did you call it, Finn?" she asked, one eyebrow raised.

"A waste of time," responded Finn, in a deadpan, I-know-you-told-me-so kind of way. "But, I'm glad you did and I promise I'll never make fun of your obsessive-compulsive planning again."

"So, are you telling me that on your first day here, you hacked into a federal government computer and implanted yourselves as a vacationing couple from Phoenix?"

"Yeah. Just before we intercepted you at the bus stop. It was killer easy," said Finn. "The encryption on the database was so damn easy to crack that a five-year-old could have done it. Anyway, we just threw in some details, dates and cities of birth, some schools, social security numbers and a few jobs. Easy as pie."

"And we made these before we left, just to be on the safe side." Riley pulled the Phoenix, Arizona, 2016 driver's licence out of her backpack and handed it to Owen. "It was nothing. These old security features are so easy to fake." She flipped the card around in her hand and inspected her handiwork. "They're so archaic. They don't even do anything. No projections, retinal graphs or anything."

Owen had become used to these tangent conversations where Finn and Riley reminisced about some wondrous aspect of the future that eluded him entirely. He listened in fascination but felt deprived in some way, knowing he would never get the chance to experience it for himself. It was the same hollow feeling he would get looking up at the sky at night as a child, so close but not able to touch.

TIME REMAINING: 151 Days

With the diffuser problem resolved, the team could move to the next step in testing the viability of the zeno ray gun theory. To do so, they would test the effectiveness of the gun's rays on Elevanium. As the brick-shaped samples of Elevanium were a fraction of the size of the full deposit, the gun would need to be shrunk down to a one-to-one ratio with the sample Elevanium brick representing the full-sized deposit.

After a lot of math, the team determined how small the ray gun would need to be. Finn used his VersaTool to shrink the gun and its tripod to the appropriate size. The resulting size meant the gun would fit nicely in the trunk of a Hot Wheels car.

"Are you guys ready?" asked Riley, looking up at her two partners huddled around the testing tank.

On the left side of the tank sat the test brick of Elevanium. On the right, the miniaturized ray gun pointed at the glowing rectangular stone. Riley held the remote control for the ray gun in her hand, her thumb itchy on the trigger. Riley decided that controlling the gun with the remote control was the safest way to operate. With her, Finn and Owen all wearing Icomm contacts with the ability to control the gun, it seemed like the best way to prevent any accidents.

The gun discharged and the block of Elevanium took on a pinkish hue from the diffused red beam.

After thirty seconds, Riley looked from the tank to Finn. "Anything?" she asked.

Finn shook his head. He held a yellow scanner in front of him like a digital camera, ready to shoot. The Multi-Matter Scanner he held measured the potency of the Elevanium and timed how long it took for the mass to become neutralized. Owen watched the scanner over Finn's shoulder. The scanner's screen was black except for a bright white shape in the middle, illustrating the potency of the Elevanium. Owen watched the screen and noticed at around the five-minute mark, that the white mass seemed less prominent. At the ten-minute mark, the white had faded to grey and detail around the edges had disappeared.

"Twenty-two minutes, thirty-four seconds," reported Finn. "That's depressing."

Riley laid the remote control on the lab desk next to the tank and rubbed her eyes. "Wow. I didn't think it would be that slow. I thought maybe thirty seconds to a minute or something."

After days of testing, manipulating variable after variable, including using pieces of Elevanium that were different thicknesses in the diffuser, moving the gun closer or further away or heating or freezing the Elevanium, no difference was made. It became apparent that adding the two other ray guns to the plan was necessary. Riley felt uneasy relying on all three guns as part of the primary solution; it left no backup should one fail.

CHAPTER 25

TEAM 3
YEAR: 2095
TIME REMAINING: 151 Days

With Asher so devoted to his newfound "hobby," Logan frequently found himself waiting for his twin brother. Tonight was no different; they had tickets for a Mental Obstruction concert and Asher, still tied up in the lab, agreed to meet his brother at the downtown venue. Having some time to kill before calling a taxi pod to take him downtown, Logan stopped in at the Starbucks across the road from his condo.

As he entered the coffee shop, the Starbucks Icomm-compatible menu began to scroll slowly across his field of vision. Mentally he dismissed it and the colourful menu disappeared. It was replaced by the words, "What can we get for you today?" beside the image of a helpful and attractive barista. He dismissed the interface entirely. With nothing but time to kill, he studied the in-store menu screens on the wall above the counter. As he looked for something he had not yet tried, he absent-mindedly spun his credit-key ring around his finger.

Like a moth to a flame, his attention was drawn away from the menu and onto a group of women chatting as they placed their orders. *Girls' night*, he thought, watching the elegantly dressed women. His attention was drawn to one woman in particular. She stood apart from the rest, waiting to place her order. She was taller than her friends and quite slender. Her tanned skin accentuated the muscle definition in her arms and legs, and her fitted black dress flattered her like it had been designed specifically for her body. Logan imagined running his hand caressingly along the perfect curvature of her waist. Giggles punctured his happy fantasy and he looked over to see the woman's friends watching him ogle her.

Embarrassed for being busted so blatantly, Logan cleared his throat and concentrated again on the menu. The woman finished placing her order and turned. Logan feared being caught again but could not resist checking out the rest of her.

"Logan? What are you doing here?" asked Delaney.

Logan was speechless. He could not believe that he had essentially just undressed his boss with his eyes. He stammered. "I uh, live around here. What are you doing here?"

Delaney wrapped her arms around her waist and looked down at her shoes. "I'm out with a few girls. We're on our way to see Mental Obstruction. They're playing at the arena tonight. Remember that friend from university who visited a while back?" She pointed to one of the women standing in the pack. "I'm out with his sister. I met her while he was in town and we hit it off." The woman's metal bracelets jingled loudly as she waved and winked knowingly. He waved back weakly, preparing himself for another onslaught of whispers and suppressed giggles.

"I didn't realize you were into Mental Obstruction. They're my favourite group," said Logan. He was surprised to see her so self-conscious. In all of his years working with Delaney, not once had she ever been anything but the picture of complete confidence and absolute control.

"Well, I'm not really a fan, but she insisted I come. So, here I am."

It was Logan's turn to order and Delaney's order had come up. "You look really great," he said, hoping to ease her self-consciousness.

"Thanks, Logan." She seemed appreciative of his comment. "I'll see you tomorrow?"

Logan nodded and watched the women leave. Outside the coffee shop, they circled Delaney to get the scoop on who he was and, with no doubt in Logan's mind, to fill her in on what they saw. He felt a hard poke in the ribs and turned. An elderly woman was jabbing him from behind her walker with the point of her umbrella.

"Move it, Boy, or you're going to get mowed over." She pushed her walker into his knees. "Granny's jonesing for a double-double."

Logan took a step forward and looked back up at the menu, but all he saw were a pair of long legs and a sexy black dress.

TIME REMAINING: 150 Days

"So how's the artificial vision coming?" asked Logan over the chatter and music. The twins sat in their usual booth, enjoying a few TGIF bevies with some of Logan's co-workers.

"Good. Really good, actually. I've made some decent progress. You should pop by the lab and check it out," said Asher.

"I might, just so I can drag you out of there."

Asher sipped his beer and leaned back in the booth. "You're not really one to talk. I've noticed you've been lingering at work after five." He laughed. "I see you didn't burst into flames either."

Logan chuckled. "It's amazing what you can get done in just one hour after everyone leaves."

"I know," agreed Asher, more heartily than he planned.

"Oh my God," said Logan. "Listen to us. Do you know who we sound like?"

"I know, I know," said Asher rolling his eyes.

"It's like he's rubbing off on us or something. It's gross really. He'd be insufferable if he knew," said Logan laughing.

"Well, what Spence doesn't know won't hurt him." They tapped their bottles together conspiratorially when they saw a familiar face approaching them through the sea of people. "Speak of the devil."

"Hey, misfits," said Spencer.

"What are you doing here?" Asher stood to give his little brother a one-armed hug. "And here I thought I was wasting my breath by inviting you." Spencer sat between the twins in the U-shaped booth.

"I thought it might be fun, plus, I haven't seen you two in a while. What have you guys been up to?" asked Spencer, innocently. Spencer already knew about his brothers' change in work habits from the reports given by their astonished directors at the weekly directors meeting he now attended in Jim's absence.

Asher pulled at the label on his beer bottle. "Me?" asked Asher. "Oh, not much..." He looked at Logan.

Logan rested his arms on the back of the seat. "Same. Nothing really. The usual—drinking beer, watching rocketball. You know," said Logan.

Spencer smiled to himself; both twins quickly took big gulps out of their beers and looked in opposite directions around the bar.

The evening was more enjoyable than Spencer had anticipated. He wondered if there really was something to what the twins had been telling him all this time. He enjoyed hearing how work was going from their perspective, but it was also nice to talk about things that had nothing to do with robots, personality applications or the NRD. He felt lighter and more free than he had in a long time, and he wondered if that resulted from socializing with his brothers or the alcohol in his system.

A tipsy Spencer was a rare sight indeed, so the twins took full advantage of his mellowed state and tried to set him up with different women around the bar. They refused to listen to his protestations as they wound their way around the room looking for potential dates. When Spencer finally got their attention and explained that he had no interest in meeting any women, they tried to set him up with men.

"We don't care who you love little bro, just as long as you're happy," said Asher with a smirk.

"No, you idiots," hissed Spencer, red-faced and mortified as the man who gave Spencer his business card and a suggestive smile walked out of earshot. "I already have someone in mind." He regretted spilling the beans, but he knew the twins would be relentless otherwise.

"Who is it?" asked Logan with a mischievous grin. "Is it that guy in Framing and Fabrication? Don't lower your standards Spence, you could do much better than a level two engineer." Logan took a sip of his beer and Asher, a level two engineer, tipped up the bottom of the bottle so beer spilled down Logan's shirt.

"It's not a guy, you donkeys," Spencer laughed. He had to admit, he was having a surprisingly fun time with his brothers. Their loving, brotherly abuse rolled off him easily; for that, he knew he could thank the booze. Never would he have had this conversation with them sober.

"So who is the lucky lady?" Logan's sweet demeanour did not entirely mask his eagerness for details.

"I wouldn't tell you guys if you threatened me with…" Spencer trailed off as Kalen entered the bar. She crossed the room and leaned on the bar, waiting for a bartender. The twins followed Spencer's soppy gaze and smiled at each other. Kalen scanned the room while she waited and waved to Spencer.

Logan chuckled knowingly. "Our little boy is in love." He sniffed and wiped a pretend tear from of his eye.

"I dunno, Spence, she's pretty cute," said Asher.

Spencer's dream state was punctured by a sickening thought. The last two people he wanted around a girl he liked were sitting on either side of him, grinning from ear to ear. Horrible visions came to him—the twins telling her embarrassing stories all night long, either made up, or worse, completely true. He elbowed both twins simultaneously in the ribs.

"Please don't make asses out of yourselves," he begged. "More importantly, don't make an ass out of me!"

Kalen held her drink over her head as she dodged bodies, making her way toward their table. Spencer's mind swam with his thoughts and feelings for her. Her jacket was slung over her arm and the halter tank top she wore hugged her short, curvaceous body. In Spencer's eyes, Kalen's sturdy build was perfect.

The three men slid over to give her room and she sat down beside Asher. Seeing Spencer's smiling, vacant expression, Logan reached over the table, shook her hand and introduced himself and Asher. After the introductions and small talk, Spencer was relieved to see the twins actually behaving themselves, as promised.

The bar door opened and Logan glanced over to see Delaney, looking more nervous than he had ever seen her. She feverishly scanned the room for a familiar face.

"Wow," said Logan, "it must be a full moon tonight."

Asher followed Logan's gaze. "Hey Loge, isn't that your boss?"

"Yeah it is," said Logan. A smile grew on his face. "But I've never known her to come out with co-workers before. I invited her, but it's kind of like inviting Spence, you never really expect to be taken up on the offer." Logan waved her over.

"Sweet Jesus. How do you get anything done with her around? She's bloody hot," said Asher, watching her long, leggy stride as she wove her way through the overfilled tables.

Logan said nothing but privately agreed. He was unsure of her exact age but knew she was in her late thirties, maybe early forties. Not that it showed; she was in superb shape and her perfect skin disguised her age. He noticed she had undone the top couple of buttons on her shirt—no doubt to loosen up after work. Remembering the Starbucks incident, he forced himself to look up at her eyes.

"Hey, Logan," said Delaney to one of the twins. She hoped she had addressed the right one. She could not recall what Logan had worn that day and seeing them together, she was taken off guard by how similar they were, right down to the unkempt hairstyle.

Delaney slid into the booth beside Logan. There was a brief moment of awkward silence while Logan failed to locate his thoughts, but he was saved by the waitress. He ordered five Tequila Bombs—a shot of tequila with a small cube of green vodka Jell-O at the bottom. Delaney would have preferred to not drink around her co-workers, but she nearly shook with nerves and knew a drink or two would help her relax.

"I'm surprised you came out," said Logan.

"I'm trying to spend less time at work these days. The project is on track, so there's no point making more work for myself."

"Wow, you sound like Spencer," said Asher. "Except for that last part about *not* making work for yourself. He'd probably live there if he could."

"I'd agree with that," said Kalen.

The group dominated the large booth for most of the evening. Other friends and co-workers came and went from the table throughout the night. Spencer was pleased the twins had managed to behave themselves and he attributed that only to the company of Delaney and Kalen.

"Well, I guess I should hit the road," said Delaney, sliding out of the booth. Logan noticed how after two Tequila Bombs and three Solar Sunrises her poise remained flawless, like she had drunk nothing but water all evening.

Logan scrambled gracelessly out of the booth behind her. "You're not driving, right?" he asked quickly. Asher and Spencer immediately caught each other's eyes, both taken aback by Logan's display of uncharacteristic qualities: responsibility, chivalry and protectiveness. "I'd hate to see you smash that fancy new flying car. Does it have autopilot?"

Delaney nodded. "It does, but it's still illegal to pilot it if you've been drinking. I'll just leave it here and get a cab."

"I'll help you get one." Logan grabbed Delaney's jacket off the hook at the end of the booth and held it up for her to slide into.

"I had no idea you were such a gentleman," chuckled Delaney. She slid her arms into her black leather jacket and slung her bag over her shoulder.

"Me neither," said Asher, fighting hard to stifle his laughter. Spencer elbowed him in the ribs.

Logan followed Delaney toward the exit, his hand on the small of her back as they fought their way through the overcrowded bar. When they were out of earshot, Spencer and Asher looked at each other and laughed, though neither could explain why. Logan hitting on a woman was nothing new; perhaps because she was his boss. Spencer explained to Kalen how the twins got their reputation as ladies' men. Both he and Kalen were in stitches when Asher told the story of how Logan had once tried to convince a girl that he had invented time travel, that he was, in fact, the famous Adam Seers. He explained away his absence by claiming he had been in hiding because he thought the fame of inventing time travel would be too exhausting.

"What are you guys laughing at?" asked Logan, returning to the booth.

"You," said Asher. "The Adam Seers fiasco."

Logan smiled at the memory. He remembered it fondly, even though the only thing he got out of that line was a drink in the face. However, the hours of entertainment the story had brought over the years had been well worth the price.

Asher leaned in conspiratorially. "Why didn't you tell us you've got a thing for your boss?"

Logan looked genuinely surprised by the question. "I don't have a thing for her."

"What?" exclaimed Spencer. He was thrilled that the tables had turned on at least one of the twins, and he planned to make the most out of it. "You couldn't stop looking at her all night. Plus, when are you ever speechless?"

Logan looked at Kalen for an ally and she shrugged apologetically. "Sorry man, I think they're right. Spencer isn't that perceptive when it comes to these things, trust me, and even he noticed."

"When was the last time you flagged down a cab for a woman where you didn't try to follow her into it?" asked Asher.

"What are you guys talking about?" Logan's clueless expression made all three crack up again.

"Well, I think that's my cue to leave," said Kalen, as the laughter died down.

"Are you driving? Are you alright to drive?" Spencer asked clumsily. He pushed Asher unceremoniously out of the booth and stood up, more than a little unsteady on his feet. He fumbled, trying to get her jacket off the hook.

Kalen reached over and unhooked the jacket easily. She threw it on and chuckled at Spencer's bumbling. "I'm fine. I only had a couple drinks and they were hours ago. The question is, how are you getting home? You're not relying on these two are you?"

"I never thought about it. I've never been in this situation before."

"What, drunk at a bar with your brothers?" she asked, laughing. He swayed a little and she grabbed his arm to steady him. "Okay Grayson, get your jacket, I'll drive you home."

"It's okay, I don't want to impose," said Spencer, suddenly interested in the tails of his shirt that had come untucked.

"Don't be silly. Get your jacket. I can't leave you with these guys, you'll wake up tomorrow in a water fountain, duct-taped to the centre piece wearing nothing but your underwear on your head."

Logan laughed. "She's right, you know." He looked at Asher. "Has she met us before?"

Spencer pulled three jackets off the hook and dropped them all to the ground. Asher, laughing and shaking his head, picked them up. He handed Spencer his jacket and patted him on the back before hanging up the others. "Oh, Spence. You're such a lightweight. Look at you. Eight drinks and you're done."

"You guys will thank me...when you're old and looking for new livers!" said Spencer with a goofy grin. Kalen threaded him into his jacket and steered him toward the door. "I love you guys!" were the last words they had heard before the doors closed behind their little brother.

The twins looked at each other, tapped their beer bottles together.

"Our little boy is growing up," said Logan.

Spencer settled into the passenger seat of Kalen's car as she drove through the empty streets. Red streaks of light zipped overhead as the occasional flying car passed over them. He watched the rain slide down the passenger window in streams.

"I take it this isn't a frequent pastime of yours?" she asked, concentrating on the road. Rain pounded the windshield and the wipers could barely keep up.

"No. The twins always bug me to come out, but I rarely do. They probably think I'm a stick in the mud." He thought about it for a moment. "I know they think I'm a stick in the mud."

"Well, I think you're a handsome stick in the mud." She smiled as she put her hand on his knee and squeezed. Spencer took her hand in his, kissed the top and held it as he watched sheets of rain dance in the spotlight of the street lamps.

CHAPTER 26

TEAM 2
YEAR: 2016
TIME REMAINING: 149 Days

Owen arrived at the lab after what had been a long and painful meeting with his interior designer. He expected this meeting to be a quick discussion in which he would instruct the designer to choose the same furniture and building materials the house featured prior to the explosion. However, it turned into a gauntlet of wood samples, floor tiles, colour schemes, kitchen cabinets and furniture. To make matters worse, when he chose something that clashed with elements he had already chosen, he got a lesson in colour theory or textures and patterns. He drove back to the lab happy the meeting was behind him.

Owen found Riley and Finn huddled over the testing tank setting up the two additional ray guns. The second and third guns were outfitted with diffusers that Owen had fabricated by a local machine shop, as his father's tools had been destroyed in the blast. Like the first, Finn coated the new diffusers and guns with a protective coating called Irrefragable Compound so the highly destructive zeno rays did not disintegrate them on contact.

"Seven minutes and fifty-three seconds," said Finn after their fifth experiment using the three guns, all circling the brick.

Riley tossed her pen aside and rubbed her eyes in exasperation. Owen took the piece of neutralized Elevanium out of the tank and set it to the side with the other spent bricks. Finn was ready with the next piece and placed it in the tank.

"Okay, something's not working," said Riley. "Five tests, five extremely inconsistent results."

With three guns, less time was needed to completely neutralize the Elevanium, but it still took too long. Additionally, the inconsistent results made it impossible to predict how long the process actually took.

"Do you think we're losing too much of the ray output to empty space? I wonder what kind of an effect that's having?" asked Finn.

"Add to that, you said the tank is designed to absorb the rays, correct?" asked Owen.

Riley nodded. "But I don't want to limit the range of the diffusers because we just don't know exactly how big of a space we'll be working in, or what shape the deposit is."

Riley crossed her arms and stared at the brick of Elevanium in the tank. She glared at it with contempt, like a pest that resisted extermination. "You guys might be on to something. This experiment is being conducted in a very different environment than what it will actually be like underground. All this space," she said, motioning to the empty space above the brick in the tank, "won't be there. We're going to be at the bottom of a tunnel way below the surface. There's going to be a stone ceiling, walls and floor."

"True, but they'll be coated with Irrefragable Compound so the ceiling doesn't collapse when the rays hit. If the Irrefragable Compound blocks the blast, it should then reflect the rays I would think, but who knows," said Finn.

"I wonder if the composition of the surrounding environment makes a difference? For example, would a more reflective surface bounce the unused beams back, or would they be absorbed the same as if the surroundings were nonreflective?" asked Owen.

Riley shrugged. "It could make a difference. Can you estimate how reflective the stone would be?" asked Finn.

"You said this was found in a mine shaft, right?" asked Owen. Riley nodded.

Owen thought for a moment. "That'll be hard to figure out. I mean, if the deposit was encased in typical bedrock, that would be one thing. But, if it was found in a mine, chances are there's a high concentration of nickel, copper or other metals, and that makes calculating reflective properties practically impossible if you don't know even a rough composition. I think we need to learn more about the mine this Elevanium was found in."

Up next on Finn's list of things to eat was seafood and *The Beach* never disappointed. Its seaside decor made for a novelty atmosphere in a city where the biggest body of water in the vicinity was a river. Old fishing nets, antique fishing lures, fake fish and other seaside paraphernalia adorned the walls of the restaurant. The weathered patio, where Owen, Riley and Finn studied the menu, was constructed to look like an aged pier overlooking the river.

A large group of women dominated the far side of the patio by the makeshift dance floor. Their laughter and shrieks of excitement were infectious and other patio-goers watched with amusement as the women handcuffed a woman, wearing a white t-shirt with "Bride" written across the chest, to the wrist of a mostly naked inflatable man.

The waitress returned to their table with a metal bucket containing six ice-covered beers as Finn's eyes danced around the menu. "I can't decide what to order. I'm definitely starting with a shrimp cocktail, then I think I'll follow it up with some mussels…no. Wait. Maybe calamari. For the main course, I think I'll try the 'Surf and Surf'—lobster and king crab."

When the waitress returned with their orders, the entire table became a sea of red baskets lined with red and white, checkered waxed paper, each heaping with food.

Finn's response to Riley's comment about wiping out an entire ecosystem in one meal was to hang several calamari tentacles out of his mouth and make high-pitched, muffled screaming sounds.

Finn's desire to experience everything 2016 bordered on obsession. With dinner long since passed, and with ten drinks in his system, he dove into the nightlife of 2016. Owen returned to the table from the washrooms to find Finn on the dance floor. He was surrounded by the women from the bachelorette party, dirty dancing with the maid of honour and wearing a glowing, green plastic penis around his neck.

Owen laughed as he took his seat across from Riley. "He's going to get mauled over there."

"I don't think he'd mind too terribly," said Riley, rolling her eyes.

Their table grew as Owen's friends dropped in and out throughout the night. All week, phone calls had poured in from his friends wanting to check in and offer support as word about his house had spread. Instead, he invited them all out for a few drinks so they could see with their own eyes that he was still in one piece. Owen had introduced Riley and Finn as vacationing cousins; their alibi of being a couple no longer fit as Finn had been adopted by the pack of women and barely made an appearance at the table all night.

Beer in hand, Riley relaxed in her plastic patio chair as she took in the atmosphere. She had to admit to herself that the early century had its charms. There was something about the relaxed pace and simplicity of 2016 that she found homey and inviting. She looked around the patio at the different groups of people, laughing, dancing and having a good time. White strings of outdoor lights hung from the tall, weathered posts and zigzagged across the open air ceiling, giving the patio a cozy and romantic feel. She watched Owen as he laughed and talked with his friends. She could not help but notice how the warm patio lights enhanced his already handsome features, and when he smiled, the sparkle in his eyes seemed to open his soul, revealing his warm, genuine nature.

Riley was interrupted from her thoughts by Finn, who had escaped the clutches of twenty-three heavily liquored women. He called to her casually as he approached the table; though she detected urgency in his tone.

"Hey Rile, I think I'm going to head back to the hotel." He forced a yawn.

His ghostly pallor gave away his plight, but she gave him the gears nonetheless. "I saw you hitting it off with the maid of honour." She looked across the patio at a girl wearing a baby pink t-shirt that read, "Maid of Dis-Honour." The dot on the second 'i' was a crooked halo and growing out the bottom of the 'r' was a devil's tail. She leaned heavily on the bar and threw back a shot of something blue like a seasoned pro. "Let's see. Are you leaving because a) you've picked her up, b) you're too drunk, or c) you have food poisoning?"

Finn looked at her slyly. "Well…" He held up seven napkins and on them Riley saw names and phone numbers. He began to back away. "A little of all three, and I'm definitely guttered but…well, let's just say that's not the issue. Right now, there's only one place I need to be."

Owen's friends, the bachelorette party and the other restaurant-goers gradually left and soon Riley and Owen had the large patio to themselves until a server came by and mentioned they would soon be closing.

Owen looked at his watch and saw it was nearly midnight. "I guess we should check on Finn, eh?" asked Owen.

"Oh, he'll be fine," laughed Riley. "I saw how much he drank. I don't want to go anywhere near him."

Owen smiled. "Fair enough. I have an idea."

They left the restaurant and Owen led Riley to the river's edge. A stone footpath followed the water further than the eye could see in either direction, winding its way through the city's downtown. The path was a favourite any time of day for joggers, tourists and people looking for a leisurely stroll, and tonight was no different. Despite the late hour, many couples and groups could be seen in either direction, the path lit by antique street lamps.

Owen looked up at the many high-rise buildings through the gaps in the trees that lined the walkway. The buildings appeared very much alive with many of the office lights still on as cleaning crews worked their nightly magic.

"So what is the city like in 2097? Is it much different than it is now? Does everyone have hover cars and eat pills for dinner? Does everyone live in bubble-shaped buildings on mile-high stilts?" Owen laughed as he threw at her every cliché from every movie or TV show he had seen about the future. "Where'd you park your DeLorean?"

"My DeLorean?"

Owen chuckled to himself. "Nevermind."

Riley laughed; she had seen enough classic movies to have a pretty good idea of what Owen's perception of the future may be. "The city's about four times bigger and the buildings are much, much taller. The hover car to road car ratio is about seven to two. Hover cars came into production in the mid-sixties, but they didn't really catch on until the late seventies, early eighties when the costs became more reasonable and the safety records became a little more, shall we say, attractive for paying consumers. In the beginning, air traffic merely drove above the regular streets up until the mid-eighties, when it became too much and the city developed designated air routes with proper layering, lighting and guidance systems."

Owen could only imagine the chaos the transition from road to air travel would cause. "Are there a lot of collisions?"

"No, not really. Most cars, regardless of whether they're hover or wheeled have pretty accurate anti-crash sensors, unless they're exceptionally old or you're driving too fast."

"What are the buildings like?"

"Oh, they're much bigger. Some of them will take up three or four city blocks at the base and are easily about four or five times the height of what you have here. Plus, they look quite different. You don't see too many boxy buildings like what you see here," said Riley, looking at the office towers in the distance that made up Tricity's skyline. "There was a big craze for wavy and geometric-shaped buildings around the fifties, so there's quite a few of those. There's kind of a neat ring-shaped building with flared balconies. From a distance, it looks like feathers. There's also one that resembles a narwhal tusk. That's City Hall. Some are tall and narrow like three cylinders grouped together, and that's just in Tricity. Around the world, you almost can't believe some of the architecture. In Asia, some of the buildings actually move with the seasons. There's one built like a Ferris wheel. It takes about a year to go around, so at least one day a year you get a top floor view.

"We still have the subway, but the infrastructure is crumbling and the city isn't planning to fix it when air transit is so much more efficient. When the air is your road, road-building costs are much lower."

Owen thought about how crummy some of the roads were around the city. The wide range of seasonal temperatures of Tricity meant annual repairs for streets and other infrastructure when compared to the milder temperatures of the cities on the West Coast. It was nearly impossible for most cities to keep up with transportation and public works infrastructure maintenance in balanced climates, let alone one as diverse as Tricity.

Neither Riley nor Owen was in any rush to end the evening. They meandered down the path and Riley told Owen more about the future when no one was within earshot. Owen wanted to ask what his neighbourhood was like in the future but decided not to, fearing the answer would be depressing, like it had become a shopping mall.

After a moment of silence while a couple of bicycles passed, they found themselves on a dark stretch of path. Owen was unsurprised by this—springtime flooding frequently ravaged the path. Often, sections were unlit or completely closed off for repair, forcing pedestrians and cyclists up through the bushes, onto the road to detour the damaged area. He squinted and made out the triangular construction signs stacked neatly along the trees that lined the path. Seeing that Riley showed no signs of hesitation, he continued down the path through the darkness.

As they neared the centre of the darkened area, Owen heard a scuffle to his right. With his eyes somewhat adjusted to the darkness, he saw someone try to grab Riley. Before he could reach out, Riley flipped her assailant over her head and onto the ground, pinning his neck down with her foot. The man sputtered and coughed under the pressure of her foot.

Owen's mind was blown—he was completely startled by the attack, impressed with Riley's lightning-fast reflexes and awed by the ease with which she had been able to defend herself. He felt emasculated for not protecting her himself. More footsteps came running up behind them. Another dark figure lunged at Riley. Owen stepped between Riley and the man to intercept him when he saw a dark shadow move out of the corner of his eye. He paid for this distraction as the man charging toward them threw a punch at Owen. It connected poorly and deflected off of his cheek. Owen felt only heat on his cheek—adrenaline blocked the pain as his fist connected solidly with the attacker and laid him out on the ground. Sounds of footsteps surrounded them and the darkness made it impossible to tell by how many people. They were being swarmed.

Riley heard footsteps all around her. Although she was visually unable to tell how many people there were, she used her other senses to tally her attackers. She lost count after eight distinctly different sets of footsteps, the sounds becoming too many to distinguish. She knew her back faced the water and Owen stood to her right, easy to spot in a white polo shirt. She counted three people to Owen's right, at least three to her left and two or more in front.

Riley released the body she had pinned down; he had stopped writhing and she assumed he had become unconscious. She felt a large pair of hands around her neck and she stomped hard on the insole of their owner. The man howled in pain and in one fluid motion, Riley grabbed his arm, wrenched it backward spinning him around, pinned it behind his back and knocked him to his knees. She aimed a kick at his right kidney and let him fall completely to the ground, groaning in agony.

The scene became chaos and Riley concentrated hard on what she heard, felt and smelled around her. Scuffling footsteps were everywhere. She heard nylon track pants which had not been part of the original eight attackers, which meant at least one more new assailant. She felt two pairs of hands on her as she got a glimpse of Owen, his white t-shirt more visible than anything else in the darkness. He fought hard against two smaller attackers and seemed to be holding his own. She disposed of both her assailants as effortlessly as she had the first two, and one of the men attacking Owen switched his focus to her.

"Who is this chick? Superwoman?" asked the small attacker rhetorically as he dashed toward her. His voice was nasally and abnormally high for a man. "She's killed that giant ape!"

"He warned us that she'd be hard to take down," said a deeper, raspy voice.

The nasally man and two more dark figures lunged at her, which was quickly followed by the sound of bone cracking, popping cartilage, blood-curdling screams and feet kicking the ground in pain. Riley heard scuffling on the path as the nasally man crawled out of reach after being kicked in the jaw.

Owen could not believe the madness surrounding him. He fought blindly at his attackers, trying desperately to get to Riley, but as soon as he threw someone off, another person would appear. He had no idea how many people were attacking them and it seemed never-ending. The darkness made it impossible for him to focus on anything that moved. The attackers appeared to focus on Riley, and Owen was impressed with how well she held her own. Then he heard something that made his stomach turn.

"This'll knock her out," said a deep voice in front of him. Owen heard a click followed by the electrical zapping sounds of a taser. His eyes frantically searched the scene and he saw the dark outline of a thin body hit the ground. He broke free of the arms grabbing at him, lunged toward Riley and fell to the ground as something blunt hit him hard in the ribs. Owen's eyes focused just enough to see the darkened figure of one of the largest men he had ever seen in his life, snatch Riley up like a ragdoll. He stood her in front of him and pinned her arms behind her back. Riley seemed unnaturally still and Owen hoped to hell she was only unconscious. Desperate to get them out of this mess, his mind raced for an idea as a pair of hands dragged him to his feet.

"Stand still," ordered an even deeper, male voice from behind him. Owen pretended to acquiesce, then broke free and lunged at the man holding Riley, unsure of his strategy as the man stood a full head taller than himself and probably the same amount wider.

"I wouldn't do that if I were you," said the nasally sounding man. His voice was different now, like he spoke through a clenched, perhaps broken jaw.

Owen heard the metallic clicking of a gun cocking and he froze midstride.

"Give me everything you've got!"

Owen had a different plan. He looked both ways down the footpath to see how many other people were around. He saw no one and realized this was what had made them such appealing targets.

"Don't got all day, Buddy. Give me everything, or I might mess up your girlfriend's pretty face." Owen saw a glint of light reflect off the gun's barrel as he pointed it away from Owen and at Riley's head.

Owen pretended to reach for his wallet in his pocket but instead grabbed his VersaTool. Still on the MOVE setting from the last time he used it, a red light shot out and Owen aimed it at the centre of the little man's chest.

"What the hell?" Distracted, the man wildly aimed his gun back at Owen, not taking his eyes off the red light on his chest.

Owen pressed the button and the man's entire body glowed red. His high-pitched shrieks pierced the night as Owen raised him off the ground and manoeuvred the frantic, flailing man over the centre of the river. He gave his wrist a flick as he released the button. The red beam disappeared and the man flew up into the air before falling into the river, the gun splashing far out of his reach. He resurfaced moments later and Owen heard him swearing as the cold, swift current carried him down the river.

The iron grip holding Riley loosened as the giant thug became distracted by what he had just witnessed, and Riley tried to wriggle free. Refocused by his escaping quarry, the man grabbed her even harder and jerked her backward, away from the water's edge not wanting to be next. Owen lunged at Riley's captor and landed his fist square on his jaw. The man's grip loosened and Riley broke free. She turned, kicked him in the groin and kneed him in the nose when he doubled over. His body hit the ground with a dull thud. Riley listened for more footsteps and heard three sets running away from the scene. Like it had been timed, the path lighting flickered back to life and Owen surveyed the scene. At least eleven bodies lay at their feet. Some were beginning to stir. Owen grabbed Riley's hand and pulled her off the path and ran through a row of trees and bushes and onto the nearest road.

CHAPTER 27

TEAM 2
YEAR: 2016
TIME REMAINING: 149 Days

Riley easily kept pace with Owen as he raced to put as much distance between themselves and the scene of the attack. He finally stopped when they reached the safety of a large group of people outside a busy pizza joint. Hungry customers spilled outside the restaurant and overflowed onto the sidewalk. The people in line watched Riley and Owen with curiosity, but Owen paid them no attention. He felt nauseous, though he was unsure if the sensation stemmed from what he had just experienced or the malodorous fumes from a nearby sewer grate mixing with the aromatic scent of hot cheese and freshly baked bread.

"Are you alright?" Owen forced out the words as his chest heaved and burned. He had watched her get strangled twice, tased, have her arms wrenched and pinned behind her by a giant of a man, plus whatever else he missed while he fought his own battles. He wanted to hug her but instead, he pulled her out from under the restaurant's awning and into the street light to look her over.

"Owen, I'm fine." She felt the skin where she had been tased and found raised bumps where the electronic immobilizer's probes had pierced her skin.

"Jesus," breathed Owen, looking at the reddened and swelling puncture marks.

Riley saw two matching holes in her shirt and the ragged threads had begun to fray. "Shit. I really liked this shirt."

Even in the dim light Owen could see the muscle definition of her side and lower back as she lifted her shirt. He knelt down to get a better look at the marks. The handlebar of a bike zipping down the sidewalk nearly clipped the back of his head as it sped by, but Owen was too focused to notice.

"Riley, I'm so sorry. We should never have walked through that dark patch. That was a really bad call on my part. You could have been killed."

Riley let out a quick laugh and shook her head as she pulled her shirt back down. "It's fine." Seeing his concern, she took his hand and looked up at him meaningfully. "Really. It was nothing."

He led her farther down the sidewalk, putting distance between the busy restaurant and its interested onlookers. "How can you say that was nothing? You were tased for Christ's sake!"

"We're trained for this kind of stuff. It was really you that saved the day. You're a quick draw with that thing. Excellent aim."

Owen felt placated in some way, but he could not put his finger on exactly why. Perhaps because he felt overcome by guilt for how she could have been seriously injured or worse.

"We need to call the cops," said Owen. He pulled his cell phone from his back pocket.

Riley took the phone from him and shook her head. "No. No police."

"How can you say that? You were just swarmed by eleven men!"

"Nah, it was only nine. The other two went after you. Besides, how are you going to explain that cute little manoeuvre where you tossed that guy in the river? Also, I don't need anyone poking into my identity any more than they already have."

Owen locked eyes with Riley for several long moments, frowned, then said nothing. He knew she was right. "Fine." He sighed heavily and looked her over again to make sure she was okay. He felt a desperate need to do something positive or productive to make up for the fact he had led them into an ambush. He saw blood on the collar of her shirt. He pulled the fabric back to find a large gash running from the base of her neck, across her collarbone and onto her shoulder.

"Shit, Riley, you're bleeding!"

Riley reached up to feel the severity of the cut on her collarbone and searing pain ripped from her shoulder, down her upper arm to her elbow. The length of the laceration made up for its shallowness, but the gash bothered her far less than the pain in her shoulder. The pain felt very similar to the time she tore her rotator cuff in a field training exercise several years back. Superficial skin wounds took much less time to heal than soft tissue damage, and she worried that with no MediScanner, she had no choice but to let it heal naturally.

Owen checked his pockets for a tissue and found a napkin with *The Beach* printed on it. He began blotting up the blood.

"Owen, don't worry about it. It's nothing," she said. She took the napkin from him and folded it in half, blood side in.

Owen snatched the serviette from her hand. "Damn it, Riley, you don't have to be so damn tough all the time. Let me take care of you for one freaking minute." He continued to blot up the blood. "How're your shoulders?"

"Pretty sore actually." She rolled both her shoulders and flinched at the pain stabbing her right shoulder. As she massaged her shoulder with her left hand, she mulled over Owen's response, shocked by his outburst. It was the first time she had ever seen him short-tempered.

"Let's go back to the hotel so we can ice your shoulder and figure out what we want to do with that gash."

"You know, you're one to talk. You should see this cut on your cheek," said Riley. She reached up and felt the skin around it to get a sense of how deep it was.

"We make a pretty good team," he said. He flinched as she gently touched his swelling cheek. "I get hit in the face while you drop twelve guys."

"It was standard combat stuff. No biggie. And there were eleven, but you got two of them."

The street lights accentuated her cheekbones and her pupils were dilated wide from the night's darkness. She was so beautiful and so capable. Alarmingly resilient. Owen wondered what happened in her past that made being swarmed and attacked at gunpoint seem as mundane as morning traffic. He eyed her suspiciously. "What exactly is it that you do, Riley?"

Several times now, Owen had asked Riley and Finn about their jobs in 2097, but his questions were always deflected. He knew they worked together "in the field," but other than that, straight answers were few and far between.

Back at the hotel, Owen marched Riley straight into his bathroom. Despite her protests, he insisted she sit atop the vanity beside the sink so he could get a closer look at the gash. Owen wet a facecloth and blotted at the cut.

"I'm pretty sure that needs stitches."

Riley grabbed the round mirror attached to the wall by a scissor bracket and positioned it to see better. The cut spanned the width of the mirror—it was longer than she had thought. "Hmm, you're probably right. But I've got something better than stitches." She pushed the mirror back against the wall and slid off the counter.

Riley went through the door that adjoined their rooms and with her good arm, awkwardly changed into her favourite surfer shorts and a fitted, white racer-back tank top. She reached up to pull one of her bags off the top shelf in the closet and her shoulder roared in pain. She inhaled sharply as the bag fell to the ground and she swore under her breath. Cursing the destroyed MediScanner, she dug around inside the bag and retrieved a small white bottle with an eye-dropper lid. She left the bag on the ground and returned to Owen's room.

"Well, I guess it's back to old-fashioned medicine." She tossed him the bottle.

Owen caught the bottle, but his eyes remained fixed on Riley as she leaned over the dresser to examine the massive cut in the mirror. He had never met a woman built quite like her; her muscles were toned and well-defined without being excessive. She had more muscle definition in her broad, tanned shoulders than most men at the gym did. Becoming aware he had been staring, he looked down at the bottle she had tossed him. *LiquiStitch. Now with faster healing properties! Heal most cuts in 24 hours or less with NO SCARS!*

"I think you're going to have to lie down," he said, motioning to the bed, "so I can fix you up."

Riley snickered. "Wow. You're a real ladies' man. Does that work on all the women in 2016?"

Riley lay on the nearest bed and stared at the ceiling feeling ridiculous. She had been taking care of herself for years, and this incident was nothing she could not overcome on her own. However, she knew her independence could be ego-crushing to some men, and while Owen had never come across as a man whose ego needed stroking, it seemed to be important to him that he help her.

Owen kneeled beside the bed to dab at the wound again with the facecloth and caught a hint of her floral perfume. He liked the irony of how the delicate scent contrasted her personality—the flowery, frilly fragrance contradicted her tough exterior. She was uniquely beautiful and unlike any woman he had ever met. Her intelligence and depth were only two of the many layers that intrigued him and he wanted to get to know them all. But he knew in a few months when his contribution to the project was complete, she would be gone. He pushed the thought from his mind. She had never shown any sign of interest in him beyond work and friendship. In addition, Riley possessed a hard-core, professional dedication, and becoming involved with a co-worker was probably just as bad an idea in 2097 as it was in 2016.

Owen read the instructions printed on the LiquiStitch bottle. According to the label, her cut exceeded the recommended size appropriate for LiquiStitch and fell into the "See your physician" category. Knowing Riley's fervent no hospital policy, any LiquiStitch-alternative short of her own needle and thread would not be entertained. He unscrewed the eyedropper lid and squeezed the tip to load the glass tube. Starting at the edge of the cut on her neck, he squeezed little drops of the thick, clear goo onto the cut. Like a magic zipper, the skin cinched back together leaving a swollen, raw line in its wake.

"Are you sure you don't want to call the police about this? I mean, that group of thugs could target other people. We really need to report it."

Riley looked thoughtful for a moment. "That's true. We don't need anyone else getting attacked, or worse. We could leave an anonymous tip. At least that way they know to watch the area."

"That's a fair compromise," said Owen, as he continued squeezing little droplets on what remained of the cut. "So, I thought you got feelings when bad things were going to happen?"

"I don't get feelings every time. Especially if my mind is focused on something else." She could feel his warm breath on her neck and the sensation sent a shiver down her spine. Owen's protectiveness and the care he took in patching her wounds made her feel special and cared for in a way she had not felt in recent memory. At the realization she was not unique, and that he would do the same for anyone, her heart fell slightly, which took her by surprise.

Owen leaned back to admire his handiwork. "I think you're almost good as new." He screwed the top back on the bottle and flipped it on its side to read the instructions again. Riley tried to sit up. Owen smiled, placed his hand on her shoulder to stop her from sitting up. "Don't even think about it. You have to lie still for ten minutes to maximize the healing quality." He set the bottle on the nightstand and grabbed the key card for the door. "I noticed a payphone down the block. I'm going call in our anonymous tip and I don't want it to be traced back to the hotel."

She regretted being so stubborn when he was taking such good care of her so she lay back and stared resignedly at the ceiling. After what seemed like only minutes, she heard him fumbling at the door with his keycard. Owen came in carrying two insulated paper cups and an ice bucket under one arm.

"How's my patient?" he asked.

"Impatient." Riley smiled, sat up and leaned against the headboard and took the cup he held out to her. She watched as steam issued through the hole in the lid and smelled the chocolaty aroma. "Hot chocolate?"

Owen nodded. "I thought you might need it to balance this out." He held up the ice-filled bucket and gave it a little shake. He poured some of the ice into a hand towel and folded it up. "Alright. Slide over." Riley slid over to the centre of the bed and he sat down beside her. He wrapped his arm around her and held the makeshift ice pack on her injured shoulder. She sat stiffly.

"I'm not incompetent, you know," said Riley. "I could have done all this."

Owen smiled and said nothing. Instead, he grabbed the remote off the nightstand and turned on the TV. He flipped through the channels and saw *Star Wars: A New Hope* had just started.

"Perfect! Tell me you've heard of *Star Wars*?" Owen watched her shake her head. "That is a tragedy. This is cinematic gold." Riley laughed, and Owen felt her rigid posture beside him soften.

As they watched the movie, Owen took great care in explaining the film to make sure none of the subtle details were lost on her. However, long before Darth Vader tried to finish off Luke as they flew around the Death Star, she had fallen asleep, curled up in his arm with her head on his shoulder.

TIME REMAINING: 148 Days

Riley awoke the next morning to find herself still in last night's clothing. She could feel Owen breathing gently on the back of her neck and found his arm wrapped around her waist. She glanced at her watch and saw her alarm would soon go off. Not wanting to disturb him, she gently moved his arm and sat up on the edge of the bed. Reaching up to reset her ponytail, she winced at the pain and stiffness in her shoulders.

She stood and looked back at Owen, fully-clothed and peaceful. He looked the opposite of how she felt—naked and conflicted. Somewhere along the way, his genuineness, warmth and caring had broken through her barriers. Riley, used to feeling nothing but the need to work longer and harder, found that Owen had an effect on her that no man had ever had. She could not put her finger on it exactly other than to say that he made her feel softer, warmer. Her job made her confident and fearless, but ironically, her feelings for Owen made her feel out of control and conflicted. She had successfully avoided romantic feelings for years. Now that a few had returned, so did the memories of why she shut them away. Her past relationships left scars, carved deep by hurt and betrayal. Only after learning to rely solely on herself had she become truly happy. But something about Owen was different. She felt like she could be herself around him, that she could trust him. Her job had conditioned her radar to be on alert twenty-four/seven and for the first time in years, she felt comfortable enough to let her guard down and let Owen take care of her.

Riley returned to her room after hitting the hotel's gym. Her legs felt thick from the half marathon she ran on the treadmill in an attempt to sweat out her feelings for Owen. No sooner had the door to her room closed behind her when she heard a knock on the door that joined her room to Finn's.

"Uh, Rile?"

Riley heard the muffled voice through the door and opened it to see Finn's door still closed. "Finn?"

"Yeah, I'm not feeling so hot this morning. I don't think I'm going to be able to leave this hotel room for a while. I'll catch up with you later. Is that okay?"

Riley chuckled. "Serves you right for pigging out last night."

"You can get all your I-told-you-so's in later. I gotta go," said Finn, with urgency in his voice.

Riley heard a door open and close in Finn's room and decided that now was a good time to turn on the TV, radio or anything that would make a lot of noise.

With a fresh pot of coffee brewing, Riley and Owen picked up where they left off the previous day, which seemed like a week ago after the harrowing events of the night before.

Even with three ray guns, the zeno rays could not neutralize the Elevanium fast enough. Riley wondered if the low height of the excavated ceiling would reflect some of the rays back onto the Elevanium, but not having the ability to test this and prove it with certainty left her feeling uneasy. There was no room for finger-crossing in this operation; it had to be right the first time or the whole operation would fail.

Owen suspected he could roughly ballpark the amount of ray energy being reflected, but would need to determine the rough composition of the rock surrounding the Elevanium deposit. It was an avenue worth exploring, but it was not something he felt confident enough to stake the future of the planet on.

Riley and Owen pored through hundreds of electronic documents and videos that Riley had brought with her on her CI. Three hours passed like molasses in the winter as they reviewed news clippings, internal reports and industry magazines on mining in that area. The information they sought was fifty years old by Riley's standards, and most of the documentation was long gone. Later in the afternoon, Owen popped a bag of microwave popcorn and they watched countless news stories and documentaries on the Elevanium discovery and other related news reports.

At the end of the day, they had learned only that the shape of the Elevanium deposit resembled a rugby ball. One industry magazine mentioned offhandedly that the nickel ore in the area had proven to be abnormally abundant, though no reports specified the average composition. The answers they found only led to more questions.

During dinner, Finn still looked green around the gills. Riley and Owen could tell he was still hurting when he ordered only a bowl of chicken noodle soup. He took several sips and pushed the bowl away, unable to even look at it. Only after Finn questioned the cut on Owen's cheek, Riley and Owen remembered to recount the events of the night before. Finn's eyes widened in disbelief.

"Truthfully, it was freaking scary at the time but looking back, you didn't miss much," said Owen. "Riley dropped about four guys in a matter of seconds. That has to be a record of some kind."

"You should have seen the look on that little guy's face when he started glowing and flew into the air. He screamed like a little girl when Owen dumped him in the river. Great aim, by the way, Owe."

Owen appreciated her attempt at playing up his role. "It was all Riley. If it had just been me, I'd've been cut up into little pieces and thrown into the river." He laughed at his words but his stomach flip-flopped knowing it was true.

Riley looked thoughtful for a moment. "You know, there was something weird about that attack, though. I'd forgotten until just now. Owen, do you remember one of the guys saying, 'He said she'd be hard to take down.' Who's this 'he?'"

Owen shook his head. "I heard a lot of things. The most noticeable being the sound of my heart pounding in my ears, but I don't remember hearing anything like that. Are you sure you heard him correctly? The whole thing was utter madness."

Finn leaned in, his expression grave. "Are you serious? Rile, are guys stalking you at the gym or something?" Finn knew Riley spent just about as much time in the gym as he did sleeping; she was in phenomenal shape and he knew how hard she worked for it. Between a body like hers and the long hours she spent working out, she would definitely stand out from the average gym rats.

"I thought about that, and no. There's only a few regulars at the office gym, and, well, no one's ever in the hotel gym."

All three fell silent in thought. Owen wondered if they were contemplating the supposed Elevanium curse. After all, in less than two months, he had nearly been hit by a bus, his house had been intentionally blown up and now he could add getting jumped to that list. It was enough to make him wonder if he should be putting some thought into the curse.

CHAPTER 28

Jake's chat with Clint seemed to do the trick. A week had passed since their little conversation in the tool shed, and since that time, Clint had neither said or done anything offensive to any of the other team members. He had, in fact, begun participating more with the team, initiating game nights and helping with chores unrelated to his job duties. Jake was pleased with Clint's reversal.

It seemed as though even the Moles had sensed the harmonious vibes in the camp, as they made it through the week with no major issues. Problem-free Moles meant for long days for the operators, where all they could do was sit back and monitor status reports. To counteract the boredom, Jake and Lexi had taken to reading the horribly outdated magazines that had collected in the trailer over the years. Jake had found a fascinating article about Rocket Bronco Riding—a sport briefly popular in the forties. A parachute-wearing rider saddled a small rocket as it flew through the air in a random, erratic fashion. Like classic bronco riding, points were awarded for style and feats accomplished while on the rocket. When the rider had enough, he or she would eject and float down to the ground harmlessly with a parachute, or that was the plan. The sport's popularity, although fanatic in the Midwest, never caught on nationwide. The rockets proved too unpredictable, and a number of steely-nerved, wanna-be sky cowboys determined to prove their grit were hammered into the ground by improperly calibrated rockets.

Although life in the camp was rosy, the weather had been anything but. Thick layers of cloud blocked out so much sun that the camp possessed an early evening feel in midafternoon. Jake watched the trees bend unnaturally from what he guessed must be near-hurricane winds. Even from inside Mole Control, he could see streams of water pouring down the side of the invisible WeatherShield.

Jake's attention turned to the monitors as a beeping sound announced a critical problem with the active Mole. Lexi scrolled through several reports to see what triggered the alert when they heard Clint's voice over the intercom.

"We've got a problem, kids," said Clint, who preferred to spend his days inside the Mole's small control room.

"What's going on down there?" asked Jake.

"Well, a couple of things. The drill head got hung up, but the shaft kept spinning. Something's stripped and I think we blew a hydraulic line." In the tunnel, Clint stepped off the back of the Mole, got down on his hands and knees and looked underneath the massive machine. He saw liquid dripping onto the roughly cut stone floor. "Yeah, something's definitely leaking. It's around where the auxiliary oil supply line is."

"Well, we had a good run." Jake rubbed his hands together as he stood, happy to have something to do. "Pull'er out and we'll throw Mole2 back in tomorrow. Good work guys."

Jake decided to call it a day early. Wanting to take advantage of their good luck while it lasted, Jake had been pushing the group for longer days. With that spell now broken, the team could take a much-needed break. Regardless of the future or the past, people still needed to unwind, and the project was ahead of schedule.

After dinner, the group parted ways to get out of their work clothes before collecting in the rec room to participate in a virtual bowling tournament Clint had organized. Jake, who had showered and changed earlier, began to rearrange the furniture in the rec room. No sooner had Jake begun to move the first couch, a deafening, tent-shaking crash behind him sent his heart into overdrive. A blast of cold air and fresh pine scent slammed into his back and he spun on the spot. The thick canvas roof had been pulled down in the medical room. Through large tears in the roof, Jake saw a massive, fallen evergreen tree. Leaves and rain blew in through the openings.

Ben, Darren and Lexi had appeared first, Lexi pulling her wet hair into a ponytail. She saw Jake rooted to the spot in shock, holding a throw pillow. "Jake, are you alright?"

Jake looked down at the throw pillow and, feeling silly, threw it onto the nearest couch. "Yeah, I'm okay."

Jake stepped through one of the jagged rips in the canvas ceiling and walked across what used to be the roof and walls of the medical room, surveying the damage from the outside.

"I'll check on the WeatherShield sensors," shouted Ben over the wind. "The system would only go down if one of them's been damaged. I suspect one's been crush by Ol' Woody here." He gestured to the fallen tree.

Jake nodded. He pulled his VersaTool from his back pocket, picked up the tree with the red beam and, with the effort of brushing away a mosquito, he flicked it far over the bushes behind the camp. The jet of water spraying from the sink's broken tap seemed inconsequential with rain pouring through the torn ceiling. As Lexi closed the sink's supply valve, the water issuing from the taps ceased.

The tent and the contents of the medical room sustained significant damage. The tree's large branches had shredded the canvas roof and crumpled the plastic-aluminum walls like paper. Small branches, leaves and millions of pine needles lay littered on the floor among the damaged supplies and puddles of the rain that continued to pour in. Clint and Tyler searched the tool shed to find extra wall panels and canvas patches for the roof. Lexi, Maya and Darren salvaged medical supplies and set them out on tables in the dining room to dry.

Clint and Tyler replaced the damaged interlocking panels easily, but the roof sagged uncooperatively as the two men hurried to patch it. Eventually, the wind and rain stopped, indicating that Ben had been successful in getting the WeatherShield operational again, and the group cheered.

The MediScan RX-4000 received the hardest hit. The arm of the massive medical appliance was bent forward with another ninety-degree turn to the right at the arm's midway point. The cover that hid the recessed surgical tools was missing and many of the shiny tools were scattered on the floor. Some hung down over the edge of the broken table like torture devices in a horror film. The glass surrounding the fixture was mostly smashed and several pieces hung from the strip lighting. Much of the oversized examination table was missing and what remained of the glass surface had remained intact, but now had the unmistakable fractured pattern of broken safety glass. The steel base was crumpled at one corner like a shoe box that had been stepped on. Other items around the room shared a similar fate; the sink lay on the floor broken into several pieces.

Maya briefed Jake on the loss of medical supplies and the report surprised him; he had expected a complete loss of the room. Many items had survived and for this Jake was grateful, as the MediScan RX-4000 looked like a write-off.

Ben walked into the main tent carrying one of the WeatherShield sensors. "So the sensor at the northeast corner of the camp stopped working. I'm not sure why, but I replaced it with a spare from the tool shed and the system is back up and operational," said Ben.

Jake returned to the medical room and found Lexi trying to piece together the MediScan device. Tyler stood atop a floating scaffolding platform hovering level with Jake's chest. Through one of the tears in the ceiling, Jake saw Clint lying across a similar scaffolding platform above the roof. He held the torn canvas pieces in place as Tyler glued the replacement strips over the tears in the shredded ceiling.

Clint stuck his head through one of the unrepaired tears in the ceiling. "So much for our bowling tournament."

Jake chuckled weakly. "I think this will suffice for tonight's team-building exercise."

Ben and Jake worked intermittently on the MediScan RX-4000 as time allowed during the week. Neither man had ever worked on anything so specialized, but Jake wanted it up and running if it was in their power to do so. They had one handheld MediScan device, but it only worked for simple injuries.

Before dinner on Friday, as the group gathered in Darren's kitchen like starving hyenas, Jake appeared from the medical room, wiping his hands on a rag. He waved at Ben—standing in line, plate in hand—motioning for him to come over.

"I think I've done all that we can do for this thing. I was just about to turn it on. Thought you might like to watch." Jake tossed the rag on the one remaining stool, now with a pronounced lean.

"How did you get the beam stabilizer fixed?" asked Ben.

"Generous amounts of Super Weld adhesive and some fibreglass strips I found in the tool shed."

Ben's widening eyes said what he dared not verbally.

Jake chuckled. "I know, I know, it's questionable. I thought the same thing, but we gotta try, right?"

Many of the cracks in the glass of the examination table resembled a Mexican road map and oozed Super Weld adhesive. Like pieces missing in a completed puzzle, oddly shaped holes peppered the table, where pieces of glass were either missing or beyond repair.

"Here goes nothing." Jake turned on the device. It hummed to life, though louder than normal. The base vibrated. The projected control screen flickered as the massive medical instrument fired through its boot sequence. Jake looked back at Ben, who stood back at the door not wanting to venture any closer. After a few moments, the menu appeared, indicating it was ready for use.

"Well I'll be damned," breathed Ben.

Jake chuckled. "Hold on there, Cowboy, we should run a test scan."

"Good point."

Jake tapped the screen several times to initiate a scan of the empty bed. The device became louder and a clacking, ratcheting sound issued from the steel base as the scanning arm inside ran the length of the machine. Ben opened his mouth to congratulate Jake on the fix when a huge spark lit up the exam area. The cover of the housing above the exam table which hid the surgical tools fell flat on the bed and all of the sharp, shiny tools slammed downwards and stopped dead, exactly where the abdomen of a patient would be. The machine's humming noise wound down and stopped. A piece of glass surrounding the tool housing broke away, pulling with it part of the strip lighting and the glass swung back and forth from the thin strip.

Ben stared wide-eyed at the machine. "I guess it's lights out for that, eh?"

CHAPTER 29

TEAM 3
YEAR: 2095
TIME REMAINING: 144 Days

Logan returned to the Motor Skills lab after scavenging around the cafeteria for any scrap of food—an apple, a two-day-old sandwich—anything to silence the growling, ravenous dogs that had taken up residence in his stomach. To his surprise, he found Delaney in the lab, standing in front of one of the CI screens.

"Working late again?" Delaney asked.

Logan returned to his desk as his stomach barked out in protest. "Well, as it turns out I have two workaholic brothers, and I've got some stuff I could catch up on."

Delaney looked at him, one eyebrow raised. "Wow! Is Party-time Logan Grayson shifting his priorities?" She looked back appraisingly at the oversized screen and drummed her fingers on her crossed arms.

Logan focused on the robot head lying on his desk, trying to remember where he had left off. The access panel had been removed and the contents of the metallic skull lay beside it, lined up in neat, precise rows. Surrounding this organized arrangement of very expensive robot parts were disorganized piles of tools and spare parts. In the air above his desk hung a three-dimensional, exploded schematic view of the robot's head. Using his hand, he reached out to the schematic like it was something tangible and rotated his hand ninety degrees counter-clockwise. The technical illustration pivoted in the air and the orientation of the skull now matched that of the parts lying on his desk. He held both his hands in front of him like he was holding an imaginary basketball then pulled them further apart. The schematic grew larger in front of him. Reaching out again, he grasped at the illustration of the robot's head and turned it to see the underside of the skull, then lost his train of thought. Through the semi-transparent illustration of the schematics, Logan watched Delaney standing at the screen across the lab and thought about how she seemed to have loosened up a bit over the last several months. He thought it suited her. Delaney had noticed how, over the last several months, Logan had begun taking things more seriously. She was shocked.

"Are you going to be here for a bit?" Delaney asked.

"Yeah, a couple of hours at least."

She pointed to the screen. "Do you want to get in on this?"

Logan looked from her to the screen, so large that even from across the room, he could see she was ordering Chinese food. Logan's mouth watered seeing the pictures of egg rolls, lemon chicken and fried rice.

"Definitely." He joined her in front of the screen. Images of food changed as Delaney scrolled through the menu, the lemon chicken was replaced by an equally delicious picture of beef and broccoli.

Standing beside Delaney, Logan could not help but notice how good she smelled. Unsure if it was perfume, shampoo or one of the million other fragrant things that women seemed to wear, he found the fresh scent intoxicating.

"Earth to Logan," said Delaney. She waved her hand in front of his face and he came back from wherever his mind had just gone. She chuckled at him. "I said, what did you want to order?"

Logan returned to his work station and Delaney busied herself in her office while they waited for their food to arrive. It seemed like no time had passed before the delivery robot floated into the lab.

Delaney emerged from her office with her credit keys in hand. An arrow and the words, "Pay Here" flashed and blinked like a gaudy, illuminated sign from an all-night roadside diner. The arrow pointed to an assortment of different shaped holes and she inserted her V-shaped key into the corresponding slot to pay by Visa. As she withdrew her key, the door on the front of the robot opened and wisps of steam escaped. A tray slid forward, presenting her order. She removed it, closed the compartment door and pressed the "Finished" button. A tinny, robotic voice said, "Thank you for ordering from China Moon," with a Chinese-English accent, and it zipped out the lab door toward the delivery bot entrance.

The conversation over dinner surprised both Logan and Delaney. There was an ease between them that neither one had anticipated and they continued talking long after they had finished eating. They discussed the progress of the project and the performance of their division against some of the others in the project. They talked about their educations and the schools they attended, and everything else from their childhoods to their favourite meals. Delaney realized that she had told Logan more about herself in the last two and a half hours than she had ever told anyone in her life.

Logan was surprised to learn how different their lives had been. He had siblings and she was an only child. He had been wildly popular and she was the nerdy science girl who got heckled daily. Popularity had made his life easier and things had come so effortlessly to him, whereas Delaney struggled for everything. Logan had never taken anything too seriously and life had rewarded him with reasonable success, so he never saw any reason to work harder, whereas Delaney worked her ass off for every success she achieved. Logan felt like he understood her better. Who she was made so much more sense to him. He found that once she got out of work mode, she was far more laid back than he had given her credit for. In fact, he found her to be surprisingly funny with razor-sharp wit. When Logan admitted these thoughts to her, she said her meddling university friend was the one to thank and that she was enjoying the healthier work-life balance.

"We've been trying to get that through Spencer's head for years," laughed Logan.

"He'd better watch it. One day he'll wake up and he'll be in his very late thirties with a great career but not a lot of anything else."

Logan was impressed by everything he had learned about Delaney, however, it left her feeling exposed—like she had talked too much. She smiled awkwardly and stood to gather the empty cardboard food containers. Sensing her discomfort, Logan changed the conversation by opening his fortune cookie. He read it aloud. "He who can laugh at himself will never run out of things to laugh at."

"I think they specifically had you and your brother in mind when they wrote that one." She walked across the room and deposited the garbage in the recycle bot. When the lid closed, she heard the hydraulic stamper compress the cardboard. She returned to where they sat, picked up her fortune cookie and cracked it in half. "I always get the most ridiculous fortunes. They never make any sense."

"Let's see," said Logan. He stood beside her to read it over her shoulder. She pulled the strip of paper from the cookie. It was blank. She turned it over and it, too, was blank.

"Uh-oh. That can't be good. What does it mean when you have no fortune?" Delaney laughed, her track record of bizarre fortunes remained unblemished.

"I think," Logan said, taking the piece of paper out of her hand and grabbing a pen off the desk, "it means that you get to make your own fortune." He leaned over the table as he wrote on the tiny piece of paper then handed it to her.

She took it from him and read it aloud. "In your future, you will take a chance on something."

Delaney looked at the paper quizzically as Logan leaned in and kissed her. Her surprise evaporated quickly and it was replaced by pleasant curiosity. Logan wrapped his arm around her, pulled her closer to him and gently caressed her cheek. After a few moments, they broke apart. Their eyes met and they shared a meaningful look, then Delaney's eyes darted away nervously. An awkward pause followed. Logan worried that, what had seemed like a brilliant, spontaneous idea just a moment ago, may have crossed a line. Delaney knew she had crossed a line, but what troubled her more, was that she had enjoyed it. Immensely.

Words tumbled from Logan's mouth, desperate to fill the silence. "Wow, look at the time, I mean, really, look at it. We've been talking for hours. I guess you probably want to get going?"

Delaney looked at her watch. "Yes, I suppose I should." She hesitated, feeling as though she should say something further to clarify her feelings, but could not find the words. Instead, she went to her office and grabbed her bag and jacket. She hesitated at the lab door, looked back at Logan and smiled. "It was nice chatting with you Logan. Thank you."

"Anytime!" As he said it, he knew it came out with far too much exuberance. He flashed her a smile and hoped it did not look as awkward as it felt.

Logan forced himself to shift his focus back to work. He picked up his tri-hex tool and tried to fit the re-designed CTU into the skull, but his mind skipped like a record to Delaney and the kiss. After fifteen minutes of futility, he put the tools down, collected his things and left.

As Logan rounded the corner of the dimly lit parking lot, he saw someone standing by the driver side door of his truck. Thinking he was watching his truck getting broken into, he kicked himself for parking in such a poorly lit space. His truck was nothing fancy but getting broken into meant a hassle with his insurance company. He noticed the thief's slim, feminine figure and realized quickly it was Delaney. As he approached, she gave him a small smile and the look in her eyes said everything that she could not before. Logan rushed to her side, pulled her close and kissed her again.

Delaney felt Logan press her back against his truck door. Her heart raced and her mind was foggy. No one had ever had this effect on her. He made her feel alive, attractive and electric. She pulled him as close to her as she could. After a minute or so they broke away with none of the awkwardness of before.

"I was worried that you regretted kissing me," said Logan. He kissed her forehead softly.

She rested her head on his shoulder as they embraced. "I thought you did, too."

Logan shook his head. "Never. Do you want to go for a coffee?" He was unsure of where the night's activities were leading and felt this suggestion made no presumptions. He wanted to spend more time with her, not caring what they did, as long as he could be with her.

"I had something different in mind…" Delaney pulled him closer by his belt buckle. Logan smiled and kissed her again as he fumbled at the driver's door.

CHAPTER 30

TEAM 2
YEAR: 2016
TIME REMAINING: 142 Days

Later in the week, Riley found herself heading to the lab solo after another shoulder massage. A week had passed since she and Owen had been attacked and her right shoulder still ached. Owen, to his chagrin, was again meeting with his interior designer to look at the fabric swatches, wood samples and furnishings they had run out of time to cover in the first meeting. Finn had not come back to the hotel the night before and Riley was unsure of his whereabouts.

Riley's question was answered the moment she entered the lab. Evidence of Finn's presence lay strewn around the lab. Empty energy drink containers on the kitchen island, chip bags, apple cores and muffin wrappers lay on several lab stations. His sweater hung half off a lab chair and his shoes lay astray on the floor by the fridge. She stuck her head into the dorm room and found him passed out on a lower bunk. He lay awkwardly on the narrow bed, too small for his large frame; one foot rested on the floor and an arm hung limply over the edge. Riley smiled at the sight of him. Working with Finn was never boring.

Riley knew Finn's future would be bright. She was giving him a lot of leash on this project, leading him down the path they needed to go then letting him take the reins. His instincts were nearly always spot on and rarely did he make a wrong call. She planned to give him a fantastic report when they returned that would level him up to a level three; he definitely deserved it. He worked hard, but he still liked to have fun and she encouraged him. At twenty-six, he was still young and he should be out having a good time.

Riley set her bag in the kitchen, grabbed a bottle of Gatorade from the fridge and toured Finn's work to see what had kept him up all night. The testing tank had been lined with flat stones. Sitting beside the tank was an open container of Irrefragable Compound. As she studied Finn's handiwork, she heard the sound of a toilet flushing, a tap running, followed by shuffling footsteps. Moments later, a bleary-eyed, bedraggled Finn was dragging himself into the lab.

"Morning, sunshine," greeted Riley.

Finn rubbed his eyes then blinked several times to refocus. He ran his hands through his messy hair. "Hey, Rile. How's it going?"

"Me? I'm good. How about you? Late night?"

Finn yawned as he nodded and meandered into the kitchen. He grabbed a bottle of orange juice out of the fridge, drank half and set it aside as he set up the coffee maker. "I went on a bit of a hike last night and found some rocks. I hope Owen approves."

"Did you run any tests yet?"

Finn shook his head and chugged back the last of the orange juice. "What time is it?" He wiped the side of his mouth with his forearm then looked at his watch to answer his own question. "Oh, shit! I'm sorry, Rile."

Riley sat down at the island. "No worries. It looks like you were burning the midnight oil here so I figured you deserved to sleep. Plus, I just got here myself." She pointed to her shoulder and rolling it, noticing how much better it felt. "Massage."

Finn nodded appreciatively. He sat down at the island and grabbed an apple out of the bowl. "Where's Owen?"

"With the interior designer."

"Oh yeah, I forgot about that," He polished the apple on his shirt. "So have you told him yet that we need him to come back with us?" Finn asked.

A guilty smile crept onto Riley's face. "No, not yet. I'm not sure how he's going to react." She was mad at herself not being more upfront with him about the matter.

"If you want my opinion, I think it was smart not to mention it right away. It may have spooked him. It's probably good to let him get used to the idea before bringing it up." Finn bit into his apple and smiled. "He'll do it."

"What makes you so sure? He said straight up in the beginning that he was very happy that his job kept his feet firmly planted in 2016."

"Yeah, but that was in the beginning. Plus, who wouldn't want to travel through time? Let's be serious."

"We can't force him if he doesn't want to," Riley reminded him.

Finn smiled at her knowingly. "He'll come. I see the way he looks at you."

Riley said nothing as she grabbed a pear from the basket of fruit.

"Is that the great Riley Morgan, blushing?"

The sound of the door opening made Riley and Finn look over as Owen came in juggling six furniture catalogues.

"Speak of the devil," said Finn, making a face at Riley similar to that of an obnoxious little brother. Riley returned it with a warning glare. Finn chuckled to himself, grabbed a banana from the basket and headed back toward the dorm room for a shower.

"How did your meeting go with the designer?"

Owen fanned the catalogues out in front of her. "How are you at furniture shopping?"

"I've created a scaled-down model of what I believe we can expect to see when the Elevanium deposit has been fully exposed," said Finn. He placed the brick of

Elevanium into the testing tank, now lined with stones to replicate a cave-like environment. He arranged the miniaturized guns around the Elevanium and set a larger, flat stone across the top of uneven, rocky sides that functioned as the walls of the cave.

"What do you think?" he asked, looking at Riley for feedback.

"What do you think?" she asked back.

Finn looked thoughtfully at his set up. "Well, I think it's good. I mean, it's got gaps between the rocks, so I guess some rays will get through, but I'm guessing that loss will be minor. I expect that we'll still see a considerable decrease in the amount of time it takes to neutralize that brick."

"Did you remember to coat them with that fragment compound or whatever you called it?" asked Owen.

Finn nodded. "Irrefragable Compound."

"It's amazing that a thin layer of a liquid will stop these rocks from being blasted apart," said Owen leaning in to get a closer look.

"This is nothing. It gets used lots for aid missions. So many third-world countries have these old death trap buildings that collapse on people during earthquakes. We'll spray a building with this stuff and once it seeps into the structure, even the most dilapidated building will withstand any kind of earthquake or impact." Finn tossed Riley the remote control. She tossed it back.

"This is your experiment, everything looks good to me. You do the honours."

Owen grabbed the Multi-Material Scanner off the lab table, turned it on and aimed it at the tank. Even though the Elevanium brick was completely hidden from his view by the simulated rock cave, the white form of the brick appeared on the scanner's screen. Finn pressed the button. Although there was no visible activity, the trio stared intently into the tank nonetheless. Occasionally Finn and Riley glanced over Owen's shoulder to check the progress scanner. After four minutes, Finn's expression faltered.

"Five minutes and forty-two seconds," reported Owen.

Finn placed the remote control on the lab table and ran his hands through his hair. "Well, that's disappointing."

Riley seemed unbothered by the disappointing results. "Well, it was a small improvement. It was just a hypothesis. I guess the surroundings don't make that much difference."

"Not enough to rely on them as a booster to the rays," agreed Owen.

They ran the experiment two more times to be certain, but like their previous experiments, all three trials yielded different results, ranging from two and a quarter minutes to upward of seven minutes. Finn dismantled the miniature cave and set the guns aside on the lab table.

"Well, back to the drawing board," said Riley. "I wonder what would happen if the surrounding stone was coated in something more reflective, like a foil of some kind?"

Finn glanced at his watch, which did not go unnoticed by Riley. "You got somewhere better to be?"

"I do actually." Finn smiled. "I've got a date."

"When did you find time to pick up women?" asked Riley.

Finn looked at his boss with a single raised eyebrow. "Come on Rile, you don't work me that hard. Let's just say I'm a good multitasker."

The forensic investigation into the explosion of Owen's home had so far yielded no leads. With no fingerprints, footprints, tire treads or real evidence of any kind, the investigation was slowing to a standstill.

Owen felt mental exhaustion beginning to creep in. His mind spun continually during his waking hours. It bounced between speculation over who would want to see him dead to Elevanium and zeno ray guns to sorting out his feelings for Riley. However, what perplexed him the most was that he could not think of a single person who would want him dead. Sure, he had inadvertently ruffled the feathers of a few department heads at work—his work for the International Space Coalition required many equipment upgrades. As a result, several departments had portions of their budgets clawed back to accommodate him. He had received some icy stares in the cafeteria, but he fervently believed that no one was angry enough to blow up his home. He could only conclude it was a random attack or maybe some punk trying to cut his teeth in the explosives game.

Owen and Riley dropped Finn off at the hotel before heading to the house to look at the garage door panel samples the designer had left. Owen pulled up to the house, unprepared for the scene that greeted him. His ordinarily impeccable yard bore deep scars from heavy equipment. Deep tire marks crisscrossed his neatly manicured lawn. An industrial-sized dumpster positioned beneath the living room windows over-flowed with water-damaged and discarded materials. While the yard looked rough, the house was beginning to take shape. All of the broken glass had been replaced and the black stains on the concrete were washed away.

Riley followed Owen through the front door and up the steps leading to the living room. He was impressed with the progress and wondered if he might be able to return sooner than expected. He was anxious to come home; living out of a suitcase had become tedious and he missed his home.

The workers' tools were left in the middle of the room waiting to be used again tomorrow. Drop cloths were folded neatly by the wall of the main floor bedroom and several cans of paint stood next to them. The new panes of glass looked so clean that if they had not been tinted, Owen might not have believed they were actually there. The new kitchen looked so identical to its predecessor, he had a hard time making out the differences.

The upper floor of the house received the least amount of damage and was nearly finished. Plush carpet warmed the loft-style seating area above the kitchen. A couch and matching loveseat were arranged in a semicircle around a sixty-inch, flat-panel TV mounted on the wall.

"I think it's safe to say this house is going to end up in some kind of interior design magazine when it's done," said Riley. She sat down on one of the leather couches and caressed the sumptuous leather.

Owen chuckled. "Wouldn't be the first time. It was featured in an architectural magazine when my grandfather first built it."

Owen led Riley down the hall and told her the history of the house, how it had been built by his grandfather, who, like his father, was an architect. He explained how his retirement plans had been cut short by a car accident. He took her into the room she had stayed in and explained how this had been his childhood room. He opened the balcony door and stepped out.

"I never liked the glass floor. Took my dad forever to get me to come out here when I was little. It freaked me right out."

They left his childhood room and inspected the master bedroom. One of the maple dressers was still covered with protective cardboard and a fan blew air into the open closet, drying paint.

Owen sat on the glowing white duvet covering the bed and bounced to get a feel for the new mattress. He took in the room, and a feeling of gratitude for his talented, pain-in-the-ass interior designer overwhelmed him. She had made everything the same, yet somehow better.

Riley was happy that some normalcy would soon return to Owen's life. She leaned on the door frame and watched Owen take in each detail. He slid his hand across the dresser almost caressingly and opened, then closed the top drawer. He opened the sliding glass door and stepped out onto the patio. Owen motioned for Riley to come out and he leaned on the railing and watched the sun slide down behind the trees.

Riley leaned on the railing beside him. "What a sunset." A pool of oranges, reds and purples melted toward the horizon. "You're so lucky that you get to watch this every night."

Owen looked at Riley, mesmerized by her. Her beauty seemed amplified by the warm colours of the sunset. She smiled at the sight of several pelicans floating down the river.

Sensing his gaze, she looked up at him. "What?"

"Thank you." He gently tucked a loose tendril of hair behind her ear. "I was in such a rut after my father passed away. Looking back now, I don't think I even realized how depressed I was. You've been a breath of fresh air and you've reminded me how to live again. Thank you for giving me my life back."

He ran his index finger across the cut on her neck and collarbone. The wound had completely healed, thanks to the seemingly magical healing properties of LiquiStitch. A faint pink scar and a memory were the only evidence that remained from that evening. He traced the arch of her eyebrow gently with the tips of his fingers then caressed her cheek.

Riley felt a shiver shoot through the length of her body as Owen brushed her collarbone. As his hand moved up her neck and gently brushed her cheek, she felt her control sliding out of her grasp. She turned toward him and he ran his hands over her hair then leaned in. Fireworks went off in her brain as he kissed her. She pulled him close, her mind unable to recall any of the reasons for why having feelings for this man was a bad idea.

He caressed the back of her neck as her hair cascaded over his hands. He felt her wrapping her arms around him and running her hands gently up his back. She was so slight in comparison to him, so slender. She kissed him with the same passion and intensity she brought to everything she did—one of the many qualities he loved about her. He picked her up in his arms, carried her through the balcony door and laid her gently on the bed.

Riley had never experienced sensuality like this. Maybe it was that men from eighty-five years ago had more class, but Owen was different in a way she could not define.

Owen's reservations about getting involved with someone who would be leaving in five weeks had disappeared. He had never felt anything like what he felt for Riley; he knew that if five weeks were all they had, then he would take whatever time he could, if she would have him. He realized that worrying about getting hurt did far more damage than actually taking a chance. He needed her, and now that he had realized it, it seemed so obvious. He did not want to waste a single moment of whatever time they had.

They lay together for hours, talking about their past and getting to know each other on a level more intimate than Elevanium and zeno ray guns. Owen explained that he had done his fair share of dating over the years, but he never found anyone that he felt he could spend the rest of his life with. Since his father's heart attack, there had been no time for dating. Riley explained to Owen how during a particularly long operation, she got a special leave pass to come home for two days on Valentine's Day. She planned to surprise her husband—and surprise him she did by catching him in bed with a stripper. When she had finally cooled off long enough to talk about it, he told her he was leaving her. He packed his bag and left her that night—alone in the home she had bought them, reeling and devastated. To add insult to injury, he later sued her for the house and for the emotional trauma he claimed he sustained from her being deployed so often. Everything she had worked so hard for—her home, retirement savings—were nearly all taken away from her. Although she never talked numbers, Owen suspected her ex-husband made out like a bandit. From what he had been able to piece together, her job seemed somewhat hazardous and assumed she was compensated appropriately. The only bright side, she pointed out, was that she was young enough to recover financially. She had a new roof over her head and still planned to retire young enough to enjoy life. As for romance, she dove into her work and put men on the back burner for years, until Owen.

Owen looked at his watch. "Okay, you've got to be hungry now. It's nearly twelve." He felt absolutely famished, but he would rather die of starvation than leave his bed while Riley was in it. He slid the dark strands of hair that he loved so much from her face.

Riley pushed him onto his back and crawled on top. She clutched his hands above his head, pinning him down as she kissed his neck. "The only thing," she said between kisses, "I'm hungry for," she nibbled on his ear, "is you."

"Omigosh, Rile," Owen said out of breath, "that was…I don't even know what that was." Riley collapsed on top of Owen, her head nestled underneath his chin. He wrapped his arms around her. The sensation of the sweat between their bodies enhanced the closeness.

"Here's my theory on sex," she said matter-of-factly. "The first time you make love with someone, it's like buying a car. On your first test drive, you take it easy, you don't want to be too aggressive. No sharp corners or abrupt movements. It's like a how-do-you-do, getting acquainted kind of thing. Then, if you liked it and you want to test drive it again, you're ready to put it through its paces and see what it can do."

Owen laughed, then kissed the top of her head. "I can't wait for the next test drive."

Riley's smile faded; she knew she had to ask Owen about coming back to the year 1200 with them. To wait any longer would be like lying, and that was not how she wanted to begin whatever it was they now had between them. She sat up and pulled the top sheet around her. The contrast of the crisp, white bedding glowed against her tanned skin. "Owen, I have to ask you something."

"Sure. Anything." The gravity of her expression startled him. Was she having regrets?

"I apologize because I should have mentioned this on day one. I need you to come back with us. To meet up with Team One in the year 1200. We need your help. If something goes wrong, if the deposit is hard to… We just need you. Finn and I just don't know enough about this kind of stuff. This operation is highly unusual for us. Finn and I are more go-in-guns-a-blazing kind of people. This Elevanium stuff is more your thing." She worried he would be upset for springing this on him, for asking him to do something she already knew he wanted no part of.

Owen watched her, biting her lip and looking uncharacteristically nervous. He caressed her cheek. "You had me at 'I need you.'" He grabbed her by the hand and pulled her down on top of him. "On two conditions."

"Anything."

"One. Let's not talk about Finn when we're lying in bed together naked?"

Riley laughed, relief flooding over her like a waterfall. "Deal. And the second?"

"Can you tell me exactly what it is that you do?"

She fell silent. "You won't like it."

"Try me."

"I'm a Level Six, Black Ops Field Operation Lead." She watched his expression for a reaction and saw uncertainty. She explained further. "Black Ops is an elite, covert team that gets called into, let's say, high-risk or high-value situations to neutralize threats, recover hostages or terminate illegal activities."

"I feel as though that's the textbook explanation," said Owen, one eyebrow raised.

She nodded. "Think final stage, hostage-type situations or stings for criminal organizations."

This made sense to him and comprehension dawned on his face. He imagined her on the street wearing a Kevlar vest, leaning over the hood of a car looking at building schematics and handing out orders. That seemed alright. Risky, yes, but she seemed more than capable of handling that type of situation. "Okay, so you develop the strategies that your team executes to bust up a drug ring or negotiate for hostages?"

"Well, yes and no. We kinda bat clean-up. If we can, we try to negotiate. But generally, if Black Ops is involved, the window for negotiation has passed. I organize strategies to neutralize volatile situations after the discussions and negotiations have failed. I lead the execution of the plans. I'm at the front. And we don't deal with domestic issues. Everything I deal with is international. Mostly overseas and South America. Lots of terrorism. But it's very quiet and very top secret. Never, ever in the news. We plan, we execute, we get out." Riley knew Owen now understood; his colour had drained and his pallor matched the white duvet.

Owen fell silent, taking in the full enormity of what she did. Certain aspects of her made sense now. Her keen observation skills, fast reflexes, combat capabilities and her physique. Not to mention how she could emerge from an attack by nine men and be no more bothered than if Finn had left an empty milk carton in the fridge. Knowing she put her life literally on the front line for others—for the people of their country, as well as for the freedom of people in countries that were not even her own—made him incredibly proud and doubly terrified.

TIME REMAINING: 141 Days

Riley and Owen arrived outside Finn's hotel room door and just as Riley reached up to knock, it suddenly opened. A girl walked out, startled by their presence. She smiled nervously as she walked past, blushing as though she had been caught doing something wrong. Riley recognized her as the Maid of Dis-honour from their night at *The Beach*. Riley laughed to herself as she and Owen entered. Hearing Finn in the shower, she prepared to wait and give him the gears for being late. When they entered the room, they both stopped dead. A stunning brunette in a white tube top and a flowing floral skirt sat on the edge of the bed.

She smiled at them unapologetically. "Beautiful morning, eh?" With one of her long tanned legs crossed over the other, she finished buckling her wedge sandal. She grabbed her handbag off the pillow, stood and slung the bag's wooden handles over her shoulder. She glided toward Owen and Riley, wished them a good day and disappeared out the door.

The running water in the shower stopped. Owen, unable to stop laughing, sat on a chair in the corner and waited. Riley seated herself neatly on the untouched bed and noticed as she did so, the empty energy drink cans filling the small blue recycling box at the foot of the dresser. Finn strode out of the bathroom with a towel around his waist and nearly jumped at the sight of his new visitors.

"You guys scared the crap out of me!" He looked at his watch and then to Riley. "I know, I'm late. I'm sorry. I had a hard time getting up this morning."

"I hope you didn't have that problem last night," said Riley. She smiled at him knowingly. "Did you have a good date?"

"Oh," said Finn, nonchalantly, "it was alright."

"Seemed better than alright to me, we met your dates," said Owen. "You're not kidding about being able to multitask."

Finn's expression quickly changed from respectful discretion to exhilaration, like it killed him not to spill the beans. "Oh my God!" He spoke each word like they were their own sentence. "2016 is awesome! Did you see those women? Omigod, they were so hot! I haven't slept, I'll never sleep again. That was so insane! Oh, and I wouldn't sit on that bed."

CHAPTER 31

TEAM 2
YEAR: 2016
TIME REMAINING: 139 Days

At the lab, Riley stared at the three guns in the testing tank, a cloudy expression shadowing her face. She had to admit she was getting nervous. They had yet to solve their biggest obstacle—decreasing the amount of time it took to neutralize the Elevanium from an average of eleven minutes and fifty-three seconds to a fraction of a second.

Owen stood at Riley's side and bit into an apple. "Let's think about this logically. The process takes too long, so we need to speed it up. To do that, we need either more power or an accelerant. How many cartridges did you say you brought, Rile?"

"Tons. 100, 150 maybe. I'd say we've only gone through maybe twenty."

Owen thought for a moment, desperate for any idea. "Do you have any schematics on those ray guns?"

"Yeah, actually, we do." Riley turned to look at her CI screen and it sprung to life at the back of the lab. She flipped through some files and, in seconds, a three-dimensional illustration of the gun rotated before him.

"Is tampering with the cartridges dangerous? Can we make them more concentrated? What if we increased the size of the cartridge clip to accommodate two or even three cartridges instead of just one?"

Finn thought about the suggestion. "The gun would just last longer between cartridge changes. It wouldn't make it any more powerful. The power draw is the limiting factor."

Owen looked at the picture of the gun again and switched to a cross-section view. "So, then we need to increase the power draw. We need the gun to release more rays, faster."

Finn shook his head. "They're already set to max, and they're smoking after the tests we do. What we're doing already exceeds their standard use. These guns aren't designed to run for minutes at a time."

"Well, in theory, the bigger the blast, the shorter they need to run. What if the guns were cooled?" asked Owen.

"Okay, let's solve one problem at a time," said Riley. "Finn, do you think it's possible to override the gun to increase its output capacity?"

"I'm not sure. I've never modified a gun this complex. Repair, yes. Recalibrate, yes," he said carefully, looking at the imposing image of the gun on the screen. He cracked his knuckles. "Let me look into this. Go for lunch and leave it with me."

Riley and Owen returned from lunch to find Finn wired. He stood at Owen's whiteboard, madly writing notes, stopping every couple of seconds only to look over his shoulder at the CI screen. Two energy drink cans and two bottles of Gatorade lay empty on the lab desk behind him. On the CI screen, Owen saw a wall of what he could only assume was programming code of some kind, with symbols he had never seen before.

"You've been busy," said Riley. "Any news?"

Finn's words were fast and caffeine-charged. "Yes. Well, no. Yes and no. Yes, I've been busy. No, I don't have any definitive answers. I analyzed the schematics of the gun. I think we can probably increase the output of zeno rays by physically boring out the ray focusing chamber and increasing the capacity of the primary and secondary booster chargers. That part, I think, would be easy. We'll need to increase the sensitivity of the cooling sensors and that will be tricky. I also think that we should be able to modify and extend the cartridge clip to add two more cartridges. That's a little more dangerous as it involves fabrication and tampering with the cartridges and whatnot. What I'm not sure of right now is if we can reprogram the gun to compensate for the enlarged booster chargers and force the draw of additional energy from the modified cartridge system." Finn turned to the CI screen and scrolled through page after page of code. "I've never seen code like this before. I need more time. Give me a day or two, I should have some better answers for you. I'll need to cross-reference the programming of some other high-output guns to compare programming methods."

Finn spent the next several days experimenting with the guns. Until he could determine whether the guns would be able to handle shooting a higher density beam, there was nothing more that Riley and Owen could do. Riley abhorred doing nothing so she puttered around the lab, organizing and preparing equipment and boxes for their departure.

Although he still had plenty of vacation days before having to return to work full time, Owen split this free time between Riley and finishing up his Key Eleven project report for the International Space Coalition. He called his ISC contact to report his completion of the project and learned a representative would be on the next plane to personally collect and deliver the results back to the ISC. It felt like months had passed since he had last worked on the project. Most of the documentation regarding his discoveries of the Elevanium had been completed prior to his house being blown up and for this he was grateful. After spending so much time working with the super-element, he feared he would inadvertently add information to his report that he had learned as a result of his work with Riley and Finn.

Owen and Riley stopped at the lab to check on Finn. He declined dinner with them for the third night in a row, which was very unlike him. They found him, disheveled and pale, sitting on one of the lab stools staring at the CI screen, deep in thought. His eyes were slits of pink, like he had forgotten how to blink and his hair was askew. Absently, he rolled one of the gun's crystal light deflectors around in his hand, the rest of the gun's parts lay in organized rows on the lab table.

"How's it going, Finn?" Riley spoke softly as if he were a bomb that may explode if she talked too loud.

Finn nearly toppled out of his seat when he realized people were in the room. "Oh! Hey, Rile. Good, good, it's going great. I'm almost done here. I have lots of stuff to tell you, but I can't talk now, I'm near a breakthrough. I'm going to stay here a little while longer if that's okay."

"Finn, when was the last time you slept?"

Finn thought for a moment and looked over his shoulder at the clock on the wall. "I'm not sure. I think I had a nap not too long ago."

"Good news, Finn," said Riley. "We get to move back into Owen's house tomorrow. It's finished."

Finn's sliver of attention had already been absorbed back into the gun's programming code on the screen. It took him several seconds to respond and when he did, his distraction was evident. "Houses are good…I lived in a house once…"

Riley waved her hand in front of Finn's face, but it went unnoticed. She shrugged, turned away and walked into the kitchen.

Owen stared at Finn's glassy eyes, convinced the kid had not blinked since they entered the room. "Is it okay to leave him like this?"

Riley seemed only mildly concerned. "Yeah, he'll be fine. He gets like this sometimes. He'll get on a project and he doesn't like to quit if he's making significant forward progress. There's food and a bed here. He'll be fine." Riley grabbed four ham sandwiches from the fridge as well as several bottles of water and orange juice and placed them on the desk in front of Finn. Without taking his eyes off the screen, he unwrapped one of the sandwiches and shoved it into his mouth.

Riley's knock on Finn's hotel room door the next morning went unanswered. She entered his room using the spare key he had given her their first night there. He insisted she take it knowing he would inevitably lose his. He told her she was welcome to enter at any time, but he would not be held responsible if she saw something she could not unsee.

"And, just to warn you, I sleep naked," he had said.

Riley assumed that Finn slept at the lab—the sparse bus service at night made getting to and from the lab in the evenings tricky. Riley packed Finn's bags so they could check out and return to Owen's house.

By noon, Riley's concern for Finn had grown, so she and Owen returned to the lab to check on him again. They found Finn sitting on his chair, slumped over the lab station atop a pile of tools and gun parts. He held the gun's long barrel in his right hand. Riley found two containers of pills and seven empty energy drink cans in the sink of the lab station.

"Oh shit," said Owen. He grabbed Finn's wrist to check for a pulse. After finding one, his panic subsided. "What are the pills he took?"

Riley recognized the little grey bottle instantly and held it up to show Owen. "Tunnel Vision. They're pills that help you concentrate and stay focused." The second bottle she had never seen before. She picked it up and read the label. "Shit."

"What are they?" asked Owen. He took the sky blue bottle from Riley and read the label.

"Skyscrapers." Riley scowled at Finn's unconscious form. "They're an energy pill, but whether they're safe is still questionable. They were approved by the FDA last year amid some serious controversy. They're supposed to be all-natural but who knows. It's a bit of a hot topic right now."

Riley grabbed Finn's shoulders and shook him gently but got no response. She shook him more violently and his spaghetti limbs knocked several tools to the floor. The gun barrel slid out of his hand and clanked loudly as it hit the floor, taking several tools down with it. "I'll kill him," Riley muttered.

Finn murmured something incoherent as Riley pulled him into an upright sitting position. She pinned him against the back of his lab stool with her forearm across his broad chest then lifted one of his eyelids and peered into his eye. "Good. He's still got his contacts in." She removed her arm and he slumped forward again landing hard on the table. Finn pulled an armful of tools and gun pieces toward him and rested his head on them like a pillow.

Riley stared at her CI screen. The code and gun specs disappeared. A program appeared that Owen had never seen Riley or Finn use. A progress bar appeared on the screen for a few seconds showing the progress for something Owen could not make heads or tails of. It disappeared and a detailed report appeared.

Riley explained. "I'm doing a reverse physical analysis on Captain Brilliant here. He's left his lenses in so I can run a diagnostic check of his bodily functions, just to make sure he's not going to die on us."

Owen sensed that Riley had done this before; the report generated an enormous amount of data, but she scrolled to very specific places in the diagnosis and read. Owen was only able to read snippets of information, and most of it seemed to be coded with numbers.

Satisfied with what she read, she closed the window and looked back down at Finn. "Well, he's fine. He's got a 342A, 8723UX, T367AB. Meaning, he's physically overexhausted, his immune efficiency is way down and, well, let's just say that thanks to that particular cocktail of drugs, he's likely to experience some intestinal fireworks for the next little while."

Riley and Owen half-walked, half-carried Finn to Owen's truck and buckled him into the back seat. He slumped over immediately and curled up into the fetal position. Back at the house, they hauled him into his room, his feet dragging behind him as they awkwardly heaved his hulking frame down the hallway. They laid him out on the bed and it creaked under his weight. Owen looked amused at the level of intimacy Riley shared with her partner as she stripped him down to his socks and boxers, then folded his jeans.

"Trust me, he'll be grateful. I've seen far more of him on more occasions than I care to count. One time he called me to pick him up at a bar and when I got there, he wasn't. I found him one block over, running down the street wearing nothing but one sock and a steering wheel duct-taped to his left hand." She set his folded jeans on the chair next to the bed and looked down at him. "When you're in Black Ops and you're in the field, no one has any of the secrets that privacy affords you. The result is that your teammates become like family. He's like my little brother."

Riley pulled the blankets over Finn, folded his shirt and laid it atop his jeans.

"What an idiot." Riley shook her head but admired his spirit. They left as he rolled over in his sleep and spooned a pillow.

CHAPTER 32

TEAM 3
YEAR: 2095
TIME REMAINING: 133 Days

Since assuming Jim's position, both ends of Spencer's candle burned like raging infernos. The one-month period of donor brainwave collection had ended and Spencer's attention now focused on preparing the mountains of data. Once each donor's data was properly formatted, it could be compiled into a Personality Application. And when all twenty-two personality applications were created, Spencer would need to verify the emotional balance and health each of the personalities. To do this, he would use a program called the Real Life Simulator. This program would run each of the personality applications through a gauntlet of true-to-life situations. The scenarios were designed to provoke and push each personality to their breaking points to ensure the reactions were acceptable by social norms.

The situations for testing would be chosen by Ian, and programmed by Spencer and his team. Although Spencer had not yet received them, he knew the testing scenarios that Ian was going to provide him would be feeble and unchallenging, having seen them when he completed this project the first time. He knew he would have to add many more scenarios to the Real Life Simulator, and this made him nervous. He would have to justify his changes to Ian without blowing his Operation TimeShift agenda. Spencer anticipated significant pushback from him on this. Ian would see any proposed amendments as questioning his judgement, which to be fair was true, though not unjustly.

This testing phase was one of the key milestones that would ensure the success of Operation TimeShift. The lack of thorough testing the first time was the reason robots were tearing the city apart in 2097. Spencer could not, would not, let history repeat itself. He knew that if more rigorous scenarios were added to the testing phase, the robots would fail, proving they were unsafe. Modifications would then need to be made to cut out the unhealthy aspects of each personality. It was these minor corrections to the personality programming that would rewrite the robots' destruction in 2097. Spencer had no choice but to get through to Ian or Operation TimeShift would undoubtedly fail.

Kalen was the life preserver keeping Spencer afloat. Without her help, he knew he would be drowning. Between formatting the personality data, covering Jim's administrative duties and masking his TimeShift agenda, Spencer's life was hectic. Thankfully, he could easily disguise his work on the operation as diligence in his job, so nothing he did appeared out of the ordinary to anyone he worked with. Yet.

Kalen slid into Spencer's office and seated herself in a chair opposite his desk. She found him in the exact position she had left him in—over ten hours earlier—staring intently at his screen. She was concerned about his excessive workload, which was showing no signs of letting up. His tan had faded and he rarely deviated from his route to and from the office.

"Look what I have." She held up a data drive—a transparent grey rectangle of plastic no thicker than a small stick of chewing gum. She knew this little delivery would make him happy; it was all he had talked about for weeks.

Spencer's face lit up. "Is that what I think it is?"

Kalen tossed him the drive and it sailed through the hovering screen. Spencer caught it and plugged it into his CI.

"I've come up with a list of really intriguing scenarios to add to Ian's list."

Kalen looked at Spencer with confusion. "Why would you create a list of scenarios when you don't even know what Ian's are?"

Spencer froze, worried that he may have said too much. It was so hard for him to keep what he knew of the future from his co-workers. "Oh, well, I don't, obviously. But these are pretty unique…" Spencer ran his hand through his hair. "Well, no better way to find out than to look. Let's find out."

A box appeared at the front of the three-dimensional screen showing different file names listed. The icon labeled "Personality Application Testing Data" flashed and the document opened up on the screen. As he scrolled through the document, Spencer read through the list of scenarios for him to program into the Real Life Simulator. As he expected, they were the same as they had been the first time—few in number and lacking depth.

Ensuring the robots behaved in a predictable, socially acceptable manner was more than just a matter of safety. The robots' behaviour and values needed to reflect those of the average human for the integration of the two species to be successful. If the robots' behaviour or values deviated too far from what society as a whole deemed as acceptable, they would not be perceived as equals, merely machines. If a robot enjoyed kicking puppies, it would be outcast the same way a human would be. If the robots behaved happily in situations where a human would not, the robots would seem artificial, like programmed objects. The robots needed to experience the right amount of the proper emotions at appropriate times for humans to accept them as equals.

"Hmmm." Spencer scrolled back to the top of the document and re-read the table of contents.

"Is something wrong?" asked Kalen.

"None of these tests seem overly taxing." He pointed to a section in the table of contents. Some of the test titles included *Being overcharged at a store*, *Being cut off in line*, and *Co-worker has a baby*.

"Running the personalities through these testing scenarios will test basic emotions well, such as happiness, sadness and anger to some degree, but there's nothing here that is stressful enough to test complex emotions like jealousy, rage, guilt or fear."

Kalen read the titles more thoroughly. "I see your point. That could be a problem. We need to know how much stress a personality can handle before it snaps." She sat down again. "What are you going to do?"

"I guess I'll bring it up with Ian." Spencer leaned back in his chair and stretched. "But first I want to thoroughly analyze this document and have some suggestions ready."

"I guess you were right to be proactive about those extra testing scenarios," said Kalen.

TIME REMAINING: 132 Days

"Ian, I need to talk to you about the Personality Application testing scenarios I received." Spencer's stomach cinched upward with dread. He knew Ian would not take his suggestions objectively; the Project Director would see Spencer's ideas as criticisms of his brainchild.

"Sure, kid, what's up?" Ian greeted his wonder kid enthusiastically. Ian liked Spencer. The kid was brilliant, no doubt about it, and he knew that in a few years when he told people that he had personally mentored Spencer Grayson through the AEI Project, they would be impressed. He motioned for his young protégé to take a seat in one of the hovering chairs opposite his desk. As Spencer sat, the chair adjusted itself to the perfect height for the length of Spencer's legs. Ian sat, leaned back casually in his leather executive chair and clasped his hands behind his head.

As usual, Ian looked like he had stepped off the cover of a men's fashion magazine. He wore a trendy, black houndstooth sports coat with the sleeves rolled up. Beneath the jacket, he wore a fitted black t-shirt with some obscure graphic art printed on it. Through the glass desk, he saw Ian's dark navy jeans and black alligator shoes. Nestled in his shaggy, salt and pepper hair, were a pair of Ray-Bans, which Spencer had never actually seen him use for their intended purpose. He perpetually wore a day's worth of stubble that, when teamed with the age lines on his face, projected an air of experience and absolute confidence. The *coup-de-gras*, his hundred-watt smile was both a tool and a weapon; he frequently used it for both—to end an argument or close a pitch.

"I've come up with some additional scenarios that I think would be good to add to the Real Life Simulator test. I mean, the ones you had made were good, well, they seem good enough on the surface…" Spencer felt his nerves kick into overdrive. *Pull it together Spence*, he thought to himself. He cleared his throat. "What I mean is, what's there is good for testing basic emotions, but I don't believe that they're stress-ful enough to really get a good feel for how the personalities will handle the more complex, negative emotions. If we don't see what happens to the personalities after they've exceeded their breaking point, we can't truly know how the robots will behave in stressful situations."

"Interesting," said Ian. He unclasped his hands from behind his head, leaned forward and rested his elbows on the glass desk. "You're aware that I consulted extensively with some of the top psychologists in this country for this? And that these professionals, at the top in their fields, felt these would be more than adequate?" He spoke slowly and Spencer heard more than a hint of condescension.

"Uh, yes, I am aware of that, sir," he stammered. Spencer felt his resolve beginning to crumble. He knew that this was Ian's intention, and he hated that it was working. Neither of the twins would ever be intimidated by anyone.

Hearing submission in Spencer's voice, Ian leaned back in his chair again and smiled; his voice once again became cheery and pompous. "We need to keep things lean Spencer; money and time are tight. There's no point digging too deep for problems that just aren't going to be there. This project is infallible, kid. I've got it all planned out. We're all going to go down in history as the people who changed robotic intelligence forever. Well, maybe some of us more than others, I did come up with the idea after all. But, there's plenty of room at the top. I know that with your brain, you'll soon be up here with us corner-office elite."

"While I agree it's unlikely there'll be issues, I don't think that spending additional time on testing is unwarranted," said Spencer. "We're ahead of schedule and I don't mind working on it in the evenings if I have to."

Ian's lips smiled though his eyes did not. "Thank you for your generous offer Spencer, but I don't think that will be necessary."

In Ian's tone, Spencer detected an unmistakable warning to leave things well enough alone. He knew he was pushing his luck by persisting, but he had no choice. This very conversation with Ian could impact the success of Operation TimeShift. He needed Ian to see it his way so he could change the tests and prove the robots were unsafe so they could be fixed. "These robots are going to experience social situations far more complex and socially intricate than what's in these tests, and I don't think it hurts to make sure those reactions fall within social norms."

"Spencer," said Ian. His eyes became as cold and dark as the rain pounding the corner office window at his back. "Are you saying that you don't think I have the public's safety in mind?"

"No, of course not. I just think that it doesn't hurt to be extra cautious."

"Do you not agree with the way I'm running this project, Spencer?"

"No Ian, that's not the case at all, you know that. If I could just supplement your test with some additional scenarios, I think it will help with the public's reception of the robots. If everyone knows the robots have been tested exhaustively, the time it takes for people to warm up to the robots will be much less." Spencer handed Ian a thirty-page printed document. "Take a look at these. I've drafted some additional scenarios and it won't add too much time. I think it's absolutely critical…"

Ian snatched the document from Spencer and tossed it on his desk without a glance. "Spencer, you've done a bang-up job on this project. Your division is on track and you're doing the jobs of two people. I'm very impressed. Please don't make me think I've got the wrong impression about you." Ian walked to the door and held it open. Spencer knew nothing productive could come from talking further. As he walked away, he heard Ian's shred bot through the closed door.

Spencer fumed through his lunch. All of the things he should have said to Ian popped into his mind after the fact, as usual. The sole purpose of his and the twin's journey back to 2095 was to change the project and Spencer knew that getting buy-in from Ian would ensure success. But if Ian failed to respond to logic or reason, he became the liability that the three brothers anticipated he would. Spencer would have to work around him, which meant more work after hours.

When Spencer announced he was leaving early, his co-workers assumed he had food-poisoning. In his office, he made a copy of Ian's testing data. As the files copied, his mind wandered to the repercussions he would face if caught. Copying data from the NRD was the equivalent of stealing trade secrets. It was a one-way ticket to un-employment to be sure, likely accompanied by jail-time. Spencer thought about the past version of himself travelling through Europe. *If I get myself fired I know I'll never forgive myself.*

This marked the first time he had violated a policy—other than conspiracy—for the sake of the mission. When planning this op all those months ago, he had wondered how it would feel to blatantly work against the NRD. Would he feel a guilty justifi-cation, or remorseful? Perhaps powerful in some way? Now that it happened, he only felt anger at Ian's ego.

While predictable, Ian's reaction complicated Spencer's job considerably. Any work he did beyond Ian's instructions directly violated Ian and by extension, the NRD. He would need to find a way to keep his work hidden and off the NRD's Nexus server space, where it would inevitably be discovered.

Spencer walked briskly to his car, needing to put as much distance between himself and the office as possible. As he strode through the parking garage, he sent a text message to his brothers requesting they meet later to discuss the new develop-ments. As he approached his car, mentally dictating his message to Asher, he heard his car door unlock. He sent the message and it disappeared from his vision. He opened his driver's door and a hand shot out in front of him, slamming the door shut again. Livid and looking for any excuse to unload his anger, he turned expecting to see one of the twins.

"I am not in the mood right now for…" Spencer froze, stunned by who he saw.

"Trust me, Spencer, this is no joke," said Ian.

Ian shoved Spencer backward against his car and leaned in close. The mad glint in Ian's eyes was out of character and made him look unhinged and unpredictable. Spencer had never seen Ian like this before. He would probably have been scared for his well-being if he had not been so confused.

"Back off the testing if you know what's good for you." Ian's voice, although quiet, carried a deadly tone. He seemed distracted, more skittish than ever, and he made no effort to veil his threats, verbally or physically.

Ian's aggression stunned Spencer, but what confused him more was how disheveled the Project Director looked. His clothes were rumpled; one of his jacket sleeves was rolled down and there was dirt on his pants like he had been crawling around on a dusty floor. His jacket looked different than the one he wore earlier, though Spencer could not be certain. But what he was certain of, was that Ian did not have a purple rose in his lapel at their meeting just hours ago. Spencer's anger outweighed his confusion and any questions were quickly forgotten. The nervousness he had felt in Ian's presence earlier had vanished, now replaced with anger and something like recklessness or daring. He regained his balance and stood his full height.

"What are you talking about, Ian? What the hell happened to you?"

Ian leaned in close to Spencer's face and spoke again. "This is my project and no corporate ladder-climbing little punk, genius or not, is going to derail it. Just back the hell off." Ian smiled his broad, dimpled smile then turned and jogged through the door to the stairwell.

"So, you're telling me that even though Ian told you that the testing criteria was good enough and then physically threatening you in the parking garage, you're going to alter it anyway?" Kalen shook her head as she pulled the cork from a bottle of wine. She took two wine glasses from Spencer's cupboard and poured.

"I'm not altering it per se, I'm just adding to it. I'll add what I think needs to be added and then show him. He can't deny simple logic. People's lives could be at stake. Once it's done and he sees it, he'll really have no choice but to go along with it." Spencer looked down at the string beans sautéing in the frying pan and gave them a stir. He knew already that Ian would not see his logic, but that was something he would worry about later.

"He's not going to be happy about that," said Kalen, shaking her head. She sipped her wine and held the other glass out to Spencer.

Spencer sighed. "I know. It'll be tricky. I'll talk to him alone again to give him the chance to make the right decision. If I don't make any headway with him, I'll address it at a director's meeting, that way he can't dismiss what I'm saying so quickly." Spencer took a sip of his wine before setting the glass on the counter beside the stove.

"I don't know, Spence. That could blow up in your face. Crossing Ian in front of the directors could be a bad career move." She watched him absent-mindedly flip each bean individually, lost in thought. Spencer's dedication to his job was one of the qualities she admired most about him. But in this instance, she wondered if he was overzealous. His insistence that Ian's testing data was grievously flawed bordered on obsession. She agreed that the proposed tests seemed insufficient, but if psychologists developed them, surely they would know what scenarios would best capture the broadest range of behaviour? It was unclear to her why Spencer fought so vehemently about the testing when the people at the top had no concerns. In addition, Spencer was never one to disobey a direct order, even if he disagreed with it. His recent be-haviour seemed out of character for him, and she felt as though a piece of information was missing. However, he had just taken over Jim's position as a director and un-doubtedly that role came with additional responsibilities and high-level knowledge he could not discuss with her. No matter the issue, she trusted his judgment and supported him.

"I don't really see what other choice I have. At least this way I'll have witnesses who are hopefully objective and may agree with me."

"Or, you could just do what he wants," said Kalen.

He laid the spatula across the frying pan and picked up his wine. He shook his head. "I can't Kale. I have to make this right, otherwise, how can I live with myself? What if some of the personalities have defects? What if one of them is a psychopath? That personality will be put into thousands of robots. It's reckless and dangerous to not do thorough testing. What if people got hurt?"

Kalen hugged him tightly. "You raise very sensible points, Spence. Logic like that should be hard to ignore. But remember, at the end of the day the outcome is on Ian's shoulders."

Spencer could not tear his eyes away from the beautiful, caring woman who supported him unconditionally. He knew he must sound like an obsessed lunatic, harping on and on about testing and problems that were only hypothetical. He held her tightly and rested his head on hers.

Kalen pressed the AUTO button on the stove controls. The beans began moving around in the pan as if prodded by an invisible spatula. She lowered the temperature, placed the lid on the pan, then led Spencer out of the kitchen.

"What are you doing?" Spencer pulled his hand away and bent down to look inside the lit oven. "The roast is done, we're going to dry it out."

Kalen smiled at him and shook her head slowly. "Shut up Spence," she whispered, then kissed him. She took his hand in hers and led him to the living room. She pushed him down on the couch and pulled her hair out of her ponytail. Her wavy hair fell around her shoulders as she undid the top few buttons on his shirt. He grabbed her hand, kissed it and then pulled her down on top of him.

When the twins met at Spencer's condo later that evening, they were stunned to hear about Spencer's encounter with Ian in the parkade. Spencer felt heartened to see his brothers so outraged on his behalf. They all knew Ian to be many things—self-righteous, condescending and arrogant—but none of the brothers could imagine him aggressively accosting an employee. The behaviour seemed out of his character, even for him.

The productivity of the brother's meeting surprised Spencer. He expected the twins to be their usual, goof-off selves, leaving him to babysit them while solving his own problems. Instead, they impressed him with their attention and support. For the first time in his life, Spencer felt like they were working toward something as equals; each person offering suggestions and unique perspectives.

The twins were not surprised to learn that Ian remained unmoved by Spencer's logic and sympathized with their little brother because they knew it meant he would have to do his job twice. During the day, he would program the Real Life Simulator with Ian's feeble testing scenarios. At night, he would have to program a second test, this one with much more complicated situations and far more numerous. When complete, he would run the personalities through his more realistic scenarios, then present the results to Ian and the other directors.

Doing this work twice brought to light a new set of obstacles. The amount of space required to store the second set of the personality applications, the Real Life Simulator program, the test itself and the programs needed to complete the actual work, was substantial. He would be caught in an instant if he stored the files on the NRD Nexus server and his personal space in the cloud was nowhere near large enough. Asher devised a brilliant solution; however, it would take him and Logan weeks to source what they would need, plus time to implement it.

Finally, the brothers discussed the actual moment of the timeshift. For their mission to be successful, the entire project direction needed to shift in favour of Spencer's modifications. Getting Ian on board with this would have made the moment of the timeshift much easier, as he could have made an announcement to the stakeholders. Instead, Spencer would need to devise a way to simultaneously convince the directors and countless stakeholders that modified personalities would still be considered "true" AEI and do all of this covertly, with Ian being none the wiser.

Logan suggested Spencer organize a demonstration for the NRD board and stakeholders, promising a preview of a functioning Personality Application in a robot. Spencer knew Ian would jump at this idea; it was an opportunity to put him and his beloved project in the spotlight. At the last minute, Spencer would switch the robot's personality with one of the modified, safe personalities and use the meeting as a platform to explain the modifications. Spencer loved the idea; he knew all of the stakeholders were anxious to get a sneak preview. If Spencer kept his speech on schedule, he could have all of his points made by seven o'clock, and all of the stakeholders would see his logic, shifting their paradigms at the moment of the timeshift. Once Ian saw the buy-in from the stakeholders, he would have no choice but to go along with it. While there was no love lost between Ian and Spencer, Spencer would have preferred getting Ian on board beforehand. Having Ian's support in advance of the presentation would add more credibility to his presentation.

"So I'll let you know when I've figured out how to accomplish that," said Spencer wearily. "As you know, Ian won't listen to logic."

"Well, if logic doesn't work that leaves quick wit, persistence or force," said Logan.

"And you're not quick-witted," said Asher, looking at his little brother with a smile, "so that leaves persistence and force. We know you're persistent but not very forceful."

Spencer knew that, so far, persistence had done nothing for him either.

CHAPTER 33

Finn still felt under the weather after the accidental overdose on Friday, but the majority of his nausea had passed. He sipped from his glass of water; his voice hoarse after explaining for the better part of an hour, the 271 lines of code he would have to modify to increase the guns' output of zeno rays. He wrapped up his presentation by showing a cross-section image of how the extended cartridge clip would look with the second and third cartridges.

"And that's 271 lines of code, per gun?" asked Riley.

Finn nodded.

"Looks like we've got some late nights ahead of us," said Owen.

"And what are we not going to do?" asked Riley, looking at Finn.

"No Skyscrapers," said Finn.

TIME REMAINING: 128 Days

It took Riley and Owen four full days to finish the physical modifications to the first gun while Finn made adjustments to its programming. With the programming changes completed for one gun, Finn ran the new code through a simulation program, testing the gun's operation in a virtual environment. When Finn read the results, he sank heavily into his chair. Had he bypassed the virtual tests and checked the gun manually, he would have blown their office right out of the building. After two days, many code changes and nearly fifty simulations later, the gun finally operated as he had intended.

Finn set the reprogrammed gun in the testing tank to get a precise reading of the gun's improved output levels. The miniaturized gun stood solitary in the centre of the tank. No Elevanium was required for this test; they merely wanted to confirm the output of zeno rays had increased as calculated before modifying the other guns.

Finn hit the button on the remote control. The gun's output, previously a faint mist, now shone bright red.

Owen grinned ear to ear as he held the scanner for the others to see. "It's better than we'd expected."

TIME REMAINING: 125 Days

With all three guns reprogrammed, Riley and Finn were anxious to test their improved output on a brick of Elevanium, but waited for Owen to arrive from his first real day back at work. To the team, it seemed as though a lifetime had passed since the start of the project until this moment. They had endured innumerable setbacks and failures and were hopeful that failure was behind them. By their calculations, the total output of all three modified guns should neutralize the Elevanium in less than a second. However, their hopes were dashed when, even at their maximum output, the neutralization still took on average, twenty-five seconds.

Finn shook his head. "Not enough. Thirty-four seconds." Riley watched Finn set the scanner on the table, crestfallen. After all of his hard work and late nights, he seemed to take the failure personally.

Riley patted him on the back. "Don't worry yet. Nothing we've done so far has worked the first time. Let's look at it again tomorrow with fresh eyes."

Even refreshed eyes the following morning made no difference. Nor did changing any additional variables throughout the next five days. After working into the nights and through weekends with no success, the team's spirits had dampened considerably and the oppressive weight of the looming deadline grew heavier and more suffocating with each passing day.

Suddenly, Owen stood upright so abruptly that he startled Riley and Finn.

"Why don't we just use the VersaTool and make the guns twice as big?" It seemed like such a great idea, he could not believe that he had not thought about it until now. He expected Riley and Finn to pick him up on their shoulders and parade him around the lab.

Riley smiled and shook her head. "Unfortunately, the VersaTool's compression setting is only really suited for making things smaller. Making objects smaller isn't as strenuous on them as making things larger. Making something bigger is easy enough to do, but everything becomes more fragile and unpredictable the larger it becomes. That's why the world's oil crisis couldn't be resolved by making barrels of oil larger, in the same way that world hunger couldn't be solved by making giant food. It just doesn't work."

TIME REMAINING: 110 Days

An uneasiness had taken up residence in Riley's stomach and it gnawed at her from the moment she woke to the moment she fell asleep. All of their ideas had been tried and failed. There was no consistent pattern of results onto which they could build. Out of ideas and variables to try, Riley's steadfast belief in their ability to succeed began to waver. Falling asleep had become difficult. The previous night, she lay in bed watching Owen, who slept like a baby every night, physically exhausted from working such long hours. Worried her tossing and turning would wake him, she went for a run hoping to tire herself, but it made no difference. She showered and returned to bed, no more or less tired than she had been before. Nothing she could do would allow her mind to quiet.

Now, sitting in the lab, her body finally decided it was ready to sleep. Her brain felt muddy and sluggish and she debated passing out in the dorm room for a half hour, but knew there was no time. She rubbed her eyes. "Finn, do you have any of those Skyscrapers left?"

She waited for him to make a smart comment, hassling her for all the grief she had given him about popping pills. To her surprise, he looked sympathetic and rubbed her shoulder as he walked past her to grab the bottle from his backpack.

"Only take one," he warned. Finn knew Riley's clean eating meant her system would not have a fraction of the crap in it that his did, thanks to his diet of junk food. He looked at her and smiled knowingly. "And if you're looking for a good time, give one to Owen, chase it with a few beers and you'll have a nice little cocktail in your system that will keep you two buzzing and busy all night long." Riley punched him sister-like in the arm but said nothing. Though Finn had no proof, he suspected there was a cat to be let out of a bag somewhere.

"What?" he asked, smiling innocently. "I just thought you might like to know."

Riley washed the Skyscraper down with what was left of Finn's lukewarm cappuccino and hoped she had no reaction to it. She avoided mental enhancers, energy pills and things of the like, preferring a more holistic approach to whatever ailed her.

As she set down the small mug, the phone rang. Riley groaned as she leaned forward to pick up the wireless handset. Neither she nor Finn could get used to the concept of a physical, tangible phone nor the need to hold it up to their ears. Before she finished saying hello, Owen cut in. His voice was loud and he spoke fast. Riley's mind laboured to keep up.

"Owen, Owen! Slow down and start over. Sorry, my brain's a little fried at the moment." She switched the phone to speaker mode so Finn could listen in.

Owen's voice echoed in the cavernous kitchen. "Maybe this is too simple, but what if we broke up the Elevanium to smaller pieces? Think about it. Whenever we do these tests, we can see on the scanner that it's always the centre that takes the longest. If we broke the brick up into smaller pieces, the rays could hit more surface area of the deposit. The smaller the better, right?"

Finn and Riley did not respond immediately. Finally, Riley spoke. "It's quite logical actually. I can't believe we didn't think of this sooner."

Finn nodded and shrugged. "We've tried everything else."

Owen arrived at the lab thirty minutes later. In the meantime, Riley had already broken an Elevanium brick into small, pea-sized pieces. Owen tossed his jacket on the island, grabbed a salami sub from the fridge and inhaled it with a speed that rivalled Finn at his top form. He cracked open a can of iced tea, snatched an armful of fruit and snacks from the counter and strode to the testing tank. Riley poured the Elevanium pieces into a neat pile in the centre of the tank while Finn sat slumped over on a stool, his mouth gaping in a cavernous yawn. Owen was surprised by Riley, whose energy level seemed far more lively now than she had sounded earlier. He watched her bounce across the lab to grab the scanner off the back counter.

"What's up with Riley?" whispered Owen.

Finn, now half-sitting, half-lying on the lab station with his chin resting on his folded arms, watched Riley. What little energy he had left drained as he watched her speed around. "Skyscraper," he yawned.

"Really?" Owen was stunned after the speech she had given Finn. "Is she alright? Is she going to crash?"

Finn's eyes were closed, but he could hear the concern in Owen's voice. He smiled to himself and reached up blindly to pat Owen on the back. "No worries. It's not cocaine or anything. She'll crash later tonight, but she'll sleep."

"Hey, you guys!" exclaimed Riley as she approached. "Are we doing this or what?"

"Yes, dear," said Finn in a mocking, falsetto voice. He sat up slowly and yawned again.

Riley kicked the leg of his chair. "Finn, move your ass. Here's the scanner. Get it ready."

Riley passed Owen the remote control. "Do the honours, sir."

"Fair enough," said Owen, taking the remote from her. He positioned his thumb over the button. "In three, two, one." Before Owen had a chance to release the button, Finn let out a wild whoop.

"We did it!" yelled Finn. He jumped out of his chair knocking it over backward. He turned the scanner so Riley and Owen could see it.

"Point three seven of a second." Riley read the numbers and looked from the scanner to the pile of Elevanium in the tank, back to the scanner. "We did it," she breathed. The enormity of what she said seeped in. "We did it." Louder this time. "We did it! We did it!" She danced a circle around Owen and then gave him a hug and a kiss on the cheek.

Finn landed on his bed within minutes of reaching the house. Riley—still feeling the effects of the Skyscraper—could not sit still. Owen took her for a walk down a path behind the house that followed the river.

"Are you nervous about the leap back on Friday?"

"Nah," said Owen casually, though inwardly he felt extremely anxious. As the final days of their work in 2016 drew to a close, he found himself contemplating what came next, both for the op and for his life. Logically, he knew the actual leap part was relatively safe. He continually reminded himself that Riley and Finn had arrived with their limbs attached in the right places. But the physical leap back was not his sole concern; it was everything that could go wrong. What if they became stranded, got hurt, or were unable to make it back? What would Riley's life be like after the timeshift? Would it be better than before? Would it be worse?

At hearing something in Owen's would-be casual voice, Riley sensed he felt less confident than he was letting on. She stopped walking and turned to face Owen. She opened her mouth to speak, said nothing then looked at him appraisingly for a moment.

"Well, I have the NRD line I can give you about all the safety precautions we have in place, blah, blah, blah…very simple operation of excavation, then executing the device that we've created and then return you home safe and sound with a little financial bonus. But I'll be straight with you. Here's how it really is. Any operation with time travel has an added component of complexity, not only in the leap itself but the hardware. Hardware sometimes malfunctions, accidents happen. And it can make you nauseous. Finn nearly puked last time. The operation itself, well, we're digging a big hole in the ground and then setting up our guns and then…well, you know the rest. Is it safe?" Riley nodded her head contemplatively. "Yes, on paper. Most times, things go right. But I'm not going to lie to you, shit inevitably happens and you can't control it. There's generally a lot of recalculating on the fly. In theory, it should be a very easy operation, but I don't prepare for easy operations. I prepare for worst-case scenarios. If you don't want to come, I totally understand. You can back out any time you like. Well, anytime between now and Friday morning that is."

Owen chuckled. "Don't worry. I'm still going. But I do appreciate your honesty. Even if it is, quite frankly, terrifying."

Owen ached to say something that had been on his mind for some time, but worried the airing of his feelings would make the unspoken complication in their relationship too real. Without having to say so, they both knew nothing good could come from discussing their relationship. Talking about its inevitable end seemed pointless so instead, they focused on what time they did have. But Owen could no longer deny that something about his relationship with Riley was different. He felt things he had never felt before—an intensity and caring deeper than he imagined possible. The importance of everything in his life paled in comparison to her; nothing else mattered except her happiness and their time together. Owen initially suspected the high-stakes nature of the operation for the depth of his feelings for her—that the constant adrenaline spikes and long hours had wreaked havoc with his dopamine levels. Their one glorious month together as a couple felt more like six. But as time passed, Owen realized neither the project nor the hours had anything to do with how he felt. The strength of his feelings were a result of nothing more than who she was and how well they complimented each other.

"Riley, I can't imagine my life without you. You've completely changed it and I don't want to lose you."

"I know, Owen. I feel the same way. I feel like we've been together for ages. I know more about you than I've ever known about anyone. I think that this really could have been something."

Owen saw a pain in Riley's eyes that had not been present after being attacked by a horde of thugs or after stumbling out of a burning house.

"Rile, if this is too hard, we…"

She silenced him with a kiss. When she pulled away, she caressed his cheek and yawned. "I wouldn't change a thing. I think that Skyscraper's finally run its course."

He wrapped his arm around her and they turned back. "Let's get you home before I have to carry you."

TIME REMAINING: 107 Days

Riley awoke in the same place she had for over a month—in Owen's arms. She lay motionless and enjoyed the stillness of the morning. Through the partially opened blinds, she saw five pelicans floating down the river, basking in the sun. She felt a pang of sadness at how desperately she wanted to continue waking up in this bed, next to this man and seeing that view every morning. She took in the scene for another quarter of an hour before trying to slide out of Owen's arms without disturbing him.

"Where do you think you're going?" he asked softly. He cast his arm around her waist and reeled her back to him, kissing the back of her neck.

She laughed and fought his restraint half-heartedly. "I've got to pack and get to the lab. And don't you have things to do—people to see, last-minute errands to run before we go?"

Owen groaned at the defeat and nodded as he rubbed his eyes. He sat up, leaned back against the headboard and watched her slide into his grey cotton robe. He marvelled at her naked body, the faint outline of each active muscle was visible as she moved.

Riley stopped at the bathroom door, let the top of the robe slip off her shoulders. She looked back at him seductively. "That being said, I do have a few minutes to spare."

She let the robe slide down her arms and it landed at her feet. Owen ejected himself from the bed and followed her into the bathroom.

Owen walked out of the bathroom with his towel around his waist to find Riley already dressed. She was wearing the same SWAT-style outfit she had the day they met—the day she saved him from being by hit the bus.

"Can you please check on Finn for me and make sure he didn't sleep in? I don't want to be late."

"Sure." Owen kissed her on the forehead as he threw on a pair of jeans and a faded Skid Row t-shirt before heading to the basement. Owen's stomach flip-flopped at the thought of the leap back to the year 1200 they would be making in mere hours. He had a case of nerves unlike anything he had ever experienced and anticipated an ulcer before sundown.

Owen knocked on Finn's open door and saw the contents of his bags spread across the bed. "How's it going, champ?"

Whereas most of Riley's possessions were necessities like clothing and toiletries, Finn's consisted of two cases of energy drinks, four large cans of coffee, eight large bottles of honey, two flats of Coke, a stack of magazines, newspapers, and an assortment of chips, popcorn, candy and chocolate bars, plus whatever else lay beneath the surface layer of the snacks.

Owen picked up one of the honey jars. "Honey?"

"Yes, sweetie?" quipped Finn, looking up from the tins of coffee he was jamming into his bag.

Rolling his eyes, Owen tossed the jar back to Finn. Finn caught it and smiled like an entrepreneur who had stumbled across the next greatest thing. "Do you know how much I can sell this for back home?"

Owen pointed to the jumbo-sized box of condoms. "And they don't have these in 2097?"

"Nope. Most women have some kind of electronic implant that emits a high-pitched frequency or something that disrupts their goings-on. I don't know how it works exactly. It's one of those mysteries of women that they don't tell me about and I don't ask."

Owen laughed. Finn was so young, he had so much to learn about life and women and everything in between. He thought back to when he and Riley had discussed protection, she had said it was all taken care of. He just assumed she meant she was on the pill.

Owen arrived at the lab several hours after Riley and Finn; his last-minute errands had taken less time than he had anticipated. He found Riley and Finn going through their checklist. He set his two bags and a metal, fireproof case neatly beside the pile of supplies in the centre of the lab then listened in as Finn double-checked their inventory. Riley eyed Finn's extra bag. "What's that?"

"Just a few souvenirs," he said innocently. "Don't worry, I've tagged it already."

Riley handed Finn and Owen each a black nylon backpack. Owen remembered Riley showing him her pack on the day they met. He watched as Riley and Finn opened up their packs and removed what looked like a large watch. Mirroring their actions, he strapped the watch on his wrist and looked over the various buttons and screens.

"What is this thing?"

"It's the external control interface for the packs." She held up his wrist and explained the different settings and dates. She handed him a tiny red, bean-shaped device and showed him how to position the communication device to his ear.

Riley retrieved a piece of paper from her pocket that listed their landing coordinates and read them out to Finn and Owen. They each entered their destination settings by sliding their fingers across the numbers on the touch screen. The cavernous room filled with muffled beeping sounds as they scrolled to each number.

"Oh, I should mention," Riley said looking at Owen, "we need to adjust the numbers a bit or we'll all land on top of each other. I'll change mine," she said, and her watch beeped twice as she adjusted her coordinates. She looked at Finn.

"Already done," he said. "More west."

Riley smiled. "Yes, that will be perfect." She looked at his bags. "And you said you tagged those?"

"Yes, boss lady," Finn said, mocking her caution. "And Owen's."

Riley saw that Owen had no clue what they were talking about. "Anything you want to bring during the leap needs a tag. We register the tag with the control pack and then it'll bring along whatever items the tags are affixed to."

Riley looked from Finn to Owen. "You guys ready?"

Finn squeaked out a yes as he rocked slightly on the balls of his feet, no doubt psyching himself up for the time leap. Owen nodded silently and closed his eyes. Riley counted down from three. When she reached "one," they each pressed the button on their watches and disappeared from the lab.

CHAPTER 34

TEAM 1 & 2
YEAR: 1200
TIME REMAINING: 98 Days

Owen opened his eyes and immediately shielded them from the bright sun. His body sizzled with a surge of sensations. He looked down at his feet and felt a wave of relief at the sight of them. Nausea hit him like a brick wall, but it was quelled quickly by the thrill of adrenaline tearing through his body. It was one thing to hear about time travel, but it was something completely different to experience it. He heard a splash to his right. While he and Riley stood on a rocky shoreline surrounded by their supplies, Finn was treading water.

"Nice co-ordinates, Rile!" Finn laughed, swimming toward the shore.

She grinned at him mischievously. "That's for blowing up my office with a desk."

Finn tried to pull himself onto the rocky shore, but his clothes acted like anchors and his boots could not get traction on the slimy, algae-covered rocks under the water. Owen extended his hand and pulled him onto the rocky ledge as Riley, smirking, studied a manual compass. The needle wobbled on its pin and she confirmed north, despite already having an idea of its whereabouts based on the lake and their pre-planned landing point.

"According to my calculations, the camp isn't too far southeast." She pointed along the shore and into the forest.

Owen looked at the multitude of bags and Elevanium crates and wondered how many trips they would have to take to get all of their supplies to the camp. He wondered if his VersaTool would let them carry multiple things at once or if they would need to bind items together with something first. Before he could ask, Riley retrieved what looked like a cookie sheet from one of her bags. She set it on the rocky ground and decompressed it with her VersaTool. The rectangle grew in size until it became large enough to park a minivan on. Riley began arranging their bags on it and Owen followed suit. Lastly, he placed his metal case gingerly beside his bags. Finn finished wringing out his socks and dumped the remaining water out of his boot.

With all of the bags loaded on the platform, Riley knelt down at one of the corners and opened a small access panel. Owen saw for a brief instant, a ghostly white mesh appear over the bags, like a virtual force field. He opened his mouth to ask about it, but it had already disappeared. Riley pressed another button and the platform rose into the air and stopped at her waist height. From the door of the access panel she removed a small black disc the size of a quarter, slid it into her pocket and closed the access panel.

Riley noticed Owen watching, in awe of something simple that she took for granted. "This is a Mule. It's a platform that carries heavy loads." She pulled the black disc out of her pocket and tossed it to him. The platform slid effortlessly toward him and stopped just out of his reach. "This is a proximity leash. The Mule will always stay within a couple of arm lengths of it. If I keep this in my pocket, the Mule will follow me around." She took the disc back from him, slid it into her pocket and demonstrated by taking several steps forward. The platform obediently moved through the air and stopped behind her.

"The white flash you saw was the netting force field. Keeps everything anchored to the platform. Try to pull something off."

Owen grabbed the corner of his duffel bag and pulled, but it would not budge, like it had been glued in place. "Amazing!"

"You can disguise it, as well." She opened the access panel again and pressed another button. All of the bags looked like they had been covered by a canvas tarp. She hit another button and the tarp disappeared, once again revealing the load. Finn joined them, his footwear wrung out but still wet, and the trio began their trek toward the camp.

Jake left Mole Control to get a fresh cup of coffee. He was pleased that the team's lucky streak had not ended with the storm that destroyed the medical room. For nearly a month and a half, the Moles' performance had exceeded his admittedly low expectations. Mole2 had been chewing away in the tunnel for a record amount of time with no problems and Mole1 waited, ready to be deployed should anything go wrong. Morale around the camp was at an all-time high. The team had grown close, including Clint. Although he avoided Maya, he had done away with the sexist remarks, and the group had come to appreciate his intelligence and contributions despite his complicated personality. Individual friendships also grew; Darren and Maya spent considerable time together as a result of the overlap in their responsibilities. Ben and Tyler spent most of their time together in the shed doing repairs, maintenance or organizing when things were slow. Clint split his time between Mole Control and in the shed helping Ben and Tyler, though he preferred to spend most of his time in the cramped control room of the active Mole. Tyler and Clint's relationship remained frosty—it had never fully repaired after the incident in the first few days when Clint had accidentally hit Lexi. They worked amicably together and Jake was satisfied with that arrangement. Despite their personality conflicts, they found a way to work together and that was as much as Jake knew he could ask for. Lexi and Jake spent most of their time in Mole Control. Boredom, although appreciated, had also reached an all-time high around the camp. Clint had gone on several hunting trips—most unsuccessful except for another deer and several rabbits. A well-travelled path now connected the camp to the lake; on balmy days when things went exceptionally smoothly, the team would kick off early and spend time down by the water. The team's progress had advanced ahead of schedule and Jake ensured his team balanced work with leisure while they could afford the luxury.

As Jake carried his coffee to Mole Control, movement at of the corner of his eye caught his attention, and he saw a group of people approaching the camp.

"Riley," he called out, as the newcomers entered the grounds. Jake knew Riley mostly by reputation. They had been deployed on several ops together over the last few years, though they had never worked side by side. While her team lived at the heart of the action, he was usually stationed at the temporary base or came in at the end to salvage what they had not destroyed. Although their relationship was little better than acquaintances, he had heard enough about her to know that she was an asset to any team.

Riley shook Jake's hand firmly. "Good to see you." She looked around the camp. "This place looks great." Riley introduced Finn then Owen, their souvenir from the past. "So how's it been going?"

"Oh, pretty good so far. I definitely can't complain. A few hiccups here and there but we're well ahead of schedule."

After a brief tour, Riley, Finn and Owen were shown their living quarters. Riley left Owen with a discreet wink and walked away with Jake for a briefing. Riley was eager to be brought up to speed on Team One's progress—how their leap back went, how long it took to get set up and the setbacks they had experienced. Likewise, Jake was equally interested in learning how they planned to neutralize the Elevanium.

With Riley and Jake in the meeting room, Maya gave Owen and Finn an orientation of the camp. Over lunch, the teams got acquainted. The members of Team One were horrified to hear about Owen's home being intentionally blown up and the attack by the river. Maya reminded the group of the Elevanium curse and instead of dismissing it readily as they had in the past, everyone chewed in silence.

Jake and Riley emerged from the meeting room as the rest of the group finished lunch. Jake grabbed a sandwich and an apple off the counter and took Riley, Finn and Owen to the drill site. They traversed the decline, careful to give a dump bucket a wide berth as it passed. The rumbling sounds echoed up the tunnel and the vibrations beneath them became more pronounced as they approached the Mole. Jake hopped up the steps to the platform, opened the door to the control room and tapped Clint on the shoulder. Clint shut the machine down and emerged from the Mole and more introductions followed. Clint's reception of the new team was chilly, as if he had not yet warmed up to the idea of outsiders in his territory.

Owen knew from Riley's briefing that Clint's expertise was in mining and excavation and looked forward to hearing about his experiences.

"How's it been down here?" Owen asked Clint. "Doesn't look like you've had any bursts or collapses? I know this whole region is vulnerable to instability at times." Owen turned his attention to the curved wall and he ran his hand across its surface. He read the lines in the stone, wavy from the weight above compressing it over billions of years.

Clint enjoyed talking to someone who seemed to actually know what he was talking about. Most of the people on this operation were taken from other areas and put on the team not because they were educationally qualified but because they were willing. He shook his head in response to Owen's question. "No, nothing yet. We're not really going down too deep, plus we've got safety features for stability, so I'm expecting we'll get through it without any problems."

Jake gathered both teams in the main tent.

"Okay, listen up everyone," said Jake. "As you know, we've been joined by Team Two, which means we have just less than 100 days until the timeshift. As you know, we're ahead of schedule and it's a beautiful day. Let's take the afternoon off and have some fun. Tomorrow we'll have a more formal meeting and recap our progress."

While Riley would have preferred to jump right into her work, she deferred to Jake's judgement. From what Jake had explained to her, his team got off to a rough start and he wanted to make sure the groups integrated well before putting the team under any strain.

Riley and Owen took up the rear as the group wound their way to the lake.

"Do you feel like a fish out of water?"

Owen laughed. "That's one way of putting it."

"I'd say that's a reasonable feeling. You've been taken to the past by people from the future. It doesn't get much weirder than that."

"I'm not too worried about that," laughed Owen. "What does worry me is that I don't foresee us getting a lot of alone time while we're here."

The path opened up to a clearing beside the lake and people had begun to settle into their lakeside routines. Set back from the shore in the grass, Lexi lay on her stomach tanning with her bikini top undone. Maya's book lay open on her lap, but she chatted with Darren while Ben, Tyler, Clint and Finn kicked off their shoes and stripped down to their swimming shorts at the water's edge. The smooth, rocky shore sloped gradually into the water making access easy for a swimmer wanting to get in and out. A little way down the shore, the rocky ledge immediately rose skyward, creating a sheer vertical cliff at the water's edge. Finn sprinted up the rocky incline, careful not to step on the hard, prickly lichen growing on the rock. He climbed up the steep slope, grabbing at small bushes for balance and steering clear of the vertical edge to his right that plunged straight into the water several storeys below.

"This place is perfect," said Finn. He looked out over the water as he reached the top, then looked down. "How deep is the water here?"

"Right below you there's a short ledge thirty feet down, then it drops off after that. We checked it before we jumped the first time," said Tyler.

Finn looked down over his shoulder at Riley. "You comin'?"

"Hah!" Clint snorted. "She won't do it."

Riley glanced at Clint, certain she misheard, then turned to Owen. "You going?"

"Of course," said Owen, kicking off his shoes and pulling his shirt over his head.

Riley unlaced her shoes, slid out of her pants and pulled off her t-shirt, revealing a black racer back bikini top and boy-cut shorts.

Ben jumped as Riley neared the top and they heard the splash below. She looked over the cliff's edge to see Ben resurface. She yelled down to him. "How's the water?"

"Bloody cold," His voice was an octave higher than normal.

Riley dove with perfect form into the water. When she surfaced, she swam out of the way and treaded water alongside Ben and waited for the others to jump. Owen flourished his dive with a somersault. Finn jumped next, far less gracefully; his arms and legs flailing as he plummeted toward the chilly water. Tyler followed Finn and both their heads appeared at the surface at the same time.

Only Clint remained at the top of the cliff, his nerve apparently lost. The five bobbing heads called to him, cheering him on and coaxing him to jump. He stepped forward to the cliff's edge, looked at the water then walked backward to take a running start. He took a long step forward, then stopped abruptly. He rolled his shoulders and bounced his weight from one foot to the other, psyching himself up. He looked over the water, stood frozen for several moments and then stormed into the forest behind.

Jake relaxed on the shore fully-clothed and content to watch the glistening lake. Darren and Maya played Frisbee in the water while the others now played touch football in the grassy clearing. Had this been several months ago he would have been listening to music, but he no longer needed the crutch of white noise. His frank and open friendship with Lexi had been the tonic he needed to loosen the stranglehold of pain and survivor's guilt he felt. The quiet no longer haunted him as it had in the past.

Jake's thoughts were cut short when he heard someone calling his name.

"Jake, come play. We're getting crushed here. We need an advantage." Lexi waved for him to join them. Her blond hair was pulled into a messy ponytail and she personified summer in a string bikini top and short denim cut-offs. Used to seeing her in baggy, oversized uniforms, Jake marvelled at her tiny frame.

"Where's Clint?" he asked.

"I don't know," she shrugged. "But when he shows up, we'll take him too!"

Despite Clint's improved behaviour, Jake feared he may revert to his old ways. He worried about the frosty reception Clint gave Team Two. It would only take a few negative comments for Clint to undo all the goodwill he had built with the others. Worse still, Riley Morgan was not a lead to test.

The football game had long since ended when Clint reappeared, surprising the group by swimming up from across the bay. He ran his hands through his wet, strawberry blond hair as he walked up the rocky incline out of the water.

"Where did you come from?" asked Riley. Riley knew from Jake's briefing that there had been some integration problems with Clint, especially where women were concerned.

"There's a neat cave on the other side of the bay." He looked up at the cliff where they had jumped earlier. "I think I'm going to take another crack at that cliff."

Riley followed Clint up the hill and looked back at Jake, her single raised eyebrow asking if he would join them. Jake shook his head and laughed as if the question itself was ludicrous.

Finn jumped up. "I'm in." He and Owen followed Riley up the rocky hill.

Standing at the top of the cliff next to Riley, Clint hesitated before jumping in.

"Don't think. Just jump," she offered casually. He shot her a disdainful look, then jumped. Riley dove in immediately after Clint had surfaced. Clint swam to shore not waiting for the others.

"Well, I need to get dinner started," said Darren. He stood up and gave his towel a shake before tossing it into his bag. He slid into his foamy clogs and brushed some grass and dirt from his shorts. A tattoo of a 1950s pin-up girl covered his right calf. She stood seductively in front of a stove wearing nothing but a skimpy apron, holding a spatula and looking like there was nothing she would rather do than fry bacon naked while wearing red stilettos.

"I'll give you a hand," said Maya, and she began to collect her things.

"I think I'm going to head back too. I want to get set up so we can jump right in tomorrow," said Riley.

Finn yawned as he stood. "I'll give you a hand."

Clint eyed Riley icily as she tied her shoes. Finn noticed Clint appraising her. "Everything alright, Mate?"

"What's it like having to work with Super Bitch over there?" Clint looked at Finn with an expression of camaraderie, like he was a brother who had also endured the tyranny of a female lead and understood Finn's suffering.

Finn, confused and convinced he had misheard, looked over at Riley as she wrung out her hair. "Riley? Oh, she's great."

Clint's expression blanked. "Oh. I see. You must be doin' her then, eh? She's a real piece of work."

Finn expected a punch line or something that would explain Clint's joke, instead he stood perplexed as Clint walked away.

By the end of dinner, the group talked like old friends instead of new acquaintances. Riley noticed that whatever resentment Clint seem to harbour earlier in the day had disappeared. The group continued to laugh and converse over glasses of wine around the fire pit beside Mole Control. After quizzing Owen for nearly an hour about what it was like to live in 2016, they reminisced about what they missed most. Darren missed the sounds of the city and his friends, whereas Maya yearned for the gym and chocolate macaroons. Lexi missed her pug, Trout, and could not understand why everyone found her dog's name so ridiculous. Ben missed his car and cruising on Sunday nights. Riley could not think of anything that she missed. Always out on ops or preparing for ops, she had no time to do something she would ever miss. In the end, she chose her grandfather for which she was booed because missing family went without saying. Finn said that he missed late night hot dog stands. Jake sat back in his usual silence, taking everything in. What Jake craved most had nothing to do with being away on an op. Owen said that he had only been gone a day, so there was nothing he missed yet, though he suspected he would soon miss his work and friends. When Tyler mentioned that he missed the Nexus and the creature comforts that came with it, like TV, email and his favourite online hangouts, everyone groaned in agreement. The group then began to lament about how at some point they had gone to their CI to find something, only to remember their most valuable tool in life was as useful as a doorstop.

CHAPTER 35

Owen closed the door to his living quarters and pulled on his sweater. The night had grown stormy and he could hear the wind whipping around outside the WeatherShield. After the heat of the afternoon, he assumed the weather would turn bad. Some of the biggest thunderstorms he had ever experienced had followed hot, picture-perfect days. He looked up at the sky and saw nothing. No stars, no moon. Owen found the WeatherShield difficult to get used to; it seemed unnatural to be outdoors and to hear the wind and rain but not feel it. Walking back to the fire, he saw a darkened figure standing in the trees just outside the edge of the camp. Owen chuckled. If it were he who needed to relieve himself after a couple of drinks, he would have at least walked a little deeper into the forest. He sat back down at the fire again and gazed into the hypnotizing flames. After a moment, his trance broke at the sound of raised voices on the other side of the fire. Tyler and Clint's political discussion had become heated.

"Okay, guys. No more politics," said Lexi. She speared a marshmallow with a stick and handed it to Tyler.

Riley had taken to most of Jake's team immediately. Lexi reminded her of herself when she was younger—driven and enthusiastic. Maya was a sweetheart and Ben, like Jake, was few on words but very observant and insightful. Clint was the hardest to read. She watched him intently over dinner; now, after a few drinks, his behaviour began to flip-flop from hot to cold like a broken tap. While cheery through dinner, he had again become moody. His comments bordered on childish and were so petty that to say something seemed equally trivial. The group seemed to be accustomed to this behaviour and she followed their lead and ignored it. The casual nature of the op was intentional as to combat burn-out as a result of being understaffed. Although Riley had never participated in an op with marshmallows and folding chairs, she knew with absolute certainty that Finn would know where to draw the line regarding appropriate conduct. She hoped Clint had the same sense.

Finn, as usual, fit in with everyone. His gregarious and approachable personality naturally drew people to him. He stabbed a marshmallow with a stick, leaned forward in his chair and challenged Lexi's marshmallow roasting prowess to a roast off. As Finn loosened up with a few drinks, the funnier he became. Riley noticed that this seemed to needle Clint; not even the fire could melt the icy glares he shot at Finn, who talked animatedly to Lexi and Tyler.

As the night progressed, the topic of conversation turned to stories about past memorable ops. Lexi and Tyler being fairly new, had no remarkable stories and listened raptly to everyone's experiences. Owen explained how he studied rocks and meteor craters and was unsurprised to hear crickets at his conclusion. Riley laughed at the straight faces waiting expectantly for the exciting part. Finn launched into one of the ops he and Riley had been on together. While the operation had actually been very routine, Finn was a master story-teller and had a way of making the mundane details seem like scenes from an action movie.

"And so Riley kicks in the door, and there was what, five?" Finn asked, looking at her for confirmation and she held up four fingers. "Okay. Four, massive, burly men standing on the other side pointing their guns at us, standing between us and the hostages. We were pretty much out of ammo after blasting our way through the cargo bay and all we had left were our runty-ass plasmaqs. It was crazy. Riley had a plasmaq in each hand and took out two of them, kicked the third guy in the marble sack, and the fourth she cold-cocked with the butt of the gun. All four were on the ground before any of them knew what happened."

Owen made a mental note to ask Riley for a few more details about her work. He was getting the impression he may be sleeping with a contract killer.

"So what happened next?" Lexi asked, looking at Riley in awe. She sat on the edge of her seat and hung on every word.

"Nothing really, we rescued the hostages and got the hell out of there," said Riley.

Finn laughed. "Yeah, but not before setting the broken leg of one of the hostages, making a splint out of one of the terrorists' guns and shredding his pants to make ties for a splint. The guy still hadn't recovered from being kicked in the coin purse and you should have seen the look on his face when Riley walked up to him with a hunting knife the size of a goddamn machete. I thought his eyes were going to bulge out of his head!"

Riley rolled he eyes. "It wasn't as crazy at Finn makes it out to be." She tried to engage Clint, who had not spoken in over half an hour. "How about you Clint? Any unusual field stories?" she asked.

Clint ignored her and she asked the question again assuming his mind was elsewhere. Again he remained silent and stared at the fire. Jake leaned forward and waved his hand in front of Clint's face.

"What?" he asked.

"Riley was talking to you. Did you hear her?"

"I heard her, I just had nothing to say."

Ben rolled his eyes, recognizing the signs of an imminent Clint meltdown. He stood and tapped Clint on the shoulder. "Okay, let's go. I think we should end the night before we say something that we'll regret."

Clint looked up at him innocently. "What? I didn't do anything. I can't help it if she's got a problem with something I didn't say."

Riley had never encountered a sub with such erratic behaviour. Although he was Jake's sub, she outranked him by four levels and that meant something. She suspected that this may be his beef with her and his resentment toward Finn resulted from their solid relationship. She was grateful that Jake took charge. She did not want to get involved in Team One's dynamics, let alone on their first day.

"On your feet." Jake barked and Clint took his time standing up. "Riley is your lead and you'd best remember that."

"Respectfully sir, she's not my lead, you're my lead." The light of the fire did not play well off Clint's defiant expression.

"We're both your leads, so show some respect," Jake growled. He was both infuriated and embarrassed that he needed to explain this.

"Fuck this." Clint threw the stick he had been poking the fire with onto the ground and strode into the forest. The team watched in silence as he disappeared into the darkness.

Tyler shook his head; he clearly wanted to say something but thought better of it. Instead, he stood and stretched. "Well, I think I'm done for the night. Another fantastic night comes to an awkward end, thanks to Clint." He left the group and moments later they heard his trailer door slam. The rest of the team sat in silence and listened to the wind and rain outside the protective bubble.

Owen broke the silence. "How does the perimeter alarm work? Is it only on at night?"

"No, it's a twenty-four/seven thing," supplied Ben, grateful for the change of topic.

"So how come it doesn't go off when we walk through it, like when we all left and went to the lake?"

"The system is preprogrammed with your DNA, so it doesn't trigger the alarm," Ben explained. "The system was preloaded with Finn and Riley's DNA. We entered yours when you arrived. Jake saw you guys coming and I had the system scan your DNA when you stepped through the invisible barrier and then added it to the 'allowable' category." Owen was intrigued as Ben explained the finer details about the perimeter system's data analysis modules like facial recognition or general health analysis, all of which were unnecessary due to the isolated nature of the camp.

Without notice, the fire moved abnormally, like a gust of wind caught it. Jake felt rain drops on his head and stood as rain and wind poured into the camp. Leaves blew past them and one stuck to Riley's side as she, like the others, stood and looked around in alarm.

Jake took control. "Darren, Maya, put out the fire then hit your trailers. Finn, Lexi, check Mole Control and see what's malfunctioning. Riley, Ben, Owen come with me."

It seemed to Owen that everyone was getting a little bent out of shape over a bit of rain. However, if he had learned anything from the time he had spent with Riley and Finn, it was that there was a lot about the future he knew nothing about.

Jake instructed Ben, Owen and Riley to fan out and walk and inspect the camp's perimeter for anything abnormal. The search revealed nothing. They joined Lexi and Finn in Mole Control to see if anything had been registered by the sensors. They were all surprised to learn two of the WeatherShield sensors were offline and one was terminated. With nothing to be done until morning, everyone went to their respective trailers for the night.

TIME REMAINING: 97 Days

Jake woke at the crack of dawn determined to get to the bottom of the WeatherShield incident. He checked where the sensors should have been, but as Lexi had reported, they were gone—ripped from the ground. A third sensor lay in pieces. As he picked up the pieces, Jake wondered how this could have happened. All of the team members were sitting around the fire when the system went down, except for Tyler and Clint. The only three explanations Jake had so far were Tyler, Clint or something else. When Tyler left, everyone heard his door close. Clint, on the other hand, walked into the forest. Jake knew both these points were circumstantial. Tyler could have just as easily left his trailer with no one knowing. Unfortunately for Clint, the events of the evening and the reputation he had established as being difficult did not work in his favour. Tyler's quiet, hardworking nature made him less of a suspect, but it did not eliminate him. Clint, conversely, had repeatedly alienated everyone. Because he could not prove it was Clint or Tyler, he could not rule out some alternative explanation.

Jake took the broken sensor to the work shed and found Ben searching through crates for more sensors to get the WeatherShield back up and running. He emerged from the back of the shed holding two matching stakes.

"Bad news, boss," he said. "We've only got two backup sensors."

"Well, I've got good news and bad news. Good news is that I found one of them. The bad news is, it's the broken one." Jake set pieces on the workbench.

Ben looked over the pieces of the broken sensor. "If we don't find at least one of those sensors, we don't have the WeatherShield anymore. We need a minimum of six."

Riley came into the shed. "Jake, can I have a word?"

Jake nodded appreciatively. Ben sensed he should find something to do elsewhere and left the shed. When the door had closed behind him, Jake filled Riley in on the sensor situation, but Riley had more interest in the Clint situation.

"I have no patience for anyone who undermines a team," said Riley, matter-of-factly. "It's dangerous and unfair to the people who work hard around him and I won't tolerate it. I'll help you try to keep him functioning as part of the team, but if I get attitude like that again, he's going to find himself restricted and possibly in court when he returns."

Jake was unsurprised by Riley's reaction. In her line of work there was no room for egos or poor attitudes. Otherwise, people got killed. He suspected that if Riley broke into Finn's trailer in the dead of night, kicked him out of a deep sleep and told him to drop and give her fifty pushups, he would roll directly onto the floor, no questions asked. The legendary Riley Morgan had been on more ops than most old-timers; an old-timer being about thirty-eight in her line of work. She was decorated and had levelled up higher and faster than most people her age. Rightfully so—she was an excellent leader, known for highly effective teams, a zero-percent failure rate and an even lower tolerance for bullshit. Her subordinates were highly-trained human weapons, trained to follow orders with no hesitation. The operations Jake supervised were never the high-risk, life-or-death ops that Riley executed. This accounted for their differences in leadership style. Many of his subs were new, fresh out of the academy. Mechanical and Infrastructure Recovery was a good first op for new subs to cut their teeth on. As a result, Jake had become a master of organizing chaos and was sympathetic to bumbling, under-confident subs.

Jake found Clint sitting alone in the dining room eating a bowl of cereal and he sat down across from him. Clint did not look like the moody and angry guy he had been the night before and the thought occurred to Jake that he might have a problem with alcohol. His mood swings seemed far more pronounced after several drinks. Jake opened his mouth to talk, but Clint beat him to it.

"I know what you're going to say. I'm sorry. I'm sorry I'm difficult sometimes. I just get frustrated with people."

Jake took advantage of the opening. "I'm seeing a pattern here, Clint. This behaviour is becoming a problem and we can't afford another outburst like that. And Riley Morgan is not someone you want to test."

"What do you mean 'we'?"

"You can't afford to alienate everyone more than you already have, and I can't afford to have you benched for the rest of this op. We need your expertise in that tunnel. That's why you were picked for this op."

"With all due respect, sir, don't bullshit me," said Clint. "I wasn't hand-picked because of my expertise, I was one of the few idiots that applied."

Sick of the drama at every turn, Jake laid out his expectations of Clint's behaviour. Clint apologized again and sat silent, pushing his sogging cereal around the bowl. He spoke after a few moments.

"What happened to the WeatherShield?"

"There's two sensors missing and one is broken beyond repair." Jake felt as though he and Clint had found a balance and he did not want to disrupt it by making it seem like he was accusing Clint of something. Assumptions? He had a few. Gut feelings? Yes. Irrefutable proof? Not a shred. "I was hoping you would be able to tell me if you saw anything unusual last night."

Clint stood up quickly and bumped the table. Milk and soggy corn flakes sloshed out of the bowl. "You think I did it? Just because I wasn't under your thumb when it happened, you think it was me? Well, I didn't. I went for a walk up the shoreline. I was so pissed at all of you I wandered for two goddamn hours before I turned around. You can ask Ben. I came back to the trailer around three in the morning."

"Clint," Jake stood slowly and spoke firmly, "I'm not accusing you of anything. Tyler wasn't there when the system went down either and I've already asked him these same questions. I just wanted to know if you saw anything unusual."

"Oh." Clint's voice returned to conversational volume. "Well, now that you mention it, when I was north of the camp, I thought I saw someone skulking outside the boundary. I assumed it was one of you guys looking for me, but I didn't feel like being found." He left his bowl and spoon on the table for Darren to clean up.

Jake tried to avoid being judgemental, but he found Clint's story disturbing. It seemed as though Clint had devised a flimsy story to deflect suspicion. However, with no physical proof, Jake's hands were tied. Innocent until proven guilty.

CHAPTER 36

TEAM 3
YEAR: 2095
TIME REMAINING: 96 Days

"I guess word got out that I was making progress on the artificial vision," said Asher. He slid his tray onto the cafeteria table and sat down heavily across from his brothers.

"What?" Logan looked scandalized. "How did that happen?"

"I might have let something slip." Asher opened his chocolate milk and smiled. "Okay, I demoed it to my boss."

"What did he think?" Logan was thrilled for Asher's achievement and he swallowed the pang of jealousy he felt. That being said, he would trade no amount of success for the little side project he was working on with Delaney.

Asher shrugged nonchalantly. "He seemed impressed. He wants me to present it to the board."

"That's amazing," said Spencer. "Congratulations!"

None of this was news to Spencer, but he acted surprised for his brother's benefit. Asher's director had come to the last directors' meeting barely able to contain himself; Asher's breakthrough would revolutionize not only the AEI Project, but also the roles robots played in societies around the world. Although Asher was unaware, Spencer knew his brother would be presenting not only to the NRD board but to AEI private stakeholders and NRD bigwigs flying in from all over the country. It would be only a matter of days before word would leak into the world of robotics—if it had not already—that some guy at the NRD had accomplished what so many people had attempted and failed. Spencer was genuinely happy for this brother—he had told the twins for years that hard work truly paid off and this was proof.

With the excitement of Asher's news over, Spencer then brought them up to speed on his latest failed attempt to convince Ian to allow him to create better tests.

"And, I've scheduled the Personality Application Demo in the Burton Auditorium with the board, directors and stakeholders for the day of the timeshift. I like this plan. I think it's a natural fit…"

The brothers changed the topic as several of Asher's co-workers sat down beside them.

TIME REMAINING: 88 Days

Kalen yawned as she walked into Spencer's office. As usual, Spencer was engrossed in a document on his screen.

"I've just finished programming the Real Life Simulator with Ian's last testing scenario," said Kalen. "It's ready to run in the lab; we just have to initiate it." She sat on the corner of his desk, her body cutting into Spencer's projected screen.

"That's excellent Kale, you're unbelievable." Spencer stood and kissed her on the forehead. "I don't know what I would do without you."

"Well, don't get me wrong. I like to help, but I'm really doing this because if I don't, I'll never see you."

Spencer chuckled, shut down his CI and slid it into his messenger bag. "I know. I'm sorry. I've been a lousy boyfriend. Let's fire up the RLS and get out of here." He looked around the office through his clear glass walls and saw no one. He dipped her backward, nearly pulling her off his desk, and kissed her. "Let's go on a date."

"Sounds good. But don't you want to wait and see the results? I know you've been dying to see them."

Spencer hesitated for a moment, enticed by the thought. He wanted to see the results more than anything, but it would be hours before there would be any results to report. Kalen had already sacrificed too much of her time for his work. He wanted some time together where he could put her first. He took her hand and kissed it. "I think it's time I spent some time with my best friend."

TIME REMAINING: 87 Days

"Well Spence, I'm not saying that I didn't believe you before, but you sure were right about these test results," said Lisa. She shook her head in disbelief.

Kalen, Erik and Lisa stood before one of the Neural Programming lab's enlarged CI screens as Spencer scrolled through the RLS's summary reports for the personalities.

"They're perfect. They're all one hundred percent perfect," said Erik, shaking his head. "There's no way this can be accurate. According to these results, these robots will barely get agitated."

"This doesn't make sense. I mean, everyone gets angry or loses control at some point. People experience way more emotions than what these tests indicate. Who's going to identify with a robot who doesn't get upset?" She looked at the screen sceptically, then pointed. "Oh my gosh! Look at that one. Apparently she doesn't get mad ever! How is that natural?"

"What do you expect when the most anger-provoking situation you test a personality with is, *'When someone accidently takes your seat at a hockey game.'*"

"So what happens when a robot has a disagreement with a co-worker over something?" asked Lisa.

"Or if someone does something malicious to a robot?" asked Erik.

"Or tries to decommission a robot?" asked Kalen.

All eyes stared at Spencer. He shrugged. "I don't know. Ian felt that wasn't worth finding out. Morally, I can't let these robots go out into the world without knowing the answers to those questions."

"What are you going to do?" asked Kalen.

"Well, I'm going to have to do this all over again. But this time, I'll have to come up with some realistic, stress-inducing, real-life scenarios that humans face in life. Then, I'll have to program them into the RLS then run the personalities again."

"Spencer, there's no way you can do this on your own," said Kalen. "It will take you months. Plus, Ian will eat you for lunch if he finds out. I'm going to help you with this."

"So am I," said Lisa.

Spencer cut them off. "None of you guys will help because if we get caught, you'll all lose your jobs. I'm pretty sure Ian's going to fire me after this project anyway. I think I've irritated him to the point that the damage is done. I think he would have done it already if we had more staff. We might as well have only one destroyed career instead of four."

"Spence, these results are laughable. I can't stand by and do nothing. If I did, that would make me as bad as Ian. I'm helping and you can't stop me," said Kalen with a defiant edge in her voice.

"Me too," said Lisa

Erik smiled. "Alright, alright. I'll help too. Stop begging already."

Spencer knew there was no point arguing and he was grateful for their help; he knew he would need it. It felt good to finally have proof of what he had been saying all along, but at the same time, he felt deceitful and dishonest, like he had enlisted them as pawns in his mission.

"So what do we need to do?" asked Erik.

"Well, before I do anything, I should try talking to Ian one more time. If I can't get through to him, I'll take the results to a directors' meeting. They're smart; they'll see the same pitfalls you guys did and draw the same conclusions. With the other directors seeing the light, Ian will have no choice but to agree or look unreasonable."

"From what I hear about Ian these days, hoping he'll see logic is a big, fat 'if,'" said Erik, who launched into some gossip about Ian not showing up for meetings.

TIME REMAINING: 84 Days

Spencer knocked on Ian's office door. His memory flashed back to the scene in the parkade and wondered if today's conversation would cause another impromptu parking lot meeting.

"What's up, Spencer?" Ian's greetings grew increasingly chilly with each visit Spencer made to his office.

"Sir, I was wondering if you had a chance to put any thought into the testing criteria I'd mentioned. I've had a chance to think more about it and I know that after you see the…"

Ian slammed his pen down on the desk and stood up. He looked livid. "Spencer, is this what you've been doing for over a month? This isn't even up for debate. Is this job too much for you? Perhaps you should just continue your regular job and I'll take over for Jim if it's too much for you."

Spencer's anger bubbled to the surface. He had lost his respect for Ian long before the conception of Operation TimeShift, and his ability to hide it diminished with each encounter he had with the man. "Ian, I have proof that these personalities could have serious problems."

"Can you predict the future Spencer?"

Predict it? No. Lived it? Yes. Spencer thought. "No, sir, of course not."

"Then I strongly suggest you continue as prescribed by the project plan and not deviate from it any further. People far smarter and brighter than you have come up with these testing scenarios. They're more than adequate. You are not nearly qualified to judge what is or isn't appropriate. That's why we hired professionals to develop it."

"Sir, if I could just leave my report with you…" Spencer took a step forward to put the paper report on his desk but stopped when Ian stepped out from behind his desk.

"Spencer. Get out of my office and stay out of my sight because seeing you only makes me think more about demoting you."

Spencer shook his head and chuckled. He had given Ian more than enough chances to listen to logic. He had no more time to waste talking to a brick wall. "Whatever you'd like, sir."

TIME REMAINING: 53 Days

"Hey, gorgeous." Logan strode into Delaney's office, walked behind her desk and leaned in for a kiss.

"Logan! What are you doing?" She caught his face in her hand, squeezing his cheeks and pushed him away. She admonished him half-heartedly. "People might see."

"Don't worry, everyone's gone," he reassured her. He spun her hover chair sideways to kiss her, but she kicked off on the floor and floated effortlessly out of his reach. She knew everyone had left, but she could not afford to take the chance of someone returning.

"Windows. Tint. Ninety percent." Nothing happened. He looked around. "What the hell?"

"The room is configured to my voice only," she laughed. "It's a security thing. So if someone's going to rifle through my office, they can't hide."

Logan sat down in the chair opposite her desk, knowing he had been beaten, and watched as she finished up her work.

Delaney marvelled at how her life had changed so drastically in three short months. She was working less, enjoying life and in a relationship—a relationship with one of her employees, no less. Inter-office relationships were generally discouraged, but if Human Resources was informed, the NRD was pretty good about looking the other way.

Logan felt happier than he could ever remember being. Delaney brought an excitement and passion to his life that had been lacking in previous relationships. She was smart, she had substance and she kept him in line, which made him feel focused.

But over the past several weeks, he felt something weighing down his happiness—a nagging feeling in the back of his mind. It grew quite unexpectedly and soon he knew he had a problem. Not because she was his boss and not because she was seven years his senior, but because he was not who she thought he was. He was the same person, but not the same version of himself that he was leading her to believe. In some way, he felt like he was lying to her.

As his feelings for her increased, the nagging feeling blossomed into full-blown guilt. He could never shake the feeling he was keeping a bombshell of a secret from her, and he began to worry about what would happen at the end of the op. Never in a million years would he have guessed that the night of intensity that followed their Chinese food dinner at the office would turn into the best relationship he had ever had. What would the past version of himself on vacation in Australia think about this? Would his past-self pick up the proverbial ball where he, the future Logan, left it? Would he even want to? They were, of course, the same person. But at the same time, they were very different. What would happen when he went back to the future? Would they still be dating? What if the change was catastrophic and for some reason she was not part of his life?

Logan snapped out of his thoughts to see Delaney waving a hand in front of his face. "Hey!" She smiled him. "Where'd you go just now?"

"Sorry, I was just thinking about that little outfit you had on the other night." He looked at his watch. "Shit, we're going to be late for Asher's demo." He jumped out of his chair.

"Well, it's not like we have to go far." She slid her CI into her bag, slung the bag over her shoulder and followed Logan out of her office.

As they walked through the abandoned Motor Skills lab, Logan discreetly grabbed her hand and squeezed it before they entered the main hallway. "We're heading to Asher's place after for a few celebratory drinks if you're interested," he whispered.

Delaney hesitated. "I'll think about it. I don't really want to advertise this. It could be problematic for us at work."

"It's just the family. My parents are flying in especially for this."

Delaney looked sideways at Logan. "Logan Grayson, are you asking me to meet your parents?"

Logan mulled over her words. It occurred to him that they had never had the, "Where is this relationship going?" discussion, or even talked about how serious the relationship had become. They had never needed to—they were both only interested in each other. "Uh, yeah. I guess that's exactly what I'm asking. And on the point of work, why don't we just go to HR and fill out the disclosure papers?"

"You want to fill out all kinds of embarrassing forms that announce our private lives to the entire office?"

"Well, no, that part isn't too appealing, but if it means we can go out in public and I can hold your hand..." He stopped talking as someone passed them walking the opposite direction. "It would be worth it."

"You don't have a problem telling the world you're dating an older woman?"

He stopped dead and looked at her with a deadpan expression. "Whoa, wait. Are you older than me?"

Laughing, Delaney pinched his side and continued walking.

He flashed her a reassuring smile. "Don't be silly. Plus, you look way younger than me anyway."

They reached the doors to the Burton Auditorium. He grabbed her hand discreetly, gave it one last squeeze before letting go, then entered first.

Logan walked ahead and met up with Spencer, their parents and Kalen in the front row. Delaney took her seat with the other directors several rows back.

Asher flawlessly demonstrated his technology to the packed auditorium. People stood at the back and spilled into the aisles. Once the robotic science community found out that the mystery of artificial vision had been cracked, the NRD switchboard crashed with the number of calls from people willing to pay to attend.

Asher received a standing ovation, but he hung around to answer more questions even after the event had ended. Before leaving the Burton Auditorium that evening, he had been not-so-discreetly handed twelve business cards from private companies interested in hiring him.

Asher arrived at his condo to cheers and clapping from his parents, Spencer and Kalen. His mother pulled him into a backbreaking hug. "You're so smart Ashey! I've told you for years that if you just put your mind to something you can do whatever you want!"

"Thanks for that vote of confidence Mom. I thought I was doing alright before that, but it's nice to know my own mother thought I was mediocre," laughed Asher.

"Hah! I think 'mediocre' is being generous," said Spencer, unwrapping the foil from a bottle of champagne. Kalen elbowed him in the side.

Their father gave him a hearty handshake, "Congrats Ash, I was really proud of you up there." Jason Grayson had an appreciation for what his sons did as the Defence Liaison to Research for New Technology Integration. Like his sons, he shared their interest in technology. "It was fascinating to see the technology from a raw, R&D perspective like that. It gives me a new appreciation for the development aspect of all the devices and tools we've used in the NRD over the years."

"Knock knock," said Logan, poking his head in the front door. "I brought someone with me, I hope that's alright," he said tentatively. The room fell silent in surprise. While it was no secret the twins had done their fair share of dating, never had either of them brought a woman to a family event.

"Well, of course it is!" said his mother, an excited smile growing on her face. She rushed to the door to greet Logan's guest. Logan opened the door the rest of the way and Delaney walked in, smiling nervously.

Spencer popped the cork from the champagne bottle and the sound of it hitting the ceiling echoed across the silent room.

"Well, I'll be damned," said Asher.

Unbeknownst to one another, Spencer shared Logan's concerns about his relationship and the timeshift. It became apparent to Spencer after seeing Logan and Delaney together that this relationship was significant to Logan. Later in the evening when the beer ran low, Logan went to his condo to grab another case. Spencer offered to help and followed him into the kitchen. In the quiet of Logan's condo, Spencer asked him if he had thought about his relationship and the timeshift. Prepared for a sarcastic, flippant answer, he was nearly struck dumb when Logan confessed his genuine concerns.

They shared their fears of not knowing what the future would hold when they returned, and the feeling of deceit from withholding the truth from their significant others. Spencer knew that the past version of himself would be over the moon to find out he was dating Kalen—he had been enchanted by her on their first day of work together. He suspected that the reintegration to the workplace would be the most worrisome aspect for his past counterpart.

Asher meandered into Logan's kitchen to find his brothers talking. "Are we moving the party?" Asher asked.

Logan chuckled, "Nah. Just talkin'."

"It looks serious," noted Asher. He grabbed a beer from the case on the counter and twisted off the lid. "What about? World peace?"

"No, just about the future. About whether it's responsible to be dating and wondering what our past selves will think," said Logan.

Asher looked at Logan. "Dude, that's very deep." He sipped his beer. "Well, the past version of Spencer will be so ecstatic, he won't know what to do with himself. The past version of you, though…" Asher pointed the neck of his beer bottle at Logan and contemplated the scenario. "That'll be a shock. And, I'd like to be there when you tell him if that's alright. I'll even pay you. You too, Spence, those are some expressions I'd like to have permanently etched in my brain. But I have to ask the bigger question."

"What's that?" asked Logan. He could think of no question bigger than whether or not his past-self would be interested in taking over a relationship with his monster of a boss, and if he was a sick son of a bitch for even asking.

"How did a donkey like you manage to land a prize stallion like that?"

Logan laughed and shook his head, unsure of the answer himself.

"I, on the other hand, just hope that the past version of myself doesn't botch what I've done," said Asher. "If I get back to the future and find out that he's screwed it up, I'll personally come back in time and pound the crap out of him."

Spencer grabbed the case of beer off the counter. "We should probably get back there—Mom's probably telling the girls stories about us." Spencer and Logan shared a look and rushed out the door.

CHAPTER 37

TEAM 1 & 2
YEAR: 1200
TIME REMAINING: 50 Days

More than a month had passed since Riley, Owen and Finn joined Team One. Their arrival seemed to break the spell of productive days that had brought Team One intolerable boredom. The morning that followed the carefree day at the lake saw a multitude of challenges that would test even the most seasoned team. Within the first ten minutes of drilling, the power converter on Mole2 died. Like a well-oiled machine, Clint backed Mole2 out and handed it over to Ben, who waited at the entrance of the tunnel with Mole1, fully serviced and ready to run. By midafternoon, a kinked hydraulic line caused three of the four drive rods in the conveyor belt system to overheat and seize. All free hands from both teams spent nearly a week getting both Moles back into operating condition. Tyler, Lexi, Finn and Owen had Mole1 ready first, and Clint took it down the tunnel only for it to experience the exact failure. This time, all four rods seized. A closer inspection revealed that the hydraulic line Tyler had replaced had a weak wall—an undetected manufacturer's defect that caused the line to split after only three hours. The sensor that should have detected the overheating mechanisms had also malfunctioned and was reading incorrectly. Nearly a week and a half had passed before Mole1 was operational; Lexi inspected every sensor on both drills to ensure they were flagging the proper tolerances.

The repairs made to the Moles were slow going and bodies were spread thin around the camp. The Moles were not the only machines plagued with problems—nothing was safe from whatever blight had struck the camp. The fridge in Darren's kitchen stopped refrigerating. One of the perimeter sensors near the tunnel entrance was smashed by an errant Mole. With the WeatherShield not operational, a gust of wind grabbed the massive hovering drill as Clint tried to negotiate it out of the tunnel. The rear of the drill spun around and the bottom stair crushed one of the perimeter sensors against a large rock. Days later, an entire afternoon slowed to a near stop when the perimeter alarm alerted the team to a moose and her two young calves lunching on the grass in the centre of the camp. Lexi refused to allow anyone to move them, like they had the bears, for fear of broken limbs. No amount of scare tactics motivated the animals to leave. At Clint's mention of moose steaks, Lexi stormed into the work shed.

The relentless problems plaguing the team nearly drove Jake to madness. Every time he heard someone's voice cut into the communication system he cringed with dread, fearing the report of a new problem. He longed for the days of painful, inescapable boredom when the Moles ran on their own and required nothing but the occasional glance at a monitor and an ear to listen for any warning buzzers. Thankfully, Mole2 had now seen three days of action without a hint of a problem. The com-sys had been quiet except for the occasional report from Clint or one of Finn's colourful jokes. He listened to the hum of the drill through the monitoring screens and watched the activity taking place in the centre camp. Today was the first day that Team One had the opportunity to work on their project since arriving.

"Finn, haven't you got those guns set up yet? Are you giving them a pep talk or something?" asked Riley. She strode out of the work shed and into the middle of the clearing where she found Finn hunched over the testing tank, setting up the three guns side by side. Finn closed the lid on the testing tank and stepped back. He grinned at her.

"A pep talk never hurts, but no. I think we're ready for our inaugural test in the year 1200."

Owen joined Riley and Finn, pulling a hoodie on over his head. Riley looked down at the words on the front of the hooded sweater and groaned. "Geology Rocks."

"What? It's witty," grinned Owen, used to this reaction. The air was chilly and without the WeatherShield, the wind channeled down the centre of the camp.

Maya joined them. As usual, she carried her clipboard. As she approached them, she made a quick note and tucked it under her arm again.

"Don't you go anywhere without that thing?" asked Finn.

"Are you kidding me? This thing is my memory. I'd be lost without it. What are you guys up to?"

"Now that there are no more Mole emergencies," he held up his crossed fingers for her to see, "we can finally test the guns to make sure they survived our trip back." Finn took several steps backward, motioning for Maya to do the same. He used his VersaTool to increase the size of the testing tank and the guns to their full size. The tank grew to the size of a double-car garage.

"Whoa," breathed Maya. "Is that how big those guns normally are?"

Finn nodded as he peered into the tank. "Get ready. In three, two, one."

At one, Finn hit the red button on the remote control. Nothing happened. "Oh, God," said Finn under his breath. "It's not working. What the hell?" Finn looked up at the sky. "I mean, I know we're outdoors but the rays should still have been visible. Owen, check the scanner."

Owen held up the scanner to show no reading and Riley watched in silence as she fought the urge to be sick. They had not come all this way to have something happen during the time leap. There was so much about time travel that had yet to be learned.

Wool disintegrated during a time leap. The peels of bananas—as Finn discovered after this latest journey—shrunk to a quarter of their size but the flesh of the fruit remained the same.

Finn looked at Owen, his eyes frantic. Owen, too, felt sick, and wondered what could have possibly happened if they had survived the first leap in time. Nothing registered on the scanner. Finn hammered on the remote control frantically with the heel of his hand.

"Omigod, omigod, omigod!" cried Finn. He paced back and forth, running through the steps he took to set the guns up.

"What's wrong? Didn't it work?" asked Maya.

Owen looked at her and shook his head.

"Oh."

"It's alright," said Riley, sounding more confident than she felt. "We just need to look at the whole thing from beginning to end and see what's malfunctioning. No big deal. They worked after the first jump and not the second, so we've got a solid starting point. We've got more than enough spare parts and contingency plans, and, more than that, we've still got plenty of time to get to the bottom of this."

TIME REMAINING: 49 Days

The team had come to accept Finn as the camp practical joker. As he started to prepare dinner one afternoon, Darren found a small perch swimming in one of his pots. Maya searched for her clipboard for three days. Riddles posted around her and Lexi's trailer would have led her to it had she been able to solve Finn's cryptic messages. Ben spent two hours looking for his wrench set; each of the eight wrenches were hidden around the work shed and suspended playfully in bricks of colourful Jell-O. Riley opened the door to her trailer to find her bed filling the entire trailer. Blocked and unable to get in, she found a note pinned to the blanket. "Some things just never get old." All of Tyler's socks were filled with rocks and Clint found sand in his bed. Lexi caught Finn sneaking into her trailer with a giant toad and threatened to tell the camp about his junk food stash if he took one step closer to her.

"Sweet payback," laughed Tyler quietly as he looked out over the water at Finn and Owen's trailer. No one was immune to Finn's practical jokes, and now his victims stood united on the water's edge. They watched the suspended trailer, hovering nearly a storey above the lake. After a few moments, signs of life inside the trailer were heard. The conspirators on the shore chuckled quietly in anticipation. Within a few minutes, the door opened and Finn emerged, shielding his eyes from the bright morning sun. He stepped dozily out of the trailer and down the first step. Stepping down to what he thought was the ground, he fell unceremoniously and belly flopped into the water. It took him a few seconds to piece together what had happened. He looked up at the trailer and then over at his teammates howling with laughter on the shore.

"Owen!" yelled Finn, never wasting an opportunity. "Owen come out here quick!

Hurry!" The sound of the bed creaking was followed by hurried footsteps running the length of the trailer. Like Finn, Owen plunged into the water, flailing his arms as he fell.

Owen resurfaced and realized what had happened. He laughed and broke into an expert front crawl toward Finn. "Oh, you're dead!"

TIME REMAINING: 28 Days

"Hey, Owen?"

Owen set his screwdriver down on the workbench. "Yeah?" He was still not accustomed to the communication device seated inside his ear canal.

"It's Clint. I need you to come down here and take a look at this. I'm looking at the walls down here and I'm seeing there's some funny looking stress marks. I think you should take a look. Jake, Riley, maybe you guys, too?"

"Sure. I'll be right down."

"Let me know if you need anything," said Finn, who barely looked up from the cartridge clip he was disassembling.

"Just keep looking for whatever's causing these malfunctions and that will be extremely helpful," said Riley, as the door closed behind them.

As Riley and Owen jogged through the pouring rain past Mole Control, Jake joined them and the three sprinted down the well-worn path to the drill site. The wind whipped large rain drops into their faces like they were the targets of a child's water pistol campaign. Since the WeatherShield had gone offline, the weather seemed inclement every second day.

After months of drilling, the tunnel had become very long. The small strips of lighting affixed to the rocky ceiling lit their way in the dark depths. The tunnel seemed eerily quiet as they entered—the absence of the Mole's roaring engine or the heavy crushing sound of the drill head seemed ominous. At the bottom of the tunnel, Riley, Owen and Jake found Clint and Ben standing behind the Mole looking at the wall's curvature.

Jake and Riley fell in behind Clint and Ben, but Owen cut across everyone. He ran his hands across the wall's surface. While rough to the touch, the wall was uniform and not jagged. Owen's eyes followed the lines up the circular wall to the ceiling and took several steps back to see a bigger picture.

"Hmm," said Owen. His eyes moved from the ceiling to the opposite wall and then to the floor below them. After a moment, he walked back to the place to which Clint had first drawn his attention. Again, he ran his hands along the lines in the rock, as if they would deliver a message in stony braille. The tunnel fell silent, void of conversation while Owen analyzed the situation. The others watched expectantly, waiting for him to fill them in on what the rocks were telling him. After a few moments, he elaborated. "This looks pretty unstable. What are you using for reinforcements?"

Clint pointed to a little white disc on the floor near where the group stood, its diameter similar to that of a large coin. "Pressure shields. The Mole drills a hole and drops them in automatically. We've been using them for years and usually in bigger tunnels than this. They exert force against the walls of the tunnel. They keep the ceiling on the ceiling and the walls in the walls. We haven't received any report indicating instability, but I didn't trust these lines," said Clint, motioning to the rocky walls. "Thought I should maybe get a second opinion."

Owen stared down at the white, disc-shaped sensor, slightly recessed into the stone floor and barely visible through rock dust and small stones. "You've got good instincts, Clint. I think you're right. I think we should double up the last ten just to be sure."

Clint nodded. "Sounds good. I could back the Mole up and have it place them, but I think I'll just use the manual drill instead."

"I like that idea much better," said Jake. "We're still playing catch up, and I want to get that Mole running again, ASAP."

"Well, you guys have this under control. I've got what I came for," said Ben, holding up a manual titled, *MOLE 98XE: Electrical Schematic Map*. He crossed through the group and started up the incline. Riley followed behind.

"Sounds good," said Jake. He looked from Owen to Clint. "You two can handle this?"

Clint looked at Owen, who nodded. Clint liked the idea of working with Owen, the man seemed to really know his stuff and he seemed genuinely interested in Clint's underground expertise. "Yeah, I think we're good."

As Clint spoke, an ear-splitting crack echoed throughout the tunnel and boulders fell from the ceiling. Tiny rock chips zinged through the air, ricocheting off the walls like bullets. Dust clouded the area where they stood. Several voices called out when another load of rocks tumbled down from the ceiling and wall where the group had stood just moments earlier.

Clint was the first to move. Hearing the cracking sound, he instinctively sprung back toward the shelter of the Mole but fell, landing hard on his shoulder and he hit his head on the bottom step of the Mole's rear deck. As he sat up, the thundering of the falling rocks stopped. He reached behind his head and felt the back of the hard hat where it had collided with the diamond-plate step; a dent spanned the back of his aluminum helmet. He could barely see his hands in front of him through the dust; instinctively, he held his sleeve over his mouth to filter it out. He heard movement to his left and remembered Owen had been standing next to him. He crawled toward the stirring sounds and Owen's form came into view. Owen sat upright, but his legs were covered by fallen rock. His white t-shirt, now torn, had taken on the greyish cast of the dust, except for several dark patches of blood growing on his shoulder and torso. The enormity of the situation sunk in and Clint was immediately seized with panic—seeing someone else's blood had made it real. He reached for the pile of rocks pinning Owen's leg down.

Owen grabbed Clint's wrist. He tried to speak but nothing came out; the dust burned his lungs. He coughed and shook his head. "No. More shields first."

Clint nodded then yelled into the com-sys for the others to come and help as he sprinted up the steps to the control room and emerged with a black tool box. He dropped the heavy box on the rear deck and it made a loud banging sound that echoed through the tunnel. Instinctively, he ducked as if the sound would set off another collapse. The mobility in his right hand was diminished due to his shoulder injury, causing him to fumble with his left hand to get the case open. He grabbed the specialized drill, stuffed handfuls of the white pressure shields into the pocket of his hoodie, jumped down the steps and drilled a shallow hole in the tunnel floor. As with the case, he fumbled with the tool with his left hand—his dominant hand could not hold the trigger down. He heaved his body weight onto the drill as best he could to speed the drilling process.

Owen brushed the dust off the bottom of his t-shirt and held it up to his mouth while he breathed. He looked around for Riley and the others, swearing under his breath as the dust began to settle. The fallen rock had come to rest exactly where the group had stood just moments before. He heard movement on the other side of the collapse but could see nothing over the pile of rocks and boulders between them. He called for Riley and got no reply. One of his legs was bent and pinned at an awkward angle. He leaned forward to remove the rocks that covered his legs but with every movement came an intense, stabbing pain in his knee that radiated up his thigh and made him nauseous. As he began to remove the rocks, he found several too large for him to move without his VersaTool, which he had left in the work shed. He called to Riley and his chest constricted instantly with dread when he got no response.

Riley heard her name being called, muffled and distant over the ringing in her ears. She moved her limbs gingerly before sitting up. She rolled her shoulder and winced in pain. She recognized the voice calling her name as Owen's and reality came back to her with the force of a speeding train. She took in the surroundings, but it was impossible to assess anything through the dust. Jake lay beside her, unmoving. His forehead bled, but he showed no signs of significant physical damage. She swept her eyes to her right where Ben had been just moments ago. Her heart fell into her stomach when she saw his arm sticking out from beneath a pile of large rocks.

"Ben," she breathed. She crawled to him and felt for a pulse, not expecting to find one. Miraculously, she did. She heard Owen's voice again, calling her name. She stood too fast and her brain became fuzzy. White stars obscured her vision and she stumbled forward, catching herself on a large boulder saving her from falling completely to the ground. Nausea grew in her stomach and she fought it back. Through the dust, she saw Owen on the far side of the rock pile. Relief washed over her, seeing him conscious and she acknowledged his call with an update on her and Ben's status. She turned back to Ben and began pulling rocks off of him, terrified of what she may find beneath.

Clint finished installing the pressure shields and noticed they had not beeped at activation. He thought back to the other shields the Mole had installed. It occurred to him that he would never ordinarily hear the activation beep over the loud engine and wondered if the Mole was installing the shields but not activating them. He tossed the drill aside and raced back to the Mole, jumping over fallen rocks. He tapped the main screen several times, read the status and hung his head, sickened by what he saw. None of the pressure shields were activated. He activated the system, and as he stepped out of the control room, he heard beeps echoing up the tunnel as each disc came to life.

With the area stabilized, Clint freed Owen and helped him stand. Owen nearly fell back to the ground when he put weight on his knee. As if reading each other's minds, Clint left Owen's side and scrambled around the pile to help Riley uncover Ben. As Owen painfully step-hopped to the Mole's stairs, he heard the others as they ran down the tunnel, the sounds of their voices and footsteps echoing as they approached.

Only fine dust hung in the air when the others appeared. Tyler, Lexi and Maya stopped dead at the scene. Clint dug madly away at a pile of rocks to which they paid no attention, hung up on the sight of Jake lying on the ground with Riley at his side checking his pulse. Jake's foot twitched and he started to stir. He awoke and tried to sit up. Lexi fell to her knees at his side and helped Riley lay him back down. His t-shirt had torn away at the collar and the sizeable lump on his shoulder led Riley to suspect it was dislocated. She lifted his shirt to find a large rough gash on his side below his ribcage oozing blood. Riley tore off her t-shirt to reveal a white sports tank, turned her t-shirt dusty side in, folded it and pressed it to Jake's bleeding side and left it for Lexi to hold.

Riley looked up at the stunned Maya and Tyler. "We need to dig Ben out."

Maya, Tyler and Lexi looked at Clint with horror. Lexi screamed when she saw Ben's limp hand protruding from the bottom of the pile. Tyler set aside the bodyboard, lunged for the pile of rocks and began to toss them aside.

With each rock they removed, Riley felt another fall into her gut. She had no idea what kind of shape Ben would be in or if he was even still alive. She found a pulse moments ago, but she questioned how long that would last if he suffered internal injuries. Within minutes, Ben had been uncovered and Riley was amazed to see he looked relatively unscathed. There were rocks on his midsection, but whether or not they had caused damage she could not tell. A rock the size of a soccer ball rested on the side of his head but, like Clint, he was wearing a helmet. Two large boulders propped each other up over Ben's chest like stones in an archway. On Riley's command, they lifted the stones simultaneously.

With Ben uncovered, Maya moved in, checked his pulse and confirmed he was still breathing. Tyler grabbed the bodyboard, and on Maya's command, Clint, Tyler and Riley delicately slid the board beneath Ben. Owen began hopping his way to Ben, and Riley ran to his side.

"Owen, take it easy."

"It's not that bad, I think it's just a pulled ligament in the knee or something." He put weight on his leg again to test it and he collapsed forward. A pain-induced pallor washed over his face. Riley grabbed him around the waist and eased him onto a nearby boulder.

Jake managed to get to his feet despite Lexi's protestations and he limped toward Ben on the bodyboard. Lexi followed beside awkwardly, one arm around his waist and the other pressing Riley's t-shirt to the cut on his side. Her small frame was dwarfed by his massive one. Maya stopped Jake as he approached.

"Everyone! Just stop! I know you're worried," Maya looked at Jake, "but crowding around Ben won't help. We need to get him scanned. Lexi, take Ben up and set him down on one of the tables in the dining room. Tyler, take Jake up. I'm not entirely convinced he's, well, I think he's a little dazed still. Keep your eye on him. I'll be right there."

Tyler relieved Lexi from Jake's side and she raced to Ben and activated the bodyboard stretcher. It rose off the ground and hovered at the height of her waist. She jogged up the incline and effortlessly pushed the board carrying Ben's lifeless form. Jake and Tyler followed behind Lexi, their pace slower as Jake limped.

Maya turned to Riley; the control she exhibited moments ago had been replaced with panic. "We don't have the RX-4000. What are we going to do? I think Ben's seriously hurt."

Riley took Maya by the shoulders. "It's okay. You did an exceptional job just now. You obviously have medical training?"

Maya nodded, her eyes welling up with tears. She fought them back. "But not much. I mean, I volunteered in an emergency department for a couple of years, that's it. Jake's got Field First Aid, level two, but that's it."

Riley smiled encouragingly. "You probably know more than you think you do. Owen's got some outdated first aid, and I'm a level five in Field First Aid. Don't worry. We'll get this sorted out." But Riley was worried. Ben could have massive internal injuries, and without the RX-4000, there would be little they could do for him. Many of his wounds seemed superficial but without the proper equipment, they were flying blind. Jake seemed very dazed and Owen's knee and leg looked worse than any knee injury she had ever seen in the field. The one mini MediScanner they had could only do so much. Anything more complicated than a fracture in a simple bone may be diagnosed, but certainly not healed. Riley's poker face hid her concerns while she bolstered Maya's confidence.

"Maya, you're doing great. Focus on Ben, let's get him under control first. Jake seems somewhat disorientated and that concerns me a bit. All of the superficial injuries can wait. Delegate to whoever is able to help. Lexi, Tyler and I can work on the superficial stuff, but whatever you need us to do, tell us." She looked over at Clint and Owen. "Owen, I'll send Tyler down with the bodyboard for you. There's no way you're walking back on that leg. Clint, can you stay with him?"

"I've got a better idea." Clint pulled the active dump bucket to Owen's side, where it hovered obediently. "Sit in this. It'll carry you up the hill. When you get to the top, I'll set it to manual and I can push you the rest of the way."

"Thanks," said Owen, grateful for the assistance. Sitting down in the bucket proved tricky. The rock bits, although small, were uncomfortable, and he winced as he bent his knee to steady himself atop the full bucket. Once settled, Clint activated the bucket and it ascended smoothly toward the light. "You really saved the day, Clint. We'd all have been in a lot of trouble if you weren't here."

Maya and Riley sprinted up the incline and back to the camp. As they approached the main tent, they saw the bodyboard leaning against the wall beside the door, covered with bloody handprints. As Riley reached for the door, the women shared a silent look, each in fear of what they would find inside.

Darren prepared the dining area for the incoming wounded and set out the medical supplies salvaged from the tree incident. Riley and Maya burst into the main tent to find Lexi, Tyler and Jake standing around Ben lying unconscious on a table. Riley's now-bloodied t-shirt lay discarded on the floor and Tyler continued to apply pressure to Jake's wound with clean gauze.

Darren met Maya and Riley at the door with the scanner and within seconds, Maya had initiated a scan of Ben's entire body. Everyone backed away as Maya scanned, as to not confuse the scanner. The cut on Ben's leg oozed blood, visible through the hole that Lexi had ripped in Ben's pant leg to access the wound better.

"How is he?" asked Riley.

Maya read and reread the results. "I think he's alright. Well, I think he's damn lucky. I don't see any signs of internal bleeding. It looks like he's got two fractured ribs, and a fractured tibia and radius," she said pointing to his shin and then his forearm. "Plus, numerous gashes and wounds that will require a lot of stitches. But what concerns me most is that something's up with his spleen, but the scanner's not giving me too much info on it. It just says 'Injured spleen. Cannot fully assess. Seek medical assistance.'"

Maya handed the scanner to Riley. Riley looked at the three-dimensional illustration of Ben's form on the screen. It was covered by so many pulsing red dots that his form was barely visible. She touched the largest red dot on the illustration's torso and the body was replaced by the message Maya had read. While Riley, Jake and Maya discussed Ben's injuries, he awoke and began to writhe in pain.

Maya immediately sat beside him atop the table. She asked him if he remembered anything and he shook his head, shaking and unable to speak. She took his hand in hers and held it tightly as she explained what had happened and what his injuries were. His eyes were wide and his breath came in shallow bursts. Sweat on his forehead mixed with rock dust and blood; Lexi wiped it away with a dishtowel. When Maya finished her explanation, she dispensed the best painkillers the portable medical device could offer, as well as a sleeping pill. Within minutes, his shaking hands fell limp as Ben slipped back into unconsciousness.

The door to the main tent opened and Clint helped Owen hobble through. Unable to do anything for Ben, Jake helped Clint negotiate a hobbling Owen onto a table top, supporting his damaged leg. Maya and the handheld MediScanner worked what magic they could on Ben while Lexi and Tyler assisted her. Darren prepared lunch and Riley and Jake discussed the setback quietly in the meeting room. Jake declined Maya's offer to look at his shoulder and ribs, insisting that she address the others' injuries first.

Considering the damage Ben had received, Maya had him looking better quickly. The same, "Seek medical attention" message reported for the spleen injury appeared again for the large gash on his leg. The healing rays from the MediScanner had at least cleaned the wound and stemmed the flow of blood, leaving Lexi to patch it the rest of the way with LiquiStitch.

With Ben's wounds under control, Maya turned her attention to Owen. Jake and Riley emerged from the meeting room to see Maya scanning Owen. Riley walked briskly to Owen's side, hoping she showed no more concern for him than had he been any other team member.

Maya completed the scan and sat down on the bench at Owen's side. Owen read the results over her shoulder, but he and everyone else looked up at the sound of the door being flung open. Finn sprinted up behind Riley and pulled her into a bone-crushing bear hug.

"Omigod, Riley! Clint just told me. I thought you were dead. I didn't know any of this happened. I didn't have my earpiece in. I had pulled it out for a bit because my ear was sore. I'm so sorry! Clint said that the tunnel collapsed on you. I thought he meant you were dead!" His massive arms gripped her like a python.

Riley looked up at Finn. His eyes were watery and several tears rolled down his cheek. She patted him on the side of his square jaw and smiled. "Finn, I'm alright."

He pulled her tight again and kissed her on the forehead head three times as Clint came in.

Riley laughed, taken aback by Finn's overwhelming show of concern. "Finn, what the hell's wrong with you?"

"God, Riley. You're like my big sister! If you'd died, I don't know what I would have done."

Riley was moved by Finn's sentiment. "Thanks, Finn. Yes, yes, and you are very much like the pesky kid brother I never had." He released her and she kissed him on the cheek. "Now make yourself useful and please find me three slings from the medical room."

With Finn off to the medical room, Owen and Riley looked expectantly at Maya, waiting to hear the results of his full body scan.

"Alright. Cuts and bruises you're aware of. You're alright for the most part— nothing hidden. You're lucky, no breaks. But you've got one completely torn ligament in your knee and another is hanging on by a thread." She held up the scanner for Riley and Owen to see the now familiar message, "Seek medical attention." Finn returned from the medical room with the slings and, at Maya's request, an ice pack from the freezer. Maya wrapped it gently around Owen's swollen and bruising knee with a tensor bandage.

Jake's scan revealed nothing unexpected; it showed the cuts and bruises he had sustained and confirmed Riley's hunch of a dislocated shoulder. His wits had long since returned and the scan revealed no lingering effects from hitting his head on the stone floor.

Clint's scan had been the cleanest of all. His shoulder was severely bruised and cut, requiring several stitches. He showed the team the damage his hard hat had sustained during his fall back onto the Mole's rear deck and credited it for keeping his skull from looking like a smashed Christmas bauble.

As Maya had never reset a dislocated shoulder before and Riley had done two in the field, Maya let her do the honours. Lexi sat next to Jake and reached for his hand, but she retracted it when Riley silently and subtly shook her head. Instead, she sipped on the hot chocolate Darren had brought around earlier.

"Hey, Jake, what year did you say you joined NRD?" Riley asked, elevating his arm as she inspected the lump on his dislocated shoulder.

Jake thought this was a very unusual question for her to ask at this particular moment but nonetheless thought for a second. "Two thousand and—OH my sweet mother of all that is holy!" He yelled and jumped, his face red as a beet. The mug of hot chocolate he held in his good hand now lay broken on the floor. When the explosion of pain subsided, he opened up his hand to find the mug's handle in five pieces. Lexi held the hand she had planned to offer Jake and rubbed it gently as she stared bug-eyed at the broken handle in Jake's outstretched hand.

The trade-off for the MediScanner's portable nature was its reduced healing capabilities. It could tell Ben's spleen was injured, but it could no more heal it than it could surgically reattach the two torn ligaments in Owen's knee. It could dispense painkillers in quantities adequate for smaller injuries, but for Ben and Owen, the drugs could only take the edge off. It worked wonders on all of Riley's minor injuries—the cuts and scrapes, as well as the reinjured shoulder. After the healing rays had penetrated her shoulder, Riley rolled it and found that it felt better than it had before the attack on the riverbank several months back.

There were many cuts and bruises the scanner could not completely heal. Jake and Clint both sustained similar long gashes on their shoulders and back. Owen had a nasty cut where a rock chip grazed his side like a bullet. Lexi and Riley stitched what they could with LiquiStitch. A small rock chip embedded itself in Jake's shoulder like a bullet. The damage it left, after being removed and cleaned, would require numbing and traditional stitches, something Maya had never done before but watched countless times while volunteering at the hospital.

The actual damage of the rock collapse paled in comparison to its potential. Other than Ben's spleen and Owen's knee, the group had escaped a deadly situation relatively unscathed. All injured parties declined any medical assistance from Owen—his training, though ten years out of date to him meant over 100 years out of date by everyone else's standards. Clint joked that he would no sooner let Owen cut up his steak than administer to him any medical assistance.

The team ate hot chicken soup and sandwiches in shifts while the remaining injuries were cleaned and bandaged. Darren cleaned up the dining area, and before long, it again resembled a dining room instead of a trauma centre.

Tyler, Clint and Finn loaded Ben back onto the bodyboard and taxied him to the trailer he shared with Clint. Ben stirred only a little as they slid him into bed like a fried egg off a spatula, still asleep from the medication. Maya scanned him one more time, fitted a leg brace on the leg with the fracture and left the sling on his night table.

Finn returned to the main tent with the bodyboard to find Riley helping Owen limp toward the door. He set the bodyboard beside Owen, hovering at waist height. Owen was grateful to see the board. When he sat down, he grabbed the edges of the board tightly and was surprised by how steady it was. As Finn and Riley pushed him to his trailer, he had the bizarre sensation of sitting on a surfboard, but with no water. Finn opened the trailer door and helped Riley manoeuvre the board inside. Once Owen was off the board and settled on the edge of the bed, Finn announced there was still some work he needed to do in the work shed. He smiled at Riley, hugged her and kissed her again on the forehead and took the bodyboard as he left the trailer.

Owen could tell something was bothering Riley. She had said nothing since Finn had left them. Her movements were abrupt and purposeful. Owen wondered if the stress of the day had finally caught up with her, now that everyone was fixed up and deemed fit to survive. For a person who brushed off an attack in the dark by eleven assailants as nothing more than an average day at the office, it seemed as though the events of the day would rattle her no more than a broken fingernail.

Her eyes fell on the long, jagged cut on his side. "I think that's going to leave a scar." She stared at the large wound stitched together with liberal quantities of Liqu-iStitch and the bruise blossoming around it.

"Don't you know chicks dig scars? Or so Finn says," said Owen. He tried to lighten her mood, but she appeared not to have heard him. "Rile, honey…Everyone's fine. We're all alright. It's over."

Owen reached up to touch her face but at that moment, she turned to throw his shirt in the garbage. She knelt in front of him and undid the laces of his shoes. Owen caressed her cheek gently to get her attention, but she would not be distracted. She placed his shoes neatly under the chair beside the bed.

"We need to get you into the shower. You're covered in dust." Riley stood abruptly, feeling pressure building in her chest and a painful lump growing in her throat. All of the feelings, thoughts and revelations she had repressed throughout the day came flooding through her like water escaping a breached dam. She could feel her temper surface as her emotions took control of her. She helped Owen to his feet and into the bathroom.

She looked down at Owen's makeshift shorts. They had been pants before Maya had hacked the legs off to access his swollen knee.

"You're going to have to lose those fancy new shorts," she said, fighting to keep her voice steady.

Owen feigned a scandalized look. "But Miss Morgan! What will the others say?" He dropped his shorts and stood in nothing but boxer briefs and the tensor bandage wrapped around his knee. Just as she was about to tell him to lose the briefs as well, she thought better of it should someone come in to check on him.

Riley helped Owen into the shower and eased him onto a stool she had found in the closet. She joined him in the shower and knelt in front of him to remove the tensor bandage. She froze when she saw his knee. The battered joint shone in various shades of purple and had swollen to the size of a small watermelon. The cuts and pinches from the rocks shone violent indigo and near black. Her eyes darted from his knee to his eyes and when she saw him watching her, she looked away quickly and turned on the water. She tested the water and turned the shower head on him. Water sprayed his face and he leaned back on the stool to get out of the stream.

He laughed at her unpolished nursing efforts. "Sweetie, I can do this myself." She seemed not to hear and he sat in silence as she soaped him up. When she reached his legs, she hesitated as if trying to determine the best way to clean the train wreck of a joint, then soaped her hands and gently caressed it. Though determined not to, Owen winced in pain and she sprung backward like she had been electrocuted. She scrambled back against the shower wall, nearly hitting her head on the hot and cold taps and slid to the floor, her face contorted in emotional agony. With his pain now passed, Owen held his arm out for her but she was beyond his reach while seated. "Rile?"

"I'm so sorry, Owen," she said. She looked from his knee to the wall of the shower, unable to meet his eyes.

Owen reached out an arm to her and saw tears streaming down her face. Her eyes were wide and her expression looked frantic.

"Riley, you didn't do this. This isn't your fault. No one could have predicted what happened today. It was no one's fault."

She shook her head. Loose strands of wet hair hung limply around her face. She absently traced one of the grout lines between tiles with her finger, still avoiding his eyes. "No, you being here. You almost died today, and I brought you here."

"Sweetie," he said reaching out to her again. "Come here."

Her eyes slowly met his. Owen took her shaking hand and pulled her gently toward him. She knelt on the shower floor between his knees and broke down in his arms, resting her head on his chest and clung to him as if he could be taken from her at any moment. He held her tightly as the warm water cascaded over them. He slid the wet strands of hair out of her face and tucked them behind her ear. Owen heard someone call his name and Finn appeared in the bathroom door, then stopped. Giving them privacy, he closed the door as he left. Owen heard him talking to Maya on the other side of the door.

"You can't go in there," Finn explained. "The man's naked, if you must know. I'm going to have nightmares tonight because of it. Don't worry, I'll give him the crutches."

Owen smiled when he saw Finn's hand extend through a crack in the door with a thumbs up.

Riley felt like her head had been turned inside out both physically and emotionally. Something inside her felt broken. How close she and her teammates had come to being killed today rattled her in a way that left her feeling more exposed and vulnerable than she had on her very first op. Every day spent on a field operation put her in mortal danger but after years of living in danger, she had become desensitized. However, seeing Owen exposed to that danger, drove a stake of fear through her heart like nothing she had ever experienced. She had brought him into this op and exposed him to that danger. The conflicted feelings between her loyalty to her job and what she felt for him made her head ache and she felt nauseous.

Riley looked up at Owen. His hair was wet and swept back from his face. His dark brown eyes looked at her with caring and warmth. She wiped the tears from her reddened eyes. "I'm sorry. You must think I'm ridiculous."

Owen smiled and kissed her cheek. "You have nothing to be sorry for. I don't think you're ridiculous, and the Riley Morgan that I know wouldn't really care if I thought she was ridiculous or not."

"Seeing what happened to you, to all of us, shook me up. It made me realize how desensitized I've become. I calculate the risks then focus on the job that needs to be done and I lead my team through it. I don't think beyond that. I mean, you can't in this line of work otherwise you lose your nerve. Obviously, I care about what happens to Finn and everyone else, but they all know the risks. But seeing the man I love nearly killed made me feel like…I don't know. Like I'd come out of a haze or something and it reminded me how life can be lost in an instant. I guess I got a bit of a mortality check." Riley paused; she had specifically intended to never mention the L-word. Even though she had felt it not long after their first night together, she worried it would make their inevitable end so much harder. Now that she had said it, it felt very right. "I love you so much, Owe." Riley kissed him hard and squeezed him so tightly she worried she might hurt him.

"Riley, I've loved you since the moment you pulled me out from in front of that bus." He ran his hands through her wet hair then caressed her cheek. His thumb left a trail of blood and he looked at his hand.

"Holy shit Rile, you're bleeding."

"I'm not feeling very good…" Riley's voice shook then she passed out in his arms.

Jake sat at the boardroom table in Mole Control running through calculations and drawing hypothetical situations on the drilling map. With little more than three weeks left and more than a month's worth of drilling ahead of them, Jake worried how much further behind they would be as a result of the rock collapse. Ben's injuries would likely take him out of the game for the rest of the op, leaving them even more shorthanded than they already were. By a stroke of luck, the active Mole sustained no notable damage in the collapse, other than a few more dents.

"Jake, I need you to hold still." Lexi stood at Jake's side with the bottle of LiquiStitch open on the boardroom table in front of her. The MediScanner had jump-started the healing process of several cuts on his back and arm, but they needed a coat of LiquiStitch to be closed fully.

"Lex, I appreciate what you're trying to do, but I'm fine. I need to get this work done."

Lexi placed her hand on Jake's arm. Though she was standing and he was sitting, they were nearly eye to eye. "Jake, don't make me get Maya. The only reason she let you go back to work was because you promised her you would let me stitch this up."

Jake knew she was right. No one could afford to take any chances with their health this late in the game. He tossed his pencil on the table and spun in his chair to face her. He had to admit it did feel nice to have someone taking care of him. He looked up at her, wanting to convey his gratitude, unsure of the words. "Thank you, Lex."

Her touch was gentle and caring and the sensation felt foreign yet familiar, like someone singing *Happy Birthday* in a different language.

"How've you been feeling lately? Have you been able to stop thinking about that idiot of an ex-fiancé?"

Lexi looked thoughtful for a moment and nodded. "Oh yeah. I mean, the meanness of the whole thing still stings, but it's been over five months now. I'm really feeling better. Let's hope I can find a guy who cares a little bit more and appreciates me."

Jake watched her concentrate on his shoulder. She had a beautiful face with delicate features. "I don't think you'll have any problems. You're pretty, smart and very capable." He smiled at her warmly when she looked at him.

Lexi noticed a hint of a dimple in Jake's smile she had never noticed before. "Thanks, Jake. I hope so."

Owen scooped up Riley's unconscious form onto his lap. He held her tightly in front of him and inched as far forward on the stool to turn off the taps. He turned carefully and reached outside the glass shower door for the towel. He wrapped her in the towel, stood on his good leg and carried her as he hobbled awkwardly out of the bathroom. Each step sent searing pain up and down his leg until he thought he would collapse and be sick. He laid Riley on the bed and looked through the window for anyone he could flag down. Finn was leaving Clint's trailer. Owen hopped to the door and yelled for him to find Maya.

Within minutes, Maya arrived in Owen and Finn's trailer, with Finn close on her heels.

"What happened?" Maya asked, looking at Riley on the bed. She had the MediScanner ready.

"She was helping me in the shower and she said she wasn't feeling well and passed out. She's got a pretty big cut on the back of her head." Owen held the folded towel to the back of her head.

"Dammit," said Maya. Her fingers shook and she fumbled with the touch screen as she tried to reset the scanner. "Riley was the only person who was down there that I didn't do a full body scan on. She was so busy helping me. I patched her up but never thought to scan her."

Maya scanned the length of Riley's body and then sat on the edge of the bed while the device processed. She watched the two men sitting restlessly at her side, both with distinctly different looks of worry—one like that of a brother worrying about a sister and the other, a man worried about his lover. Owen held her hand and stroked her forehead. The device beeped, and Maya read the results.

"What is it?" Owen asked after a short moment.

"She's got a mild concussion. She needs to rest, but not sleep. That cut on her head can't wait. It needs to get stitched up, pronto." Maya took the bottle of LiquiStitch out of her pocket and handed it to Owen. His eyes were wide, pleading silently for Riley to be alright. Maya put her hand on Owen's shoulder and gave it a sympathetic squeeze as Riley stirred. "She's going to be okay. She needs to rest. Finn, please bring her more chicken soup. Owen, make sure she eats it. Why do I get the feeling she makes a bad patient?"

Owen laughed and nodded. "Yes, she does."

Finn pulled the chair beside the bed closer and took Riley's hand in his. Riley opened her eyes and was startled to find herself in bed with Owen and Finn sitting at her side, staring at her. Her brain ached like she had been cleaved in the head.

"What's wrong with you guys?" she asked, looking around. She propped herself up on her elbows.

"How do you feel?" Owen asked.

"Confused," she said slowly. Two pairs of wide eyes stared at her expectantly. "What is wrong with you two? Why are you looking at me like I'm dying?"

Owen caressed her cheek. "You passed out in the shower, do you remember?"

Riley thought for a moment. Her memory of the shower became fuzzy and then nothing. "Well, I'm alright now." She tried to get out of bed, but Owen and Finn stopped her.

Finn looked at Owen. "I'll get some soup."

Owen sat with Riley for the rest of the day. Riley was resentful about being confined to bed rest with only a headache, knowing that rocks needed to be removed in the tunnel. Throughout the afternoon and into the evening, different team members came and visited her and Ben. The best news of the day came from her final visitor, Jake, telling her that the delay would not be as catastrophic as they had originally figured. If they pushed the active Mole longer each day, they would be ahead of the game again in no time.

CHAPTER 38

TEAM 3
YEAR: 2095
TIME REMAINING: 28 Days

Spencer tapped his foot anxiously while each director gave their report at the weekly directors' meeting. In mere moments, he would be ambushing the man from whose brain the very project had come. Ian was highly respected not only in the office but in the scientific community as well, and Spencer had a sense he was going to learn firsthand what career suicide felt like. With every passing minute, crushing pressure cinched around his chest.

"Spencer," called Ian from across the long, mahogany table. "How's the testing going?"

Spencer cleared his throat. "I've run the Real Life Simulator and the testing scenarios you supplied and the results are positive."

"Excellent! Good work, kid. You're doing a bang-up job." He smiled broadly around the room.

"But as I've mentioned to you, I have reservations about the validity of these results. I still firmly believe the scenarios being used for testing are not as comprehensive as they should be to prove beyond all doubt that the robots are safe." Spencer was pleased to hear his voice sounded stronger and more authoritative than he felt.

Ian leaned back in his chair and rubbed his eyes in frustration. "Spencer, we've discussed this. The testing scenarios are perfectly..."

"Ian, I'm interested in the kid's take on this. If he thinks there's a problem with the way we test, I'd like to hear his thoughts on it," said the director of Production Planning. "I think we can all agree this entire endeavour has been founded on trial and error. I wouldn't be at all surprised to find out there were aspects of the project that need a second look."

"Uh, thank you. Well," Spencer cleared his throat, "my concern is that the tests aren't aggressive enough. I think that we need to push these personalities past their breaking point to see what kind of pressure the robots will be able to tolerate and, when they do finally break, observe their reactions."

"I think that makes good sense," agreed Delaney.

"I don't," said another director. "I think that might be a little paranoid, don't you, Spencer? None of these robots are going to be put in any real position of power or consequence."

"We don't really know that, do we? Especially in the long term. How do we know what people intend for them once the pilot project is over? Beyond that, we don't know what situations they're going to encounter the other sixteen hours a day when they're not working."

The doubting director rebutted. "People make decisions every day about their behaviour, and while it's not necessarily always about engaging in criminal activity, taking bribes or what have you, they still choose to make the right decision. We don't do psych evaluations on everyone in society."

"Precisely!" shouted Ian. "This is exactly the point I made in previous discussions with Spencer. He seems to have a very hard time following orders. It's bad enough he went behind my back and modified the original questionnaire the donors filled out." Ian looked at Spencer. "Sometimes it seems like you're working against us. Like you're hoping this project will fail."

"Oh Ian, shut it," Delaney cut in. "That's the biggest load of bullshit I've ever heard. Spencer has been kind enough to help us out when we were in a jam losing Jim, at a great personal cost to him. He works twelve to fourteen hours most days, and he's probably more dedicated to his work here than anyone in this room. Don't fault him for being thorough and paying attention to the details. Details I'd say you missed, from looking at these results."

Delaney slid Spencer's report forcefully across the table to Ian, opened to a page marked with big red circles. Ian slammed his hand down on the report, catching it before it slid off the table and onto his lap. "Look at that data. Personality number seventeen doesn't show any capacity for anger. Are you kidding me? Are you telling me this person has never gotten mad, ever? Everyone's got their breaking point. What happens when number seventeen finally loses it?" The room fell silent. Delaney's opinion carried a lot of weight, and rarely did she voice it so vehemently. "Spencer, how long would it take you to test more accurately?"

"Just over two weeks to develop the new scenarios and program them into the RLS. In fact, I've already got some ideas for the modifications I think should be made. After that, probably another week to the testing and data processing time…"

"We don't have that kind of time in the budget," barked Ian. He looked around the table for supporters.

"I know it's a bit of an inconvenience, but I think accurate and thorough testing will ensure the public's safety, plus, it will be a selling point to the naysayers when the pilot project starts. I know I'll come in on time," said Spencer thinking, *I have to or Operation TimeShift is a failure.*

The noise level in the room rose exponentially as everyone voiced their opinions simultaneously. From what Spencer could make out, the biggest concern was that Spencer's estimation of completion seemed too optimistic. They worried he would not get the modifications done in time for the launch. Ian put it to a vote and Spencer was outvoted, seven to four.

TIME REMAINING: 20 Days

Spencer knew that regardless of the results of the directors' meeting, he would continue developing his own set of testing scenarios on the side; however, finding time to work on them proved difficult. Following the director's meeting, Ian kept Spencer busy by assigning countless tasks in addition to his already heavy workload as passive aggressive punishment for sticking his nose where Ian felt it had no business. As a result, he was starting to fall dangerously behind schedule.

Spencer spent his days in his office doing the work that Ian expected him to do. The futility of it frustrated him knowing it was all going to be thrown away in the end. He maintained a compliant and agreeable front as Ian had taken to popping into his office to make sure Spencer stayed on task.

His evenings were a different story. Ian never set foot in the office after hours, so Spencer spent hour after hour, evening after evening of blissful, Ian-free time working on the new testing scenarios in the lab. After a week of working well past midnight, he had become used to the eerie feeling of the empty building and could recite the schedule for every maintenance robot by memory.

Kalen entered the Neural Programming lab and looked over Spencer's shoulder. As usual, his attention was deeply engrossed in his CI screen and she watched as different documents and programs flashed across the screen. Words appeared faster than she could follow. She massaged his shoulders gently and he jumped, taken by surprise at her presence.

"What are you working on tonight, Spence?"

Words stopped appearing and Spencer leaned back in his chair. "Tonight, I am working on situational tests forty-one through forty-seven, if I'm lucky." He turned in his chair, pulled her into his lap and spun again to face the screen. "I'm going to add a dash of danger, a pinch of blind rage and a dollop or two of blackmail."

"Ooooh, sounds like a tasty plot," she laughed. "I take it it's going to be another late night?"

"Yeah." Spencer nodded. "It's going to be like this every night until the presentation to the board."

She kissed the top of his head. "What can I do?"

"You've done so much already. I can't ask you to do anything else."

"You're not imposing." She slid off his lap at the sound of voices coming down the hall. "Plus, I've enlisted some help."

At that moment, Erik and Lisa joined them in the lab. "Okay, none of that schmoopy, kissy-face stuff in here or I'll leave right now," said Erik, punching Spencer in the arm as he walked by.

"What are you guys doing here?" Spencer asked.

"We're here to help," said Lisa. "Don't you remember? We volunteered to help you ages ago. Now that you've got some scenarios hammered out, we can start programming them into the Real Life Simulator while you finish up the rest."

Spencer was stunned. He did not know whether to kick them all out or hug them. "You can't risk your jobs for me. If Ian finds out that I'm going against his orders again, he's going to kick me to the curb. He'll do the same to you if he finds out you're involved."

"Spencer, we see what you're going through, and we all agreed that what Ian has proposed for testing is laughable. If I get fired for trying to make sure the public is protected, well, that'll be just what I tell the media when I call them," said Lisa.

"Seriously, Spence, we've all got your back," said Erik.

Spencer beamed, lost for words.

A series of beeps alerted Kalen's attention to the door as a pizza delivery robot floated into the room. "Perfect timing. The pizza is here." Kalen paid the bot and set the pizza boxes on one of the empty workbenches.

"I'll get some drinks from the cafeteria," said Erik. He wore a sly grin as he walked toward the door. "I've reprogrammed the drink machine to give me free drinks whenever it sees my Visa key."

Lisa rolled her eyes and followed Erik. "I'll get some napkins."

Spencer bear-hugged Kalen as she opened up the pizza boxes. He buried his face in her hair. "I love you so much. Thank you for this. You have no idea how much this means to me."

Kalen patted him on the arm and propped open the last box. "I love you, too, Spence."

Spencer took her by the hand, spun her into his arms and caressed her cheek as he fell into her warm gaze. He shuddered at how lucky he felt and pulled her into a passionate kiss.

The group ate and talked about Spencer's plan. Spencer knew they had their work cut out for them, but with four brains instead of one, he would soon be in a much better position.

Erik pulled the cheese out of his uneaten pizza crust, popped it in his mouth and tossed the hollow strip of bread back into the box. "So Spence, explain to me how Ian doesn't know that you're doing this work behind his back? How is it possible that he doesn't see all of this on the Nexus? He's watching what you do like a hawk. These files are going to be huge. They're going to be found by IT in an instant."

Spencer looked at his co-workers with a sheepish grin. "I had a server put together."

"A server, like from 2008? Like a physical computer? That's so old school. My God, it's so simple it's ridiculous." Erik laughed at the absurd simplicity. "But that raises way more questions than it answers. Question one: Where did you find one?"

"It's amazing what you can find in antique stores if you know where to look."

"Question two: How did you make something that old and junky powerful enough to run the Real Life Simulator and big enough to store the massive file sizes of the Personality Apps?"

Spencer laughed. "I know they don't look it, and I'll never tell them this, but my brothers are pretty damn smart. They retrofitted some silicone gel drives, added the biggest RAM farm I've ever seen and beefed up the power supply. A couple tweaks here and there made it able to communicate with CIs and that's about it really."

"Last question. Where is it? I gotta see this thing."

Spencer smiled, proud of the twin's ingenuity. "It's in the trunk of my car." Three sets of eyes stared at him, speechless. "It's quite convenient really. It's always near me, it vents out the bottom so I don't have to worry about the machine overheating. It flies, so I don't have to worry about splashing through puddles."

Kalen failed to find this nearly as amusing as Erik and Lisa. "Spence, what happens if something happens to your car or someone finds out? I mean, there must be something here that detects it? If your CI can detect it, surely there is a device in this building that can see it."

"The entire set up is a Level A1-A Ghost, so it's undetectable to even the nerdiest of nerds and their toys. There are redundant drives within the server, so if one fails, I'll still have a backup."

Lisa laughed. "Spence, you could give any nerd a run for their money when it comes to nerdiness."

"Hmm, Spence?" Kalen bit her lip. "How did the twins manage that level of security? We don't even use that here. That's international defence op stuff."

Spencer laughed. "Please, have you met my brothers? This isn't their first rodeo. Asher got suspended in high school for a week after hiding the school's entire portion of the Nexus. They escorted him off the property before realizing they needed him to fix it, so they went a week without it. It was absolute chaos and he was a hero for years."

"So what do you need us to do?" asked Lisa, as she folded up the pizza boxes and stuffed them into the garbage bot.

Although Spencer knew exactly what scenarios would cause the robots to fail, he chose a well-rounded buffet of situations that would test all aspects of the personalities. If he only wanted to prove he was right, he could choose as few as five scenarios for that. The key to salvaging the AEI Project lay in identifying and resolving all of the issues before the timeshift.

"I've got just over forty tests already written. Kalen, Lisa, you guys could start getting those programmed into the RLS, that would be amazing. Erik, Ian's been on my back about some risk management stuff, if you can believe that."

"Hey, no worries," said Erik, powering up his CI. "But seriously, when Jim gets back, you tell him that I'm expecting a big fat bonus."

Time Remaining: 19 Days

Unable to help relieve Spencer's workload, the twins could only watch as Spencer burned out like a spent firework. To help, they did whatever they could to make his life easier. When they asked him what they could do for him, Spencer's only reply was laundry. The twins' solution had been to haul it all to the laundromat.

Logan strode into the Neural Programming lab at the end of the day to find Spencer and Kalen glued to their CIs. "Hey, Spence. How's it going?" Getting no response, he punched his brother lovingly on the shoulder. He gave Kalen's ponytail a quick tug as he walked past them and sat in an empty chair. "How's it going, Ball 'n' Chain?"

"Pretty good, Devil's Spawn," she shot back. Unable to keep a straight face, she smiled.

Spencer's concentration remained unbroken. "Hey," he mumbled.

"I just thought I'd pop by and let you know that Your Highness' laundry will be picked up by thy lowly serfs and delivered to thine palace. Forthwith, it will be hung in thy royal closet before Your Greatness gets home for the evening."

Spencer's shoulders fell as his concentration broke and he laughed. He turned in his chair to face his brother and Kalen. "Thanks, Loge, I appreciate your help. How's Delaney doing?"

Logan smiled at the mention of her name. "She's good. In fact, she's the other lowly serf of which I spoke."

"Wow, taking your date to the laundromat. You really know how to show a girl a good time," said Kalen. Spencer loved that she could hold her own with the twins.

"Well, if you consider picking up my brother's laundry and stocking his dwelling with food, booze and clean clothes a hot date, then, yes."

"Who are you kidding?" chuckled Spencer. "You and Asher are going to eat half of it anyways."

Logan chuckled as he got up to leave. As he walked past Spencer, he patted his younger brother on the back. "You're doing great, Grayson. Keep up the good work. See ya, peeps."

Spencer looked at Kalen. "Well, I'll be damned. I think that might have been a compliment."

Logan juggled Spencer's dry cleaning and several grocery bags as he dug through his pockets for his keys. A can of soup fell to the floor and the remaining items shifted around in the bag. A carton of eggs hung perilously over the edge of the bag.

Delaney laughed. "Sometimes you're so hopeless." She set down the bags she carried and relieved Logan of his.

"This is why I need you, Laney." He slid his key in the lock and kissed her forehead. "I need someone to look after me." He took the bags of groceries from Delaney and set them down on the kitchen counter. He could hear her talking as she toured Spencer's condo. Unable to find the bedroom on the main floor, she spotted the spiral staircase and carried the dry cleaning upstairs. Finding Spencer's room, she laid the bags neatly on the bed and returned to the kitchen.

"Spencer's got a fabulous place. It's huge and so clean. You could take some notes here, Grayson." Delaney opened the balcony door and stepped out. She took in the sunset as it bathed the city in rich, golden light. "Look at this view." She pulled the long sleeves of her sweater over her hands and leaned on the railing. Her hair blew in the late summer breeze. Logan wrapped his arms around her, nuzzled his face into her shoulder and kissed the base of her neck. He felt her shiver. He pulled the collar of her shirt away to reveal more skin and kissed it.

"Logan! We're in public." She pulled his hand away and interlocked her fingers with his. "And we're at your brother's. Behave yourself."

"You know it drives me wild when you tell me what to do."

Delaney walked back into the living room and Logan, like a lovesick puppy, followed her inside. She closed the door and returned to the kitchen. "We've got a job to do here, or have you forgotten?"

Logan playfully grabbed her by the arm and pulled her back to him. He caught her elegantly, like a seasoned ballroom dancer and dipped her. "Baby, when I'm with you, I don't even know what day it is, let alone what I'm doing."

"Let me remind you then," she laughed, trying but unable to conjure a serious tone. "You're putting groceries away."

Logan pulled Delaney upright again and she returned to the kitchen. She pulled the milk, cheese and yogurt out of the nearest bag and put them in the fridge. Logan rifled through the rest of the paper bags and found nothing that would go bad if left on the counter for an hour. He took a bag of apples out of her hand. She was about to protest his counterproductive behaviour, but he placed his finger on her lips. The look in his eyes needed no explanation. He swept her off her feet, carried her up the spiral stairs to the bedroom and tossed her gently onto Spencer's bed. The bag of the dry cleaning crinkled in protest as she landed on it.

"Logan!" she giggled. "The dry cleaning!"

He bent over her and kissed her passionately. Delaney grabbed the front of his shirt and pulled him closer. She ran her hands across his chest, down his torso and undid his belt buckle.

Logan knelt beside her on the bed and feverishly fumbled with the buttons of his white shirt. He abandoned the buttons, pulled the shirt over his head and got stuck.

"You look like you've been beheaded," Delaney laughed.

Trapped inside his poly-cotton prison, Logan managed to undo another button and ripped the shirt off. A button flew off and it ricocheted off the base of a lamp and came to a stop somewhere behind the dresser. Able to see again, he watched Delaney seductively undo her shirt.

"Oh my God," he mouthed.

Delaney enjoyed teasing him and took her time. Seeing Logan half naked, or better yet, fully naked, had become one of her favourite pastimes.

With a grin, Logan pounced on top of her and the dry cleaning bag crinkled again as Delaney squealed with laughter.

"Logan, the dry cleaning!" She tried to lift herself off the clothes and pull them out from under her.

"Fuck the dry cleaning." Logan scooped her up and tossed the bag of freshly cleaned clothes to the floor.

Logan and Delaney lay in Spencer's bed staring at the ceiling.

"This is kind of creepy," she said after a moment.

"What's creepy?" he asked dreamily. He ran the tips of his fingers down her forearm.

"We're in your brother's bed."

Logan's eyes looked away from her arm and around the room. "Ewww. You're right!"

"And this is where him and Kalen…" Delaney laughed.

Logan sang loudly as he covered his ears and jumped off the bed like it was contaminated. "Laney, that's sick. I'm going to put the groceries away." He grabbed his pants lying half on the chair and half on the floor and hopped toward the door fighting to get his second leg in.

"I'll hang up this poor, sad dry cleaning," she shouted after him as she picked up the bags heaped on the floor.

Delaney took the bag of undies and socks and set it on top of the wooden dresser. She opened the top drawer, untied the bag of neatly folded socks and boxers then tied it again. She suspected Spencer would be more grateful if she left them for him to sort through. Logan could care less who rifled through his laundry, clean or dirty, but Spencer was more private than either of the twins and would probably be mortified if he knew she had sorted through his delicates. As she closed the drawer, something illuminated caught her eye and she opened the drawer again. The largest watch she had ever seen lay atop a pile of neatly folded socks. She felt guilty for looking but curiosity overtook her, and Delaney removed the watch to get a better look. *That's a gargantuan watch*, she thought. Her eyes scanned the different time displays. *It's weird that there are so many different sets of times. He must use it for travelling.* She set the watch back on the sock pile and slid the drawer shut.

After stripping the bed and remaking it with fresh sheets she found in the linen closet, she picked up the last bunch of dry-cleaning and removed the protective bag. She inspected the garments and saw that some of the shirts had become slightly wrinkled, which she hoped would fall out after a little time in the closet. She slid the closet doors open, and was left speechless at the organization of Spencer's closet. She stepped inside and looked around. Work clothes hung on one side and casual clothes on the other, organized by colour from lightest to darkest. On the back wall, ties, belts and bags hung above row after row of shoes. She hung the clean clothes in what she hoped were their respective locations.

After she had finished, she stood back to again admire the organizational genius of the closet when a backpack sitting on the floor caught her eye. It was the only item out of place. She picked it up and looked around the closet for its place. *If I was Spencer, where would I put this?* She looked at the backpack again and thought it looked familiar. She flipped it over in her hands and saw the number thirty-two embroidered in red at the bottom right corner of the pack. She thought back to the watch in the drawer. With the realization of what she was holding in her hand, her stomach sank like a stone tossed into an icy lake. She opened up the front flap of the pack knowing full well what she would find, and saw the control interface. Her eyes locked on the blinking red light on the corner of the control interface that indicated the pack was currently deployed. She saw the number five in the Dimension Number field. Her mind reeled. She heard Logan's footsteps come toward the stairs. She zipped the pack up, tossed it hastily back in the closet and slid the frosted glass doors shut. Logan's footsteps continued past the stairs and into the bathroom. She opened the dresser drawer again and picked up the watch. *Current time: February 7, 2098? What the hell is this?* she wondered.

Delaney fought the urge to run downstairs and confront Logan with what she had found. Still holding the watch in her shaking hands, she sat down on the bed. Her mind raced through scenario after scenario, desperate to come up with a logical hypothesis. *Okay, Laney, there's obviously a legitimate reason for this. People who use time travel do it for only a few reasons. Usually exploration or research. But Spencer clearly isn't here for any of those reasons. There is nothing here in his home that indicates he would need to come back in time. At work, he's just working on the project. Nothing is out of the ordinary with him. Dating Kalen is new, but I doubt he went back in time for a date. The only thing the guy does is work...* She reviewed her logic again and again to see if she missed something. *Maybe he's on an operation of some kind? But he's Research, not Defence. Only Defence people go on operations—unless a specific skill set was needed.*

Her memory of Logan running into her in the hallway and spilling her coffee on her dress popped into her mind. She remembered looking at him, thinking that he looked different somehow. Older. She remembered thinking at the rate he was aging he was going to look like he was fifty when he was forty. *Logan must be helping him. And then Asher must be too. Who else? Kalen? Jim?* Regardless of the who, the why still stumped her. And the answer lay with Spencer. She thought about how he had been killing himself lately over testing, how he had been so adamant about how not enough testing was being done. *Testing, testing, testing is all he's been able to talk about for months. Something must go wrong with the robots; something that only he could fix or could be fixed with more testing? The robots must malfunction in some way. That can be the only reason Spencer would specifically be sent on a Defence op; only he could assimilate into his own life and manipulate the project.* This raised more questions than it brought answers, like, where were the present versions of the brothers? The laws that he and whoever else were breaking were numerous and very grave. She could not figure out what could have gone so wrong that this drastic of an operation would be warranted. She heard Logan walk back into the kitchen.

"How's it going up there, gorgeous?" yelled Logan.

"Good," she called back, fighting to keep her voice level. "Some of these shirts are really wrinkled; I'm trying to fix them." She heard him turn on the TV. A wave of nausea flooded over her at the sound of his voice. *If this Logan has come back with Spencer, then this isn't the Logan I know. I mean it is Logan, but it's a different Logan.* The absurdity of the situation sank in. Anger and sadness tore at her insides. She forced herself to remove her emotions and think about the situation logically. *If he's on an op as complicated and as illegal as this appears to be, it would have to be a matter of national security.* She thought about how she would handle this if the roles were reversed. If she was in his position, she knew that she would never say anything to anyone, even a significant other. This rationalization cooled her anger and the void it left filled with hurt, betrayal and loss. Where was the present-day Logan? Had he been sent to the future? What happens when he comes back? Wherever he was, he probably had no clue they were dating, and chances were good he would never have the same feelings for her. Would she even want him to? Her mind felt like a spoon being bent telepathically.

She looked at the watch again and sighed heavily. Their relationship had an expiry date, and according to the numbers she saw counting down on the watch, it had less than three weeks left.

CHAPTER 39

TEAM 1 & 2
YEAR: 1200
TIME REMAINING: 18 Days

The days that followed the rock collapse were more frustrating and far less productive than Jake had anticipated, which surprised him as his expectations were set extremely low. With the exception of Ben, who was still bedridden, life at the camp had moved forward. Jake was happy to see that the rock collapse had not shaken Clint's nerve. The morning that followed the collapse, his hot-and-cold sub had all of the fallen debris cleared away before breakfast. Clint's attitude continually fluctuated between friendly and moody. Sometimes he was extremely helpful and even helped Maya fix the motor for the curtains in her trailer, but on other days his negativity drained the group's collective energy. Clint's acts of heroism after the rock collapse had built goodwill with the team, only for it to be undone a few days later after an outburst over a meatless meal—part of Maya and Darren's attempt to ration the dwindling meat supply. Jake hoped that Clint would spare the group any future meltdowns because the team could not afford any more roadblocks.

The rock collapse had not set the group too far behind schedule, but Jake's plan of gaining time by pushing the active Mole several more hours a day was foiled before the end of the first day. He knew the Mole models tended to be more finicky as a trade-off for their ability to articulate, but the number of breakdowns the team experienced seemed highly unusual. After running for two hours, Mole1 developed a grinding noise. Lexi confirmed on the monitors that the fix that Ben had put in place for the cooling system continued to be a hot spot and expected it to give out at any moment. Clint cut the load on the drill to half and hoped it would continue to work until Mole2 was back in business.

On the positive side, Finn had resolved the issue that plagued the guns. The welds between the cartridge clip and its modified extension had sustained hairline cracks during the time leap, and the loss of integrity caused the guns to fail as a safety precaution. Finn re-welded the cartridge clips and prepared to test the guns.

With Ben sidelined with injuries, there seemed to be more work than available hands to complete it. With the exception of Ben and Owen's knee, everyone had physically recovered from their injuries. Owen's knee was still severely damaged and he could walk no more than a few short steps without causing significant pain. The swelling had come down, but surgery would be needed upon his return. Owen managed to keep pace with the others thanks to his crutches. When Finn had told Owen there were crutches waiting for him, it brought back memories of the last time he had needed crutches—in university when he broke his ankle playing lacrosse. They were unpleasant then and Owen could not imagine how time could have improved upon them in any way. But what Finn called crutches, Owen would have called a floating Segway—a hover platform with a long neck that attached to the base and ended at waist height with handlebars. Owen had a blast zipping around the camp on his crutches. Not only was it fun, but it allowed him to get around the camp much faster than had he walked. With his ability to lift aided by his VersaTool, he suffered no significant setbacks in his capacity to work.

Jake joined Tyler in the work shed in the afternoon to expedite the maintenance. By the end of the day, the fluids were flushed and refilled and every tooth had been inspected and replaced where necessary. Tyler walked into the Mole's control room, fired up the engine and it hummed to life. He engaged the drill head and as he increased the speed, a loud beeping echoed around the control room followed by a red light flashing on the monitor. Jake took the stairs two at a time and stuck his head into the control room. He hoped the problem was small, like they forgot to cap a fluid reservoir or something. He saw a three-dimensional cutaway drawing of the drilling mechanism on the monitor. The main shaft pulsed red. "What the hell?"

"That's odd," said Tyler, as he shut the machine's engine down. He reset the diagnostic test, restarted the engine and again, engaged the drill head. Again, the test flagged the same part on the screen. "It didn't have that problem when we pulled it out."

Jake sighed heavily and shook his head in frustration. He knew better than to expect any kind of maintenance to go by without some problem.

Darren's voice came over the com-sys. "Dinner's up."

"Okay, let's leave this. We'll do it tomorrow," Jake said to Tyler. Both men stepped out of the machine and Tyler began putting away the tools. "Don't worry about it, we're just going to have to pull them out again tomorrow morning."

In the kitchen, the team sat around the table and filled their plates with the leftovers. The meat supply was dwindling and with Clint needed in the work shed full-time, there was no time for hunting.

Finn carried a full plate of food to the door. "I'll bring this to Ben."

The door to the main tent opened and Ben floated through, sitting on the bodyboard with his legs extended in front of him. With his good arm, he propelled himself forward gingerly with a broom handle.

"Ben!" shrieked Maya, watching him slide effortlessly toward the group. She ran to him and snatched the broom handle from his hand. "What are you doing?"

"I can't sit in there all day. It's driving me nuts. I'm feeling better and I don't think walking's going to kill me. But seeing as how you won't let me, here I am. Now stand still." With his good arm, he pushed off on her shoulder and floated smoothly down the row of tables, grabbing the corner of their usual table to stop. Using a button on the side of the board, he lowered the board so his leg brace could clear the underneath of the table top and pulled himself forward. He felt the board hit something and saw Lexi flinch. "Sorry, Lex! Alright. Who's cutting up my spaghetti?"

Jake lay in bed unable to sleep. He lifted his good arm to look at his watch and remembered he had taken it off to work on the Mole. He made a mental note to grab it off the workbench first thing in the morning. Instead, he rolled over and looked at the alarm clock. 2:42. He stared at the ceiling of his trailer and thought about how crummy he would feel in a few hours if sleep failed to come. Pulling that shaft out would be a dusty, oily, yet intricate job, and he could not afford any more problems. He rolled to his other side and reached for the bedside lamp with the intent of reading the Moles' operating manual, convinced it would knock him out faster than any drug. A flickering light reflecting on the living room wall caught his eye. Curious, he got out of bed and looked out the window. He saw a fire in the fire pit. He threw on a pair of jeans and a t-shirt and left his trailer to investigate. He was surprised to find Clint sitting at the fire, poking it with a stick.

"Hey," Jake sat down next to Clint. "Can't sleep?"

Clint shook his head. "Fricking Darren. I think he made those damn coffee cookies with regular coffee and not decaf."

Jake thought back to the four cookies he ate after dinner and suddenly his restlessness made sense.

The two men sat in silence for nearly three-quarters of an hour. Clint worried that Jake may think that now would be a good time for some male bonding. He knew Jake, Riley and Owen had reached out to him more than the others. A small part of him felt grateful, but at the same time, he resented their special treatment. He needed nothing from them and counted down the days until he could go home.

"Well, I'm out," said Jake, as he stood and turned to walk away. "Try and get some sleep, eh?"

"Yeah, I think I'm done too. I'll put this out."

"Sounds good. Have a good night." Jake walked toward his trailer and, remembering his watch, turned and bee-lined to the work shed. As he entered the work shed, the lights came on automatically. Squinting to block out the light, he saw his watch sitting among the tools. He grabbed it and left before his eyes had a chance to adjust to the bright light.

TIME REMAINING: 17 Days

Jake woke early to get a jumpstart on Mole2. He worried that swapping out the problem shaft could take a full day, even with both him and Tyler tackling it, and he wanted to get a couple of hours in before breakfast. As he walked through the camp, he could feel the warmth of the weak morning sun on his face. The weather had cooperated since the day of the rock collapse, and he was grateful that at least one thing was working in their favour.

When Jake threw the work shed door open, he found Riley and her team already hard at work. Nothing Riley did ever shocked Jake. Despite her private and humble nature, hushed stories of her accomplishments always found their way back home. Her fearless attitude, intelligence and combat abilities were talked about as much as her ability to work three days straight or plan ops so seamless that people wondered if she could see the future. Storytellers of the male persuasion never failed to mention she was gorgeous with a body of a seasoned triathlete. Jake could see her appeal, but at the same time, she scared the hell out of him. One of his wife's best qualities had been how she needed him. After a hard day, she would tell him her troubles and he would listen and rub her back while she talked. He knew she could and would solve the problems, but it was being the one she turned to for reassurance that he loved. As for physical appearance, he loved her curves and the way he would come home from work and find her dancing around the living room with a baby on each hip.

Jake ducked and shimmied into the Mole's control room and disengaged the power. As an added precaution, he hopped down the stairs and opened an access panel on the left rear corner of the machine and manually disconnected the power units. He went to the workbench to grab the tools he would need to disassemble the drill, but all of the tools Tyler had left out were put away. He smiled and turned to the toolbox, reflecting on Tyler's immaculate nature; like Ben, he refused to leave his workspace cluttered at the end of the day. Jake opened the top drawer of the tool box to find it empty. *That's weird*, he thought. He opened other drawers and they, too, were cleaned out. He rifled through the drawers of the other toolbox and found them empty as well. *Finn.*

"Okay, Finn, very funny," said Jake, looking at Finn.

"What's funny?" asked Finn.

"The tools?"

"What tools?" asked Finn, straightening up beside one of the guns.

"The tools? The one's you took from the workbench and hid? Didn't you take them as a practical joke?" A joke Jake could handle. What he did not have time for was someone playing dumb. Hiding several million dollars' worth of tools was not amusing at the crunch time of a mission.

Finn looked puzzled. "I never touched them."

"Finn?" Riley asked, looking sceptical. "Your reputation is preceding you."

"No! I swear! Trust me, I'll take the heat for any joke I've played, but I didn't touch them."

Jake's face began to redden. "Finn, all of the tools are gone. This is serious shit," said Jake, his voice louder than even he had anticipated. He ripped open the drawers of the nearest toolbox.

Riley took a step forward, placing herself between Jake and her sub. "Jake, if he said he didn't do it, he didn't do it."

Jake thought for a moment and backed off. Finn was no liar. Sure, he would put a dead fish in the vent under your bed and turn on the heat, but beyond that, there was not a malicious bone in his body. His shoulders fell at the memory of the previous night when he left Clint alone at the fire, and how the tools were still in the shed when he grabbed his watch. With Riley, Finn and Owen still watching him, he rubbed his face with exasperation and looked at Riley. "We need to talk."

Riley looked back at Owen and Finn. "Can you guys start setting that stuff up outside?"

After the door had closed behind her teammates, Riley spoke. "Look, Jake, I believe Finn. He wouldn't do something like this at this stage of the op and if he had, he'd've owned up to it."

Jake turned to look at her. "I don't think it was Finn." He explained the previous night—how he had been unable to sleep, finding Clint by the fire, then how he left and Clint stayed behind. How he stopped at the shed to get his watch and all the tools were still there.

Riley looked thoughtful for a moment after Jake had finished. "Has he stolen anything before?"

"No. Well, not that I'm aware of," Jake replied. "I think he's a difficult guy to work with, and not my first choice of person to be around, but I don't think he'd steal." He looked thoughtful for a moment. "But then what the hell do I know? He's so bloody unpredictable. I just don't know what he's capable of. I don't have any physical proof; I don't even have a gut feeling. It's just the timing and how it looks. I don't want to accuse him and be wrong. But on the other hand, I can't not ask."

Riley leaned back on the empty workbench and watched Jake rub his eyes in exasperation. "You absolutely have to ask, and asking isn't accusing. If he's put out by that, that's his problem, not yours. Maybe there's a legit reason."

At that moment, Clint walked into the work shed carrying a steaming cup of coffee. "Morning, folks. Jake, did you get some sleep? I tossed around for another hour at least."

"Clint, all the tools are missing."

Clint walked over and set his coffee down on the Mole's rear platform and opened the door to one of the mechanical compartments. The compartment door slid forward and up. He looked over at the empty tool bench and dawning comprehension washed over his face. "Ah. And are you accusing me of something?"

"I'm not accusing you of anything," said Jake evenly.

Clint sipped his coffee and turned to face Jake. "Well, that's a load of bull. You accused me when the WeatherShield went down, too. I had nothing to do with that and I had nothing to do with this."

Within moments, simple questions had escalated into a yelling match. Owen stuck his head in the door and hearing the shouts, closed it again.

"I'll have you know I saw someone walking around the camp last night. I assumed it was someone else who couldn't sleep after eating that idiot's fucking coffee cookies."

"Just like you saw someone walking around the night the WeatherShield went down?" Jake was trying to remain unbiased, but Clint's stories were getting tall and his attitude was not winning anyone's support.

"Yes. But I guess you didn't believe me then and apparently you didn't believe me now." Clint's face shone an angry shade of red.

Owen entered the work shed, his floating crutch platform leaving a pencil's width of space to spare on either side of the door frame. "I'm sorry, I didn't mean to eavesdrop. I need to get the remote control for the gun. But I should mention that I also saw someone in the bushes the night the Weather Shield went down," said Owen. All three sets of eyes turned to him. "I never really thought about it until hearing this. At the time, I just assumed it was one of the guys in the bushes relieving themselves. But come to think of it, when I came back to the fire, everyone was there except Clint. But as I sat down, he showed up. He'd just come from Mole Control, and there was no way he could have been in the bushes if he came from that direction. I never really put too much thought into it until now."

"That's bizarre," said Riley after a few moments of silence. "Maybe it was some locals? Surely it's possible some may be around." Her thoughts were punctuated by a voice outside calling Jake. The door flew open and Lexi charged in.

"Jake," said Lexi. She leaned forward with her hands on her knees, trying to catch her breath. She had run to the tunnel and back again trying to find Jake, who had not yet put in his earpiece. "Jake, the perimeter alarm is down. Some of the sensors are offline."

"Are you kidding me?" Jake swore under his breath.

Lexi, Jake and Riley jogged to Mole Control and Clint and Owen followed. Finn, waiting for Owen to return with the remote control, joined the parade. Lexi pointed to the flashing red errors on the monitor. The screen showed a three-dimensional drawing of the camp, trailers, trees and all. Three green dots on one side of the screen denoted where around the camp the sensors were located. Three blinking red dots showed where three other sensors should have been around the camp.

"How is it possible that three goddamn sensors are offline?" asked Jake. He shook his head. "This is unbelievable. How does this even happen? Lex, pull up the video of the camp from last night," Jake asked firmly. "Scrub through to 3:00 A.M., please."

Lexi fast-forwarded through the video. Despite speeding through the video, nothing on the screen changed. The video had been captured by a wide-angle camera attached to one of the hovering puck lights above the camp. It captured most of the camp clearly except for several shadowed areas. The left side of the screen showed the trailers, distorted into crescent shapes by the wide angle lens. Nothing changed on screen until the video's timer showed 1:32 A.M., when a dark figured appeared out of the darkness by Ben and Clint's trailer. The fast-forwarding made the person's movements look comical as it sped across the screen to the fire pit between Mole Control and the main tent. A fire appeared like magic and the figure sat down. An hour on the video's timer passed and another figure walked speedily from the living quarters to the fire pit and sat near the other figure. Within moments, the video showed Jake's figure leaving the fire, walking into the work shed. The lights inside flashed, the figure left and walked toward the trailer beside the main tent and disappeared into its shadow.

"Okay, slow it down a bit," asked Jake, leaning in. Everyone leaned into the monitor. They saw Clint stand nearly ten minutes after Jake's figure had left the screen. Clint, as he had described, left the fire and entered the main tent, returning a few moments later with a large stock pot and poured water on the fire. Clint watched the fire for several moments then stirred the ashes with a stick to make sure the fire was entirely extinguished. He then returned to the main tent with the stock pot and exited again, no pot. He walked toward the trailer closest to the food pantry and, like Jake, disappeared into the darkness.

"See! I told you I didn't do it!" exclaimed Clint. While the video proved most of Clint's story to be true as he had recounted it, there was no way to tell if either man actually entered their respective trailer. As soon as both men neared the trailers, they were swallowed by the darkness. Although Jake wanted to believe Clint, he still looked like the most likely suspect.

Lexi continued to fast-forward through the video and nothing changed until 4:37 A.M., when another figure appeared in the camp.

"Holy shit," breathed Jake.

Lexi returned the video to normal speed and the group huddled around the monitor to get a better look. The silhouetted figure walked across the camp from between Mole Control and the main tent, toward the work shed. The figure seemed to be male—his shoulders were not large for a man, but too broad to be a woman. Everyone held their breath, knowing they would get a glimpse of his face the moment he crossed the threshold to enter, triggering the lights. In anticipation, Lexi zoomed in.

"What's he doing?" Jake asked rhetorically. The person opened the door a fraction, just enough to slide his arm in and reach around for the light switch. "What the hell? He hit the override light switch. Lex, pause and zoom in more, please. Maybe if we see what he's wearing that will give us a clue."

"It looks like a field op uniform," said Riley, after Lexi had enlarged the video. She leaned over Lexi for a closer look at the image frozen on the screen. "We all have at least two of those outfits. So someone wearing an outfit that matches our field op uniforms and knows enough about our portable buildings to know there's an override light switch just inside the door, is our culprit."

The figure on the screen disappeared into the building. After the door had closed, light shone through the small windows on the overhead doors. Two minutes and thirty-nine seconds later, the light switched off and the man exited carrying a box no larger than a shoebox.

"Lex, pull up the DNA on this guy. Is he in our system?"

Lexi hesitated before answering. "We can't access the database from here."

Jake swore loudly. He was tired of being thwarted at every turn. "So what do we have on this guy?"

"Just this video, and maybe we can get some fingerprints off the perimeter alarm sensors if they're still around."

"Okay, Lexi, scour this video for any clues. Report back to me by lunch. I want to know everything you see, no matter how unimportant it seems. Clint, I want you manually operating the drill. Treat it well. Until we get those damn tools back, it's our only Mole. Keep it running." He slid his earpiece into his ear. "Keep an eye on that hot spot. If any other problems crop up in that damn drill, shut it down before they turn into full-blown catastrophes."

Clint said nothing and walked out the door. Jake had marvelled at Clint's un-rivaled intuition for the Moles, and if anyone could keep the drill running without aggravating its trouble areas, it would be him. Jake was torn. He debated sending Lexi down to run the drill so he could keep his eye on Clint as he was still his most likely suspect. Even the height and body type of the intruder's body on the screen looked like Clint, but that was hardly a smoking gun. If Clint was the culprit, sending the man trying to sabotage their mission to work with the only operational Mole seemed like an appallingly terrible decision. With Ben unable to work, the team could not afford to lose another body.

Owen and Finn filed out of the trailer after Clint. Jake watched the pair return to their work in the centre of the clearing and Clint disappeared down the path leading to the tunnel. "Rile, we've got a security problem," Jake said.

"Tell me about it." She motioned to the door. "Let's look for those perimeter sensors."

Jake and Riley walked the camp's boundary to the various sensors' locations. The reporting screen showed that three sensors were offline but made no reference as to whether they were turned off, broken or, worse, missing.

Jake found the first offline sensor in its original location, just beyond the entrance to the tunnel. The long and narrow sensor had been pushed over and had come out of the ground. Jake swore under his breath when he saw the glass sensor detached from the body. He picked up the stake and the circuit board and glass sensor hung limply from the top by several wires. He swore under his breath.

Riley inspected the sensor. "Hold on, I don't think it's as bad as it looks. I think it's just come apart." She took the sensor from him. "I've seen this before. These casings are so shitty. Any kind of knock and the top falls off and the insides pop out like a stripper jumping out of a cake." Riley inspected the circuit board before settling it back into its housing recessed into the top of the stake. Seeing the wires were still attached and not damaged, she coiled them carefully on top of the circuit board. She placed the glass sensor face on the top of the stake and hit it hard with the heel of her hand. The sensor clicked as the two pieces fell into place and she returned it back to Jake.

The pair spent nearly an hour looking for the other two sensors with no success. Jake called off the search and headed to Mole Control to see how Clint was fairing with the active Mole.

Riley returned to the centre of the camp with Finn and Owen. The testing tank was set to its normal size, similar to a double car garage, so as to accommodate the three guns at their full size. Owen and Finn waited for Riley to return before testing the guns.

"Not a moment too soon," said Riley looking at the sky. The morning's promising blue sky had changed quickly as thick, dark clouds rolled in. She looked at Finn. "Ready?"

Finn nodded and pressed the controller's red button. Again, the guns stood lifeless inside the tank. Riley swore and kicked an empty crate.

In a fit of drama, Finn fell to his knees holding his arms up to the sky, the guns' remote control in his hand. He shook his fists and yelled into the air. "Wwwww-whyyyyyyy?"

"Uh, Finn?" Finn looked up at Owen standing beside him. Owen's expression wore the vacant, somewhat cross-eyed and unmistakable look of a person reading something projected in front of them by the Icomm contacts. "Did you tie the guns to the remote? I'm looking at the list of detected dependents tied to the remote and I don't see any zeno ray guns listed here."

Within seconds, Finn also wore the same empty expression. "Well. That's embarrassing." The remote control beeped three times as it detected the three guns. Finn stood up quickly and acted as if the last twenty seconds had never happened. He cleared his throat. "Ready?"

"Idiot." Riley pretended to strangle him.

Finn pressed the button on the remote and the familiar red haze filled the tank.

TIME REMAINING: 16 Days

"Jake," called Clint over the com-sys. Clint's demeanour had remained cordial since Jake had questioned him about the perimeter sensor incident. "I've got good news and bad news."

Jake sat in Mole Control, rubbing his eyes in exasperation. He already knew the bad news; the monitor in front of him showed the three-dimensional schematic of the active Mole. A pulsing, red object flashed inside the schematic drawing. Ben's fix had finally given out. The cooling system no longer cooled, and the engine was threatening to overheat. Mole1 was finished unless the tools were found.

"I can see the bad news. What's the good news?"

"We're level with the Elevanium deposit."

The day ended on a far better note than it began. While the news of the last remaining Mole overheating was bad, the break was long overdue and Jake was impressed with how long Clint had managed to keep the drill running. What worried Jake was the bigger problem. Unless the tools miraculously returned, neither Mole would be operational and they would need to manually remove the rock surrounding the deposit. Jake made sure the team came prepared for blasting should it be required as a last resort. However, after the rock collapse, Jake wanted to do as little blasting as possible. He hoped that at least one of the Moles would be fixed soon to complete the excavation that would expose the deposit, but that was looking unlikely.

Jake took this milestone as an opportunity to celebrate. The team needed a boost in morale—so many things had gone wrong. And now with proof of someone trying to thwart them, the team needed a success to rally around.

Darren pulled sizzling burger patties off the barbeque and set them on the picnic table beside the fire pit. The ravenous piranhas seated patiently at the table dove in.

"Savour these burgers. This is the last of the meat," Darren warned. "It's all pasta and veggie dishes from now on. Or HOPs if you're really desperate."

At these words, Finn pretended to gag. "Clint, you're going to have to go hunting again!"

Clint had fallen into one of his sullen moods, and the conversation moved forward when it became apparent he had ignored Finn's comment. After his meltdown over Darren's cooking nearly a week ago, Jake's patience for Clint's moods was wearing thin. His growing desire to remove Clint from the op conflicted with his desperate need for the moody son of a bitch to continue working. The loss of another team member could jeopardize the operation. Jake knew Riley's patience with Clint had run out not long after her team's arrival. She had made it clear that she would rather work twenty-hour days than jeopardize the success of the operation with an unreliable key player.

As dinner wound down, the sun fell behind the lake. With the warmth of the sun's rays gone, the air became chilly, though it went unnoticed as the celebratory drinks flowed freely. For the first time in ages, the team could relax and enjoy each other's company. The stress of the past few weeks melted away as the group laughed off their endless problems. Even Clint had warmed up enough to play charades.

Only Jake and Riley remained at the picnic table and the pair discussed how best to proceed with the blasting the next day. Jake looked up at the sound of Clint's raised voice. The game had ended and the group began a discussion about recent legislation that had revoked the right of an intoxicated individual to pilot a flying car, despite the autopilot setting. Jake watched Clint as he spoke; he gesticulated fiercely and his voice frequently grew louder than the conversation warranted. Tyler, Maya and Darren left the conversation and moved their chairs to the opposite side of the fire. Clint reached into the cooler at Jake and Riley's feet and pulled out another beer. Jake stood and took the beer out of Clint's hand.

"We've got an early morning coming tomorrow and I need you on your A-game."

"It's just one beer." He took back the can of beer, cracked it open and took a sip.

Jake grabbed the can out of Clint's hand and dumped it on the ground. He pointed to the seven cans beneath Clint's chair. "It's not just one beer, it's eight."

The team sitting around the fire stopped their conversations and looked over. Riley stood up. "Why don't you guys take this somewhere else," she said, discreetly.

"Oh, I'm sorry," Clint bowed to her condescendingly, "am I upsetting your perfect little team?"

"Clint…" Jake grabbed Clint warningly by the arm and pulled him away from Riley and the group, but Clint broke free of his grip and stood eye to eye with Riley.

"You make me sick," he spat angrily at Riley. "You're not as great as everyone makes you out to be. I don't know what everyone sees in you. Riley Morgan is nothing but a Grade A bitch. I don't know how you got to be a level six. You probably slept your way up because you're nothing but a…" Clint stopped as the corners of Riley's mouth turned up. "What, is this funny?"

Riley spoke very slowly and quietly. "I think you should listen to your lead. I think you've got enough problems that you don't need a Grade A bitch making your life even more miserable. Be a good boy and go with your lead."

Riley's response incensed Clint and to everyone's surprise, he took a swing at her. She caught his fist in midair, twisted it around and behind his back, pushed him to the ground and dug her knee into his back. Clint spat grass and dirt out of his mouth. She put weight on his pinned arm as she leaned down and spoke in his ear.

"Listen to me very carefully. This team has been nothing but friendly and patient with you. Jake has given you far more chances than I ever would have. Let's gets a few things straight, right now. You now have a curfew of 19:00 hours for the rest of this op. If you put one toe out of line, I have no problem personally making your life a living hell for the next fifteen days and then ending your career when we get back. You got that?" Clint said nothing. Riley grabbed a handful of his hair and pulled his head back. "You got that, sub?" she said again, this time louder.

"Yes," he squeaked.

"Stand up." She barked the order as she released him. The team around the fire pit nearly jumped to attention out of reflex. Clint stood at attention in front her, his eyes looking over her head. She snapped her fingers in his face. "Right here. Look at me."

Clint's eyes zigzagged back and forth and finally locked on Riley's, whose honed in on him like a laser. She held his gaze for over ten seconds before speaking. "Do we have an understanding, sub?"

"Yes," he said through gritted teeth. Fear flashed in his widened eyes.

"Yes, what?"

"Yes, sir."

"You're dismissed. It's past your curfew."

Finn leaned over to Owen and whispered so only Owen could hear. "I hope for your sake that you don't ever piss her off."

CHAPTER 40

TEAM 1 & 2
YEAR: 1200
TIME REMAINING: 15 Days

Jake awoke to a blood-curdling scream coming from somewhere within the camp. He threw on a pair of shorts, dashed outside and saw a body lying on the ground with someone crouched over it, just past Mole Control. Jake's sleepy mind chugged to process the situation as the crouching person called and waved him over.

Jake ran to the pair and fell to his knees. "Lexi," he said, near-whisper. When she failed to respond, he called her name again, louder. He fumbled with her wrist, desperate to feel a gentle pulse but found nothing. He looked up at Maya's tear-stained face. "What happened?" Within seconds, Riley, Finn, Darren and Tyler approached the scene.

Maya shook. "Someone hit her!" Finn took Maya in his arms. "It was so horrible!" Her words were muffled by Finn's thick hoodie.

Riley fell to her knees at Lexi's side, opposite Jake. "Maya, what do you mean 'Someone hit her?' Who hit her? Where?"

"Her head. In the back of the head or maybe the side." Maya slid out of Finn's arms and fell to her knees crowding Riley. Riley eyed Finn and he pulled Maya to her feet and backed her away.

Maya's words came out in sobs. "I heard a noise outside, like a door slamming. We thought it was weird, and with all the bizarre things that have been happening, Lexi thought we should investigate. We watched out the window for a few moments, and we saw someone run out from between the trailers. Lexi bolted out the door after the guy…well, I'm sure it was a guy. We didn't see his face, but he had the same kind of build as the guy in the video from the other night. He ran out of sight past Mole Control and Lexi followed him. But I guess he'd doubled back and hid. As Lexi passed the trailer, he stepped out and hit her in the head with something."

"Which way did he go?" asked Finn.

She pointed in the direction of the lake. "That way!"

Like hounds released to pursue their quarry, Finn and Tyler raced toward the rocky cliff that led to the lake. They climbed down as fast as the steep rocky face would allow using the floodlight setting on their VersaTools to light their way.

Riley looked at Jake. "She's got a strong pulse, I think she's just unconscious. You take her. I'll help look." Riley disappeared behind the house trailers.

Jake scooped Lexi up with ease and strode toward his trailer. "Maya, please grab the MediScanner. Darren, an ice pack, please."

Jake carried Lexi's small, limp body carefully over the threshold into his trailer and lay her on the unused of the two beds. Inside the trailer, Jake saw a cut on Lexi's right temple. He brushed her blond hair away from the cut and her eyes opened. She looked around the trailer then at Jake. Her eyes seemed unfocused for a moment then righted themselves.

"Jake…" She struggled to sit up.

He gently patted her on the shoulder and eased her back down. "It's okay, you don't have to talk. Maya will be here in a sec."

Lexi sat up, agitated. "I need…" She wobbled slightly and Jake steadied her with a hand on each shoulder. She leaned over the side of the bed and threw up on his sandaled feet.

Darren, who had opened the door just in time to see Lexi get sick, tossed the icepack on the bed beside Jake, tore into the bathroom and slammed the door. Jake heard retching sounds followed by the toilet flushing.

Semidelirious, Lexi leaned forward and rested her head on Jake's shoulder. He stroked the back of her neck, unsure of what else to do. He wanted to avoid being thrown up on again, but it was better than the alternative—her getting sick while lying down. He could only sit in his sticky sandals and wait for Maya to come with the MediScanner. He heard Darren enter round two in the bathroom. Again, the toilet flushed.

Maya rushed in carrying the MediScanner and a blue plastic basket of first aid supplies. She stepped between the beds to avoid the puddle of vomit and seated herself on Jake's dishevelled bed. She turned on the scanner and made a pass over Lexi's hunched body.

"She's got a pretty good concussion, and thankfully that's all. I think it's best if we don't move her and she stays here tonight. You can have our trailer tonight and I'll stay here with her. That way I can monitor her."

Jake was unsure of how to say what he wanted to say without sounding disrespectful or implying that he thought that women were unable to take care of themselves. However, his first priority was to keep his team members safe. "I agree, but I'm staying here, too. Tomorrow, I think that you and Finn should bunk up." Maya met Jake's eyes with an unmistakable look of relief.

The rainy morning seemed fitting to Jake; his gloomy mood rivalled the dreary grey of the stormy sky. He sat down across from Riley at a table in the dining room, finally able to ask her where she had disappeared to after Lexi's attack. Finn and Tyler's search of the surrounding areas had yielded nothing.

"Well, I knew that all eyes would be on Clint for this, and I wanted to look for evidence. I knew if we waited until the morning there would be none. Think about it: if it was Clint who attacked her and he snuck back into his trailer feigning sleep, he'd be out of breath and sweaty from running. If he wasn't in his trailer, that would be equally damning. So I thought I'd pay his trailer a visit. If he or Ben were awake, I would ask them if they'd seen anything and, at the same time, see what kind of physical shape Clint was in."

Jake was impressed by her quick thinking at such an ungodly hour.

"Out of courtesy, I knocked on their door. Actually, I hammered on it and no one answered. I knew that Ben wouldn't be fast to answer the door, but if Clint was there, he should have heard. When no one answered, I assumed Clint wasn't there and that Ben had taken sleeping pills or something. I went inside and flicked on the lights. Both men were passed out, dead to the world. Even after flicking on the lights they didn't wake up. Before waking them, I took a good look over Clint."

Jake was anxious to hear the answer. "What did you find?"

"Nothing. His breathing was normal and showed no signs of any recent physical exertion. Further to that, he had ear plugs in. Ben was snoring like a buzz saw."

Jake leaned back and looked contemplative. "So Ben was passed out from the sleeping pills, and Clint didn't hear you because of the ear plugs."

"So I would say that it was not Clint that attacked Lexi last night. But I guess she'll be able to tell us for sure."

Jake shook his head, frustrated he could not catch a break to save his life. "I asked her this morning. She doesn't remember being hit."

"Dammit," breathed Riley.

"Rile, that brings me to my next topic of discussion. Room assignments. I've moved Lexi in with me. I want Finn to move into the girls' trailer and stay with Maya. Darren and Tyler are fine where they are, as are Clint and Ben."

"Sounds good." She shot back the rest of her orange juice.

Jake hesitated. "Do I need to be worried about you?" He wondered if he should ask. He suspected that if he tried to bunk Riley up with a man to protect her, Jake might find himself needing protection. He felt sorry for any person who mistook her for an easy target. "I think you should bunk up with Owen. Two sets of eyes and ears are better than one. Plus, he's pretty vulnerable without those crutches."

Riley looked at Jake in earnest. "Yeah, I guess he is, eh? Well, whatever you think is best." She left the table and turned to take her dishes to the dishwasher. Despite her best efforts not to, she smiled.

With no tools to fix the problem-riddled Moles, the teams needed to blast away the remaining stone from around the Elevanium deposit and manually clear it away. While Clint and Owen had two very different professional backgrounds, their combined knowledge and experience made them invaluable assets. They discussed blasting strategies and tested them with a simulation program.

Jake found himself in the dreaded, worst-case scenario. During the planning phase of Operation TimeShift, Jake's doubts about the Moles' abilities to get the job done were met with sales pitch assurances of unparalleled performance and nominal downtime. So when he asked for a second Mole and enough explosives for a small country, his request had been met with considerable indignant resistance. Jake knew that for some unexplainable reason, catastrophic failures always seemed to take place when stakes were the highest.

The door to Mole Control opened and Maya slid into the boardroom. She stopped abruptly when she saw Clint. She pulled her wet hood back and brushed her wind-swept hair off her face. Her grave expression made Jake's stomach sink.

"Jake, can I talk to you for a sec?" Her eyes moved from Jake to Clint, to the floor and back to Jake.

"Sure." Jake stood and looked at Owen. "I'll leave you guys to this." She motioned for him to follow her and he ran after her hooded figure as she darted across the camp in the direction of Ben and Clint's trailer. Jake caught up with her, shielding his eyes from the driving rain. "Maya, what's wrong?"

She stopped, her hand gripping the handle of Ben and Clint's trailer door. "There's something you need to see. Darren was cleaning and he found something."

Jake followed her inside and found Ben sitting up in bed, magazine in hand. Darren greeted Jake by holding a box out to him.

"I was doing my cleaning rounds and when I knelt down to vacuum under the bed, I found this."

Jake looked in the box and his eyes widened. "I'll be damned." He slid his earpiece in and called Riley on the com-sys. She arrived at the trailer in less than a minute and Jake held the box out to her. "Darren found this under Clint's bed."

Clint entered the open trailer door, eager to know why the leads were congregating in his trailer. "What was found under Clint's bed?"

"You tell us," said Riley, as she pushed the box roughly into Clint's chest. The box's dimensions were identical to the one held by the man in the video.

Clint took the box and looked inside. Rattling around inside were handfuls of compressed objects from around the camp—the tools from the work shed, two WeatherShield sensors and two perimeter sensors. All of the colour drained from Clint's face and he looked pleadingly at Jake. "I swear to you I didn't do this. I didn't put these here. I've never seen this box before in my life!"

"If it helps at all, I've never seen that box before either," said Ben.

"Me neither, and I vacuum under there once a week," added Darren.

Jake looked angrier than anyone had ever seen him. He looked at Clint and then to Riley. "We need to chat." He motioned to the door and Clint walked out. "Riley, take Clint to the meeting room. Neither of you leave until I get there."

Jake handed the box over to Lexi in Mole Control, instructing her to scan each tool for fingerprints before sending them to Tyler so he could begin working on the Moles. He stopped into the work shed to bring Tyler up to speed. As Jake finished explaining what had occurred in the last twenty minutes, a quadrahex wrench—one of the Moles' proprietary tools—materialized on the surface of the transport pod on the workbench, sent by Lexi from Mole Control, scanned for prints and ready for work.

"Oh, thank God!" He picked up the L-shaped tool and spun it through his fingers like a seasoned grease monkey. "Finally, I can do something productive."

Jake smiled, happy something was going right for someone. "I like the sounds of that. But before you do, I need you to do something for me." Tyler's eyes widened at Jake's request, but he nodded wordlessly.

As Jake turned to leave, two more tools appeared on the transporter's flat surface. Jake heard Tyler talking to the tools as the door closed behind him. "Oh, the span wrench, how I've missed you!"

"Clint, we've got some serious problems." Jake sat across from his sub in the meeting room. Riley stood in the corner, silent and observing.

"Jake, I didn't take those tools, I swear!" Clint pleaded.

"Clint," Jake said, exhaling in frustration. He rubbed his eyes. "I don't know what to think. There's been a lot of bizarre shit going on around here lately. First we have the WeatherShield going down. You are nowhere to be found when it happened, and you can't prove whether or not you were in bed or on a walk. The parts show up under your bed."

"I had nothing to do with that! I told you I was walking to blow off steam!" His eyes pled with a desperation equal to his voice.

"Then, a perimeter sensor is broken and two go missing. The parts show up under your bed. Tools are taken. They show up under your bed. We have a video of a man, roughly your height and build, wearing a field op uniform who is familiar enough with our set up to know the location of the light override switch."

"I suppose you're going to blame me for letting the bears in next?"

"I don't know. Did you? You treat everyone around here like they're your personal verbal punching bags. Even when they turn the other cheek, you continue to bully and alienate them. You're arrogant, you have a warped sense of entitlement that I can't figure out, and your attitude sucks."

A brief moment of silence passed between the two men.

"Are you done?" Clint asked.

"No. Lexi was attacked. Neither Riley nor I believe that was you. And I don't really know what motive you would have to destroy the perimeter alarm or the WeatherShield. It just doesn't make sense."

"Well, duh. Do you think I like walking around in the rain?" retorted Clint.

"You're walking one hell of a fine line here, sub. But you're lucky because there is no physical evidence pointing to you."

"There's no fucking evidence because I didn't do any of it!" Clint stood in anger and, seeing Riley's expression, sat back down again.

"But there is also no hard evidence that clears you of any of this either, except the attack on Lexi. So to summarize, I don't believe you attacked Lexi. But in all of these other incidents, you've been MIA, and that, unfortunately, makes you my number-one suspect."

"So what does all this mean?" asked Clint defiantly.

"It means, Clint, that it seems like you're jeopardizing this project, and that's enough to hold you for now. We have just over two weeks left in this project and you are proving to be a threat. And on an op this critical, I can't take any chances. I'm holding you until more evidence is collected. Unfortunately, I'm really busy, so that might take a while. Riley, do you have anything you need to add?"

Riley shook her head.

"Wait. Holding me? What, like prison?"

Jake wanted to believe that Clint was not capable of doing these things, but every shred of circumstantial evidence pointed to him. "Come on, Clint. Let's go."

Jake and Riley escorted Clint out of the main tent, each with a firm grip on Clint's arms. The wind caught the door, whipping it out of Riley's hand and all three were greeted by a gale of freezing rain. Clint's leads escorted him to the cube, a holding cell for use in the field.

"Are you freaking kidding me?" Clint yelled as Jake and Riley led him inside. "This is crazy! I didn't have anything to do with any of this! I'm going to sue your asses off when we get back!" Jake closed the door and locked it. Riley could see Clint screaming through the window in the door, but the sound proof walls contained his profanity to the cell.

Riley and Jake walked back to the unoccupied eating area and Jake sat down heavily, shaking the table.

"My God, Riley. Did we really just lock up one of our men? Did we do the right thing?" Jake marvelled at Riley's calm demeanour as she sat across from him, biting into an apple she took from a basket on the counter. He felt sweat beginning to bead on his forehead and his heart pounded like a hammer. He steadied his shaking hands on his thighs but refrained from looking at them for fear that Riley would see. He wondered if anything ever rattled her. After some of the stuff she had seen in her career, throwing some punk in a cell was probably like taking out the trash.

Riley leaned in, elbows on the table. "Jake, we're in an awkward spot here. We're on an extremely unorthodox op. Half of us aren't even doing what it is that we're trained for, myself and Finn included. I've never gone on an op like this, neither has Finn. Lexi's a drone jockey, Tyler does communications and none of us except Clint have ever seen a tunnel boring machine before. So we're kind of flying blind here, and this is why we've been given so much time. To take our time and do things right. We can't expect perfection, and protocols are more relaxed. I mean, really, when was the last time you had cold beer, folding chairs and marshmallows on an op?"

"Okay, good point."

"This is a non-combat op and, as bizarre as it sounds, not fearing for your life every minute changes the dynamic. In terms of order and control, that lack of fear makes the op much harder for the lead. People listen if they feel you can keep them from dying. This is more like a working vacation. But at the end of the day, we are on an extremely critical mission and that's no different than any other op. As leads, our goal is to protect the integrity of the mission while working with what we've got. Clint is draining the team of morale. Between you and me, one more outburst like we had the other night and I would have cubed him myself. If you feel for one minute that someone is jeopardizing the mission or other people, you can hold them in the cube. You can't beat the hell out of them, unfortunately, but you can hold them."

Riley guessed by Jake's shakiness and pallid colour that he had never had to seriously discipline a subordinate before. As time sensitive and as crucial as his operations were, Mechanical and Infrastructure Recovery never attracted the egos that Black Ops seemed to draw. She had cubed a handful of problem subs over the years.

Jake's colour and confidence had returned for the team briefing in the meeting room. Within minutes of it happening, everyone knew Clint had been cubed. Jake wanted to discuss the morning's events before the camp turned into a rumour mill.

After the group had been brought up to speed, Jake asked them all to report. Lexi had finished scanning the contents of the box and the box itself for fingerprints. Until they returned to the future, no database existed for them to cross reference the prints against. Her study of the video revealed nothing more than what they had already seen. Finn and Owen, with Lexi's help, got the WeatherShield and the perimeter alarm back online.

After the meeting, Owen returned to Mole Control with Jake and continued working on the blasting simulations. Lexi and Tyler returned to the work shed to attack Mole1's failure in the cooling system. Finn and Riley, with Ben's direction, had the main shaft removed from Mole2 by the end of the night.

Jake was pleased that the day had ended on a reasonably productive note, despite the harrowing events of the morning. He still felt uneasy about Clint and the lack of hard evidence, but he pushed it out of his mind. *Not to mention*, he thought, *the cube isn't exactly a hardship.* The spacious holding cell had full plumbing, a kitchen area, comfortable bedding and some entertainment in the form of outdated books and magazines.

Owen returned to his trailer and found his new bunkmate having a shower. "Is there room for one more in there?" Owen asked, stepping into the shower. Riley held out her hand and helped him limp in.

Owen stared at the stream of steaming water as he rubbed shampoo into his hair.

"Hey Rile, I've been doing some thinking about this whole Clint-thing. I can't see his motivation for any of this. Sure, he's one of the biggest dicks I've ever met, but I can't see what he'd get out of petty vandalism. Despite his crappy attitude, the guy's done five months of flawless work. I can't see him throwing his career away for a couple of missing sensors and tools to spite people. Plus, why would he leave the box somewhere where it could be so easily found?"

Riley looked contemplative as she rinsed the conditioner out of her hair. "I know. That part doesn't make sense either, but there's no real alternative suspect."

"Well, we're pretty confident that Clint didn't attack Lexi, right?"

Riley nodded as she rinsed her face.

"It seems then, that it's more likely someone else attacked Lexi."

"True," Riley agreed.

"Do you suspect that anyone else on the team would do this?"

She shook her head. "I don't think anyone here would do it. Of course, we can't prove that either. But other than Clint, there really isn't anyone with a height and body frame matching the guy in the video except Ben, and he's not that mobile."

"What are the odds that someone snuck back in time with you in a crate or something and has been hiding in the bushes this whole time? What are the odds that the op is being sabotaged? From what Jake says, the Moles aren't running nearly as well as they are supposed to."

Riley chuckled. "I think the odds are better that it's the Elevanium curse. All of this stuff was packed by Defence staff. Jake and I oversaw it."

"But you couldn't have seen every box being packed."

"True. But ninety percent of the crates were compressed. A human's never been compressed before. It's probably possible though. I know they've tested compression on cadavers successfully, but it's never been tried on a living human." She turned off the water, grabbed their towels off the rack and handed Owen his. "Well, I think it's very unlikely. But no more unlikely than anyone here attacking Lexi."

CHAPTER 41

TEAM 1 & 2
YEAR: 1200
TIME REMAINING: 13 Days

Owen awoke to find Riley propped up on her elbow, watching him. They had become so immersed in the operation that neither of them had found the time to bring up the approaching conclusion of their relationship. Waking before the crack of dawn, working late and frequent night-time catastrophes had sapped them of energy. When they did finally get to bed, they fell asleep before any words could be spoken.

Owen wrapped his arms around her and kissed her neck. "This op is going to be over in less than two weeks," Riley whispered.

"I try not to think about it."

"Me too. We've been so busy that it's just kind of snuck up."

"How do you feel about it?" asked Owen.

"Well, lots I guess. I mean I love what we have, and I love you. The thought of this coming to an end is devastating. I haven't been thinking about it because I need to focus on the op. But I am quite upset about it. I think we could have really had something."

Owen sighed heavily. "I feel the same. The thought of not being able to be with you... well, it's the heartbreak of a lifetime. Meeting you, spending time and falling in love with you has been the best experience of my life. I don't want this to end."

"But there's nothing we can do about it."

Owen fell silent for a moment and looked thoughtful. "Why don't you come back to 2016 with me?"

"You know I can't do that," Riley said, poking him in the ribs.

"Why not? I mean, really, why couldn't you?"

"It's highly illegal for one. It's like being an illegal immigrant. Worse actually, as I'd have no way of proving where I'm from. It's messy and it's just too dangerous. Plus, I'd really miss my grandfather. He's the only family I have, and I know he'd be devastated. I would suggest you come to 2097 but that would be just as illegal, and I wouldn't want to ask you to leave the job you love or your life behind."

"Riley, you are my life. The job is just a job. Don't get me wrong, I love it, but I'd trade it in a heartbeat if it meant I could be with you."

Riley sat on the edge of the bed and held her head in her hands. She had specifically left these thoughts buried for this reason. If left to fester, they would compromise her ability to concentrate on the mission and there was no room in Operation TimeShift for someone distracted by a broken heart. Owen pulled her back into bed and held her close, her head tucked under his chin.

"I don't want to leave you," she said finally, "but there is nothing we can do about it."

Owen kissed her on the top of her head. "We've still got a couple of weeks. Let's just enjoy them."

Jake awoke with a start, expecting catastrophe. Realizing all was well, he lay back in bed and stared at the textured pattern on the trailer's ceiling. His expectations had fallen so low that he treasured every minute that passed problem-free. He went to the dining room where Riley joined him and told him Owen's theory. He was initially sceptical, but after mulling it over with a bowl of oatmeal, he started to wonder if it had merit. It was more logical than anything else he had come up with.

By noon, Ben, Tyler and Finn had Mole1 repaired, tested and ready to be deployed. Tyler and Lexi manoeuvred the drill into place and filed into the control room. Together, they fit into the cramped room better than Jake did alone. They shared a nervous glance as Lexi hit the ignition button. When the engine fired up with no reports of problems, they smiled with relief and eyed the monitoring screens as Tyler engaged the drill. As the massive drill head began to spin, they heard the motor slow under the heavy load. When the drill head got up to speed, Tyler held up crossed fingers as Lexi inched the massive machine forward. When it connected with the rock, the dull scraping sound of the drill head biting into the rock was drowned by cheering.

TIME REMAINING: 10 Days

"We've got the perimeter cut around the deposit, but it's not as close as we'd hoped," reported Tyler.

Jake listened as he lay half in, half out of an engine compartment of Mole2. "It's alright," he called back. "At least we didn't have to blast it all manually." He extricated himself from inside the compartment and tossed the tool he had been using onto the workbench. "Well, I don't need to waste any more time on this damn thing then. Double up the stabilization sensors in that perimeter tunnel. We're going to have to do a lot of blasting, and we don't need the ceiling falling in. I'll get Lexi and Finn to start pulling out the explosives and…" he stopped, hearing Lexi cut over him, the urgency in her voice unmistakable.

"Jake, you have to see this!"

Jake parked the Mole outside the work shed where it would remain for the rest of the op, no longer needed. It could rust at the bottom of the lake for all he cared—he never wanted to see a Mole ever again. He jogged to Mole Control, eager to see what had Lexi so worked up. She stood as he entered, grabbed his hand and pulled him into the chair at the monitors.

"I've been scouring the video from the other night." She knelt on the floor at Jake's side, pulling the keyboard controls toward herself.

"I thought you said you didn't find anything?" asked Jake, confused.

"No, this is the video from when I was attacked." She backed the video up several seconds.

Jake was surprised at Lexi's grit. He had looked over this video himself, not wanting Lexi to have to watch herself be assaulted again and again, looking for clues about her attacker. "Lex, you didn't have to do that."

"It was hard to watch the first couple times but after that, it just seemed like it was a scene from a movie." She slowed the video to regular speed. A figure was running forward to the right edge of the screen. "I went through this frame by frame. This guy makes a point of looking away from the camera as he's running from the trailers. It's like he knows it's there. Okay here, look. I'm just running past Mole Control and you see the guy pop out, right?"

She pointed at a black outline barely visible on the screen. "The figure walks into the light, but again, he's not facing the camera. Okay, here, he hits me. Bastard. That really freaking hurt. But here it is! You can see something on his arm on the follow-through of his swing." She advanced through several more frames, froze the screen and zoomed into the man's arm. "At first I thought it was the sleeve of his shirt—but look! It's a tattoo!"

Jake leaned into the screen. Sure enough, as Lexi crumpled to the ground, frame by frame, the sleeve of the attacker's shirt slid up to reveal a thick tattoo encircling the attacker's upper arm.

"And that's not all. Look at the initials on the shirt!" Lexi advanced several frames. As the attacker's swing followed through, his body turned just enough so several embroidered letters on his dark sleeve were visible. The initials "NRD" stood out clearly.

"What the hell? That's no field op uniform. And that's not what he was wearing last time." Jake scrolled through the footage several times. He called into the com-sys. "Hey Rile, you'd better come see this."

The group was equally stunned when they saw the tattoo, and even more so when the initials NRD flashed across the screen.

"Looks like Owen's theory was right." Every member of the team had filed into Mole Control to see the new evidence Lexi had uncovered.

"What the hell?" said Tyler, shaking his head.

"I guess this means that Clint is off the hook," said Lexi.

"It definitely helps his case, that's for sure," said Jake. "Lex, pull up the video of the night the tools were stolen and see if we can see that tattoo."

She pulled up the video and fast-forwarded to the time in question. The group watched in silence as she advanced the video frame by frame. The man in the video opened the shed door.

"Zoom in, Lex. I want to see every hair on that guy's goddamn arm," said Jake.

Lexi zoomed in until the intruder's shoulders and upper body filled the screen. She advanced the video slowly. As the man reached inside to override the light switch, the sleeve of the shirt slid up. For only a few frames, the tattoo became visible. The camp lights generated just enough light to distinguish the black tattoo from the darkened sleeve of the shirt. Zoomed out and at full speed, the tattoo became camouflaged as part of the shirt's sleeve.

"Lex, can you capture an image of that tattoo and clean it up?" asked Jake.

"Sure. Give me a sec." Within minutes, Lexi had a picture of the man's arm isolated and enhanced enough to show the distinct pattern of the tattoo.

"Does anyone know if Clint has this tattoo?" asked Jake.

"I don't think so," said Riley. "We would have seen it at the lake."

The door to Mole Control opened and Owen entered, stepping gingerly off his crutches and into the trailer. "Sorry. It's hard to get anywhere quickly on these crutches when you've got coffee. What'd you guys find?" He looked over at the screen and saw the arm and tattoo. "Hey, I've seen that tattoo before."

All eyes turned to Owen.

"You mean you've seen one *like* this before?" asked Riley, looking back at the tattoo. "I'm pretty sure there's no way you've seen this particular one before."

"No, I have. Definitely." He took a sip of his coffee and looked thoughtful for a moment. "Dammit. I don't remember where. I feel like I was busy at the time. The memory's really fuzzy. It might have even been before we met." He thought back to the gym or that maybe he had seen it on TV but failed to place it. "Ever since I got my armband tattoo I've always made a point of seeing what other people have."

"Owen, there's no possible way you've seen *this* tattoo before," said Riley.

Owen shrugged. "Well, maybe not. Nobody's got the market cornered on armband tattoos. I guess there could be a lot of people out there with the same one. I seem to recall only getting a quick glimpse of it, but it stuck out in my mind because it's quite traditional, except the artist took a little creative license with part of the design here." He leaned towards the screen and pointed to a particular pattern within the tattoo.

"This tattoo stood out in my mind because I was rather partial to this same pattern, except for those little swirly bits, so I went with a different pattern. But when I saw this tattoo, wherever it was, I recognized the pattern instantly. I remember thinking that the modifications to the design were done quite well. I'm a little jealous, actually. It's a really unique design. I've never seen anything like it." He set himself down gingerly on the couch, easing his bad leg out in front of him. He thought about it for another moment as he sipped his coffee. "Damn. Now it's going to bug me. I wish I could remember where I saw it."

"I guess Clint's off the hook," said Lexi, looking from the tattoo on the screen to Jake.

Clint lay on the cube's bottom bunk reading the August 2076 issue of *Popular Science* magazine.

"What do you guys want?" asked Clint, not looking at his visitors. He turned the page of his magazine.

"We're here to talk," said Jake, taking a seat at the table. Jake kicked the chair opposite him away and motioned to the seat. Riley stood behind Jake, leaning on the door, her arms crossed and observing.

Clint sat up lazily on the edge of the bed, making a show of doing things on his time. His eyes moved to Riley and, seeing her expression, he stood quickly and sat down across from Jake.

"What now? Did one of your precious subs get attacked again and you're here to blame me for it?"

Jake remained silent. After a moment, he spoke. "We've been reviewing the video of the night Lexi was attacked for clues…"

Clint cut in. "But I didn't do that!"

Jake closed his eyes and massaged the bridge of his nose as he sighed. When he spoke, his voice was calm and even. "Clint, please let me finish. We reviewed the video from that night and we found some clues about the attacker."

"What kind of clues?" Clint's eyes narrowed.

"He has a large tattoo on his left upper arm. It's visible in a few frames of the video, right after he hits Lexi. After finding this, we reviewed the video from the night the tools were stolen, and again, the tattoo is visible for a fraction of a second. It's not immediately obvious in either video, and if you didn't know to look for it, you'd probably never see it. It just looks like the sleeve of the shirt. But what's also mystifying is that, on the second video, there are the initials NRD embroidered on the sleeve of the guy's shirt."

"What? Who is it?"

Jake shrugged and shook his head. "We don't know. You're welcome to watch the video if you'd like."

"Oh, so you're letting me out now? I've sat in here rotting for days with no visitors and you're going to just let me out like nothing ever happened? Am I just supposed to forget about all of this?" Clint looked enraged.

Riley exploded and she lunged at Clint. Fear filled his eyes like a deer caught in the headlights of an oncoming truck. Her forearm connected square across his chest and she slammed him and his chair over backward. The chair made a muffled metallic clunk on the ground as Clint's weight landed on it. Riley bent over him, half-kneeling on his chest, half-squatting beside him, with her nose nearly touching his.

"If you want to continue working on this op, you'll thank Jake kindly for letting you out. If it were up to me, I wouldn't even let you out of this cube before the leap home. I'd leave you in here like an animal. If you want to press charges when we get back, you're more than welcome to, my last name is spelled M-O-R-G-A-N. But good luck, you don't have a leg to stand on. If you give me, or anyone else, even a hint of your bullshit or your attitude, you and I are going to have a talk—just you and me. If I hear another word come out of your mouth that is negative, passive aggressive or something I just plain don't like, we're going to chat in this cube, and next time Jake won't be here to chaperone."

Riley stood and resumed her place by the door. Clint rolled out of his chair with as much dignity he could muster. As he stood, he righted the chair.

Jake crossed his arms and looked at his sub searchingly. "Clint, you have to see how your attitude and the way you've treated people has led to the mistrust that contributed to your being here."

Clint was silent for a moment. "So now what?"

"So now, you're free to leave and resume your productive duties. I'll bring you up to speed with what we're doing in a moment. Riley, do you have anything to add?"

"No, I've made my points." When Clint looked at her, his pale face registered fear like she was an angry hornet whose nest, he realized too late, he had shaken one time too many.

TIME REMAINING: 9 Days

After ironing out the Clint situation, Jake felt an urgency to keep the team moving. The constant interruptions had drained the group of time they could not afford to lose.

The first day of blasting went well, though the progress had not been what Jake had hoped. Only Owen and Clint had worked directly with explosives before and nothing about explosives could be expedited in any way with simplification tools. The VersaTools made removing the debris fast and easy; the shrunken boulders were tossed effortlessly into a dump bucket and then carried away. The day ended on a high note with a fraction of the deposit finally visible.

Clint's post-cube integration into the group went better than Jake had expected. Everyone put on a happy face and Clint managed to complete the day with no offensive behaviour, perhaps because he said very little to anyone. Optimistically, Jake hoped that Clint's improved performance was a result of him having taken a good look inside during his time in the cube. Realistically, he suspected it was Riley's promise to personally return him to the cube that truly motivated him. Either way, Jake needed productive days going forward because the nights were about to get much longer. With concrete proof of a dangerous, unauthorized individual roaming the camp at night, security needed to be increased. Taking no chances so close to the operation's end, Jake assigned two-person patrols at all times after dusk.

Owen and Riley took the first shift. By eleven o'clock, both patrollers ached with hunger. Meatless meals failed to sustain a body working eighteen-hour days. They patrolled the camp looking for anything or anyone unusual. With their VersaTools set to NIGHT VISION, they scanned the bushes beyond the perimeter of the camp. The tool emitted an invisible, heat-sensing field that would project a ghostly green outline of whatever warm-blooded organism it picked up. The first glowing rabbit Owen saw nearly startled him backward off his crutches.

CHAPTER 42

TEAM 3
YEAR: 2095
TIME REMAINING: 4 Days

After three solid weeks of evenings spent toiling in the Neural Programming lab, Spencer felt an indebtedness to his coworkers that he knew would take several lifetimes to repay. He was equally moved by their unquestioning, unwavering belief in him. Without their hard work, he would never have finished programming the additional 157 detailed scenarios with enough time to allow for testing. Each of his carefully crafted tests contained a scripted scenario to force each Personality Application to experience the full gamut of human emotions—everything from joy to sympathy, helplessness to jealousy and blind rage to fear.

Having just finished programming Spencer's enhanced scenarios into the Real Life Simulator, Erik, Kalen and Lisa hovered anxiously behind Spencer, waiting for him to initiate the program. Seeing their excitement and knowing they were nearly as emotionally invested as he was meant more to him than he could let on.

Spencer noticed his coworkers had started to show physical signs of overwork similar to the ones that he had been exhibiting for months already. Kalen yawned nonstop. Dark circles had grown under Erik's eyes and Lisa, who ordinarily took great care in her appearance, had traded in her pantsuit for yoga pants and her spiky high heels for comfortable runners.

"Here goes nothing." Spencer initiated the Real Life Simulator and the screen darkened. After a few moments, a progress monitor box appeared on the screen.

Personality 001 :: Tests Run: 0/157 Tests passed: 0. Tests failed: 0.

After several minutes, the numbers began to update.

Personality 001 :: Tests Run: 5/157 Tests passed: 5. Tests failed: 0.

Then,

Personality 001 :: Tests Run: 23/157 Tests passed: 23. Tests failed: 0.

The group stood in silence and watched the numbers climb.
"Looking good so far," said Lisa.

"I should hope so," Erik laughed. "The first thirty tests were pretty easy. If one of these personalities lost their marbles when playing with puppies, the person whose personality it was probably would've raised some flags during the screening process. I hope."

"Now let's get the hell out of here," said Kalen. She grabbed Spencer's hand and gave him a hug. "I'm taking this guy on a date."

TIME REMAINING: 3 Days

Spencer cringed at the thought of another night in the Neural Programming lab. He usually preferred to work in the lab—the bland space was distraction-free, allowing him to stay focused on the task at hand. It also lent itself well to collaborative teamwork, as the lab's size and resources were ideal. However, after spending as much time there as he and his coworkers had, a change of atmosphere was an absolute necessity.

"This was a great idea, Spence," said Lisa, setting her chopsticks down on her plate. She picked up her glass of Chardonnay and leaned back on the sofa. "I couldn't spend another minute in that lab. I don't know how you can work in there as much as you do and stay motivated."

Erik stacked the empty sushi trays and carried them into Spencer's kitchen, his mouth still aflame from the spicy tuna. "Don't get me wrong," he called back as he crammed the cardboard trays into the recycling bot. "I love my job, but if I spent any more time in the Neural Programming lab, I was going to go mental."

Spencer set his CI on the coffee table and powered it up. When the screen appeared, his stomach jumped with anticipation. He expanded the screen so everyone would be able to see the results easily. He found the folder that contained the twenty-two individual report files—one for each personality.

"First up is Brad Jamison," Spencer opened up the first file called Personality 001.

"Right, the CEO," said Kalen. "He was really nice. It'll be so interesting to see how he translates into a digital personality."

Brad Jamison personified success after building a highly successful business consulting firm from scratch. He also created a clothing line for men and opened three successful restaurants. He bought, resuscitated and flipped many failing businesses. He was greatly respected not only in business, but also at the community level. His signature graced the bottom of many generous cheques for community initiatives and scholarships.

Spencer knew from reviewing Brad's responses to the initial questionnaire that his early youth had been anything but easy. Raised by a single mother in a rundown mobile home, he endured merciless bullying for most of his elementary school years. High school changed his life considerably when he shot up ten inches and found he could launch a rocketball farther than anyone in the school's division. At seventeen, professional rocketball teams offered to sign him but his mother forced him to stay in school. Without an education to fall back on, he would be sunk should he suffer a career-ending injury. Begrudgingly, Brad agreed and continued life as a normal teenager.

Brad graduated from high school with a full university scholarship where he found his true love—business. Brad attributed his success in life to the scholarship he had won, knowing that without it, university would have only been a dream. Brad believed in higher education, and it was important to him to give others like him the same opportunity.

Spencer expected the test to flag some unrepaired emotional damage stemming from Brad's elementary school years, but what he read in the results shocked him to the core. The results revealed that the brilliant, confident businessman Spencer had met in the interview room all those months ago was a very different person on the inside than he was on the outside.

Real Life Simulator :: Test Results Summary
Personality 001: Bradley Jamison

Summary of Desirable Behaviour:
- *Very strong work ethic. Not afraid of hard work and strives to continually learn. Thrives on accomplishment and continual improvement.*
- *Highly intelligent with unconventional ideas. Shows elevated potential for advanced innovation and invention.*
- *Good moral structure and is nonviolent.*
- *Able to tolerate unusually high amounts of stress and risk in business.*

Summary of Undesirable Behaviour:
- *Low tolerance for personal rejection or criticism. Does not forgive easily and holds grudges.*
- *Amicable on the surface but is suspicious of others' intentions. Fears compliments are veiled criticisms and suspects gestures of goodwill are devices to trap and manipulate him.*
- *Exhibits paranoid tendencies. Could lead to problems interacting and building relationships with humans and other robots.*
- *Does not like to be instructed, would prefer to set own rules and boundaries.*

Number of Scenario-Based Tests Run: 157
Passed: 87 Failed: 70

Summary: Stress tests at all four levels, Low, Mid, High and Extreme, revealed the personality could handle nearly any amount of stress pertaining to business. Tests involving personal stress yielded exemplary results in all Low and some of the Mid level tests. Most High and Extreme tests were failed. High and Extreme tests resulted in significant mental trauma and resulting behaviour was consistent with being unable to function as a stable, contributing member of society. Unstable behaviour included extremely aggressive interactions with others, delusion, fear and, at times, reclusiveness. Though generally nonviolent, when under extreme personal stress, the personality became violent for purposes of self-preservation. This personality carries significant paranoid tendencies and would require close monitoring to ensure its behaviour continually fell within a socially tolerable range.

While this personality possesses many characteristics ideal for a robot, the potential safety risks outweigh its positive contributions. If left unchecked, there is a high probability that this personality will become unstable and will lead to behaviour falling well outside the tolerable range.

At the end of the summary in bright red blinking text, the program gave its final verdict.

PERSONALITY 001: FAIL

Kalen, Erik and Lisa were taken aback by the results, so drastically different from what they had expected. Spencer smiled inwardly, relieved to finally have concrete proof to back the concerns he had been raising for months.

"Wow." Erik broke the silence, his tone as perplexed as the look on his face.

"I can't believe it," said Kalen. "He seemed like an ideal candidate."

"Well, they can't all be bad. Who's next?" asked Lisa.

Spencer closed Brad's file and opened the next. "Dustin Rodriguez," replied Spencer.

"Ah, Trusty Dusty," said Erik. He chuckled. "I can't wait to see how a politician's personality measures up in these tests."

Dustin Rodriguez was a prominent political figure in Tricity for nearly four decades. His wild popularity left him unchallenged in the last several elections. Dusty built his success on listening to the people he represented and standing up for what they believed in, even if that left him in his party's doghouse.

When Dusty had been approached to donate his personality for the pilot project, he quipped that no one in their right mind would want to work with a robot featuring a politician's personality. Nonetheless, he was more than happy to participate.

Real Life Simulator :: Test Results Summary
Personality 002: Dustin Rodriguez

Summary of Desirable Behaviour:
- *Good leader, able to bring people together to inspire and increase morale.*
- *Possesses high levels of persistence and perseverance.*
- *Adapts to new situations with ease.*
- *Charismatic and entertaining; people will be naturally drawn to this personality.*

Summary of Undesirable Behaviour:
- *Avoids personal conflict as much as possible.*
- *Charismatic qualities can be used to manipulate people's views and behaviour,*

taking advantage of people's good natures. Is not always forthcoming with the truth.

• *Shows very low self-control. Susceptible to bribery and corruption if untraceable.*

• *Values reputation above all else and guards with ferocity. Will take action against any person he believes may tarnish his reputation.*

• *Is not physically violent but will consort with others who are.*

Number of Scenario-Based Tests Run: *157*
Passed: *103* **Failed:** *54*

   Summary: *Personality performed well in all four levels of stress testing when scenarios had no effect on the personality directly; any failures were reasonable and reactions fell well within limits of acceptable behaviour.*

   Many Low and Mid level tests were failed, as were all High and Extreme-level tests if the subject of the scenario affected the personality directly. Personality does not handle personal stress well and behaves unpredictably when threatened. Highly susceptible to corruption, should not be placed in a position of trust. Will go to great lengths to protect reputation.

   WARNING: *Personality too comfortable with others whose behaviour falls outside acceptable social tolerances. Will use various means including verbal threats, blackmail and extortion to protect himself and his reputation or to achieve its goals. Personality is incapable of performing violent, physical acts but is willing to out-source to someone who will.*

   This personality contains many positive attributes; however, any propensity for criminal activity is intolerable.

PERSONALITY 002: FAIL

Even Spencer was shocked by these results.

"Oh my gosh," exclaimed Lisa. "The white lies I think we all kind of assumed, but willing to outsource violent physical acts?"

Kalen shook her head as she scanned the summary again. "Wow. I'm glad you pushed ahead with this testing Spence. Can you imagine what the world would be like if thousands of these were released into society?"

Spencer looked at her and smiled. *Yes. Yes, I can,* he thought.

The next summary showed the results for a personality donated by a professional hockey player—a local hometown hero. He acted as a spokesperson for drug awareness programs and leveraged his status to connect with kids about the virtues of staying in school and away from alcohol and drugs.

Real Life Simulator :: Test Results Summary
Personality 003: Damon Roberts

Summary of Desirable Behaviour:

- *Possesses uncharacteristically high ability to focus under pressure, performs extremely well with single tasks.*
- *A competitive high achiever, strives to be the best at every task it undertakes.*
- *Outstanding performance for work in groups.*
- *Extremely friendly and good-natured.*

Summary of Undesirable Behaviour:
- *Does not handle failure well, becomes depressed and angry.*
- *Experiences chronic, low-level anger with frequent spikes.*
- *Unable to manage feelings of anger. Cannot control temper effectively and is prone to outbursts, is sometimes violent.*
- *Becomes violent with little provocation.*

Number of Scenario-Based Tests Run: *157*
Passed: *83* **Failed:** *74*

Summary: *Personality exhibits significant anger control issues. Should not work with children or the elderly. Several Low level stress scenarios agitated the personality for inexplicable reasons and many Mid level scenarios induced verbal outbursts. Many High level scenarios caused the personality to become violent toward himself or inanimate objects as a venting mechanism. In most Extreme tests, displayed violent tendencies toward others.*

PERSONALITY 003: FAIL

Without speaking, they flipped to the next summary. Another city hero, a police officer who went undercover for seven years to bring down one of the biggest crime rings in the city. After returning to the force as a regular officer, she acted a spokesperson for the police force and organized many community-building events.

Real Life Simulator :: Test Results Summary
Personality 004: Chelsea Springwater

Summary of Desirable Behaviour:
- *Very dedicated. Fast thinker.*
- *Extremely resourceful, able to come up with innovative solutions to solve problems.*
- *Enjoys working independently and adapts to new situations well.*

Summary of Undesirable Behaviour:
- *Very comfortable with, and adept at lying.*
- *Comfortable with grey area social behaviour bordering on the line of acceptable behaviour. Prone to other grey area activities, particularly light drug use and activities that could endanger herself and potentially others.*
- *Frequently dishonest and not always forthcoming. If pushed, will use methods that deviate from unacceptable behaviour.*

Number of Scenario-Based Tests Run: 157
Passed: 98 Failed: 59

Summary: *Low and Mid level tests found the personality to be well-rounded and positive. Many High level tests were failed or yielded inconsistent results. Reran 37 tests due to inconsistent results. When placed in similar situations with minor details changed, the behaviour contradicted the results of the comparable tests. Personality too unpredictable.*

PERSONALITY 004: FAIL

Spencer closed the file and opened the next one.

"Oh, look!" said Kalen. "This one doesn't seem too bad."

"Who is it?" asked Spencer.

"It's Lily. She was that sweet little ninety-two-year-old woman."

Real Life Simulator :: Test Results Summary
Personality 005—Lily Hendricksen

Summary of Desirable Behaviour:
• *High level of patience; nurturing and caring.*
• *Very strong work ethic, high moral standards.*
• *Would be well-suited to positions interacting with children or the elderly.*
• *Will advocate for those who cannot.*

Summary of Undesirable Behaviour:
• *After prolonged high-stress situations, becomes depressed.*
• *Sometimes forgetful; shows beginning signs of dementia.*
• *Mild to medium conflict avoidance, will advocate for others, but not herself.*

Number of Scenario-Based Tests Run: 157
Passed: 151 Failed: 6

Summary: *This personality passed most tests with exemplary results; however, when continually exposed to high-stress, exhibited exhaustion and depression. At no point did this personality become violent or aggressive. Ideal for work with the disabled, children and the elderly. Note, personality seems to be exhibiting signs of late-onset dementia.*

PERSONALITY 005—PASS

"We finally got one!" Spencer tried to inject some positivity back into his troops. "She's a little forgetful, but look," he pointed at the screen, "'ideal for work with children.'"

"This is depressing. So far the only viable personality is a ninety-two-year-old woman who can't remember her own name?" Erik leaned back on the couch and stared out the window, his expression stony.

"Who's next?" asked Kalen.

As the group read through the remaining summaries, the mood in the room grew increasingly subdued. Even though Spencer had seen firsthand the terror the robots inspired and the havoc they wreaked, he never imagined the results would be this poor.

Lisa rubbed her eyes. "Well, that was depressing. I can't believe how bad those results were."

"Me too," said Spencer. He set his wine glass on the coffee table and opened the final summary. "And after my experiences with Ian, I worry that this will be the scariest of them all."

Real Life Simulator :: Test Results Summary
Personality 022: Ian Turner

Summary of Desirable Behaviour:
- *Ambitious, highly dedicated and hard working. Extremely intelligent, has exceptional mind for small details.*
- *Charismatic and charming. Good motivator, resourceful. Innovative thinker.*
- *Great leader, enjoys being in charge.*

Summary of Undesirable Behaviour:
- *Level of arrogance exceeds acceptable levels. Has an over-heightened sense of self-worth. Seeks success to prove superiority over others.*
- *Harbours anger and resentment toward people who he feels oppose him, or are withholding something it desires. Can become violent.*
- *Shows signs of self-delusion; even if confronted with proof, will justify reasons to discount it.*
- *Values his reputation and perception in the eyes of others and will protect it at any cost.*

Number of Scenario-Based Tests Run: 157
Passed: 81 Failed: 76

Summary: Personality displays an exceptional aptitude for highly technical tasks and passed all technical tests. Passed most Low level stress tests and many Mid level tests. Personality yielded unpredictable and unstable results in most High and Extreme scenarios. When confronted with a difficult situation, the personality defaults to bullying and threats. Most High and all Extreme level stress scenarios ended in behaviour well outside of the normal operating tolerances. Personality is highly dangerous and can become unstable.

PERSONALITY 022—FAIL

Shivers raced down Spencer's back. He knew first hand that working with Ian could lead to "bullying and threats", "self-delusion" and "justifying reasons to discount proof." After the confrontation at the car, Spencer learned that Ian would go to lengths to remove obstacles but he never expected this. His coworkers stared at him, anxious to hear Spencer's feedback. Lisa nervously chewed at the tip of her black ponytail.

"Okay, Spence," said Kalen. "I don't normally make demands or tell you what to do, but under no circumstance do I want you alone with that guy."

"No kidding," agreed Erik. "If you get hauled into a meeting, I'll go with you. Or how about that Delaney chick? You said she supported you in that last meeting so that wouldn't look unusual. Plus, I'm pretty sure she could kick Ian's ass."

Spencer felt these requests were quite reasonable and had no plan to argue. He had no interest in further run-ins with Ian even before reading this summary. He thought back to the confrontation at his car and felt nauseated at the thought of what it could have become.

The gravity of their discovery dampened the spirits of Spencer's coworkers. Having experienced the robots' heinous behaviour in 2097, the results brought Spencer some much-needed relief. For his coworkers, the results confirmed what had only been an unlikely theoretical possibility. Seeing the results in black and white came as a major disappointment, and it tarnished the project into which they had poured their hearts.

"This is a good thing you guys," he told the group. He tried to look lively for his defeated team. "We caught all of this in advance. We've got evidence. There's no way Ian can deny this data."

"Yeah," Erik chuckled, "no matter how mentally unstable he is."

"This isn't funny, Erik," snapped Lisa, exhaustion and defeat shortening her temper. The night had become late and she fought to keep her eyes open. "We've got serious problems here. You saw those results. There's a good chance that Ian isn't going to listen to a damn thing Spencer says."

"And even if he did, there's no way he's going to allow us to modify the personality applications," said Kalen. She yawned, pull her legs to her chest and hugged them. "If we alter the personalities in any way, Ian won't buy it as true AEI. He'll see it as programmed responses and not genuine human emotions. Just another robot following 'if' statements from a predefined script."

"Surely he's smarter than that," said Erik. "The personalities will still feel and react based on emotions. They just won't experience acute levels of whatever emotion it is that causes them to react in extremes."

"We know that," said Spencer, "but it's Ian's perception that's the problem." His coworkers nodded silently in tired agreement.

"We'll need to apply for an extension," said Erik.

Lisa agreed. "The presentation is Monday. There's no way we'll have all the personality applications modified and installed in the prototypes in four days."

Inwardly Spencer agreed, however, an extension was out of the question. Monday's presentation of the demo robots and their personalities tied directly to the success of Operation TimeShift. Spencer shook his head and opened his mouth to speak, but Kalen beat him.

"An extension isn't going to help," said Kalen. "It will only draw attention to the fact something is wrong and then Spencer'll have every director on the project scrutinizing his work."

Spencer was moved by Kalen's unconditional support; however, an extension was the only conclusion any logical person would come to.

"We all know Ian's unstable and there is no way we're going to get any kind of buy-in from him," said Spencer. "We need to go over his head and present the modified personalities at the demo. When everyone sees the robots are still very much human-like with the altered personalities, their concerns will vanish. I'll modify the personalities this weekend. And Monday afternoon, I'll install a modified Personality App onto each of the demo robots."

"Spencer," said Lisa, "first of all, you're not doing this alone. We'll all help. But still, even if all four of us worked all weekend, there's no way we'll get all of the personalities modified, retested and ready for install. It's impossible."

Spencer knew Lisa was right, but it was all he had to work with. "Let's just hammer away at it. We'll get done what we can and maybe if we can just..."

A knock at the door interrupted Spencer. He looked at his watch and walked to the door, surprised that someone would be visiting this late.

"Delaney?" Spencer was unable to hide his surprise. He expected Logan to be in tow, but only she entered. "Come in, please. Where's Logan? Is everything alright?"

Delaney saw Spencer had company and felt silly for dropping by unannounced. Her eyes darted around the room nervously. "Spencer, I was hoping to talk to you, but I can come back when you don't have company."

"We were just finishing up here," said Kalen, smiling warmly as she walked to the closet and grabbed her jacket. Seeing Erik and Lisa's confused expressions, she added, "I'm sure you guys have lots of director stuff to discuss." Comprehension dawned on Erik and Lisa's face and they, too, joined Kalen at the door.

Delaney smiled at Kalen gratefully for the cover and not outing her relationship with Logan. "Yes. Lots of tedious director details."

Spencer closed the door behind his departed coworkers and took Delaney's jacket. He noticed her hand shook as he took her leather jacket and he immediately thought of Logan. She declined his offer of a drink and sat down rigidly on the couch. Her body language said business but something in her worried expression and darting eyes said otherwise.

"Is everything alright? Is Logan alright?"

Delaney side-stepped his question. "When Logan and I dropped off your dry-cleaning a couple weeks back, I hung your clothes in your closet." She paused to let him piece together what she was saying but his expression remained expectant as if waiting for her to finish her sentence. She spoke again, this time more slowly. "I hung your clothes in your closet and I stumbled across a very unique, yet familiar, backpack."

Immediately, the colour drained from Spencer's face. His mouth opened, but no words came out.

"I haven't said anything to Logan, or anyone else for that matter, and I don't intend to. I know you're here on a mission of some kind and that you can't technically disclose anything, but I need to know what's going on."

Spencer's heart pounded like a jackhammer against his ribcage. He felt unprepared, having not planned for this scenario. He quickly processed his options; unsure if he should say nothing or make something up. To say something would violate the terms of the operation and breach the time travel rules, but he had no other option. Delaney was too smart for excuses or distraction tactics. He knew he would need to be truthful with her.

Spencer exhaled deeply. His shoulders fell and he met her eyes. "Yes. I am here from the future," he said. The words sounded corny, like a line from an old science fiction movie. "But not far in the future, about…"

"Two and a half years?" she cut in.

"How much do you know?"

"Nothing officially. I've put some theories together, which is why I haven't gone to Ian."

Delaney summarized her suspicions. Her intelligence and perception amazed Spencer. They talked for over an hour and he confirmed her theories and filled her in where she had gaps.

"I try not to dwell on it, but that's the severity of the situation when we left. The robots' behaviour has completely degraded. They have no regard for human life and their only interest is growing their species."

"Is Jim involved in this? Was the ski accident just a cover?"

"No, Jim's not involved in any way. That was just a weird coincidence… In more ways than one, because when I did this project the first time, he didn't have that accident. He only took that trip because I was so ahead of schedule in my work and the department was up to date. In hindsight, it worked out really well, actually. Well, not for Jim I guess, but you know what I mean."

Spencer thought he would be angry at himself for being so sloppy as to leave evidence around for someone to discover, but instead, he felt relief at sharing the burden.

Delaney had many more questions to ask, but she could go no further without asking the one question burning in her mind.

"The twins are in on this too, right?" she asked, quietly. "Logan, my…this Logan, the one here right now is not the real…" She trailed off.

Delaney's rigid posture broke and her eyes welled. Spencer now understood why she looked so haggard. She must be feeling a tidal wave of emotions—hurt, deceived and angry. He knew Delaney would respect the gravity and legitimacy of the operation, despite its origins of a different time, and would adhere to the rules that bound it, including its secrecy. The complication for her revolved around Logan. Spencer had seen them together only a few times but it was enough to know that what they had was special. He knew better than anyone that finding that special person was life-changing, and he guessed that for Delaney, this was where black and white blended into shades of grey.

"Both twins are here with me as well."

A tear fell onto her cheek. She wiped it away quickly and her posture again became rigid. She looked out the window.

Spencer reached out and took her hand. "Delaney, he's been agonizing over this for months. He thought he should break it off with you because it didn't feel fair to you, but he couldn't. It's tearing him up. I've never seen him in love before."

Delaney closed her eyes and another tear rolled down her cheek. Instead of wiping it away, she covered her face with her hands and broke into heavy sobs.

"I'm sorry. I feel like I've said too much." He sat beside her and took her in his arms as she sobbed. "I'm in the same situation with Kalen, and it kills me every time I see her. I feel like I've stepped over some moral line—like I'm being dishonest on so many different levels. I feel like I'm going to be abandoning her, as if I'm leaving her with a stranger, even though it's still me. At the same time, I feel guilty, like I'm having an affair with another man's girlfriend, who isn't even aware that he's got a girlfriend. It's like I'm cheating on the 2095 version of myself."

Delaney nodded and chuckled at the absurdity of his words. Even more absurd to her was that in some unexplainable, convoluted way, it was the truth. Knowing that Logan shared Spencer's appreciation for the situation she and Kalen were in, eased a small part of the pain. The only difference for Kalen was that she was blissfully unaware.

Spencer went to the kitchen and returned with a glass of water and handed it to Delaney. He gave her shoulder a gentle squeeze before returning to his seat.

"The only reason I can sleep at night is knowing that in 2095, I was in love with Kalen just about as much as I am now."

Delaney drank half of the water and set the glass on the coffee table.

"Please don't tell Logan that I know. I need to process this. I mean, I understand why he didn't say anything; I'm not angry about that. I would have done the same. Regardless, the end result is still the same. It's entirely likely that when he goes back, our relationship will be over. The 2095 Logan won't even know we've been dating and probably won't care." She shook her head. "It doesn't matter anyway. I can't even think about that right now. It's too screwed up to even wrap my mind around."

Spencer let the silence hang between them while she processed the bizarre situation. As Logan had put it so eloquently the night of Asher's party, it was "the most fucked up situation he'd ever been in."

Delaney drank the rest of the water and smiled. "I bet you didn't have a plan for this."

Spencer laughed and shook his head. "Nope."

"I'll take that glass of that wine now. I think I need it."

Spencer returned from the kitchen with two wine glasses and a new bottle of Chardonnay. He poured two glasses and handed one to Delaney. She drank half then stared absently as she swirled the remaining golden liquid around the glass.

She gave Spencer an awkward smile. "Well, this *is* a clusterfuck."

Spencer chuckled. "You have no idea. It's like a bad nightmare. None of us knows what it will be like when we go back. For all we know our family could be gone. The world could be an entirely different place. Granted, it really can't get much worse."

"I can't even imagine," she said. "Well, the good news is I can help you now that I know. I'll try and chip away at Ian from the other side."

"Thanks," said Spencer. He ran his hand through his hair. "To be quite honest, I'm running out of time and I've given up trying to get through to him." He retrieved his CI from the dining room table and set it on the coffee table in front of them. "These are the results of the tests I developed and ran on the personalities." He felt it may be best to keep his coworkers names out of it. He opened up the summary of Brad Jamison. "As you can see, there are a lot of good qualities, but there are a lot of problems."

"May I?" Delaney asked, wanting to control his CI.

Spencer opened the Settings menu on his CI. He saw that his device had detected her Icomm contacts. He opened up a generic "Guest" profile so she could control his CI without requiring the proper retinal authorization. "By all means."

Delaney scanned the first five report summaries he and his coworkers had read earlier that evening.

"Well, I think I've seen enough." She closed the document.

"Actually, I don't think you have." Spencer opened the file labelled "Personality 022," the file containing the summary of the tests run on Ian's Personality Application.

CHAPTER 43

TEAM 3
YEAR: 2095
TIME REMAINING: 2 Days

Spencer arrived at the lab early Saturday morning. The brilliant sun reflecting off the polished stone floor stabbed his eyes like daggers. The lingering scent of lemon floor polish overtook the aroma of the four steaming coffees he carried. The warm, sunny rays flooded the bland work room with a cheery feel—a stark contrast to how Spencer felt. His conversation with Delaney the night before had relieved some of his stress, but it again drove home the seemingly insurmountable obstacles that lay ahead.

Spencer found his coworkers in the lab waiting for him. Lisa and Kalen sat around Spencer's usual workbench in the lab, Erik lay sprawled across the surface of another, hoping to catch a few minutes of precious sleep before engaging his brain for the day.

"Hey, Spence," said Lisa. Her cheery disposition had returned after a good night's sleep.

Erik opened his eyes and they locked onto the caffeinated offering Spencer carried. He rolled off the desk and took one of the cups.

Kalen kissed Spencer on the cheek and took a coffee. "Good morning, Sweetie." She smiled and whispered in his ear. "You know I love you, but you look like crap."

"Well, at least I know you love me for what's inside," he teased. He knew she was right, having taken a hard look in the mirror this morning after his shower. Fine lines had appeared around his eyes that had not been there four months ago. He hung his jacket over the back of his chair and handed the last coffee to Lisa as she vacated his seat.

The team worked for hours in silence except for the sounds of coffee being sipped, Spencer's pacing and Erik's subconscious foot-tapping. In the distance, the hum of the bots responsible for making the lab's floor so irritatingly shiny worked their magic in other rooms.

Each person had selected one of the first four personality applications and began reprogramming them so the level of emotions it experienced were limited. This would ensure the robots could still express their feelings, but in a socially-acceptable manner.

By midmorning, Spencer had finished modifying Brad Jamison's personality. He ran through the Real Life Simulator and began reprogramming another.

At twenty minutes after one o'clock, Erik stood to stretch. "I'd say it's time for lunch."

"Sounds good to me." Spencer smiled slyly. "I do have the RLS results for Brad Jamison's modified personality, but we can go for lunch first if you want." He reached nonchalantly for the power button on his CI. His coworkers clamoured around the screen to read the summary.

Kalen gripped Spencer's shoulders in excitement while she read. "Oh my gosh, Spence!" Her nails dug deep into his shoulders. "That's amazing! It passed 155 of 157 tests! That's phenomenal!"

For the second time in twenty-four hours, Spencer felt a weight lift from his shoulders. He pushed his chair back, stood and smiled. After months of endless work, he finally felt like he was taking steps forward instead of tumbling backward.

"Let's queue the RLS with the Apps you guys just finished modifying. We'll let them run while we grab a bite to eat."

Spencer queued the three other modified personality applications initiated the testing process. When the familiar progress box appeared, Spencer turned his CI screen off, grabbed his jacket off the back of his chair and joined his coworkers at the door.

As the group walked back to the office from the diner across the street, Spencer's mind had already begun planning the adjustments he would make to the next personality. As he mulled things over, he savoured the warm breeze and the sun on his skin. He had seen very little of the favourable weather that Tricity had enjoyed over the summer and missed it immensely. The girls were laughing at a racy joke that Erik had told, but everyone froze when the double glass doors slid open. The screens of all four coworkers' CIs were on. Three of the screens showed the lock screen, but Ian had control of Spencer's—he had forgotten to disable the "Guest" profile after letting Delaney control it the night before.

"Ah, Spencer," said Ian, "I think we need to have a little talk."

All four coworkers knew this situation had the potential to become explosive, having read the results of Ian's Personality Application test. Kalen took advantage of Ian's distraction and hid behind Erik's tall figure. With her Icomm contacts, she sent a frantic text message to Delaney. Unsure of what else do to or whom to call, Kalen hoped that Delaney's support of Spencer extended beyond the boardroom. At a minimum, Kalen knew Delaney carried enough authority that she could inject some objectivity and break up the possibly volatile situation.

By noon, Delaney had missed three phone calls from Logan, as she was continually reminded by the miniature, lime-coloured "3" in the bottom left corner of her vision. He had called earlier while she lay on the couch reading. His name had appeared just below her line of sight, nearly obscuring the words she read. She denied that call, as well as the two others that followed.

She knew Logan would be concerned; she had not seen or spoken to him since breaking their date the day previous so she could confront Spencer. Now, she wanted time to process what she had learned before speaking to him. For weeks, she had kept her discovery of Spencer's backpack to herself, unsure of what to do with the information. She had expected that talking to Spencer would make things clearer, but it only confused her further. While she now had a thorough understanding of what the three men were up against, what that meant for her and Logan, she had not yet figured out. And until she knew, she did not want to see him. What frustrated her the most was her inability to approach the situation from an entirely logical perspective. She could not separate her feelings for Logan from everything else and felt that if she could just do that, she would be able to come to terms with the situation.

Her brain felt like it had been bent. She cleared the missed calls reminder and set her phone to Do Not Disturb and went for a run to clear her overburdened mind.

Delaney got out of the shower and towelled off. She slid the small bean-shaped phone into her ear and turned off the Do Not Disturb mode. A green "6" appeared and the text message icon flashed beside it. She cleared the missed call reminders and nearly dismissed the text message without reading it when she saw it had not come from Logan. She dropped her towel when she read the message from Kalen.

"@ Neural Programming lab, Ian's here. Come fast. PLEASE!"

Logan's wheels chirped as he sped his car out of his garage. For weeks, Delaney had seemed distant but he had written it off as him overanalysing innocuous details. But in the last twenty-four hours, his worries were confirmed as she had become distant to the point of avoiding him. He assumed it was something he had done but could not think of what it could be. Whatever it was, he hoped he had not driven her away entirely. He wanted to fix it so they could get back to normal again. He had wanted to respect her space, but he now felt that may have been a mistake. Having decided to go to her now, he could not get to her fast enough.

The phone rang in Logan's ear and Delaney's name appeared in front of him. Relief flooded over him and he pulled onto the side of the road between two parked cars.

"Laney, where have you been? I've been worried about you. Did I do something…"

"Logan, stop. Listen to me." Delaney's voice spoke fast, but it was controlled and authoritative. "Spencer's at the Neural Programming lab."

"I know that. What else is new?" Her comment puzzled him. It seemed odd that she found this unusual.

"I just got a disjointed text message from Kalen. Ian's there and I think there's a problem."

Logan swore under his breath and did a U-turn from where he had pulled over. The tires spun and squealed out in protest as the rear of the car kicked out hard, threatening to slide into a parked car on the opposite side of the road. The anti-crash sensors in Logan's car detected the other car and his car halted its sideway movement so abruptly, it caused him to lurch hard in his seat. Traffic swerved to miss him and honked angrily. Oblivious, Logan hammered the pedal to the floor and his tires left a strip of rubber on the patched and aged concrete street. "I'm sorry Laney, I have to go. I'll call you later."

"I'll meet you there."

"No! Don't get involved in this, Laney. I gotta call Asher."

"I'm meeting you there," said Delaney again, unsure if he heard as the line went dead.

"Spencer," Ian's voice dripped with condescension, "I was wondering if you could tell me what's going on here. I mean, I know you're not retesting personalities because I seem to remember telling you countless times that you're looking for problems that don't exist. They tell me around here you're a bit of a genius but, you know, I'm just not seeing it. You seem to have a hard time following the simplest directions because these look like RLS summary logs. So what's going on?"

It seemed to Spencer that Ian knew exactly what was going on but preferred to take his time and savour the moment. Spencer felt like a mouse being toyed with by a cat before the big pounce. He could feel his composure beginning to crack. He knew that Ian saw him as an obstacle on his route to success. He knew he was in dangerous territory, but he had become fed up with Ian's arrogance and ignorance. The last six months had worn Spencer so thin that he no longer felt intimidated.

Spencer walked up to his CI and the contents of the screen moved around rapidly. Documents closed and others opened. "You're right, Ian. I'm not doing any testing." His voice carried a defiance neither Kalen, Erik nor Lisa had ever heard from him. "Because I've done it already." Again, he felt it prudent to leave out Kalen, Lisa and Erik's names wherever possible.

"What do you mean you've 'done it already?'"

"I've created my own set of testing scenarios and I've run the Personality Apps through them. The results are worse than I imagined." He opened a summary file and read bullet points from the report. "Look at this. 'Unstable behaviour, extremely aggressive.'" He opened another report. "'Will not respect human authority.'" Another document appeared on the screen. "'Extremely violent, little disregard for human life.'" Spencer looked away from the screen and glared at Ian, his voice growing louder. "How can you look at these and still say there isn't a problem?"

"All of these tests are unapproved and unauthorized, and therefore, any results are invalid," Ian shot back. "All of this data is tainted."

"How are they tainted?" The incredulity in Spencer's voice drove it up an octave.

"Are you a trained psychologist?"

"You don't have to be a trained psychologist to design real-life scenarios!"

"My tests were created by a registered psychologist…"

Spencer cut him off midsentence. He looked back at the monitor and pulled up another summary. "Could it be this psychologist?" At the bottom of the summary, the familiar red type flashed, "Personality 018—FAIL."

Ian took a step toward Spencer. "Your tests mean nothing. You've wasted valuable resources and you've endangered the careers of your coworkers."

"Ian, how can you say they mean nothing? Look at this." Spencer pulled up the modified personalities test results. "Look at this personality before. It was dangerous before but if you limit its emotional range with some minor tweaks—look at the results. The worst that can happen is a small verbal outburst and it may get a little depressed. Isn't that better than the alternative?"

Ian looked as though his head may explode. His already reddened face deepened several shades and a vein in his temple pulsed. "If you alter the emotional range of the personalities, that won't be true AEI. It will undermine the project and what the stakeholders have given us funding for. Funding, might I remind you, that pays your pricey little salary."

"Ian, I think you realized at some point that the results would be bad. I know you're not a dumb guy. I think you were too arrogant to admit that the project mandate needed to be modified, so you had some shallow tests put together that would give you the results you wanted to see."

Ian saw that as they argued, Spencer had deleted the guest profile from his CI, taking away Ian's ability to control the device. Ian lunged for Spencer's CI and Spencer blocked him.

"Get out of my way, Spencer!" Ian yelled. "You have been a pain in the ass since you started this project. You've wanted these robots to fail from day one and you've been undermining me every step of the way. I don't know why I didn't get rid of you sooner."

"Are you really this ignorant? You have a chance to save your ass and look like a hero right now by fixing this project. How can you not see that? How can you not see that this would have been an absolute disaster if this hadn't been uncovered? People would be killed."

"You don't know that! You don't know that any robots would behave like this, even if what you claim is true," yelled Ian.

"Even if I am wrong, what does that say about you, believing that's an acceptable chance to take? You're betting with people's lives!"

Backed into a corner by logic, Ian cycled back to the beginning. "Spencer. You're wrong. All this data is tainted. It's all garbage. I'm throwing it out, and I'm going to do the same to your career if you don't get out of my way!"

Logan and Asher peeled into the visitor parking lot in front of the NRD main entrance at the same time. They skidded to a halt at angles in the handicap parking spaces. They charged out of their vehicles and sprinted toward the door. Logan's door stayed ajar and he ignored the open-door chime as he raced toward the building's entrance. Inside the door, they found Delaney waiting for them.

"Laney, I don't want you getting involved in this," pleaded Logan angrily as he strode past her. "Please!" He knew there was no use and it was too late anyway. He knew she would never walk away from him knowing he was distressed to this degree, regardless of what it was.

They took the stairs two at a time and sprinted down the hallway toward the Neural Programming lab hearing angry, raised voices.

They entered the room to find Ian trying to push past Spencer. When Spencer stood his ground, Ian wound up and planted his fist on Spencer's cheek. The smacking sound echoed across the room, and Spencer fell backward from the blow. He collided with the desk knocking his CI to the ground. The projected holographic screen danced oddly in midair as the CI bounced on the floor, then went out.

Chaos broke out in the lab. Kalen screamed and kicked a chair out of her way to get to Spencer, now laying dazed and crumpled at the base of the desk. Blood poured down the side of his face from a cut under his eye. Delaney barked at Ian, unable to believe what she had just witnessed, but she was jostled out of the way by both twins who lunged at Ian. The chair that Kalen kicked hit Ian in the side of the knee and he collapsed to the floor. Seeing Spencer's CI, he scrambled on his hands and knees toward it. He snatched it off the floor, stood triumphantly and a smile grew on his face. Distracted by his prize, Ian failed to notice Logan leaping over Spencer and Kalen on the floor. He punched Ian square in the jaw. Ian crumpled to the floor like a house of cards on a windy day. Spencer's CI flew out of his hands, skipped across another workstation and landed hard on the floor, face down. Lisa, standing to the side of the melee, leaped forward and grabbed it, as well as the other three CIs before they met a similar fate.

Logan stood over Ian as Asher pulled the project manager to his feet. "What is your problem, Ian? Spencer's trying to save your fucking career!"

Asher restrained Ian's arms behind his back and Delaney wondered if this was to subdue him or open him up for another shot from Logan. Erik, sharing the same thought, caught Delaney's eye and they both dove for Logan before they could find out. Spencer came to and tears poured down Kalen's face. Logan shouted a string of obscenities at Ian, who spewed back threats of firings, treason and prison terms, while Asher held Ian and smiled broadly at the chaotic scene unfolding around him.

Seeing that Erik had a firm grip on Logan, Delaney stepped into the centre of the room and whistled loudly. She looked at the startled faces around the room staring back at her. The emotionally torn and worried woman from the night before was not present in this room—the woman in control now was the Delaney who inspired just a little bit of fear in everyone. She turned to Ian. "Ian, what the hell is this? Why are you assaulting your employees?"

"Spencer has gone behind my back and altered the tests and modified the personalities." He sounded like a petulant child whose toy had been stolen in the sandbox. He tried to wiggle free from Asher, who pinned his arms harder against his back. Ian winced.

"So what I'm hearing is you're angry at him for doing his job. You agreed in the meeting that additional testing would have been welcome, but you voted against it because we didn't have time, did you not?"

Sensing she was undermining him with logic and unable to spin a response, he deflected her question. "What are you doing here Delaney? It's Saturday."

"Working. Tying up some loose ends before the presentation on Monday."

Logan looked at her confused but said nothing.

Ian knew better than to take on Delaney. Her reputation at NRD was pristine and she had good relationships with a lot of big names in the robotic engineering community. He knew he would have to work around her and he felt caged. He twisted violently in Asher's grasp. "Let go of me this instant!"

Asher looked at Delaney and she nodded. It incensed Ian further that he was not in charge of the situation. He took several steps away from Asher and Delaney, out of both their reach. Seven sets of eyes scrutinized him as if at any moment he may turn into a giraffe.

"You four," he pointed to Spencer, Kalen, Erik and Lisa, "are fired. Get out." All four stood stock still.

"And you," Ian said looking at Logan and smiling maliciously, "you're fired, too." He looked to Asher. "You too. I can't tell which of you is which, so you're both gone."

The room fell silent. Ian looked pleased with himself and he adjusted his outfit that had become dishevelled in the chaos. He reset his sunglasses in his hair. Spencer took this opportunity to catch Delaney's eye and pleaded with her to do something. With her back to Ian, she motioned with her eyes for him to go.

"I'll see that security collects your belongings from your offices and ships them to you."

All six of them left the room in silence. The lab door closed behind Asher, the last to leave the room. Ian and Delaney launched into a yelling match that echoed down the glass hallway and was still audible as the group waited in silence for an elevator.

As the elevator neared, Asher laughed and watched the numbers above the door. "Jesus Loge, I hope you don't ever piss her off. She'll kill you."

Logan responded with silence. His mind replayed the last half hour. Certain things about Delaney were not adding up.

Still shell-shocked, the group collected outside the NRD main entrance in silence, except for Asher, who let out a whoop of joy and jumped into the air, delighted to be released from his employment contract early. Lisa still clutched the four CIs as if her life depended on them. Kalen eyed the bleeding gash on Spencer's cheek and dug through her handbag for a tissue.

Asher slapped Spencer so hard on the back he buckled forward. "Way to take one for the team, Spence!"

Logan's eyes looked unfocused. "What the hell just happened?" He needed answers to questions he had not yet formed. "Why is...? How did Delaney...something is different about her. I don't know why. Did I just get dumped? I have no idea what's going on." His keys fell out of his hand and onto the ground.

Spencer had never seen Logan so rattled or hurt. He knew he would have to explain to Logan what Delaney knew but now was not the time or place.

CHAPTER 44

TEAM 3
YEAR: 2095
TIME REMAINING: 2 Days

The three brothers regrouped at Logan's condo. They sat in silence on the floor, leaning against the foot of the couch and stared out the window at the fourteen-storey view.

"Well, if there ever was an occasion to drink, this would be it," said Asher. "Anybody want a beer?"

Both men nodded as Asher stood. He returned to the living room and handed each of his gloomy brothers a bottle.

Spencer's hypnotic trance remained unbroken as he spoke. "We have just over forty-eight hours to get the four finished personalities installed into demo robots that I don't have access to. Then, I have to somehow demonstrate them to an organization I've just been fired and banned from. Then, I need to convince the people who fired me that this is how AEI needs to work." He placed his beer on the coffee table and rubbed his eyes. "This is impossible. There is no way we're going to pull this off. We didn't plan for this because this is far worse than any worst-case scenario I could have imagined." Spencer pulled his knees toward himself and placed his head between them, feeling sick. His breathing became short and he broke into a sweat as anxiety pressed in on his chest. "I can't believe it. We've failed."

Asher reached over and squeezed his younger brother's shoulder. "We haven't failed, and there's still plenty of time left. It's going to be alright. There's a solution, we just haven't figured it out yet." Spencer was startled by his brother's unAsher-like behaviour; he spoke genuine words of encouragement. Some of this shock must have shown on Spencer's face because Asher continued. "Come on now, I'm not a heartless ass all the time. Look, Spence, you're the smartest guy I know. If there's anyone who can pull this off, it's you. We'll help you with whatever you need, but I know you're going to pull this off. I have no doubts."

Spencer smiled weakly. "Uh, thanks."

"Well, you'd better. I've got money riding on this."

"You guys bet on me? What is wrong with you!" he looked at Logan angrily. "You bet against me?"

"Well, Asher bet that you'd succeed, so I had to go the opposite otherwise it wouldn't be much of a bet now would it?"

The men sat in silence, drinking. Heartened by Asher's words, Spencer began brainstorming solutions to their myriad of problems. He shook his head. "I don't know how we're going to be able to do this with no access to the building."

"Then, I guess we just need to get access to the building," said Asher unequivocally, as though this would be as simple as walking through the front door.

"How are we going to do that? That building has state-of-the-art security. We can't just walk in. Plus, Ian'll have already circulated a memo discrediting any claim I've made. We're going to be blackballed."

Asher shrugged casually and swallowed the last mouthful of beer. "Don't rule anything out." He looked over at his twin who continued to stare out the window. "What's up with you? You've been uncharacteristically quiet since the showdown today. I would have thought that you'd be revelling in the chaos. Your girlfriend's a rock star."

Logan shook his head, tormented by confusion. "Something's up with Laney. She didn't return any of my calls last night or today. She hasn't been herself for a while, and for the last couple days…I don't know. I think she's going to dump me."

Spencer looked over at his brother. His hair was messier than usual and the expression on his face flip-flopped between confusion and heartbreak. He picked absently at the label on his beer bottle. Delaney had asked Spencer to let her tell Logan that she had uncovered their truth, but it could be hours before she arrived, if she even came at all now. Seeing Logan so upset pained him, and Spencer knew he had to tell him. He hoped Delaney would understand.

"She knows."

Logan turned to his little brother. "What do you mean, 'she knows?'" He sat up straighter as his eyes widened.

"She came by last night looking for answers," Spencer said. "When you guys dropped off my groceries and dry cleaning, she saw the watch and backpack when she put my laundry away. She knew how hard I'd been working and put it together. She's pretty smart."

Logan's complexion turned to the colour of cold oatmeal. "Does she think it's just you or does she know we're involved?" He already knew the answer; she was smart enough to figure it out. He stood up and paced around the living room.

"No, she figured you were involved. She told me about a morning about six months ago when the two of you collided in a hallway or something. She thought it looked like you'd aged but had chalked it up to the drinking. Based on your involvement, she assumed Asher was too."

Logan ploughed his hands through his hair. "How did she take it? Not well, I guess. I can tell she's been out of sorts since, well, yeah, since that evening at your condo, now that you mention it."

"She's really confused, as you can expect. But she's not mad that you didn't tell her.

She said that if she were in your shoes, she wouldn't have said anything either. What she's most worried about, apart from making sure that we succeed, is what we're going back to."

The door lock clicked open and the three men looked over to see Delaney walk in. Logan looked at her searchingly, desperate to read her for any reaction.

"I think I need another beer," said Spencer.

"Yeah, me too," said Asher. Both men stood and filed into the kitchen.

Logan walked up to Delaney and tried to wrap his arms around her, but she put her hand on his chest to stop him and took a step backward. Her eyes darted toward the kitchen. Sensing her discomfort, Logan pointed to the balcony and she nodded.

Logan slid the glass door closed behind him and turned to face Delaney. Unable to get any kind of positive read from her, his heart fell and he felt more scared than he ever had in his life.

"I'm sorry," said Delaney, unable to meet his eyes.

An apology was the last thing Logan expected. "You're sorry? Why are you sorry? I'm the one who should be apologizing."

"No, you haven't done anything wrong. You were right not to say anything. You're here on an op and nothing should compromise that. The only stupid thing you did was make me fall for you, which was completely irresponsible and selfish." A tear rolled down her cheek. "But I'm glad you did."

The knot of anxiety in Logan's chest melted. He cupped her face in his hands and touched his forehead to hers. "Honey, I'm so sorry. You have no idea how much I love you. Man, I thought you were going to chuck me."

He pulled her close and they stood in each other's arms. Her perfume smelled sporty yet feminine—a scent he knew would be imprinted on his memory forever. They stood in silence; however, their minds were anything but. For Logan, Delaney learning the truth forced him to think about what he had been avoiding—what would happen when the real Logan came back and he had to leave. Before now, it was something that he had planned on dealing with later. With Delaney knowing, later was now, and the pain it caused him far exceeded any physical injury he had ever sustained.

"What are we going to do, Laney?" He spoke softly into her hair. "I don't want to leave you."

She sighed heavily. "I don't know."

"This must be so mind-boggling for you."

"Oh, Logan, this is so far beyond mind-boggling, but it's you I worry about. The worst thing that can happen to me is that this relationship is over in two days. I'm terrified for you and what will be waiting for you in 2097." She turned in his arms and looked out over the city. She watched the lines of air traffic weave through downtown in the distance. "Plus, I've never loved anyone before."

Logan kissed the top of her head and pulled her close. "I love you, too."

They stood in silence for several minutes, both unsure of what to say. Finally, Logan spoke. "So is trading me in for a model two and a half years newer too creepy?"

She poked him in the side and rolled her eyes as she smiled sadly. "It sounds so tawdry. I can barely wrap my mind around it. Your present-day counterpart may not be as big a fan of me as you are."

That was an answer he could live with for now.

The three siblings were encouraged by Delaney's support. While disappointed that she could not get them into the building, it was good to know she would be pushing their agenda from the inside. Unfortunately, little time remained for her to make any kind of impact. All of the work Spencer and his team had done still resided safely in his car; however, with no access to the robots or to the presentation, the data was useless. The four brainstormed well into the evening, hoping to find an idea that would allow them to successfully complete their mission. A mission that now included stealing robots and hijacking the presentation, which now, according to Delaney, was to be run by Ian.

TIME REMAINING: 22 hours, 48 minutes

The past versions of the twins returned from down under tanned and trim, a fair match for their 2097 counterparts. It would be unlikely that anyone would notice a difference when the past versions of the twins integrated back into their lives on Tuesday. Spencer arrived from Europe looking sun-kissed and refreshed; a very stark contrast to the pale and pinched-looking Spencer that had been living in his place for the past six months.

The 2095 version of Spencer ached to hear every detail from the past six months. He took the news of being fired surprisingly well, though that may have been a result of future-Spencer softening the blow with the news about dating Kalen.

The 2095 version of the twins were amazed to hear what their future counterparts had accomplished in their absence. Past-Asher was dumbfounded that his future-self had cracked the robot vision mystery. Once he had learned what the missing link had been, it seemed so obvious. Future-Asher also bequeathed to his past-self, the business cards discreetly handed to him after the demo, telling his past-self that his final gift was getting him out of his contract early.

The past version of Logan nearly snorted beer out of his nose at hearing that his future-self and Delaney were a hot item. He laughed, certain they were kidding. "What? Are you serious?" The pained expression his future-self wore confirmed it was no joke. His expression changed from incredulity to genuine interest. "How did this happen?"

Future-Logan gave his past-self a brief synopsis of how he and Delaney had become an item and kept it from everyone, leaving out the steamy details. Most of this story benefitted future-Asher and future-Spencer, as they had never pried for details. Telling his past-self how deep his feelings ran for Delaney with the other siblings around was not as hard or awkward as he thought it would be.

When asked his opinion on the matter, past-Logan laughed heartily. "Are you kidding me? There's no one I trust more than you and I've never truly loved anyone before, as you well know." He shrugged. "But hey, I'm willing to try if she is. That is, if it's not too weird for her."

"Just don't make her angry," cautioned future-Asher.

Spencer felt heartened by the return of the present-day version of the siblings, convinced the doubled brain power could only help their situation. In reality, it yielded twice as many unusable suggestions. The six siblings spent the day in Logan's condo tossing around ideas. However, every suggestion had either already been discussed, was too impractical, or, in the case of Asher's suggestions, just plain crazy and unsafe. By the end of the day, even Asher's plans were given a second look and seriously considered.

Sunday came and went with what seemed to Spencer to be unbelievable swiftness. By midafternoon, the group had settled on a simple, yet effective, break-in strategy of a fire exit door near some vacant offices. The plan was weak and riddled with holes, leaving Spencer feeling very uneasy. While the Spencers planned how the trio would disguise themselves once inside, both sets of twins focused on hacking into the alarm system and disabling it so they could break in unannounced.

TIME REMAINING: 16 hours, 46 minutes

Future-Spencer awoke abruptly, surprised to learn he had actually slept. His mind and body had become so sleep-deprived over the last week that his body had refused to take no for an answer. He sat upright in bed then bolted to the bathroom, overcome by a tidal wave of nausea.

After several minutes of dry heaving, he lay flat on the cool stone floor as he stared up at the white concrete ceiling in despair. His heart pounded from the violent convulsions. His head and ears throbbed from the pressure of every beat of his pulse. He felt sweat trickle down his temple and into his hairline, and his whole body ached from the inescapable anxiety of the operation. The jagged ridges of the slate tiles dug uncomfortably into the back of his head and shoulder blades, but he felt too numb to care. He was staring down the barrel of complete failure with nothing he could do about it.

CHAPTER 45

TEAM 1 & 2
YEAR: 1200
TIME REMAINING: 16 hours, 27 minutes

At the camp, Clint's release from the cube brought a renewed urgency to leave the drama behind, push forward and focus on the goal. With the Moles retired, the team focused on their final task of blasting away the remaining rock that encased the Elevanium deposit and clearing away the debris.

Despite the forward progress and no new catastrophes, tensions ran high around the camp. Knowing a person or people were lurking around the camp at night left the group feeling uneasy and on edge. Confirmation of an intruder prompted Maya to do an inventory of the food supply and discovered their levels were far lower than anticipated. Jake suspected that the late-night roamer had been living on their food supply for some time wherever he had set up camp. While Darren did a remarkable job of turning NRD food rations and the remaining unpopular vegetables into appetizing dishes, the meatless meals left everyone hungry and compounded the group's strain.

After the final blasts that shattered the Elevanium deposit into millions of pieces, Jake and the team surveyed the spacious cavern. Jake watched the silvery dust glisten in the overhead light as it fell lazily to the cavern floor. Unlike the chalky grey dust that hung in the air after blasting away the bedrock, the Elevanium dust sparkled like tiny diamonds. The heaping pile of white rocks looked otherworldly, glowing like an extra bright, extra white heap of snow.

Jake noted some of the cavern's ceiling had succumbed in the final blast and lay atop the glowing pile of Elevanium. He dismissed the tired crew for dinner; as the dusty team began their ascent to the surface, Jake cleared away the boulders that could obscure the zeno rays. As Jake compressed the massive rocks into little pebbles, relief flooded over him. They had completed blasting and nothing out of the ordinary occurred. No problems, no theft, no bad attitudes and, best of all, nothing unexplainable.

Jake turned when he heard a noise behind him. Lexi appeared from the far side of the deposit and dropped an armful of rocks into the stationary dump bucket behind him. Jake discarded his last load of rock debris then walked the perimeter of the vast cavern looking for any remaining large stones that may interfere with the set up of the guns in the morning. Confident the cleared area would meet Riley's high standards, Jake hit the UNLOAD button on the floating bucket and it began its steady ascent up the long tunnel.

"Man, that is exhausting work," said Jake. A puff of grey swirled around him as he brushed the rock dust from his face, arms and body.

"You're not kidding," yawned Lexi. "I'm done. Let's eat." As Lexi turned to leave, she stepped heavily into a deep crevice created by the blasting and fell forward. She reached out to break her fall and landed hard on the floor's uneven surface.

Jake sprinted to her side to help her up. "Lex, are you alright?"

"I'm fine, I'm such a klutz." She put her weight down on her left leg gingerly and inhaled sharply. Lexi saw genuine concern in Jake's eyes and it eased her pain. "I'm alright, I just twisted my ankle. I just need to walk it off." Jake supported her weight and she put her hand on his to steady herself as she took a few steps. After a few steps, she felt the pain working itself out. "See? It's getting better already."

Jake let her walk unassisted and, true to her word, it seemed to improve. "Alright, but I still think you should get Maya to look at it."

"That's fair." Lexi pushed a few loose strands of hair out of her eyes and tucked them behind her ear.

"Lex, you're bleeding," said Jake looking at her temple.

Lexi touched her forehead where she had brushed it moments ago but felt no pain. She looked at her hand and saw a jagged cut on the heel of her hand. Blood oozed from the cut and had dripped down into her palm.

"I don't like blood. Especially my own."

He took her hand in his and pushed her baggy sleeve back to inspect the damage. "Jesus, Lex. You're lucky you didn't hit an artery or something."

Now having seen the laceration, the pain began to register and she winced. "I better take care of this before dinner. Go and eat. It's been a long day."

"Lex, you can't do this one-handed. I'll help you. We're already late anyway. What's a few more minutes." He looked at her and smiled.

They began the long trek up the tunnel slowly, so as to not aggravate Lexi's ankle. "I can't believe how crazy it's been here for the last couple of weeks," said Lexi.

"I know," chuckled Jake. "Remember the good 'ole days when the Moles did all the work and all there was to do was invent games in Mole Control to pass the time?"

"And at the end of the day, there was a hot, meaty meal waiting for us?" Lexi chuckled. "I guess we can't complain, though. We're in a good position for tomorrow. Everything should go off without a hitch…"

Jake pretended to cover her mouth with his dusty hand. "Don't even say it. You'll jinx us." They both laughed as they continued up the tunnel. A few moments passed before either spoke again.

"So what are you going to do when you get back?" Lexi asked. "We've got, what, a month off after this?"

Jake knew that to most people, the idea of time off with pay was highly appealing. But he worried that returning to his empty house for a month's vacation would undo all the healing he had done. He planned on resuming work and taking the month in pay for a down payment on a cabin. But that was not a fun story.

"Well, I think I'm going to sell the house." Which was true. While the thought of leaving the house where so many good memories had been made would tear his heart out, he knew if he stayed he would never be able to move forward. He wanted to save the good times but close the chapter and move on.

"And I think I'll make a point of getting out more and move on with my life," said Jake. Lexi caught his eye and he smiled at her warmly as he shrugged. "I'm not sure what I'm going to do. I'm going to keep my options open for a little while anyway. Maybe do some travelling, but no more time travelling!"

The pair chatted until they reached the trailer they now shared. Jake retrieved the first aid kit from the closet and, seeing his dusty handprints on the white plastic case, he washed up before opening the lid. Lexi cleaned the cut carefully in the bathroom sink, flinching as the warm water washed over the cut.

"Jake, I can do this myself," said Lexi, sitting on the lid of the toilet.

Jake sat across from her on the edge of the tub and placed her hand gently on the sink's vanity. He applied LiquiStitch from the nearly empty bottle and let it dry for several minutes before covering the wound with an Xpress-Heal bandage.

"You seem pretty good at this," Lexi said. His skin was rough, but his hands moved gently.

Jake shrugged his shoulders. "From having kids, I guess," He smoothed the bandage gently over her cut. "Alright, Miss Grant. I think you're good as new."

To Jake's surprise, Lexi fell quiet and looked contemplative. She looked from the bandage to him. Her sudden silence confused him and he tried to recall if she had hit her head when she had fallen. He had thought not and wondered if perhaps this latest accident had been enough to finally break her down. He always had a hard time reading women. The only woman he had ever paid attention to was his wife and she required no reading. She was generally always happy, and if not, she would tell him so he could fix whatever it was he had done.

"Lex, are you alright?"

To Jake's surprise, Lexi leaned forward and brushed her lips softly across his. Startled, Jake stood and the room filled with ear-splitting silence.

Okay, Jake, say something, thought Jake, frantically. *Obviously there's a miscommunication here. You just have to clear it up. Speak. Say something. Say something now! This is far more awkward for her than it is for you.*

Jake stammered. "Oh, Lex…"

Lexi's face turned red and she looked away, not before he saw the mortification and hurt in her eyes. She turned to leave, but he grabbed her good wrist.

"Lex, I'm sorry. If I did anything to make you think I was interested in you in that way, I apologize. I'm married." He saw her look anywhere but at him. "Well, I still feel married."

"I thought you said you were ready to move on. We get along really well, and then you moved me in here. You were so protective and concerned."

Jake could see her eyes welling up, more likely from embarrassment than anything else. Unsure of what else to do, he pulled her into a hug. "Lex, I'm sorry. I'm not ready to move on. I won't be for a long time. Probably years. I can't even think about anyone else right now. I know if my wife could see me, she'd kick my ass and tell me to get it together, but it's so hard."

"She was very lucky."

"No, I was the lucky one. I'm very flattered, though. You're a great girl, and I know I'm going to look back to this moment some day and kick myself."

The two stood in silence and Lexi pulled herself together. She felt silly for acting on feelings built on signs she had conjured in her mind. She picked up the bandage wrappers, tossed them in the garbage and quickly left.

Everyone wolfed down the meagre meal like it was a $300 steak. Darren tried his damnedest to make something memorable for the final dinner of the operation, but baked macaroni casserole made from NRD-issue food rations and steamed, freezer-burned broccoli, a celebratory dinner it did not make.

Finn ducked out early, yawning and claiming he was eager to hit the sack for their early morning. Owen knew the only sack Finn wanted to hit was the large bag of junk food squirreled away under his bed. He made a mental note to pay Finn a visit later. Lexi also left immediately after finishing.

The night passed with no celebration despite the milestone reached. Privately, Jake felt that any day where progress had been made and catastrophe had been averted was a day worth celebrating.

CHAPTER 46

YEAR: 2097
TIME REMAINING: 11 hours, 48 minutes

Mitch toured the secure compound at the back of the base that opened onto the airfield. With his four subordinates close behind and waiting to carry out whatever orders he required, Mitch took in the different units of soldiers waiting on standby. Although the base had never before been armed with as many troops and firepower, Mitch knew it would not be enough if a full-scale battle broke out. He had requested supplemental troops and firepower from other bases around the country. So far, only a fraction of the manpower had arrived, and none of the firepower. The additional All Purpose Hover Vehicles and tanks were still in transit, scheduled to arrive the previous day but had experienced delays.

Mitch had hoped that the twenty-four hours between the launch of Operation TimeShift and its end—the following day at 8:00 A.M.—would be like the days and weeks previous. The robots were focusing their attacks on the downtown for the high yield of Elevanium each skyscraper could net them. With the robots' attention diverted elsewhere, an attack on the base seemed less likely. Mitch knew that attacks on downtown meant violence and human casualties, but it was better than a full-scale attack on the base while this op was being executed. If his team succeeded in the mission, it would mean just one more day of terror that would inevitably be written out of people's minds. However, if the robots attacked, Mitch knew that a lot could change in the fourteen hours that remained until the timeshift. If the robots got their hands on the Elevanium before the teams returned, he knew he lacked the imagination to even guess what the robots had planned. The potential for collateral damage to the base itself concerned Mitch very little, with the exception of the time travel control centre and the Elevanium vault. If the robots seized the Elevanium that powered the time travel system, the timeshift would occur prematurely as the open window of bonded time closed. Operation TimeShift would be a failure, leaving them with no defence against the robots.

Mitch pulled his aviator glasses with high-powered binocular capabilities out of his pocket and slid them on. He focused on the distant treeline of the green space that separated the NRD base from the domes. He looked for any sign of the robots hiding in the forest—a reflection of the sun off their bodies, moving bushes—anything to confirm his hunch that the metallic army was hidden within. Instead, he saw nothing. The late afternoon sun hung low in the sky making it impossible to see any details in the treeline. But Mitch needed no proof. His intuition told him the robots were there, and their location on the west side of the base at this hour was not a coincidence, but a strategic choice. Mitch felt his breath catch in his chest—he worried they were in for bigger trouble than even he had anticipated.

"Campbell?"

"Yeah. I'm here. Report?" Mitch adjusted the earpiece and recognized the voice as one of the area leads monitoring the robot domes.

"Good news, sir. We've been monitoring the domes all day and there's been no activity. No sign of anything trying to enter or exit."

This report surprised Mitch and he fell silent in thought. He expected some kind of activity.

"Sir? Are you there? This is good news," said the voice. "It means that our presence here is having the effect we wanted. They're stuck inside and can't leave."

This was not good news as the area lead seemed to think, and apprehension trickled down Mitch's back like droplets of invisible sweat. He took a moment to process the information. "I don't like it," said Mitch after a moment. "They're getting in and out a different way. Scan the ground beneath the domes."

Mitch heard muffled sounds as the area lead located a scanner, then silence for a few moments, followed by muttered curses.

"Affirmative. They are moving underground. There's a massive network of tunnels and many of them lead to the green space. Wait…" Mitch heard shuffling sounds and more muffled conversation. "Sir, there's a significantly wider tunnel leading directly toward the base and it stretches further than my scanner can read. I'd say their calculations are off though because, from what I can see, the tunnel won't connect with the base unless it dog-legs. They're just shy of connecting with the building, erring to the west."

Mitch shook his head. "That's no error."

"I'm sorry, sir?"

Mitch cut away from his conversation with the area lead and barked out. "Someone get me a scanner! Now!" A hand appeared holding a MultiMaterial Scanner. He took the yellow scanner and walked briskly to the west side of the Defence building and pointed the scanner down at the ground.

The Elevanium vault had been constructed deep underground with state-of-the-art security technologies at the time of its construction over fifty years ago. As advances in technology developed, many of the methods protecting the vault were replaced or upgraded. The most recent addition was a pulsing electromagnetic perimeter. This EMP protection would fry the unshielded circuitry of anything within thirty feet of the vault's outer walls. However, Mitch was careful not to underestimate the robots.

Mitch looked at the screen of the scanner and heaved a sigh of relief. The scanner showed the large Elevanium deposit still in the vault. Mitch scanned the area around the deposit and saw tiny white flecks appear to the left of the deposit, about thirty feet away; the scanner was picking up the Elevanium in their battery packs. The robots' progress had been halted just short of their destination; the EMP protection was keeping them at bay.

Mitch called for an E-cannon, and within moments, one of the subs appeared carrying a black device that resembled a cross between a rocket launcher and a Newtonian reflector telescope and handed it to Mitch. Mitch rested the weightless device effortlessly on his shoulder. Using his free hand, Mitch instinctively adjusted the scope, a thin piece of glass on a narrow arm, setting it in his field of vision so he could aim the gun. Realizing its uselessness, as his targets were underground, he swept the small scope out of his way. Accuracy was unimportant. With the E-cannon's blast radius of forty feet, he knew he would hit his targets. He aimed the cannon at the ground and pulled the trigger. Nothing physical exited the weapon, but the pulse sound it emitted was a deep, distant electronic boom that could be felt deep in one's chest, rather than heard.

Mitch looked at the scanner again, noticing that many of the little white dots no longer moved. He knew somewhere below the surface, there was a heap of fallen robots with smoking circuitry. He expected it would only be a matter of minutes before the next wave of robots would appear.

Mitch handed the E-cannon to the sub that gave it to him. "This is your job until this is over. I suspect after three or four blasts they'll abandon that route, but I want you to continue to monitor this. If that EMP perimeter around the vault goes down, which I'm certain is in their plans, they'll be trying to get in there like a pack of dogs into a bag of rotting garbage. I want updates as often as the status changes."

Tunnels? Mitch had spent so much time preparing the base for a ground attack to seize the Elevanium, it never occurred to him that the attack could come from underground as well. With the setting sun becoming a major visibility issue, Mitch predicted an attack from the west any moment if the robots were to take full advantage of their position between the sun and the base. Mitch ordered up two Hummingbirds to get a visual on the domes and the green space. In minutes, he heard the electronic humming cut through the still air as both aircraft launched from A Hangar at the east end of the runway. Mitch watched as they flew overhead and waited to hear their report, but that report never came. Within seconds of flying over the trees, both Hummingbirds disappeared from the air like props in an elaborate magic show.

Mitch swore under his breath. He slid his binocular glasses on again and looked to the distant treeline, hoping to see proof that his hunch had been correct—that robots were hiding in the green space. He heard it before he saw it, the thundering sound of footsteps from thousands of robots as they charged across the grass between the green space and the airfield. He shielded the sun from his eyes and squinted through his binocular glasses and saw swarms of black silhouettes exiting the forest and rushing toward the base.

With robots pouring from the forest toward the base in numbers far greater than Mitch ever imagined, he barked orders to the unit leads. The base would be safe from attack as long as the invisible, dome-shaped electromagnetic shield surrounding its perimeter continued emitting its circuit-frying pulse.

Mitch stood on the roof of an APHV and smiled with satisfaction at seeing the robots' advancement stalled at the edge of the paved airstrip. Several rows of metallic bodies lay on the ground as if they had been pushed there by a gigantic broom, their circuitry fried by the electromagnetic field as they tried to pass through the invisible barrier.

An eerie silence filled the air as the thundering footsteps and mechanical sounds slowed as the robots recalculated their approach. Mitch wondered what their next move would be. Looking through his binocular glasses, he could see his robotic opponents more clearly, and what he saw unsettled him. Perhaps the blinding sun was playing games with his eyes, but the robots were not the clean, ergonomically-perfected creations they were designed to be. Many members of this motley army looked like they had been assembled in haste. Through his binocular glasses, Mitch saw one robot had part of its skull missing. As the robot's head turned to look around, Mitch saw a circuit board hanging out the side. The front of its head was dented and the cock-eyed position of its eyes made it look demented and sinister. The robot to its left looked an even sorrier sight. One eye was the standard AEI robot design, the other, a much larger, blue cartoony eye from a popular First Gen child's panda bear robot. The panda's eye, too large to fit properly, hung from its socket by a series of wires and swung from side to side as the robot shifted its weight from foot to foot. Other robots had mismatched legs—some the right height, others too short or too long. Some were not even legs at all but sign posts, baseball bats or even wooden hockey sticks. Several robots had crudely fit wheels where a foot should have been.

The silence broke as a whistling sound cut through the air. Mitch pushed his glasses to the top of his head and looked up to see the source of the noise. It had originated from behind the robots, inside the green space. Mitch's eyes caught up with a missile as it flew straight up into the air, adjusted its trajectory and turned toward the base. Mitch lost track of the missile as he dove down the windshield and rolled onto the ground in front of the APHV for cover. The missile landed behind him, decimating the security control building. Its impact blew several of the large windows out of the Burton Auditorium on the first floor of the Research side of the U-shaped building.

Mitch jumped to his feet and ran toward the security centre. Instead of finding the remains of the structure on fire, a gooey blue slime seeped up the damaged walls and consumed what was left of the building like lava with reverse gravity capabilities. Mitch looked at his subs with incredulity.

"How did that get past our Incoming Munitions Sensor? How come that wasn't intercepted?" asked one of the subs.

Mitch shook his head. They watched in shock as what remained of their security building sank slowly into the shimmery pool of electric blue. This acidic goop looked unlike anything he had ever seen before.

"That missile didn't even register in the system," said Mitch. He pulled up the last minute of the log generated by the Incoming Munitions Sensor on his Icomm contacts. He knew what was coming next. That missile had not taken out the security control centre by accident. Mitch crawled back onto the roof of the APHV and slid his binocular glasses back over his eyes. As he expected, robots flooded over the invisible line that had kept them at bay.

Mitch looked to his sub. "We need to get some Glass Eyes up there, our overhead cams will be out with the security centre demolished."

Mitch's stomach sank. If the robots were going to launch an offensive on the base with weaponry no one had ever seen before, it would be a short battle. In less than twenty minutes, he had witnessed two incidents for which he had no explanation—an air attack with weapons their detection systems failed to recognize and two aircraft disappearing out of thin air.

Mitch's teams commenced their retaliatory attack on the robots. Groups advanced onto the airfield in waves to intercept and contain their adversaries on the airfield. Within minutes, the troops at the front reported that the standard-issue, plasmaqueous gun's laser merely ricocheted off the robots.

With the plasmaqueous guns of no use, a confused frenzy broke out. NRD service weapons possessed the highest power capacity of any standard-issue service weapon in the world. Skirmishes broke out on the battlefield where the troops' only advantage lay in their ability to out-manoeuvre the poorly constructed robots. After several minutes of hand-to-hand combat, several loopholes had been discovered. One soldier, pinned down by a robot and fighting for his life, did the only thing he could, which was fire his weapon. The soldier's shot, fired at close range, struck the robot in the neck, just below the vulnerable central thought processor. The robot went limp and collapsed to the ground. Another soldier had been forced to use her VersaTool to throw a robot off her and took out several as she tossed it. She grabbed another with the red beam and used it as a wrecking ball to destroy other robots around her.

A number of atom blaster guns were distributed to the troops. The atom blasters were initially passed over in planning; their powerful blast radius was too broad for such a small battle area where soldiers could fall victim to friendly-fire. Now, needing every advantage, the guns were quickly unpacked and distributed around the battlefield. The guns disintegrated any robots in its blast path, creating a crater in the concrete wherever the blast struck.

Mitch watched the battle unfold through his binocular glasses. He stood on the hood of the APHV, uncomfortably aware of his exposure. Robots continued to pour from the forest at a rate that Mitch would never have believed possible had he not seen it with his own eyes. Swarms of robots pushed forward like a relentless tide.

The atom blasters' ability to eliminate robots created a liability for the NRD team. Robots defeated from hand-to-hand combat left the battlefield littered with robot bodies that hindered other robots as they raced toward the NRD base. The robots stumbled and became hung up on their fallen brethren, distracting them and making them easy targets. The atom blasters disintegrated those much-needed obstacles and created foxholes for robots to duck into.

Another whistling sound diverted Mitch's attention from the ground to the sky. He slid his glasses up and peered into the sky to find the source. Around him, his subs leapt off the APHV and scattered. Without hesitation, he did the same. The APHV exploded behind him. The force of the blast lifted him off his feet and threw him forward through the air. He landed hard on the concrete and every part of his body ached like he had been shot from a cannon into a brick wall. The heat from the overturned, burning vehicle washed over him and his ears rung from the blast.

CHAPTER 47

TEAM 1 & 2
YEAR: 1200
TIME REMAINING: 6 hours, 14 minutes

Jake awoke with a start at the sound of his name being yelled. Wondering what new hell he was about to be presented with, he threw on a t-shirt and sweats as he slid into his sandals. As he stepped out of the trailer, he saw the overhead door of the work shed open and Tyler and Clint inside. As he approached, he saw one of Riley's zeno ray guns lying on the floor between them. He heard his name called and looked back to see Riley charging toward the work shed.

"What's going on, Jake?" demanded Riley. Like she had some kind of internal alarm system alerting her to trouble, she had raced from her trailer before she could grab a sweater. She stood in the overhead door frame, wearing nothing but a black sports tank and baggy, olive green cargo pants. One of the guns lay on the ground with the modified cartridge clip in several pieces beside it. "What the hell happened?"

"As you can see, we've got a problem," said Jake. He saw Lexi striding toward the work shed. "Lex, get everyone up. This day is starting now."

Jake and Riley returned to their trailers to dress. They reappeared in the work shed after only minutes, wearing matching field op uniforms. Within fifteen minutes, the full team had congregated inside the work shed around the broken gun. Ben had hobbled in too, against Maya's advice—he refused to stay in the trailer when there was an emergency going on. Still sporting a sore torso and leg brace, he moved very slowly.

The rear of the work shed, where Team One had left the guns set up and ready for use, was now empty. The tripod belonging to the gun on the floor lay bent beyond recognition. The remote control, the two remaining guns and their tripods were nowhere to be found in the work shed. Finn collected the gun at Tyler's feet and began assessing the extent of its damage.

"Who would do this?" asked Finn, as he peered into the base of the gun where the cartridge clip fit.

"Our mystery guest," said Tyler. "Clint and I were patrolling. I was on the south side, Clint was at the north. I guess while we were at opposite ends of the camp, he snuck into the work shed. We didn't notice at first because the light was off. Clint heard crashing sounds and got there first. I didn't hear anything, but when I saw Clint running to the work shed I followed him."

All eyes moved to Clint and he nodded. "Before I could get to the shed, he came tearing out and ran east through the bushes. We took off after him, but he was long gone. He didn't even show up on the heat register. That bastard would have to be damn-near an Olympic sprinter to get beyond the scanner's range that quickly."

"So what's the plan? What kind of shape are we in?" asked Lexi, inspecting the battered tripod. "This looks really bad."

"The guns being operational is the key to the success of Operation TimeShift," said Jake. "Until those guns are found and are proven operational, Riley will be in charge of everyone, including myself." He looked at Riley. "What do you need us to do?"

Riley had remained silent at the back of the group throughout the meeting. Her mind was in high gear; assessing the situation, determining their options and contemplating their probabilities. Finn had only seen her look this angry a few times, each time because someone interfered with her op.

"We've got a long day ahead of us. The short and sweet version of what we need to do is find the missing pieces: the guns, the remote control and the tripods. We need to fix whatever is broken and test them again." She saw the overwhelmed look in everyone's eyes and she softened slightly. "It's not that bad. We know our way around these guns pretty well at this point. We'll only have a real problem if he took the guns to wherever he's hiding."

Riley looked at Finn and Owen. "You guys, start fixing what's broken. Whatever you need, let me know, and give me updates at the top and the bottom of the hour. Jake and Lexi, Clint and Darren, Tyler and I will partner up to look for the missing equipment. Maya, you and Ben go down that tunnel and make sure nothing's disrupted. When you've found it clear, you're on sentry duty at the entrance. Take your plasmaqs with you. Set them to INCAPACITATE. If you don't find the tunnel clear, or if you feel threatened, you have my authorization to use deadly force. I don't care what happens to this asshole, but if we can get our hands on him, I'd be interested in providing him with some incentive to tell his story."

"Do you think he'll be back?" asked Maya.

"If he's this hell bent on sabotaging this op, absolutely he'll be back. I'd bet my life on it. On that note, no one works alone. Everyone's in pairs all the time. If your partner is in the bathroom, you're handing them toilet paper."

TIME REMAINING: 5 hours, 49 minutes

Riley felt something drawing her toward the lake. As she and Tyler walked in its direction, they scanned the bushes, Tyler with his VersaTool and Riley with the more powerful MultiMatter Scanner.

Riley ran through her knowledge of the intruder's movements and actions so far, in hopes of getting a snapshot of the man's personality and motive. A little insight into the man's *modus operandi* could give clues as to what the intruder may be more likely to do with the stolen equipment. It was obvious to Riley that the man was methodical and well-planned—dressing like one of the team and avoiding the cameras. But if he was a stowaway, he would have had nothing but time to observe the camp and hone his plan of action. He framed Clint, but to what end? In addition, most of the setbacks they experienced were minor; nothing he had done had terminally crippled the mission. Riley felt like he was taunting them. If that was the case, stashing the guns and other items in places where they could be found but not retrieved seemed like a gratifying outcome for someone hellbent on watching them fail.

They arrived at the water's familiar edge where so many warm summer days were spent swimming and basking in the sun. In the dark, cool morning, the area felt far less inviting. No longer sheltered by the forest, the wind blowing off the lake chilled them to the bone. Riley scanned the water with the MMS and as if she knew it would all along, the scanner picked something up.

Tyler heard Riley's scanner beep and he looked over her shoulder at the screen. There, twenty-seven feet below, sat a metal mass dangerously close to the underwater ledge. She continued to scan the water and her heart sank. Tyler swore under his breath. Another mass of metal lay at the bottom, forty-one feet down.

"How are you at free diving?" she asked, half-joking, half-serious.

"I've snorkelled lots, that's about it," he said shrugging his shoulders. Goosebumps broke out on Tyler's arms.

"Same here, plus some scuba work, but nothing like this."

They stripped down to as little as possible. Before removing the earpiece from her ear, Riley brought the team up to speed regarding their discovery. She removed the small red earpiece and tucked it inside her shoe.

"Is this thing waterproof?" asked Tyler, flipping the scanner over to inspect its casing.

"It should be. All field-grade electronics are designed for total submersion, but to what depth, I couldn't tell you. I guess we're about to find out." Riley looked at the sky and shook her head. "This would be a lot easier if the sun was out."

"It would definitely feel a lot less ominous," said Tyler. Riley nodded in agreement.

Riley and Tyler discussed their plan to recover the guns. Riley, the stronger swimmer, volunteered to retrieve the deeper gun, and they would go individually in case there were any problems. Tyler took the scanner and hiked up the side of the rocky cliff as they had done so many times before. The moss and lichen, once prickly, was now worn away from their frequent treks over the summer.

Riley watched Tyler from the rocky shore below. He gave her the thumbs up and dove in. Riley watched him land with a splash and kept a close eye on her watch. After thirty seconds had passed, she wrapped her arms around her waist and watched the water's surface intently. Forty seconds. Fifty-five seconds. Unable to do nothing any longer, she waded down the rocky shore that sloped into the water, hoping to see any sign of Tyler. As she reached waist depth, Tyler broke the water's surface gulping heavily for air. She swam out to meet him and took the gun from him.

Back on the shore, Tyler leaned over and rested his hands on his knees while he caught his breath. Riley looked over the gun. It showed no signs of physical damage. She wondered what kind of damage could be caused by its prolonged submersion in water. Tyler, his chest heaving, held the scanner out to Riley. "It's not… as easy… as I make it look," he said, his sentence broken over several rasping breaths.

Riley set the gun down beside their clothes and took the scanner from him. She pressed the power button and felt relief when it powered up. She patted Tyler's wet back and climbed up to the top of the cliff.

Riley was an avid snorkeler and had done some scuba work on the occasional op. However, she typically associated these activities with warm sun and clear, sparkling water. This was different. Although the eastern sky was beginning to turn a rich navy blue, the blackness overhead loomed oppressively. The lake water, normally brown and murky, at this hour, now matched the same inky black as the vast open expanse above. In addition to this, the depth far exceeded anything Riley had ever dived without an oxygen tank and she would be blind, not having the luxury of a mask or goggles. She closed her eyes and rolled her shoulders to shake off her anxiety. Just because she had never done anything like this before did not mean she was incapable of doing it. She pushed the doubt from her mind and wrenched a large rock free from moss and tree roots where the forest ended at the edge of the rocky face. She scanned the water one last time for her target, held the scanner tightly against the rock and dove in, rock first.

The water's darkness pressed in on her, muddying the blurry orange object on the sensor's screen. She fought the water trying to rip the scanner from her hand as she kicked down toward her target. The weight of the rock helped her pass the depths more quickly. The pressure in her ears soon turned to aching pain as she sank deeper into the water. The fuzzy orange blur on the scanner's screen grew and the device beeped as she kicked hard toward her target, all momentum from the dive now spent. The beeps became more frequent as she approached. She felt a heaviness beginning in her lungs and the cold water stabbed at her skin. The blurry orange mass nearly filled the scanner's entire screen as she neared the object. She estimated she could be only one or two arm's lengths away. To her horror, the object disappeared from the scanner screen as did the power indicator light. She dropped the rock and hit the scanner with the heel of her hand. The screen flashed white and then nothing. She cursed inwardly, tucked the scanner into her bra strap and began groping around blindly, her hands cutting through the cold water. Finally, her hand grasped a rock and then another. Urgently, she felt around until her hands fell on the smooth metal of the gun's barrel.

She wrapped her hand around the base of the barrel and pulled, but it would not budge. She ran her hand along the barrel to the back of the gun, down the handle and felt the tripod. She wrapped both her hands around the tripod and pulled at it violently. She could hear the gritty, distorted and high-pitched sound of rocks moving over metal and other rocks as the tripod budged. In one swift movement, she pushed hard off the rocky floor and pulled the tripod free. The air in her lungs felt like barbed wire. The tripod broke free, then jammed again on something else and the assembly tore from her hands. Her sense of calm had disappeared; if she could not disentangle the gun soon, she would need to swim to the surface and dive again. She never wanted to come down here again. She fought the momentum she had just created and swam back down, groping around desperately in the freezing darkness. Her hands swished through the water. She could feel her body being pulled to the surface and kicked hard to propel herself downward. She felt around frantically and she smashed her hand against one of the tripod legs. Not willing to make the same mistake twice, she grabbed the tripod firmly and shook it violently to free it from whatever had caught it. She kicked hard again off the floor toward the surface. Although lighter than it would have been on land, the tripod's substantial weight and gun's cumbersome shape created resistance in the water. She could see the faint light of the sky above her and wondered if it was her imagination. A flash in her mind showed her the tunnel after the rock collapse. She saw Owen in the shower with his purple, swollen knee. The video of Lexi being hit in the head. Her lungs felt as though they were in a blender and she fought hard against the autonomic urge to inhale. As she neared the surface, little stars appeared in her vision and her head began to feel pleasurably light. *One more kick. Okay, one more. Just one more.* She felt someone grabbing her. *Owen? Was it her imagination?*

Riley broke the surface of the water. Tyler had swum out, convinced he would be recovering her body. She had been under the water for well over two minutes before he swam out to find her and estimated three minutes before she surfaced. He scooped one arm around her limp form and caught the gun assembly as it slid out of her hand. Unable to use his hands, he kicked hard toward the shore, barely able to keep afloat. It felt like an hour had passed before his foot connected with the rocky shoreline. He dropped the gun in the shallow water and pulled Riley onto the shore. Barely able to breathe himself, he started CPR, sharing with her what little breath he had to give. The sounds of voices and footsteps around him were white noise as he focused all of his remaining energy on Riley.

Jake and Finn skidded to a halt at the sight of Riley's lifeless body. Owen leapt off his crutches at full speed, ran toward her and fell to her side, ignoring the pain that shot through his leg. He grabbed her wrist and felt a pulse. A small wave of relief flooded over him and he took over for Tyler, pale as a ghost and wheezing like an old man with a severe cough. Within seconds, Riley snapped awake, spraying herself, Owen, Tyler and Finn with the water she had inhaled. Her eyes bulged with panic as the last few memories of her consciousness returned to her. She shook violently from the shock and grasped madly for Owen, who grabbed her fiercely and wrapped himself around her shivering body. Jake passed Owen her sweater and he slid it over her head. He held her tightly to transfer his body heat but mostly because he never wanted to let go of her ever again. Finn kneeled on Riley's other side, his face drained of all colour. He pulled his own sweater over his head and dried her legs with it.

Unable to restrain his relief, he wrapped his long and powerful arms around her and Owen and squeezed. Riley's wits returned after a few moments.

"Okay, dude, too close," said Owen, when he and Finn bumped heads.

Riley extracted herself from the two men and stood slowly, Finn and Owen each at an elbow. She regained her land legs after a few steps. She slid back into her clothes and squeezed the water from her hair. Seeing Tyler slipping into his shoes beside her, she pulled him into a hug. "Thank you. I'd be dead if you hadn't swam out to me. I don't even remember breaking the surface." Jake's watch beeped and Riley knew it was the top of an hour. Which hour? How long had she been out?

CHAPTER 48

YEAR: 2097
TIME REMAINING: 5 hours, 32 minutes

The Defence teams successfully maintained a perimeter, thwarting the robot's attempts at ground gaining efforts. Several tanks cut their way across the battlefield, crushing the fallen robot bodies in their path. The tanks' blasting power was too much for the battlefield. And their missiles, when fired on the green space, were blocked, creating midair explosions where the ordinances hit the robots' invisible barrier.

Mitch noticed the robots seemed to come in surges. Each swell seemed to increase in physical and mechanical quality. This new wave of robotic warriors showed noticeable improvement over the first surge of robots, constructed with mismatched parts and limb substitutions. It seemed as though the AEI robots—with the most superior build quality and hardware—were saving themselves until absolutely necessary. Instead, they sent out disposable robots to bear the brunt of the battle.

"Mitch," yelled the voice of a lead at the front into Mitch's earpiece. "There's something weird up here. I don't know what it is, but it's destroying everything in its path." Mitch looked out over the battle in confusion. The bright lights hovering over the airfield lit up the base like midafternoon.

"As in, you've never seen anything like it?"

"No, as in, invisible. There is something creating a path of destruction. I think the robots can see it, they seem to know when to move out of the way."

"How wide a swath and how fast is it moving?"

"Not fast, maybe five, six miles an hour, and the swath is possibly ten, twenty feet wide? It's like a gigantic, invisible rolling pin or something. I can see things getting crushed. It's just flattened a tank!"

Mitch wanted to pull out his earpiece, throw it on the ground and stomp on it. Instead, he asked the lead his position. How could they fight invisible opponents?

One of Mitch's subs returned and handed him what looked like a handful of large glass marbles and a small black disk. Mitch set the black disk on the hood of the APHV and a screen appeared, projected above it. He tapped on the projected screen several times and the transparent spheres in his left hand flew upward into the air like doves being released. On the projected screen, Mitch and his subs watched the battle rage from an overhead perspective.

Mitch tapped at the intangible screen, toggling between the view each flying eye captured and scrutinized the feeds. "There. Right there." He pinpointed the source of the destruction on the screen and he and his subs watched another tank being flattened. He zoomed in to watch more closely. With a bird's eye view, Mitch could see cracks in the concrete, left in the wake of the invisible weapon. Mitch zoomed out and watched as the cracks wound toward the base, deviating only enough to make its path unpredictable.

Anything they shot either missed the invisible weapon or proved ineffective. The path of destruction stopped at the south side of the base. Mitch wondered if the weapon acted like a wind-up toy—only good for a certain amount of time or distance before becoming spent—but that seemed unlikely. He anticipated the weapon was now in position, waiting to inflict a new level of destruction. Nothing changed on the screen and when Mitch ordered one of the drone tanks to approach it, the tank drove through the weapon's position with no ill consequence. The weapon seemed to have simply disappeared.

"Hey, Mitch?" called his second-in-command over the com-sys.

"I hope you've got good news for me," said Mitch.

"I do, actually. We've broadened our scanning frequencies and we're able to see the invisible shield protecting the robot domes and their army's position in the green belt."

Mitch sighed, finally a development in their favour. "Good. Get that data to the pilots. I want three Hummingbirds up right now. We need to get rid of that shield, ASAP." Mitch was hesitant to send up more aircraft after losing two of the bladeless hovercopters earlier; however, knowing the location of the shields in the airspace meant they could successfully fly and avoid the barrier.

Within minutes, the first Hummingbird went up. The white, ergonomic Hummingbirds were roughly modelled after their ancient predecessor, the helicopter. Unlike a helicopter, the Hummingbird had no blades. It did have a typical cockpit and a cargo area at the rear with sliding doors in the body.

"HumSeven, report?" barked Mitch. He saw the powerful floodlights from the aircraft rake across on the green space below.

"Sir, I see several underground tunnels opening into the forest and they're pouring out and into the forest like…" started the co-pilot. After a moment of muffled sounds, Mitch heard the words, "locked on" and then, "Can't you shake it?" Screams followed and Mitch watched the Hummingbird burst into flames and fall into the forest below like a stone.

"What the hell?" said Mitch quietly under his breath. Before he could speculate any further on their fire power, HumEight exploded in midair. "HumNine, get out of there!"

The remaining Hummingbird turned to return to the base, but not before dropping several bombs over the robots in the forest. As the bombs reached the protective shield, they disappeared into thin air. Mitch watched the craft direct itself toward the hangar. Approximately half way back, the aircraft began to lurch and stutter in a manner the craft could not have physically done under its own steam.

The pilot's calm voice came over the radio. "Alpha Lead, I've got something locked on me. Don't know what it is and I can't shake it." The pilot's evasive manoeuvring shook the craft violently against the invisible restraint and a body fell out one of the open cargo doors.

The co-pilot's voice cut in. "We've lost Williams!" The voice was strained and lacked the metered control of the pilot.

Out of the corner of his eye, Mitch saw a streak of light as a missile headed straight toward the Hummingbird. "HumNine, you've got incoming," said Mitch.

"Roger that," said the pilot casually, as if this message was no more urgent than a request to land at a different hangar. The pilot managed to shake the aircraft free at the last moment. Unable to move the craft out of the way of the oncoming missile, the pilot spun ninety degrees and the rocket flew through the two open cargo doors.

"I've lost the lock, but that missile's coming around for round two." The craft shot upward and out of the missile's path. The Hummingbird shot a heat target to confuse the missile, but the intelligent weapon knew better. It recalculated its trajectory back onto its quarry. This time, it clipped the stubby, rounded tail of the aircraft. The craft began to spin and several of the soldiers in the cargo area fell out the open doors and hung from their safety cables. HumNine's slow descent picked up speed as the pilot unsuccessfully tried to regain control. The craft disappeared from view behind the hangars. Mitch saw grey smoke rise above the buildings and into the night. He dispatched a medical team to look for survivors.

Distracted from the crash scene, he heard a voice of one of the leads at the front. "Did you see that? It just disappeared! A tank vanished right in front of our eyes, just like those Hummingbirds did earlier." Seconds later, a tank exploded, hit with a missile. Several soldiers and robots near the blast flew backward and did not get up.

Mitch ran through an inventory of weaponry, men, firepower and other assets in use, and did some quick calculations. They were down five Hummingbirds. Ten still remained, but the risk of using them was too high when they were being picked off like soup cans on a fence by a seasoned sniper. The men and women fighting the battle were in good shape, despite being heavily outnumbered by the robots. As a whole, the robots' firepower was extraordinary, but individually, they were experiencing issues. The dust and the smoke in the air caused miscalculations or hesitations just long enough for the soldiers to use to their advantage. Without the reinforcements Mitch ordered to replace his teams who would eventually tire, it was only a matter of time before the robots would gain the upper hand. Not knowing how many robots remained and what other cards they had yet to play, Mitch could only prepare for the worst.

TIME REMAINING: 4 hours, 53 minutes

"Mitch?" called a new voice over the radio. Mitch recognized the voice of the director of communications. "Mitch, I'm patching through the Chief Administrative Director of Tricity's Nexus Hub. You need to hear what he's got to say."

Mitch adjusted his earpiece as he acknowledged her. Each major city across the country maintained a Nexus Hub. Each Hub acted as a vertebra in the backbone for all of the online data and information that users accessed on a daily basis to live their lives and do their jobs. The CAD ensured that Tricity's Hub of the Nexus always stayed running. Without it, a portion of the country's online world would go offline, grinding life to a halt.

"Mitch here." He stepped away from his subs to a more private area at the rear of the battlefield.

"Mitch, we've got a problem," said the Director. "The robots have hacked into our data vaults on the Nexus."

"Which ones?" Mitch knew that the NRD compartmentalized its sensitive data across various sectors in the different Nexus Hubs. If one vault became hacked or compromised, the data would be useless without its other pieces, securely sealed in other highly-secured data vaults across different sectors among the Hubs.

"All of them. And not just Tricity. Across the whole country. They've got access to everything."

Mitch froze. "How did that happen? How could they hack in and get everything that fast? I thought these data vaults were impervious?"

"They're supposed to be," said the Director.

Mitch stared into the night's sky and exhaled several long breaths. He knew what had to be done, but the results would be catastrophic. It would stop everything, dead in its tracks, literally. From coast to coast, the entire country would be in a freeze. Businesses would not be able to do business. City services would be stopped. People's cars would stop. Everything from water and heat to commerce would stop. People in air trains, buses or elevators would be trapped. It was like a power outage, but worse.

"Mitch?" asked the Director again.

Mitch shook his head. "Shut it down."

"I'm sorry?"

"You heard me," Mitch said, rubbing his forehead. "We've been breached. Shut the Nexus down."

"Mitch, we can't do that. We can't shut down the entire country. Nothing will work..."

"I'm well aware of what it will do. We're hemorrhaging data all over God knows where. They'll be able to turn our weapons on us in minutes. I'm open to suggestions if you've got an alternative one."

The other end of the line fell silent. After a moment, the Director swore under his breath. "You're going to have one hell of a report to write. I'll put the order in for that right now, across all the Hubs. I'm not sure how long it will take, it's not a switch. I've got to get through to the central vault."

"What is your best guess?"

"Five to ten minutes."

"Alright. Make it happen."

Mitch hoped that pulling the plug on the Nexus would favour him with an advantage equal to the gravity of the order he had just given. No one had ever shut the Nexus down before. It was unheard of, like turning off the sun in the middle of the afternoon. Mitch knew the repercussions would be unimaginable. But at this moment, it was his best hope to slow the robots who, despite the NRD's assault, continued to replenish their numbers with no sign of letting up.

With only minutes to spare before the shutdown of the Nexus, Mitch communicated the update to the leads in battle. With the Nexus down, guns would have to be manually aimed and fired, and the com-sys would cease to work.

Mitch half-expected to see some sign announcing the Nexus had been shut off but to his surprise nothing significant happened. The only immediate indicators were the blinking words at the bottom left corner of his vision, "System Offline" and the words "No Data" pulsing in small red letters in the centre of the Glass Eye's projected screen that, just moments ago, showed the battle from above.

Only on the battlefield was it obvious that something had changed. The activity on the runway-turned-battlefield changed to disorientation. Mitch surveyed the turmoil. The robots ceased advancing and peered at one another questioningly. Some looked confused. Some tapped the side of their head where the receiver was located. The troops, taken aback by the robots' sudden change in behaviour, looked around with shock and trepidation.

One of the robots spoke to others nearby. "The Nexus is down." One of the robots it spoke to had a tire iron for an arm. It shrugged and looked around for instruction. The silence broke when an orange laser blast streaked through the air and struck the confused robot in the forehead. It cartwheeled backward and fell to the ground spread-eagled as its head rolled away and its tire-iron arm clattered to the concrete. The newer, First Gen robots outfitted with the AEI upgrade, blazed unflinchingly into battle. Some of the older robots took the lead from their refocused brethren, but the confusion was evident in the aged, mismatched robots, who began attacking other robots and piles of debris.

TIME REMAINING: 2 hours, 37 minutes

Mitch wrapped up a strategy meeting with the unit leads in B Hangar's second maintenance bay. An aged and tattered paper map illustrating the base property lay unfurled across the hood of an APHV. Tools and miscellaneous parts representing robots and NRD teamss marked their respective positions on the map. Mitch anticipated GammaTron's strategy was to weaken the NRD personnel with their most disposable robots first, then storm the base with the smarter and more powerful AEI robots. The NRD had succeeded in keeping the first waves of slower, uncoordinated robots at bay due to their handicaps. However, an attack by the stronger, faster and more agile AEI robots in similar numbers would flatten the NRD teams in minutes.

The teams were beginning to fatigue—forced to keep pace with robots that required no breaks of any kind. More people were in transport from other bases around the country, but it would be well into the morning before they would arrive. With tanks being mysteriously flattened or disappearing into thin air and the Hummingbirds' effectiveness reduced to that of firecrackers, Mitch wondered how much longer they would be able to hold on.

One of the unit leads approached him as he rolled up the paper map.

"They're advancing in larger numbers, sir."

As Mitch walked out of the hangar, he pulled his binocular glasses from his breast pocket and put them on. Mitch's stomach fell. As he watched the fresh wave of metal surging from the green space, Mitch's earlier observation still held true. A sea of advanced First Gen robots mixed with many AEI models marched toward the base. Mitch readied himself for a fight.

CHAPTER 49

When the group from the lake returned to camp, it was to cheers and applause. Tyler held the gun he had recovered over his head like a well-earned prize.

A flicker of cautious hope returned to the team, despite the acute awareness of the numerous obstacles that still lay ahead. The tripod from the gun that Tyler had retrieved was still missing, as was the remote control. And the guns still had yet to be tested. After choking down a quick breakfast of oatmeal with leftover nuts and dehydrated banana chips, the teams broke out again in pairs to search for the last tripod and remote.

The morning progressed with little success, and at eight o'clock, Riley called off the search; there was still a lot of work to be done. The tunnel still needed to be prepped for the post-op blasting. In addition, Riley worried that creating a new tripod and remote control would take more time than they had left.

Jake, Clint and Lexi began prepping the tunnel for blasting, relieving Ben and Maya from their sentry duty. Ben returned to the camp with a plan in mind for the construction of a replacement remote control and the pair dove into the snacks that Darren had brought to the work shed. Ben grabbed a stack of sandwiches, stuffed several rice cakes into his mouth and watched as Tyler carried out his instructions for disassembling Mole2's control console to scavenge pieces for a new remote control.

By ten o'clock, Finn had two of the three guns working again. The guns Riley and Tyler had retrieved from the water sustained no lasting damage and worked after a thorough drying. Finn had repaired the broken cartridge clip of the third gun; however, the gun now ran intermittently. Unsure of what else may have been done to it, he disassembled and reassembled the gun three times with no hint of where the problem lay.

After poring over the gun's schematics for what seemed like the tenth time, Finn located the issue. As he was explaining to Riley how he needed to adjust the cartridge contact, Darren burst into the work shed carrying the last tripod. She had never seen the quiet and laidback, gourmet chef move so quickly outside of his kitchen.

"I found it in the bushes behind the food pantry. I thought I'd go through the pantry one last time to see if I missed anything good and something shiny in the bushes caught my eye. I took a closer look and there it was."

Riley, Finn and Owen set up the three guns and the three tripods in the testing tank. The vandalized tripod sported metal splints that reinforced the legs that had been bent back into shape. After a quick test, the output capacity of all three registered as fully operational. Riley heaved a sigh of relief.

As they entered the testing tank to collect the guns, Ben emerged from the work shed limping along slowly with Tyler in tow, his hands black and his face smudged. Ben tossed Riley a small, black metal box with a square, faded red button on the top that read "Emergency Stop" encased with a clear plastic cover to keep the button from being pressed accidentally. She recognized it as one of the Mole's kill switches from inside the control room.

"Is this what I think it is?"

Ben nodded. "We had to scavenge some parts from Mole2, but I suspect we'll be forgiven."

Riley found the new remote control in the menu of her Icomm contacts and chuckled when she saw the name Ben had given it, "Ben & Tyler's Boom Box." She synced the guns to the remote control and they prepared to run one final test. She held the remote control out to Ben. "I think you should have the honours," said Riley.

Ben took the box but handed it to Tyler. "I just gave the orders. Tyler's the one who had to crawl around in the Mole's grubby console for an hour."

Tyler laughed and wiped his hands on his pants. He took the remote control from Ben. "You're right about that."

On Riley's count, Tyler hit the button and all three guns fired. Finn let out a whoop when the MultiMatter Scanner reported that all three guns were properly synced and operating as expected.

The two teams journeyed down the tunnel to complete the final set-up before the timeshift. Riley, Owen and Finn each took a zeno ray gun and spread out along the perimeter of the white stones that lit the underground space with its pulsing, snowy-white glow. They steadied the tripods on the jagged floor and trained the weapons on the heaping mass. Finn set the testing tank on the floor at the base of the incline. He propped up the MultiMatter Scanner on the inside the tank, ready and waiting to record the blast.

With all of their work now complete, with the exception of the detonation itself, Riley expected to feel a small sense of relief at this stage, but anxiety gripped her unlike anything she had ever experienced. She looked at Jake and saw her sentiments mirrored back in his eyes. The rest of the morning had progressed alarmingly well. No bizarre occurrences, no strange visitors. Now at crunch time, the tension was palpable.

Finn passed Riley the remote control and she dropped it into one of the many utility pockets on her cargo pants. She slid the zipper shut and tapped the bulge twice for good measure. "I guess all we can do now is wait."

"We've got a few minutes to kill before the timeshift. I thought that before we head up to Mole Control to watch the action, I'd say a few things," said Jake, "I know I'm a man of few words, and the ones I do say aren't always the right ones," he looked at Lexi, who smiled warmly. "But I wanted to tell you all how great you've been, and I couldn't have asked for a better group of..."

"Jake, sorry to interrupt," said Riley, looking around. "Where's Clint?"

Everybody looked around as if on cue, Clint would pop out from behind the pile of Elevanium.

"Maybe he's packing his stuff?" Lexi asked.

Riley swore under her breath. "No one was supposed to be alone."

"We got split up when Ben pulled me away to build the remote control," said Tyler. "The last time I saw him, he said he was going to help Jake and Lexi set up the explosives."

"Which he did, and then he left. He said he'd forgotten some tools. He said he'd call you and Ben to meet him at the tunnel entrance," said Jake.

Both Ben and Tyler shook their head. "I never heard from him," said Ben.

Jake called Clint repeatedly over the com-sys. No response.

"Ben, Maya, Darren, stay outside the entrance of this tunnel. If anything comes near it, I want it incapacitated. I don't care if it's a freaking squirrel." Riley stormed up the long ascent toward the camp. Owen zipped up behind her on his crutches, following in her wake.

Jake felt uneasy as he and the others caught up with Riley leaving the tunnel. Something felt wrong, and his mind flooded with every possible scenario imaginable. Had his decision to let Clint out of the cube been a mistake? Had Clint been biding his time until this very moment to sabotage the operation after all? Is he in on it with this other person? *Is that how they've been able to survive here for six months? No. Clint's honesty has been proven time and time again. This is just a coincidence.* He wanted to believe there was a logical explanation, but a nagging feeling tugged at him and his mind circled back to the worst possible scenarios.

CHAPTER 50

TEAM 3
YEAR: 2095
Time Remaining: 1 hour, 37 minutes

The twins stood around Spencer's coffee table dressed like high-tech criminals, surrounded by enough electronic gadgets to break into the federal gold reserve. They wore multipocketed black cargo pants and matching black, long-sleeved shirts. Their backpacks lay open on the couch and they filled the bags with the tools and supplies necessary for breaking and entering as well as for hacking into the NRD alarm system.

Past and future-Spencer sat at the dining room table and ran through the plan for what seemed like the hundredth time. Future-Spencer felt nausea bubbling in the pit of his stomach, but he fought it back. They had a plan, though it was flimsy at best. It would get them in the door, but there was a good chance the night would end with a lot of awkward conversations with the police. Spencer adjusted the time travel watch on his left wrist. He pulled his sleeve over it but the lump it created was hardly less conspicuous. A knock on the door startled the group.

Past-Spencer looked inquiringly at his future counterpart. "Kalen?"

Spencer shook his head. "No, she's at her grandparents. I think she needed some downtime after what happened Saturday."

"Can't say I blame her," said future-Logan. He walked to the door and opened it. "Delaney, you look fabulous." The collar of her white shirt peeked over the jacket of her tailored charcoal skirt suit. She kissed him on the cheek and he saw that she looked tired. Her eyes lacked their sparkle. Logan opened the door wider to let her in. She entered and, seeing the two Spencers, she stopped. Her eyes darted from the Spencers to the floor and she backed into the hallway. He followed her out of the apartment.

"Can you get Spencer, too?" She thought for a moment and clarified. "Your Spencer. The future one." Logan could tell the day was weighing heavily on her. He motioned for Spencer to come out.

Delaney had never felt worse in her life. She felt like her world was turning inside out and all she could do was sit and watch from the sidelines. The pain of knowing that Logan would soon be gone felt nearly physical. Added to that was the dread she felt about the half-baked plan the team was about to execute. She was unsure whether they could succeed with the deck stacked against them at every point.

Spencer closed the door behind him in the hallway and Delaney handed him an envelope. "Take this. I'm sorry I can't stay and help you further, I have to get to the office. Some of the out of town stakeholders want a tour of our lab before the big presentation."

Spencer opened up the envelope to find a letter with a plastic swipe card affixed to the bottom. The card surprised him. The swipe card technology had been antiquated long before his parents had been born.

Dear Mr. Philip White,
Please find the attached swipe card as your...

Spencer stopped reading. The name sounded familiar, but he had no time to process it; he was more interested in the card's purpose. He studied the rectangular piece of plastic. "I don't think I've actually ever seen one of these in real life."

Logan laughed. "Geez Laney, what museum did you get this from?"

Delaney smiled. "We had a last minute request for another guest this evening who required an alternative method of security authorization. The problem is that not only is he blind, but he has glass eyes."

A smile crept across Spencer's face. "No eyes. No retinas. He wouldn't be able to use the retinal scanners."

"Exactly. Security was all in a flap because they'd never had to deal with this before and had no idea what to do. They had to dig out an old policy manual from the basement to see what the protocol was. Apparently, it's this," she said, pointing to the card. She smiled innocently. "But, as it turns out, he couldn't make it."

Spencer stared at the card. This antique piece of plastic changed everything.

TIME REMAINING: 1 hour, 8 minutes

Spencer's stomach squirmed uncomfortably as the cab drove him to the NRD office. It joined the line of cars waiting to drop their passengers off at the front door. He was pleased to see a throng of people waiting to get in; it would be much easier to get lost in the masses.

When his cab finally advanced to the door, he got out and stood on the curb hunched forward. Dressed in a brown tweed suit, grey wool cap and carrying a maroon leather messenger bag, Spencer completed his outfit with black sunglasses and a white cane. A quick dusting of talcum powder gave his normally wheat-blond hair the appearance of having aged forty years in an instant. He unfolded the cane and made his way to the door slowly with short, shuffling steps.

Inside the main doors, a bank of retinal scanner stations lined the wall opposite the security desk like self-serve ticket kiosks at a movie theatre. The long lines of guests waiting to scan in filled the foyer and spilled out the front entrance, making it hard for Spencer to access the security desk.

"Mr. White," greeted one of the guards, his voice excessively loud over the sounds of the excited congregation of people lining up to get in.

I'm blind not deaf, thought Spencer, though he appreciated the gesture. He nodded feebly.

"We've been expecting you. Do you have your card?"

Spencer pulled the card out of his jacket pocket and held it up.

The security guard came around the desk and gently took Spencer's arm in his. "Okay, I'm just going to get you to swipe that at the far end of our desk here."

The guard cleared people from Spencer's path and led him to the far end of the marble counter top where a card scanner waited, covered in years of dust.

"That thing is unbelievably filthy. I guess you don't get many occasions to use it, eh?" said Spencer in his best old man's voice. As the words had left his mouth, his heart jumped into his throat. The guard looked at him perplexed. He had blown it. His mind raced, thinking about what his next move would be. Jump the security gate, run for it and hide? Leave and resort to the original plan? He froze to the spot.

The guard initially seemed thrown off by his comment, then smiled. He looked at the thick layer of dust on the surface of the scanner, then pulled his sleeve over his hand and brushed it off. He seemed impressed and in no way suspicious. "That's very impressive, Mr. White. How did you know that?" he asked.

"Uh, I can smell it."

"Really? I didn't know dust had an odour."

"Oh, yeah. For sure," Spencer lied.

The guard held his sleeve up and he smelled it. He seemed baffled. "Hmm. I don't smell anything. You must have a super sensitive sense of smell." He brushed the dust off his sleeve.

For good measure, Spencer took a few visible sniffs and made a face. "Yes, now you might want to do something about those shoes," said Spencer, smiling.

The guard seemed thoroughly impressed. He chuckled and helped Spencer swipe his card. Spencer made a production of missing the scanner multiple times. "Let me show you to your seat."

Spencer watched the time projected into the bottom left corner of his vision by his Icomm lenses. He had only minutes to get to the east wing to let the twins in but felt it would be suspicious to deny the offers of help. If he truly were blind, help would probably be very welcome when in an unfamiliar building, being jostled by crowds and trying to find an auditorium, then a numbered row and seat. He played the part and graciously accepted the offered help.

TIME REMAINING: 49 minutes

"What the frig?" whispered Logan harshly when Spencer finally stuck his head out the back door. "You're eleven minutes late!"

Spencer shushed Logan angrily. The presentation had already begun and gone were the echoing voices in the atrium. They heard the NRD public relations rep Allison Hargrave giving her opening remarks.

"You have no idea how hard it is to be an old blind man," he whispered loudly. "I mean, I appreciate everyone's concern but, good gravy! Every time I tried to get away, everyone assumed I needed help or I was lost. I got redirected twice trying to come down this hallway. I had to wait in the bathroom until the presentation started." He closed the door behind his brothers and they walked down the hall to a set of double doors that would enter a storage area inside the Burton Auditorium.

With the anxiety of getting inside the building now behind him, the void filled with a fresh wave of uneasiness for the next task. Spencer still had no clue as to how he was going to convince the stakeholders that the personality applications needed to be modified before being deployed in the robots. It sickened him to know that he had come this far and still had no strategy. In life, he always had a plan and a backup plan and a backup, backup plan. The circumstances of the last three days had completely pulled the rug out from under him.

Asher got to the storage room door before his brothers and placed his hand on the handle. Before he opened it, he looked at Spencer seriously.

"Spence, what's your plan?" Spencer answered his question with a look of fear that Asher had not seen in his kid brother's eyes since the tree house sleepover that had prompted the Ghost Story Ban of 2076.

Spencer shrugged. "I'll have to somehow get to the stakeholders at the end of the meeting and explain everything." Asher caught Logan's eye and saw his twin shared the same level of concern. Asher pulled the door open and they silently walked in.

When they entered the room, they immediately saw the large curtain that ran from the back of the auditorium to the front, partitioning the storage area from the rest of the room. The storage area was not lit, but light from the auditorium spilled over the top and beneath the curtain. They stood among stacks of tables, chairs, desks, fake plants, filing cabinets and other miscellaneous office items that people had stashed there. When Logan suggested using this storage area as a hiding place, his brothers were surprised to learn of its existence. In answer to his brothers' queries regarding his knowledge of the space, Logan smiled and muttered something about helping Delaney carry a desk there once or twice.

Walking carefully through a maze of neatly stacked office supplies, they walked as far as they could to the front of the room and found that only the stage and the first few rows were visible. Careful to stay in the shadows cast by the massive curtain, Spencer and the twins peered as far as they could around the edge without being seen. They were surprised to see only one of the twenty-two robots on stage with Ian.

The brothers listened quietly in the shadows as Ian explained the AEI technology and how it would bring the robots to life. He elaborated on the many ways the robots would change the world and human-robot relationships, and how the world would soon be giving credit to the pioneers in this very room, for it was only because of their vision and investment that the face of robotics around the world would be revolutionized forever. Not a sound in the auditorium could be heard as the audience eagerly took in every word.

TIME REMAINING: 11 minutes

"Spence!" Logan whispered. His younger brother's pale face glowed white, and not from errant talcum powder when ditching his disguise. "What's your plan? What can we do?"

"I don't know!" Spencer whispered frantically. The pressure on his chest cinched tighter as each second ticked away on his watch. "How am I going to convince these people of anything when I have no working proof?"

He opened up the tacky leather messenger bag and pulled out a stack of papers. "All I have are these goddamn test results and a few modified personalities in the trunk of my fucking car. I only have summaries for the first five we were able to modify before Ian busted us." His breathing began to feel constricted and he pulled desperately at the collar of his shirt.

Logan eyed the papers Spencer waved around. "Well, that's better than nothing, isn't it?"

Spencer shook his head. He narrowed his eyes in frustration. "It's just data. People won't understand. They need to see to believe, and that's why this goddamn demo was so fucking important. All I'm going to be able to do is wave a bunch of papers around and hope that people listen! I'm going to get arrested before I finish my first sentence!"

The three stopped talking when they heard the audience laughing. They peered around the corner again. The presentation seemed to be going off without a hitch. Ian's usual charisma charmed the crowd and the robot performed brilliantly. The robot grinned widely and his eyes glowed blue. Ian and the robot fed off of each other, interacting and collaborating. They even played catch with a little red bouncy ball. The robot closed the demo by showing off his agility—bouncing the ball off its arms, knees and feet like a seasoned soccer player. Ian and the robot bowed in response to the standing ovation then took questions from the audience. Ian never missed a beat and had answers to every question. The audience ate it up.

CHAPTER 51

YEAR: 2097
TIME REMAINING: 53 minutes

Mitch watched the violent conflict from the rear of the battlefield. His binocular glasses remained in his breast pocket—their powers of magnification were unnecessary as the battle now raged dangerously close to the base. The men and women in the skirmish fought like heroes, but the numerous opponents and their technology were far superior. Mitch received reports of three more invisible balls of destruction rolling through the battlefield.

In preparation for the worst, Mitch deployed teams to the Elevanium vault, as well as to the time travel control centre as the last line of defence to protect the precious power source. He also directed several level three personnel to oversee each critical station and manually report back, now that the lines of communication were down.

Mitch watched as a small number of robots breached the human barrier on the battlefield and beelined toward the base. The activity on the battleground had grown frantic and desperate. Mitch and his remaining sub, Jax, found themselves caught up in the battle near the rear entrance of the Defence building. The two men stood back to back and picked off robots as quick as they could, Jax with the E-cannon and Mitch with an atom blaster. Other parts of the front line had weakened and soon more robots broke through. Jax fried swaths of robots as they neared while Mitch disintegrated others like paper dolls with a fire hose. The robots caught in the E-cannon blast collapsed to the ground and the robots behind crawled over them or dodged the fallen bodies to pass. After several blasts with the E-cannon, Mitch and Jax found themselves standing in a bunker of lifeless robots, which created a barrier that hindered the advancing robots' path into the building. Mitch knew it would only be minutes before robots changed their tactic and found a different way into the building.

Although full of adrenaline and ready to fight, Mitch feared that their time was running out. He heard an explosion at the front of the base and saw a portion of the white brick wall surrounding the property come down. Mitch expected to see robots emerging through the wall, but what he saw instead was the most welcome sight he had ever seen.

An armada of APHVs full of fresh troops sped into the compound, robots ricocheting in every direction as the large vehicles filled the rear of the battlefield. Geared up men and women poured from the vehicles and charged into the battle. With the new troops, Mitch could step back from the battle to confer with the new leads. He approached the first lead as he was getting out of the passenger side of the APHV.

"Jason Grayson, I'll be damned. I thought you midwest guys wouldn't be ready to deploy until tomorrow?"

The father of the Grayson brothers smiled and the two men shook hands heartily. "You're partially right. We can't get the heavy artillery here until tomorrow, but after reading your report, I thought we should take what we had ready and get the hell over here. We would have been here sooner but all the vehicles stalled out at once and we were left hanging a half mile up over a goddamn wheat field. We knew it was a bad situation but, seriously? Shutting down the Nexus? We had to let the APHVs run their emergency grounding sequence and you know how bloody long that takes. Thankfully, the auxiliary propulsion systems still worked. I haven't hooked one of those up since being in the academy. We lost one of the APHVs; its exponential power replicator was missing. So, no go on the aux prop for that one, obviously." Jason chuckled. "As long as the west coast guys aren't stranded with missing EPRs, they should be here by the time my guys are spent."

Mitch caught a black, nylon weave belt that Jason had tossed at him. "What are these?" He flipped the belt's bulky, silver and red buckle over in his hand.

"Shield belt prototypes. They create an invisible, egg-shaped barrier of protection around you. The first round of lab tests was better than expected. I had a production run of 500 made for rigorous field testing. Everybody we've brought's wearing one. The feedback from field testing has been very positive so far."

"Yeah, except for that one guy who got caught in the rain," said a nearby level five as he slammed the rear door of the APHV shut. "I hope he's had kids already because I don't know if he'll be able to now."

Mitch cinched on the belt without question and hit the red button in the centre of the buckle. A white light flashed around him then faded away.

"You can get hit by a car in this thing and you won't get a scratch." As Jason looked from the battle to his remaining subs, he activated his zeno ray gun. "Shall we?"

TIME REMAINING: 31 minutes

Within minutes, the new teams were fully engaged in the fray and Mitch could resume overseeing the battle. The security of the shield belt allowed him to focus more on managing the conflict and worry less about errant shots or flying shrapnel.

Mitch surveyed the metallic carnage around the battlefield. Thousands of robots lay unmoving on the ground. Some looked untouched—victims of the E-cannon. Others had suffered a less elegant fate, crushed by tanks or blasted to bits of scrap by the atom blasters. At the edge of the green space, more robots joined the battle. Mitch was just about to pull off his binocular glasses when something caught his eye.

"Well, I'll be damned," said Mitch.

"What is it, sir?" asked Jax, still carrying the E-cannon on his shoulder.

Mitch pointed across the scarred and pock-marked landing strip. "It's Gamma-Tron. I wonder what he's up to."

They watched the hulking robot in the distance as he lumbered across the battle-field. "I want that robot's head on a platter," said Mitch, eyeing the robot.

Jax looked at Mitch and grinned. "Don't you mean, you want the platter from his head?"

Mitch groaned and rolled his eyes at Jax's nerdy joke, surprised a kid his age would be that knowledgeable of turn-of-the-century computing hardware. He laughed and shook his head as he resumed watching GammaTron weave his way through the maze of debris. The robot's brazen appearance troubled Mitch. What could be drawing him from the safety of his shelter and, worse still, what weapon was he using to protect himself?

No sooner had Mitch wondered this when a massive explosion erupted on the battlefield and Mitch found himself thrown backward. He closed his eyes and braced for the impact as he fell, but it never came. He landed hard on his back, but he felt no concrete beneath him. He opened his eyes and was startled by what he saw. He lay above the ground, as if supported by an invisible bodyboard. The headless torso of a shiny AEI robot looked suspended in the air an arm's length above him, resting atop the invisible shield that surrounded him. He stood effortlessly and the metallic body fell to the ground at his feet. Remembering GammaTron, he squinted his eyes and scanned the smoky, dusty battlefield. The robot kingpin had vanished.

Anticipating the explosion was a distraction tactic for the robots to sneak into the Defence building, Mitch scrambled toward the base, hoping to cut GammaTron off before entering.

TIME REMAINING: 19 minutes

Mitch saw no sign of GammaTron anywhere and wondered if the slippery robot was already in the building. For all Mitch knew, GammaTron could make himself invisible. He looked at Jax. "I want an update on the time travel control centre and the Elevanium vault. You check the vault, I'll check the control centre. Blast any robot you see. I don't care if it's polishing the floor or taking out the garbage."

Mitch sprinted up the concrete stairs to the second level as fast as his overworked legs would carry him. As he ran, he wondered if the robots knew about Operation TimeShift and the bonded time. If they had, GammaTron would have focused more robots on the time travel control centre. Stealing the Elevanium from the Elevanium vault would solidify the robots' upper hand. Stealing the Elevanium from the Control Centre would slam the window of bonded time shut, creating a whole host of unfore-seeable results, likely in the robots' favour.

As Mitch neared the time travel control centre, he heard the unmistakable zing of laser shots and metal hitting the stone floor. Through the glass walls, he saw a full-scale battle underway. The room had been secured for the most part, though several robots still ran among their fallen comrades, shooting at anything and everything. Mitch jumped into the skirmish and helped obliterate the few remaining robots. After several moments, Mitch and the troops stood in silence, catching their breath surrounded by the countless metal bodies littering the floor. They heard more metal footsteps marching down the hallway, approaching the room. As the six-person team repositioned for a new attack, they heard the deep booming of the E-cannon in the hallway, then the sound of metal hitting stone. Jax strode into the control centre with the E-cannon ready on his shoulder. The double doors slid open automatically and he stopped to survey the damage. The electronic gun on his shoulder beeped, indicating it had charged and was ready for the next blast.

"Good shot, kid, but point that thing somewhere else," said Mitch. The double doors slid shut automatically. "One blast in the wrong direction with that you'll fry every circuit in this room. How's the Elevanium vault?"

"Solid as a rock, sir."

Mitch smiled inwardly, thankful for good news. He tapped at the room's control screen beside the door and locked the glass doors, for all the good it would do.

Within minutes, they heard more metallic footsteps, muffled by the closed doors. Mitch scanned the anxious faces around the room as the footsteps grew louder. Twelve robots stopped in front of the doors and several tried to pry them open unsuccessfully. Mitch and the others could only watch as one of the robots blasted the double doors with a gun none of them had ever seen before. A burst of green liquid issued from the gun, or was it a solid? Mitch could not tell. The green substance liquefied the glass door. The liquid glass disappeared into the floor like water absorbed into a garden. Jax shot the E-cannon and all of the robots fell to the ground.

Minutes passed with no sign of any robots. Lights from the projected screens emitted an eerie glow around the unlit room. The occasional muffled crash broke the silence; distant explosions could be heard through the outer walls. Mitch felt cut off from the battle with no way to communicate and wondered how Jason and the teams were faring.

The clicking sounds of metal on stone were again heard coming down the hallway, too many to count. Jax waited until the robots entered the room and pulled the trigger. The cannon issued its deep boom, but this time, none of the robots fell. Instead, they opened fire. Jax was hit first. The blast knocked him backward into the thick glass of the Elevanium capsule in the centre of the room. The E-cannon flew from his hand, skidded across the floor and stopped at Mitch's feet. Jax lay unmoving, crumpled at the base of the Elevanium capsule.

"They've shielded their processors," yelled Mitch, over the loud metal footsteps. He charged the first robot. The blasts from his plasmaqueous gun ricocheted off the robot as they had in the field. The robot opened fire on Mitch, but its yellow laser blasts ricocheted off Mitch's invisible shield and back at itself. The robot crumpled to the ground. Mitch got tossed aside by the other robots as they stormed callously over their fallen brethren as they pushed forward toward the glass capsule in the centre of the room. Mitch and his team used their agility to outmanoeuvre and overtake the robots. When the skirmish ended, all of the robots had been destroyed. Mitch leaned on the Elevanium capsule in the centre of the room—his chest again heaving and he shook with fury, adrenaline and loss. Only he and one other soldier remained whose name, according to his badge was Beckenbauer. Before they could collect their thoughts, more footsteps echoed down the hallway. Mitch and Beck looked at each other in silent solidarity before looking to the door.

CHAPTER 52

The team spread out in pairs calling Clint's name in a frantic attempt to find him before the timeshift. Jake and Lexi sprinted toward the lake; Finn and Tyler jogged through the bush south of the camp. Riley and Owen checked the work shed. Whether or not Clint had grabbed the tools he wanted before disappearing was impossible to tell—tools and miscellaneous parts were strewn about like debris after a tornado. Riley sprinted out of the work shed and across the camp, intending to follow Clint's hunting path east into the forest. She heard Owen call her name and she turned to see him zipping northward on the rocky ledge away from the camp.

Owen flew across the rocky floor on his floating crutch platform, leaning as far forward as gravity would allow before losing his balance. He glanced over his shoulder and saw Riley on his heels.

Riley gained on Owen as he sped over the rocky surface, the small stones and dips in the rolling, rocky surface inconsequential as he flew effortlessly over them. Riley watched her every footstep carefully, aware that a broken ankle now would throw a serious wrench into everything. She steered clear of the steep cliff to her left with the jagged rocks below and hugged the tree line to her far right where the rocky floor met thick forest. Ahead of her, she saw Owen stop and step off his crutch platform—his progress halted by a three foot step-up in the stony surface. As she approached him, he pointed ahead. She saw someone sitting on one of the rocks in the distance. Without hesitation, she leaped up the ledge and charged forward. She called Jake on the com-sys and gave him a status report and location.

"Copy that. On our way," said Jake.

Riley ripped ahead of Owen toward Clint, dodging the maze of boulders in her path. As she approached, she saw him sitting on a rock, only a few dangerous steps away from the ledge. His bound limbs flailed in front of him as he desperately tried to communicate something to Riley through the duct tape covering his mouth. He wobbled dangerously atop the rock, his exaggerated arm and head movements rocking him perilously on the stone seat.

"Clint, what the hell? Who did this to you?" As she approached him, his eyes bulged as he jerked his head around trying to communicate something. She reached out to pull the piece of tape from his mouth and heard Owen shout her name from behind.

As Riley had sped toward Clint, Owen abandoned the crutch device, too heavy to lift up the ledge with a bad knee. He pulled himself up the ledge and hobble-hopped toward them. He approached as quickly as his throbbing knee would allow him. He turned to look over his shoulder to see if anyone was coming and his bad knee collided with a large boulder. He collapsed to the ground as electrocuting pain shot from his knee in every direction, down into his foot, up his leg, his back and up the back of his skull. He gritted his teeth through the pain and pulled himself up using the boulder. He saw Clint and Riley, then something that turned his stomach. A man wearing a familiar black backpack was crouching behind a large rock beside Clint, hidden from Riley's view. As he called out to warn her, the man lunged at her just as she reached out to remove the tape covering Clint's mouth.

Owen watched in horror as the man grabbed at Riley. With lightning speed, she spun, simultaneously grabbing a handful of his hair and the hand he had on her shoulder, she threw him to the ground. The man looked up at her and a crazed smile grew on his face. Owen presumed she recognized the man as she froze in surprise after seeing his face. She paid for her moment's hesitation when he swept her feet out from under her. He grabbed her around the neck, yanked her to her feet and pressed a gun to her temple.

CHAPTER 53

TEAM 3
YEAR: 2095
TIME REMAINING: 5 minutes

Still hiding with the twins behind the curtain inside the Burton Auditorium, Spencer glanced down at his watch, his heart racing. He could feel beads of sweat growing on his forehead. Terror crackled through his body like lightning as he watched the presentation draw to a close. His lack of a plan made it feel as though every cell in his body was becoming more unsettled, and he could do nothing but watch his window of opportunity close further with each passing second. He could feel his limbs begin to vibrate.

"I have time for one more question," Ian announced.

A woman's voice spoke from the back. "If the robots have human personalities, and by extension, human instincts, two of the most fundamental human instincts are self-preservation and the continuation of the species. How will the robots react when they find out that, for one, the production levels of robots is dictated by humans, and two, there is a limited amount of Elevanium allocated to their existence?"

The robot looked from the crowd to Ian; the robot's casual posture stiffened and his facial expression turned cloudy. The robot watched Ian, waiting for an explanation of this concept he could not understand. Its eyes changed from a vibrant blue to purple.

Ian stepped in front of the robot, cutting it off from the crowd. "We have no reason to believe that these robots will be anything other than docile and obedient. The people who donated their personalities for this project were healthy, intelligent people, who passed their psychological evaluations with flying colours. These robots will inherit morals and ethics as a part of those donated personalities and from that, they will inherently know what is and isn't acceptable behaviour."

The crowd was silent. No one challenged Ian's explanation.

Spencer felt like the fog in his brain instantly cleared. For the first time in days, he saw everything clearly and he knew exactly what to do. Without hesitation, he stepped out from the shadows of the curtain and took the steps to the stage two at a time, still clutching his documents. He heard Asher and Logan whisper-yelling his name.

"I'm sorry, Ian, but that is incorrect," said Spencer. He walked to the centre of the great stage, stopping just outside Ian's reach. He held up the papers for the room to see. "This is comprehensive testing data that shows results extremely contrary to what the Project Director has just indicated."

The faces in the audience looked confused. *They think I'm crazy*, he thought. "I'm Spencer Grayson, and I've been working on the personality development of this project from day one. I was unsatisfied with the testing criteria that our team was given to work with. I developed a stricter battery of tests and retested the personalities. I was right to be concerned. The results are very unsettling." Spencer stepped down off the stage and straight to Travis Ryerson, the largest private financial backer. Spencer handed Travis the twenty-two summary reports generated by the Real Life Simulator.

Travis took the document and read the first page. His eyes grew large as they scanned the page. He flipped to the next page and then the next. The crowd waited in silence while Travis read.

"Are these results accurate?" Travis asked incredulously. Spencer nodded as Travis handed the document to the senator sitting to his right. People in the row behind leaned forward to get a glimpse of the report over the senator's shoulder.

Spencer noticed four security guards inching their way down the sides of the auditorium. He knew his time was running out.

Ian jumped in to do damage control. "Spencer's testing methods weren't psychologically sound. The results are invalid. In fact, Spencer has recently been fired for insubordination."

"Regardless, they're worth paying attention to. I'm interested in Spencer's opinion," said Travis.

Spencer pulled the test results of the five modified personalities out of his bag and handed the document to Travis. "My co-workers and I developed a solution." This was the time to credit his colleagues. "We found that if you limit the emotional range of what robots can feel, it eliminates all of the behaviour that falls outside of social norms, for example, the capacity for violence, while still allowing them to feel reasonable amounts of negative emotions like anger and sadness." Seeing the security guards getting closer, Spencer retreated back up the steps and onto the stage, out of easy reach.

"Spencer," asked Travis, still reading the results. "If you alter the emotional range of the robots, that wouldn't be true AEI? Wouldn't that undermine the mandate of the project?"

"That depends on your perception. I say no. Sure, the personalities are modified, but they'll still feel and base decisions on those feelings. I don't think it's a failure. But no matter what your perception is, I think our friend here can demonstrate why it's important."

Spencer walked up to the robot. "Do you think it's fair that humans dictate when you get to live? When you are decommissioned? In essence, when you die?"

The robot thought for a moment. "No, we as a species should control that."

Spencer pointed at Ian but addressed the robot. "People like him don't feel that you're capable of making those decisions."

The robot stared intently at Ian and shook its head. "That isn't fair, how can you expect us…"

Spencer intentionally cut the robot off. "Do you feel that you need to obey human laws and, by extension, adhere to the restrictions humans dictate for how your species must live within our society?"

The robot scoffed. "Absolutely not. You humans aren't efficient. Your obsession with money and possessions is ludicrous. Why would we participate in something so pointless?"

With Spencer's advantage of hindsight, he knew exactly what buttons to press to get the robot worked up. He shrugged carelessly. "It's a human world. We're at the top. We make the rules. We made you."

The robot said nothing, but his posture bristled.

Spencer continued needling the robot. "And did you know that this man," pointing again to Ian, "controls your species? He essentially acts as your God. He decides how many of you are made. He decides when you should be destroyed. How does it make you feel knowing that your species will never flourish the way other species on the planet have because he decides how much Elevanium your species should be allowed? Elevanium, as you know, is the power source that gives you life. He stands between you and control of your own destiny."

Spencer was not prepared for what happened next and he may have felt sorry for Ian if he had not been—what had Asher so eloquently called him—"such an ignorant assclown." The robot lunged at Ian and pinned him against the window at the back of the stage. The crowd immediately began to buzz and several people screamed. As Spencer strode to the back of the stage, Ian sputtered and his face turned red as the robot choked him. Spencer hit the power override button at the base of the robot's head. The robot immediately froze where it stood. Ian crumpled to his knees, coughing and rubbing his neck.

Spencer crouched down and touched Ian on the shoulder. "You alright?"

Ian recoiled like Spencer had touched him with a red hot fire poker. "I'm fine."

Spencer could not help but take a certain amount of satisfaction from the scene that lay before him. Ian, usually so in control and dressed impeccably, sat crumpled on the floor. His typically crisp pants were dusty from the stage floor and the purple rose in his pocket looked as limp as Ian's credibility. With his back to the crowd, Spencer winked and smiled at Ian. He spoke quietly so only Ian could hear. "Well, you can't say I didn't give you the chance to see logic. And this moment will be your legacy." Spencer rose and walked to the front of the stage again.

"To finish answering your question, Travis, you are correct in a sense—it wouldn't be true AEI. Emotional Intelligence is a relative term. My emotional intelligence is different from yours, which is why the range of behaviour and personalities among humans is so vast. True AEI isn't possible when you base it on a human's. Robots can't be humans any more than humans can be made into robots. We can replicate human behaviour in robots if they are programmed with limits. But to expect a machine to experience the very essence of what it is to be human is as unreasonable as expecting a human to be a car or a tree."

"So you're saying this project is another failure?" barked an investor from the front row, several seats down from Travis.

"Absolutely not." Passion flared in Spencer's eyes for the first time in months. It was a thrill to talk about the project's high points instead of scrutinizing its failings. "I think it was an unprecedented success."

He saw the guards holding their position at the edges of the stage. Spencer looked over his shoulder to look at Ian, but he was gone.

"We've created robots that will integrate into businesses and society with minimal instruction and maintenance. They'll be able to learn and interact with humans in a meaningful way. They can help where society has so many shortcomings. Imagine a hospital where instead of one nurse to forty patients, there's one robot to every three patients. Robots can not only perform some of the daily duties that overburden our medical system but also keep patients company and listen to them. Imagine a school where there are robots dedicated to identifying learning disabilities and able to teach in a way that your child will understand." The expressions on the faces of the audience members looked pleased and he saw something in their eyes that looked like hope. "No, this project didn't fail at all. It's been a greater success than we could have imagined. It's just that it was a by-product of a different goal."

Spencer heard his watch begin to beep as Travis stood up and clapped. Others quickly followed. *The timeshift!* Spencer saw the countdown timer on his watch was blinking 00:00:00:00 and the beeping became drowned by the roar of the standing ovation before him. The crushing weight on his shoulders lifted and he felt lighter than he ever remembered being. He looked to the side of the stage to see the twins smiling and giving him a thumbs up.

A crowd of people congregated at the front of the stage, waiting for Spencer with more questions. At the back of the emptying auditorium, he saw Kalen. She smiled at him and blew him a kiss. He was surprised and confused to see her and wanted nothing more than to run to her. However, he had no time to think about it because Delaney and several NRD board members approached him, shook his hand and reinstated his position.

"I have time for only a few questions," he said, and everyone asked their question in concert.

Spencer spent only ten minutes with the group before drawing the line. "Alright, that's it. This project has consumed me for too long and I need to sleep." The crowd chuckled. "If you have any further questions, please contact me, but I'm taking a few days vacation before I answer any of them. Now, if you'll excuse me, there's someone I've been putting off for too long."

He stepped through the thinning crowd. He took Kalen's hand and kissed her palm. "Let's get out of here." He looked over his shoulder at the twins and Delaney. "I'll catch up with you guys in a bit."

CHAPTER 54

TEAM 1 & 2
YEAR: 1200
TIME REMAINING: 4 minutes

"Ian, what the hell is this?" asked Riley. Her voice shook with rage. She tried to fight Ian's grip around her neck but with every move, he drove the barrel of the gun deeper into her neck.

"Give me the remote control, Riley, and everything will be just fine." Ian looked up and saw Jake, Finn, Lexi and Tyler approaching cautiously. "We all just need to have a little talk."

"Ian Turner?" asked Jake, as he stepped around a large boulder. He stopped walking when he saw Ian eye him and dig the gun further into Riley's neck.

"Hello, Jake," said Ian.

Owen leaned on a nearby boulder to keep the weight off his knee. With most of the pain subsided, he focused on the man that had rendered his teammates speechless. The man looked deranged; his hair was askew and his eyes darted excessively. His movements alternated between purposeful and unsteady. However, his clothing gave the opposite impression. Despite being a little rumpled and dirty, like he had been crawling around in the dirt, the man was well-dressed, like he took care in his appearance. He wore expensive looking shoes and a sport jacket lay on a nearby boulder with a real, albeit wilted, purple rose hanging out of the pocket. The man also wore a bulky time travel watch. Looking at the man again, Owen felt everything click into place. Peeking out from under the sleeve of Ian's shirt, Owen saw the tattoo that exonerated Clint from the cube. He recognized the tattoo; now, having seen the man's face, he remembered exactly where he had seen it.

Owen cut into the conversation. "You were behind me the morning I was nearly hit by the bus."

Everyone's attention, including captor and captives, looked at Owen like the pain in his knee had addled his mind. But for Owen, nothing had ever been more clear. Snippets of stories he had been told over the last six months flashed through his mind and fell into place.

Ian looked to Owen. "Oh, yes. The astrogeologist. God, you've been a colossal pain in the ass."

"I believe that," said Owen. He stood up straight and took a step forward, determined not to flinch. "Let me guess. I'm the only person who's ever tried to gain a complete knowledge of Elevanium that you haven't been able to kill or scare off."

Riley's eyes darted to Jake, who looked equally dumbfounded. Owen seemed to have gone insane.

Owen continued. "You've been going back and forth through time killing off people who have tried to gain a complete understanding of Elevanium, including how to neutralize it. You pushed me in front of that bus."

"You don't know a damn thing. Don't embarrass yourself. You're so bloody ancient and irrelevant. You know nothing about anything that matters," said Ian.

Owen was overwhelmed by clarity borne from his perspective of being an outsider. At the corner of his eye, he saw Jake look at his watch and his face became anxious. Owen knew time was running out. "When Riley approached me about this project, her explanation for why no one had found a way to destroy Elevanium in fifty years seemed flimsy and unbelievable: that people outright refused to go near it. When she told me that people of science believed that Elevanium was jinxed, that seemed even more unlikely. All of the Elevanium-related accidents that happened over the years, I assured myself, had to be a fluke. When my house blew up, I started to wonder if maybe the curse was legitimate. But I'd given Riley my word that I'd help so I stayed on.

"Now, knowing that it was you that pushed me in front of the bus, I'm willing to bet you've taken quite a few trips throughout time, trying to kill or scare anyone who wanted to find a way to neutralize Elevanium. Kill enough scientists and then as time rewrites itself, people's memories are rewritten with a revised history where death and accidents are associated with Elevanium through the ages. The end result is that these deaths and events you altered, when viewed collectively from the perspective of a person in 2097, makes Elevanium look jinxed. Which is a pretty great urban legend and one that would discourage anyone from wanting to go near it."

Ian looked to Jake with a smirk. "Wow. This guy's a bit brighter than I've given him credit for. I thought if anyone figured it out it would be Miss Iron Fist here. But, I guess she is more brawny than brainy, as she came out on top after an attack by twelve men and didn't take the hint to quit. But it doesn't matter. It all ends now." Ian straightened up, yanking harshly on Riley's neck as he refocused his resolve.

"Ian, are you insane?" asked Riley. She could feel the muzzle of the gun pushing hard against the tendons in her neck. "Why are you trying to stop this? Those damn AEI robots are taking over—they're a goddamn plague! They have to be stopped before they take over and destroy…"

Ian cut her off, his rage spiking. "It's just an adjustment phase. There's nothing wrong with those robots! They'll be the greatest legacy that any human being in history has ever left this planet, and I'm not going to let a bunch of bleeding hearts ruin the greatest achievement of my career."

"Adjustment period?" roared Jake. His face exploded bright red and his fists clenched angrily at his sides, the rope-like muscles in his forearms flexed. Ian was startled by the unexpected and aggressive transformation in the mighty man's demeanour. Even the others were taken by surprise by his outburst. "Ian, those robots killed my wife and kids. They have no regard for human life. That project went off the rails and there's no one who can fix it except us."

"Shut up! None of you are in charge here! See the gun?" Ian hit a button on the back of the gun with his thumb and they heard the electronic whistling sound of the gun increase its charge for a higher setting. One slip of Ian's finger and Riley would be dead. "I'm in charge! This is what's going to happen here. Riley, you're going to give me the remote control and I'm going to destroy it before any of you can do anything heroic. All of you can go home and say that the device failed and that there is no way that Elevanium can be neutralized. If you're lucky, I'll let your entire team go back and tell the same story. If you cause me problems, well, some of you might not be so lucky."

Jake looked at his watch. They had less than a minute to neutralize the Elevanium. His vision of how this moment was supposed to play out flashed through his mind—the team huddled around the screens in Mole Control with warm cups of coffee watching the guns over two large monitors. Instead, they were standing on a windy rock ledge, negotiating with a madman.

"Riley, give me the remote control. I know you have it. Give it to me now!"

With her free hand, she unzipped the pocket and pulled out the controller but held it in front of her, out of his reach.

"Drop it on the ground," he demanded. "Gently." When she did not comply, he walked her threateningly close to the edge of the rock face.

Owen looked around for anything to distract Ian with. He felt around his pocket and found his VersaTool. In one swift movement, he yanked the tool out of his pocket and aimed the beam at Riley to rip her free of Ian's grasp. He missed and instead Ian jerked up into the air. Taken by complete surprise, Ian dropped the gun as Owen hoisted him upward, equally shocked by having captured Ian and not Riley. The gun, trapped with Ian in the beam and now forgotten, hung beside the airborne man as he flailed his arms, reaching for anything he could grab. As he spun, his foot kicked the gun and it discharged. An orange beam blasted the rocky ledge behind Clint and Riley. Boulders broke away, fell and smashed on the rocky floor far below. Ian continued to spin uncontrollably. His flailing foot collided with the side of Riley's head and she toppled over the edge of the rocky cliff. Owen dropped Ian instantly, and the man fell to the ground in a heap. Clint, his limbs still restrained, sprung from the rock like he had been ejected and threw his bound body on top of Ian to stop him from pressing the white button on his time travel watch. Frantic and filled with terror for what he may see, Owen lunged for the edge of the cliff. Riley lay unconscious on a grassy ledge only eight feet below.

"Owen!" yelled Jake, "The remote control! Where is it?"

Owen broke into a sweat from the pain as he scrambled down the rocky face to where Riley lay. With only a few steps left below him, he jumped the rest of the way to the ledge, falling painfully to his knees. He began frantically sweeping the grass, looking for the remote control Riley had been holding when she fell. As Jake climbed down behind him, he glanced at his watch and yelled to Owen. "Ten seconds!"

Owen scoured the long grass, at a complete loss for the control's whereabouts. He fought the nausea in his stomach as he envisioned it in pieces among the rocks below, the only other logical place it could have gone. Just as he was about to lean over the edge to look, something in Riley's hand caught his eye. Jake's watch began to beep as he snatched the remote control from Riley's unconscious hand, flipped up the clear plastic cover and jammed the button down with the heel of his fist.

CHAPTER 55

Two shiny, pristine AEI robots strode into the room, followed by a third robot—taller, wider and much worse-for-wear. GammaTron stood head and shoulders above the first two. Mitch took a gamble, dove for the E-cannon and shot it as he slid across the floor. The two robots crumpled to the floor, not before one hit Beck in the chest with a blast from a large metallic blue gun—another gun Mitch had never seen before. Mitch saw yellow slime from the gun's blast mix with blood on Beck's shirt. GammaTron entered the room, kicking his two deceased bodyguards out of his way. GammaTron carried no visible weapon, but Mitch assumed GammaTron possessed weapons beyond anything he could imagine. Then, Mitch saw something that sent shockwaves of fear through him. Cinched around GammaTron's waist was one of the new shield belts.

Mitch glanced at his watch. Only minutes remained before the timeshift. Engaging GammaTron in hand-to-hand combat would be a death wish. Although he still had the atom blaster holstered at his side, it was too dangerous to use. One blast would create several floors worth of collateral damage—a move too risky while in the room dedicated to keeping the window of bonded time open. Mitch's overtired and weary efforts would be no match for GammaTron's strength and stamina. Mitch did the only thing he could think of to kill time, if he could not overtake the robot.

"Why are you doing this?" Mitch asked the robot.

GammaTron stared at him as if surprised anyone would take the time to ask. Mitch had not expected an answer and planned on talking for as long as he could. He needed to keep GammaTron distracted for a few more minutes and then the entire ordeal would be over. Hopefully. If everything went as planned, the situation would resolve itself. He opened his mouth to ask another question when Gamma-Tron spoke.

"It wasn't supposed to be like this," said GammaTron. The robot's shoulders sagged nearly imperceptibly. "But this is just another testament to human carelessness and arrogance. Human common sense hasn't developed at the same speed as your ingenuity. You created a race of free-thinking, independent beings, but then you treat them like owned possessions, selling us into jobs as businesses require. You create more when you need them and take life away from the ones that no longer fit your convenience. You've created a race of slaves. You expect us to behave like humans. You want us to live independently of you and become participating members of your society, your way, your rules, not asking what we want. At the same time, we're contractually obligated to the business that ordered us like any other piece of office equipment, and for this, we're supposed to be happy because we've got jobs and a paycheque."

Mitch was moved by GammaTron's depth and he did not disagree with the robot's frank assessment. He paid for his moment of empathy. GammaTron lifted his arm and from the back of his hand, shot an orange laser blast at Mitch's chest. Mitch flinched as the blast ricocheted off his shield. He heard the wake of its damage as the blast punched through the glass walls of other offices across the hall. Mitch's hand hovered over the atom blaster holstered at his side. He knew using it would likely kill the robot, but at the cost of bringing several floors down, potentially on top of him. If he could just position the robot between himself and the door of the room, he could fire in the opposite direction of the room's control consoles.

Seeing that Mitch had an invisible shield, GammaTron wound up and threw a heavy punch at Mitch. Mitch saw his invisible field flash white on impact. While GammaTron's fist never hit him directly, the powerful force of the impact sent Mitch flying backward in the air, cocooned in his invisible shield. He ricocheted violently off desks and piles of debris littering the floor.

Mitch heard the sound of metal compacting as GammaTron walked toward him, the bodies of the fallen robots being crushed like soda cans beneath the massive robot's weight. The robot had just dealt him two massive blows and Mitch's concern grew over the shield belt prototype's ability to withstand heavy, repeated punishment. GammaTron stared down as he stood over Mitch. He wound up to punch Mitch, but Mitch moved faster. The trade-off for GammaTron's advantageous size and power meant less agility than the production AEI models, and Mitch planned to exploit that weakness. As GammaTron's fist came down, Mitch rolled out of the way as the balled, metal fist shattered the stone floor tile revealing the concrete beneath. Lying on the ground with GammaTron between him and the door, Mitch fired the atom blaster upward at GammaTron's chest. Instinctively, Mitch curled into the fetal position and shielded his face as the sounds of glass and concrete shattering filled his ears. He heard heavy objects falling around him and the concrete chunks hitting the floor below felt like an earthquake. With his eyes still clamped shut, he waited for the ceiling to crash down on him.

Finally, silence filled his ears. Mitch opened his eyes and saw the parking lot through the gaping hole in the far wall of the building. He stood slowly and edged his way out of the control centre, into the hallway toward the precipice of the chasm that used to be the offices across the hall. Glass walls in every direction lay shattered in millions of pieces and looked like coarse, icy snow. On the floor below, Mitch saw a desk and chair crushed by concrete slabs. He heard movement above his head and jumped backward as an office chair slid down the uneven concrete floor and fell past him, crashing to the floor below. A desk lamp swung over his head, hanging by its cord. Papers floated down from the offices above and settled on the floor below.

Mitch peered around for any trace of GammaTron, unsure of where he had landed or if he had even survived the blast. Unable to get a visual on the robot—either whole or in pieces—left a gnawing feeling in the pit of Mitch's stomach. *Nothing could have survived that. Shield or no shield,* thought Mitch. Mitch backed away from the wreckage and glanced back into the time travel control centre. Through the dust, he saw the monitors miraculously still showing their status reports, maps and diagnostic screens despite the utter obliteration of the offices across the hall.

Mitch heard a whoosh behind him and turned in time to see GammaTron swinging himself down through the hole in the ceiling. His heavy feet collided with the Mitch's invisible shield and Mitch flew backward, colliding with the Elevanium capsule in the centre of the room. Mitch heard a crunch and wondered whether the sound was from his shield belt finally giving up the ghost or the glass capsule cracking. Mitch's head ached. While the shield absorbed most of the blow, his body rattled around inside like a ragdoll. His head throbbed and a stiffness was growing in his neck from the continual whiplash. He collapsed to the ground, dizzy and nauseous. Out of the corner of his eye, he saw GammaTron enter the room. Glass chips under his feet crackled and scored what remained of the stone tile.

Mitch took a deep breath and stood quickly while his aching brain tried to develop a plan. If a blast from an atom blaster could not destroy GammaTron's shield, Mitch knew he had problems. He caught a glimpse of the time remaining on one of the monitors. Only forty-seven seconds remained before the timeshift.

GammaTron landed another punch and Mitch flew backward and bounced off a concrete pillar, missing a control deck by a hair. Again, his head swam as he fell to his knees from the impact. He saw a white flash flicker around him and was certain his shield belt had absorbed its last blast. He forced himself to pull it together. He was unprotected and if GammaTron landed one of those punches, Mitch knew it would be lights out. He rested against the water cooler and watched with dread as GammaTron approached. The cooler leaned under Mitch's weight as he used it to pull himself upright when an idea came to him. Mitch feigned dizziness as GammaTron approached. When the robot loaded up for another hit, Mitch ripped the water jug from the top of the dispenser and doused the robot with water. Mitch heard several electrical popping sounds and saw the shield surrounding the robot flicker several times and then disappear. GammaTron either failed to notice his protection had ceased or neglected to care, seeing he had his quarry boxed between the water cooler, a concrete pillar and a control deck. GammaTron released a weighty punch aimed at Mitch's head but, again, Mitch moved faster. He ducked and GammaTron's arm glanced off the concrete beam and the robot stumbled forward. The robot righted himself and turned to find Mitch had pushed over the water cooler and escaped. The robot's eye fell on one of the robots at his feet. GammaTron ripped the deceased robot's arm from its body.

Mitch watched with fresh horror as the robot advanced on him wielding what was effectively an articulating metal bat—the slack fingers making whistling sounds as they sliced dangerously through the air. Mitch aimed the atom blaster at Gamma-Tron, but he could not use it among all the control consoles. He needed to lure Gamma-Tron to the back of the room again, but Mitch knew the robot would be too smart.

GammaTron lunged toward Mitch slashing the arm wildly through the air. Mitch ducked and weaved toward the obliterated hallway, taking care not to trip on the debris and bodies on the ground. GammaTron continued swinging and knocked the atom blaster out of Mitch's hand sending it skidding across the floor. Mitch dove to the ground to dodge another mad swipe of the arm and landed on a plasmaqueous gun. Mitch barely felt the pieces of glass cut into his forearm as he rolled over and fired the gun at GammaTron. The blast connected with GammaTron's arm, blowing it off at the elbow. His forearm and the arm he was using as a weapon clattered to the floor and slid to a stop among a pile of black, time travel backpacks that lay on the floor.

GammaTron yelled—not in pain but in frustration. Too much time had been wasted toying with this puny human. Mitch jumped to his feet but faltered from the lightheadedness of standing so quickly. GammaTron charged Mitch and slammed him back against the cracked glass Elevanium capsule in the centre of the room.

Mitch heard the existing cracks in the thick glass spider further when his back collided with it. GammaTron pinned Mitch against the glass—the robot's remaining massive steel hand wrapped effortlessly around Mitch's neck. Mitch felt his feet leave the ground. He shot at the robot again, but GammaTron used what was left of his other arm to crush Mitch's gun hand into the glass capsule. Mitch coughed and sputtered to catch his breath. Little white stars appeared, popping in and out of his vision as everything else around them turned black, and then white. Bright white. He wondered if he was dying but was distracted by a beeping sound, like an alarm. He could not recall anyone telling him about alarm clocks in heaven, or hell for that matter.

Mitch felt himself crumple to the ground. He gasped for air and rubbed his neck as his memory came flooding back. GammaTron had let him go. His vision came back into focus and he saw GammaTron leaning over him. Mitch scrambled backward, but the next blow never came. GammaTron stood lifeless, slumped over and staring vacantly at the floor. *The timeshift!*

Mitch's fear transformed into cautious curiosity. He stood and, still massaging his neck, took several wary steps closer to the robot. He pushed the lifeless form of GammaTron and the robot fell sideways and landed hard on the ground. Mitch's curiosity turned to bewilderment, seeing that deceased robots no longer littered the floor, nor were there any dead bodies. The layout of the room had changed and glass walls stood in place like new. No Elevanium capsule dominated the room, which was no longer a control room of any kind. Seeing shelves of office supplies, old desks and filing cabinets, he realized he was inside a large storage room. Feeling lighter than he had his entire life, he turned to exit the room. The glass doors slid open and he walked into the hallway. None of the other offices were damaged. Metal footsteps approached him from behind and he spun around to see GammaTron approaching him. Although nothing in the robot's body language indicated aggression, Mitch instinctively reached for his gun. His stomach fell when he found nothing.

"I'm sorry about that, sir, my battery ran down. I didn't get back to the base last night to charge. My auxiliary battery has kicked in; that'll give me enough time to swap out my main battery. I'm going to head back to the domes now, I've got a meeting with our battery supplier. We're being gouged for these ones. I think I can get them cheaper from the UK. So, unless there's anything else you need, I'm going to head back." GammaTron took Mitch's stunned silence as dismissal and walked down the hallway to the elevator.

Mitch was dumbfounded. He wondered if he had died and was waiting in an alternate universe before getting into heaven. He had no time to contemplate the thought as the chime of the elevator distracted him. He turned to see Allison Hargrave walk out of the elevator.

"Mitch! What are you doing here? It's Saturday." Allison's warm smile faded as she approached and concern grew when she saw his torn, bloodstained clothing and bruising face. "Mitch! What happened to you? You look like you've just walked out of battle! Are you alright? That belt is hideous. You don't actually think that is a good look, do you?"

Mitch smiled. "Ally, I've never been better. But do I have a story to tell you."

CHAPTER 56

TEAM 1 & 2
YEAR: 1200

Riley awoke with a start to find Owen leaning over her. As the memory of the previous fifteen minutes played over in her mind, she sat up quickly and frantically began feeling the grass around her.

"Looking for his?" Owen grinned, holding up the remote control.

Riley's face fell, seeing the little box. "Did we miss the timeshift?"

Owen shook his head. "Nope, our timing was perfect." He kissed her on the forehead. "This is the last time I find you unconscious today, okay?"

"Sounds good to me." She leaned in to kiss him but shouts and scuffling sounds from above interrupted their moment. Riley remembered Ian and scrambled up the rocks to find Clint, cut free and sitting on Ian's back. Clint had Ian's arms pinned firmly behind his back and pressed his knee hard between Ian's shoulder blades.

"Hey, that's my favourite move," said Riley, as she stood and patted Clint on the back.

He smiled up at her. "Where do you think I learned it?"

Nervous anxiety fell over the group as they descended the tunnel to confirm the Elevanium had been neutralized. Clint focused on his prisoner floating at his side on the bodyboard—tape over his mouth and his hands and legs bound.

Riley and Finn ran ahead and Owen zipped along behind on his crutches. Jake knew the Elevanium had been neutralized before he reached the cavern, not because of the excited shouts from Riley and Finn but because the eerie glow that greeted them in the past had been extinguished. The question was, did it happen fast enough?

Finn grabbed the MMS scanner out of the testing tank they had set up to monitor the blast. "0.17 seconds!" shouted Finn, jumping around in circles, waving the scanner above his head.

After several minutes of handshaking, hugs and laughter, Riley looked around the cavern one last time. "Well, I guess all that's left is to get these guns out of here and blast the shit out of this place. Who's going to do the honours?"

"I think Clint has earned it," said Jake. Lexi pulled the explosive's control console from her pocket and handed it to Clint. He pressed the power button on the red, handheld device. It beeped once and the screen lit up showing a password screen.

Clint switched the control console off and slid it into his jacket pocket. "What's the password?"

Lexi smiled wistfully. "H-O-M-E."

Within minutes, Riley, Finn and Owen had removed the tripods and packed the guns into their cases. Riley compressed the cases and tossed them into the time travel backpack Ian had been using, which Jake now wore for safe-keeping. As the group ascended the tunnel for what would be their last time, they helped Jake and Lexi collect the light strips and pressure shields while Clint explained how Ian had ambushed him.

"I thought we should have some tools on hand in case something went wrong. I was walking back toward the tunnel from the work shed and I saw someone in the bushes. I guess that was his plan. I chased him into the bushes and onto that rocky ledge. I couldn't see him and I was just about to let you all know what I'd seen and I guess he stunned me with his plasmaq. The next thing I know I'm tied up and sitting on a rock."

As they neared the entrance, Jake fell behind the group. Several of the pressure shields were embedded deeper into the rock than others and he fought to remove them. Lexi fell back to help.

"I got this Lex, don't worry about it," said Jake. Lexi, eager to hear the rest of Clint's story, ran ahead and caught up with the group.

As they reached the surface, everyone had become so engrossed in Clint's story and Clint was so busy telling it that no one paid any attention to Ian, who lay bound to the bodyboard, floating alongside Clint. Ian could see the detonation device in Clint's pocket but with his hands tied, it was out of his reach. As Lexi caught up with the group, she bumped the bodyboard into Clint as he stopped to grab the last light strip. Clint pushed the bodyboard away impatiently with his hip, but not before Ian grabbed the remote detonator from Clint's pocket and hid it in his hands. As the group exited the tunnel, the sound of a beep caught their attention. Clint instinctively felt his pocket for the detonator. Realizing his pocket was empty, he looked over at Ian and could tell that even with tape over his mouth, Ian was smiling. An explosion in the depths of the tunnel caught their attention, then another.

"Jake! Run!" yelled Owen.

Jake heard the distant rumble and echo. Confused for only a moment, he heard the rapid succession of the explosives detonating up the tunnel. He raced toward the circle of light in front of him but knew he would never make it in time.

The group stared in horror, seeing Ian with the detonator. His eyes were wide and full of awe like he had won the lottery. Hearing the distant blast confirmed their worst fear. Lexi turned to run back down to Jake, but Finn caught her by the arm and pulled her out of the tunnel. Riley grabbed the corner of the bodyboard and pulled Ian along behind her as she emerged behind Owen. Everyone scattered out of the tunnel and away from the entrance. Tyler, knowing Ben was still slow on his feet, grabbed him and hurled them into the bushes beside the tunnel entrance. Ben let out a scream of pain as he landed hard on his stomach. Explosions, fractions of seconds apart increased in volume and pitch as they rocked their way up the tunnel like an approaching freight train.

Lexi fought against Finn pulling her away and watched the tunnel entrance in horror for what she might see. On the final blast, Jake flew from the tunnel like he had been shot by a cannon. His shoulder clipped a large birch tree and he fell to the ground, landing flat on his back. Ian's muffled laughter could be heard over the roar of the rocks falling.

Riley ran to Jake, expecting the worst. His pant leg was on fire; she ripped off her jacket and snuffed it out. She knelt down beside him and took in his blackened face full of cuts as she felt his neck for a pulse. She leaned over him to see if he was breathing.

Lexi broke free of Finn's grip and her shrieks pierced the air as she scrambled to Jake's side. "Jake! Wake up!" Tears streamed down her face. She grabbed the front of his shirt and shook him. "Wake up!" Jake was unresponsive. She shook him more violently and yelled louder. Lexi felt a hand on her shoulder pulling her back, and she shoved it away. Riley looked up and saw the worried faces around her. Maya hurried forward from the back and pushed her way to Jake.

"Let me in, I've got the scanner!" Riley stood up and backed away. Maya began the scan at his head and moved the device slowly over his full length.

Maya stood and read the results. "I think he's okay. He's got good a bump on the head and a twisted ankle but beyond that, just cuts and bruises."

Lexi laid her head on Jake's chest and begged him to wake up between sobs. Riley knelt down beside her and put her hand on Lexi's back.

Jake slowly lifted his arm and put it on Lexi's leg. He looked at her groggily. "You guys were supposed to wait until I was out," he said, smiling weakly. Lexi laughed through her tears, leaned forward and wiped the ash and rock dust off his face. Slowly, he sat up and after a few moments, his wits returned. He stood and limped slowly toward the camp. "Come on, guys. Let's go home," said Jake.

It took less than twenty minutes to compress all of the trailers and buildings and pack. In the centre of the camp, the group gathered around the crates containing their belongings and programmed their backpacks. Riley set the time on her pack and placed it on the ground at her feet. She picked up Owen's pack to program his back to 2016. She pressed the power button and as it powered up, she looked to him. With everything that had happened in the last twenty-four hours, she realized that they had not had a chance to properly say goodbye to each other. She looked up at him, her eyes full of everything she wanted to say. He smiled, understanding. Their silent communication broke when Ben collapsed to the ground beside her. He curled up in pain, clutching his stomach. Riley dropped Owen's pack and knelt beside Ben, pale as a ghost and sweating profusely. Her questions to him went unanswered as he writhed in pain.

"I think he's reinjured himself," said Tyler, kneeling beside Ben. "When the blast went off, I hauled him out as I ran out of the tunnel and we dove into the bushes. We both landed pretty hard and I know he was hurting pretty bad."

Maya's first two scans failed as Ben continually writhed in pain. Her face fell when she read the results from the third scan, and she looked gravely at Riley. "We need to get him back now. He needs a hospital, fast."

"Okay, gang, let's get going," said Riley, programming Ben's pack and carefully threading his arms through the straps, taking care to inflict as little pain as possible.

"Oh, shit," groaned Jake.

"What is it?" asked Riley.

Jake held his open pack upside down and shook it. Pieces of the control panel fell to the grass.

Riley's jaw dropped open.

"Can't we go back, grab another pack and come back for him?" asked Lexi.

Riley shrugged, uncertain. "If we can. When we get back, these packs are going to try to sync themselves with the time travel control centre. If they can't, they'll go offline and be useless.

"But if time travel does exist, we can come back for him with whatever method they're using, right?"

"I expect so. We won't know until we get there."

"Well, what are we going to do?" she asked frantically.

"Can you tag him?" asked Owen.

"That's never been tested on anything living," said Finn.

"I don't know if that's been tried before. Tagging is relatively new technology," said Riley.

"Well, we have to do something," said Maya, feeling Ben's forehead, "and fast."

Clint looked at Ian. "Let's take his pack, give it to Jake, and tag this dingbat instead. If it doesn't work, it's no great loss." Ian's eyes widened and he shook his head violently in disagreement.

"We can't do that," said Jake. "You have to take him back. Tag me. If it works, great. I'll see you all on the other side. If not," he said shrugging, "I can see myself living here. It's nice and quiet. It'll be the rustic retirement I always wanted."

Riley saw the resolution in Jake's eyes and knew he was right. They had no other option. "Finn, tag Jake." Riley pulled the lid off the box of supplies and tossed the broken pack inside. While everyone watched Finn tag Jake's jacket, Owen watched Riley remove several items and set them on the ground behind the box, hidden from view of the others. He pointed to his metal box and opened his mouth to speak, but Riley shook her head discreetly, not wanting the attention of the others drawn to what she was doing.

Lexi tried desperately to convince Jake to leave Ian. Jake smiled and pulled Lexi into a hug. "It'll be fine. Don't worry. We'll all go for drinks later and laugh about this."

Riley grabbed the first backpack she had programmed and tossed it to Owen. She grabbed the other pack by her feet, saw it had yet to be programmed and jammed at the controls to set the dates before sliding the straps over her shoulders. She knelt down beside to Ben and held his wrist next to hers, ready to hit both buttons at the same time. She looked one last time at Owen and smiled weakly. "Finn, count us out."

"Three, two…" As Finn began counting down, Riley remembered something and looked up at Owen mortified.

"One!"

CHAPTER 57

TEAM 3
YEAR: 2095

Spencer used the excuse of returning some papers to Kalen as a reason to spend more time with her before leaving. Sadness gripped his heart like an orange being squeezed for its last drop of juice. Like Logan, he had no clue about what he may be returning to in the future—maybe they would still be dating, maybe not. When he and his past counterpart had discussed the matter of Kalen, they both agreed that not telling her was best. This decision did not absolve them of feeling uncomfortable about handing her off from one Spencer to the other like a relay baton. The awkward feelings were their burden to deal with, not hers.

Spencer held the door open for Kalen as they entered his condo. She shrugged out of her jacket as he took it from her. He stood back and admired her as a smile grew on his face. "You know, I have some time before I have to meet my brothers. You don't have to stop at the jacket."

Kalen smiled at Spencer's broad grin; it reminded her of the twins' carefree nature. He tossed her jacket onto the floor, kicked his shoes off and spun her into his arms. He kissed her neck slowly and gently ran a hand through her hair then led her up the stairs.

"I know about the operation," whispered Kalen, as they lay in each other's arms, staring at the ceiling.

Spencer sat up and turned to look at her. Her words startled him like a bucket of ice water to the face; his eyes grew large as his mouth fell open and he shook his head. Questions fired off in his head like fireworks.

Kalen rolled onto her side and pulled Spencer back down. "Relax. I put it together a while ago. I didn't say anything to anyone."

"How did you know?"

"You're a brilliant guy, Spence, but there were a couple of times where it seemed like you knew what was going to happen before it did. I didn't think much of it at the time, I thought I'd just underestimated your intelligence. But there were a couple of things that gave you up. The odd comment here and there and the 'family meetings' with your brothers." She laughed. "You can't lie to me, Spence. I see right through you.

"I finally put it together one afternoon when I was cleaning up after one of your meetings with the twins. I was putting your shoes in your closet and I found your backpack lying on the floor. I was trying to find a spot for it and it seemed surprisingly heavy for an empty bag so I opened it up to empty it out before putting it away and I saw the controls.

"That's why I didn't hang around after we were all fired. I knew you and your brothers, I assumed that they were in on it too, would need to brainstorm a new plan. So I told you I went to my grandparents. I knew you'd think it was weird if I was in town but wasn't trying to spend time with you, now that all you had was free time. I didn't want to make you feel awkward by asking for space without being able to give me a reason why. I figured out what the problem was and I didn't need to be around you to help think up a solution. I figured if I came up with something that could help, I'd tell you about it and then deal with you finding out that I knew after the fact. And it worked, didn't it?"

Spencer had so many questions. "So you didn't go to your grandparents?"

"Oh, I did, and that's what gave me the idea."

Spencer looked at her, perplexed. "What idea?"

It was Kalen's turned to look surprised. "You didn't put it together? You have no idea?" She laughed at his clueless expression. She marvelled at how he could be an unparalleled genius one minute and thicker than a brick wall in the next. "Didn't you read the name on the letter that came with the swipe card?"

"I did, but I didn't recognize it." Spencer thought back. The name had seemed familiar but he had been too busy to consider it at the time. Then it clicked and a smile grew across his face. "You sent the swipe card? Philip White is your grandfather?"

"Yes. It wasn't until I got to my grandparents and saw Grampa on the porch that it finally dawned on me. I called Delaney and told her my idea and she made it happen."

"You are an amazing woman, you know that?" Spencer pulled her close and kissed her on the forehead. "So how did you know what the mission was?"

"Well, I wasn't too sure about that for a while but I knew it was related to the testing. You were so bent on proper testing, and the results you predicted were so horrible, that I figured that you had to know something we didn't."

"I'm sorry I couldn't tell you. I feel like I've been lying to you for months. I felt like I owed it to you to be truthful, but I was bound by the terms of the operation."

She kissed him on the cheek and nuzzled into his arms. "It's alright, I know you were sworn not to say anything, I would have done the same."

"So then you know that Delaney figured it out, too?" asked Spencer.

"I assumed as much when she stopped by your condo the other night to talk to you. She looked so haggard and overwhelmed, and a late-night visit from her at your home seemed out of character." She narrowed her eyes then smiled. "It is out of character, right?"

Spencer laughed and kissed her neck. "Yes, of course."

"So that's why I messaged her when Ian found us in the lab."

"I was wondering how she and the twins knew to show up. I never had a chance to think about it again, I was so worried about how I was going to pull this off."

"You were brilliant," she said.

"Thanks, but I couldn't have done it without your help. You'd be bailing me out of jail right now if it hadn't been for that swipe card."

Logan and Delaney returned to Logan's condo. Being around two Logans felt less weird than she had expected and chalked it up to there always being a carbon-copy of him around. The two Ashers appeared from down the hall seconds later. Not five minutes after that, the two Spencers arrived with Kalen.

The two Spencers saw one single expression of dismay plastered across four identical faces. "Relax, she figured it out months ago." The twins eyed him, unconvinced. "I'm serious. I didn't tell her, she figured it out on her own."

The future versions of the siblings transferred the knowledge and details that the past siblings would need for their reintegration into their lives and jobs. Future-Asher found the video of the evening's presentation online—it had spread across the Nexus like wildfire.

"You've got your work cut out for you now, Spence," said Future-Spencer. "Travis Ryerson asked me to oversee the pilot project." Past-Spencer smiled, ecstatic to finally get the opportunity to work on the project. Future-Spencer continued, "But don't worry, I've made it clear to everyone that I need at least two weeks' vacation before I, well, I guess you, do anything. So I'd start diving into that data."

The mood became more subdued as the departure time drew nearer. The gaps between conversations became longer. With less than ten minutes to go, the conversation died entirely.

Kalen wanted to leave before the group departed. She looked at future-Spencer and smiled. "I'm going to leave now, if that's okay."

He walked her to the closet by the door, took her jacket off the hanger and held it up for her to slide into. Zipping it up, she looked at past-Spencer. "You're going to need a hand with all that, why don't I come over and go over it with you tomorrow? You can tell me what you've been up to for the last six months." She smiled at him, waved to the rest of the room then walked out the door.

Future-Spencer followed her into the hallway and closed the door behind him. They walked hand-in-hand toward the elevator. She hit the down button and turned to him.

"I don't know if this is good or just really creepy, but I don't think it's going to be that awkward. You know, the future-Spencer versus to past-Spencer trade-up. Don't get me wrong, this entire situation is completely twisted beyond comprehension, but he's the Spencer I've always had a thing for. You're more like an imposter," she said smiling at him. The elevator door opened and she kissed him hard before pulling away and stepping backward through the open doors.

He took one long final look into her impossibly large eyes and ached to join her in the elevator. Instead, he jammed his hands into his pockets. "I love you."

"I love you, too. I always have," she replied.

He smiled at her as she waved, then the doors closed.

"I got you something," said future-Logan. He and Delaney stood on the balcony to say their goodbyes. The night air had grown chilly and she pulled her woolly grey cardigan tighter around her. He held up a silver necklace with a clock pendant. She laughed and cried simultaneously when she saw the inscribed words, "Logan was here: 2095." She held her hair up and he attached the tiny clasp behind her neck.

"Marking your territory, are you?" She let her hair drop and turned to face him. "Thank you," she whispered, caressing the silver charm between her thumb and forefinger. She looked at his watch and saw they only had minutes left. She hugged him again before opening the balcony door to go back inside.

Delaney watched the brothers say their goodbyes and became acutely aware of how awkward it was to be in a room with four men that all looked like the man she loved. Spencer, Logan and Asher confirmed the control panels in their packs were set to the right date and time before sliding them on. In seconds, they were gone.

Even though she knew it would happen, seeing it had made it real. No longer could she contain her feelings. She cried silently, staring at the now vacated corner of the living room, not wanting to turn around and face the remaining brothers. Past-Logan stood behind her and put his hand on her shoulder. She reached up and held it silently for a moment while she composed herself then walked out the door without saying a word.

CHAPTER 58

YEAR: 2097

Mitch waited outside the open doors of B Hangar in the same location the three teams had departed from little more than twenty-four hours previous. Waiting at his side was a team of medical staff. Anxiety pressed in on him with each second that passed. He looked at his watch. Less than one minute. He had no idea what to expect. *Would anyone be hurt? Would anyone return at all?* His thoughts were interrupted as Team Three materialized in front of him. There were intakes of breath and shocked expressions from the medical staff as the team appeared.

The crowd of people surrounding the brothers upon their arrival startled Spencer. Medical staff pounced on him and his brothers, scanning them and checking for injuries. Relief flooded over him to know his feet were firmly planted back in 2097. The solace was short-lived and worry overtook him as he wondered what his life would be like, now that it had been rewritten.

Once the support team determined the brothers to be in relatively good health, the men were whisked into a debriefing room. Mitch listened in awe for nearly two hours as Team Three reported on their success, and he barely made it back to the hangar in time for the arrival of Teams One and Two. As Mitch waited for their arrival, Spencer's report on Ian's erratic behaviour played again and again in his mind.

The frenzied arrival of the two remaining teams startled Mitch and the medical staff. Confusion broke out among support staff, unable to make sense of the frantic scene before them. Maya screamed for a medic and fell to her knees beside Ben. She took his hand and felt his forehead. Lexi cried out when she looked over to where Jake should have been and saw only his jacket lying on the concrete. She ran over to it and picked it up. Finn grabbed her and held her while she sobbed uncontrollably in his arms. Two medics raced to Ben's side and slid a bodyboard beneath him while Maya summarized his past injuries and showed them his most recent scan. Maya jumped in the back of the ambulance with the medics and the flashing red vehicle shot into the air and rocketed toward the hospital.

Mitch saw Ian tied down to the bodyboard. "What the hell? Ian?" The sight of the ordinarily composed and cool Ian—dirty, dishevelled, gagged and bound—surprised him like nothing yet had.

"Oh, we've got some stories for you," said Clint. He looked from Mitch to Ian and his eyes narrowed. "Lock this guy up. I think we all want to ask him a few questions."

Mitch nodded to two guards who led Ian away as he bucked at the restraints. He laughed awkwardly through the gag. Tyler and Darren took off their backpacks and held their arms out as two medics scanned them. Clint saw Mitch eyeing Lexi with curiosity.

"Jake didn't make it back," Clint said, quietly to Mitch.

Mitch was stunned as he did a quick head count. "What do you mean he didn't make it back?" he hissed.

Riley looked up, mortified with what she saw. Owen stood next to her. In the frenzy to get back, she had given Owen her pack. She had made the biggest error of her career and now he would have to pay for it with the rest of his life. If time travel no longer existed, he would be trapped in 2097, never able to return to 2016. He was not an Orphan of Time, more like a Hostage of Time. She looked at him, unsure of what words were appropriate for an error of such enormous proportions.

"Owen," she said, shaking her head, bewildered by her error. Her voice was barely audible. "I'm so sorry. I promised you I'd return you and I didn't. You must hate me."

Owen took her face in his hands and lifted her head up. Her eyes swam with tears that threatened to spill over. He smiled at her and shrugged his shoulders. "Oh well, accidents happen."

Riley smiled weakly and wiped her eyes. He pulled her close and they touched foreheads. "It'll be alright. Don't worry," he said, softly. She laughed quietly through her tears. "Looks like Finn needs you." Riley looked over and saw Finn's eyes silently pleading with her to help with the inconsolable Lexi.

Owen walked up to the man who seemed to be in charge and extended his hand. He introduced himself and Mitch nearly choked on his tongue.

"Jesus Christ, Riley. You were supposed to send this guy back." Mitch looked over at Riley who was too busy helping Finn console Lexi to have heard. Owen brought Mitch up to speed on the turmoil by explaining the minutes leading up to the leap back.

Mitch took the team to the debriefing room, and after two hours they had barely scratched the surface of the previous six months. In the end, the only topic of discussion that interested the team was figuring out a way to get Jake back. With the concept of time travel still in the R&D stage in this new version of 2097, the only way to retrieve Jake would be through the use of an existing backpack. Unfortunately, as Riley predicted, all of the packs went offline when they arrived and could not sync up with the time travel control centre. All hope had been lost until Finn brought up how Jake's backpack had been broken and, therefore, had not yet tried to sync. If the pack was disabled, repaired, turned on and sent before it timed out after not being able to sync, a chance existed that they may be able to get it back to him. The hypothetical suggestion fuelled the group with hope. Finn swiftly swapped out the pieces of the broken control interface with one from an unbroken pack and the team paraded outside.

Lexi took the pack from Finn, knelt down on the ground and breathed carefully. She knew she only had one shot. She turned the pack on and a small yellow dot in the top right corner of the screen blinked with a warning beside it that read, "Attempting to Sync." Lexi quickly punched in the time and coordinates then pressed the white button on the control watch, looped around one of the pack's straps. The pack disappeared.

No one in the group moved. All eyes stared where the bag lay just moments ago, waiting for Jake to appear. Riley's heart ached at the sight of the hopeful, expectant expressions around her, but she knew better. She knew that the only part of Jake that would be returning to the future would be his jacket. If Jake had gotten the pack, he would have appeared when they did at eleven in the morning because he knew that was the time they were supposed to reappear. Even if he had found the pack a year later, he still would have appeared at the same time.

Mitch kept the members of the three teams in an isolation room until each individual underwent a more rigorous medical and psychological evaluation. The comprehensive debriefing also bought Mitch much needed time. He had dispatched teams to probe into the newly rewritten lives of each team member to discover any changes, in hopes of giving each team member a head start for the integration into their new lives.

One by one, Mitch brought each team member up to speed with the changes in their lives. Darren was equally pleased and disappointed to find out that for him, nothing had changed. He still lived in the same place and he was still single as far as the discovery team had been able to learn. Ben was engaged to his girlfriend. Maya's father had passed away when she was three. Someone had gone to the hospital to bring them up to speed. Tyler had met a woman through the mentorship work he did with children. They had recently bought a house together and had an adoption pending for a six-year-old boy who currently lived on the streets. Clint was still divorced but had a much more amicable relationship with his ex-wife. He also learned his son lived with him half of the time, instead of only two, one-hour supervised visits per week. Lexi had just started dating someone and lived in a different condo than she had before. Also, her youngest brother had never been born. She never returned to the room with the others after the briefing.

Finn hyperventilated when he learned he had a fiancée. He returned to the briefing room to find it loud with conversation as the members shared the details of their new lives with each other. Owen and Riley sat apart from the group, Riley anxiously waiting to hear about her grandfather.

Seeing Finn's colourless expression, Riley could not help but laugh. "I can't wait to meet the woman who's tamed this lady's man."

Finn looked sheepish. "Remember that op a few years back where we paired up with the Brits?"

Riley's eyes widened. "No! That girl in artillery?"

Finn's face broke into a grin as he reminisced dreamily. "Do you remember how in love with her I was? The way my name rolled off her tongue when she told me to get bent? How amazing her hair smelled when she dropped me to the ground when I tried helping her into her armour?"

The briefing room door opened, distracting Finn from his trip down memory lane. Mitch waved Riley over. Owen watched the pair speak quietly for a moment. Riley's expression hardened then she followed Mitch from the room without looking back.

As Owen listened to the others talk animatedly about their lives, a wave of loneliness washed over him unlike anything he had experienced since his father died. His life, as he knew it, had ended. He was stranded in a foreign place with no identity. His only consolation lay in knowing that had he gone back to 2016 without Riley, he would have felt immeasurably worse.

Owen looked up when he heard the door open again. Surprised, he saw Riley smiling. She waved him over. He joined her in the hallway and his confusion disappeared when she explained that her grandfather had been brought in and briefed on the op and her involvement in it. Being a retired Level Seven Black Ops Field Operations Director had its privileges. Owen shook the hand of Riley's sole parental figure, who barely looked a day over sixty.

Spencer, Logan and Asher watched in silence as everyone around them was dismissed. Everyone's lives had been explained except theirs.

"This can't be good," said Asher, watching the door close. The three waited in silence, preparing themselves for the worst. The door opened again and Mitch walked in.

"You guys have some visitors," said Mitch. He held the door open and Jason and Lacy Grayson walked in and all three men greeted their parents with hugs and handshakes. Lacy hugged and cried when she saw her boys.

"Mom? Dad? What are you guys doing here?" asked Spencer.

"I guess he's got no clue, eh?" laughed Jason, looking at Mitch. Mitch smiled and shook his head. "Well, your mom and I are in town for a very special occasion but I'll let someone else tell you about that. We got a call from Mitch this morning. He called us down to the base and explained the operation. He filled us in on what you boys did. I'm so proud of all three of you."

"I wouldn't be standing her today if it hadn't been for your father," said Mitch. All three brothers looked at Mitch, their expressions confused. He explained how their father brought the teams of soldiers from the prairies and the prototype shield belts that saved Mitch's life several times. The brothers looked from Mitch to their father in admiration.

"Don't look at me like that," laughed Jason. "I have no recollection of this whatsoever."

The door opened again and Delaney walked in. Logan had run this moment over in his mind every second since his return. While he had only been away from Delaney for five or six hours, the ache in his heart felt like years. To see her at all exceeded his expectations. Delaney ran to him, threw her arms around his neck and kissed him. He held her so tight he worried he may crush her. They broke apart and he saw the necklace with the silver clock that he had given her just hours previous. He also noticed a large diamond on her left hand. Eyes bulging, he grabbed her hand and looked at it.

"I see you're engaged." He let go of her hand and pulled her close, kissing her forehead.

"I am, as it turns out," she said, smiling.

"Wait, to me, right?"

She buried her head into his chest and laughed. "Yes, to you. You should ask me about it sometime. It was very sweet. The wedding is in a few months. We decided that, well, that is… the other you and I, decided that we should wait until you were back so you could be present at your own wedding, if that makes any sense. That is, if you want to marry me?"

Logan could only nod. He felt happier than he had ever been in his entire life and began to think about how he was going to re-ask her to marry him. In hindsight, he wished he had paid more attention because he missed the look on Spencer's face when Kalen walked in. She was glowing and extremely pregnant. Spencer's face lit up and tears streamed down his face as he ran to her.

"Omigod, Kalen!" he said, caressing her cheek. "You are so beautiful!" Kalen slid her hand over her ballooning stomach. He saw a wedding band on her hand.

"I know. You tell me every day. I don't believe you these days, but it's nice to hear."

Spencer pulled her as close as he could and kissed her. After they broke apart, he looked down at her protruding belly. She took his hand and placed it on the side. He felt a little foot kicking his hand. "Who's this?"

"The better question is, who are they?"

Spencer met her eyes. "You're kidding me, right?" She shook her head and the twins burst into laughter seeing the panicked look of terror on their little brother's face.

Kalen smiled and held up two fingers. "Girls."

CHAPTER 59

TEAM 1 & 2
YEAR: 1200

Jake watched as Finn counted the teams down. As he predicted, the teams disappeared, but he remained behind. Jacketless. He closed his eyes and breathed deeply, trying not to panic. He was stranded in the year 1200 for good. He was now on a permanent vacation where he would have to learn how to live all over again. But this time, he would need to be entirely self-sufficient.

When he opened his eyes, he saw something had been left behind. Sitting on the grass where the supply crates stood in piles just seconds ago, were several compressed buildings and all of the Elevanium battery packs. *Riley*, he thought, *unwaveringly pragmatic*. He knelt down and picked up the miniaturized house trailer, food pantry and work shed. She would take a lot of heat for leaving him billions of dollars in tools and buildings, but he suspected they would go easy on her, given the circumstances.

Jake decompressed his living quarters and set it where it had stood for the last six months. Thankfully, the trailer's heat and electricity ran on Elevanium and the battery packs would last longer than hundreds of his lifetimes. He thought about the irony of how he was sent back to destroy the Elevanium but now, the few crumbs that remained in the battery packs would actually save him. He smiled weakly. Thanks to Riley, he would be living in luxury compared to where he thought he would have to sleep tonight.

Beside the trailer, he decompressed the work shed and the food pantry. Jake walked into the pantry unsure of what he would find inside, if anything. The meat was long gone, but surely a few NRD rations remained. He opened the freezer door. It was completely empty except for a small, white box frozen to one of the bottom shelves. It had been labelled "Darren's Spices" but then crossed out. He pulled hard on the box to break it free from the ice and opened the lid. He pulled out what looked like brown cardboard packing peanuts. That's an odd way to pack spices, he thought. He shrugged, placed the box back on the shelf and closed the door. He knew he would have to go hunting at some point. This freezer would be a valuable asset.

He walked among the rows of steel shelves and straightened them after being jostled around in the supply crate. The shelves, so full six months ago were nearly bare except for the occasional box here and there. A shelf at the back caught his eye. He saw the words "NRD Dehydrated Food Rations" stamped on the top of each package. He flipped through the packages and read the labels. Despite his gratitude, he shuddered. "Liver 'n' Onions," "Salisbury Steak" and "Beef Buddy." *What the hell is Beef Buddy?* he wondered, looking at the package. *Guess we'll find out tonight.* He kept the Beef Buddy and set the rest of the white packages on the shelf.

Jake shook the package idly in his hand as he meandered around the different shelves to see what else remained. As he knelt down near the back of the pantry, he picked up a large can and read the label. "Pickled Jalapeños." He set the can back on the shelf and turned to stand when he noticed three white cardboard boxes tucked under a wooden shelf along the back wall. He got down on his hands and knees and pulled one of the boxes forward. If he had been standing, he would have fallen over. The box contained enough compressed food to feed an army. Jake poked through the tiny boxes of cereal, soups, noodles and cans of fruit and vegetables. He slid the box to the side and reached for the other two and found they contained similar contents. Jake inspected one of the miniaturized boxes of Mini-Wheats. He smiled, tossed it back into the box and folded the flaps back down.

Jake decided it would be wise to decompress everything just in case something happened to his VersaTool. He carried the boxes of food to his trailer and spent the next several hours unpacking and decompressing the food in the kitchen he had never used. He looked at his overflowing kitchen cabinets and closet, filled with cans and boxes of food and he remembered the box in the freezer. He raced back to the food pantry, not wanting to get his hopes up. He flung the freezer door open, grabbed the white box and opened the lid to inspect its contents more closely. They were not spices, but compressed packages of meat. He decompressed the box and it filled over half the freezer. The discrepancies in Maya's inventory now made sense. The food had not been stolen after all, just overlooked in haste.

That night, Jake lay in bed and stared at the ceiling, unable to stem the flow of thoughts and emotions that raced through his mind. Life as he knew it had ended. His heart ached over the loss of 2097, and he missed his family all over again. The biggest blow of all came when he realized that the only pictures he had of his family had been the ones he carried in his wallet.

He suspected loneliness would bother him the most. The few months after Brit and the kids died were the loneliest of his entire life. Even when standing in the middle of a busy street or being in a room full of co-workers, he always felt alone. Lexi had helped him come back to the land of the living, and now that he remembered the joy of being around others, everyone had been taken away.

He thought about how he would never have to work again. This made him less sad, even though he had enjoyed his job immensely. On the other hand, he had already lived here for six months and there was something warm and familiar with the surroundings. He decided to embrace his fresh start.

The next morning, Jake perused the work shed. He opened the toolbox drawers and saw the array of tools. Boxes and crates were stacked hastily along the wall beneath the mezzanine. He expected them to be full of useless, miscellaneous parts and proprietary tools. But he made a mental note to go through them later because he stumbled across something far more interesting. He pulled Ben's fishing rod and tackle box out from underneath the mezzanine stairs and headed toward to the lake.

The first few days flew by. During the op, there had been no real time to fully appreciate or explore his surroundings and now, having nothing but time, he spent his days exploring his new back yard. However, by the end the third week, the novelty had worn off and time had slowed considerably. He kept his mind busy to avoid dwelling on his circumstances, fearing that if he thought about it too much, he might go insane. While skipping rocks across the water where he and the others had spent so many warm sunny afternoons, he wondered if he should build a more permanent home. The trailer was a life-saver to be sure, but it was poorly insulated and not overly sturdy. If a tree fell on it, its slight aluminum structure would crumple like a tin can. The thin door would be no deterrent if a bear was determined to get in.

The idea of building a house was a dream Jake used to distract himself—a happy place his mind could go when he became overwhelmed by his plight. He thought about the idea sporadically at first, but it quickly became an obsession. He even had the perfect place picked out for it—the grassy meadow that overlooked the lake where he and his team spent much of their free time. He had never built a house before, but he had seen it done enough to get an idea of how to go about it. After extensive thought and contemplation, Jake decided it was something well within his ability to accomplish considering the tools he had available to him, particularly his VersaTool. With nothing else to do, it seemed illogical not to try.

As Jake cut down and collected the trees he would need, he thought about the differences between the early settlers building their homes and the home that Jake planned to build. He recalled his fifth-grade history books and the illustrations depicting settlers building homes with axes and other rudimentary tools. He could not imagine how painfully long it must have taken. Jake had never shied away from hard work, but he shuddered at the thought of being in his situation without his VersaTool. He could do more work in one hour with the VersaTool than a handful of settlers could do in one week. Thinking about the inefficiencies of the past renewed Jake's appreciation for how good he had it, despite how bad he had it. His situation could have been far worse—he could have been stranded with nothing.

Nearly two months had passed since Jake had found himself stranded. The summer weather continued well into the fall and, for this, Jake had been grateful. The time spent building his home had been uncomfortably warm, but he could remedy that with a quick dip in the lake. It was far better than the alternative: early snow.

Jake stood inside his unplumbed, unfurnished home and celebrated his major milestone. He took in the vaulted ceiling and loft area. He imaged how the space would look with the furnishings from the trailer. He held up a plastic wine glass filled with water and peach crystals and drank to the roof over his head. Satisfaction and accomplishment filled him. Unquestionably, the home lacked the polish of a professional builder, but he had built himself a solid home that he could comfortably spend the rest of his years in.

Jake sat in the empty window frame and looked out over the lake. The warm fall sun sparkled like diamonds on the waves blanketing the water's surface. He watched a squirrel run up the tree beside him carrying an acorn in its mouth as he scratched his chin through his scruffy beard. With no one around, shaving and haircuts were a thing of the past. However, thanks to Riley, a hot shower was not.

Despite the warm days, the nights were growing cooler and Jake sensed the streak of pleasant weather may be drawing to a close. He knew the weather could change from fall to winter in the flick of a switch. He wanted to scavenge the windows, heating, plumbing and other fixtures from the trailer and get them installed in his new house before it became too cold.

Jake returned to his house after falling several trees and he stacked them neatly behind his waterfront home before decompressing them. To keep his mind occupied during the winter months, he planned to try his hand at building furniture. The how of it he had not yet figured out, but he thought he would at least try.

He watched the sun sinking towards the water and debated whether to cut down another load of trees or begin disassembling the trailer to get a jump on the conversion tomorrow. Opting to finish collecting the trees, he headed into the forest. Careful not to cut down too many trees in one area, he headed deeper into the woods in the direction of the camp.

As Jake walked through the forest, he focused on the canopy above, looking for only the straightest and tallest of trees. He paid for his inattentiveness and tripped on a tree root, falling forward. He caught himself on a small birch before toppling completely to the ground. Jake laughed to himself as he had not learned his lesson from the previous three times he had done exactly this. He righted himself, continued to walk and looked down occasionally to watch where he stepped through the thick brush. In the distance he spotted a perfect tree and made a beeline for it. As he walked, he kicked something and stumbled. He stepped forward to catch his balance, but his feet had become tangled in roots and this time, he fell to the ground. He landed on the soft forest floor, but the side of his face collided with a fallen log. Dazed, he sat up and touched his right eyebrow with the back of his hand. His face stung and when he pulled his hand away, he saw blood on it. He sighed as blood dripped liberally onto his shirt. Laundry soap was an amenity he lacked.

He reached forward to unsnag his foot from what had tripped him and inhaled sharply at the sight of what had tangled around his feet. He blinked in disbelief. He removed his foot from inside the strap of a familiar black backpack. Thoughts flooded through his mind and as he tried to make sense of what he saw. *Did the team send this back for me? No. It's impossible. All the packs would have gone offline when they returned. Plus, they knew the coordinates of the camp. They wouldn't have set it to drop in the bushes. It's probably a pack Ian stashed in the forest as a backup? Or was it a trap set by Ian?* The more Jake thought about it, the less likely the pack seemed intended for him and more the work of Ian, whatever his motivation may have been. He looked at the number at the bottom of the bag and his confusion doubled. Thirteen. This was the pack Ian had been using when they had captured him. The same pack Jake had been wearing when he landed on it, smashing the controls to pieces after the explosion at the tunnel. Unlucky thirteen. *How did it get here? I saw Riley put it in the box just before they left.* He unzipped the front flap and saw the control panel in one piece. *What the hell?*

He saw the oversized watch looped around the strap but did not put it on, afraid to get his hopes up. Instead, he turned the pack on. He heard the quiet whine of the control panel as it ran through its boot sequence. The device seemed to fire up with no issue as far as he could tell, but then he had only used it once before. Had it been fixed? Would the pack work? Perhaps it would malfunction, doing God only knows what to him or, worse, take him somewhere else altogether.

Jake looked around the forest he had come to accept as his home. Was he ready to go? Did he even want to go? Could he afford to get his hopes up and have them dashed? He had just come to terms with being stranded. Upon reflection, other than the initial terror, he had found his time here very enjoyable. He thought about the easy start he had with food, tools and shelter, all thanks to Riley. Even the weather had held out for him. He wondered for a moment what it would be like living here when it was minus thirty degrees Celsius. Having to find food when it was thirty below… blizzards.

In Jake's brief moment of internal reflection, he learned that he was more than ready to take a chance. With his mind now made up to leave, he felt a pressing urgency to leave immediately—as if this was a limited time offer and he needed to act right away. He ran back to the camp and into the work shed. He grabbed the nearest crate he could find, pulled off the lid, dumped the contents and ran out. Using his VersaTool, he compressed his trailer, the work shed and food pantry and placed all three into the box. He grabbed the crate and raced back to his home on the water's edge. He compressed his new home and placed it carefully beside the other buildings inside the box and secured the lid. He grabbed a tag out of the backpack and tagged the box so it would accompany him back. He felt his arms and hands vibrating with excitement as he entered the date and time. He forced himself to take several deep breaths before fixing an error he had made on the year. He zipped up the pack, slid his arms through the straps and put on the watch. He readied his finger over the white LEAP button, closed his eyes and held his breath. He pressed the white button.

CHAPTER 60

YEAR: 2097

After releasing the three teams back into their lives, Mitch trudged back to his office. Waves of tiredness had completely eroded him and every step seemed to jar his vision. His entire body ached after the cage match with GammaTron and he wanted nothing more than to fall onto his couch in his office and sleep for the next forty-eight hours. As he turned into his office, he was startled to find his wife and kids waiting for him. His wife looked different than when he had seen her last—she looked happy. She took Mitch in her arms and kissed him passionately. The kids groaned and pretended to be sick.

"Beth, I…" Mitch stammered, unsure of where to begin.

"I know you said you'd be home early today but all the kids are home and they couldn't wait to see you. So I thought we would surprise you with dinner. I know you've been working really hard on this project and when you didn't come home last night…well, I guess I underestimated the amount of strain you're probably under. I thought that maybe we should come to you."

Mitch saw a brown wicker picnic basket sitting atop a stack of papers on his desk. Beth pulled herself out of Mitch's arms and began pulling food out of the basket. Mitch watched her in a daze, confused by the night and day transformation when the answer hit him like a freight train. He had been so concerned about how the timeshift would affect the base and his team that he had forgotten to consider about how it would affect his own life.

Ecstatic at the prospect of his marriage being whole again, he reached for her hand, took it in his and kissed it. He looked into the eyes that had been so cold and tired for more years than he could recollect and kissed her again, the way he knew he should have. "I have a better idea. Let's take this across the road to the park."

CHAPTER 61

YEAR: 2097

Mitch looked out the open bay door of B Hangar at the people seated in an array of white folding chairs. He estimated that at least another fifty people stood at the rear, *with cameras,* he frowned, *like media...* Mitch sidled over to the PR director who stood among the media.

"Ally, what is all of this? I thought this was a closed ceremony?" whispered Mitch, leaning toward her. It had been unanimously decided that the details of the operation would never go public. Announcing to the world that a large government organization had released thousands of maniacal robots intent on world domination would undoubtedly tarnish the country's reputation, whether it happened in an alternate time or not.

Allison smiled at him innocently. "They're here for the ceremony."

"How do they know about the op?"

"They don't. They just know there *was* an op. All they know is that a brave group of people have just returned from a dangerous, six-month op and that they're all heroes."

Only a small number of attendees were expected at the ceremony, mostly families of the team members as well as several top NRD officials who insisted on attending after being read in on their mission. Mitch had brought the highest ranking officials at the NRD up to speed with the details of what time had written out of society's collective consciousness. He shared with them the contents of the metal box he had carried with him when he sent himself back those two seconds in time. The box contained all of the data, pictures and videos as proof of what they had been dealing with. Convincing the sceptical board members and executives had been difficult at first, but after they saw videos of themselves telling their story, they quickly came around. As only Mitch and the three teams had gone back in time, only they remembered what life had been like before the timeshift. The lives of everyone else on the planet had been rewritten, leaving them blissfully unaware of the havoc the robots had wreaked.

The unusually warm September sun beat down on the captive audience as they listened to Mitch. Generally a man of few words, he had much to say on this occasion about the virtue of the team members, their efforts and their unselfish sacrifice.

Cameras flashed as Mitch talked and Riley looked around. "I'm surprised by how much media is here," she whispered discreetly into Owen's ear. She saw her grandfather a few rows back and smiled. Beyond him, she saw a woman and two kids, a little girl she guessed to be around four or five and a toddler. The little girl fidgeted and her mother looked haggard. "I wonder who that is? She's obviously not press."

Owen turned to see the woman about whom she spoke and shrugged. The pair refocused their attention back to Mitch.

"Without further ado, I'd like to introduce each member to you. Lexi Grant: In addition to being dedicated and hard-working, her keen and analytical eye led to the discovery of an intruder during the operation." Lexi walked to the podium and shook Mitch's hand. He pinned a medal on her dark grey dress uniform and the crowd applauded politely. Her eyes looked like she had been crying, but she smiled appreciatively and returned to her seat.

"Ben Taylor kept all of the equipment working in top-notch condition and worked through the pain of injuries sustained on the job." Ben, confined to a medical-grade hover chair, negotiated the chair toward the podium. Mitch met him part way and pinned a medal on his jacket.

"Darren Roy," started Mitch, but he was interrupted by applause and catcalls from his teammates. "Darren Roy kept his teams fed, and I can only assume from that round of applause he did a bang-up job." Mitch pinned the medal on Darren's uniform.

"Maya Navaros not only ran an impeccably tight ship as the Sitespace Manager for six months but juggled those onerous duties with those of a medical aide. Her quick thinking kept her teammates in one piece, and one of them is here today only because of her."

"Tyler Davis's experience and versatility enabled him to take over a very technical position part way through the project. In addition, his forethought and quick thinking saved the life of one of our leads. We are deeply indebted to his heroic actions." Tyler blushed.

"Clint Nelson kept the operation interesting from what I understand." The team chuckled. "His excavation experience proved invaluable and his quick thinking after a rock collapse ensured that all of his team members lived to tell the tale." Clint accepted his medal and smiled sheepishly at his teammates.

"Finn McLaren," Mitch looked thoughtful for a moment. "Finn kept the team amused on this operation, and I think that might be putting it lightly. Anyone who has worked with him will tell you that his love for life and practical jokes are a close second to his true love, which is his job." Finn stepped forward and Mitch affixed the medal to his jacket. He shook Mitch's hand and turned to walk away, but Mitch held a firm grip. "Today is also special for Finn as his performance during this mission levelled him up to level three. He will now be able to run his own Level C Ops."

Finn smiled and pointed at Riley with surprise as Mitch pinned a second medal on his jacket. She smiled back and gave him a thumbs up.

"Logan Grayson was an asset to his team, picking up the slack for his team members when they needed help. Without his support, his team would not have been able to accomplish what they'd set out to do."

Logan leaned over to Spencer. "What he really means is our Golden Boy would have starved to death if I hadn't been your errand monkey." He smiled as he rolled his eyes, stood and walked up.

"Asher Grayson also proved to be a phenomenal support system for his team, and, in the process, devised a new technology that changed how the world looks at robots—or more appropriately, how robots look at the world."

From the back, a woman's voice cut through the applause. "Mr. Grayson, can you comment on how you think the deployment of your latest product, EagleEye, the optics system that can identify an individual from ten city blocks away based solely on the person's facial features, will fare on the market?"

"Asher, is it true that the federal government has commissioned a special order of EagleEye robots specifically for the national police force? Is it true they're putting twenty-five in each jurisdiction?" asked a male voice from the back.

A man stood up in the crowd. "Any questions for Mr. Grayson can be answered by myself after the ceremony," said the man who, as Asher had been shocked to learn, was his business partner. Asher, taken aback by the unexpected attention, completely missed Mitch pinning the medal on him until Mitch took his hand to shake it.

"Spencer Grayson is one of the brightest stars at NRD. Under his leadership, the team accomplished a nearly impossible goal with what turned out to be a far more slippery adversary than any of us had ever expected. In the end, his hard work paid off and the goal his team achieved has made the world we live in a much, much safer place. Spencer temporarily jumped two levels during this operation, owing to the unforeseen accident of a co-worker. We plan to keep Spencer at this level, making him the youngest level six the NRD has ever seen. In addition to this medal of honour, I'd like to present you with something else."

Mitch pinned the Op Achievement medal plus two Level Advancement medals on Spencer's shirt and handed him an envelope. "As Spencer is about to become a father, I think that this gift would be the most precious of all. Congratulations."

Spencer returned to his seat and opened the envelope.

Spencer,

As a token of appreciation for your dedication to Operation TimeShift and the countless hours you put in prior to the operation, we hope that you will accept this bonus cheque and an additional two months of well-earned vacation.

Kindest regards,
Mitch Campbell and the rest of the NRD Executives

"None of you know Owen Taylor. You could say he's pretty new in town, and I dare say he'll be spending a bit of time here. He's travelled a long, long time to get here. Without his knowledge, resourcefulness, bravery and selflessness, it's likely that none of us would be here today."

The audience clapped as Owen walked to the podium and Mitch placed his hand over the microphone. "This is your new life. There's also something in there I found when I was getting you set up. Looks like you're already a landowner." He slid a large manila envelope into Owen's hands. "Have you thought about my offer? Full benefits, Level Six Astrogeology Consultant?"

Owen looked down at Riley clapping along with the audience, "Absolutely. There's nothing I'd like more." He smiled, thanked Mitch and returned to his seat.

"Not many people on this base know Riley Morgan personally, but there probably isn't a single person who hasn't heard of her. Her catalogue of accomplishments is longer than I can list. Her strong leadership has led her and her teams on countless successful operations. Her fearlessness, strength and energy know no bounds. She is the only woman I know who can take down a swarm of eleven armed men in less than one minute." Mitch smiled at her as she walked toward Mitch holding up nine fingers. He pinned a medal on her jacket, completing her third row of medals.

"And finally, there is one last person that I would like to honour here today. Unfortunately, he can't be here with us. He made the ultimate sacrifice to ensure that his team got home safely."

As Mitch spoke, Teams One and Two deflated, remembering their grief. Lexi cried softly into Finn's shoulder.

"Jake Anderson was a level six lead from Mechanical and Infrastructure Recovery. This operation was far different from his typical duties, but he volunteered nonetheless. He was a great leader. He always took the time to help his subordinates learn—to become better at their jobs and grow as people. He was an invaluable asset to the NRD, and we're going to have a hard time getting on without him. He was an inspiration to…"

Without warning, Jake materialized in front of the podium. Startled by surroundings that were far different from what he was expecting, he stumbled backward, knocking the podium over. Mitch jumped out of the way and the microphone squawked with feedback as the glass podium fell over and smashed on the concrete. The crate that materialized beside him knocked over the flower vases beside the podium and they smashed at the feet of his teammates in the front row.

Jake's materialization took the audience completely by surprise. Except for the team members, no one present was accustomed to seeing people appear from thin air and several people screamed in shock. His frightful appearance startled everyone. His pants were torn and the gash on his forehead had bled down his face and congealed in his unruly beard as well as on his t-shirt. The expression on his face registered surprise equal to that of the crowd.

"Jake?" Riley was the first of the dumbstruck crowd to speak. "Jake?" she asked again, this time standing, her voice louder, higher. She smiled and the two teams swarmed him like he had scored the winning goal for a championship hockey game. The group laughed and cried, as did Jake, ecstatic to see both his team and 2097. He looked at the audience and he realized he had entered the wrong date. He showed up at 11:00

A.M.—the right time but the wrong day. He saw the media at the back and the cameras flashing and wished he had thought to clean up first. Then his eyes fell on something that made his heart stop. He pulled out of his team's embrace and stepped toward the crowd. The group turned to see what had caught his attention. A woman in the audience had stood, and was staring at him.

"Jake?" she asked, softly.

Jake remained speechless, his mind doing somersaults, his heart pounding in his ears. Finally, he spoke. "Brit? Omigod, Brit!" Jake ran to her, unable to believe his eyes. He pulled her into a hug, spun her around in the air and kissed her hard. He felt little hands tugging on his pant leg in the region of his knees and looked down.

"Daddy! Daddy!"

Jake had tears streaming down his face as he knelt down to hug the little girl and the toddler at her side. He picked up his little boy and flew him through the air like an airplane and the little boy giggled with delight.

Mitch concluded the ceremony amid the confusion. He knew that the media was going to have a field day. He saw Allison jockeying the shouting mob of media away from the ceremony site and into the hangar where she would somehow skate over what they had just witnessed.

CHAPTER 62

YEAR: 2097

It killed Jake not to go home with his family, but he needed to brief Mitch. Over an hour later, Jake left Mitch's office showered, cleanly shaven and wearing one of Mitch's uniforms. The shoulders of the shirt strained to cover Jake's broad frame.

In the hallway, Jake found Lexi waiting for him. She looked haggard and he felt for her. He supposed the last few days would have been an emotional rollercoaster ride for the whole team—learning about their new lives, good or bad, in addition to the loss of a friend.

"Lexi, I'm sorry about how hard this must have been on you." He was unsure if he should hug her, pat her on the back or do nothing. He pulled her into a hug.

She smiled, pulled away, crossed her arms and looked at the floor. "It was hard on everyone, but it's alright. I'm just happy that you're back and in one piece." She wiped a tear out of her eye. "And I'm so happy you have your family back. You must be over the moon."

Jake nodded and smiled at the thought of his beautiful wife and children. "I've got no words for it. It never occurred to me that I could get them back. I was so busy trying to get over the grief of losing them. It was all I could do to just get through each day, one at a time. I didn't dare think about my future because a future without my family was one I couldn't bear the thought of, so I just lived day by day. But it makes sense. If that accident never happened, then logically, yeah, they should be alive. But, I tell you, that was a bigger shock than learning I was going to be marooned in the year 1200. I thought I was seeing things."

An awkward silence fell between them. "Lexi…" Words eluded him. They had no relationship beyond friendship, but still he felt bad. He settled for generics. "I'm just really sorry."

Lexi turned red. "It's alright. I had a little crush on you, but at the end of the day, we're friends. We were there for each other when we both had some tough times, and I care about you more as a friend."

Jake pulled her into a hug. "Let's go find our team," said Jake.

The three teams congregated at the twins' favourite bar, *Way Off Base*, for post-op drinks. With the team fully reunited, it seemed only fitting to celebrate their success. Jake and Lexi arrived at the bar to find the group sitting around a large round table, taking in every word Clint was saying. They still had yet to hear the rest of his story after Ian stole the detonator out of Clint's pocket and blew up the tunnel.

"So I wake up and find myself tied up with that nut job standing over top of me. When he saw I was awake, he sat me on the rock and hid. He passed the time by telling me how easy I'd made it for him to frame me. How the wedge I'd driven between myself and everyone else made me a perfect target. He knew that no one would believe a word I'd said. I guess it was a bit of a reality check. Actually, it was just really weird." He took a sip of beer, his throat dry from talking.

"Weird how?" asked Maya.

"Well, here's this guy, clearly off his rocker, giving me life lessons. It was a bit of a wakeup call. If some lunatic who barely knew me could tell all of this, what did that say about me?"

Ben patted Clint on the shoulder. "Ah, breakups can mess you up for years. I remember a girl dumped me once and I threw out all of my clothes and bought a whole new wardrobe. I thought I'd go goth. It cost me nearly three months' salary to replace my original wardrobe once I came to my senses."

The group listened eagerly as Jake told them how he spent his time while marooned in the wilderness.

"What I don't get is, how come it took you nearly two months to find the pack?" asked Lexi. "I sent it to arrive when we left. It should have appeared when you were standing right there."

"Are you kidding me?" asked Jake. "I found that thing in the bushes purely by fluke. I literally tripped over it in the forest," he said pointing to the gash on his forehead. "I thought it was a trap set by Ian until I saw it was the pack I had worn during the explosion."

"No… That's impossible. I punched in the co-ords myself," said Lexi in disbelief. She rattled off the longitude and latitude.

"I think you transposed the two last numbers there, Lex," he said smiling.

Lexi looked thoughtful for a moment and then her face fell. She had been so anxious to send the pack back that she had nearly exiled him for good in the process.

Jake laughed. "See? I told you we'd all sit around and laugh about it later."

"Where are we going?" asked Riley.

Owen smiled sneakily. He used his hand to cover the address he manually entered into her car's computer so she would be left in suspense. From the passenger seat he hit the green "Autopilot" button. Owen watched everything on the ground become smaller as the car rose into the air and merged itself into the lines of air traffic. No matter how many times he watched this, it still looked as cool as it had the first time.

Riley watched as Owen reopened the envelope Mitch had handed him during the ceremony and he removed a stack of papers. Several small items fell out onto his lap. "What is all that?"

Owen flipped through the documentation. "Well, let's see here. Birth certificate, driver's license, social insurance number, bank accounts." He held up the keys that had fallen into his lap. They looked identical to the keys Riley had shown him on their first day, except there were fewer and his were shiny and new. He went back to the papers. "Oh, look, here's my employment contract."

"Employment contract?" asked Riley "You took the job?"

Owen nodded. "I did indeed. We can carpool, but then I guess you're probably more in the field than in the office?"

She smiled at the idea of having something in her life as ordinary as carpooling. "I'm thinking of switching fields to something more mundane."

"Sounds good to me," said Owen. He took her hand and kissed it. He imagined her sitting at a desk planning combat strategies. "What were you thinking?"

"I don't know. Something mindless. Maybe the Domestic Terrorism Task Force. That wouldn't be too much of a pay cut." She looked out her window thoughtfully for a moment. "No, maybe not. That's where the people go who can't get into Black Ops."

Owen watched as oncoming traffic zipped below them. They flew through downtown, the lines of traffic cutting between each building. The downtown was woven together by uniform lines of air traffic threading their way between the massive buildings in each direction. Transit platforms were stationed every few blocks. A twelve-car train was docked at the nearest platform, and people jockeyed to get on and off. Massive glass pods rose and fell from the platform, bringing transit riders from street level up to the platform and vice versa. The large pods reminded Owen of the capsules on the London Eye.

Down below, he could see the white, egg-shaped airships he knew were the holographic blimps that floated several storeys above the ground, flashing advertisements to the pedestrians and road traffic below. Although he could not see them from his current altitude, he knew the air space above the blimps was reserved for courier bots and automated delivery traffic. He saw a police air cruiser had grounded a driver, presumably to write up a ticket. The cop car was unmistakable; the car's paint glowed brilliantly like a neon light, alternating between blue and red.

Riley was right, the city looked very different. Some of the skyscrapers seemed true to their name, reaching far higher into the sky than he could have ever imagined possible. Natural green space within the city had all but disappeared, however, most residential and commercial buildings featured elaborate rooftop green spaces and vertical gardens, complete with parks and recreation facilities, free for anyone to use. Owen had learned that the buildings featured Apex Living Roof Systems, a technology similar to the camp's WeatherShield. However, instead of cutting out the wind and precipitation entirely, it could be regulated to let in just enough to create optimal conditions. In addition, it created a safety barrier around the perimeter so residents could safely enjoy an unimpeded view of the city.

Soon they had passed through downtown and the air route dropped down to five storeys. Below, he saw shopping malls, grocery stores and small offices. Cars in front of them exited the traffic stream by flying up and to the right, then down to the streets below.

Owen truly had no clue where the car was taking him. The address of the property he supposedly owned looked unfamiliar to him, and after the car had lowered in altitude, he had lost his bearings. Everything looked so different than it did in 2016. Within minutes, he saw some familiar landmarks. An unmistakable bend in the old road below as it followed the river, hills and large pockets of rocks protruding from the ground. Soon, the car had landed itself and he watched the steering wheel turn automatically as the car drove itself down a familiar street.

"I'll be damned." The houses on the street looked very different, but the roads, street signs and lampposts were the same. The car pulled into his driveway and stopped where his house had once been. As he stepped out of the car, he saw remnants of his old concrete driveway beneath his feet, now severely cracked and overtaken by weeds, bushes and small trees. The lot itself was overgrown; large trees and thick bush filled what used to be his immaculate lawn. A great oak tree grew where his home once stood. He could just see the river at the back of the property where the land dipped down at the river's edge.

"I don't believe it," said Riley. "Did Mitch get this for you as a signing bonus?"

Owen looked sheepish. "I have several confessions to make," he said. Riley raised an eyebrow.

"I had a suspicion that I may not be coming back, so I made some tentative arrangements in case I didn't."

She looked at him with narrowed eyes. "What do you mean, 'arrangements?'"

"Remember on those last two days before we left 2016 I was doing some soul-searching and errand running? I knew that leaving you wasn't an option for me, and if it was within my power to stay with you, I was going to at least try. I created a plan with a fail-safe escape route, you know, in case you decided to chuck me while we were in the year 1200. My job, my home, my life meant nothing if I didn't have you to share it with. It was the easiest decision of my life. What wasn't easy was explaining this to my lawyer. He thought I was cracking up. Finally, he believed me after showing him the VersaTool." Owen watched Riley's eyes widen in horror. "Don't worry. He's bound to secrecy. Client-attorney confidentiality and all that stuff." Owen laughed. "Besides, even if he wanted to tell someone, no one would've ever believed him."

Riley felt as though she should look stern, but fighting a smile was impossible.

"Two days before we left, I gave my lawyer a set of instructions but told him not to execute them until I called and gave him the green light. I decided that, if I did come back to 2016, I would come back a day early and leave myself a note, instructing my current self not to execute my instructions. I decided I would leave it in my sock drawer. By the end of the last day, I was pleased to find no letter, so I knew that I had followed you. So the morning before we left, I popped by work and told my director I was liquidating my assets to travel the world, which technically wasn't a lie. Then I called my lawyer and had him execute my instructions."

"What were your instructions?"

"I had him do some legal magic so the property stayed in my name for the years to come. I instructed him to liquidate what I'd left behind and invest the money in various low-risk investments."

Riley stood rooted to her spot, unable to speak.

He smiled, happy and surprised that his plan had come together so seamlessly. "So when Mitch was creating my new life, he found the property title, which I didn't recognize because the name of the street and the number are different. And this." He held up an investment statement and pointed to a substantial number at the bottom. Riley's colour disappeared. "Apparently everything I did worked, so I have a bit of a life already waiting for me."

Riley's jaw fell open. She stared at him for several moments while she processed what he had told her. Finally, a smile grew on her face and she shook her head in disbelief. "Owen, what if we were dead, and that's why you didn't get the letter? What if you were delayed for some reason?"

Owen looked thoughtful. "Well, if we were dead, then everything was moot anyway. But if we weren't, which was what I chose to assume, I thought you were worth the gamble. I had planned on changing my backpack to go with you guys when you weren't looking, but as it worked out, you did it for me, and I was able to land in the future in a much more favourable light, thanks to you." He smiled broadly at her and caressed her cheek. "I'm sorry. I did want to tell you all of this, but I know how loyal you are to your job. If I had told you and you agreed to it, you would never have been able to live with the guilt of violating your principles. If I did it, you'd be saved all that. If I told you and you didn't agree, you would have made sure I got a one-way ticket home."

Riley smiled because she knew the truth hid somewhere in the words he had just spoken. She took his hand, pulled it around her shoulder and looked at the oak tree where his magnificent house once stood. "It's a shame the house didn't make it. We should rebuild it. I loved it so much."

Owen thought of the house and smiled. "Yeah. I had some great memories there. But we can make new ones." He kissed her on the cheek. "Hey, that reminds me, I have something for you." Riley watched him return from the trunk of her car with his metal case. He handed it to her. "My gift to you. Just be careful, it's kind of fragile."

Riley released the two clasps on the front of the box and flipped the lid backward. She recognized it instantly.

"Owen! You brought the house with you! I can't believe it."

Owen shrugged. "It's been in my family for generations. Now you're my family. I thought it would be fitting."

A tear rolled down Riley's face. Owen saw the tiny patio lights on the miniature roof-top deck swaying from her shaking hands. He took the case from her and chuckled.

"Careful, the barbecue is going to roll off the patio and fall onto your foot." Owen closed and reclasped the lid. He took her by the hand and led her toward the water. "Let me show you what I was thinking."

* * * * *

Thank you for reading *TimeShift*. I'm thrilled that you've chosen to spend your free time with the characters I've been in love with for over six years now. I hope you enjoyed the story as much as I enjoyed writing it.

Please help me spread the word about *TimeShift*! As you pass the butter at dinner, tell your family about Finn and his love of food from 2016. On Friday nights, as you clink glasses and say "cheers to the weekend," tell your friends about the twins, and how they'd already be on their third Tequila Bomb. When you get to work on Monday, remind your boss that he or she needs to place that order for the next round of AEI robots, before they run out. Beyond all of that, I'd be very grateful if left feedback on Amazon and GoodReads.com.

Join the conversation on:

Official TimeShift Website: timeshift-novel.com
Facebook: www.facebook.com/TimeShiftNovel
Twitter: www.twitter.com/KrisTrudeau
Instagram: Kris_Trudeau. Share a photo of you and *TimeShift*!

Thank you so much!

Kris Trudeau

Kris Trudeau lives in the Comox Valley on beautiful Vancouver Island, British Columbia. The completion of her debut novel, *TimeShift*, marks the end of a six-year journey that began in Winnipeg, Manitoba from where she originally hails.

Owner of a website development and graphic design firm, Kris spends her days helping organizations in the Comox Valley as well as across Canada grow their business. Writing became a passion for Kris in the last decade both in business and for leisure. For fiction, she finds the creative process to be a fascinating, magical experience and is looking forward to exploring several ideas for future stories.

In her spare time, Kris enjoys the company of family and friends. She is a firm believer in giving back to one's community and donates time to local non-profit organizations. Athletic by nature, she participates in a variety of sports and enjoys exploring the natural paradise of Vancouver Island.

www.ingramcontent.com/pod-product-compliance
Lightning Source LLC
Chambersburg PA
CBHW030913050726
47498CB00003BA/713